PRAISE FOR *BLEAK HARBOR*

"Bryan Gruley's *Bleak Harbor* is an electric bolt of suspense, packed with twists and surprises. Gruley's plot races along, powered by characters—big and small—who truly crackle. A masterful follow-up to his Starvation Lake trilogy."

—Gillian Flynn, #1 *New York Times* bestselling author of *Gone Girl*

"The best book Gruley has ever written and unlike any other crime book I've ever read."

—Steve Hamilton, two-time Edgar Award–winning author of
Exit Strategy

"Bryan Gruley creates a fascinating calamity of flawed characters, each hiding secrets in the haunting town of Bleak Harbor. His portrayal of an autistic boy's kidnapping, and the subsequent efforts to find and rescue him, gradually and brilliantly exposes the decidedly dark underbelly of both the town and all those living in it. I dare you to put the book down. I couldn't."

—Robert Dugoni, #1 *Wall Street Journal* bestselling author

"The myth of the happy family! Bryan Gruley dives deep into twisted psyches, well-hidden secrets, and dark, explosive desires. Welcome to Bleak Harbor. Be afraid."

— Tess Gerritsen, *New York Times* bestselling author

"Vivid, spellbinding, and laced with tension, *Bleak Harbor*'s labyrinthine mystery is packed with characters so real you want to buy them a beer—or hide under your bed to pray they don't come for you. If you're not reading Bryan Gruley, you're missing out."

—Marcus Sakey, bestselling author of *AFTERLIFE* and the
Brilliance trilogy

BLEAK HARBOR

OTHER TITLES BY BRYAN GRULEY

THE STARVATION LAKE TRILOGY

Starvation Lake
The Hanging Tree
The Skeleton Box

NONFICTION

Paper Losses

BLEAK HARBOR

BRYAN GRULEY

THOMAS & MERCER

Published by Thomas & Mercer, Seattle
www.apub.com

Amazon, the Amazon logo, and Thomas & Mercer are trademarks of Amazon.com, Inc., or its affiliates.

ISBN-13: 9781503904682 (hardcover)
ISBN-10: 1503904687 (hardcover)

ISBN-13: 9781503904675 (paperback)
ISBN-10: 1503904679 (paperback)

Cover design by Shasti O'Leary Soudant

Printed in the United States of America

First edition

For Joel, Miles, and Sawyer

PROLOGUE

"You won't hurt the boy?"

"Not if I don't have to."

"Do not hurt him."

"How 'bout his mother?"

"I didn't hear that."

"Heh. I'll take the kid for a milkshake. Least that's what I'll tell him."

"He's a troubled young man."

"Dude, he's fifteen. You weren't fucked up at fifteen?"

"He'll be sixteen soon. That could be our deadline."

"Serious?"

"Things appear to be headed in that direction."

"Which things?"

"Again, none of your business. You need to worry about getting him to the safe place. He won't throw a fit or something?"

"The kid's got issues, but he ain't crazy."

"You've been in touch with him?"

"I told you, him and I are good. And there ain't no neighbors. Bank took the one place, and nobody's ever at the other one."

"Should we go over the details once more?"

"I got mine. What about you? The bitch is gonna call the cops."

"Once they realize the boy's really gone, of course they'll contact the police. Remember, though, he ran away before. They called the police, and it was embarrassing for everyone."

"That was then."

"It's the Bleak Harbor Police. By the time they get a clue, the boy will be in the safe place, and you will be long gone with your money."

"Better be."

"Plus, there's the festival in town. The cops will be busy."

"Who the hell has a dragonfly festival anyway?"

"Remember: do not contact me. Just wait. Don't change a thing about your life. Keep working where you work."

"I'll be glad to get the hell out of there."

"Not until the job is done."

"Don't even think about trying to pin it on me."

"That would be foolish for everyone involved."

"Don't forget it."

"Trust me—my client is a much bigger fish than you."

"Your client better just have my money ready."

"The initial payment was transferred fourteen minutes ago. The rest will be tendered when the job is complete."

"Tendered?"

"You will have it."

"A hundo now, two and a half later."

"As agreed upon."

"And your boss, whoever the hell he is, gets to be the hero."

"Not your concern. Now, you may find it tempting—"

"Is this client screwing my ex, by chance?"

"—to take the down payment and run. That would be a bad idea."

"Don't worry."

"Just as we can help you disappear, we can find you. You saw the photos from North Dakota."

"Seen 'em. Nice dogs. Pits or rotts? I'm a rott guy myself."

"Those people thought they were home free with a semi full of catalytic converters. They were mistaken."

"I seen worse. My boss ain't no shrinking violet, you know."

"Once you have the boy, use the disposable, and text the number I'm about to give you. Do you have something to write with?"

"Putting it in the phone right now . . . got it."

"Did you write it down?"

"It's in the phone, man."

"Write it down, please, then delete it from the phone."

"All right, Jesus, hold on . . . OK. Written down."

"Send one letter: *Y* for yes, you have him. *X* for no."

"Yo."

"After that, wait for us to contact you. My signal could come at any moment. When this is done, we will never speak again."

"Fuckin' A. Fine by me."

THURSDAY

1

Danny sits at the end of the dock, watching.

The dragonfly appears to his left, skimming a flat line one foot above the glassine surface of the bay.

It skitters up as if on a wire and takes the first mosquito without slowing. Danny pictures the cruelly efficient jaws and serrated teeth tearing the prey into a gooey black mash while the dragonfly plots the geometric path to its next target.

"Pretty pretty pretty dragonflies . . . pretty pretty." Danny sings softly into the sunshine, the lilting ditty his mother made up when he was a little boy. He stops and listens. He knows he was singing a little off-key. He closes his eyes.

And smiles, feels the sun warm on his cheeks.

He adds the mosquito to the running tally in his head: 694 since Saturday morning, heading for a record by sundown Friday.

Which will be Danny's sixteenth birthday.

"Sweet sixteen," his mother told him.

"What's so sweet about it?"

"It's just a saying, honey. You're sweet every day."

No, Danny thought then. *I don't think I want to be sweet.*

The dragonfly vanishes into the cloudless blue to his right. It will soon be back for more. Danny dips a toe into the bay and kicks up some water, watches the scatter of beads settle back into the bay, many becoming one again.

Down the pebbled-sand shoreline that winds around to downtown Bleak Harbor, the upper arc of a Ferris wheel juts above the shops and bars along Blossom Street. Danny imagines the smells of hamburger grease and powdered sugar, the impatient shrieks of children, the contorted faces of clowns and drunks. The Twenty-Eighth Annual Southwestern Michigan Dragonfly Festival begins tomorrow.

Twenty-eight years ago, Danny thinks, *the Cubs should have won the World Series.*

The festival was what first interested him in Anisoptera, the dragonfly, when he and his mother came from Chicago to visit her parents. He sometimes wonders whether any of the people attending the festival actually know what the dragonfly is about, how its flitting beauty, wings aglint in sun, masks the bloodless killer within. Probably not.

He shifts his gaze across the bay to the Joseph E. Bleak Public Library, between city hall and a parking lot that will be crammed all weekend with cars and trucks and SUVs bearing out-of-state license plates. Danny was at the library yesterday and other days before that, stationed at a microfilm machine, reading local history. He'd taken a liking to the library since moving to Bleak Harbor.

Zelda, the librarian, always helped him when the microfilm roller got stuck, as it often did. And Danny would watch as she fiddled with the machine, fixated on how Zelda had put on her makeup that day, whether she had smeared her red lipstick or layered her mascara so thick that it clotted. She had recently separated from her husband, and Danny had noticed that since then, her mascara was usually not right, and some days she skipped it altogether.

Sometimes he would imagine Zelda at her vanity mirror, calling out orders to her four children—Gregory, Helen, Ronald, Alex; names Danny knew because he'd asked her—as she did her makeup, noticing a fresh gray strand in her blonde waves, making a face at it. She never made a face when Danny asked for help. He was used to people making faces at him. But Zelda's smile was patient and true. "It's no trouble,

Daniel; that's why I'm here," she would say. He liked the way she said "Daniel."

When he was leaving the library yesterday, he stopped at the desk where Zelda was sorting returned books. She didn't notice him at first, and he just waited and watched until she looked up and saw him. "Oh, I'm so sorry, Daniel," she said. "How long have you been standing there?"

"I'm fine."

"Is the machine giving you trouble again?"

Danny shook his head and said, "I just wanted to say something, Mrs. Loiselle."

"All righty," she said, "and what is that?"

"You are a very beautiful woman."

She blushed, and for a second, Danny thought she might cry. "Oh, my," she said, "you're such a nice boy."

"I don't know. Thank you for your help. I hope to see you again."

———

Pete didn't know how much time Danny spent at the library because he wasn't home a lot during the day. Today, though, he had stopped at the cottage to check on him. Danny was out on the dock.

"I gotta go to this meeting, or your mother will have my nuts," he told Danny. Of course Pete didn't want to go. He wanted to spend the afternoon praying customers would come to his medical marijuana shop downtown. But Danny's mother was ninety-seven miles away in Chicago and wouldn't be home till after five o'clock.

"Dulcy's at the shop in case you need something and you can't reach me," Pete said. "Coverage sucks inside city hall."

"How is Dulcy?" Danny asked.

"She needs to work on her English. And her punctuality. Why? You got the hots for her?"

Pete thought that was funny. That's how he was.

"She's nice."

"Nice and late, every morning."

"Maybe she's not a morning person."

"Unfortunately, some of our clients are morning people. You gonna pack the cooler?"

"Yes. For fishing. When will you be home?"

"Sixish. Gotta stop back at the dope den after the meeting."

No, Danny thought. *You gotta stop at the bar.*

"The cooler will be ready," he said.

"You feeling up to it?"

"I feel fine. The sun's been good today."

"OK. Pack a whole six-pack. I'm gonna need it."

———

Danny stands and walks back toward the house. He likes the sting of the nailheads in the sunbaked planks on the bottoms of his feet.

Stepping off the dock, he crosses the sand to the deck attached to the cottage. He finds his cell phone on the picnic table next to his book. He turns the phone on and taps in his password.

There's a new text message:

milkshakes at 5 al right >?

Danny doesn't really like milkshakes. But he answers:

K have to be back before 6.

The reply comes immediately.

c u soon

2

Carey fights the tears until she hits the Skyway Bridge into northwest Indiana. She catches a glimpse of downtown Chicago in her side-view mirror. A flash of sunlight off a window high on one of the skyscrapers looses the sobs. They shake her so hard that she almost jerks her car off the road. She closes her eyes, feels the soggy burn of her tears, tries to wrest herself out of the nightmare.

She picks up her phone and rereads the text, wishing it would disappear:

we know about v day

The blurt of a horn startles her. She glances up and sees the trucker's frown as his semi pulls up on her right. She looks at the phone in her hand and realizes she's been gliding along below the speed limit in the left lane of Interstate 94 East.

"Sorry, sorry," she says, thinking, *I am such a wimp.*

The trucker slows and holds steady alongside her, staring from behind mirrored glasses. *He doesn't know*, Carey thinks. *Don't be ridiculous.* She waves him on and flicks her blinker and eases into the right lane. The trucker pulls away, shaking his head.

Bitch, she tells the rearview mirror. She sets her phone aside, picks it up again immediately, glances in her rearview, sees nobody close, starts typing with her right thumb while steering with her left:

talk to my lawyer

The phone pings with a response:

better get one ms peters

Fuck you, she thinks. *Fuck me. Fuck everybody.*
Everybody but Danny.

Carey is in over her head. She knows this as clearly as she knows the distances from the Loop to exit 21 at Interstate 94, from there to the Michigan border, from the blue **Welcome to Michigan** sign spanning the highway to the sandy bluffs along the big lake and the little cottage in Bleak Harbor where Danny waits. She knows it as clearly as she knows how much she loathes making this drive.

She takes a breath. Everything will be all right, she tells herself. One way or another, she will gain the freedom to put her life where she wants it, away from her husband and Chicago and Michigan and everything but her son. She isn't about to give up this time. She isn't about to settle again.

She flips the sun visor down. The snapshot paper clipped there was taken five years ago, when Danny was ten. He's wearing his auburn hair the way Carey loves it, long and curly down the sides of his narrow face, his saucer eyes the green of Lake Michigan on a crystal summer morning. He is standing beneath an enormous silver sculpture in Chicago's Loop, an ice-cream sandwich melting in one hand as he gazes up at the countless reflections of himself in the sculpture's shiny skin, all the ice-cream sandwiches dripping in the heat.

And he's grinning. The photograph is too small to see the thin gap in Danny's front teeth or the pale freckles on his cheeks, but Carey imagines them and allows herself a fleeting smile. She loves this picture.

She sees herself in Danny's face, his eyes, his curls. He's happy. She wants to be happy. She wants to be happy with him again.

She tries to remember, as she does whenever she's feeling down or overwhelmed—a lot, of late—how hard he squeezed her this morning when he hugged her goodbye. Then she recalls—she'd almost forgotten—that he whispered in her ear, "Be happy, Mommy. OK?" She just laughed and shook her head. She wishes now that she had squeezed him right back and said, "You too, my beautiful boy."

Or was that yesterday? Or last week? Between her commute and working and nights falling asleep on the sofa watching shows about couples buying homes in exotic foreign cities, Carey loses track of time.

People tell her how beautiful Danny is. Because he *is* beautiful, as beautiful a boy as Carey could have hoped for. But also, she thinks, they say so as some nebulous means of solace, as if his looks are a trade-off for the things about her son that they will never understand, as if it is a tragedy that Danny is so lovely a boy at the same time that he is so unattainable to them. Carey has taught herself to tune them all out, even the various doctors with their various, supposedly well-intentioned labels—autism, apraxia, on the spectrum, pervasive developmental disorder, high functioning and low. None of them matter anymore.

Tomorrow, she will have Danny to herself. She will work from home and make him his CoCo Wheats with maple bacon on the side. She will tell her husband to go to his pot shop and stay there, busy or not. She and Danny will walk the beach to the channel and count the boats chugging out to Lake Michigan, maybe stop for a cold pop at the little shop at the channel's mouth.

Back home, they'll sit in the adirondacks on the deck and pass the book back and forth, reciting Danny's favorite poem. They'll recall again how Carey mistook the palm in the poem's opening line for a hand instead of the tree it is. Carey will raise an open palm and point at it and shake her head, and she and her son will laugh again.

And Danny will point past his mother across the bay, past the drowsing sloops and catamarans, the festive tavern decks, beyond to the stolid pink mansion looming above it all, judging the town from one side, Lake Michigan from the other. Once Carey called it "the wedge of space," mangling a line in Danny's favorite poem, "because," she said, "that's it—there's nothing in the world after that, nothing but the big damn lake."

It made Danny laugh. "The wedge of space," he said. "Yes. Between town and the lake."

Her phone beeps in her hand. She starts to look at the text, changes her mind, sticks the phone in a cup holder.

There was a time when even her short absences from home were intolerable for the boy, even if Pete was with him. Carey would return to glass shattered across the kitchen floor, smears of peanut butter and grape jam spelling obscenities on the walls, Pete rushing to clean up, Danny adept at timing his tantrums so that Pete would have to share the blame.

Where were you? Carey would demand of Pete when she thought they were out of Danny's earshot. Pete would shrug and make an excuse about a business call he had to take or a fishing reel he had to rig. *No,* Carey would say, *no excuses,* Pete wincing at the submerged pique surfacing in her voice, averting his eyes, apologizing partly because he was sorry but mostly to make her stop.

Then they would not speak for a day, maybe two or three. Sometimes Danny himself would go quiet, withholding even one-word replies, and Carey would wonder if it was because she had been gone or because he'd overheard the words she'd hurled at Pete or if it was just Danny being Danny, retreating into himself.

She picks up the phone, reads the text, wishes she had never gotten involved with the feds:

u have until end of the week. then i'll be at your door. v day
betwn us——for now.

She remembers how cold it was on February 14, how the Chicago
wind clawed at her cheeks after she left Randall Pressman's building to
hail a cab just after midnight.

He had taken her to Alinea to celebrate her promotion to executive
assistant, finance, at Pressman Logistics. Randall Pressman didn't believe
in glorified titles; his four executive assistants, all women under the age
of forty, were the most important and best-paid people at his company
except, of course, for himself. The chef had come by their private table
to shake Pressman's hand with both of his, explaining the unexplainable
food. After dinner, Carey had vowed to go back to her studio rental
alone, but there was Dom Perignon on ice and red roses in the back of
the limo, and Pressman, without asking her, had the driver take them
to his building on the Chicago River.

Forty-five minutes later, she had fucked her boss.

Now, as she eases back into the left lane and pushes the speed
higher, she hears his contented moan as he rolled off of her, sees his flat-
ted palms smoothing the mat of wiry white on his chest. She remembers
how she wrapped herself in a blanket and went to the floor-to-ceiling
windows, staring into the reflection of her porcelain skin, her wide eyes
set off by the angular sculpt of her cheekbones, the things that made
men like Pressman want her. She looked through the reflection to see
steam swirling out of the stacks atop a steel-and-glass tower across the
river and wished she could fling herself down the seventeen floors into
the water, all the way to the cold black bottom.

That night had been a slip on her part. A bad one. A terrible one.
Though she had to admit, in retrospect, it was one she'd made all but
inevitable. She'd let herself get caught up in the client dinners, the Gold
Coast pied-à-terre Pressman had insisted on having the company lease

for her. So she didn't have to worry about the commute, he'd said, and she'd let herself believe it. She'd let herself be taken in by the idea that she was valuable, even indispensable, to Pressman Logistics. In fact she was good at her job. But there was only one indispensable employee at that company.

His palms, she thinks, *oh God, dear God*, his sandpaper palms pressing on her shoulders as he groaned his climax. She shudders with disgust. He was old enough to have said that maybe one day they could have a "nooner," a word Carey once heard her philandering late father use. She flips the visor back up and rolls her window down, welcoming the rush of wind.

"I'm sorry," she says, to no one.

She picks up her phone and punches 1. She hears Danny's end ringing, hoping he will answer, knowing he probably will not. The voice mail comes on after five rings. "This isn't exactly Danny," his voice says, followed by silence, then a beep.

She wishes Danny's reply said something about leaving a message, something welcoming to those few who reached out to him. He seems steadier these days yet still absents himself from—she struggles for the word, reluctant to land on it—from life. She ends the call, hits 2. The phone rings on without going to voice mail. Pete isn't answering, no surprise. She hopes he isn't out on the deck with a cooler of beer but in the city council meeting she asked him to attend in her place. Pete certainly would not enjoy the meeting, but it was the least he could do while she was driving back and forth from Chicago to Bleak Harbor two or three times a week.

Another call comes in, one she was half expecting and dreading at the same time. "Carey Peters," she says.

"Why so formal?" The caller chuckles.

"You think this is funny?"

"No."

"You have till tomorrow," she says. "After that, I hand the stuff over, and you deal with the feds."

"You're not really going to go through with this."

"I am, and I will."

Pressman goes silent for a few seconds. Then, "Think about it, babe. Some of those documents have your name on them too. You're in this as deep as anyone."

"No, I'm not. And do not call me babe."

"You're going to blow up a bunch of lives, including your own."

I have every intention of blowing up my life, Carey thinks, *just not the way you assume.* "You can keep that from happening, Randall."

"Come on. This is extortion, plain and simple. What if I go to the police?"

"Go ahead."

Pressman gets quiet again, then says, "So this is really just about that one night."

No, Carey thinks but does not say. She can't hold that frozen Valentine's Day against Pressman entirely. He didn't rape her. Not literally. But he responded to her subsequent declinations and refusals by moving her from the office adjoining his to a smaller one on the floor below and supplanting her with a younger woman, his new executive assistant for transportation. He hinted that he might need Carey to move to one of the company's satellite offices, in Cleveland or, worse, Duluth.

He was too smart and too cowardly to simply fire her and face the publicity of yet another sexual harassment claim from yet another younger subordinate. Instead, he'd make sure that Carey's job slowly turned to shit.

Lucky for her, Pressman had gotten sloppy as his net worth grew and his stature in the business pantheon climbed: cover of *Fortune* magazine, Executive Club honoree, *Crain's Chicago Business* CEO of the Year. He'd gotten too busy, too worshipped, too much in demand.

Although he'd moved Carey's office, he had neglected to change the passwords he'd given her to attend to certain sensitive business activities. She'd spent two long nights in the tiny office beneath his using those passwords to fill her email inbox with company documents she wasn't supposed to have. She couldn't read all of them—some had been stamped in an Asian script—but she suspected, if she didn't outright know, that they showed Pressman Logistics wasn't always transporting legal cargo.

She had briefly considered giving the documents to the man who's been texting her, at the risk of losing her job and her benefits. Instead, she had determined that the documents she possessed were worth $10 million. She'd picked the number out of an article she'd read in *Us* magazine about what a famous and talentless actor had been paid for a two-minute cameo in a vampire flick. With $10 million, she and Danny could live off the interest for the rest of their lives. She wouldn't have to work. She could focus on being her son's best mother.

And $10 million would be a pittance to Pressman. It was less than half the bonus he had paid himself the year before. She really wasn't being greedy. Extortionate, yes, criminal, yes, but not greedy.

"How many times do I have to say I'm sorry?" Pressman says. "Can't you—we—just let it go?"

"You obviously couldn't. Anyway, this isn't about that anymore. It's about freedom, for both of us. You can afford it. And I'll disappear. Think of it as severance."

Carey hears the guttural whoosh of a boat passing on Pressman's end of the call. She pictures him on the veranda of his condo, sipping a martini. She lowers the phone, looks at the texts again. How the hell did this guy know about Valentine's Day?

"Sweetie," Pressman says, "the limp-dick feds have been trying to nail me for years. It will never happen."

Being called sweetie doesn't rankle Carey as much as her growing suspicion that Pressman can detect how desperate she is. It's precisely that cynical sense of the way things really work that makes men like Randall Pressman so rich and powerful. Carey had learned that from her father. How could she have forgotten?

Ten million, she thinks now. *Too much.* She should have demanded one or two million, no more, and Pressman would have paid her in fifties and hundreds to make her go away. Ten million drew some line he would not cross, not with a woman, not with a woman who worked for him, not with a woman he'd had between his sheets.

What had she been thinking?

She knows what she'd been thinking. She'd been thinking about that night, about how ashamed and furious she'd felt.

She tries now to summon some of that revulsion to steel her nerve. "Stop with the bullshit, Randall," she says. "Get me the money, or you and your company will be screwed."

"Carey, rich guys don't go to jail. You know that. You read the *Wall Street Journal.* Little guys go to jail. And little girls."

"Fuck you."

"What do you think the jury's going to think when they hear the star witness slept with the defendant?"

"They're going to put you in jail."

"No. Think about this, Carey. You're in over your head here. You know you are. But you have time. You don't have to burn this bridge. Call me tomorrow if you want—"

She ends the call and flips the phone onto the passenger seat. "Go to fucking hell." The phone bounces off the seat onto the floor. She starts to reach for it, decides not to, mutters, "Damn it."

The phone zizzes. A text. Maybe Danny. Again she stretches out her right arm, but the phone is out of reach. She takes a deep breath. Everything will work out, she tells herself. In the morning, she will call Pressman and tell him, *All right, you win, one million.* Or maybe two million. Two million will get him off the hook and her and Danny out of the country. He'll go for that. He'd be stupid not to. Two million will be enough.

She looks at the odometer. Sixty-nine miles to Danny. She steps on the gas and lurches into the left lane, thinking, *Two million, just two million, and everything is going to be fine.*

3

Pete feels the phone vibrate in his shorts pocket. Usually, on a July afternoon like this one, clear and blue with a breeze wafting off the lake, swirling down the channel and across the bay, he likes the buzzing sensation against his thigh, its comforting reminder that the world outside Boz's Bayfront Bar and Grill demands his attention and he can choose whether to grant it.

He yanks the phone out. Carey's calling. He'd rather not speak to his wife just yet, so he silences the phone and takes a sip from his vodka and tonic. He'll be seeing her soon enough. He did his duty, went to the city council meeting as she insisted. He can tell her all about it, what there is to tell, after he takes Danny fishing.

"So, Petey," Boz says. "Fun downtown?"

Boz leans his forearms on the bar. He grins, and tomato cheeks squeeze his eyes nearly shut beneath a cotton-white flattop. Boz is an ex–Chicago cop who took early retirement after a bullet splintered his left femur. He bought a plot of land, razed a defunct orphanage, and built a shack of knotty pine and four-chair tables with a wall of windows and screens opening on to a porch set on the beach. Pete appreciated Boz spelling *Grill* without an *e*, unlike the fancy joints on the downtown promenade across the bay. No ampersand either.

"Fun's not quite the word," Pete says. "Got there early and still couldn't get a seat. Found a nice wall to lean on, though."

Boz takes a drink from the plastic sport bottle filled with his early-evening rum. "The old lady show up?"

"No, never. Just her lawyers. A dozen or so, sitting up front, watching the circus."

"Buncha clowns, all right. They oughta sell peanuts."

———

The circus revolved around a peculiar proposition made months before by Serenity Meredith Maas Bleak, Pete's mother-in-law and Carey's mother.

Serenity was reputed to be the richest person in Bleak Harbor, perhaps in all of western Michigan, heiress to the fortune handed down through the descendants of Joseph Estes Bleak, the pointy-nosed New Englander who'd come to a shore of dune and swamp on Lake Michigan, dredged a channel, carved out a bay, and erected a harbor that birthed a shipping yard, a timber mill, a daily newspaper, and a burg of sturdy churches and families. The early Bleaks went so far as to build a massive steelworks across the Indiana border.

The timber mill was long gone; the steelworks shut; the tugs and barges replaced by sailboats and twin-screw cruisers; the downtown a flowery haven of cobblestone streets dotted with boutiques and galleries, overpriced restaurants, shops selling flip-flops for a hundred dollars a pair, even a bookstore. The cobblestone, made from a synthetic version of concrete, had been laid only in the past decade over the old, chipped, authentic stuff.

"Quaint," the travel catalogues inevitably called Bleak Harbor. "The Southampton of the Midwest." It was "renovated" and "refreshed" and a place where many of those sturdy families no longer could afford to live. Once a home, now a summer way station for people who wanted little to do with each other unless alcohol was handy, and plenty of it.

The main remnants of the city's past were the local newspaper, the *Bleak Harbor Light*, and Serenity herself, widow of Jack Bleak, who had died of a heart attack last Thanksgiving. Serenity hadn't been seen in public since being diagnosed with terminal cancer not long after her husband's passing. Local gossips speculated the cancer was cervical, the consequence of her late husband's playing around. Others thought it had to be liver cancer from Serenity's years of quiet, disciplined drinking. Nobody—not even Carey—really knew.

In a one-page statement released by her lawyers, Serenity had offered the city, the township, and the surrounding county, upon her death, her entire estate, rumored to be worth $200 million to $300 million. But there was a catch that was tripping up the politicians. As Serenity undoubtedly had expected.

"You gotta hand it to her," Pete says. "It's kinda like she gets to watch her own funeral, all these guys fighting over her money."

Boz nods. "She loves to mess with people. Like when I was trying to get my liquor license. I ever tell you that story?"

"Fifty or sixty times."

"Yeah, yeah. If only I could pull up and get the hell out of here."

"Any bites yet?"

"Nah, you know, I don't wanna just give it away."

"Smart."

"So tell me—why does Carey give a damn about those meetings? She ain't getting any of that money. She and the old lady don't even talk, do they?"

"Not much. But it's family. I do as I'm told."

Jack Bleak's will left Carey and her brother, Bleak Harbor mayor Jonah Bleak, nothing but a few acres of duneland set so far back from the shore as to be worthless. Serenity's lawyers are contesting even that paucity.

The rift between Serenity and her children dates back so far that nobody can recall its specific origins, except that Serenity didn't feel her kids defended her amply enough against the many slights and embarrassments her wayward husband inflicted upon her. Pete never understood exactly what she'd expected Carey and her brother to do. Their father was an asshole. They had to live with it too.

The year-round residents of Bleak Harbor are well aware, via the grapevine, that Carey and Jonah have been zeroed out of the family estate. Because of the locals' barely disguised feelings of pity and schadenfreude, Carey defiantly attends every public meeting concerning the disposition of the estate, when she isn't stuck working in Chicago. Pete suspects she goes partly to demonstrate that her pride is intact but also in search of something even she isn't sure of, some idea that she did what she could to close the chasm between her and her parents, especially after it turned out that Danny was not the perfect grandson they believed was their right.

Boz grunts. "You know, those numb nuts are already spending her money. The township ordered a Humvee last week."

"Today the council was talking about getting surveillance cameras."

"Keeping up with the Joneses."

"And, of course, a helicopter. Gotta have a helicopter."

"Shitbags. What in God's name for?"

"Emergencies."

"Like some asswipe at the festival gets drunk and falls down?"

"Or maybe they get high."

"Noooo," Boz says, mugging. "How is business anyway?"

Pete looks into his drink, shakes his head. "That shop in New Buffalo is killing me."

"New Buffalo sucks anyway. What's going on?"

Pete glances around the bar. Though he's been in the medical marijuana business for almost a year, he still isn't quite used to the idea that it's legal. "Their stuff's good," he says. "Maybe a little too good. Not that anybody uses it just to get high."

"No way." Boz points at his bad leg. "Totally therapeutic."

"And they're selling it for pennies."

"Undercutting you? Hey, man, that's what I do to the bars here." He waves at the row of taps on the bar. "Three bucks for a Schlitz pint—can't beat it, baby."

"Yeah, well, their stuff's more like Heineken. Anyway, I've been working with a new supplier."

"Local guy?"

Pete immediately wishes he hadn't brought it up. He squints toward one of the TVs mounted over the back bar. "Cubs up? I can't see the tube down there."

Boz ambles over and peers at the screen. "They were ahead 6–1. Now it's 6–5, and the Giants got the bases loaded, nobody out in the eighth."

"That's what my Cubbies do."

"Another cocktail? You know, you can't fly home on one wing."

Truth is, Pete wouldn't mind another drink and another and another. But then Carey would know he'd had another shitty day at the pot shop.

"A light one," he says. "Going fishing in a while here."

———

Pete couldn't tell whether Danny was genuinely happy that they were going fishing that night. He had left his shop downtown around three, putting Dulcy in charge so he could check on Danny before going to the city council meeting. He'd found his stepson standing on the dock, hands folded into the curls atop his head, gazing into the water. The boy's laptop was open on a picnic table on the deck.

"Ready to go out tonight?" Pete said.

Danny didn't move at first, as if he hadn't heard; then he slowly turned around, hands still on his head, and said, "I will have the cooler and the bait ready."

"Good," Pete said. "Going to that meeting. Back around six. I love you."

Again, Danny didn't seem to hear. Then, as Pete was going through the glass double doors to the house, he heard Danny say, "Peter."

It was a little joke. Pete's real name was Andrew Michael Peters. "Pete" was the nickname almost everyone called him. Pete stopped and turned around. "Yeah?"

Danny was looking right at him. "I love you," he said. Not *I love you too*, like he was answering Pete. Just *I love you*. He didn't say it often, but Pete sure appreciated it when he did.

"I love you too, pal."

Danny appeared to consider that for a moment. Then he said, "That's good. Do you love my mom, Peter?"

"Do I love your mom?" Pete laughed. "Of course."

"That's also good. Do you think my mom loves you?"

Pete cocked his head. "Come on, pal. Why wouldn't she?"

Danny turned away then. "Look," he said, pointing. "That one has taken sixteen mosquitoes since noon."

Pete looked, grateful for the distraction. He couldn't find the dragonfly Danny saw.

"Wow," he said anyway. "That a record?"

Danny didn't respond. But conversations with Danny often ended abruptly. Pete didn't take offense.

"OK," Pete said. "We'll get us a pile of fish later."

They fished two or three evenings a week in summer, anchoring in the deep middle of the bay or, when the water wasn't too rough, out on the lake a quarter mile from the seawalls flanking the channel. Pete would plunk his line on the port side, Danny on the starboard. Sometimes they caught enough for dinner, sometimes not a single fish. It didn't seem to make a difference to the boy. He threw back everything he caught anyway.

In the past year, Danny had gotten this thing about perch. Pete figured it had something to do with the baby perch that swam beneath the dock where Danny spent much of his summer afternoons. He was mesmerized by those damn little fish. Sometimes he'd ease into the bay and stand as still as he could, legs apart, staring down into the water. Once Pete asked him what he was doing. Danny kept staring. Pete waited.

"I want them to swim through," Danny said.

"Through your legs?"

Danny nodded. "They're afraid."

"Afraid of what?"

"Afraid of everything."

Pete smiled. "How can a little tiny fish be afraid of anything but a big fish?"

"They're all alone. Where are their parents?"

"Out there, I hope," Pete said, pointing toward the lake. "Waiting for us to catch them."

But now, when they were out fishing, Danny didn't like hooking perch at all. He'd read that the lake perch, a docile species that simply submitted once a hook was set in its mouth, might not survive the ascent to the boat if it was more than sixty or seventy feet. It could drown. So Danny would be tossing a dead fish back into the lake. It was impossible to avoid, of course, but it bothered him anyway. "Drowning fish," he'd say. "Not optimal."

Still, Danny went out with him. Pete liked to think it was because the boy liked spending time together. Just before dark, the two of them would reel in their lines and sit in silence watching the sunset, a quivering ball of orange and scarlet plunging the day into the water. *Listen,*

Danny would say, and they'd both smile, waiting for an imaginary hiss of steam, hearing only the cries of gulls. *Maybe next time*, Danny would say.

———

Pete takes a swallow from his second vodka tonic. He sees his phone on the bar, decides not to check it again until he's outside. He glances at his watch. If he walks into the house in fifteen minutes, he and Danny can be out on the dock untying the boat when Carey arrives home from Chicago. They can wave goodbye from the water. He can tell her about the meeting later, before bed, hoping she's too tired to ask about the pot shop. She might even be asleep by the time he and Danny get back.

"Closing early tonight?"

"Festival's on—deck closes at six," Boz says. He's never liked the festival, partly because it lures customers away, partly because he loathes anything involving "foreigners," as he refers to out-of-towners. Even though he's from out of town. Every year at festival time, Boz shuts his porch before nightfall and draws the shades so neither he nor his regulars can see the fool goings-on across the bay.

"I'll be out on the lake with Danny," Pete says.

"How's he doing?"

"Good. He's a good kid. Most of the time," Pete says.

"Hey, he's a teenager. Hormones."

That too, Pete thinks. The truth is, he doesn't always feel worthy of his stepson. Sometimes he wonders if Danny sees him less as a stepdad than a lovable fuckup of an older brother.

Boz nods toward the bay. "Saw him out on the beach just today."

The phone on the wall behind the bar starts ringing.

"Yeah? He talk to you?"

"A little—hang on." Boz twists to grab the phone. "Boz's Bar and— whoa, slow down there. OK, hold on."

Boz presses the receiver against his Hawaiian shirt and mouths the word *wifey*. Carey is calling Boz's landline because Pete didn't answer his cell. Jesus.

"Gimme," Pete says. He takes another swig of his drink as Boz passes him the phone. The cord isn't long enough, so Pete has to step up on the footrail and lean across the bar.

"Hey," he says. "You're early."

"You're not."

"I went to your—the meeting. Did you have a good day?"

"Fine. What happened at the meeting?"

"Not much. A lot of talk. No actual votes."

"Did Jonah make it?"

"He was wielding the mayor's gavel."

"How long have you been at the bar?"

"Just got here."

"And?"

"And I'm just leaving."

"Right."

Pete hears something thud on the great-room table at home, probably Carey's purse.

"Did you let her go?" Carey says.

"Did I what?"

"Dulcy. You said you were going to fire her."

"Tomorrow. I had to go to the meeting, and I couldn't just close up. That's a good part of the day."

"Uh-huh. Is Danny with you?"

"No. He's there."

"I don't see him."

"When I left for the meeting, he was out on the dock in one of his trances. Is his laptop out there?"

"Hold on. Yes. On the picnic table. Open."

"Good thing it didn't rain. What about the cooler? That ready?"

"Your precious cooler is here on the snack bar."

"So he's ready for fishing. Maybe he went for a walk."

"Why couldn't you have just come straight home?"

"I stopped for one," Pete says. He tries to bend away from Boz, who is pretending not to eavesdrop, but the phone cord won't stretch that far. "I went to the meeting. I could've taken Danny, but that might not have turned out so good."

He hears her sigh. He tells himself Carey means well. She's been under a lot of stress. She doesn't love her job at Pressman Logistics, especially lately. She certainly doesn't love the commute. Sometimes he wonders what she does love, besides Danny.

Do you think my mom loves you? he hears Danny say.

"So you're coming home now?"

"Yep." He waves at Boz. "Just settling up."

Carey hangs up. Pete hands the phone over.

"Everything OK?" Boz says.

"Who knows?"

"Bring me some fillets."

———

Outside, Pete starts up the rise to the road that encircles the bay, then changes his mind and lopes down past Boz's patio, peering down the crescent of pebbled sand bending toward his house. *Danny's gotta be there somewhere*, he thinks. *He was going to have the bait and cooler ready.*

Pete's flip-flop straps dig into the gap between his toes as he trudges. Across the bay, off-key voices warble "Peaceful Easy Feeling." Pete turns to see the broad decks outside the bars and restaurants, the pastel blue and pink umbrellas, the shapes of people drinking and laughing in the early-evening sun. Few of them live there year-round. Most are from

Chicago or Detroit, two hundred miles to the east, even Indianapolis, a bit farther to the south, and spend summers in Bleak Harbor.

From here, Pete can see his cottage. The rear half is shielded by the supposedly soundproof fencing Carey insisted on installing after some trouble with Danny. The boat is still covered. Danny usually has the tarp folded on the dock by now.

A hundred yards from the house, Pete stops and checks his phone. No new messages, but he rereads the text he saw as he was leaving city hall:

hows the fam?

Something like rubber bands grips his belly. He feels angry, then helpless, then angrier still for feeling helpless. The text came from a phone number he doesn't recognize, an area code he's never heard of. He searched it online, came up with codes in Cuba and Canada.

hows the fam? the text says.

The fam's fine, motherfucker, Pete thinks. *Why don't you stick to business, leave me and my family the hell alone?*

He looks up from the phone and sees Carey standing on the deck in her business suit, silk scarf bunched at her neck, arms folded, eyes on Pete. Those big green eyes that swallowed him whole when he first saw her sitting on a packed Chicago city bus a decade ago.

"Aren't you going to offer me your seat?" he'd said then, grinning. Carey had looked at him like he was a panhandler with sewer breath.

"Excuse me?"

"Your seat. I'm standing here, and I'm way older than you."

It had taken her a minute, but she had smiled, a little, trying to hide it, and Pete had put up his hands like he hadn't really wanted the seat anyway, just as the bus lurched to a stop, pitching him backward over a massive woman in a wheelchair.

That's how he and Carey had gotten started, with him apologizing to the annoyed woman and Carey with a hand over her mouth as she tried not to laugh, saying, "I guess you got your seat."

She's not smiling or laughing now. Pete deletes the text before dropping the phone back into his pocket.

"Hey," he calls out, waving.

4

Carey watches Pete pause to mess with his phone. She counts as he stands there: three seconds, seven, eleven. *Come on*, she thinks. *Get your ass home.*

He pockets his phone and starts walking again, waving at her, calling out. She doesn't wave or shout back. His cargo shorts sag on his skinny waist. He needs a shave and a T-shirt without a hole in an armpit. She imagines him showing up at Pressman Logistics looking as he does, how the receptionist would assume he was a bicycle courier.

She takes out her phone, deletes the texts she read in the car, then remembers the one that swooped in when the phone was on the floor. She can't find it. She's sure she heard it come in, but there's nothing to see. Then, as she's holding the phone in one hand, a fresh text pops up, from a number she doesn't recognize. Working for a logistics company, Carey knows plenty of area codes by heart, but she can't recall what place this one might be attached to. She opens the text. It's blank. No words, no pictures, nothing. She closes and opens it again. Still there's only an empty window. Probably a wrong number.

Pete comes up the four steps to the deck. He's grinning that effortless grin and pushing back the unruly salt-and-pepper mane.

"How was the commute?" he says.

"Fine until I hit Michigan. Some idiot ran out of gas, so of course the state cops had to block an entire lane."

"That sucks." Pete leans down to kiss her cheek.

"I appreciate you going to the meeting, but I wish you'd come straight home," she says.

"Sorry."

"It's late in the day and—"

"I know, I know, sorry. Danny's not here yet?"

"No. And he didn't leave a note. He knows he's supposed to."

"Sometimes he forgets stuff."

"Selectively. Where was he when you left?"

"I told you, right out there." Pete motions toward the dock. A minnow bucket dangles from a piling into the water. "Maybe he's at the library."

"No. Library's closed for festival parking. I called his phone when I got home and heard it ringing out here."

"Huh. You check for his meds?"

When Danny disappeared two months ago, he'd taken his prescription drugs with him. It was at once a relief and a fright to Carey. He could last awhile on his own if he had his meds. Without them, there was no telling what he might do.

"Yes," she says. "They're on his nightstand."

"And his chair's there by the window where he waits for me. So it's all good. He would've taken the drugs and the phone if . . . you know. Like I said, he probably just went for a walk."

"He would've taken his phone."

"Not necessarily."

"He doesn't miss fishing, Pete. It's burned into his schedule like brushing his teeth at eight fifteen. If you say you're going and you don't go, he throws a fit—you know that."

It pains Carey to say that, because she isn't always on Danny's schedule anymore. Not like Pete with the fishing. Her overnights in Chicago have disrupted their daily time together. She has rationalized that she can't help it, they need her income until Pete gets the pot business going. But she hates herself for it anyway.

34

"Sorry," is all Pete says, and she hates herself for that too, that sorry is all he ever seems to say.

———

One afternoon a few weeks ago, she came home after being gone for two days and poured glasses of iced tea with orange slices and asked Danny to bring the Wallace Stevens collection out to the deck. He was in the kitchen assembling the cooler for fishing.

"Never mind," he said. "It's going to rain."

Carey looked through the glass doors facing the beach and saw the southwestern sky churning purple and gray. "So we'll bring the chairs under the eaves. Or we can sit at the table with the umbrella."

"Poems aren't good at that table," Danny said. He was fitting Pete's cans of Old Style into the cooler with the labels facing up, one can one way, the next the other.

"Honey."

"I told you, I'm not 'honey' anymore."

It raked at Carey's heart. He'd said it before, but without so much conviction. She couldn't help but call him honey. Honey was the color of his eyebrows and the hairs on his forearms.

"Danny, if it's going to rain, why are you packing the cooler?"

He looked up from the cooler and gave her one of those stares that made her feel as if he were looking into her skull, reading words streaming across the front of her brain.

"The rain's not going to last *that* long."

"So you don't want to read poems today."

"Maybe not."

"*Maybe* not?"

Danny used his fist to tap the cooler lid into place.

"Not."

Carey turned away and gulped the rest of her iced tea, letting the sorrow drip down with the drink. She knew not to press it. Instead she went to the liquor cabinet and refilled her glass with vodka and went out to the deck alone as the sky began to spit, letting the first drops prick her forehead and cheeks.

———

Now Pete is telling her that maybe Danny has just gotten a little off schedule, that he'll probably come strolling in any minute. His words float around her head as she turns away toward the bay.

The sun beams through a crooked break in the cumulus towering over the hills of trees and sand across the water. Her family's mansion perches atop the bluff that separates the heart of town from Lake Michigan. The people of Bleak Harbor who aren't Bleaks can access the lake only by taking a boat along the serpentine channel out of the bay, or a car to the public beaches beyond the channel, as if they aren't worthy of having the sand and surf at their feet.

One of the pink turrets on each of the mansion's four corners juts up through the green. Carey slept in a bedroom in that turret as a girl. She hears a mewling pop song floating across the bay, the clanking of sail cables against masts in the evening breeze.

"He's not going fishing tonight," she tells Pete.

"You're punishing him? Come on."

"Call it whatever you like." She goes to the picnic table and gathers up Danny's laptop and phone. "He has to learn he can't just leave us hanging like this. He knows what he's doing."

"Look, how's about I get you a drink? When he gets home, we'll have a talk with him."

"You just want to go fishing so you can get the hell out of here and not have to explain why you didn't fire Dulcy."

"For Christ's sake, Care."

She slides the glass door aside and steps into the house. She sets Danny's laptop and phone on the kitchen island and kicks her heels off. Seeing them askew on the hardwood floor, she sees them again on the floor of Randall Pressman's condo kitchen, where he first pressed her back against the counter and kissed her. Her stomach turns.

Danny, she thinks. *Just come home, honey, and everything will be all right.*

5

Malone stares into her bedroom wall mirror, tucking the royal-blue button-down into her navy trousers for the fourth or fifth time. She wants it smooth and tight all the way around her waist before she straps on her gun belt, but the tail keeps bagging out above her hips. It looks sloppy, unprofessional.

She's lost too much weight since she last wore the uniform, probably should have asked the department for a new one. Probably shouldn't have subsisted for a year on 7-Eleven coffee and Cheez-Its. The not sleeping, the sitting up watching *Friends* reruns, the listening to her house creak and groan. Maybe should have just quit.

"Whatever," she says, stepping away from the mirror. Nobody's listening. She has been alone in the house for fourteen months, two weeks, four days. The particular hour of her young daughter's death passed fifty-seven minutes ago, while Malone was sitting on her bed, trying not to stare at the photographs crowding her dresser and deciding whether to even put the police uniform on.

Her phone rings in the kitchen. Radovich again. The chief has been good about the whole thing, let her take the extra leave of absence, stopped at the house now and then to see how she was doing. She really did appreciate it, even if sometimes she ignored Radovich's calls or sat still and quiet in the bathroom when he knocked at her back door.

She wishes he'd waited just one more week to ask her to return. "Gotta get back on that horse," he'd said again and again. She knows what he meant, and he meant well. She also knows he needs every cop he can find for the Dragonfly Festival.

Already the RVs with the out-of-state license plates are lining up on the Blue Star Highway along the lake south of town, the drivers waiting in traffic with cocktails hidden between their legs. Already the downtown pubs have their YOU CAN'T DRINK ALL DAY IF YOU DON'T START IN THE MORNING banners up. Already the cruisers and speedboats from Chicago and Milwaukee and Traverse City are swarming the harbor.

She has the midnight shift, 11:00 p.m. to 7:00 a.m., though Radovich asked her to come in a few hours early to get reacclimated. She'd requested the night duty, though it's a toss-up as to whether it's worse patrolling in the sticky heat—tomorrow's supposed to hit ninety-four, with 99 percent humidity—or dealing with late-night out-of-towners who've spent nine hours in the beer tent. She just wants to get off work in time to make her dawn cemetery visit.

Her phone is ringing again. She goes to the kitchen, picks it up, hesitates, then finally says, "Chief?"

"How are you?"

"Fine."

Radovich has been chief since Malone was in high school. Maybe grade school. He's ready to retire but still has two of his seven kids to put through college. His cheeks look pinker and baggier now than they did a year ago.

"I hate to do this," the chief says. "But listen, do you mind coming in right away? I got a heckuva mess on my hands already. Goddamn festival. Tell me, Katya, who frigging cares about dragonflies anyway?"

She's staring at her Bleak Harbor Police hat resting upside down on the table. It brings back a memory of herself, sitting in her uncle Smitty's lap, wearing his Chicago police hat, which brings another memory, of Louisa dancing around in the shade of the beach gazebo on her seventh birthday, wearing Malone's police hat.

"Katya?"

"Sorry, Chief. Sure. Of course. I guess so."

"Crazy stuff's going on, and the festival hasn't even started yet. Somebody got into the bars' sound systems, and they're all playing the same song over and over, and nobody can stop it. Some frigging Eagles tune."

Malone doesn't care. She picks up her hat, lifts her car keys from a hook next to the fridge, closes her eyes. "Ten minutes," she says.

6

The sun is gone. Pete and Carey sit in the adirondacks overlooking their beach, Pete on his fourth Old Style; Carey, her second scotch rocks.

They haven't said a word in an hour.

The cooler sits at Pete's feet. He went through it hoping for a clue as to where his stepson might have gone. He found the two salami-and-cheese sandwiches, the pop and beer, the bag of pretzels neatly packed around the plastic container of worms. At the near end of the dock, a bait bucket is filled with fresh, wriggling minnows. Two fishing poles lean against a bench. Danny must have untangled the line that had knotted when he hooked a bullhead two nights before. The boy had done everything he always did to prepare for fishing.

Carey gets up from her chair and flings the last of her drink at the beach. A moist smear on her left cheek glistens in the moonlight. She sees her phone move on the deck, picks it up.

"Goddamn it," she says.

"What?"

"This is the third text I've gotten that has nothing in it. I keep thinking it might be Danny, and then I pick it up, and there's nothing there."

Pete feels his Adam's apple bounce up to the back of his mouth. He swallows. "Who are they from?"

"I have no idea."

She shows him her phone. He sees the number, the same odd area code as hows the fam?, and a shock of heat radiates from the base of his neck through his shoulders down into his arms. "Should I call the police?"

"They were useless last time, remember?"

"What else are we going to do? It's dark. Danny could get lost. He could get hit by a car. Lots of drunks—"

"Don't talk like that, Pete."

His phone beeps on his armrest. Carey leans in to see, pulling hair away from her face. "Is it Danny?"

"He doesn't have his phone, remember?" Pete snatches the phone up and holds it close to his face. He hopes Carey can't see the tremble he feels in his fingers. There's a new text:

alarmed?

"What is it?" Carey says.

"This—just this guy."

"What guy?"

Pete deletes the text with a swipe of his thumb. "Some typical rich Bleak Harbor jag-off. Thinks I'm a twenty-four-seven dope-vending machine. Got his card because he has a sore shoulder from riding his Jet Ski six hours a day." Pete stands, feels faint, briefly holds himself still. "Want anything while I'm up?"

Carey turns away. "I want my son."

———

In the kitchen dark, Pete stares into the open fridge.

alarmed?

It seems too pricey a word for the person he suspects is harassing him. Why not *afraid* or, better, *scared shitless*? Pete is those, for sure. He turns to the window on the back door, hoping Danny will be there, smiling in at him. There's only the faint amber glow of a streetlamp on the bay road.

"Shit shit shit," he whispers. He thrusts his head deeper into the fridge and sucks in the cold, trying to calm himself. His family might be in danger, and it could be his fault, a poor choice he made, one questionable judgment. He'd made it with good intentions, but that makes little difference now.

He straightens, willing his heart to beat slower. He pulls the freezer door open. Inside is a lavender-and-white box from Kate's Kakes holding the strawberry cream pie Pete picked up for Danny's birthday celebration. Staring at it helps to calm him down. He closes the freezer.

When this is over, he tells himself, when Danny comes home as if nothing happened, as if he just went for a stroll nobody should have worried about, then Pete will take Carey aside and tell her everything, tell her he went a little too far, took too big of a risk, and he'll never do it again—he'll shut the damn pot shop down if she wants, and they can go back to Chicago and figure things out.

It makes him feel better. He grabs a can of Old Style from the fridge, snaps the tab back, takes a long gulp standing in the fridge light. Wherever Danny is probably has nothing to do with this asshole on his phone. He takes another pull of beer. "OK," he says.

He goes back outside. Carey is standing at the deck railing, staring out at the water. Pete regards his wife silhouetted against the softening sky. The ringlets of hair on her shoulders sometimes remind him of Danny. He wants to wrap his arms around her, but he doesn't want to feel her twist away from him.

"What do you want to do?" he says. "Did you check his room?"

"I glanced in to make sure he wasn't there. But I haven't—no. I haven't really looked yet."

Pete steps close enough to touch her, without touching her. "I suppose he'd probably walk in when you were in there and be all pissed off."

"I don't care if he's pissed off. It's going on eleven. I'm pissed off."

"You don't think this is still about Paddle, do you?"

"I hope—oh Jesus."

"What?"

She's looking at her phone. "What the hell is this?"

"Danny?" Pete says.

Carey twists her phone around her neck for Pete to see. There's a new text, this one with a photograph. A hard-backed chair stands in a pool of shadow. On the seat is an object the color of dull silver. Maybe a roll of tape.

Pete hears his heart start to thump again. "A chair? Who's sending you pictures of a chair?"

She turns to face him now. Her eyes are filled with fright. It gives him a start. "How the hell do I know? What's that thing on the chair?"

Pete takes the phone, squints at it. "Can't tell. Maybe it's"—he starts to say *somebody's idea of a sick joke* but changes his mind—"some kind of hacker or something."

"Gimme." Carey takes her phone back. "What's going on around here?"

"Maybe we should call the police," Pete says. It comes out half-heartedly. The cops might ask questions he'd prefer they didn't.

"Wait," Carey says, pressing the phone into his chest. "Just wait." She rushes past him and into the house.

"Carey. What—I'm going to call."

"Just wait."

"What are you doing?"

"Where are my sneakers?"

"Care."

"Where are my goddamn sneakers?"

7

The last time Danny left, it was about Paddle.

In early April, Carey stood next to Danny beside the foam-padded table in Dr. Torrent's examination room, Paddle lying on his side, groggy with sedation. Pete watched from the other side of the table. It was their sixth or seventh visit to the vet's since Christmas, none of them routine.

Dr. Torrent explained that the cancer had moved to Paddle's liver. She said he was in constant pain, although he would never show it because dogs so craved approval. *Like boys*, Carey thought. Danny kept his eyes closed as Dr. Torrent spoke. Carey recalled how nice he'd been to the vet when she first started diagnosing Paddle's illness, trying to make eye contact and smile, as if he could charm her into a positive verdict.

Now she said she could fix Paddle, but only for a short while. "I'm afraid a cure is not a realistic possibility," she said. Danny leaned toward Paddle, and Carey stared at the back of his head, imagining his brain at work. He had told her recently that, by his rough calculation, the many doctors in his life were no more than 62 percent sure of anything they said. "Which leaves considerable room for error," he had said. Even when it became clear that their assessments were off, they never admitted they'd been wrong. "There are always 'unforeseen circumstances' or 'uncertainties,'" Danny had said. "How convenient those are."

Carey remembered bringing the little dachshund with the floppy ears home to their Chicago apartment on Danny's sixth birthday. Each morning, Danny would descend the stairs with Paddle in his arms, turn onto Madison Street, and walk exactly two hundred steps to the café, where he waved through the window at the pretty young women making lattes. Paddle would rear up on his hind legs, smudging his wet nose on the glass as Carey watched from the corner.

Likewise, in Bleak Harbor, the first thing Danny did each day was take Paddle for a walk on the beach, exactly two hundred steps out, returning in the footsteps he'd left in the sand or snow. Paddle would curl up on Danny's feet while he washed his face and brushed his teeth; then Danny would share three level tablespoons of his CoCo Wheats with the dog.

Carey had to admit to some envy at Paddle's seeming ability to translate with ease Danny's sometimes frustrated, sometimes frustrating efforts to make himself understood. With a nod or a look or a shift of his shoulder that meant little to his mother or stepfather, Danny could make Paddle jump into his lap or go scuttling off in search of one of his fuzz-worn tennis balls. Paddle seemed to know intuitively when Danny was ready to play and when Danny needed to be left alone. She wished her son could be so simpatico with another boy or girl.

Paddle had begun to have trouble walking in January, started dragging his hind legs in February. Danny had had to carry him on their morning walks, help him up and down the steps to the beach. "I like it," he'd said. "He keeps me warm." He'd cleaned up Paddle's diarrhea without a word, swabbed the dog's chafed butt with baby wipes he'd bought himself at Meijer. Carey bought Paddle a bright-red coat that made him look like the dog in the Grinch cartoon. That made Danny smile.

Now Dr. Torrent laid a hand on Paddle's hindquarters and said he had only weeks to live, "Unless, of course, you choose to graciously put him out of his suffering."

Carey saw Danny wince before opening his eyes. She moved toward him, but he raised a hand to ward her off.

"Paddle does not want to be graciously killed," Danny said. "We will take whatever time Paddle has left."

"I understand," Dr. Torrent said. "As I'm sure your parents do. But it isn't that simple. You see . . ."

Carey wasn't listening but watching Danny watching the vet. She knew he was staring at the beauty mark on Dr. Torrent's left cheek. He'd told her how fetching he found it, how it subtly and beautifully disrupted the symmetry of her face. "Is that the only reason you like it?" Carey had asked him then, suspecting there was something else, and when he didn't answer, she'd said, "Don't stare at it, Danny; it will make her uncomfortable," and her son's knowing smile, his eyes averted, answered her question.

Now Dr. Torrent asked Danny to step outside. "I just need a few moments to discuss this with your parents," she said.

"Do you have children?" Danny said.

He knew Dr. Torrent had three children. He had shown them to Carey on Facebook.

"Why, yes, I do," Dr. Torrent said. "Two sons and a daughter."

"Are they perfect?"

"Danny," Pete said, "this really isn't appropriate."

Carey looked at her son. "Danny," she said, "you're perfect."

Danny ignored them. "You live in Saint Joseph, right? With all the rich Whirlpool executives. Your husband is a rich Whirlpool executive."

"I think we should talk about your dog," Dr. Torrent said.

"Paddle. Your commute is approximately fourteen miles then. Maybe twenty or thirty minutes, depending on traffic?"

"OK, Danny, that's enough," Pete said.

"That's about right." Dr. Torrent tried on a patient smile. "Now—"

"So you never leave your three children alone for long."

"Jeez oh pete, Danny." Pete came around behind his stepson. "Come on—let's go."

As Pete gripped Danny's elbow, Carey saw Danny tense and worried for an instant that he might wheel around and take a swing at Pete. Instead Danny just yanked his arm away.

"It's my dog," he said. "I take care of him—you don't."

"Honey."

"I'm not 'honey.' I am fifteen."

He swiped Dr. Torrent's hand away from Paddle. She moved back, clutching the hand he'd touched. "Paddle," he said. "It's Danny. I'm here."

The dachshund lifted his head, one ear flapping over an eye. His hind legs shifted. His head dropped back to the table. The doctor started to say something, but Danny cut her off.

"Shut up."

"Danny," Carey said.

He looked at Pete, then Carey, then at the door. "She is no oncologist," he told the door. "She doesn't have a single oncology degree on the wall in her office."

"I'm sorry, son. I am certified—"

Danny turned to the vet. "You didn't do a biopsy?"

Dr. Torrent's eyebrows hitched up just enough to suggest the question surprised her. "It wasn't necessary."

"How so?"

Carey slid between them. "I'm sorry, Doctor," she said. "Danny, it's time to go."

"No, it's all right," the vet said. But Carey could hear the trill of annoyance in her voice, how it really wasn't all right. "Danny, the dysplasia—I'm sorry, that's like a change in—"

"I know what it is. Even a kid like me can use Google."

That stopped her for a second. Carey could see that she'd had enough of Danny and that that was perfectly fine with him. "Anyway," Dr. Torrent continued, "the dysplasia was so extreme that further tests weren't indicated. He—Paddle—has liver cancer; there's no doubt about that."

"But there's doubt about what's next, isn't there?"

Dr. Torrent shoved her hands into her smock pockets. "There is almost never certainty."

Danny stood looking at her for a long moment; then he bent and kissed Paddle on the head and left the room, brushing Carey's hand off his shoulder.

———

The next morning, Carey sat Danny down. Paddle was lying in Danny's bed, where he'd slept for one of the last times. She told Danny that, although there were things the vet could do to make Paddle more comfortable, they were not cheap. "Some things are meant to be," she said, knowing as the words left her mouth that they were bullshit and Danny would hate her for it.

Paddle's last vet appointment came three days later. Danny cradled the dachshund in his arms as Dr. Torrent gave him the shot. "Pads," Danny whispered, rocking back and forth as he wept. "Pads. Pads. Pads." The dog went limp. Carey and Pete gathered Danny into an embrace. "No," he said, wriggling free.

At home, he locked himself in his room. For three days, he refused to come out or eat or bathe. He emerged the fourth morning and brushed his teeth and ate his CoCo Wheats at the usual times. Carey and Pete thought he'd come around. That afternoon, he went for a walk. He didn't come home.

Pete was at dinner with one of his weed suppliers. He wasn't answering his phone. At ten o'clock, Carey called the police. The dispatcher told her to call back when her son had been missing for twenty-four hours.

"Tell you what," she replied, loathing what she was about to say, "in twenty-four seconds, I will be on the phone to Serenity Bleak. You sound young, so if you don't know who that is, ask the chief."

She had no desire to involve her mother, nor did she believe her mother would care to be involved. But within minutes, two bored-looking men, one quite a bit younger than the other, materialized at her door. The older one, in a police uniform, asked her a series of perfunctory questions about when she and Pete had last seen Danny, whether he used a phone, who else he might know nearby, Pete's place of work, hers. The other one, wearing a polo shirt, belly straining at his khakis, scribbled with a ballpoint in a small notebook. When the uniform finished, the pudgy one said, "Can I ask you something, ma'am?"

"You just did."

"Yes, ma'am. I'm sorry to ask this, but—"

Carey knew what was coming. "No, you're not."

"Excuse me?"

"What do you want?"

Fatso is out of his league, she thought.

"Uh, I just—you and Dan didn't—"

"Danny."

"Of course. You and Danny didn't have an argument or anything like that earlier today, did you?"

"Anything like what? Who are you, anyway? Where's your uniform?"

"I'm sorry, ma'am; I thought I said. Will Northwood. I'm a—"

The uniform interrupted. "Will's kind of a plainclothes guy, Ms. Bleak."

"Peters."

"Peters. Yes, apologies. We're short-staffed."

"What's your question, Will?" She pointed past them. "You want to know why we put that fence up? Is that it? Spit it out."

Carey had heard echoes of the vile rumors around town, the whispers of screams coming from the house. Danny's tantrums invariably involved screaming. His screams had gotten louder as puberty arrived, or so she believed. Sometimes she thought he amplified his shrieks to embarrass her. Then she felt guilty for thinking it.

He had thrown a fit a few weeks before in the frozen foods section at Meijer. It was ostensibly over Carey's refusal to buy chocolate chip mint ice cream that contained casein, something his doctors said contributed to autism. Danny had never made such a scene about ice cream before, so she assumed he was really reacting to Paddle's deteriorating condition. It was clear, she thought, that he wanted his flip out to be public and he wanted to draw his mother in. So she had stood and watched in arms-folded silence as he emptied a freezer case of its Popsicles, scattering them across the floor while other mothers furtively pulled out their phones. Later, Carey forced herself to watch some of the videos the bitches posted online.

"Sorry, ma'am. I'll take that as a no," Will told her.

"It is a no," Carey said. "He's a fifteen-year-old boy. He doesn't agree with every single thing his parents tell him."

"It's just routine, Ms. Peters," the uniform said. "Do you have any idea where your son might have gone?"

She didn't, at least not then. The uniform and the chubby guy left. Carey stood out on the deck watching cop flashers flicker across the bay, waiting for Pete to call, hoping to God her mother wouldn't find out. Her brother, Jonah, called, asking if he could help. Carey told him thanks, but it would be better if he stayed away for now. That's when her mother beeped in.

"Carey, is that you?"

"Mother." Carey imagined Serenity Bleak lying in bed with a TV remote in one hand, a half-full glass in the other, cubes clinking.

"What is the matter with that boy now?"

"His name is Danny."

"Tell me, dear, why am I seeing our family's good name on the eleven o'clock news?"

"Feel free to turn it off."

"Why is Daniel wandering around in the middle of the night? If you can't keep track of your son, then perhaps he needs to be somewhere professionals can."

"You're slurring your words, Mother."

"It will keep him safe from the world."

"That's a big help. Thank you."

"You are in denial, dear. You need to get out of denial."

"You are certainly an expert in that. Good night."

It was the first time Carey and Serenity had spoken in months, and they had not talked since.

Around midnight, Carey was out scanning the beach again when she recalled how Danny had once remarked that he didn't like seeing the old Helliker place next door shut up and abandoned, how he wished he could go in and open windows to let it breathe. "No," she said aloud. Then she walked down to the dock and looked back at the Helliker house.

Curtains were fluttering in two open windows.

Ten minutes later, she found Danny curled into a paint tarp in a corner of the house's basement, asleep. He looked like a little boy again as she knelt over him, holding her breath against the odor of turpentine. He came awake as if she had roused him in his own bed. "Oh," he said, then broke free of her embrace, bounded up the stairs, out of the Helliker house, and around the security fence into his own house, where he locked himself in his bedroom until morning.

Pete finally appeared just after 1:00 a.m., stoned, apologetic, insisting his phone had run out of power. Carey dragged him out to the end of the dock, where she hoped Danny couldn't hear her telling her husband that she could not do this alone now that he was fifteen and able to do enough on his own to get himself in real trouble. Pete, as always, had nothing to say but sorry, he would try to do better.

8

Carey jogs up the driveway toward the bay road, around the far end of the security fence, then back down the driveway next door through dandelions and quack grass jutting up through ruts in the asphalt.

She despises the fence even though, or maybe because, she's the one who insisted on having it built, to keep the neighbors from hearing Danny's tantrums. She hears Pete call out as he rounds the end of the fence: "Carey. What the hell? He won't be there again."

The Helliker house is empty. Streaks of tar-black mold mar the siding. Screens on the wraparound porch are shearing away from their frames. There are gouges in the shingled roof and shattered windows in the clapboard walls.

The house was probably built in the 1940s or '50s, like a lot of the houses on this side of the bay, weekend getaways for the steelworkers then employed at the Bleak plant across the border in Indiana and other blue-collar laborers. The bank had reclaimed the house after the owner, a Chevy plant manager named Helliker, lost his job and stopped making payments. In town, of course, the rich rabble delighted in tales of a fractious divorce and the Helliker children taking sides. That's how those rubberneckers were.

After Danny's earlier escape, Carey had paid a locksmith triple his usual fee to fashion her a key to the Helliker house's back door. Just in case. Now she locates the key where she hung it on a withered forsythia near the porch. She swings the screen door open, unlocks the inner door, steps inside, and throws the deadbolt to lock it behind her.

She steps into the kitchen, and her nostrils fill with the reek of mildewed blinds and drywall rot. She remembers coming here the night Danny last disappeared. She'd used a rock to break the door's window and gashed her thumb as she reached in to undo the lock. She recalls how panicked she'd felt, how angry, how guilty for feeling such anger toward her son.

She hears Pete twist the doorknob. He bangs on the repaired window. "Carey," he says. "Let me in."

"Why don't you go down to the bar?"

"Seriously?"

Her phone vibrates in her pocket. She pulls it out. There's a text from Pressman:

think about what youre doing, C. it's your family. u have time.

She starts to type a reply—*you are the one running out of time*—but stops herself, thinking she does in fact have time—let him sweat for now. She turns and unlocks the door. Pete pushes it open.

"What are you doing?" he says. "We're in this together."

Carey ignores him. Using her phone as a flashlight, she steps across bubbled linoleum through the kitchen into the living room. Sheets of particleboard cover windows facing the bay. Cable wires snake out from a wall where a television once was mounted. The indoor-outdoor carpet is furrowed with tracks of the oven and water heater the Hellikers hauled out hours before the sheriff showed up with the foreclosure notice.

Carey stops and listens, as she did the last time she was here, swearing she can hear something in the walls, chipmunks or cockroaches or mice.

"Danny?" she calls into the gloom. "Where are you, honey?"

"He's not gonna answer to 'honey.'"

"Just shut up."

"Please don't tell me to shut up," he says.

As Carey shines her way through the shadows, the realization buried in the back of her mind pushes forward like a light cutting through dark: her husband, however charming and well meaning and even, on occasion, intelligent, is essentially unnecessary.

Yes, he's good for the fishing with Danny, the jabbering about the Cubs. But she has had to reluctantly conclude that he'll never be much good at the real work of bringing up her special boy. Pete, alas, is too much a boy himself, a six-foot-five-inch boy of thirty-nine, and not a terribly special one.

"Why don't you go down the hall and check the bedrooms?" she says.

Pete is her mistake. He is, at the core, a decent man, a better one than any others she was with before or after Danny, certainly better than Danny's birth father, whom Carey hasn't seen in years. She'd said yes to Pete for reasons that seemed at the time like the right ones, or at least the most convenient ones. She knows he will be heartbroken when she finally leaves with his stepson. It will pain her too, to a point, but the ache will fade in time, and she will be left with a new life with Danny. She just needs the money and the space to start it.

"He's not in the bedrooms," Pete says. He emerges from a hallway into the living room, where Carey is closing a closet door. "Do you really think he'd come back here again?"

"Here," she says, angling her phone up so it illuminates the ceiling. "Pretty sure that's a ladder."

Pete aims his phone's glow upward. Two sheets of mottled plywood are nailed haphazardly around a pull-down door to an attic. He goes into the kitchen and returns with a chair, which he places beneath the hatch. "Hold this steady, OK?" Carey grips the chairback with both hands. Pete steps up and reaches over his head for the handle to the door. He pulls. Nothing happens.

"It's stuck."

"Pull harder. Here, let me."

Pete uses both hands this time. "Damn old cottages," he says just as the hatch door attached to a fold-up ladder tears away from the ceiling and comes crashing down. He keeps it from hitting him or Carey by swinging it out to his left as the chair keels out of Carey's grasp. Pete pitches onto the floor, landing on his elbows and knees in a cloud of drywall dust.

"Sonofabitch," he says, blinking white shreds from his eyes.

"You OK?"

"Shit." He looks up. "Whoa."

Carey twists around to see the ragged hole in the ceiling and another hole shorn in the roof above, a crescent moon shining in its middle. "Come on," she says.

She turns and goes to the basement door. She raps on it a few times, hoping Danny will hear.

"I'll go down," Pete says.

Carey tries the door. The knob turns, but the door seems trapped on the jamb. "Danny, it's OK," she shouts. "I'm here."

"Let me in there."

"Get away."

"Carey."

She steps back. "Just do it. I'll go down."

Pete tries the door. "Wood probably warped in the heat." He wraps both hands around the doorknob, leans back on his haunches, and pulls. The door groans, budging a quarter of an inch. Pete stands, muttering under his breath, squats, and pulls again. Just as the door jerks open, a high-pitched squeal begins blaring from somewhere in the house.

"What the hell?" Carey covers her ears.

"An alarm? What the shit for?"

Carey starts down the stairway, right hand on the railing, her lit phone shoved out in front of her. The dead air scrapes at the back of her throat. She hears a phone ringing beneath the squealing house alarm.

"Danny, are you down here?" she yells. "Danny! Honey!"

"Carey, we gotta get out of here."

She trips on the bottom stairstep and slams into the concrete floor, feeling skin on her kneecap shred. "Danny, where are you? Please."

Pete scrabbles past her. "Look right. I'll go left—hurry. I think I heard a police siren."

They bustle around the basement, throwing open closet doors, rummaging through a pile of blankets, looking behind a furnace the Hellikers didn't take. Danny is nowhere.

"He isn't here," Carey says. "Damn it."

"Should we just wait for the police?"

"That's all we need. Come on—let's get out of here."

She bounds up the stairs, Pete behind her. As they go out the door they entered through, she sees police lights in the sky over the bay road. "This way," she says, trotting toward the water through the weeds along the side of the house.

They make the beach and curl around the end of the fence, then back toward their house as the police cruiser headlights shine on the Hellikers' roof. Ducking down, they slink onto their deck and into the house. They slide the deck door closed, lock it, close the blinds, and stand in the living room, gasping.

"You're hurt," Pete says, nodding at the smear of blood on Carey's knee. He takes his phone out, the glow playing on his face.

"Was that your phone ringing in there?"

"Looks like." He hits a button and raises the phone to his ear, listening. "Holy Christ," he says. "Now what?"

"What?"

"Another fucking alarm. At the shop."

"What do you mean?"

"Got a voice mail from the alarm company saying there might be a break-in."

"Could be drunk kids."

"On the third floor?"

"Or maybe it's Danny."

Pete considers this. "Yeah. Maybe. I'll go."

"I'm coming."

"No. What if he comes back here?"

Carey hesitates. "All right. Then go. Hurry. Call me."

"What if the cops come over? What are you gonna tell them?"

"Fuck them. I'll figure it out."

Pete starts toward the garage.

"Not that way. That's where the cops are."

"Right. I'll run down the beach."

"Hurry, but don't run. You don't want people—"

"Yeah, yeah, right."

Pete slips out through the glass doors and crab scuttles across the deck to the sand. Carey watches him move down the beach silhouetted against the distant downtown lights, his scarecrow shoulder blades jutting in and out of shadow. She reaches down and presses a thumbnail into the scarlet goo on her knee. It stings. She wants it to.

9

Three cottages short of Boz's bar, Pete veers left and creeps up the grassy sand slope to the birch stand along the bay road, hoping no one will notice. He looks back and sees the cop lights flickering at the Helliker place. He calls the alarm company, supplies his code, tells the operator everything is fine, no need to send police to his shop. Once he's far enough past Boz's, he scrambles back down to the beach.

He's tired and a little drunk and trying to think. If somebody is trying to mess with his head, they're doing a splendid job. *Alarmed? Funny,* Pete thinks. *So you break into my pot shop? Fine, fine, get it over with.* He knows he cut a deal he shouldn't have. He thought he had good reasons, but the reasons evaporated when the other guy kept changing the deal. And not at all in Pete's favor.

So now what does he do?

He thinks about the alarm inside the Helliker place. It has to be a coincidence. At least he hopes so. This guy who's taunting him, trying to intimidate him, is obviously a reprobate—what the hell did Pete expect from a drug dealer anyway?

But is the guy smart enough to have triggered both alarms, the one at his shop and the one at the house, at the same time? And how could he have known Pete was in the Helliker place? Unless the guy's been watching him. Or maybe he read about Danny's previous running away in the *Light*. But even then, how could he know Danny would be gone on this particular night?

Unless.

He starts to run. As he nears town, he hears "Peaceful Easy Feeling" playing again from one of the harbor taverns. *Those people*, he thinks.

———

The redbrick office building stands a block up from the bay at the intersection of streets named for two of Joseph Estes Bleak's three daughters, Lily and Blossom. That Eagles song is still blaring from the beach down Lily. Some sadist must have a bucket of quarters.

Pete scans Blossom. The darkened galleries and boutiques and pottery shops—Strawman Drug, Casurella Fudge, Kate's Kakes, Bascolino's Soda & Sandwich—all slumber beneath striped awnings, the sidewalks washed in the milky glow of faux gas lamps. The cars parked on both sides of Blossom all seem to be convertibles, all red or black—BMWs, Mercedes, Porsches—except for one silver Jaguar.

A ladder left leaning against a lamp pole reminds Pete the town is preparing for the Dragonfly Festival. Danny loved the festival as a younger boy. He still loves dragonflies. The kid knew more about those bugs than anybody Pete knew, even the dude from the Bleak County Nature Center who had been one of Pete's customers until he decided the shop in New Buffalo had better, cheaper product.

Pete approaches the entrance to the redbrick building, four stories of glowing glass atrium wrapping from Blossom around to Lily, the windows speckled black with mosquitoes, moths, other bugs that give him the willies. He can feel the radiance on his face as he takes a plastic card from his wallet and presses it to a black plastic panel. He hears a beep, then a click. He pushes the door open.

He uses the card again to open the elevator, and again to tell the elevator to take him to three. He can't imagine how Danny could gain entrance to this digital fortress, but maybe, just maybe—but no, there's no one in the elevator lobby or the corridor to his office.

At the door to AMP Botanicals, Pete punches a six-number code into a keypad. He hears another click and steps inside, flicking on a light, closing the door behind him.

———

A year before, Pete lost his job trading corn and soybeans for O'Nally Bros. & Co. in Chicago. He'd done OK as a trader, at least for a while. Had a few big days, then got on a bad streak that just wouldn't stop. In retrospect, he had panicked. His employer couldn't afford panicky guys playing with millions of dollars.

After leaving O'Nally Bros., he had enough in severance pay and savings to pay for lawyers, licensing fees, the office lease, and a $20,000 vending machine that kept track of his weed inventory and how much in taxes and fees he owed various government authorities. He sublet the office from a retiring dentist and reopened it as a medical marijuana dispensary, offering smokable weed, edible brownies and cookies, and salves and oils infused with supposedly therapeutic cannabinoids.

He'd gotten the pot idea from a couple of trader buddies over drinks one late afternoon. Zeus and Byrd were talking about how easy it had to be to make money selling legal reefer. By then Pete knew he probably wasn't long for the trading business anyway. After his fourth whiskey and Coke, he'd started scratching numbers on a napkin. He couldn't read much of the smudged ink the next morning, but he thought he remembered enough. He got on Google and in a few hours had sort of a plan.

When he first broached the idea with Carey, she actually seemed tickled at the idea of Pete, a semiofficial member of the Bleak family, peddling pot to the puckered asses on the rich end of the bay in Bleak Harbor. Maybe she didn't think he was serious, because she wasn't too tickled five months later when he announced that he'd leased a cottage and an office in Bleak Harbor and was just waiting on a license to launch the business.

"You are joking," Carey said.

They were having coffee and cold cereal on a Friday morning in their Chicago condo. Danny had finished his CoCo Wheats and gone into his bedroom.

"No. I'm going out on my own. I took the initiative."

"'Initiative'? How about your job?"

"Quit." It was a lie, but an irrelevant one, as Pete saw it. "You know I've been bored shitless since they took me off the floor and put me in that cubicle."

"When exactly did you quit, Pete?"

"The other day."

"What day?"

"Last week, or actually the Friday before. I've been so busy getting this new adventure going that—"

"Exactly when did you plan on telling me about your little adventure?"

"I'm telling you now. I wanted to have a good plan in place. I took the initiative, babe."

"You took the initiative to move us to Michigan?"

"You can't sell pot legally in Illinois yet, but you can in Michigan. But you gotta live there to sell there."

Carey gave him one of those looks that made him want to leave the room. He held his ground, though, tried to fill the silence. "Come on."

"'Come on'? I honestly can't believe this, Pete."

"I really thought it would be a nice surprise. It'll be good for Danny. He loves the lake. He'll be closer to family."

"We are his family. My mother doesn't give a damn about Danny."

"Keep your voice down. Danny loves Jonah."

"What about his school?"

"There's an excellent school in Saugatuck. You're not—we're not happy with the school here anyway. You're always saying that. You hate your job. This is an opportunity for us, Carey."

"Pete, what do you know about selling marijuana?"

"What does anyone know? I've done tons of research. I've done my homework. Really, I'm gonna kill this. It's a huge business. There's so much pent-up demand. They'll be lined up."

"And you're the only one in the world who knows that?"

The rest of the conversation had not gone well. Nor had the next few months. Pete had tried to get Carey to quit Pressman Logistics and move full-time to Bleak Harbor, but she'd gotten the promotion she wanted, and she told Pete she wasn't going to let his initiative interfere with hers. She would commute once or twice a week. The pot shop was barely a mile from the cottage, and Pete would hire an employee or two so he'd be free to be with Danny. Just for a while. It would work itself out.

Pete hadn't liked keeping his pot-shop plan from his wife, hadn't been proud of it, but he'd convinced himself that she'd come around when the money started rolling in. How hard could it be? All the experts were forecasting a multibillion-dollar business, with twenty- and thirtysomethings wanting to get high and older folks yearning for something other than opioids to salve their aching knees and shoulders. Pete would no longer have to fret about uncontrollable bullshit like floods and droughts and currency fluctuations and idiot traders on the other side of the world screwing up the markets. Selling marijuana was no different from selling hot dogs, he kept telling himself. Just sell a lot of dogs for more than it cost to make them. Get rich.

———

Nothing looks amiss in the customer area of AMP Botanicals. The antique dentist's chair with its twin porcelain spittoons stands in one corner, the plastic palm tree in another, the leftover Georgia O'Keefe print on the wall between them, all untouched.

The glass display case is empty, as Dulcy left it after closing that evening. The vending machine behind the counter looks undisturbed. Pete uses a key to open it. Seeing all the different products lined up in their cellophane wraps and plastic vials produces, as it does most mornings when he slinks into the shop, a twinge in his belly that reminds him how little he knows about what he's doing.

This was not hot dogs. This was pH levels and proper temperatures; building a brand and interpreting web analytics; coddling cranky customers and suppliers; and endless ass-covering, mind-freezing paperwork for the regulators and politicians with their hands in Pete's pockets. And hiring people he could trust who could multiply six by twelve and get seventy-two.

He had a good staffer for a while, an ever-smiling guy named Hank who knew the ins and outs of the business after working it in California. But Hank had left, smiling, for the shop in New Buffalo. He'd said it was because it was closer to his home in Union Pier, but Pete figured Hank could see he was flailing. Pete then settled for hiring a young woman named Dulcy who'd recently moved from Detroit, had a head for computers, and showed a lot of enthusiasm for the job until she actually had to start showing up.

All those people who had helped Pete open the business and cashed his checks and clapped him on the back and told him to remember them when he made his first $10 million were gone now. He had no more money to give them. He was on his own.

All of the inventory appears to be in the vending machine. Nothing is stolen. Which, in a way, disappoints Pete. He wouldn't mind if there really was a break-in and the guy who's been harassing him just took everything—the reefer and edibles, the fingerprint-matching machine, the card readers, the throwback roach clips. Then Pete could file an insurance claim or even bankruptcy, what the hell, and be done with this mistake. That way he'd also feel more certain that this guy hadn't done anything to Danny, that Danny had simply run away and would come home in the morning looking for his CoCo Wheats, stirred evenly and constantly so that not a single lump bubbled up on the surface.

Christ, Pete thinks, *I don't even know the guy's real name.* All he knows is what he calls himself over the phone: Slim. He wishes he could turn back the clock, tell Slim, "Sorry, we can't do business, no hard feelings, just go away—I'll have to fail all by myself."

Too late for that.

"Buddy," Pete says aloud. "Danny. Where are you, man? Danny! Come on. Help me out here."

He moves along the wall toward the door to his back office. If there was a burglar, maybe he didn't want the weed; maybe he went looking in the office for cash. Though there wasn't much of that.

Pete taps another code into another keypad. Maybe somebody's waiting for him back there. Or maybe the alarm was bogus. As he pushes the door open, something to his left catches his eye. He skips back from the doorway and waits, listening, hearing nothing but the quickened thrum of his heart.

Wimp, he tells himself, *it's your goddamn office.*

He reaches around the jamb and hits a wall switch. The office floods with fluorescent light. It looks as he'd left it. His gray hoodie hangs from a hook next to the file cabinets, a pair of his running shoes curled on the floor beneath. His desk is its usual clutter of unpaid bills and pistachio shells. Everything's normal, except for his computer monitor.

The screen, which should be black, is flashing. That's what Pete glimpsed from the doorway. The screen turns blue and then red and then black, blue and then red and then black.

Pete walks over, sits, takes the mouse in hand. When the screen goes red, he thinks he sees something at the center of the view. He waits for the next red flash. He sees the same something, a little clearer, though he still can't make it out. He leans closer, waits, squints. There:

hereheis

The screen goes black again, then blue. Pete doesn't see any words on those screens. Then the red returns. Pete sees the word again. Not one word, he thinks, but three:

hereheis

"No."

The red screen reappears. For the hell of it, Pete left-clicks his mouse. The flashing stops. The red remains, the words a white smear at the middle of the screen. Pete looks at his phone. Should he call Carey? Or the cops? And tell them what? There's a funny screen on my computer? Somebody's fucking with me, and he might have done something with my stepson?

Now the red begins to bleed away from the center of the screen toward each side, like a theater curtain opening. The revealed backdrop is newsprint gray. An irregular black shape forms around the words. The words begin to blink inside the shape.

Pete left-clicks again. The words vanish. After a moment, the black begins to peel away from the bottom of the shape, revealing a color photograph.

Pete feels a sledgehammer in his chest.

"Jesus."

At the bottom of the unfolding photo appear two feet. One is bare. The other wears a green high-top sneaker. Duct tape secures each of the hairless shins to the legs of a chair. The roll of tape sits on the floor between the chair legs. It looks like the thing that was sitting on the empty chair in the picture on Carey's phone.

It takes about a minute for the photo to reveal itself in full. Pete hits the print command again and again. A few seconds after the photo is complete, the screen goes black. Then three words in two-inch-high letters appear in white at the center of the screen:

DO NOT TELL

Pete taps Carey's number into his phone. His hands are shaking so badly that he has to do it three times.

"Is he there?" Carey says.

"Oh God."

"Pete, what?"

"Somebody—"

The texts flit again through Pete's mind:

how's the fam?

alarmed?

"Pete, goddamn it."

He can't catch his breath.

"Somebody what? Pete?"

"Fuck. Oh Jesus, oh Jesus."

"What is it?"

"Somebody has Danny. Somebody has our boy."

FRIDAY

10

Danny sleeps.

The room is dark. The room is hot. The room is stuffy. He feels the scratch at his throat. He swallows.

He is standing on the beach. His toes touch the water. The dragonflies are bigger than gulls. They are blacker than crows. They hover and glide, skitter and dart. Their shadows darken the water.

Anax junius, Enallagma civile.

Predator in emerald, damsel of the swamp.

Tramea lacerata, Libellula vibrans.

Spotted black killer, sapphire king.

Danny hears his mother singing:

> They flit about the sunny sky
> Like flowers that can fly
> Pretty pretty pretty pretty
> Their wings are sparkly gossamer
> They wear diamonds on their eyes
> Pretty pretty pretty pretty
> Pretty dragonflies

The dragonflies want the fishes. The baby fishes. They swoop and dive. Their wings make a murmur of clicking. The dragonflies disappear into the water. Some are damselflies. *Argia apicalis, Nehalennia irene.* Nobody knows this. Danny knows it. They emerge from the water with their jaws full. Their terrible jaws, their knives for teeth. They crunch and slurp and dive again.

His mother's voice fades, and Danny hears the music. It's close but far away. People are singing along. They don't care about the dragonflies or damselflies or baby fishes. Danny tries to speak. His jaw will not work. He tries to reach out and stop the dragonflies. His arm will not move. A fog descends. Danny can't see anything. He hears the splash and crunch and slurp.

He turns to the house. It has moved away up the beach. It is shrinking. Then it's gone, splintering into the trees across the bay road, the trees becoming the Willis and Hancock and AON buildings of Chicago. He hears her again: *Some things are meant to be.* As if he didn't know, couldn't comprehend it.

Danny remembers.

He was drinking coffee on the deck. It was 8:34 that morning. He had brushed his teeth nineteen minutes before.

His mother hugged him from behind. She kissed him beneath an ear. She was running late. She had broken a nail. *The goddamn traffic. Tonight you are all mine*, she said. *I love you.*

Yes, Danny said.

He drank his coffee. He heard the kitchen door slam shut. He heard it open again. He heard his mother call out, *Please, Pete, don't forget the meeting.* He heard the door slam again. He put a finger to his neck. He put the finger to his lips. He tasted sweat mixed with lavender body wash.

He made the two sandwiches, salami and muenster. He creased the folds of the sandwich bags. He arranged the cans of Squirt and Old Style in the cooler. He packed the pretzels and the worms. He hung the minnow bucket from a chain into the water next to the dock. He leaned the poles there. He left the boat covered.

His mother called. He watched the phone ring five times. He thought of Paddle trotting on the beach, ears of charcoal and copper fluttering back along the sides of his head, limp hind leg tracing a squiggle through the sand.

He didn't want to talk with his mother then. She would be home in a while.

Danny's eyes are burning. The room is hot. His cheeks are damp. The room is dark. Danny knows he is crying. He knows where he is. He wonders if he will see his mother and Pete again.

11

"You don't ever call him Danny boy, do you?"

Bleak Harbor Police lieutenant Katya Malone directs the question to Danny's mother. Carey Bleak Peters is facing Malone across the oaken table in the Peters cottage on the southeast corner of the bay. A dimmed overhead lamp splays yellowish light, leaving the rest of the room in shadow. Sitting in the middle of the table is a tin Ernie Banks lunch box, its edges fringed with rust.

"We do not," Carey says. She's staring at the tabletop, the fingertips on her right hand idly tapping the side of a glass of melting ice. Her husband sits two chairs to her right.

"No," Pete says.

Malone doesn't want to look at her watch while she's interviewing two parents about their missing son. She guesses it's a little after eight. The husband called the station around seven thirty. Malone had just finished her shift and was planning to visit the Bleak Harbor Cemetery before going home.

Malone had taken the call. She could tell Peters was talking with his mouth close to the phone. In the background she had heard a woman shouting, "He said not to tell anyone. He'll hurt—" Then Peters had hung up.

Malone had skipped her cemetery visit for the first time since the February blizzard buried her car. After scanning the police report from Danny's previous disappearance, she had gone straight to the Peters place, where she was presented with two printouts: one a screenshot of Danny tied to a chair, another of an email sent to Carey Peters at 6:45 a.m.

The email came from jeb@jeb.com and was signed "Jeremiah." It rests on the table between the lunch box and Malone.

"You don't know anyone named Jeremiah?"

"Not that I can think of," Pete says.

Malone slides the lunch box to the right, clearing the space between her and Danny's mother. The woman looks tired. Malone thinks of a handwritten note pinned to a bulletin board in her kitchen. The note came in the weeks after Louisa's death, slipped inside a sympathy card, the envelope bearing a Chicago postmark. "I can't imagine," the inscription said. "I'm so sorry." It was signed "Carey Peters."

"You don't really think a kidnapper would sign a ransom note with his real name?" Carey says.

"I don't want to assume anything at this point, Ms. Peters. It could be that this person who claims to have your son is trying to implicate someone else."

"I have a distant cousin or two named Jeremiah. It's a Bleak thing."

"We'll definitely check them out. Could you please—"

"They've been dead for years."

"I see. What about this email name, 'jeb'?"

"Family initials. Every male Bleak has a 'J' first name, middle name Estes, after the patriarch, Joseph. Jonah Estes Bleak, Jonathan Estes Bleak, et cetera."

The husband interrupts: "What's this guy mean by our 'sins'?"

"It doesn't say *your* sins, Mr. Peters. It says, 'Everyone gotta pay for *their* sins.'"

He wraps himself in his arms. Carey gives him a sideways glance, not especially kind. Malone jots this in her notepad. She inches the printout closer, scans it for the tenth time:

To who It Better Concern—

I got yr Danny boy.

He is OK for now. if u know what I mean

5145000 dollars.

11:46 tonight

details coming

Get the cake or that's the last of Danny.

every one gotta pay for there sins.

Jeremiah

Malone does the math in her head. They have a little less than six-teen hours till 11:46 p.m. The email arrived at 6:45. There's also a 45 in the odd ransom amount. On a whim, she counts the words in the email: 45. Could the 6 in 11:46 be a typographical error?

Maybe these echoes have meaning, Malone thinks. Or maybe they're random. Most criminals aren't nearly as clever as the ones on television and in books. Prisons are packed with people who think they're smarter than they really are.

"Your son was home alone yesterday afternoon, yes?"

"Danny," Carey says. Again her eyes slide sideways at her husband. "He was here, yes."

"I was just downtown," Pete Peters says.

Just, Malone thinks. *Feeling some guilt?* "Was he left alone on a regular basis?"

"He wasn't *alone* alone, Officer. I was—"

"The answer is yes, he was alone," Carey says. "Danny was alone at times." A shadow crosses her face. "Oh Jesus."

"Ms. Peters?"

"Danny was born at 11:46 p.m. Sixteen years ago. Tonight."

"I see."

Pete says, "That can't be a coincidence."

"Maybe, maybe not," Malone says. She's thinking not, but she wants to get back to the boy. "Ms. Peters," she says, "you were saying Danny was alone sometimes."

Carey takes a breath, then says, "Yes, sometimes. His issue isn't functioning on his own; it's functioning with—functioning well with others."

"So he's fine alone."

"We're both here on weekends, and I try to work from home at least one day a week. Danny isn't lacking for companionship."

Malone wants to ask about his grandmother but hesitates. She's aware that the relationship between Carey and her mother is fraught. The last time the boy disappeared, Serenity Bleak's assistant called the chief to express Mrs. Bleak's concern, less with the boy's whereabouts than the publicity surrounding the incident. The assistant didn't mention the hundreds of millions of dollars Serenity Bleak was dangling. He didn't have to.

"There was nobody else here?" Malone says. "A nanny or someone who—"

"No," Pete says. "Nobody else."

"Until recently, he had a dog."

Malone hovers a hand over the lunch box. "Here."

"Yes, Paddle—the dog's ashes are in there."

Malone looked inside earlier, saw the clear plastic bag secured with a twist tie, the doughy contents.

"That's the dog's name?"

"Paddle, yes."

"And Danny was quite fond of him."

Again Carey shuts her eyes. She appears determined not to cry in front of Malone or even her husband. Malone knows the feeling.

"Danny loved Paddle," Pete says. "He doesn't have a lot of friends—"

"That's not his fault," Carey says.

"—and Paddle was sort of his best pal."

"Thank you. And you found this lunch box where, exactly?"

"On his bed."

"When you checked his room earlier."

"Yes."

"We had to put the dog down," Pete interrupts. "Paddle was old and sick and, you know, he could barely walk. It was a lousy day for all of us."

"Of course. Did Danny always keep Paddle's ashes on his bed?"

"No," Carey says. "I'm actually not sure where he had them. Maybe in his closet, or one of his desk drawers. I know he keeps a little baggie of them in his wallet. But otherwise, this lunch box was out of sight."

"What about the wallet? You don't have that, right?"

"No. He probably had it on him."

"I have to say," Carey says, "I was kind of glad when I saw the lunch box on the bed because I thought maybe Danny was ready to finally do something with the ashes."

"Get some closure," Pete adds.

"Did Paddle—when did you put him down?"

"Around the last time."

"The last time?"

"The last time Danny left."

Malone recalls the *Light* story about Danny's earlier disappearance. She remembers feeling the story was unkind to Carey Peters, but she can't recall precisely why. She wishes she had reread it before coming over.

"I see. Do you think the dog's death had anything to do with Danny's leaving then?"

"Maybe," Carey says. "Probably. Danny didn't say, really."

"Has anything—"

"No, he's been fine. He's been good lately."

"We go fishing a lot," Pete says. "We were supposed to go last night. You can see the cooler—it's right over there—the sandwiches—"

Pete, apparently choked up, looks away. Carey eases back into her chair without looking at him. They don't seem like the happiest couple. But then who is the happiest couple but for a few scant years? On top of the usual, natural distancings over time and space, Carey and Pete Peters have had some of their own complications: the commuting, the new business, and of course, whatever challenges Danny must present.

"Danny's surname is Peters; is that correct?"

"We had it legally changed," Carey says.

"For any particular reason, may I ask?"

"Well, I'm a Peters too. And it's just easier not being a Bleak in Bleak Harbor. We're not the most beloved clan."

"I see. And Danny is autistic; do I have that right?"

"They asked us last time, Officer. He hasn't been cured."

"I'm sorry, Ms. Peters. I'm just trying to get a clearer sense of how Danny behaves."

Carey sighs. "I'm sorry," she says. "Danny is on the spectrum, as they say. What that means depends on which doctor you talk to. What we know for sure is that he's very bright. He likes to read, especially history."

"He likes the library," Pete interjects.

"He goes there on his own?" Malone asks.

"Yes," Carey says. "It's a short walk along the shoreline."

"He likes fishing," Pete says, "he likes poems, he loves the Cubs, as you can see. He's very interested in dragonflies. He can stand out on the dock for hours watching them."

"That all sounds fairly"—Malone stops herself from saying *normal*—"ordinary. What are Danny's, I'm not sure how to say this—"

"Deficits?" Carey says. "Shortcomings?"

"All adolescents have those."

"Problems? Danny's problem is he's not in love with people in general. He has trouble being around people he doesn't know well."

"And even the ones he does, sometimes," Pete says.

"Unless," Carey says, "he sees some purpose in them, something he needs."

"For instance?" Malone says.

"That's his mind-blindness," Pete says.

"For instance, the librarians," Carey continues, without acknowledging what her husband said. "They help him when he's there, and he actually talks about them when he comes home, especially a Mrs. Loiselle. It's—" Carey stops to compose herself—"quite sweet, actually, *especially* in an adolescent."

"He isn't just living in a shell," Pete says. "He's actually come out of it some."

"What about school?"

Carey keeps her eyes on Malone. "He was in a good place in Chicago. He had an excellent one-on-one aide—"

"Excellent," Pete says.

"—until she lost her job to budget cuts—"

"Politicians."

"—and Danny just wasn't the same after that. We tried a different school, and then, of course, we came here, and it wasn't working out, he wasn't engaging, so we took him out in February, and he's been working on a GED course online and, like I said, going to the library."

"Is he in therapy of some sort?"

"Yes. Occupational therapy, some speech, though speech isn't the issue it once was."

"I'll say," Pete says.

"Mr. Peters, what was that word you used? Some kind of blindness?"

"Mind-blindness?"

"Yes. What did you mean by that?"

Carey speaks up. "A state of mind. Danny will focus on one thing or idea or person to the exclusion of all others."

"He lacks sympathy," Pete says.

"Empathy," Carey corrects him.

"I see. Is that typical for someone with autism?"

"Is it typical for cops to eat doughnuts every morning?"

"Excuse me?" *She's annoyed*, Malone thinks.

"There is no 'typical.'"

"OK. Sorry." Malone flips a page on her notepad. "Ms. Peters, can you tell me again where you were at approximately five o'clock yesterday afternoon?"

"I was driving back from Chicago. I was probably, I don't know, more than halfway here. Traffic was a mess."

"You still work for the logistics company?"

"Pressman Logistics."

"And you, Mr. Peters?"

"I was at the council meeting at city hall. Everybody noticed me because I spilled coffee on Mrs. Naughton. I left around five."

"So you were back here at, what, five fifteen?"

"No, he had to stop at Boz's," Carey says, eyeing her husband again.

"The bar up the beach? Is that right, Mr. Peters?"

"Call me Pete, please."

He's avoiding his wife's gaze.

"Pete. Did you stop at the bar?"

"I had a tough day."

"Did you close your shop, or was someone—"

"I have an employee who was taking care of things."

"And who is he, please?"

"It's a she. Dulcy—I think it's actually Dulcinea—Pérez."

"Does she know Danny?"

"A little," Pete says. "He saw her at the shop a couple of times; no biggie."

"And when you got home, nothing seemed out of place?"

"Danny wasn't here," Carey says.

"Is that unusual?"

"Not really," Pete says.

"Yes, it's unusual."

"He goes for walks sometimes late in the day."

"Not for twelve hours."

"To answer your question, Officer Malone, no, nothing was amiss. You can see the cooler over there."

"The boat was still covered," Carey says. "His phone was here. He always takes his phone wherever he goes. We insist on it."

"And you checked his room."

"Yes. Everything seemed normal."

Malone had made a cursory check of the house when she arrived. She had pulled on disposable gloves and followed Carey and Pete around. The cottage was cozy, simple, well kept: two bedrooms, two bathrooms, a kitchen, a great room that opened on to the beach deck and the boat dock. A low-ceilinged basement devoid of anything but a furnace and water heater. Malone had looked for signs of a disturbance as well as evidence that one had been tidied up. She'd seen neither.

Carey had hesitated before opening her son's bedroom door, saying, "He doesn't like us going in here." Malone's thirteen-year-old, Louisa, had been the same. Danny's room looked as undisturbed as the rest of the house. Half-full vials of prescription pills sat on Danny's nightstand. The parents said that probably wasn't a good sign.

"What about this, Officer?" Carey points at the screenshot printout in front of Malone. "See his cheekbone?"

In the photo, Danny is wearing most of what he had on when Carey left him that morning: gray cargo shorts, a faded purple Prairie Surfers T-shirt, one of his green high-tops. His right foot is bare. Danny's eyes are obscured by a blindfold that looks torn from a pillowcase. His arms are behind his back, presumably duct-taped like his feet. His head lolls to one side.

"I see. Our lab will take a closer look, make sure it isn't just—"

"It's a bruise," Carey insists. "He fought back, and they hit him."

"Or, forgive me, Ms. Peters, they made him up to make you think they hit him."

"To scare us," Pete says.

"That's the same chair that was in the picture I showed you on my phone," Carey says. "Don't you think? And the roll of duct tape."

"Very possible," Malone says. "Again, I don't want to presume anything. We'll be checking that number."

"Danny can hit, so it has to be a man," Carey says. She seems angry all of a sudden. "Women don't steal other women's children."

The lump that rises in Malone's throat surprises her. "Excuse me, Ms.—Carey. Can I just say something?"

Carey sits up. "Go ahead."

"You sent me a note. A very nice note, last year, when my daughter was—when she died."

Pete turns to his wife, puzzled. Carey leans forward, recognition gradually widening her eyes. "Oh. Yes. I was—I'm so sorry."

"That was very kind of you. Thank you. It came at a particularly good—well, not good, but you know."

"Of course. You're welcome."

"So," Malone says, "we will assume for now that whoever this is did strike Daniel."

"Danny, please."

"Danny, pardon me. Even so, the boy appears to have left the house willingly."

"So he probably knew the kidnapper," Pete offers.

"Possibly. It would be helpful for you to give us a list with contact information for any friends or family who might be able to help us."

"I'm sorry," Carey says. "Nobody in my family gives a shit about my son, except for my brother. I'm sure you know him."

"I've met Mayor Bleak. What about your mother, and . . . is there any chance this could have anything to do with her"—Malone reaches for a word—"her proposal?"

Serenity Meredith Maas Bleak had offered the local municipalities her estate if they met one seemingly simple condition: that the town, the township, and the county, after 140-odd years as the namesakes of Joseph Estes Bleak, rechristen themselves as Serenity Bay, Serenity Township, Serenity County.

It seemed like a no-brainer to Malone. Hardly anyone liked what the place was called anyway. But the no-brainer had become mired in tiny-*p* politics and threats of litigation as the fiefs bickered over who would collect how much of Serenity's booty before any of them would relinquish their sole leverage, endorsement of the new name.

That's where the diabolical final sentence of Serenity Bleak's New Year's Day proposal came in. It stated that, if Serenity died before the names were changed, her entire estate would be placed in a trust that would in turn be bequeathed to the towns of South Haven, Saugatuck, Grand Haven, Union Pier, and New Buffalo, all lakeside resorts that vied for tourist business with Bleak Harbor.

"What would that have to do with this?" Pete says.

"It's been on the national news. A lot more people know about your mother and her wealth than a few months ago."

"So it could be just some random stranger, somebody Danny doesn't even know?" Carey says.

"Possibly. Though without any sign of a struggle, probably unlikely. Excuse me, but can I ask why you didn't call when you first determined Danny wasn't here?"

"You guys won't look for missing persons until they've been gone for twenty-four hours," Pete says.

"Actually, no, that's TV."

"No, that's what you told us last time," Carey says.

"Plus, we were worried maybe Danny was pulling another of his disappearing acts, like last time."

"So you looked for him."

"Yes. We even went next door, like last time."

"You set that alarm off?"

"We were in the house then," Pete says. "Why would an alarm be on anyway?"

"The bank probably wants to keep kids out."

"Exactly how many child abductions have you been involved in, Officer?"

One too many, Malone thinks.

"Pete," Carey says. "What's the matter with you?"

"It's all right," Malone says. "Plenty of children get taken in custody disputes." She recalls now what that *Bleak Harbor Light* story insinuated, and the rumors of tensions—potentially physical ones—between Carey Peters and her son. Sitting here, looking at the woman, Malone finds the whispers hard to believe. She decides not to ask about that, for now. "Ms. Peters," she says instead, "you wouldn't have any issues with your ex, would you?"

Carey sits back in her chair, hair falling away from her face, and Malone notes how much she looks like her son, the big eyes, the cheekbones. With a bit of makeup, either could pose as the other.

"I don't have an ex," she says.

"The record from the previous incident indicates your husband is Danny's stepfather."

"Pete is my first and only husband."

"I see, but what about—"

"I haven't seen him in years."

"—Danny's birth father?"

"I have no idea where he is."

"His name, please?"

"Bledsoe," Pete says. He sits up straighter, seemingly buoyed by this turn in the questioning. "Jeff Bledsoe. Loser."

"Jeffrey?"

"Yes," Carey says.

"Oh, he could've done this," Pete says, nodding. "For sure."

"Is that with a *j* or *g*?"

"*J*," Carey says.

"R-e-y or e-r-y?"

"R-e-y."

"Middle initial?"

Carey thinks. "I don't remember. I'm not sure I ever knew."

"I ask because this email is from J-E-B-dot-com," Malone says. "Could be a coincidence. You don't know if his middle name started with an *e*?"

"I didn't really know him all that well, unfortunately."

"I'd say fortunately," Pete says.

"Do you know this Bledsoe person, Mr. Peters?"

"Just what my wife's told me."

"Have you ever met him?"

"No. No desire to either."

Malone looks at Carey. "Apologies for asking, ma'am, but was this a brief, shall we say—"

"One-night stand? No. A fling. A month or two."

"And this was when?"

"Danny will be sixteen tonight, so almost seventeen years ago. I was working in Detroit, just out of U of M."

"And how did you come to know this man?"

"He was a client."

"A client?"

"I was working at the Wayne County Department of Social Services in Detroit. I helped people kick drug habits."

"Jeffrey Bledsoe had a drug habit?"

"Habit's a nice word for it."

"What was his drug?"

"What wasn't?"

"I gather he didn't kick it."

"For a while he did. Then he didn't. I told him to go away. By then I was carrying Danny."

"So, forgive me, but to be clear, you had an affair with a known drug dealer."

Carey opens her palms on the table and looks into them as if the right words might be written there. "I was young," she says. "I was bored. I don't know. He was, you know, my project."

"Something a little wild."

She turns her palms back over, looks up at Malone. "Something like that."

"I wouldn't think your department would allow fraternizing with clients."

"Of course not. I got suspended, actually, because after I told him to get out of my life, he ratted me out. I took my son and got out, came back here for a while, then to Chicago, and then"—she gives her husband another look—"back here."

"Do you know where he is now?"

"I know he was in prison. I think he got out."

"Why do you say that?"

"He contacted me."

"He did. When?"

"Late last year."

"Really?" Pete says. Malone studies his face, now turned to his wife. He had not known until this moment.

Carey's face is in her hands now, her elbows propped on the table. "He emailed me at my office. I told him to go away or I'd call the police."

"What did he want?"

"I don't remember exactly. Something about him coming to Chicago or something. So I guess he was out of prison. I erased it from my mind. I don't like thinking about Jeffrey."

"You didn't tell me about this."

Carey answers from inside her hands. "I didn't need to. It was bullshit. Jeffrey loves to fuck with people."

"Do you still have the emails?" Malone says.

"I doubt it. We wipe our servers clean every month."

"He sent it to your company email? At Pressman Logistics?"

"Yes."

"Did you ever hear back from him?"

"A week or so later. He told me he could just show up at my work if he wanted, make trouble."

"And what did you do?"

"I blocked his email."

"You didn't take it seriously."

"No."

"Did he ever just show up?"

"Not that I know of."

"And you didn't go to the police."

"And tell them what? I got a nasty email?"

"Jesus," Pete says. He should be upset with his wife, but the way he slumps back in his chair suggests to Malone that he's somehow relieved. "So it could be this asshole who took Danny."

"You don't know where Bledsoe was, which facility? Jackson?"

Carey thinks about this. "I'm not sure, but I think I may have heard Muskegon."

"Not too far from here," Pete says. "Goddamn."

"We'll track him down." Malone picks up her phone, sends a text to a colleague outside the cottage.

Pete says, "Isn't that a weird number?"

"Which?"

"Five-point-one-four-five million. I mean, wouldn't it normally be five million or ten million, something round?"

"There's no normal in these situations, but I take your point."

"Well, we don't have it. Not even close. And whoever took Danny, if he knows us, has to know that."

"But this person might think you could get it."

"My mother's not about to come to the rescue, Officer."

Malone wants to say, *It's her grandson, for God's sake.* Instead she closes her notepad and sets two business cards on the table.

"We will do everything we can to find your son as quickly as possible," she says. "We'll contact the FBI and alert other departments nearby. If you think of anything, don't hesitate to call me. My cell number is on the card. If for some reason you can't reach me right away, call the station and have me paged. Do you have somewhere else to stay?"

"Why?" Carey says.

"I'm afraid this is now a crime scene."

Pete says, "Are we suspects or something?"

Malone waits a beat. "No."

"Do we have to leave this minute?" Carey says. "What if Danny comes home and we're not here?"

Malone considers, then says, "We'll be back. Please do your best not to disturb anything in the meantime. It'd be good now if I could have Danny's phone and any other electronics, tablets, computers, whatever."

Pete's phone bleats.

"Why?" Carey says.

"It could tell us things—"

"Like?"

Out of the corner of an eye, Malone sees Pete turn sheet white as he looks at his phone.

"Like whether somebody was communicating with him."

"I will go through it and tell you."

"Danny's devices are evidence, Ms. Peters. We need them."

Carey's phone starts to shimmy across the table, a call coming in. Malone watches her check the phone. She knits her eyebrows as if the call is from someone she doesn't recognize. Carey stands. "I'll drop everything at the station later," she says. "I want to take a look first. I won't change anything. I'm sure that you can understand, Officer Malone."

Malone thinks of the note in her kitchen again. She could get a search warrant, but it would take longer than having Carey just bring the stuff in. She gets up from her chair. She has a bad feeling about all of this—the picture of the kid, the mark on his face, the ex-convict. She hopes Bledsoe was in for something like drug possession, nothing violent.

"All right, but please drop it off by ten o'clock sharp," she tells Carey.

"Eleven," Carey says. "We've been up all night."

Malone nods reluctantly. "Eleven," she says. She picks up her hat and fits it onto her head. "Mr. Peters," she says, "would you mind walking me out?"

"Uh, sure," Pete says, standing. "But I gotta hit the john. Meet you out there."

12

Pete closes the kitchen door behind him so as not to alert the neighbors on the side opposite the Helliker cottage. They probably aren't there, but he doesn't want to chance them seeing. His phone is in his back pocket, so he's less likely to look again at the image that appeared on it a few minutes ago.

In the bathroom, he locked the door and sat on the closed toilet seat with his head in his hands, wishing he could stay there until Danny showed up and the cops went away and everything went back to normal. Standing outside, he feels like he does in the foggy middle between sleep and waking on a hungover morning. None of this can be real: the photographs, the ransom email, the taunting texts, the silvery walking-away footprints left by Malone in the dewy grass.

How could it feel real? Who could ever imagine these sorts of things happening before they actually did? The phone blasting you out of dead sleep in the pit of night, the marines like ghosts on your front porch, the doctor whose look of pained resignation devastates you before he utters a word. Nightmares, that's what every parent calls them. Pete is in one now.

He sees Malone standing next to her police cruiser, talking with a heavyset young man in street clothes. He's holding something in his hands that he moves out of sight when Pete approaches.

"Got nothing for Jeremiah," the young man is saying.

"And you tried Bledsoe?"

"Excuse me?" Pete says.

"I'm sorry, Mr. Peters—Pete—this is my colleague, Will Northwood. He'll be assisting with the investigation."

"Sorry for your trouble," Will says.

"Will likes anagrams. I asked him to try *Jeremiah*. I figured this guy, whoever he is, might think he's clever."

"I see." Pete notices another car, unmarked, parked on the shoulder across the street. "Have you been out here all this time?"

Will Northwood is studying him. It makes Pete feel uneasy. He wants to go back in the house. But then he'll have to show Carey the new picture on his phone.

"Just checking things out," Will says. He turns to Malone and points down the high fence between the Peters and Helliker houses. "Found a turtle shell, pretty big one, cracked like someone whacked it with a hammer. Some empty beer cans. Two loose boards in the fence, fifteen up from the beach."

"Maybe that storm a few weeks ago," Malone says.

"That was a wicked one. I walked through the house next door too. It's pretty much gutted. Found what looked like blood at the bottom of the basement stairs."

"That was my wife's," Pete says.

"Looked fresh."

"She fell."

"Dangerous in there, sir. I wouldn't try that again."

"Mr. Peters," Malone says. She looks more official, even intimidating, with her police hat pulled down just above her eyebrows. "Do you have something you want to tell us?"

The "Mr. Peters" again, the questions, the "something," catch him off guard. "What do you mean?"

"I understand how you might want to protect your wife."

"Protect her from what?"

Will says, "Why the soundproof fence?"

"For privacy," Pete says. "To keep out nosy people." He had never wanted the damn fence anyway. Two grand, and it already has two loose boards?

"OK, Will," Malone says, taking a step in front of him. "I had to ask, Mr. Peters. I'm sorry."

It seems genuine, but Pete is still leery of the fat guy with his arm behind his back. "What kind of cop wears a golf shirt on the job?"

"I'm not an officer, Mr. Peters."

"Will's our tech guy," Malone says. "He's going to help find your son."

"Carey wouldn't harm a hair on Danny's head. Why are we even talking about this? What about Bledsoe? Are you going to look for him?"

Will and Malone exchange glances. "He got out of Muskegon in December. Paroled for good behavior."

December, Pete thinks. Wet and cold. Carey was bitching more than usual about the commute.

"I see. How long was he in?"

"Almost six years."

Pete recalls that Bledsoe called Carey once not long after they were married seven years ago. He can't remember much but that she'd told him to go to hell. He wishes now that she'd said something about Bledsoe's more recent contact, just so he would've known, though he's not sure what difference it would have made.

"We'll know more soon," Malone says. "Will, can you show him the shoe?"

From behind his back Will produces a clear plastic bag. It contains a green high-top sneaker, right foot.

"Jesus," Pete says.

"This is your son's?"

"Looks like it. Where did you find it?"

"Out by the road. Size eight and a half."

"Is there any . . . ?" Pete can't finish.

"No blood that I can see. But we'll run some tests."

"But the fact that it came off—Danny must have resisted." Pete can't decide whether this is a good thing or bad.

"Found this too." Will shows Pete a smaller plastic bag containing a phone. "Found it in the grass beneath the windows on the side of the house. Ever see it before?"

"No. It doesn't look like one of ours."

"It's a burner—a disposable phone, one you buy with prepaid minutes and throw away when it's used up. Your boy wouldn't have had one, would he?"

"Not that—no. Why would he?"

"You're in the drug business, aren't you, Mr. Peters?"

"What's that got—I'm in the legal marijuana business."

"How's it going?"

"Fine."

"I read it's a money-printing business," Malone says.

"I'm just getting started. What's this got to do with anything?"

"From what little we know so far," Northwood says, "it sounds like Bledsoe may have been involved in the same business in Detroit."

"I don't know about him, but my business is perfectly legal."

"Yes," Malone says. "You'll be closed today, by the way. We'll be cordoning off your office as a crime scene."

Icy droplets of sweat prickle Pete's temples. Could these cops possibly know about the illicit dealer he's been buying from? What might they find in his office? He mentally scours his desk for any scribbled scraps or sticky notes that could get him in trouble.

Maybe he should just tell them. But what's he going to say? *Find a dude who calls himself Slim?* Pete has never laid eyes on the guy. What good would telling do anyway? It would just confuse things, he tells himself, might even put him in jail when Carey needs him most. Better to focus on the ex-convict, Danny's real father, Bledsoe.

"I better get back to Carey."

"Can I ask you something, Pete?" It's Will again. Pete wishes he would go away. "Why did you go to the bar yesterday? Why not just go straight home to your son?"

He pictures Boz's, the TVs leaning off the top of the back bar like they might pitch onto the floor, the queue of beer taps beneath the fake reindeer head with the blinking red nose on the knotty pine wall, a Christmas decoration that stayed up all year. "I just sat through two hours of bullshit at city hall and I wanted a drink. What's the big deal?"

"We didn't say it was a big deal," Malone says.

"Officer Malone said you seemed kind of relieved to hear Bledsoe's name."

"Relieved? I'm not relieved about any of this. Christ." Pete takes a backward step toward the house. "I'm glad there might be a suspect. Could that phone, that disposable thing, could that help?"

"You've never met him, have you?" Will asks.

"Who?"

"Bledsoe."

"No, I've never met him."

"Inside, you called him a loser," Malone says.

"He is a loser, based on what Carey has told me. Didn't you just say he's a drug dealer?"

"Incidentally, Pete," Malone says, "when we were inside, it looked like you got something on your phone that upset you."

Pete tries to keep his breathing steady as the image returns to him. He considers showing them. But he doesn't want to make the same mistake twice. It'll be bad enough showing it to Carey.

"Everything is upsetting, Officer. It was nothing. It just reminded me that yesterday, we were—everything was fine."

"OK. You said you had an employee keep your shop open while you were gone yesterday," Will says.

"Pérez?" Malone says.

"Yes, Dulcy, Dulcy Pérez."

Will says, "Got a cell number for her?"

Pete takes out his phone, reads out a number for Will, who punches it into his own phone.

"All right," Malone says. "Can you think of anyone besides this Bledsoe who'd have the slightest motivation to do this?"

"We will definitely think about it, Officer."

"Don't think long. We have about fifteen hours."

As Pete turns for the house, he sees the blinds on the kitchen door flutter. He thinks again of that reindeer nose blinking red on the wall at Boz's. There's a man standing in front of it, with a stark, bony face. Pete thinks of the bruise on Danny's cheek. He thinks of what he's about to show Carey. He tells himself he will make the call he does not want to make.

13

Carey squints through the blinds on the kitchen door.

It's hard to see through the morning haze. The young man in the polo shirt is showing Pete something inside a clear plastic bag—it looks, from afar, like a shoe—then another similar bag containing something Carey can't quite make out. She remembers this man. He came to the house and asked the upsetting questions the last time Danny vanished.

She had forgotten about sending that sympathy note to Officer Malone. It was more than a year ago, when she and Pete and Danny were still living in Chicago. Carey had read about the accident in an online news story her brother had sent. Perhaps Carey imagined it, but sitting across from her at the great-room table, Malone appeared much older than the woman Carey remembered from photographs the year before.

Even now, Carey isn't sure why she took a sheet of Pressman Logistics stationery and jotted a message on the back to the bereaved mother. She isn't one of those people who are constantly dashing off little missives about birthdays and baptisms and such. But maybe she felt a distant kinship because Malone was in Bleak Harbor and the death of her daughter had, in a way, isolated her from everyone else there. Carey knew that feeling.

She catches a glimpse of Pete's face as he turns to come back into the house. It's creased with guilt. She lets the blinds close, steps away from the door, waits. Pete enters the kitchen and shuts the door behind him. Carey's not surprised when he chokes out a sob.

"I'm sorry," he says. "I shouldn't have called them."

"Who?"

"The police." He covers his face with one hand and gives Carey his phone with the other. "Look."

Carey's legs go rubbery when she sees the image on the phone screen. It's framed like the earlier one of Danny tied to the chair. But now the chair is in pieces, the seat and back askew on the floor, a leg snapped off and thrown aside. In the background shadows, a green high-top sneaker is lying on its side, and farther back, she can see the heel of a hand. Tiny white letters are printed at the bottom of the screen:

u told

"Bastard," she says.

"I'm sorry."

Carey feels herself starting to hyperventilate. "Fuck it," she says. "Just fuck it, fuck this asshole. Did you show the cops?"

"No. Should I have?"

"Probably. I don't know. I know I said they're worthless, but how could we not call them?"

They were sitting in the great room, silent, just waiting, dawn nearing, when the kidnapper's email arrived. Carey had closed her eyes for one second, dozed off. She woke to Pete on the phone with the cops.

"How could this guy know we called, anyway?" Pete says.

"Maybe he heard it on a police scanner?"

"Or maybe he hacked our phones somehow. Carey. What are we going to do?"

"Pete, you have to settle down."

"Carey."

"Come here."

Pete steps into her embrace. She feels the trembling along the backs of his arms. Closing her eyes, she conjures a memory of Danny. He's two years old on the crowded beach at North Avenue in Chicago, a steamy Sunday in August. He's jumping up and down at the water's edge. The pebbles at his feet glisten like black diamonds. He's jumping and laughing, the sand squishing up between his toes, and Carey is jumping and laughing herself when Danny's soaked diaper undoes itself and tumbles off. Carey shrieks another laugh and hurries to grab him up, but Danny is already running away down the shore, his lightbulb butt bobbing between the beach walkers.

Carey draws away from Pete. She feels, all of a sudden, unexpectedly calm. The panic and fear that gripped her driving home yesterday and then later when she knew Danny was gone have, for now at least, leached away. Which is good, because if Pete is falling apart, she has to stay as composed as she can so someone is figuring out what to do next.

"Maybe those photos are staged, like the officer said," Pete says.

"It's possible. He can't—whoever this asshole is, he wants his money. He has to keep Danny safe."

She hopes this more than believes it.

"The police found a disposable phone outside. It's got to be the kidnapper's. Maybe they can trace it or something." He pauses. "They found a shoe too."

"I saw."

"One of Danny's high-tops, out by the road."

"So maybe he tried to resist."

"Maybe. They said Bledsoe got out of prison in December."

"All right."

"So maybe it's him. The police will find him. I'm sorry."

Enough with sorry, she thinks. "I left a message at Mother's."

"You don't think Serenity's going to help."

"I'll worry about her. You need to reach out to Oly."

Carey suspects that Pete was actually fired from O'Nally Bros. Yet he maintains a relationship with one of the brothers, Oly, so maybe he really did just quit because he was bored. Oly has at least as much money as Serenity Meredith Maas Bleak.

"What about the 'do not tell' thing?" Pete says.

"We can't just sit here. And the cops already know. We need to raise the money somehow in case they can't find him."

Carey's phone goes off.

"Oly doesn't use a cell, you know," Pete says. "That Serenity?"

Carey looks at her phone. It's the second call from a Bleak Harbor number, but not her mother's. Bledsoe? She doubts it—or wants to doubt it.

"No," she says. "I'm going into Danny's room. Get with Oly, please."

14

Everything in Danny's room looks to be in its place. The blue Cubs bedspread neatly folded beneath the pillows, the pillows stacked in their checkered blue-and-white covers, the Wallace Stevens anthology on the nightstand, four of Danny's five pairs of sneakers and sandals lined up at the foot of the bed, toes out. His green high-tops, always second from the left, are missing.

Danny doesn't like his parents going into his room when he isn't there. Carey finds this endearing, perhaps because it makes him seem like a normal fifteen-year-old.

At the window facing the bay, she sees sun bleeding around the edges of the drawn blinds. Most summer dawns, she likes to leave Pete in bed, pad barefoot out to the deck, and stand shivering in the last moments of dark to wait, first for the caress of warmth on the back of her neck, then for the glimmers of light skipping across the water.

Now the light reminds her that Danny has been gone for—she glances at her phone: 9:29—something like sixteen hours. She's been without him, and he without her, for longer than that many times in the past year, since Pete had them move to Bleak Harbor. She tells herself yet again that she couldn't help those absences. She wishes now, more than ever, that she could have them back. She wishes she were sitting with Danny on the tiny balcony of their Chicago condo, drinking tea and watching the sun rise through the skyline, the wind making it impossible to read the *Tribune*, Danny trying anyway, his eyes needle-points of focus as he halves and quarters the pages.

She feels tears coming, squeezes them back. *I will find you, honey.* She promises herself that when she does, she will take Danny away—whether she has the money or not, whether Pressman calls her bluff or not—she will take Danny away, alone, just the two of them, forever.

She reminds herself that Randall Pressman's Chicago number has also appeared on her phone twice in the past hour. Maybe he's feeling desperate. As she is. He could help her now. The ransom, five million bucks, is chump change to him. But she hesitates to call him back after what Pete showed her on his phone. What if someone really is listening in? At the same time, the thought of it, the wrecked chair, the hand in the shadows, infuriates her.

Hurt my boy, she thinks, *and I will hurt you.* And then decides if Pressman calls again, she will answer.

Danny's twin desks, spotless but for identical black blotters fitted with calendars, stand on facing walls. One wall is covered with posters of fish, the other with photographs and drawings of dragonflies that Danny made. He alternates between the desks, rolling from one to the other on his swivel chair, laptop propped on his knees. Carey and Pete have tried in vain to discern some pattern to his choice of desk on a given day; Danny has told them, shrugging as if it was obvious, that some days one desk works better than the other.

Carey pulls the chair over to the desk beneath the fish, where she set Danny's laptop and phone. She opens the laptop. As she waits for the password prompt, she notices something stuck in the groove between the keyboard and screen, at the very middle, as if Danny placed it there on purpose. She takes it out, holds it up in front of her face. It's a cherry stem. Danny doesn't even like cherries. She sets it aside.

She demanded Danny's password after his previous vanishing act, promising to use it only in an extreme emergency. He protested, but Carey wouldn't relent. He stalked into his room and emerged with his Wallace Stevens collection open to a dog-eared page at the back of the book. Carey knew the poem. She had read it hundreds of times, had listened to Danny recite it at least as many. He held the book up in front of her face. He had circled one word: *unhappy*. His password.

She types the seven strokes now for the first time since that night, feeling the savage swell of her emotions. Danny could be cruel that way. His anger, as sudden as it was fierce, frightened her sometimes. She had to remind herself that he wasn't always in control of himself, that he could be as much at the mercy of his unexpected compulsions as she was, that she couldn't blame him for being what—that is, who—he was.

As his doctors and her therapist had repeatedly told her, although his tantrums were usually aimed at her rather than Pete, they weren't always a direct response to something she had done or said or failed to do or say. They were merely Danny's way of purging his feelings without hurting himself. She should not fault herself. She should ignore anyone who did.

None of which made Carey feel any better when Danny flung himself and his fists and elbows and knees at her, screaming as if he, not she, were enduring the blows. Once in a while he would apologize. But first he would descend into his own quiet mourning for what he had done to his mother. At least that's what Carey imagined, what she hoped.

Once, after he bit her so hard on her forearm that she had to sponge droplets of blood from the kitchen hardwood, Danny locked himself in his room and refused to come out even to pick up the food Carey left for him outside his door.

After a day and a night, he appeared in the front room, where Carey and Pete were watching a movie.

"Look who's here," Pete said.

"Danny, honey," Carey said. Before she could get out of the recliner, Danny had crawled onto her lap as if he were six years younger. He hadn't done that in a long time.

"Mom," he said. He touched the bandage on her arm. "Mommy."

"It's OK."

He put his arms around her neck and buried his face in her shoulder. "No, no, no," Carey heard him saying, and it was all she could do to keep from crying. She gently rocked him, feeling his warm tears on her neck, telling him it was all right because it was, because Danny was the son she had made and she loved him more than anyone or anything in the world. He kept mumbling. Finally, Carey understood.

"Who is it?" Danny was saying. "Who is it?"

"Who is what, honey?" Carey said, and then in a terrible heartbreaking flash, she understood that he was asking about himself. "It's all right," she whispered into his ear. "It's going to be OK." Then her own tears came. Pete got off the sofa and came over, but Carey shook her head and held Danny tighter as her husband stepped back.

———

While the laptop starts, Carey lifts her eyes to the poster over the desk. A banner in gold atop a field of blue announces, THE GREAT FISH OF THE GREAT LAKES. Below it are pencil sketches of fish: bloaters and alewives, Chinook and coho, yellow perch and white, muskellunge, pike, smelt, burbot. They all look pretty much the same to Carey. Some are bigger or longer or skinnier than others, some a little grayer or greener. They're all swimming in the same direction, toward the left edge of the poster. They're all wearing the same faint, ironic grins. Sheep, not fish.

Carey reaches for Danny's mouse and tentatively inches it around, following the arrow-shaped cursor as it darts about the screen. She halts the white arrow in the middle. Her eyes stray to the edges of Danny's laptop, flecked with yellow and orange scraps of paper, the remains of torn-off two-word sticky notes he writes to himself in precise block lettering:

TROUT BOOK. MOM SCHEDULE. PADDLE TREATS. PETE CALL.

The rows of icons on the laptop screen are aligned as orderly as the dutiful poster fish. Carey wonders if she should have just handed the laptop and phone over to the cops, to someone who might actually know how to find what clues could be hidden within. Yet, clicking into Gmail, Carey knows she's not as curious as she is afraid. This computer is a window into her boy's mind. She doesn't know what it might reveal, and she's reluctant to have strangers, even police officers, see.

The email program opens. The expanse of white space inside the inbox saddens Carey. She knows Danny doesn't get many emails or texts or calls, because he has few friends. Really none she knows of. Most of the kids on this side of the bay are here on weekends only. Most are younger. Sometimes Carey hears them chortling like chipmunks as they build sandcastles, and she wishes Danny were still eight or nine so maybe he would join them. He's good at sandcastles when he's in a patient mood.

Sometimes Danny seems fine with it all, and Carey takes a chance on thinking he's feeling more comfortable with himself. Then he flies into one of his fits, and Carey has to ask herself again whether she has given him a real chance at a normal life.

No, she has to answer. By marrying Pete, she bought her son financial security, or what she thought would be security until Pete's trading went south and he had his preposterous, un-thought-through notion of becoming a marijuana magnate. Before Pete, it was all she could do as a human resources nobody at Pressman Logistics to get the rent paid and fill the fridge halfway after paying for Danny's schooling and therapy and medical bills.

The blast of a horn outside startles her. She pictures the tourists crowding the tour boat's gunwales, the brims of floppy hats and baseball caps shading their sunscreened foreheads. She takes the mouse in hand again and whispers, "Danny."

Three opened emails wait. One is harmless, from a Cubs fan site peddling T-shirts and caps. The other two make Carey sit back. "Oh God," she says. The sender of each is "bleeds0." *Jeffrey.* He probably thought the reference to blood was funny. Violence to him was an occupational hazard, an occasionally entertaining one.

When she'd met him, she was twenty-one years old, a recent graduate of the University of Michigan, pondering tattoos and a master's in social work, disgusted with her parents, planning to save the world or at least some shadowy corner of it along Detroit's gentrifying Cass Corridor. Who better to save than Bledsoe, a supposedly recovering addict who was taking banjo lessons at Wayne State and had pecs of quivering bronze?

Bledsoe was her rebellion, Pete her surrender.

She recalls Bledsoe's face the last time she saw him—Detroit, Indian Village, Danny's baby things in cardboard boxes. He stood behind a locked screen door.

"I ain't the daddy, am I?" he said.

"If only," she said. "Go away."

Do not hurt my boy, Carey's thinking now. *Just give me my boy, and we will disappear forever.*

How the hell would he know how to contact Danny anyway? She clicks on the earlier of the two emails. It arrived at 9:27 a.m. on April 8. The date is familiar, in a scary way. Carey scours her memory. A shiver runs up her forearms. April 8 was three days after Danny ran away and hid at the Helliker place.

She doesn't know whether she's more upset that Bledsoe contacted her son, or that Danny didn't tell her about it, or that Danny chose to save Bledsoe's email, not delete it. *Easy*, she tells herself. She closes her eyes, takes a breath, opens her eyes again.

The email subject line reads "YOU."

Champ,

This is your real daddy. Sorry about what's goin on. Glad u are OK.

Carey hates that word, *champ*. Jeffrey had used it to label any male he encountered, friend or stranger, unless it was *ace* or *bro*. Or *pussy*. That was another favorite, reserved for those whom Jeffrey felt either absolutely superior to or absolutely threatened by.

Men are so fucked up, Carey thinks.

The email went on:

Here for u, my man. Hope u know that.

Fuck you, she thinks. She wonders what Jeffrey knew or knows about what happened the day Danny ran away. Maybe he just read what that bitch wrote for the *Light*. Or, as much as Carey doesn't want to think it, maybe Danny told him. Maybe he was so furious with her and Pete that he sought out his birth father.

Why, Danny?

She remembers Bledsoe sprawled on a chair in her cramped office in Detroit with its odor of baseboard mold and scalded coffee. He would show up at her office unannounced and grin and flash his fingers for the number of days he'd been clean and sober. Carey would nod and smile and get off whatever call she was on. He made it to seventy-seven days. Or so he said.

———

She banished him from her life on what was supposedly Sobriety Day 81. It wasn't just that he was lying to her about using again. It was what it did to him that night as they hunted for parking on a Corktown side street before a Tigers ball game.

Carey drove her Ford Fiesta with the shattered side-view mirror. Jeffrey sat in the passenger seat with his rottweiler, Pip, curled at his feet. He brought the dog whenever they were out in the city. "Nobody fucks with Pip," he liked to say. "He's been expertly trained." Carey didn't like Pip much, but she tolerated him and supposed he tolerated her too.

Jeffrey was uncharacteristically quiet as they trolled the neighborhood that evening. Carey almost asked if something was wrong but wasn't sure she wanted to hear the answer. He had recently picked up that surly voice he adopted whenever he was around certain people. He'd had it when Carey first met him at social services. It had slowly disappeared as he got sober.

She saw the spot on Plum Street first, but a Civic full of young men coming from the opposite direction swerved to block her. "Jerk," she yelled out her window as she slowed going past.

By then Jeffrey and Pip were out of her car. She watched them in the cracked kaleidoscope mirror on her left and hand rolled the window down, shouting, "Jesus, Jeff, leave it."

Bledsoe walked to the Civic, Pip snarling beside him. The kid had made the mistake of rolling his window down. "What the fuck, old man?" he said, his pals laughing. Bledsoe reached through the window and dragged the kid—he couldn't have been twenty-five—out by his hair. Doors flew open, and Pip vaulted into the back seat and sank his teeth into a gym-popped bicep. Carey froze, her foot planted on the brake, as the bicep guy screamed and the driver yelled, "Dude, what the fuck?" while Jeffrey yanked him across the potholed street and rammed his head into the backseat window of a Buick, then pulled the kid's head back, blood spurting, and slammed it into the driver's window.

The kid's other two pals pulled Bledsoe away—he was laughing now—but they didn't have time or the balls to retaliate. They were yelling at Carey to call 911 as she pulled the car forward and screamed at Jeffrey to get in, goddamn it, get in before the cops show up. "Pipster, now, boy," Bledsoe shouted, and the dog sprang out of the Civic and scrambled with his master into Carey's Ford.

She screeched her way down the street, fishtailing so the kids might not pick up the license plate. She smelled the blood spackling Bledsoe's hairless arms, heard the sickening wet click of Pip licking his jaws. "What the hell are you thinking?" she said, but Jeffrey just grinned and said, "Serves 'em right, driving a Japmobile—don't it, Pipster?"

For the next few days, she avoided her office and ignored his calls and emails until, a week later, she felt like she had to tell him she was pregnant. It was his child, after all. Maybe he'd come around if he knew he was a father. She was mistaken about that. Bledsoe told her she must have fucked around on him. She told him goodbye. He told her good riddance, whore.

———

Carey skips to the more recent email from Bledsoe. She's trying to ignore the creeping realization that she's in the middle of one of those pathetic kidnappings that aren't really kidnappings, or that people don't count as kidnappings because they involve an ex-husband or ex-wife using a child as a human shield. But this is Jeffrey, she tells herself. If he'd learned nothing in prison, if he'd only grown angrier, if he's using, there's no telling what he might do.

The email's subject line says "Re: YOU." Carey assumes it's part of a string connected to the first email. She wants to see how Danny responded. The email opens. All prior messages, including Jeffrey's first, have been deleted.

The email had come the night before Danny was taken. *Oh fuck fuck fuck*, she thinks. The time signature says 10:29 p.m. Danny's bedroom door would have been closed and locked, but he probably would have been awake.

The email says only:

Y not, Danny boy?

Carey reads it again, then a third time, then picks up the mouse and slams it back down.

"Goddamn you, Jeffrey, goddamn you."

She scrolls to see what else is in the email. There's nothing. She can't see what Danny said to prompt Bledsoe's response. He apparently rejected something Jeffrey had requested or suggested. But what? A call? A visit? Had he pissed Jeffrey off enough that he would come to take her son by force? If Danny was unwilling to see Jeffrey, why would he have gone with him without a fight? She remembers the shoe the cops found discarded outside. Maybe there was a fight.

She returns to the first message, rereads it, then clicks back to the more recent one. There had to be emails in between. Why did Danny save only the two? She slides the cursor to the Sent folder, thinking she might find the entire string there. But there are only a dozen or so sent emails, all to the Cubs fan site, nothing addressed to bleeds0. If there was a string, Danny erased it.

She reads again:

Y not, Danny boy?

Why not what?

She picks up Danny's phone, fumbles it to the floor—"Damn it"— bends over, picks it up, turns it on. It wants a password. Carey didn't have the heart to demand Danny's phone password after the way he reacted to giving her the one for the laptop. She tries the laptop password: *unhappy.* Incorrect. Tries again. Wrong.

Her own phone is ringing. It's Pressman. She starts to answer, then calls out, "Pete? Are you still out there?" Deciding he's gone, she lets the phone ring once more before picking up.

"Carey Peters," she says, trying to sound tough, afraid she doesn't.

"Working from home today?" Pressman says.

"What do you want?"

"Wow. Right to the point. All right. You know what I want. I want to work this thing out."

Carey looks around the room as if somebody might be listening. "My son," she says.

"Your son?"

"I'm not at work because of my son."

"What happened?"

She thinks, for a short moment, about ending the call, then says, "He's been taken."

"What do you mean, 'taken'?"

"Kidnapped. For ransom."

The phone goes silent. Finally Pressman says, "You're serious."

"Dead serious."

"You obviously don't know who?"

"He calls himself 'Jeremiah.' And no, we don't know, but he wants five million dollars, or Danny—"

She can't finish.

"Five million? Have you called the police?"

"They just left."

"Jesus. Do you—do they have any ideas?"

She isn't sure what to say. She knows what she needs. She knows what Pressman will want in return. That's the way it is. Unless her mother helps. Which she can't count on.

"Carey?"

She imagines Pressman sitting in his office at company headquarters, a gray, three-story brick building hunkered like a dead hippo on a brushy bank of the Chicago River. Pressman took an absurd pride in keeping his gritty business of trucks and container ships and boxcars in that decrepit building on the river. He said he liked to count his money on the cargo boats chugging by. He took equal satisfaction in having a drab third-floor office with a plain steel desk, the two cheap angle-iron chairs facing it, the threadbare sofa, the Kmart lamp, the single window with its slatted perspective on the river. One black-and-white photograph hung on a wall to the right of the desk. A man with Pressman's dimpled chin stood in grease-smeared coveralls, holding a wrench the size of a baseball bat in his thick arms. It was Pressman's father, who had worked in a plant in northern Indiana, where Pressman grew up. Carey knew the plant. Her family had once owned it.

"I have to have five-point-one-four-five million dollars by 11:46 tonight. Which means right away, Randall. Are you going to help?"

He doesn't respond immediately. Then: "Sorry if I find it a bit surprising that you'd ask me."

"You called me."

"Your mother's loaded. What about her?"

"She's loaded, all right."

"It's her grandson."

"Who she hasn't seen in months."

"How do I know this isn't just another shakedown, with a discounted price?"

Again Carey feels the urge to hang up the phone, forget Pressman, pray the Bleak Harbor cops get lucky. "You prick. You don't have a choice."

"I have a choice, Carey. I can choose to just hang up now."

He's bluffing. He wants to be rid of her, the documents she stole, the threat she poses.

"Go ahead."

"And we'll all just take our chances."

"Go to hell."

"Sure. You can hold the door for me." He sighs. "Look. You don't have any idea who might have the kid?"

"His name is Danny."

A fresh email pops up in Danny's inbox. The From field says jeb@ jeb.com. Subject: Danny boy. Carey grabs the mouse, clicks the email open:

> boy safe for 14 hrs 3 minnits.
>
> that's all

She skims the rest quickly, her heart thrumming. This person somehow knows she's in Danny's computer? Does he know she's talking to Pressman? She scrolls down as far as she can. No new images of Danny, thank God.

"Danny. Yes. Sorry. You have no idea? Carey?"

She does, of course. But all Pressman needs to know is that she'll turn him over to the authorities if he doesn't pay the ransom. If Bledsoe really is the abductor, the cops will have to find him. If he's not, she'll have Pressman's money to pay whomever it is.

"I don't know," she says.

"All right. We can help each other here, Carey."

"Tell me how, Randall."

"OK. Can we just forget about everything up to this point? Wipe the slate clean? No more blackmail games?"

She's reading:

> U will get instructions on cash soon
>
> 5mill 145 grand

"It's possible," she says.

"Do you have something to write with?"

She pulls open a desk drawer, finds a legal pad and a box of sharpened pencils. Danny prefers pencils to pens for drawing because he likes to erase his mistakes and start over clean.

"Got it," she says.

"Write this down."

She hears the beep of a new call coming in as Pressman gives her the address of a restaurant across the Indiana-Michigan border. "How soon can you get there?"

She's reading the rest of the email:

> yr bitch mama could pay with tens and 20s or maybe hit up randy bossman (get it?) if u haven't already
>
> nummnuts cops aint gonna find danny boy
>
> Jeremiah
>
> ps. what I hear u don't deserve a kid anyway

She sits back straight, thinks, *You fuck.*

Another beep comes. She leans back into the desk, swallows hard, tells Pressman, "Hold on," flips to the other call.

"Roland," she says.

"Miss Carey."

It's her mother's personal assistant. *Your bitch mama*, she thinks. She has known Roland Spitler her entire life. She imagines him in his seersucker and bow tie, sitting at his little rolltop desk down the hallway from her mother's bedroom, his face as pale as if he lived his life in a closet. Which, in a way, he does.

"Have you found Danny yet?"

"No. You haven't heard from him?"

"We have not. I'm sorry. This is frightful news, of course. Miss Serenity is beside herself."

"Please, Roland."

"You really need to have more faith in your mother."

"I would love to. But now I need to call you back. I'm on the line with the police."

"We hope to be in position to help."

Hope, she thinks. *In position*. She taps back to Pressman. "Why am I going to a Mexican restaurant?"

"So I can help you."

"Randall, I need five million one hundred—"

"You will have it if we need it. But first we're going to find this scumbag who took your—Danny. He had—has a computer, right? Can you bring it with you?"

"A laptop." She hesitates. "The cops took it."

"Gimme a second."

She thinks she can hear irritation in Pressman's voice. He puts Carey on hold. She hears a piano plinking Devo. Pressman comes back on. "Does Danny have a portable hard drive?"

"I'll have to look." Carey knows what a hard drive is because she never remembers to use hers. "Why?"

"You'll be meeting Quartz. He works for me."

"Who?"

"Quartz. Like the rock."

She knows the names of most of Pressman Logistics' 153 employees. She thinks she'd remember a "Quartz."

"He's on my personal budget," Pressman says. "You don't know him."

"Do I want to?"

"Remember those boxcars of catalytic converters that disappeared from the rail yard in Roselle? How we tracked them down and had the bad guys in jail in under twelve hours?"

She recalls that one of the bad guys wasn't fortunate enough to get to jail. "In North Dakota. I remember."

"That was Quartz. My hunting dog."

She hadn't expected this. She just wanted the money. "This isn't a train, Randall. If this Quartz screws up, my son—"

"We're going to find your son. And if we don't, I will pay. And you will do your part. Just get to Valparaiso. Bring the hard drive. And there'll be no more discussion of documents or talking to the feds."

Carey looks up at the dumb grinning fish. *Dear Lord*, she thinks, *how did I put myself in this position?*

"Fine. And you will never touch me again."

"All right."

"And I will have my job as long as I want it."

"So be it. Quartz is an acquired taste. But he'll help you."

"He better. Or all bets are off—do you understand?"

"Get going."

She reads the new email again: "randy bossman." *Real funny*, she thinks. This bastard, too, seems to know about her Valentine's Day mistake. Would the police now know? Would Pete? Or, worst of all, Danny?

Carey rereads the postscript. *The hell with it*, she thinks. *The hell with all these people and what they think they know about me and my son. I'm gonna get him back and get out of this place forever.*

She looks again at the "randy bossman" line. This one she wishes she could delete. Just that one. Just those words. What difference would it really make to the cops or anyone? The rest of the email is what matters, not this random bullshit taunt.

But of course there's no way to selectively obliterate that phrase. She'd have to erase the entire email. She could delete it all and then go to the trash file and delete it again. The police would never see it, Pete would never know, Danny would never know.

Do not tell, Jeremiah had ordered.

She shuts her eyes, puts her fingers on the keyboard. Hits the print command.

She pushes away and rolls across the room to the other desk. Danny's portable hard drive, a black box about the size of a wallet, is in a drawer with other electronic paraphernalia. She grabs it, slides over to Danny's printer, snatches up the printout of Jeremiah's email. She gets up and walks back to the other desk. She shuts the printout in the laptop and picks up Danny's phone.

On her own phone, she punches the speed-dial number for her brother.

"Carey," he answers. "I've been trying—"

"Jonah, shut up—sorry, I don't have time."

"What?"

"I want you—I need you to meet me at the fork north of town, by Billy's Bait. I have something you need to take to the police."

"Right now?"

"Three minutes."

Arms full, Carey is leaving Danny's bedroom when something to her left catches her eye. She turns and stumbles back, bumping the door shut as she expels a yelp of fright. She fumbles for the doorknob behind her, eases the door back open. Sunlight from the hallway creeps across the pencil drawings pushpinned to the wall.

There's one Carey hadn't noticed until now.

The dragonfly's silver-dollar eyes are dense with fine, crosshatched strokes. Inside its mouth she sees two more eyes, a smaller insect being crushed in the dragonfly's dark maw. "My God, Danny," she whispers. She steps out of the room and closes the door.

15

"What the fuck, Quartz? I thought Bledsoe—"

"No names," Quartz says. He's sitting in an angle-iron chair across from Pressman, who just got off the phone with Carey Bleak Peters. "You don't know who's listening."

"I thought you hadn't heard from him."

"I have not."

"He got the kid."

"Obviously. But he hasn't yet alerted me as he was clearly instructed."

Idiot probably didn't write the phone number down, Quartz thinks.

"And you haven't heard from him otherwise?"

"We agreed we would not communicate, lest people make connections you don't want them to make."

"So he's just gone?"

"No. He's probably lying low. You know I will find him if it's necessary."

"Where the hell did he get that number? Five-point-one-four-five million? That's not what you told him, is it?"

"I told him the ransom would be what you and I agreed upon, a nice round one million dollars."

"So he just decides on his own to quintuple it? What does he think he's doing?"

Quartz shrugs. It's amusing to see the captain of industry sweat over a few million bucks. "It's possible he thinks he can shake us down. That might be a potential downside of hiring convicted felons for contract kidnappings."

"Fuck you, Quartz—"

"Names."

"—you said this guy would be fine."

Quartz doesn't know a great deal about Carey Bleak Peters's ex, but enough. Or so he thought.

Before Jeffrey Bledsoe went to prison, he had managed the boys, most of them no older than fourteen, who ran pot, coke, meth, and heroin for a Detroit entrepreneur named Vend. Bledsoe had supposedly professionalized the operation with sales metrics charted on Excel spreadsheets and quarterly bonuses bestowed on top performers, according to a *Detroit Free Press* clip. Bledsoe had also meted out discipline to those who failed to hit sales targets. Quartz hopes Bledsoe's time in prison had served to temper his more vicious impulses. He hopes, for the kid's sake, that Danny Peters did not put up any fight.

"My record is perfect so far," Quartz says. "But I'm actually not surprised. Now that he has the boy, he has more leverage. Or at least he thinks he does."

"You put the fear of God into him?"

"He knows."

Pressman swivels to face the single window in the office, shakes his head.

What a fool, Quartz thinks.

If Pressman hadn't insisted on banging Carey Bleak Peters, he wouldn't be sitting here now, wondering whether he might be indicted for conspiracy to commit kidnapping as well as whatever the feds would have on him if they saw those documents Carey stole.

If he hadn't taken Carey to his condo, he wouldn't have been confronted with her threat to blow the whistle on his less-than-legal activities, wouldn't have hired Bledsoe to kidnap Danny Peters so Pressman could swoop in to rescue the kid and save himself in the process.

Quartz knows Pressman sees things differently than most people. The rich and powerful always do. To Pressman, bedding Carey Peters, the milky lusciousness of her taut belly beneath him, was something to which he was entitled as her benefactor and, as the local gossip blogs noted, the most eligible bachelor in Chicago. The rest was bad luck and circumstance that he now has no choice but to deal with.

"Do you think she suspects our guy?" Pressman says.

"I couldn't tell from what I heard, but I doubt it. Far as I can tell, she and our guy haven't spoken more than once in years."

"Well, maybe they're speaking now. Maybe he cut his own deal with her. Maybe she knows we hired the guy. Christ, she'd have us by the balls."

Not quite "us," Quartz thinks. Pressman doesn't know it, but an FBI agent is hovering. Quartz's days as the rich guy's Mr. Fix-It are numbered. He just has to make or steal enough money to afford a pristine getaway.

"If you think that," he tells the back of Pressman's head, "then don't you also have to consider that he may have made an arrangement with her husband?"

"Peters? No way. The guy's a drip."

"A desperate drip, therefore unpredictable."

"His wife has no clue he's been buying illegal pot?"

"As far as I can tell, no."

It had been Quartz's job to figure out how to pull off the abduction. Hiring some random thug to grab the boy was too risky. It had to be someone Danny knew, so he was less likely to resist. A fifteen-year-old boy wouldn't necessarily be easy to subdue. And Quartz couldn't be sure how the kid's autism would affect things.

A little research led him to Bledsoe, who'd recently been released from prison and was living only an hour from Bleak Harbor. A phony email about local MILFs looking for one-nighters got Bledsoe to click on a link, and the malware Quartz had attached let him rummage around in Bledsoe's tawdry digital existence. At one point he estimated that Bledsoe spent almost all of his weekly diner paycheck on porn of both genders and all ages. Bledsoe's email account also was littered with scraps of evidence that he had another income stream, from his old boss in Detroit.

Quartz couldn't believe his luck when he discovered that Bledsoe, under some preposterous false identity, was selling illegal weed to Pete Peters. Credit to Bledsoe, he'd thought. Even after Quartz induced Peters to bite on a bogus email about low-interest loans and hacked into the wide-open computers at AMP Botanicals, he couldn't tell whether Peters actually knew with whom he was dealing. There were no direct emails between Peters and Bledsoe, but enough oblique refer-ences that Quartz was able to add things up. He had two conversations with Bledsoe, sent him a few texts from a disposable phone, and the snatch was on.

Yet Quartz prides himself on never being surprised. He cer-tainly didn't expect trustworthiness from a criminal. But he thought $350,000 in cash and a safe exit to a distant country would secure Bledsoe's loyalty. Not to mention the threat of Pressman's personal gestapo coming after him.

And "Jeremiah"? What was that? When he tracks Bledsoe down, he'll ask him what he was thinking, if *thinking* is the word. He's been trying for hours to get back into Bledsoe's computer, to no avail. Bledsoe must have changed a password or installed some sort of defensive soft-ware. Quartz isn't sweating it. Bledsoe knows how bad it will be for him if he skates on Pressman.

Pressman spins back around to face Quartz. "You know we have to find that kid before the cops do."

"You can't be a hero if you don't deliver the kid, right?"

"How bad is this guy really?"

"He's a felon convicted of aggravated assault for putting an unconscious man's mouth on a parking block and kicking the back of his head repeatedly. I told you this. Somehow the man lived, or Bledsoe would still be in prison."

"He isn't some kind of perv, is he? He's not gonna, you know?"

Bledsoe's past treatment of his young charges isn't reassuring on this point—neither is the porn—but Quartz says, "It's his son. But we will find him. Before the cops. The boy's mother can't have much faith in them, or she wouldn't be meeting me. I'll size her up. She might know something she doesn't know she knows."

"Jesus, what the hell are we doing?"

"We're doing what you decided to do a month ago when you were soiling your pants over Carey Peters and whatever she has on you."

"Fuck me." Pressman slaps his palms flat on his desk. "All right. We just—you don't think her old lady will bail her out?"

"I can see why that makes you nervous. If you're not the savior, maybe Carey goes back to the blackmail plan."

"That cannot happen."

"Serenity and your honey haven't been on speaking terms in ages. And I don't think Grandma's seen the kid in at least a year, even though she lives ten minutes away by stretch limo."

"She dislikes her daughter that much? Because the kid's retarded?"

"He's not retarded. He's autistic." Quartz searches Pressman's face for a hint of empathy. Unsurprised to find none, he continues. "The boy's condition doesn't help matters. But she and her mother haven't gotten along for a long time."

"That is one fucked-up family."

"Aren't they all?"

Pressman looks at his phone. "Son of a bitch," he says. "We gotta get this into the outbox, Quartz. We have other bullshit to deal with. The goddamn gooks are trying to get between me and the Chinks."

"The Vietnamese and Chinese never did get along."

"Shouldn't you get going? You gotta beat her there."

Quartz stands. "I am your loyal hunting dog."

"Why Valpo anyway? You can't find a Mexican dive in Chicago?"

"Best fish tacos in the Midwest."

16

Michele Higgins slides the ficus away from the window so she can see the cottage across the bay.

For some reason the weekly cleaning guy keeps parking the tree where it blocks the window facing the water. Michele likes the distraction of the view during the long hours she spends putting out the online-only *Bleak Harbor Light*. But this morning in particular, she wants to be able to see the Peters cottage if and when Carey Bleak Peters finally answers her phone.

Michele lifts the window and wedges the frame open with the ancient pica pole her editors had once used to lay out her articles before everything went digital. She'd rather use the air-conditioning, but it shut down two days ago, and the repair guy has yet to appear. She returns to her desk for her tea and her phone, then goes back to the window and sets her foam cup on the sill. She taps Carey Peters's number into her phone but doesn't hit the call button just yet. She'll wait the eight minutes till ten thirty.

The morning is as still as midnight. Across the mirror of water, the Peters cottage sits on a creamy lick of beach curling into the channel that winds out to the big lake. Three green adirondack chairs and a picnic table with an unopened umbrella stand on a wooden deck a few feet above the beach. The deck stretches across the sand to a dock where a small, covered fishing boat is tethered.

Michele tried Carey Peters's number twice earlier. She called the first time after getting out of bed a little after eight, checking her phone, and seeing the astounding bcc from someone calling himself "Jeremiah." The email had also been sent to Carey Peters.

Michele, who had never seen an actual ransom note in thirty years as a cops-and-courts reporter, immediately figured it as a malicious prank. The internet was full of trolls who for spiteful kicks would send a phony ransom demand to the mother of an autistic boy. But Michele couldn't discount the email entirely. She called Carey Peters, who didn't answer.

Michele went back to bed. Couldn't sleep. What kept her up was that, after the initial shock of seeing it, the ransom email didn't really surprise her. Subconsciously, she'd been expecting something more to happen with Danny, or to him, since she'd written her story about his earlier disappearance. Part of her hoped the ransom really was a twisted hoax. Another part told her something bad was happening. After so many years of mucking around in the dark slime of Detroit, she was inclined to believe the latter.

It didn't help that the whole extended Bleak family was reality-show weird. Michele had been posting stories for months about "Serenity's Gift," what Michele saw as the bitter old bag's way of entertaining herself on her deathbed, dangling a windfall Michele didn't believe she had any intention of delivering. At public meetings of Bleak Harbor City Council, there was Carey Bleak Peters, the estranged daughter destined for not one dime of her family estate, taking notes, saying nothing. And there was her castrated older brother, Jonah, nodding and rapping his little gavel as mayor. They'd grown up wealthy in a mansion on a bay, and there they were, at the pathetic mercy of their mother's cynical bidding.

Now Michele sits at the window of the old Victorian that houses the *Light* newsroom. Her phone shows 10:30. She hits the call button.

Come on, she thinks. *Pick up.*

Carey Peters answers. "Who is this?"

"Ms. Peters?"

"Who is this?"

"Michele Higgins of the *Light*."

There's a pause. For a second Michele worries she'll hang up.

"Aren't you done tormenting my family?" Carey says. She hadn't liked the article Michele wrote about her son's April disappearance.

"I'm sorry you feel that way."

"Why are you calling me?"

Michele hears a car horn in the background, wonders if Carey is driving somewhere. "I understand there may be a situation with your son." Michele waits, finally says, "I got a disturbing email concerning your son, Ms. Peters. I wanted—"

"What are you talking about?"

"The email says your son has been kidnapped."

"You don't have any email. You're lying."

"I'm afraid I do."

"I'll get a lawyer. You can't write this."

Confirmation, Michele thinks. *Not 100 percent, but close.* "The email comes from someone calling himself Jeremiah. It isn't a prank?"

Again she waits for the phone to go dead. She's hoping Carey is considering whether Michele can help her. Though it's not her job to help the people she writes about, if there's a kidnapping and her reporting helps bring a kid home, that would be fine. But really it's just a great story, the thing journalists call the terrible tragedies that befall other people. Michele hasn't had a great story since the *Free Press* purged her and fifty-two of her coworkers two years ago. But she has learned over the years that a great story goes a long way toward making a girl forget her life hasn't turned out exactly as she had hoped.

"I don't trust a word you say," Carey says.

"Ms. Peters—"

"Leave my family alone."

She hangs up.

Michele drops her phone into her lap. She understands. She'd almost decided not to post the brief story she wrote about Danny Peters in April. A kid found unhurt after a few hours wasn't much news, after all. But she'd dutifully posted anyway:

Boy's Disappearance Gives Bleak Clan a Fright

By Michele Higgins

Fifteen-year-old Daniel Peters, youngest member of Bleak Harbor's founding clan, gave his family a scare Thursday night when he disappeared from home and couldn't be found for several hours.

"We were terrified," said his mother, Carey Bleak Peters, 37. She declined further comment, as did her husband, Andrew "Pete" Peters, 39, owner of AMP Botanicals, the new medical marijuana clinic in town. Roland Spitler, spokesman for Bleak family matriarch Serenity Meredith Maas Bleak, issued a one-sentence statement: "Ms. Bleak is both relieved and dismayed to hear of this development."

The young Bleak was found sometime after midnight, asleep in the basement of an abandoned house next door to his parents' home at 39878 South Bay Drive, said Bleak Harbor Police Chief Booker Radovich. "He was lucky he didn't get hurt in there," Radovich said. The boy has been diagnosed on the autism spectrum.

Radovich said the police consider the case closed. A separate investigation by the Bleak County Department of Social Services is continuing, he said.

The last, innocuous sentence was what got Michele into trouble with Danny's mother. Michele had heard that complaints had been lodged with social services about screams and other noises coming from the Peters house. A county source had confirmed that department staffers were looking into it. Plus, there was that security fence going up along both sides of the property. To a former Detroit cop reporter, it all reeked.

Maybe Michele wouldn't have included the sentence if she'd had an editor to press her for more details. But for the most part, it was just her, a computer, and her cell phone. Technically, she had a boss in Grand Rapids, a woman named Gatti, who chimed in about what to cover, especially during the festival. But almost everything Michele wrote went on the *Light* website as she'd typed it.

Carey Bleak hadn't bothered calling Michele to complain. She'd gone straight to Gatti, who ordered Michele to delete the sentence. Gatti had no desire to mess with the Bleaks. Michele had obeyed, but the damage was done.

The next day, she started watching the boy.

Each morning at ten o'clock sharp, Danny emerged onto his deck, barefoot in droopy shorts and a T-shirt, a laptop under one arm. He positioned the laptop just so on the picnic table.

He never went near the water in the morning. He sat tapping on his laptop, two-finger style, for two and a half hours, stood, went inside, and reemerged with lunch on a paper plate. After Michele started using the cheap binoculars she'd bought at Crova Hardware, she could see that the plate always held a sandwich, potato chips, and a cookie. Some days, the boy's stepfather joined Danny for lunch. Michele watched to see if and how much they talked. The boy seemed to dictate this. Some days he couldn't shut up. Others, he simply ate and looked at the bay while Pete Peters talked.

After eating, Danny would pat his lips clean with his napkin and roll it up in the plate. If it wasn't raining, sometimes even when it was, he walked out to the dock. Some days he sat and read a book. Michele couldn't make out the book's title, but it looked like the same book, the same green-and-black cover, every day. She wondered why he didn't finish it and read something new. He never seemed to even turn a page.

Some days he left the book behind and walked out to the end of the dock. He peered into the water as he shifted from one side of the dock to the other, or he gaped at the air around him, his head twitching back and forth, following something he apparently saw that Michele couldn't make out from afar. Other days Danny walked the beach. Sometimes that white-haired bartender hailed him.

Almost nobody came to see Danny besides his mother and stepfather. Once, though, Michele had seen a short, buxom woman emerge onto the deck late in the afternoon while Danny was out on the dock. The woman had a dark complexion and wore a blue sweatshirt emblazoned with the Detroit Tigers' big-*D* logo. She carried a package under one arm. She waved at Danny. He pointed at the house. The woman went inside. Danny stood where he was for a moment, looking around as if to be sure no one had seen. Then he went into the house. Michele never saw the woman again.

She was beyond feeling pity for children after seeing the rib cages of twelve-year-olds blown to bloody shreds by shotguns. But, looking at Danny, she felt something. He reminded her of her adolescence, how she had wriggled out of her parents' embraces, not understanding why she felt angry or whether she was upset with them or herself or merely the idea of being fifteen years old and wanting desperately to be on her own while knowing she needed these adults, these suddenly repulsive total strangers, for almost every single thing that kept her safe and warm and fed. She supposed Danny felt that too.

She takes her phone and foam cup back to her desk, dumps the rest of the tepid tea in the trash. She can already feel the day's heat like glue on the insides of her elbows. She wants to write something about what she knows, but she knows she doesn't know enough. She picks up her phone, dials.

"Police."

"Hey," she says to the dispatcher. "Michele Higgins."

"Good morning. We don't have any crowd counts yet—the festival doesn't officially start till noon—but let's just say, oh, ten million or so."

Dragonflies, Michele thinks. Why would anyone celebrate a spooky insect that flits this way and that on those skeletal wings? To her they seem more like lizards.

"At least," she says, acknowledging his joke. "That's not why I'm calling."

"There's something more important than the festival?"

"Who's around?"

"Uh, let's see, the chief, but he's on a call. Will, Malone—"

"Katya Malone? She's back?"

"Yeah."

"How's she doing?"

"Fine, far as I can see. But I'm not supposed to comment, you know."

"Don't worry. Can you have somebody call me?"

"I'll try."

Normally Michele would stroll down to the cop shop and wait around, but she's supposed to meet one of the festival organizers. Gatti, who arranged the meeting for Michele, has made it clear she wants the *Light* website full of updates on how fabulously the festival is going and photos of people in painted faces gobbling funnel cakes and guzzling beer.

She clicks her mouse to get her computer going, check the website before she goes. The thing's been balky lately. Michele hasn't called the tech guy in Kalamazoo yet because she doesn't want to admit that a week ago she fell for an emailed link offering cheap Vegas flights that turned out to be bogus. She hopes it's just a glitch. She hopes nobody has hacked her. Gatti would not be happy about that.

Michele looks at her phone: 10:44. The computer screen comes alive, though not in the normal way. It starts flashing—blue and then black, blue and then red and then black again. Michele taps the mouse on her desk. The flashing continues. "What the hell?" she says. Now she'll have to call the tech guys.

She shoves away, grabs her backpack, and glances a last time through the window at the Peters place before heading out.

17

Carey waits, knees beneath her chin, atop the picnic table facing the lake, a brown paper shopping bag at her feet.

She hears him coming, doesn't turn around because she's waiting for his arms. And then, there they are, embracing her shoulders. "Jonah," she says. "Thank you—thanks . . ."

She can't get it out.

"Carey, my God."

Her older brother slides onto the table next to her. She keeps crying. She feels a sob shake him, pushes in closer to his embrace. A minute passes, maybe two, before they separate and look out at the water.

They would come here when they were children and didn't want to hear their parents fighting. Bicycles carried them away from the mansion and the shoulder of Blue Star Highway to the small cut of thin grass and sand where the waves sloshed up over pebbles and driftwood. They would sit at this picnic table and tell each other that they would leave Bleak Harbor someday, never to return.

"I talked with the chief," Jonah says. "They're on this."

Carey just shrugs.

"Who could this be?" he says.

She shakes her head. "Somebody who thinks they can get at Mother's money?"

"The thought crossed my mind. Goddamn it." Jonah lays a hand on her knee, squeezes. "I understand why you wanted to come here, but now we have to get back to town."

She hands the brown bag to Jonah. "I need you to get this to Officer Malone," she says. "It's Danny's laptop and . . ." Again she can't finish.

"I don't understand. Why don't you just take it to her?"

"I have somewhere—something to do."

"What?"

"It's for Danny."

"Carey."

She usually told her older brother everything. He was her Irish twin, born in January, ten months before she was. Their father had insisted the boy be named Jonah because he said Serenity grew as big as a whale while carrying him. Pregnant again six weeks later, Serenity decided her new child, boy or girl, would be named Carey.

Jonah had been Carey's rock when she left Detroit and Bledsoe behind and returned with baby Danny to Bleak Harbor, where she would eventually learn that her parents wanted little to do with her afflicted youngster.

He had picked her up at the Amtrak station in Kalamazoo that night. It was raining, and Carey cried at the sight of her brother while Danny twitched in his fevered sleep. Jonah took him from her, and immediately he settled down. She drove while Danny slept in Jonah's arms.

When Carey decided to leave Bleak Harbor again, Jonah loaned her enough money to set herself up in Chicago, and he came to visit weekend after weekend. He'd take Danny in his stroller up and down the city blocks while Carey went shopping or got her hair cut or just stayed in her apartment, reading and napping. He accompanied her on many of the doctor appointments when it was beginning to become clear that there was something different about Danny. "Different is not wrong," Jonah told her over and over. "Different can be better."

He taught Danny backgammon when he was six. Soon Danny was doing the schooling. Jonah marveled at how the boy's eyes darted back and forth, from one die to the other, as he calculated the possibilities before a hand emerged from his lap and he slid the stones around the board with the decisiveness of a croupier, his eyes never leaving the board until he looked up at Jonah and said, "You."

Jonah took Danny to the Chicago museums, the art institute, the music festivals, Wrigley Field. There were Friday evenings when the two of them would make the long walk to Millennium Park and sit in the pavilion, listening to the symphony orchestra. It was on one of those evenings that Jonah introduced Danny to the book of poems that would become his favorite, *The Palm at the End of the Mind.*

Carey gets off the table. "It's almost eleven," she says. "Malone is expecting this stuff."

"Chief said the ransom deadline is 11:46 tonight. Isn't that about when Danny was born?"

Carey remembers calling her brother from the recovery room at Henry Ford Hospital, downtown Detroit. He was at her bedside the next morning.

"Exactly when Danny was born," she says. "I have to go."

"Carey, why don't you just come back with me now?"

"We don't have time. Just take that and go."

She starts toward her car, hears Jonah call out. As she's getting into the car, she turns and shouts at him, "Do not follow me. I love you."

18

Pete shoehorns his SUV into the last remaining spot in the subterranean lot of Johnny's Ice House. He slides his window down halfway and listens for the click and scrape of skate blades carving the ice surface on the floor above him. Oly O'Nally won't be off the ice until 11:50. Pete doesn't mind waiting. The garage feels safe. Nobody knows he's here.

He's been driving aimlessly for the past two hours, avoiding festival roadblocks, listening to the radio for news, trying to work up the courage to make a certain phone call. He's also tried Dulcy a few times to let her know the store is closed for the day, but she isn't answering, and her voice mail box is full.

"All right," he says. He taps a number into his phone. He hears one ring, quits the call, drops the phone into his lap. He has no idea what he's going to say. Part of him is praying that Jeffrey Bledsoe or somebody else, anybody else, took Danny. But he knows that it's more likely that the kidnapper is the man Pete does not want to call.

He picks up the phone, dials again. Slim answers, as always, just as the fourth ring is ending, before the call bounces to voice mail. It's a code Slim has insisted upon, ostensibly so Pete will know he hasn't mistakenly called someone else before saying something that could get Slim in trouble. "Trouble for me is trouble for you," Pete has heard him say more than once.

"Yessir," Slim says, his standard greeting. As always, his voice gives Pete a small jolt of fright.

"It's me."

On the trading floor Pete had the ability to set his fear aside to get done what needed to get done. Not with Slim.

"Got the money yet?"

Pete doesn't know Slim's last name. He has never met the man and has no particular desire to. He pictures Slim as a mass of brown sinew, with a shaved head and a T-shirt that looks painted on, a character he has seen on a TV cop show, a dangerous black man running dope for a dangerous white man.

Slim has mentioned his boss only once, the first time he contacted Pete. Mr. V, as Slim referred to him, is the reputed head of a midwestern pot-growing syndicate that for decades has supplied illegal marijuana dealers from the Mackinac Bridge south into Ohio, Indiana, and Illinois. The weed is supposedly grown in vast underground greenhouses beneath the dense forest of Michigan's Upper Peninsula.

Mr. V's operation has slowly taken hold of the state's legal marijuana business while the legislators and regulators argue over how to spend all the new tax income they expect to reap from medical pot. The marijuana Slim delivers is truly killer, with at least the punch and staying power of any of the legal stuff. And it's cheaper. The politicians set price minimums for legal dope so high and tacked on so many taxes and fees that the illicit suppliers could undercut the legals and still make almost as much profit as before. If you didn't stock the contraband, your customers would find a state-licensed shop that did. Like that one in New Buffalo.

The first time Slim called him cold, introduced himself, said he could save Pete's business with Mr. V's "primo" product. "Same stuff your competitor down the road's kicking your ass with." Pete told him thanks, he'd go it on his own. Slim provided a number, just in case. A week of slow days later, Pete convinced himself he could go in with the guy just long enough to dig AMP Botanicals out of this start-up hole. Then he'd go street legal again.

Next came midnight deliveries of primo and drop-offs of cash-filled piggy banks in dumpsters behind Burger Kings. Things for AMP Botanicals improved. Customers liked the new stuff, liked the lower prices. Pete started paying down his debts.

Then Slim disappeared. Stopped answering calls. AMP Botanical's inventory of primo was down to a few ounces when he finally showed up on Pete's phone one evening. He said Mr. V was sorry for the delay, but he was experiencing "regulatory issues," and while he would never raise prices, he would need an up-front payment for "security" purposes.

Your security or mine? Pete thought.

The next call came after Pete didn't pay by the specified deadline because he didn't have the cash. Slim informed him the security advance would now be $12,000, going up $3,000 each week Pete failed to pay. Pete said he couldn't afford that; sales weren't going up that fast. What if they just ended their relationship amicably? "You have that option," Slim replied. "But I will require a personal visit to tie up loose ends, if you know what I mean."

Pete wanted no loose ends with Slim. He could imagine the guy waiting for him behind the shop some night, tire iron in hand. He accepted a new shipment of primo, paid for that and half the security advance. Slim wasn't happy about half. He said he'd do what he could for Pete, but he couldn't guarantee that Mr. V wouldn't take "more decisive action."

That was two days ago. Then Pete started getting the texts from that weird area code threatening his family.

Then Danny was gone.

His chest feels like it might explode.

He hears a grinding whine—maybe a machine?—in the background on the other end of the call. Slim must be outside somewhere. It makes Pete think of a car trunk, a body duct-taped hand and foot inside, wheezing in the heat, a welt on the forehead.

"Slim," he says. "I will get the money. I promise. Just give me a day. But this—you can't do this. You can't . . . this is, this is . . ." He can't get the words out he's breathing so hard.

"I can't what?"

"You can't do this."

"What the—speak up, pussy. I can't hear you."

"I do not have five million dollars. I will never have it."

"Shitfuck. Hold on a second."

The whining sound is muffled for a moment, but Pete hears Slim yelling, "Can you shut that thing down for a minute?" The sound grows louder again, and Slim addresses Pete.

"Fucking idiots. So you"—he pauses—"so you got the money or not?"

"You sent me texts."

"What? Goddamn it, speak up, man."

"Don't lie," Pete says, then lies himself. "The police know."

"Police? Are you out of your fucking mind?"

"I'll get you the rest of your twelve thousand, I promise, but give our son—"

"I can't hear a damn thing. I suggest you get us our money, pussy. You don't want to deal with Mr. V—trust me."

Slim hangs up. Pete stares at the phone, thinking, *Something's not right—there's something different about this guy.* When he was yelling at somebody to shut off the noise, it was Slim's voice. But it wasn't. Pete replays what he heard in his head. As Slim was shouting, his voice sounded different. And when he came back on with Pete, he sounded different until he stopped and repeated himself.

Pussy, Slim said. It propels Pete back to December, Boz's bar, a Monday night, the Packers killing the Lions on TV, Carey still driving back from a weekend in Chicago with Danny. The Packers were lining up for an extra point when Pete's gaze wandered, and he was startled to see a stranger staring at him in the mirror behind the bar. He had an almond-shaped head that craned forward from a long neck, giving him the look of an ostrich. Pete couldn't tell whether the bluish swirls along his neck were veins or old tattoos. Behind him, the red nose on a plastic reindeer's head blinked.

Pete tried to act casual as the guy hung a thin-lipped grin over his longneck Bud. Pete glanced down the bar, and the guy's eyes slid sideways to meet Pete's. He raised his bottle in a toast. Pete nodded and drank, then slipped off his stool for the men's room, where he locked the door.

When he emerged, the stranger was gone, and so was Pete's Sam Adams Octoberfest. In its place stood a fresh Bud and a note scrawled in ballpoint on a damp napkin:

"Get real beer. Pussy."

It kept Pete up that night and the next. He avoided Boz's for a time. But the guy never showed his face again.

Pussy, Pete thinks again.

It's four minutes after noon. Oly O'Nally is probably in his dressing room by now. Pete will go up in a minute. But first he summons Google on his phone and enters "jeffrey bledsoe." He wants to know what he doesn't want to know.

The top results are all for a man who oversees a global mining empire from Vancouver. Pete moves to the next page. Halfway down is a link to a six-year-old *Detroit Free Press* story. The headline says, "Man Linked to Drug Boss Sentenced for Vicious Assault." Pete clicks the link. The man in the story is Jeffrey Bledsoe. There's a black-and-white mug shot. Pete stares at it, then closes his eyes. The guy in the photo is the guy who leered at him in the mirror at Boz's, the guy standing in front of the blinking deer head.

Pete lets his head drop to the steering wheel.

Slim is Bledsoe, he thinks. *Bledsoe is Slim.*

How utterly stupid could he be, not just to fall for Slim but to think he could keep everything from the cops while Danny's life hung in the balance? The only consolation is that he did not know that Slim was actually Bledsoe. Idiotic, he knows, but he really didn't. How could he have known?

Now he knows. And now, though it could destroy his marriage and his business, maybe even land him in prison, he has to tell the cops about Slim and Mr. V, the illegal dope, the piggy banks, the demands for security payments. All of it.

Pete pulls out Malone's card and dials her cell as he climbs the stairs to the rink. He hears the sound of a Zamboni groaning its way around the ice. He doesn't really expect Oly to help. The old man fired Pete, after all—one more thing Pete didn't make clear to his wife. But Oly is a good man. He might take pity. And Pete promised Carey he'd try. So he will.

Malone's phone rings three times and goes to voice mail. "Leave a message" is all the recording says. Pete, feeling relieved, is about to end the call without leaving a message when he realizes she'll see he called anyway. "Officer, I'm sorry," he says, then wishes he hadn't. "It's Pete Peters. I have to . . . call me, please."

19

"Katya?"

Malone spins, phone to her ear, and sees Mayor Jonah Bleak on the sidewalk where they agreed to meet outside Nucci's Tavern. He's carrying a brown shopping bag. "Mayor," she says, holding up a finger for him to wait.

She had almost made the cemetery when the call came for her to meet the mayor, who was bringing Danny Peters's laptop. She considered going to see Louisa anyway, if only for a minute, but reluctantly turned her cruiser around and headed back into town.

Malone half turns away from Jonah and tells Will, "Gotta go— mayor's here, Danny Peters's uncle." The sweat trickling down the back of her neck makes her think of the boy taped to that chair. She wonders if he's hot too, if he's suffering, wherever he is.

"This Pérez woman who works for Peters?" Will says. "The only address I find for her is in Detroit."

"Detroit?"

"I'll run it down. Weird, though, she did not show up for work this morning."

"Maybe Peters told her the store was gonna be closed. Or maybe she saw the cops and got the hell out of there."

"Or maybe she never planned to show up at all."

"You tried the cell number Peters gave us?"

"No answer—voice mail's full. Sent a text."

"Stay on her. Anything more on Bledsoe?"

He tells her about the circumstances of Bledsoe's assault conviction. She listens, holding her grimace inside. Then Will says, "One thing I read connected him to a dealer in Detroit, guy named Vend. So both Bledsoe and Pérez have Detroit ties."

"Great. Let's hope it's a coincidence. What about his middle initial?"

"Far as I can see, he didn't have a middle name."

Malone's phone beeps with a call. She ignores it. "Stay on the parole officer too, OK? We have to find this Bledsoe."

She stows her phone and turns back to Jonah. He's a slim man, a head taller than Malone, in a white button-down shirt open at the collar, khaki shorts, rimless spectacles, a goatee the color of snow-flecked wheat. His shirt pocket is stuffed with a cell phone, pens, a folded-over Dragonfly Festival street map.

They're standing behind a face-painting station on Lily Street, flanked on both sides by arts-and-crafts booths. Malone smells popcorn and kielbasa, hears the canned merry-go-round calliope, the shrieks of kids on the Tilt-A-Whirl. An oversized plastic dragonfly, lime green and gold, totters from a light post behind Jonah. Across Lily stands a tent where out-of-town strangers have started quaffing crappy beer and dancing to Tom Petty covers.

"Mayor," she says. "I'm sorry about your nephew. We have officers from here, Allegan, Berrien, Cass, and Kalamazoo Counties looking everywhere, going door-to-door, searching the dunes. The FBI is on the way. Alerts have gone out all over the Midwest."

Jonah is nodding, trying to keep his composure. She's seen it before. "Chief filled me in," he says.

Many of Bleak Harbor's year-rounders wonder why Jonah Bleak ever bothered to run for mayor. He's long divorced, childless, a real estate broker who could do the same anywhere, no less estranged from his whacked-out mother than his sister, Carey, is, with no compelling need to stay in Bleak Harbor. There were rumors that his father wanted a Bleak babysitting things, if not actually running them—that was

Jack Bleak's job—and that Jack Bleak had threatened to revoke Jonah's inheritance if he didn't step up.

Then Jack died, and his widow concocted the bizarre quid pro quo that the media labeled "Serenity's Gift." Jonah, who would get none of the gift himself, was left to wrestle with his counterparts at the county and township for his city's share of the loot.

He hands Malone the shopping bag and says, "Danny is a resilient young man. But I'm very . . ." He stops to collect himself. "I'm very worried about this person who may have taken him."

"Bledsoe? Do you—did you know him?"

Jonah briefly looks away. "Not much, but enough, unfortunately. He's a bad character. Really bad."

"He dated your sister a while back?"

"Not sure *dated* is the right word. What did he go to prison for?"

Malone thinks of Bledsoe's parking-block victim, jaw torn in bloody halves. "Assault," she says, leaving out the "aggravated" part.

"Carey told me he had a mean streak. And unpredictable as all get-out, just would snap at the slightest provocation. Which is what—I mean, I just keep thinking, if Danny doesn't—you know, he's not always, shall we say—"

"Don't," Malone says. "We're going to find him."

He takes a breath, then says, "And Pete was at the bar."

"Apparently so. Do you know him well?"

"Pete's Pete."

"Reminds me: Would you happen to know his employee? Name's Dulcinea Pérez."

"Dulcy. I've heard Carey complain about her, but I've never met her."

"Complain about what?"

"Nothing, just . . . coming in late, not being reliable. What about Bledsoe? Do you have any idea where he is?"

"Not yet, but we will. We're trying to reach his parole officer, who should at least—Jesus."

Both their heads snap around at a sudden blast of guitar chords from the beer tent. A band is warming up with a song a lot older than Malone. "Sorry, the parole officer should have Bledsoe's address. We've left messages."

"The parole officer can't be the only one who knows."

"There's a duty guy at the parole office, but he can only give it out if Bledsoe is under official investigation, and—"

"He's not? Do I need to call the chief?"

"Mayor, listen. It's probably unlikely he'd take Danny to his listed address anyway. But we're on it—we will find him."

"I'm sorry. I know you're doing your job."

"Don't be sorry." Her phone keeps blurting with texts, probably from Will. "By the way, Chief heard from your mother's assistant. Spitler? He asked that we try to keep this quiet, no publicity."

"Of course." Jonah's cheeks flush. With anger, Malone decides. "What could be more important than the Bleak reputation?"

"It's all right." She glances inside the shopping bag, sees a laptop, a phone, a knot of electrical cords like rat snakes. "I thought your sister was going to bring this."

"She had—has other things to do."

Malone chooses not to ask, *Like what?* "I've been trying to call her."

"I think she's with our mother. We may need her help."

Malone has a feeling he doesn't know where his sister is. She lets it go for now.

He looks at his watch. "I can't believe I have to go meet some damn festival donor."

"Don't hesitate to check in with me or Chief."

"I won't. So what about you? What's it been now, a year?"

"Pretty close. Chief asked me back early for the festival."

"Well," he says. "I'm glad you're here."

"Don't be afraid, OK? We will bring Danny home safe."

Jonah hurries off. Already the street is more crowded than it was ten minutes ago. Malone waits a few seconds, then sets the bag down, takes out her phone. There's a voice mail from a number she doesn't know and two texts from Will:

chief talking to dep warden in Muskegon . . .

Good.

might have a bead on bledsoe

Better.

But still, Malone thinks as she starts walking toward the station. She breaks into a jog, squeezing left and right through the gathering throngs, recalling what Jonah just said about Bledsoe's mean streak, feeling a spoil in her gut, feeling afraid.

20

The fingernails on Quartz's left hand are gnawed to slivers. Carey noticed it the minute she sat across from him at the restaurant in Valparaiso. Her father, too, had been a nail-biter, chewing the ones on his right hand until they bled. For a long time it was his only visible flaw. The others were hidden, until they weren't.

"I already ordered," he says.

"Traffic," she says. "There was an accident on 94." She's lying. After leaving Jonah, she drove down the beach road a mile and pulled over to cry again.

"Do you want anything?" Quartz says. "Randall's buying."

"No," she says. "Do you work for the company?"

"I get paid by the company."

"What are you doing here, in Valparaiso?"

Carey has been wondering that about herself since she pulled into Valparaiso's main square. What is she doing here? Sitting at a high-top table in a recess of gaudy gold-and-burgundy tile, in a place called Xochimilco that's empty but for a table of four across the room, this stranger Quartz, and a waiter in a red vest and black bolo tie. Danny's not here, the police aren't here—what is she doing here?

As she was driving from Bleak Harbor, questions swirled around her brain, tightening like a tourniquet: What is Danny eating? Is he warm? Is he dry? Has he slept? Has the bruise on his cheek spread? Did the kidnapper ice it? Are there other bruises, other scars? Is Danny scared? Is he crying? Just the disruption in his daily routine has to be horribly upsetting. Is the kidnapper aware of Danny's condition? What about his meds? Oh God, does Danny wonder if he's going to die? Is he begging for his mommy? The last question made her eyes well, and she nearly sideswiped a panel truck.

"I generally like to work from home," Quartz says. A sheet of paper rests facedown beneath his left hand. He has a can of Tecate with lime. He's waiting on fish tacos. "Thank you for coming down."

"Do you have a first name?" Carey says.

"Quartz. Tell me about your son."

"Your name can't be Quartz."

"I'm going to find your son."

"Is Pressman going to pay the ransom?"

"I'm going to find Danny. I need your help."

Carey wraps her arms around herself. The air-conditioned relief from the heat outside is too much. "So you're not going to tell me."

"Tell me about your son."

Quartz is a wire of a man in a black button-down shirt. The shirt has two button-flap breast pockets and two below those, one low on the left side above his belt. Slight bulges in each. Black jeans. Black sneakers. He's in his mid to late thirties, going-away hair wisping around a face pale as skim milk, a skimpy afterthought of a beard, green eyes not unlike Carey's. Or Danny's. Tiny scars curl from the corners of each eye. The scars appear identical, as if they'd come not from an accident but something purposeful, maybe surgery.

Carey unwraps her arms, takes a drink of water from a plastic cup. Jumpy, she sets the cup down hard enough that it splashes drops on Quartz's hands. He gives no indication of feeling it.

"Is Pressman going to pay?" Carey says.

"Have you looked online? People are talking about you."

"Already?"

"Are you kidding? It's been hours, not minutes."

"So?"

"Some people think maybe you and your husband—Pete, yes?—are faking the kidnapping to get your mother to pay the inheritance you're not supposed to get."

"That's it. You got us. But you forgot the part about where we beat Danny up before we faked his kidnapping."

"I didn't say I believed it."

"Who are you?" She half stands in her chair. "Am I here to amuse you and Pressman? I can get that federal agent on the phone in ten seconds if you and your boss would like."

"Sit. Please. I'm merely trying to eliminate possibilities and—"

"And you think that I could put my son through this?"

"Fair enough."

"Those people are disgusting."

Carey wanted to track down every single one of the vile gossips and smack them across their faceless faces at the same time that she wanted to hide inside her house for a year.

"I agree. There's one individual on Twitter who's really been going after you. Do you know anyone named Drew?"

"Drew who?"

"Not sure. It's a Twitter handle."

"So you don't know if it's his real name."

Quartz nods in agreement, takes a sip of beer, then says, "Here's a real name for you: Jeffrey Bledsoe."

Carey sits up straight, feeling the blood rush to her head.

"Your ex," Quartz says. "The guy who fathered your son."

"I know who he is."

"Then you know he got out of the state prison in Muskegon last December after serving a term for aggravated assault. He was emailing with Danny quite recently. Did you know that?"

"No," she lies. "How do you know?"

"Let's just say I'm good with computers."

"You're one of those hackers?"

"That is such a crude term."

"You hacked into my son's computer?"

"No. Bledsoe's computer."

"Already?"

"Seemed obvious. Did you bring Danny's hard drive?"

Carey reaches into the purse hanging on her chairback and pulls out the portable hard drive, sets it on her side of the table.

"You don't monitor your son's email?"

"You don't have children, do you, Quartz?"

"Danny is—what's the politically correct word, *special*—is that it?"

"He's on the autism spectrum. That's the label the doctors use. No label, insurance doesn't pay."

"So, does he have things that, you know, interest him in particular?"

"Because all autistic people have obsessions, right?"

"All *people* have obsessions, Ms. Peters; they just don't display them all the time."

"Yes, Danny has obsessions. The Chicago Cubs. Lake fish, especially perch. Dragonflies. This one Wallace Stevens poem."

"Wallace Stevens? In college we used to get high and read his stuff aloud. No idea what it meant. I remember something about a blue guitar. Is that the poem?"

"No."

"But just one, over and over, the same one?"

She pictures Danny sitting across from her on the deck, shaking his head no like a metronome. A whispering drizzle had claimed that late March afternoon. It was too cold and damp to be outside, but Danny had opened the umbrella on the picnic table and insisted. Carey, wrapped in a wool shawl, had agreed on the condition that he consider just one of the other Stevens poems. The poem he loved—or perhaps *loved* wasn't quite right; perhaps *clung to* was more accurate—was a beautifully elusive verse, but Carey wished her son would, as she put it, "expand" his view of the world.

"My view of the world is right here," Danny said, gesturing toward the lake, the water boiling with the rain. "That's enough."

Carey picked up the book from the table and paged to a poem she thought Danny would like. "This one, look; it's about ice cream," she said. "Let's just try it. Please?"

Danny took the book from her, looked at the page she'd opened it to. "Ice cream?" he said. "You are not serious."

"Danny. No."

He gripped the page at the top and tore it out, then balled it up and tossed it at his mother. She let it bounce off her shoulder. "I'm going in," she said.

"Yes," she tells Quartz now. "Just the one poem. What does it have to do with anything?"

"Probably nothing."

He slips a phone from one of his pockets and with a stylus scratches something onto the screen, then returns the phone to its pocket. "OK, so Danny is connected to money, your mother's money, or Bledsoe figures he is. So he gets out of prison and gets a bright idea, and here he is."

"That's what you think?"

"If you saw their emails, you might. Do you think this guy's smart enough to pull this off? Does he have the, I don't know, the guts, the will? If he gets caught, he's fucked."

The man in the bolo tie appears at the table and sets Quartz's plate in front of him. "Gracias," Quartz says.

Carey stares at the plate as Quartz drenches the tacos in hot sauce. "I don't know," she says, but she's recalling the blood, how it geysered up and out, spattering Bledsoe's face, when he shoved that punk's head through the car window.

"Have *you* heard from Bledsoe recently?"

"Not until the ransom note. If that's really him."

"Any idea where he might be?"

"How would I know?"

"How about the police?"

A stab of guilt punctures Carey just below her collarbone. She doesn't know what the police know, because she's here with this stranger and his pockets instead of in Bleak Harbor.

"I don't know."

Quartz swallows half a taco in one bite. When he finishes chewing, he says, "Do I assume correctly that you and Bledsoe didn't part on good terms?"

"Things weren't good between us," she tells Quartz. "But he disappeared from my life, which was fine with me."

Quartz points at the hard drive. "Can I have that?"

She pushes it to him. Quartz shoves it into a pocket, then flips the sheet of paper in front of him faceup and turns it so Carey can read it. "Recognize this guy?"

At the top of the page it says, "LOCKE, Allen Philip." A snapshot shows a man with smooth brown skin marred only by a scar like a thread stitched from below his left earlobe to the corner of his mouth. He's unsmiling, bald, perhaps in his fifties. His tinted glasses sit slightly askew, so that his face appears unbalanced, as if one eye is set lower than the other. Carey scans the guy's job history beneath the picture while Quartz forks rice into a taco.

"This is your contact, right?" he asks. "Your federal agent? The guy who wants those documents you have. Stolen, by the way."

"The people I hand them to won't give a damn how I got them."

"Ha, yeah," Quartz says. "They're not better than any of us, are they? I mean, look at your guy Locke here. He had quite a career. DEA, Customs, ATF, FBI. Apparently couldn't hold a job."

Carey looks up. Quartz is wearing half a grin. He plays it cool, she thinks, but inside he's wound up like a jack-in-the-box. And he's here for more than just Pressman. He has his own plan. She doesn't know what it is—she just knows in her gut that Quartz isn't in this for anyone but Quartz. She wonders if Pressman has surmised the same. Maybe not. Pressman doesn't think anyone can put anything over on him.

"What's your point?" she says.

"Reach your own conclusion. You want to trust this guy? Apparently none of his previous employers did. I'm told the DEA pushed him out after they found a baggie of coke in his pickup."

"Why didn't they put him in jail?"

"That would've cost him his pension, got the DEA a bunch of bad publicity. It's quite a club, federal law enforcement. They just moved him somewhere else."

"Pressman could have told me this."

"Randall keeps his own counsel. But he knows Allen Locke is greasy. Hell, the guy's been trying to take him down for years."

"Why?"

"Who knows? Wants to catch a big fish? A way to resuscitate his career? Locke almost got him on a mail-fraud thing last year. I made it go away."

"This isn't going away."

"It is if you want your boy back."

"How do I know you didn't kidnap my son?"

Quartz grins. "So you'd have something else to blackmail my boss with? Randall's impulsive and a little full of himself, but he's not stupid."

"A *little* full of himself? Just pay the ransom."

"Tell me," Quartz says. "How did you hook up with Locke anyway?"

Carey heard from a young woman at the company—another of Pressman's conquests; she'd worked late one night and wound up beneath him on his office sofa—that a federal agent had contacted her out of the blue. Without saying anything about her Valentine's Day encounter, Carey let the woman know that she too might like to speak with the agent, whose name was Locke.

That was two months ago. By then the digital files with the Asian stamps she had stolen were stowed in her computer at home. It took her most of a bottle of Shiraz to work up the courage to return Locke's first call.

She isn't about to tell Quartz any of this, though. "Just pay, get my boy back, and Pressman will be clear," she says.

"Maybe you're bluffing."

"Don't you dare fuck with me, Quartz. My son . . ." She feels the sob rising in her throat, stops to collect herself. "Fucking pay, and we'll all go our separate ways."

Quartz finishes his second taco, drinks the last of his beer, sets the can down. "Relax. Randall's going to pay most of the ransom."

Carey feels an urge to slap Quartz across his face. "Most?"

"Two million will be plenty—trust me. We just need to lure the kidnapper out into the open so we can get Danny. Has he said yet how you're supposed to pay?"

"Two million's not enough."

"When you know how he wants the money, let me know. We will dangle the two mil. I guarantee he'll take it. He's in no position to negotiate, especially if it's this Bledsoe."

"And what if it's not?"

"We'll worry about that then." He taps the pocket containing Danny's hard drive. "I have other work to do."

"Pressman's condo alone is worth five million dollars."

"Exactly which condo would that be, Carey?"

Her cheeks flush. "I don't care. I just want my son back."

Quartz shoves his plate aside, reaches into a pocket near his belt and pulls out a purple sticky note, hands it to her. She notices his bitten-down fingernails again.

"Call me at that number if you must," he says. "It's very difficult to trace." He gets out of his chair. Carey's phone is ringing inside her purse. "Do not contact Pressman. I'm your man now."

"Just find my son."

"I will. Gotta hit the head."

She watches him move along the bar toward the back of the restaurant. "Quartz," she calls out.

He stops and turns, standing across the bar from the bolo-tied barkeep.

"Do you think I'm weak, Quartz?"

Quartz exchanges a look with Bolo Tie, who smiles.

"Who the fuck are you?" Carey shouts at Bolo Tie. He stops smiling, picks up a rag, goes behind the bar into the kitchen.

"You think I'm weak, Quartz?" she repeats. "Is that what you think?"

"I doubt you're weak."

"Uh-huh. I better see that two million by"—she hesitates, choosing a deadline—"by five o'clock, or I'll be talking, if you know what I mean."

"I need more time. You know Pressman's finances are complicated. Give me till—"

"Six then." Carey slips the sticky note with his phone number into a jeans pocket. "You have about five hours."

"It will be better for everyone concerned," Quartz says, "if we find Bledsoe before the police do."

"Why do you say that?"

He starts walking away again. "I'll be in touch."

21

Jeffrey Bledsoe snaps the deadbolt shut on the restroom door. LaBelle's Family Diner is busy. Petunia will have to deal with it.

He chooses a photograph from his wallet and props it on the back of the bathroom sink, then stares at it as he sets his phone atop the paper towel dispenser, strips off his T-shirt, drops his jeans, and whacks off into the sink. His gaze alternates between the photo and the mirror over the sink as he dry pumps his cock. He likes to watch his pecs flexing. The joint was good for getting in shape.

He finishes, a guttural squeak squeezing from his throat just as his phone vibrates off the dispenser and clatters to the piss-spattered tiles. "Shit." The vibrating stops. Bledsoe picks up the phone, stuffs it in a pocket. He gives the sink a perfunctory swab with a wad of tissue, then takes a last look at the photo of the girl before returning it to his wallet. "Sweet Amelia," he says. She can't be more than thirteen but has the rack of a broad twice her age.

He steps out of the restroom and glances into the diner. Petunia is behind the bar, bobbing her head in that annoying fucking way of hers and scribbling on a green pad as a guy who has each of his butt cheeks on its own counter stool orders his daily breakfast. *Eight eggs over medium, links and patties, double hash browns, rye toast, a banana, a bacon patty melt with three kinds of cheese*, Bledsoe thinks. *Fucking pig thinks a banana will save his fat ass. I am so fucking out of here.*

His phone starts to hum again. He moves down a back corridor and through a door marked EMERGENCY EXIT. Pussy Pete Peters is calling.

After four vibrations, Bledsoe puts the phone to his ear and slips into the voice he reserves for guys like Peters, the dropped-two-octaves growl he'd taught himself growing up with the thugs and skanks, white and black and brown, in his Detroit neighborhood. His *triple-badass* voice. What else did a bony-assed white guy who drank faggy beer expect to hear from a dope dealer?

"Yessir."

"It's me," Peters says. At least that's what Bledsoe thinks he says. He can barely hear because of the caterwauling of a giant tree shredder working in a cemetery behind the diner.

"Got the money yet?"

"Slim," Peters says. Over the shredding, Bledsoe gets only bits of what Peters says next. "I will get . . . me a day . . . you can't."

"I can't what?"

Peters says something else inaudible.

"What the—speak up, pussy. I can't hear you. Shitfuck. Hold on a second."

Bledsoe stumbled onto AMP Botanicals while stalking his bitch ex, Carey, on the internet. He'd located her after paying a website $27.50 for a personal file. It wasn't long before he learned that her hubby was in the pot business in one of those fancy towns on the lake, not too far from where Bledsoe had taken up after leaving prison.

The discovery had tickled Bledsoe even as it had pissed him off. All these preppy motherfuckers thought they were just gonna waltz in and take business from guys like Mr. V who'd been hauling ass for years; sweating the cops, Colombians and Mexicans, ATF and DEA; dodging the border dicks and IRS pricks; scrapping with the assholes on the other side of town or the state or the country for every last corner they could make a few bucks on. Jesus, what these new fucking guys didn't know.

Bledsoe had sized Pete Peters up one night at Buzz's or Biff's or whatever that beach dive was with the knotty pine and shitty Christmas decorations. Seeing Peters's string-bean ass drinking his pansy beer convinced Bledsoe that he could do business, so long as the guy didn't know who Bledsoe really was.

A few phone calls and texts later, he was leaving pounds of primo pot and picking up piggy banks filled with cash. Pussy Pete, scared shitless of the faceless voice named Slim on the phone, was none the wiser. The best part was that "Slim" was also what Bledsoe called his pecker.

He pulls the phone away from his ear and takes a few steps toward the guys operating the shredder. "Hey," he yells. "Can you shut that thing down for a minute?"

One of the men glances in Bledsoe's direction and cups a hand behind an ear. "Fucking idiots," Bledsoe says. He speaks into the phone again. "So you—so you got the money or not?"

Peters starts talking, but the only thing Bledsoe hears is the word *police*, to which he says, "Police? Are you out of your fucking mind?" He can't hear the rest, and he doesn't want to talk inside because Petunia is the nosiest bitch he's banged since he got out of prison. He probably should have gone to his car out front, but he didn't want Petunia to see. The last thing he shouts at Peters before hanging up is, "You don't want to deal with Mr. V—trust me."

He tries the emergency exit, but it's locked. He gives the door a kick and the shredder an angry over-the-shoulder glance, then walks past an overflowing dumpster and around to the front entrance of LaBelle's. Things are fucked up. This was supposed to be an easy job: grab the kid, shut him up, drop him at the safe spot, collect the second chunk of the cash, get the hell out of Dodge. Nobody was supposed to be calling cops. Bledsoe can't afford cops.

He wants to call Quartz, but he must have dropped the goddamn disposable Quartz gave him rushing to get out of the kid's yard the day before. He hopes nobody found it, but what the hell were they gonna find anyway but a bunch of shit nobody but him and Quartz could understand? Real problem was, the only number he had for Quartz was in that lost disposable. He hadn't actually written it down.

Of course Petunia is waiting beyond the double-glass-door entrance. She has an overdone boob job and a mousy face that looks better with his cock stuck into it. She's been hot to trot ever since he let her in on this caper. He just wishes he hadn't done it on email. Really fucking stupid, but he was flying on Crown and Percocet, and Petunia was emailing how she wanted him to blast on her titties, and before he knew it, he'd hit "Send," and she was on the phone cooing about beaches in Rio and how this was all so cool like a TV miniseries. He told her to double delete those emails. He hopes she did.

"Is everything OK, baby?" she says as he steps into the diner. She looks concerned. Bledsoe ignores her for a moment and scans the place for cops and anyone else who might have nothing better to do than eavesdrop. The double-wide dude is using the patty melt like a trowel to shovel eggs into his face.

Bledsoe gives Petunia his phoniest grin. "Everything's fine, sweet stuff. Went out for a smoke and locked myself out."

"Silly boy," she says, her face brightening. Then she whispers, "The kid's OK?"

"He's fine. Yeah."

"So when do you think, you know, we can skedaddle?"

Her lipstick isn't right. Never is. Even with a wake-up hummer every day, Bledsoe knows he won't be able to stand Petunia for long. He doesn't want to take her, but he sure as hell can't leave her behind. "How about now? Blow this pop stand forever?"

She frowns, looks over a shoulder. "I can't just leave this minute. We're the only ones here."

"Putter's in the back. He can handle it."

"Honey, Putter couldn't microwave a pizza without burning the place to the ground."

Bledsoe thinks for a second. "All right, then how about—what time do you get off?"

"Four."

"OK. Meet me in Schoolcraft at four."

"Schoolcraft? Can't we make it my place?"

"You know it's gotta be Schoolcraft."

"All right, but can we make it five? Fiveish? I have to pack."

Petunia lives a mile from the diner. Bledsoe gave her address to his parole officer even though he's been sleeping most nights in a place in Schoolcraft that only his old cellmate knows about.

"Four on the dot," he says. He undoes the apron around his waist and hands it to Petunia. "Done with this, eh, babe?"

She licks her lips, and Bledsoe feels himself getting hard again. Maybe he'll have time for one more before he has to do what he has to do.

He's about to pull out of the LaBelle's lot when he remembers the police scanner. He reaches over and jerks it out of the glove box, plugs it into the cigarette lighter, sets the volume to high. Then he reaches beneath the passenger seat and pulls out a foot-long piece of rusted rebar hacked off and honed to a jagged point at one end. He sets it at his feet.

So he fucked up losing that phone, and Pussy Pete fucked up calling the cops, if he really did. Fuck it. Bledsoe has the $100,000 down payment from Quartz's boss, whoever that is. It won't be long before he'll be sipping a fruity cocktail somewhere warm, savoring the memory of fucking with his bitch ex. He pulls onto Marcellus Highway, driving with one hand, working his phone with the other. He has a couple of errands to run and a few texts to take care of.

22

"Glory be," Oly O'Nally says. He's in the locker room next to the Zamboni garage. "What in God's name are you doing here?"

"You heard," Pete says.

"Good lord, Andrew, come here."

Oly rises from his folding chair, naked from the waist up, gray hair a sweaty tangle, and takes Pete into his pale old arms. Oly is the only person in the world, besides Pete's mother, who calls him by his given name. When Oly fired him from O'Nally Bros., it was bizarre to hear him saying, "Andrew, you have to learn from this," as if it were some other person who was being canned and Pete just happened to be there, watching.

Oly sits again. "Heard it from one of the youngsters," he says, nodding toward the dressing room on the other side of the cinder-block wall. "Was on his phone."

"I'm sorry to bother you. I would've called, but—"

"It's OK. I'm glad you're here."

Like a lot of Chicagoans, O'Nally summers at a beach house not far from Bleak Harbor, directing his trading crews by landline from afar. He doesn't carry a cell phone or bother much with the internet. Although he is the genius behind the long success of O'Nally Bros., he now leaves much of the firm's management to his son. Declan O'Nally had taken the necessary steps to modernize the business, which in turn had helped precipitate Pete's demise.

Pete knows Oly plays pickup hockey Friday mornings with some local guys. Afterward, they convene at Boz's to argue over beers and Italian beefs about who had the best hour and fifteen minutes on the ice. Oly has enough money to have written a big check for the rink's construction, and most Fridays he picks up lunch too. In return, the younger guys let him have his own dressing room and, once in a while, the puck.

Oly's mold-mottled shin guards and elbow pads are scattered across the rubber-mat floor. White curls carpet his sagging chest. In his seventies, he's on his third wife, with a thirteen-year-old son named, like the rink he paid for, Johnny.

"You want to shower first?" Pete says.

"Nah, I'll catch up with the youngsters later." He bends and picks a skate off the floor, wipes a frayed rag down the length of its blade, stuffs them both into the red-and-black bag at his bare feet. "They'll wait for my credit card."

"I need your advice."

"I'm thinking more than advice, son."

He sits up straight, looking right into Pete's eyes. It sends Pete back to his biggest day in the soybean pit at the Chicago Board of Trade. He made O'Nally Bros. almost $470,000, and Oly himself came down to the pit to thank him. Pete had some good days after that. Never any close to that good. Then one day Declan plucked him from the pit and planted him at a desk.

"Listen up, son," Oly is saying now. "What happened between us before happened. It's just business. But as I said before, and I'll say again, we'll always be friends. Now sit down, will you?"

Pete sits in one of the steel cubbyholes lining the room's walls. The place reeks of tape and sour leather. He's not sure why he came. Maybe just because Carey told him to. He doesn't expect Oly to give him anything more than that hug. How the hell do you ask anyone—let alone someone who fired you—for five million bucks?

"Tell me what you know, son."

Pete gives up most of it, leaving out, for now, the stuff about his dealings with Slim. Oly listens while peeling off the rest of his hockey gear. Pete can hear the profane jawing and guffawing of the younger players next door. They probably have worries about jobs and girlfriends and kids and wives, but Pete thinks they really have no worries at all.

———

If only Pete hadn't lost his shit, he and Carey and Danny might never have moved to Bleak Harbor. They wouldn't be in the danger they are now. And maybe, he thinks, Carey would still love him as she once had. If she had.

They'd had a good life in Chicago. They had their fourth-floor condo with the rooftop deck in the West Loop. Carey went to early-morning Pilates classes. Pete and Danny could walk to Bulls games at the United Center. Carey took Danny to school most days, while Pete hopped a bus to the Board of Trade. Because he traded ags, mostly corn and beans, he was done early and able to collect Danny from school.

Pete did well at trading not because he was better than his pit rivals at divining the market's next wriggle or because he had a stronger stomach for riding out a wrong turn. He did well because he was tall. At six feet five, Pete could see across the pit more clearly than anyone else. He could make his hand signals seen and his voice heard. He could spot the creased eyebrows and bitten lips that signaled a trader in trouble. That was someone you wanted to do business with.

His edge vaporized when Oly's son yanked him from the pit and stuck him in front of a semicircle of computer screens in a storefront cubicle a few blocks from Wrigley Field. Other such trading boutiques had sprouted in lofts and warehouses and office towers all over Chicago, even in the suburbs. It was the new, less costly, more efficient way to trade, abetted by ever-changing algorithms fed into computers a thousand miles away and reached by T-1 lines leased for $10,000 a month.

At first Pete was just bored. Declan kept saying he was going to send another trader or two, but for weeks he was the only trader in the shop, his sole companions the blind, oscillating screens. He couldn't even entertain himself by watching passersby, because Declan insisted on keeping the shades drawn, lest someone spy on O'Nally trading strategies. As if algorithms had discernible strategies. Pete felt less and less like a trader and more like an automaton executing commands delivered by faceless, faraway masters.

Then he started to lose. He had one pretty bad day—lost $172,000—followed by a really bad one—$293,000—then another and another, the losses mounting to a million bucks, a million two, to the point where Pete thought the only way he could stop it was to stay home.

Bad days happened sometimes, even to the best traders. But Pete couldn't understand why they were happening to him. He was following instructions. He was making the trades the algorithms told him to make. Declan suggested he take some time off. He took two weeks and returned to work thinking his luck—what else could it be but luck?—had to change.

He didn't say much about it to Carey. He told her once that he was bored, and she shrugged and said, "Try logistics." She had her own problems at work and with Danny's increasing recalcitrance with his teachers and fellow pupils. They were running out of schools where he would be welcome.

On the day that Pete finally took his $6.99 Walgreens umbrella to his eight computer screens, he was down almost $200,000 by 10:30 a.m. His height did give him an advantage swinging the umbrella. Later he wouldn't remember much except that, for a while at least, it felt good. He'd recall the sight of his CPU suspended in midair as it flew from his hands and through the plate glass window; how he felt the urge to grab it back a second before it shattered the glass and crunched to the sidewalk; how the yuppies peered through the jagged hole in the window with are-you-fucking-crazy looks on their faces; how he stood there in his sweat-drenched T-shirt waving and grinning at their picture-snicking smartphones, waiting vaguely for a police siren that never came.

Declan wanted him gone, of course. Oly said he'd take care of it. He sat Pete down. Pete apologized only because he liked Oly. "Apology accepted," Oly said, then fired him. "Those damn computers. I don't get them either, but I don't have to."

He called the $25,000 check he gave Pete severance pay. Later Pete noticed that it had been written on Oly's personal account. Pete used it to pay the attorneys who helped him open AMP Botanicals.

"Tell me, Andrew," Oly says now. "Why dope?"

"It's therapeutic. Really."

"For guys with a Fritos deficiency."

"You have arthritis, right, Oly? It'll help."

"I'll pass, thanks. Andrew, I know you believe your troubles at O'Nally were mostly about luck."

"I really don't know what I think."

"Well, there's certainly a bit of luck involved in buying low and selling high. And yes, it didn't hurt that you're a tall drink of water out there on the floor. Maybe we should've just left you there as long as we could have. But what you're doing now, there's not a lot of luck there, son. You've got to do the work, stay with your plan, make your own luck."

Pete's thinking about Bledsoe now. "You're right."

"So. You and your boy. Danny. You have a good relationship?"

"I think so, yes."

"He gets along with his mother?"

"He loves her. Sometimes they fight."

"He's fifteen, right? Who doesn't fight with their mom at fifteen?"

"Shit." Pete looks around the room, down at the floor. "Shit."

"What is it, son?"

"Listen. I'm sorry."

"Just say it."

Pete tells him about "Slim" and Bledsoe. As he does, Oly cocks his head to one side. Pete has let him down yet again.

"Jesus, Mary, and Joseph," Oly finally says, slapping his knees. "I never should've let Declan take you out. But you can't fix what you can't fix. So you know what we need. We need a hedge."

"What do you mean?"

"Think, son. The police will do their very best to find Danny, I'm sure. But this isn't Chicago; it's Bleak Harbor."

"I know."

"You don't have much time. You need a hedge."

"The ransom."

"Right. In case you can't—in case things don't work out with the cops, you've got to pay. You've got to be ready to pay."

Pete laughs a pathetic little laugh. "I don't have five million bucks. I barely have five thousand."

"Have you spoken to your mother-in-law?"

"We don't really speak."

"What about your wife?"

"Carey's calling her today. We're not expecting much."

Oly twists his body away and rolls his long johns down his legs. He grabs a towel from his cubbyhole and knots it around his waist. "Boz has a landline, doesn't he?"

"Yeah," Pete says. Carey called him on it the day before. It reminds him of Boz saying he'd seen Danny on the beach that day, sometime before he disappeared. They had talked. It probably meant nothing. But Pete had to ask about it. Or tell the cops.

"I'm gonna call your mother-in-law. Serenity. Her guy there—what's his name?"

"Spitler?"

"He's been trying to get me to come out publicly in favor of her little plan. So she's going to take my call. You got a pen?"

Pete feels around in his pockets. "Uh."

"Never mind." Oly takes a toilet kit from his bag, zips it open, digs in it for a ballpoint, hands it to Pete. "Find something to write on. Put down your bank account number, and stick it in one of my shoes."

"Jesus, Oly. My bank account?"

"You know," Oly says, "I had a Daniel too."

Army ranger Daniel B. "Boomer" O'Nally was killed by sniper fire in Mosul. No trading was allowed at O'Nally Bros. each year on the anniversary of his death. On what came to be known as D-Day, Oly would rent out Tufano's, and the whole firm and their families would toast Boomer long into the evening.

"Of course."

Oly reaches for Pete's hand, shakes it, holds on. Pete sees a glisten in the old man's eyes. "We're going to get your boy back, Andrew."

Oly goes through the door to the shower room. Pete scratches his account number on the back of an expired car registration slip and tucks the scrap beneath a Velcro strap on the old man's right sneaker.

Pete lets himself feel a shred of relief as he descends the stairs to the garage. Until he takes out his phone and sees that Malone called him back. Now that Oly might bail him out, he wishes he hadn't left her that message after all.

23

Carey steps outside the restaurant into a wall of mushy heat. Across the avenue, people jog up and down the steps of the county courthouse, lugging briefcases and backpacks, going about their lives.

Her phone says it's 1:17. There are missed calls from Jonah and some reporter from Battle Creek. A text from Jonah says, Can't hold off cops much longer. She skips to the next text, from that area code she doesn't recognize.

Tacos in valpo??

An icy ripple of fear crosses her shoulders. Carey looks around, as if she might see whoever it is who knows where she is. Of course there's no one. She goes to the next text, gasps at a photograph of two black-faced dogs, their dark jaws open and drooling over a green high-top sneaker:

rotts hongry too. daisey and hoho likin danny boy

She closes her eyes, tries to collect herself. Thinks of old Pip, expertly trained Pip, huffing wetly in the back of her Ford Fiesta, the blood stink on his breath, his nails scratching on the vinyl seats.

There are more texts. She doesn't want to open them but reads:

Blackmailing yr boss huh . . . ill take that cash 2 . . . ransom now $7.388 mill . . . payment direx coming . . .

"No," Carey says.

danny boy safe fr 10 hrs 29 mins . . . or not . . . everyone gotta pay . . .

"You can't do this."

She stumbles back against the door to the restaurant, palms her belly, thinking she might be sick there on the sidewalk.

"God. God."

She pushes away, steadies herself, taps a reply:

JEffrey if it's you . . . you can't do this . . . or whoVer this is . . . we will have 5 million . . . it's your son. Please stop pleaxe

She sends it. Waits. A reply appears almost immediately:

5373642445 is a landline #. Reply Y to send all TXT messages to this # as voice messages for 0.25/msg + std msg fee.

24

Quartz shuts the door inside his apartment above the Mexican joint and raps out a text to Pressman:

Witness not telling whole truth. Got curves though.

Then a second:

must address rogue, yes?

He fishes Danny's hard drive out of his pocket and tosses it on the kitchen table, a mess of devices connected by a jumble of white and black wires winding over the table edge and converging into a single red cord plugged into a knee-high rectangular box.

He glances up at the wall beyond the table. It's covered with thirty-six black-and-orange bull's-eyes aligned in columns and rows, six by six. Each is perforated by tiny holes he made at a local shooting range with a pistol that is now resting in his nightstand drawer. Quartz had gone most of his life without even touching a firearm until deciding that, in his business, he'd feel better having a gun handy in certain situations. He recalls he has a shooting lesson scheduled for this evening. He isn't going to make that.

He starts biting the nails on his left hand as he watches for Pressman's reply text. He's wondering why Carey never asked to see the emails between Danny and Bledsoe. Quartz had seen them after hacking into Bledsoe's sieve of a laptop a while ago. He mentioned them to Carey partly to show her he was on the case, partly to see her reaction. No way she wouldn't ask for those emails unless she already knew about them.

She can't be trusted.

He can't trust Pressman either. Which is why he won't tell Pressman about Carey Peters's walking-out-the-door threat. If Pressman thinks the whole thing is going to blow up in his face, Quartz could easily be collateral damage.

Pressman's text appears:

proceed as nec

25

"Officer Malone."

"Carey. Where are you? I've been trying to call."

"My phone's acting up."

Bullshit, Malone thinks. She glances into the corridor outside the break room at the Bleak Harbor Police Department. The chief is there on the phone, his double-wide back to her, moving around like he's agitated. She hasn't seen Radovich this worked up since those shit-faced teenagers set fire to the Saint Wenceslaus rectory eight years ago.

A woman Malone has never seen before stands against a wall behind him, waiting. She's wearing a navy pantsuit and a look that says someone should have gotten her a coffee or a chair or something by now. Probably FBI.

"We're working every angle," Malone tells Carey. "Nothing much to report yet, sorry to say. Are you coming in? Your brother gave me Danny's laptop."

Malone turns to a Bleak County wall map dotted with red push-pins where firefighters, paramedics, and volunteers have searched without finding Danny, green ones where they have yet to look. Searchers have combed the dune bluffs, the beaches straddling the channel from Bleak Harbor Bay to the big lake, the woods along the bay's southern shore. The red pins have started to outnumber the greens. Two Bleak Harbor cops scouring the Peters place have been calling in. So far they've found nothing helpful. The place is filled with fingerprints, of course—Danny's and his mother's and stepfather's.

"Have you located Bledsoe?" Carey says.

Watching the chief on his phone, Malone wants to say, "Maybe soon." Instead she says, "We're on it. Where is your husband? He tried to call me, but now I can't raise him."

There's a pause on the line, then, "I'm sorry; I don't know. I'll be there soon. I'll find him."

"Have you heard again from the kidnapper?"

Malone listens as Carey tells her about the higher ransom demand, the menacing dogs, the message from the landline. She detects a tremor in Carey's voice. "You're doing great, Carey," Malone says, trying to reassure her, even as she wonders why Carey isn't sitting here with her. She cups a hand over her phone when she hears Radovich's shout echoing in the hallway: "You don't give a good goddamn if this kid dies? Is that what you're telling me?" She assumes he's trying to get someone to give him Bledsoe's address. He's swinging his girth this way and that, and now he waves at the suit, and she hands him a pen, and he leans into the wall across the hall and scratches something on a piece of paper just as the dispatcher squeezes past and leans into the break room.

"Katya," the dispatcher says.

She tells Carey, "Hold on one minute," presses the phone to her chest. "What?"

"You want to talk to Michele Higgins?"

"Michele who?"

"Reporter from the *Light*."

"About the festival?"

"The Peters boy."

"We have nothing to report at this time."

"We've had calls from TV in Grand Rapids and Kalamazoo too."

The dispatcher is a twentysomething who wears ear expanders that Malone finds painful to look at. "No for now, but keep them on the hook. We might need them later."

"Will do. You heard about the rides and stuff?"

"The what?"

"Festival's all kinds of messed up. Rides aren't working right; lights are going on and off. People are pissed."

"I don't care." She waits for the dispatcher to leave, puts her phone back to her ear. "Carey, I'm sorry. I need to ask you about that email."

"Go ahead."

"Was there a particular reason you printed that one out?"

"I wanted to make sure you saw it. It's new, from this morning."

Malone sits at a table in the middle of the room and reads yet again the printout of the 9:43 a.m. email that Carey left with Danny's laptop. It's peculiar that the email was sent not to Carey or Pete but to Danny. Jeremiah wouldn't have directed it there unless he knew one of the boy's parents would see it. He knows more than Malone is comfortable with. She wants to hear what Will has learned from the laptop and the email addresses and the phone and internet companies he was supposed to call.

"All right. I'm going to get back to work. When will you be here?"

"Soon," Carey says. "I have to take this other call."

Radovich is still pacing with his phone. Impatient, Malone picks a photo of Danny from a scatter on the table. He's sitting in a small boat with a fishing pole across his lap. He's smiling, but Malone doesn't know enough about him to say whether he's happy or posing. Still, she's drawn to the photo because it reminds her of Louisa. Louisa liked to fish and had agreed to go with Malone's ex on the day when, in truth, he was planning to steal her away. Or so Malone had believed.

With her other hand she pulls out a prison mug shot of Bledsoe. It's a grainy, colorless scan, but his face, with its hatchet-blade cheekbones and smirk of empty defiance, registers on one look: *He's gotta be the one who took Danny.*

But if he isn't?

Goddamn it, Chief. She looks out at Radovich again. His face is tomato red. She picks up her phone, puts it down. She could try Pete

Peters once more, but she doesn't want him panicking. He knows something he's not telling, may have wanted to come clean when Malone missed his earlier call. Other officers are searching AMP Botanicals, so far to no avail.

Will steps into the room, closes the door. He has some paper in one hand. "Volunteer got hurt searching the Helliker place. Chunk of ceiling fell on his head. Just stitches, luckily."

"Who's Chief talking to?" Malone says.

"The warden at Muskegon."

"What about Danny?"

"I've run down every 'Jeremiah' within a fifty-mile radius. Not a lot, but a sex offender in Fennville. I let Allegan County know."

"A sex offender's not going to demand ransom."

"I also found four Jeremiahs in the Bleak family, all long dead."

"Any kidnapped?"

"Not that I can tell."

"What about the domain name?"

Will shakes his head. "Jeb.com is registered to one Morton Needelman," he says.

"Who's where?"

"In the ground. Since 1968. He apparently was once a prosecutor for the county."

"Great. How exactly does a dead man register a domain name?"

"I think somebody else took that liberty. Trying to track that, but so far I'm getting nowhere."

"What about the burner phone we found?"

"A single incoming text: '1ovrEZ@5.'"

"Huh?"

"Could've been a butt dial."

"Can you trace it?"

"How?" Will says. "No."

"What about the thing on Carey Peters's phone, the landline message?"

"That's not a landline; it's a ruse. Anybody could have cut and pasted that message in there."

"Can the phone companies help us?"

"They need a wiretap order."

"Right. Don't tell me—the judge is out of town. Or he's in the goddamn beer tent. Fuck. What about Peters's computer, from the pot shop?"

"Working on it. Obviously hacked. But hackers generally try not to leave trails."

"Damn it. I should've taken Carey Peters's phone when I had the chance."

"Maybe so."

"Jesus. What about"—Malone knows she's reaching now—"Jeb or Jeremiah or jeb.com as an anagram. Anything there?"

Will spends his lunches on a website fiddling with anagrams. He hasn't solved any crimes with them yet, but he's made Malone laugh, and cringe, a few times.

"You must be desperate," he says. "No, nothing yet. I gotta tell you, though: I'm worried about the kid's drugs." He nods at a bench behind Malone that holds two clear plastic bags. One contains Danny's green high-top. In the other are three drugstore vials, the boy's medications. "I don't know about autism, but I lost my epilepsy meds once on a bike trip, and it wasn't good. Had a seizure." He holds up his arm to show a scar zigzagged down the back of his elbow. "That's how I got this."

"And Danny's electronics?"

"Here," Will says, brandishing the papers in his hand. "Looks like he may have emailed with Bledsoe."

"No."

"Afraid so."

Will sets two printouts in front of Malone. Reading them, she feels torn between wanting Bledsoe to be the culprit and not wanting to see Danny unwittingly setting himself up. Oddly, the emails include only Bledsoe's end. The first, from April, suggests he and Danny were having a conversation. The second, from the night before Danny was taken, says only, "Y not, Danny boy?" Maybe Bledsoe was trying to arrange a meeting. Maybe Danny resisted. Maybe he eventually relented.

"Where's the rest of the chain?"

"That's it."

"So Bledsoe initiated this?"

"Hard to believe the kid—"

"Please call him by his name."

"Sorry. I doubt Danny would've known where to find Bledsoe. But it's impossible to know based on what we have so far. The kid's—I mean, Danny's phone looks cleaner than most kids'. Either it's new, or he was just anal about deleting stuff."

"Not was, *is*. He *is*."

"Yes. Is."

There's a sharp knock at the door. It opens, and the woman in the suit steps in. She's taller than Malone by half a head and carries herself with the stiffness of a steel girder. "Officer Malone?" she says. "Stefanie Hamilton, FBI." On her head a pair of sunglasses looks stapled into the tight, dark curls of her hair. Malone wonders if she wears them to bed.

Malone stands and gestures. "This is Will. You're in from Chicago?"

"Indeed," Hamilton says. She glances at the wall map dotted with pushpins, shakes her head. "Chief gave me the basics. You're looking for a felon named Bledsoe. But you don't even know where the boy's parents are at the moment? Is that correct?"

"I just talked to Carey Peters. She's on her way. Take a look at these." She hands the emails to Hamilton, who takes them without looking at her.

"Any skeletons in their closet?" the agent says.

"Not much, at least officially. An indecent exposure."

Hamilton looks up, hands the emails to Will. "Details?"

"Apparently they had sex on that big Ferris wheel in Chicago," Will says. "Eight years ago, before they were married. Peters got arrested; they let Carey go."

"How in the world do you have sex on a Ferris wheel?" Not expecting an answer, Hamilton looks again at the pushpin map, then at Will. "I'm sorry," she says, "are you an officer?"

"He's not," Malone says. "But he's the best we have at rooting around in computers."

"Agent Hamilton," Will says, "we think we can connect Peters to a Detroit drug dealer."

Hamilton turns to him. "Which Peters?"

"Pete."

"And?"

Malone reaches back to the table for a photo and hands it to the agent. "This is Peters's only employee. Dulcinea Pérez. Twenty-three. Moved here last year from a Hispanic neighborhood near the bridge to Canada in Detroit. She's been in and out of juvy and jail: petty theft, pot, cocaine, obstruction of justice. Used to work for a dealer named Vend."

"Might still, for all we know," Will says.

"We think Bledsoe worked for Vend too."

"Vend is Vendrowska," Hamilton says. "Jarek Vendrowska. Criminal right out of the womb. Certified shithead. I had the pleasure of dealing with him on a tour in Detroit a while back. He's mostly drugs, predominantly pot and coke, but also strip clubs, money laundering, politician greasing."

"Never convicted?"

"Oh, no."

"Pérez got an associate's in computer science three years ago from Henry Ford Community College. Then spent a year in code school."

"Computer code?"

"Yes."

Hamilton knits her brows, thinking, then says, "Christ. Petruglia."

"Who?" Malone says.

"Vincent Petruglia. Old-school mob boss in Detroit," Hamilton says. "He and Vend got into it over territory now and then. Vend—or one of his crew, maybe this Pérez—hacked into Petruglia's computers, got all sorts of stuff Petruglia wouldn't want law enforcement to see."

"They blackmailed him?"

"Looked that way. We knew about it—hell, Vend teased us with it—but could never prove anything. He and Petruglia settled up somehow. Nobody got killed, at least not over that."

"But Pérez could've been in the middle of it, helping with the hack," Will says. "There's definitely some hacking going on here."

Malone looks at the photo of Pérez again. In it, she appears younger than twenty-three. Peters said she knew Danny "a little," saw him at the pot shop a few times. Maybe she knew him enough to lure him into a trap. "Maybe it's just a coincidence," she says.

"And maybe it's a coincidence that Peters's employee is connected to the same Detroit dealer that Vend is, huh?" Hamilton says. Malone doesn't appreciate her sarcasm but can see her point. "I don't suppose you've picked Pérez up yet?"

"The only address we have is an abandoned house in Detroit," Will says.

"Wonderful. Maybe Peters knows. But you don't know where he is either, am I right?"

You're right, Malone thinks. *So help us, or fuck off.* "We will bring him in. What about Vend? Should we try him?"

"The only cops he talks to are on his payroll," Hamilton says. "Loves the press, though. He's a so-called colorful character, so they kiss his ass."

"You know," Will says, "when I was looking up Vend, I ran across some articles by that *Light* reporter. She used to work in Detroit."

"Michele something?" Malone asks.

"What's the *Light*?" Hamilton says.

"Local paper, online. And yeah, Michele Higgins."

Damn it, Malone thinks, and Louisa's face, dark bangs on her forehead, appears unbidden in her mind. "I'll give her a call after this," she says. "Maybe she knows him. And we ought to—"

The door to the room swings open, and the chief leans his bulk in, waggling a slip of paper. "Bledsoe's in Bridgman," he says. "Got an address. State police and Berrien County are on the way."

Hamilton steps up and snatches the paper from the chief. "Nice work," she says. "I'm on my way."

"I'm going," Malone says.

"You have jurisdiction there?" Hamilton asks.

Radovich gives her a look. "Far as I'm concerned, Agent, she does."

Hamilton turns from the chief to Malone and back again. She shrugs. "Fine," she says. "Officer Malone, let's get this Bledsoe."

The hell with Bledsoe, Malone thinks as she follows Hamilton out. *Let's get Danny.*

26

The officer sounds anxious.

"Now we're off the record," Malone tells Michele Higgins.

"No. Why?"

She'd called as Michele was walking back to the *Light* after shooting photos at the festival. Malone had confirmed that Danny Peters had been kidnapped for a ransom of more than $5 million.

"I just helped you on the record, Michele. Now we're off, or I'm hanging up."

"Go ahead."

"Do you know Jarek Vend?"

Vend. A reptilian coil of muscle that holds still and calm until it snaps free and dangerous. "I did once."

"We need you to get in touch with him."

"I can give you his number."

"No. We need you to call him."

Michele is half a block from the Victorian that houses the *Light*. An unmarked panel truck is parked in the side drive. A man is standing on the front porch, swiping his phone.

"You can call him yourself. Or ask the Detroit cops—"

"He's not going to respond to a cop in Bumfuck. I hear he likes you."

"Trust me—he doesn't. He really doesn't like anyone."

"Michele, you're going to call him the minute you get off this phone—do you hear me?"

"Why? Do you think he has something to do with the Peters boy?"

Vend is many despicable things, but Michele has difficulty seeing him as an abductor of autistic children. Not worth the trouble.

Then again, Vend is in essentially the same business as Pete Peters. She's seen the cop message boards speculating that illegal dealers are exploiting their no-tax, no-fee advantage over the neophytes selling legal stuff. Maybe Peters crossed Vend somehow. That would have been a mistake.

"Tell him we have one of his employees in custody."

"What employee?" Michele says. "Give me a name."

"Just tell Vend, and have him call me."

"I'm not sure I'm comfortable—"

"Don't even pull that shit." Malone's voice rises a pitch. "A boy's life is at stake." Then she's gone.

Michele isn't in the habit of helping cops do their jobs. But she's not so sanctimonious about her barely breathing profession that she's going to ignore Malone. She scrolls through the contacts on her phone, stops at "JV." She starts to call, then changes her mind and thumbs a text:

Cannot believe you'd kidnap an autistic boy.

Vend will respond. He's always had a thing for Michele. Michele never had a thing for him. Meanwhile, she has to post her first story on the kidnapping of Danny Peters. She feels remiss; even the local radio mopes have already picked up on it. But her boss, the ever-texting Gatti, has had Michele hopping on festival stuff.

The man on the porch is a good twenty years younger than Michele, his head enrobed in a green wool cap that puts her in mind of a grasshopper.

"You here for the air-conditioning?"

He looks up from his phone and sizes her up, top to bottom, lingering briefly on her breasts. She doesn't begrudge him that because her boobs are still pretty great, but the glance at her naked ring finger feels creepy.

"You're Michele Higgins? The reporter?"

"Did you fix the AC?"

"I don't have the right part yet."

"Then what are you doing here?" She bounds up the porch steps past him. "Come back when you have the part."

She hears him from over her shoulder. "Think I got a scoop for you."

———

Her computer screen is blinking blue and black and red again, as it was when she'd left earlier. Michele sets her phone aside and clicks her mouse. The blinking stops.

The screen goes gray, then black, before unfurling the image of a boy in a hard-backed chair. "Holy shit," Michele says. It's Danny Peters, blindfolded and wearing a single high-top sneaker. His legs are secured to the legs of the chair. There's a shadow on his cheek.

"Fuckin' A," comes the voice from behind Michele. She spins to see the Grasshopper looking over her shoulder.

"That the kidnapped kid?" he says.

"What are you doing? Get out."

"That's goddamn cool."

"Do I need to call the police?"

"They're pretty busy. But I might have something you'd be interested in." Canting his head, he gives Michele a smile that probably works on the bimbos he chases at Tuesday night happy hours. "About that kid on your computer."

"Uh-huh," Michele says. "Wait outside. We'll talk in a minute."

He leaves, and she returns to the computer. Danny has vanished from the screen. Another image, a rectangle of white and black and gray, is slowly coming clear, a ghost emerging from shadow. As it sharpens,

Michele thinks it could be something scanned from the files at the city library.

Centered at the top of the rectangle is the familiar *Light* logo. Beneath that is the date: Friday, May 18, 1945. The lead story on the page concerns two local soldiers returning from France after V-E Day. The story that catches her eye runs down the right side of the page in a single column:

Inquiry Concludes Drowning of Young Bleak Accidental

Teenager's 'Eccentric' Character May Have Contributed to Death

What is going on? she thinks.

Her phone buzzes. There's a new text from Gatti:

how bout a pic of someone in a d-fly hat on home page?

Michele ignores it and returns to the 1945 *Light* story: A fifteen-year-old boy, a great-grandson of the town's founder, died that May 1 in a sailboat on Lake Michigan. His name was Jeremiah Estes Bleak.

The story describes him as "ornery, unpredictable, and barely manageable from the day he was born." He was on the boat with his father, James Estes Bleak, and his brother, Jonathan Estes Bleak, known as Jack. The Jack who'd been married to Serenity until he died last Thanksgiving.

Something about the story feels familiar. She can't come up with it just yet. She reads on.

A squall rose up out of nowhere on that May afternoon. "As the waves crashed like thunder and the boat tossed about, young Jeremiah, who had inexplicably doffed his life jacket, pitched into the swirling waters," the article says. "His father, Mr. Bleak, almost drowned as he heroically tried to save his son." In the penultimate paragraph, an unnamed law enforcement official suggests the boy may have intentionally thrown himself into the lake. "Nevertheless," the story's final line says, "police were unable to definitively conclude that it was suicide."

Nevertheless. Definitively. To Michele, they're winks and nods that would nudge readers to the suspicion that the "unmanageable" boy had in fact flung himself to his death. It strikes her as gratuitous, unless the police hoped to absolve the boy's father—and by extension, the Bleak family—of any blame in the tragedy.

Her phone goes off. Gatti again:

WTF is on home pg?!!!

Leave me alone, Michele thinks. She's guessing Gatti doesn't like the photo of disgruntled festivalgoers standing in a too-long line for beer because the coolers shut down. Whatever.

She clicks the icon for the *Light* home page. It takes a minute to open. There is no photo of a beer line, no festival stories, not even the current *Light* masthead. That day's page is gone. In its place is the 1945 page with the stories about the returning soldiers and the drowning of Jeremiah Bleak.

"What the—oh, shit," Michele says. Not knowing what else to do, she grabs the mouse and starts clicking. Nothing happens. If Gatti is seeing this decades-old page, then anybody looking at the website is seeing it too. She texts her boss back:

not me can you ask techs? Looks like a hack.

She goes into her email and calls up the message that arrived at 6:45 that morning. The signature at the bottom explains what nagged her when she was reading the old story: Jeremiah.

Is it coincidence? Or did the kidnapper intentionally take the name of that drowned boy? And if so, why? This kidnapper is not your run-of-the-mill bad guy. She clicks out of email back to the *Light*. The 1945 front page is still there. Gatti is buzzing Michele's phone again.

She calls out to the porch, "Hey, you."

The Grasshopper returns. Michele gets out of her chair. "Whatever you have better be good."

He actually laughs. "Yes, ma'am. You know the kid's house?" He gestures at the window facing the bay. "That big fence? I put that up."

"You're an HVAC guy."

"I freelance other stuff."

"And?"

He grins. "What are the odds of us meeting at the beer tent later on?"

She wants to say, *Are you fucking kidding me? Get out, and don't show your invertebrate face here again.* But she wants to hear whatever he knows more. "We'll see. What about the fence?"

"You know," he says, "that family ain't exactly the Brady Bunch. No wonder the kid's a retard."

"He's not a retard, asshole."

"I thought he was autistic or something?"

"What's your name?"

"Nathan."

"Last name?"

"Barringer."

"If you know something about Danny Peters and you don't tell me and he gets hurt, I guarantee that 'Nathan Barringer' will be in the paper and your skinny ass in the county jail."

"Skinny ass?"

"Spit it out, Nathan."

"Chill, eh? So, one day, it started raining like hell, so I knocked off early. Then a couple hours later I remembered I left some tools over there I needed, so I went back to get them." He yanks his hat off, and a thatch of carrot-colored wires springs free. Maybe that's why he wears the thing. "He had this sort of girlfriend."

"'Sort of' girlfriend?"

"Looked Hispanic, a little chunky, definitely older than the kid."

"And?"

He shrugs, grins again. "They were screwing."

Michele recalls the woman she'd seen through her binoculars on Danny's deck that one afternoon. She was wearing a Detroit Tigers hoodie.

"How do you know this?"

"I could hear them. Or, at least, her. I kinda envied that kid."

"That's disgusting."

"It was accidental, honest. I left my tools under a tarp along the side of the house where the kid's bedroom happened to be."

"So you heard, but how did you see?"

"Curtains were open a little. I thought maybe someone was getting hurt in there."

"Did you recognize the woman?"

"I happen to buy pot from her."

"At the shop in town?"

"Yep. She works for the kid's old man. Name's Dulcy."

Michele makes the connections in her head: the Tigers, Detroit, the Hispanic enclave beneath the Ambassador Bridge, the Jarek Vend Community and Health Center on Vernor Avenue. Vend threw a lot of charity cash at that neighborhood and hired a lot of its young people. Like maybe the one Malone is looking for.

"So Danny was having sex with a woman who works for his father."

"Yeah. That help?"

"Dulcy? What's her last name?"

"Not sure."

Her phone again. It's a text. From Vend.

"Why did you say what you said about the Brady Bunch?"

"Well, his parents, they don't seem to like each other much. They sure didn't agree about the fence. I was a little worried they wouldn't pay me. She wanted it more than he did, and he would tell her she was paranoid, what did she care what people think?"

"But you never saw any physical stuff?"

"You mean like abuse? No. Nothing like that."

"Why didn't you go to the police?"

The Grasshopper looks sheepish as he pulls his hat back on. "I don't always get along so well there. Besides, you were here."

Right. The beer tent later. "Have you told anyone else?"

"Maybe a couple of buddies, but they were drunk—they won't remember. So, am I gonna see you tonight?"

"How late's the tent open?"

"Officially, eleven. But I know a guy."

"I'll bet." She gives him enough of a smile to keep him loyal for now. "I better get back to work so I can finish up in time."

———

As he leaves, Michele grabs a notebook and writes down everything he told her. Then she looks at the text from Vend:

ahh michelle my bell . . . long time . . . sorry no idea what you talk about

She starts to reply, decides to let him wait, returns to her keyboard. She clicks out of the screwed-up *Light* home page, opens Wordpress, and taps out the story she should've written hours ago:

Bleak Descendant Kidnapped for $5 Million Ransom

By Michele Higgins

Fifteen-year-old Daniel Peters, youngest member of Bleak Harbor's founding family, was taken from his parents' cottage on Bleak Harbor Bay yesterday and is being held for a ransom of $5.145 million, local police confirmed.

The abduction is all the more tragic because the boy, known as Danny, has reportedly been diagnosed on the autism spectrum. His mother, Carey Bleak Peters, daughter of Serenity Meredith Maas Bleak, declined to comment.

The boy left home on his own in April and was found hours later in an abandoned home next door to the cottage where he lives with his mother and stepfather, Andrew "Pete" Peters, at 39878 South Bay Drive. Peters is the owner of the new medical marijuana shop in town, AMP Botanicals.

Anyone with information on Danny Peters should call the Bleak Harbor Police Department, 269-551-4060.

Michele sits back in her chair, thinking about what Malone told her, then about Vend, then about Danny having sex with the woman from the pot shop. She wants to talk to this woman. The cops have commandeered Peters's pot shop; she doesn't know where else to find Dulcy.

For the first time since leaving Detroit, she can feel that thing she used to feel when she was in the *Free Press* newsroom after making her cop rounds, long after last call at the Anchor Bar, alone at her desk, the newsroom silent but for the burps and screeches of the police scanner, staring out the window at Lafayette Street, wondering how she was going to get the story she wasn't supposed to get, knowing that eventually she would. It wasn't about the byline or the money, which was shitty anyway, or even the editors telling her how great she was. It was really just about the chasing and the catching.

A name pops into her head: *Lengel.*

She picks up her phone and texts Vend back:

your friend Dulcy says hello

Michele opens her contacts, scrolls to Lengel.

Vend's reply appears:

hm poor dulcy if you see her tell her to call I miss her

She can't remember the last time she spoke with Lengel, but it won't matter. She competed against him when she was at the *Free Press* and he was covering federal courts for the *Detroit Times*. He kicked her ass on a story or two, maybe three; she kicked his on a few others. They became friendly, and he took on the distinction of being the only single male reporter who never once hit on her.

Lengel also is amazingly gifted at finding hard-to-find people. Michele texts him with their standard greeting: Big deal. Seconds later comes his standard reply:

Bigger than you think.

27

The old Bleak steel mill squats in a field of waist-high weeds a few miles south of the Indiana-Michigan border. Carey had passed it without noticing on the way to Valparaiso. But coming from the other direction, it's impossible to miss the FUCK BLEAK someone slopped in black over the faded Matsunaka logo on one of the idle smokestacks. Carey really can't blame the vandals. If she wasn't on her current mission, she might stop and take a picture, post it online with a smart-ass comment.

Her phone has been zizzing with texts from the kidnapper: A photo of Danny's shoe blotched with dark stains. Audio of a dog's growls and snorts. An accusation: u quit on people its in yr blood. She has read and tried to push each one from her mind, focused on the road and the deadline she gave Quartz.

Now the phone rings. She picks it up and says, "Jonah."

"Carey," he says. He sounds excited. "The police think they've found Bledsoe. They're going after him."

"Is Danny there?"

"We'll know soon. Let's hope. Where are you?"

"On my way back. Where are the cops going?"

"Chief wouldn't say; he doesn't want a screwup. But he gave me a heads-up that they got a break."

"Good. I just—" She has to stop for a moment. "I just want to hold him in my arms again."

"You will."

She knows it troubles Jonah that Danny doesn't know his grand-parents better. He had tried on several occasions to make peace between Carey and their parents. It was as much his nature to seek appeasement as it was Carey's to stiffen her neck and turn away. She knew Jonah meant well. But she had decided long ago that her mother and father were not the best for her or Danny.

Jonah knows all about her disillusions with her marriage and her daily frustrations with Danny. But Carey hasn't told him anything about her attempt to blackmail Pressman. Jonah would have tried to talk her out of it. She would have gone ahead, and she wouldn't have wanted her brother connected in any way, in case the authorities found her out. If she had to go to prison, she would feel all right leaving Danny in Jonah's care.

Now he asks again, "Where are you?"

"I just passed the old plant," she tells her brother. "I can't believe it's still there."

Their great-great-grandfather built it in the 1880s. Carey was eight, Jonah nine, when her father sold it to the Japanese company that would close it only two years later. It would take another two years of litigation for the unions to discover that the worker pensions had been dissolved.

"Why the hell are you in Indiana?" Jonah says.

"I told you, for Danny. Do not tell the cops—do you hear me?"

"Damn it, Carey, all right, I won't, but just tell me."

"We'll talk about it later."

Jonah sighs. "Come right to the police station, OK?"

She drops the phone in her lap and peers into the rearview mirror at what was once J. E. B. Steel. The receding vision beckons a memory Carey wishes she did not possess.

———

The dinner table at the Bleak Harbor mansion was an expanse of var-nished mahogany set along a wall of French doors rising to the high ceiling. On a clear day, the blurry trapezoid of the Chicago skyline was visible on the horizon across Lake Michigan.

Carey's father sat at one end of the table, seven or eight feet to her right, her mother the same distance to her left, Jonah directly across. Roland Spitler stood at one end of the room, near a double door that led to the kitchen, wordlessly awaiting orders.

Carey was twelve, a seventh-grader home from Cranbrook for fall break. The dining room windows were closed to shut out the megaphone catcalls of the protesters from the street below.

Jack Bleak didn't look at his daughter when she asked him why the workers' pensions hadn't been secured before he sold the mill to Matsunaka. Reaching for the scalloped potatoes, he said, "You know dinner is not the time for this, young lady."

"Carey, please," Serenity said.

Carey sneaked a look at Jonah, who gave her the slightest of nods. She put her fork down. She hated pork roast anyway.

"When is it time?" she said.

Her father ignored her.

"Tell me, Father. Did the pension money really have anything to do with the improvements at the marina?"

He stabbed a slice of meat, keeping his eyes lowered, giving no indication that he would answer.

"Did your bookkeeper really—"

"Controller," her father said. "He was the controller. He was supposed to have full control of the finances." He looked up from his plate. He didn't look angry or exasperated. He looked as sure of himself as if he was observing that the glazed carrots were overdone. "Unfortunately, he did not have full control. He's been dealt with. And that is all I will say on this topic at the dinner table."

"So one guy made a mistake, and all those people out there"—she waved an arm toward the windows—"they just have to lump it? What about the marina? Is that how you, I mean we"—she glanced at Jonah, who was pretending to be focused on his food—"paid for the new boat lift?"

Serenity addressed her husband. "She's been reading the Chicago papers, which I blame on that history professor, Krier. I don't know why we spend so much on that school."

"Sociology."

"I truly do not care, dear." Serenity did in fact look exasperated, as she often did with her adolescent children. "This isn't some classroom exercise."

"No, it's not. It's people's lives."

"What do you know about people's lives?" her mother said. "You don't know anything, little girl."

"Don't call me that."

"All right—why must you be such a bitch all the time? Is that language preferable to you?"

Carey felt her insides coil, hoping it didn't show on the outside. Her mother could have been her ally against her father. He wasn't worth it anymore. Carey's rants against her father's greed just complicated life for Serenity, who desired nothing more than to curl up alone in her noiseless vodka cocoon.

"Right back at you, Mother."

"Enough, all right? We pay for your book learning; please do not bring it into our home, if that's quite all right."

"It's not quite all right." Carey got out of her chair. "It's not all right at all."

"Sit down," her father ordered. "I'm trying to have my dinner. Goddamn it, can't we have five goddamn minutes of peace around here?"

Carey turned to her father. "You hurt those people. You knew the pensions weren't paid up. You knew that Matsushita company—"

"Matsunaka."

"—Matsu-whatever, you knew they were just going to shut the plant down so they could raise prices."

"So you're a business expert now? Sit. Or leave."

Carey started to sit, then recalled that morning, watching from her turret bedroom as the police wielding dark batons herded the demonstrators away from the house. "No," she told her father. "You shit all over those people."

"Watch your language."

Carey spun on Serenity. "And you're no better, living off of it."

"Miss Carey?" It was Spitler. He had stepped closer to the table. "Shall I bring your dinner up to your room?"

"It's fine, Roland," Serenity said. "This is none of your business anyway."

Spitler flinched as he stepped backward and then turned and disappeared into the kitchen. Carey's father set his utensils on his plate with a loud clink, snatched his napkin from his lap, and stood. That's when Jonah finally spoke up.

"Jeez, Dad," he said. He wore the weary, cocked smile of a thirteen-year-old who knew more than he should have. "Maybe you oughta stick with fucking women instead of fucking over your employees."

Jonah's father held his son's gaze for a second before shifting his glare down the table at Serenity. "Are you happy now?" He pointed Carey toward the kitchen. "Excuse yourself, young lady."

Carey took the kitchen elevator down and slipped out to the boathouse. She sat on the stern of one of the Chris-Crafts, knees beneath her chin, watching the cumulus tumble across the late-afternoon sky, hearing the angry shouts of the protesters on the other side of the mansion, her eyes hot with furious tears.

———

A few minutes after crossing the border into Michigan, Carey dials her mother's assistant, Roland Spitler.

Over the past few hours, her phone has filled with texts and voice mails from colleagues who've seen the news of Danny on social media. Carey hasn't bothered with them. And she has ignored the reporters promising that their outlet can help her find her son.

"Miss Carey," Spitler answers. "May I return your call in fifteen minutes?"

"No. I need to see my mother."

"I'm sorry, Miss Carey, but Miss Serenity isn't feeling well. Could you please call me—"

"Roland, I have my mother's cell number."

Spitler pauses before responding. "Please let me get off this other call."

Carey recalls the email Spitler had sent after Jack Bleak's death expressing "sincere regret" that Serenity "lacks the liquidity in her current portfolio" to assist with private school tuition for Danny. Carey had replied, "My mother doesn't know the meaning of *regret*." To which Spitler wrote simply, "Yes, Miss Carey."

She waits. At the click that announces Spitler's return, Carey says, "I don't have time for this. I need to see my mother, or if you can't arrange that, then I need her help with this ransom."

"Of course, Miss Carey."

"Which is it?"

"Tell me again what the ransom is."

She gives him the new one.

"That is a peculiar number."

"Serenity can handle it."

"I'm afraid it's not quite as simple as that, what with Miss Serenity's bequest."

"Explain, please?"

"Your mother's liquid assets are in an escrow account, as a demonstration of good faith to the various qualifying entities."

"I've been at every meeting about her money, and I haven't heard anything about escrow accounts."

"Correct me if I'm wrong, Miss Carey, but I don't believe you attended yesterday's city council meeting."

"Pete did. He didn't say anything about an escrow."

"It was briefly discussed. Perhaps Mr. Peters left early?"

That was entirely possible. "So what? Are you saying you can't violate some stupid escrow to save my son's life?"

"Miss Carey, the escrow was established at the behest of—"

"I will see Serenity, Roland."

"Of course, but you realize you haven't called your mother in at least six months. She hasn't—"

"I will see my mother this afternoon. You will call me with a time. If I don't hear from you in fifteen minutes, I'll be on the phone to the city attorney to ask about this escrow account."

"Please, Miss Carey."

"Fifteen minutes."

28

A ragged circle of officers, some in blue-and-gold and some in brown-and-mustard uniforms, surrounds the clapboard house on Beechnut Street in Bridgman. Something isn't right. The officers aren't crouching or moving in a way that suggests danger is imminent. Their guns are holstered. They're standing around talking.

"Shit," Hamilton says.

She's out of the car almost before she puts it in park, walking toward the house. Malone follows a step behind, scanning the yard. The grass is spotty with dust patches, the bowed hydrangeas a crackling brown. Whoever lives here doesn't give a damn.

A cinder block standing on end props the front door open. She can see cops moving around inside. Maybe Bledsoe is dead. That would be fine. But what about Danny?

She starts to jog and overtakes Hamilton, who calls out, "Hey, where you going?" A hatless state cop emerges onto the front porch with a phone to an ear. "Delacroix," the officer is saying as Malone stops at the porch steps. "Petunia? What about the landlord?"

"Danny Peters," Malone says. "Is he here? Is he alive?"

The state cop holds up a hand to quiet Malone. She's nodding at whatever she's hearing on her phone. "All right. One of their people just got here—I'll let her know."

Malone's heart sinks. "They're not here."

The trooper drops her phone to her side. "Afraid not. This Bledsoe either bolted or never was here."

"Wrong address?"

"Yes and no. It's definitely the address Bledsoe gave his parole officer. But the only trace of him is a pair of socks that might or might not be his and a used condom under a bed. The actual renter here is one Petunia Delacroix."

"And we're running her down?"

"Her landlord says she works at the diner in town. Berrien County has two officers there now. If Petunia knows Bledsoe, and I'm betting she does, we'll find him."

Malone checks her watch. A little more than nine hours remain to the ransom deadline. "Can I help?"

"I'd get back to your station and hope we get a break soon."

"This Bledsoe is a bad guy."

"Ten-four, Officer. Got a fifteen-year-old at home myself. She can sure be a handful, but I'd do anything for her."

An image of Louisa running on the beach, arms pumping, ponytail bobbing, feet leaving tracks in the sand, materializes in Malone's mind. She lets it go.

She walks around the back of the house, looking for Hamilton, invisible to the officers poking around in the bushes. She looks at her watch again. What if Bledsoe isn't anywhere nearby? What if he really is running a vile errand for that Detroit dealer? What if this Dulcinea Pérez somehow got to Danny? What does Peters know about it?

She moves away from the house and makes a call. "Chief," she says, "have you heard from Peters yet? No? Screw him then, eh?"

She finishes with the chief and circles to the front of the house, telling herself that Petunia at the diner will lead them to Danny. She keeps walking, circles the house, the yard. She can't find Hamilton. She turns to the street. The FBI agent's car is gone.

"Are you kidding me?" she says aloud.

"Looking for Agent Hamilton?"

Malone turns to see a dark-skinned stranger in a gray mock turtleneck and a black leather jacket. He has a crescent scar on his left cheek, and his tinted glasses are askew.

"Special Agent Allen Locke. Indianapolis."

"Katya Malone, Bleak Harbor Police."

"Need a ride?"

———

"Don't feel bad about Hamilton leaving you like that," Locke says reassuringly. "She doesn't play well with others."

"What's her problem?"

Locke is a cautious driver. He hits the turn signal whenever he changes lanes. He never looks over at Malone as he speaks.

"I don't know her that well, but supposedly she got a pretty big head after that Hayek kidnapping a few years ago. She's now the FBI abduction queen. Wants those cases all to herself."

"Hayek," Malone repeats. "Where was that?"

"Saint Louis. You probably saw it on the tube because it involved a rich guy."

"Ah, right, the pesticide exec."

"Hell hath no fury like a GMO activist. Anyway, Hamilton was the one who talked that idiot out of dropping the guy from the top of a building. And then there was the straight-to-DVD movie."

"No."

"Yeah."

"Why are you here all the way from Indy?"

"Ma'am," he says. "I could tell you my bosses sent me, which wouldn't be the whole truth. The whole truth is, I don't like people who mess with children."

Malone watches the trees flying past, wishing they were back at the station already. She wants to do something but doesn't know what.

"Can I ask you something?" Locke says.

"Go ahead."

"The mother—Carey Peters, right?—doesn't she work for that Pressman gentleman in Chicago?"

The randy Randall Pressman, Malone thinks. "Yes," she says. "Pressman Logistics."

"Have you checked in with him?"

"With Pressman himself? Why would we?"

"I've had reason to cross paths with him. He's involved in some unsavory activities."

Malone's phone goes off. "At a logistics company?"

"Contraband has to get somewhere somehow."

"It's Chief." She answers her phone. "Yeah?"

"This frigging guy," Radovich tells her. "Now we got him."

"Where?"

"Schoolcraft. He gave his parole officer his girlfriend's address while he was holing up at his old cellmate's place."

"The cellmate gave him up?"

"Yes, he did. How far are you?"

Malone points the phone at Locke. "Stop the car."

"Why?"

"We got Bledsoe. Pull over."

Malone's seat belt digs into her shoulders as Locke's tires scatter the shoulder gravel.

"Kalamazoo County's going," Radovich says. "Where are you?"

"On our way. Keep this off the scanner. Bledsoe might know we were in Bridgman."

"You gonna be OK?"

Malone knows what he's getting at. "I'm fine. Talk later." She undoes her seat belt and jumps out of the car.

"What are you doing?" Locke says.

"Switch seats. I know a shortcut."

Sliding behind the wheel, Malone maps the route to Schoolcraft in her head, seeing again the elbow bend where Louisa was sitting in the pickup next to her father as Malone gave chase. She closes her eyes but sees for the hundred thousandth time the tailgate fishtailing left and right before the truck skids sideways and lurches over the shoulder into the unyielding oak.

She slams the accelerator down and screeches out onto the road, her heart breaking a thousand different ways as she thinks, *Danny, please, just be there, alive.*

29

Bledsoe's trying to keep cool. He can't afford to get pulled over for speeding, but he's got to push it as fast as he can. He exited I-94 the minute he heard the scanner croak the order for Berrien County deputies to get to 1626 Beechnut in Bridgman. Petunia's place.

They're coming for him.

He kept the speedometer just below the 45 limit on Flowerfield and tapped it up a few miles per hour after turning north onto 131. He slows entering downtown Schoolcraft. Passing Bud's Bar, he wishes he could while away the hot evening with a bucket of cold ones, but he has to get out of here, out of Michigan, out of the country. Fuck the kid and his asshole parents. Fuck the rotts. Bledsoe is outta here.

He turns right on Clay, sees the gray box of his apartment building three blocks away. Corrigan, his Muskegon cellmate, had told him he could rent apartment 302 from a sister-in-law for fifty dollars a week. He wound up paying her in other ways she seemed to prefer and he didn't mind much either.

He sees no police cars in the lot but circles the block just to be safe. He swings behind his building and parks next to a dumpster just as an email from Petunia dings on his phone. That's not right. She's a texter, not an emailer. The subject line is empty. He clicks on a link to her Facebook page, and a wave of dread washes over him.

"Are you fucking kidding me?" he says. He looks around to see if anyone is watching or listening. "Dumb fucking cunt."

He has seen the photo before. Petunia in a too-tight yellow bikini. He took it on the sand at Warren Dunes. That's not the problem. The problem is that she pasted it into some kind of postcard graphic that shows her sitting on a different beach beneath a palm tree. "Ola!" the caption reads. "Time for a new adventure!!"

It's already been "liked" twenty-eight times.

Bledsoe looks at the dashboard clock. Petunia could be on her way to this very spot, with the cops on her rear bumper. He hopes like hell she didn't stop at her place first. Brainless bitch.

He skulks into the building's rear entrance, rushes up the stairs. Inside 302, he secures both deadbolts and goes directly to the laptop sitting open on the kitchen table. He has to clean out a few items he neglected to wipe the night before.

He signs on and slides the cursor to a folder labeled "bitch." It contains an email exchange from seven months earlier, a week after Bledsoe had left prison and bought that file on Carey:

C,

how u? got a minute for an old pal coming to chicago? give a shout

Jeff B

He'd looked at her blunt reply once every few days, more if he'd had a lot to drink. At first it had just pissed him off. Lately he's begun to regard it as a source of inspiration:

Jeffrey,

If you contact me again, I will call the police. I assume you don't need any more trouble.

Good Bye.

Bledsoe hadn't forgotten the night he was sure he'd knocked Carey up. Halloween damp seeped through the cracked-paint window frame above Carey's bed. Bledsoe wore a flannel nightshirt, a fresh condom in the pocket. She was the one who wouldn't stop. She was the one who'd guzzled the white Russians at the Elwood. She was the one who had raked her nails across his skin and shook her head when he offered to pull the balloon on. "Don't stop fucking me don't stop fucking me." Bledsoe had merely done what he did so well.

He reads her latest words one more time. The bitch couldn't even sign her name. She had to drag out the goodbye, using two words, like she got off telling him to stay out of her precious life. He had told himself to let it go. Of course he couldn't. He couldn't let anything go. Sometimes that was a good thing, in the way rich guys liked to say they never gave up and that's how they got rich. Sometimes it wasn't, like when you pushed too hard on a guy in the joint who didn't give a shit if you lived or died or if he did.

Bledsoe deletes the emails, erases the files, goes to the trash bin, deletes them all again.

He'd never thought of trying to contact his son until Petunia pointed out the online article about the runaway kid named Danny in Bleak Harbor. "Looks like his mama might've been knocking him around," she said. That was all Bledsoe needed to hear.

One night, after four beers and a Vicodin, he found Danny on Facebook. The kid had all of four friends. One was his bitch mother. The others were members of some dweeby Cubs fan club, one of them in a foreign country Bledsoe hadn't heard of. No wonder Danny responded right away. Bledsoe had emailed him with the subject line "YOU." What fifteen-year-old wouldn't bang on that?

> Champ,
>
> This is your real daddy. Sorry about what's goin on. Glad u are OK . . .

Danny had replied:

> I am glad too.
>
> Did you know that the dragonfly is one of the most vicious killers in the animal kingdom?

Bledsoe had not known that. He wondered why a teenaged kid would bring that up, then reminded himself that Danny wasn't right in the head. And yet, for a kid who was supposedly messed up, he turned out to be a hell of a lot smarter than Petunia. After they started texting instead of emailing, Danny listened to Bledsoe bitch about hauling paint buckets of grease in his trunk to the dump, creeping low in the night because LaBelle's owner wouldn't pay to have the stuff disposed of properly. Bledsoe listened to Danny gripe about his stepdad spending more time at that bar than with Danny. He started thinking, *Shit, this kid ain't retarded or agnostic or nothing. He's just shy and lonely and ignored. Goddamned if he isn't me.*

Now he double deletes the Danny emails and wishes he'd taken a last look at Petunia's computer. Too late now. He's about to shut the laptop when he decides to check his Sent email folder, just in case the cops happen to catch up with him. Which they won't.

He leans into the screen, squinting at the sent email four down from the top. It went to Danny's Gmail address. It contains the subject line "Re: YOU." But Bledsoe hasn't sent an email to Danny in weeks. It's been all texts since. The date on the email says he sent it two nights before. *No fucking way*, he thinks. He opens it:

Y not, Danny boy?

"Danny boy?" he says. "I didn't—what the fuck?" He wonders if Petunia was in his email. He thinks back to the last time she was in Schoolcraft. Sunday. Five days ago. Too stupid to be her.

He hears two knocks at the door, thinks, *Petunia already? She must have left work early.*

He goes back to his main email page, then to the trash bin, then back to the sent folder. He thinks back to Wednesday night. He was watching porn. He can remember the white-haired guy going down on the hairless kid with the skin like wax paper. But he can't recall sending a single email, certainly not to Danny.

He hears three more knocks, rapid and hard.

He remembers the text from Quartz—1ovrEZ@5—that sent him from the diner to collect the boy.

Wishing now that he had ignored it.

He gets up and tiptoes to the locked bedroom door. You could hear a mosquito breathing through the shitty particleboard. Bledsoe hears the twin rottweilers huffing and snarling and scraping their nails on the other side of the door. His nose tells him they've shit all over the floor. He's not about to clean it up now. The cops will find what they find.

He looks into the kitchen. From the window it's three floors to the ground. Too far to jump, but maybe there's a car or a trash can down there to break his fall.

There's another knock. Bledsoe edges sideways toward that door. It has no peephole. "Baby?" he says.

He pulls up short when no answer comes, takes a step back, glances over his shoulder at the kitchen window. He waits. Hearing nothing, he leans into the door again. Without touching it, he sniffs the air as quietly as he can. He wants to smell Petunia's perfume. At the diner he could smell it even over sizzling onions.

Now all he gets is sweat. He takes another backward step, then another, and reaches behind him for the doorknob to the room where the dogs wait.

"Petunia?" he says. "Who the fuck's out there?

30

Pete downs the double vodka tonic in one languid guzzle. He doesn't care about tasting it—he just wants to feel it, to drown himself in it for half a minute before resurfacing. The last drops trickle off the back of his tongue, bitter. He sets the glass down.

"Another?" Boz says.

Yessir, Pete thinks. And another and another. He pushes the glass across the bar. "Diet Coke."

"Sure?"

"Yeah. Needed that, though."

"I can imagine."

Pete left Oly at the rink and drove into downtown Bleak Harbor to check on his office. He couldn't get close because of traffic and pedestrians and blocked-off streets, but he really didn't want to get close anyway. He'd pulled into a pay lot three blocks up the rise on Lily and slumped low in the driver's seat, blasting the AC, as festivalgoers in "Anisoptera Always" T-shirts streamed past. Some of them paused on the sidewalk to peer into the building that housed AMP Botanicals. Police tape ringed the semicircular glass entrance, and sheriff's deputies were hauling boxes out to a police van parked in the middle of the street. Pete made a quick inventory in his mind. He'd been careful about packaging the illegal dope in the same vials and cellophane baggies as the legal stuff. He couldn't think of anything that would get him in trouble. *I'm not the criminal here*, he thought. *Why aren't they out finding Bledsoe? Why aren't they out finding Danny?*

He thought of Danny standing in their kitchen, wrapping the salami-and-cheese sandwiches in wax paper, how careful he was to make the wrap tight, the creases sharp. And then Pete started to cry. At first he tried to slump lower in his seat so the passersby wouldn't notice, but then he didn't care—he let the sobs shake him, let the tears drip off his chin. "Oh God," he said aloud. "My man, my man, my little man. Come home, Danny. Please come home."

Boz sets a tumbler of ice and Diet Coke in front of him. Pete says, "Traffic is a pain in the ass today."

"And will be until Monday."

"Listen, Boz, gotta ask you something, then I gotta get to the police station."

"They were here, you know. A couple hours ago."

"The police were here?" he says.

"Sheriff's deputies. Routine stop. Did I see the boy yesterday, see anything unusual at your house?"

"You did see Danny. You told me."

"Yeah. He was outside."

Pete waits, expecting more, but Boz moves down the bar to the sink without saying anything. "And?"

Boz shrugs. "Like I told the deputies, not much. I mean, I was in the dead spot between lunch and happy hour. He walks by every now and then; we talk."

"What'd you talk about yesterday?"

"Not much. The storm that's coming tomorrow. My new boat. Kid likes that boat. And we did some bitching about the festival, of course."

"Danny loves the festival."

"Huh." Boz takes his cell phone off the back bar, punches something in, sets it down again. "What do I know about kids?"

Pete picks up his own phone, considers trying Carey again, instead hits the app for their bank, types in the username and password. The numbers pop up again. He swipes to make them bigger. He has to look at the pending total three times before he believes it: $5,150,122.98. *Thank God for Oly*, he thinks as he sends Carey a text:

Oly came thru w5 mill+!!

He wants to show the bank entry to Boz, show him he's doing something for Danny. Instead he clicks out of the bank app, looks up, and says, "What do your ex-cop instincts tell you?"

"They have any leads?"

"Looks like it might be Danny's real father." Pete glances down the bar at the stool where Bledsoe stood mocking him months before. The reindeer decoration is still on the wall. "Guy just got out of prison."

"They have a bead on him?"

"I guess they're working on it."

"You guess?"

"Like I said, I gotta get over there."

"Right."

Boz busies himself at the cash register. The air in the room has shifted like it does when Pete and Danny are out fishing and a squall comes up. Pete looks over his shoulder through the picture windows at the empty beach, the bay lying still and silver in the humid afternoon. Down the beach, yellow tape is looped along the deck railings at his house. He presses his eyes shut, wishing it all away, seeing Danny strolling out to the dock with a fishing pole and minnow bucket, bobbing his head to a tune only he can hear.

Just find him.

When he opens his eyes, Boz's face is screwed up with what looks like emotion, maybe regret. Pete hears a door opening somewhere behind the bar, then footsteps, two people.

Boz leans forward and grips the bar hard with both hands.

"Something wrong?"

"Jesus," Boz says. "I'm sorry, man."

"Sorry for what?"

They both turn to see a woman and a man in Bleak County Sheriff's uniforms. Pete feels a little surge of hope.

"Oh my God, did you find Danny?"

The male deputy stays behind, standing stiff with his arms folded beneath the reindeer head, while the woman steps forward and says, "Andrew Michael Peters?"

Pete turns to Boz. "What's going on?"

"Sorry, buddy."

Pete smiles in his confusion. He turns back to the woman. "Yes," he tells her, then looks back at Boz. "Once a cop, always a cop, eh?"

The handcuffs pinch Pete's wrists. He feels guilt leach through him as the officer ushers him out the back door.

31

Boz watches through a window in his kitchen as the sheriff's cruiser pulls out of his lot, siren wailing. *For Christ's sake*, he thinks, *you don't need the damn siren.*

He likes Pete, and not just because he's a regular. The guy knows his Chicago sports, leaves a decent tip, agrees with Boz about most of the political bullshit that rules this town.

But the guy's in over his head. Way over. Boz saw guys like him all the time in his years on the Chicago force, retired cops especially, thinking they could do what they couldn't. Dreaming of that one big strike, getting themselves in trouble. As the cop flashers disappear around a bend in the bay road, Boz half smiles at himself. After all, he's doing the same thing, isn't he? The big strike is at hand for him now.

Pete will understand one day, if he ever finds out.

Boz walks back into the bar. Two regulars are waiting at a high top inside, three more at a picnic table on the beach deck. They've probably seen Pete Peters before, but Boz doesn't think any of them know him. They're going to ask about the deputies, and Boz is going to smile and zip his lips like he did when he wore a badge, tell them he's going to close the deck pretty soon—everyone come inside; first round's on him.

His phone is waiting where he left it on the back bar beneath the Schlitz sign. He leaves it there, opens a cabinet beneath the back bar, and takes out a disposable phone.

"Parched over here, Mr. Boz," a high-top customer calls out.

Boz waves at the customers, says, "One sec," then taps out a text:

pete in cuffs coast clear cops know nothin

32

Danny listens.

The echoing drums, the church bells, the tinny calliope.

He imagines the tack of cotton candy on his lips. Hears a rock song, something about Montreaux, Frank Zappa, a flare gun. The singer flat, the cymbals hissing, the bass too loud.

Hears Pete.

That one's a keeper, Danny. Do you think your mom still loves me? We'll sneak out to the big lake one of these nights. Do you think she ever did?

Hears Carey.

No lumps, my baby, eat your breakfast. Early meeting. The goddamn traffic. This goddamn place. I'm so sorry we brought you here. But soon, someday, someday soon, I will take you away.

Maybe she thought he couldn't understand. Entirely.

Does not hear the wet chuff and growl of the rotts.

Hears Paddle. Paddle barking at the dragonflies. Jumping and yapping at the end of the dock.

I'm sorry, honey—there is nothing we can do.

Paddle wheezing. The dragonfly wings aflutter. The veterinarian's perfect children will learn one day that a cure is not a realistic possibility.

There is nothing we can do, son.

Paddle hushed.

There was nothing we could do.

Did they think he wouldn't understand?

The dragonflies hover.

We will get a new dog, a new Paddle. I promise, honey. As soon as we're out of here.

Danny sees the face of Jeremiah, the one the newspaper used back then, not on the front page, inside the paper, black-and-white, the longing stare, the head canted ever so slightly.

Imagines him speaking:

The time is near. The perch are rushing to the hooks. You see, Danny, the summer is ours. This place is ours. The dragonflies are here, jaws agape with blood and fire.

33

"Where's the kid?"

"One thing at a time, Randall. Our immediate problem is solved."

"That was our guys?"

"Our guys."

"In broad daylight?"

"Inside an apartment building. It had to be done."

"What about the cops?"

"They'll think it's the Detroit dealer."

"How do you know that?"

Quartz doesn't. "Relax."

"I'll relax when we know where the fucking kid is."

"Working on it."

Quartz hunches over a table in the kitchen of his apartment above the Mexican café in Valparaiso. He has emptied his many pockets, and the table is strewn with laptops, Danny's hard drive, and other boxy black devices. Quartz speaks to Pressman through a Bluetooth earpiece as he works a mouse and a keyboard.

"I suggest you work harder," Pressman says. "Do you realize how many different ways we're screwed if we don't find that kid?"

Let's see, Quartz thinks, *the hundred grand to Bledsoe is long gone, and you promised two million dollars to Carey Bleak*. If the cops stumble onto what's really going on, Pressman could go down for conspiracy and kidnapping and murder.

Quartz will have disappeared by then, possibly with that two million bucks in one of his overseas bank accounts. He has considered leaving immediately but has been digging up things in his current digital excavations that are keeping him here for now. At this instant he's prowling the servers of the *Bleak Harbor Light*, trying to figure out how that 1945 page wound up on the website and what the hell it means.

"Let's focus on the positives, shall we?" he tells Pressman. The sweat beading at the backs of Quartz's ears itches. He tried to open a window, but it got stuck in congealed paint. "Bledsoe is dead. Nobody has a clue we're involved."

"Can't they trace what we paid Bledsoe?"

"I made sure that trail leads nowhere."

"Have we given Carey Peters any money yet?"

"I set up a timed transfer for close of business. But that could easily be explained as a magnanimous boss helping out an employee." Quartz stops typing to gnaw on a fingernail. The blood hasn't come yet.

"I don't like it."

"You don't like what?"

"All of it. Like, Jesus, why the hell did they have to kill dogs?"

Quartz looks up at the bull's-eyes arrayed on the wall across the room. He thinks about the .22-caliber pistol in the drawer next to his bed.

He hopes he doesn't have to use it.

"Forget the dogs, Randall," he says. "I'm actually getting somewhere."

34

The woman is sobbing so hard that Malone can't make out what she's trying to say.

"Why . . . ?" she keeps saying. "Why did they . . . ?" But each time her wailing swallows the rest of her words. Blood splotches the frills along the low scoop of her blouse. Her perfume smells as sickly sweet as dying flowers, with an incongruous hint of bacon.

Her driver's license identifies her as Petunia Marie Delacroix, age thirty-seven, of Bridgman. She's standing with Malone and Agent Allen Locke in the parking lot of an apartment building in Schoolcraft. Four Kalamazoo County sheriff's deputies are inside, service weapons drawn. Two others patrol the grounds. A pair of ambulances waits by the building's rear entrance. Locals gawk from a weedy playground next door.

"Ms. Delacroix," Locke says. "Would you like to wait in my car?"

Petunia shakes her head. Rivulets of mascara bleed into the lipstick smears along one of her cheeks.

"Is Jeffrey dead?" she says.

"We don't have confirm—"

"Yes, he is dead," Malone says. "How did you know him, Petunia?"

Locke takes a tissue from a back pocket and hands it to Petunia, who balls it up on her face and says, "Who killed him?"

The first officers to arrive found Petunia slumped against the wall outside Bledsoe's open apartment, a splat of vomit on the floor near her high-heeled feet. Bledsoe had three bullets in his head, two in his back.

"We don't know yet," Malone says. "Was Jeffrey Bledsoe your boyfriend?"

She gazes past Malone and Locke at the building. "We had some good times. He's—he was—"

"He gave your address in Bridgman as his, ma'am," Locke says.

"He did?"

Malone steps closer. "Why did you come here, Petunia? You need to tell us. We're running out of time."

Her face scrunches up as if she's going to start crying again. "I understand."

"Do you understand that a boy's life is on the line? Was he here? Did Bledsoe have a boy with him?"

"Maybe I should get a lawyer."

"Officer Malone?"

Malone turns and recognizes the sheriff of Kalamazoo County, a man named Krasean. She tells Petunia, "Stay where you are."

She and Locke and Krasean move a few steps away. The sheriff speaks softly. "There's no sign of the Peters boy."

"Nothing?"

"So far. The techs will be here any minute."

"No signs that he might have escaped?"

"I think we'd have heard by now," Krasean says. "We've checked every public area in the building, and now we're going door-to-door." He looks over his shoulder at the building. "I have to say, it looks like a professional job. These people didn't fool around. And the deceased was one disturbed person."

"How so?"

"You'll see. Bunch of snapshots on the wall in the bathroom, all around the sink mirror."

"Snapshots of what?"

"Girls. Young. Boys. Black. White. Brown. Mostly naked."

"So our number-one suspect was a pervert," Locke tells Malone. "And now he's dead. Could someone have killed him and taken the Peters boy? This guy in Detroit? Or what?"

Or we were all dead wrong about Bledsoe, Malone thinks. *Or the kidnapper is someone we haven't imagined, a depraved stranger toying with us while he gets ready to—*she forces the thought from her mind, hears Petunia blubbering again.

"I'd like to slap her," she says.

"Please don't," Krasean says.

"I want to ask her something," Locke says.

Petunia is shaking with sobs again as she dumps pills from a plastic vial into one of her hands. She jams them into her mouth, still crying, and tosses her head back to swallow.

"Ms. Delacroix."

She starts to gag, pitching forward, hands going to her mouth. Locke continues: "Did your boyfriend ever say anything about a man named Pressman?"

The pills are burbling out through her lips now. Malone catches one, the saliva slimy in her hand, starts to drop it, then squeezes it, opens her palm, stares at the gooey blue thing.

"Wait," she says. She remembers Will worrying about Danny's meds. She turns to the sheriff, points toward the building. "Did you find any sort of prescription pills in there? Anything that would have been Danny's?"

"Some Percocets, I believe, but we assume those were the deceased's."

"Nothing else? Nothing marked for Danny Peters?"

"Negative."

"OK, Sheriff, can you do me a favor and get Agent Locke back to Bleak Harbor?"

"Pardon me?" Locke says.

"Of course. Agent, do you want to take a look inside? We're also searching the deceased's car, in back."

"Yes, he does," Malone says, then tells Locke, "I'm taking your car. I have to get back now."

Locke looks from Malone to Petunia and back. "Should I bring her?"

"She's useless, but whatever."

Malone heads toward Locke's car, looks at her watch, starts running, hears Petunia bawling again. "Why?" she's wailing. "Why did they have to shoot the dogs?"

35

Carey flings the door to Radovich's office open and flips her phone onto the chief's desk.

"You arrested my husband?" she says. "Are you fucking kidding me?" She scans the room, heads swiveling in her direction: Chief, Jonah, Will, an official-looking woman she's never seen before. "Where is Officer Malone?"

"Ms. Peters."

"You're all fuckups. It's not Bledsoe, is it? What the fuck are you all doing?"

She knows she's out of line. She knows they've been waiting on her, trying to reach her. She'd planned to come in as calm and polite as she could be under the circumstances. Then the video had appeared on her phone, courtesy of Jeremiah. She had pulled into a rest area to watch it. It took her a while to settle down enough to drive again.

"We understand you're upset, ma'am," the woman says.

"You understand shit," Carey tells the woman, then looks at the chief, sitting at his desk. "For all you know, Danny's riding the merry-go-round with a box of popcorn."

"Ma'am—"

"And the ransom, incidentally, is now up to seven million something, according to this goddamn Jeremiah." She doesn't mention Oly O'Nally's contribution; the cops don't need to be bothering the only person who has helped so far.

"We'll need to see that phone."

"Who the hell are you?"

"FBI. Stefanie Hamilton." She offers her hand. Carey ignores it. "We've been trying to reach you."

"Watch the video," Carey says, nodding at her phone.

Will takes it from the desk.

Jonah comes over and joins Radovich and the FBI agent leaning over Will's shoulder. Carey knows the video by heart by now. It was black-and-white and slightly out of focus. There was no sound.

It opened on what looked like a living room, with a television on a stand near an open doorway. Discarded cans of energy drink littered the floor. The arm of a man, limp in front of the doorway, jutted into the bottom of the frame. The middle halves of two men in dark garb moved in and out of the scene. Neither acknowledged the camera, as if they had no idea it was there.

The arm twisted one way, then turned over and pushed the upper half of its body up from the floor. The head and shoulders of a man lurched into the picture. His face was turned away, but Carey recognized the tattoo on his neck.

He dragged himself toward the doorway. The barrel of a gun appeared at his back. There was a small flash of light. Bledsoe collapsed, black liquid pooling around his head.

Two more flashes followed. The dark-clad men left the room. At fifty-seven seconds, the screen went black. A timer at the bottom of the screen said twenty-three seconds remained. The black turned to blue, then gray. The gray began to peel back from the left side of the screen, revealing a backdrop of white and then, gradually, in the middle of the screen, Danny's thin, anguished face, in color.

The camera pulled back until Danny's shoulders and chest came into view. He was awake. He no longer wore a blindfold. The shadow remained beneath his left eye. He appeared to be sitting, his arms pinned behind him. He looked offscreen, then nodded.

His lips began to move. He was speaking, but there still was no sound. It took Carey a few views to read his lips. He wasn't saying much. Just three words, spaced about a second apart: "Mom. Pete. Why."

Then Danny bowed his head briefly before raising it to say, "What are you doing?"

The image flickered before engulfing Danny in black.

Now Jonah and the others move away from Will, who taps the phone screen, watching again. Carey is fighting tears. She feels Jonah's fingers on her elbow. He's whispering: "Calm now. Calm." She closes her eyes as she would when she was a child, Jonah's hand on her shoulder, her mother and father down at the deck overlooking the big lake, their choked-off shouting and cursing audible but blessedly unintelligible.

"Bledsoe's computer must be fitted with a miniature video camera," Will says. "Probably for women he brought back. Or—never mind."

"But Bledsoe didn't make this video of him getting shot," Hamilton says.

"No. It looks like someone accessed the cam remotely."

"A hacker."

"Is Danny in the same room as Bledsoe?" Jonah says.

"Doesn't look like it," Hamilton says.

Carey remains silent. Her brother speaks up again. "How do we know those men didn't take Danny with them?"

"We don't."

"Damn," Will says, working his own phone now. "This thing's all over the web. This guy—@drewthenobody—tweeted it like ten times."

Mom. Pete. Why.

"Are you going to bring Pete out here?" Jonah asks.

The chief turns to Hamilton, who says, "We need to ask Ms. Peters a few questions first." She gives Carey a practiced look that's probably intended to comfort. Carey takes her in: Early forties. Tai chi classes. No wedding band. "Ms. Peters—"

"Carey, please."

"Carey. As we understand it, you last heard from Jeffrey Bledsoe late last year—is that correct?"

"Yes. I told him to go away."

"Understood," Hamilton says. "Now, are you aware of any recent contacts between Bledsoe and your husband?"

The question slams Carey like a forearm to the breastbone. She repeats it once in her mind, then again, catching her breath. She knows the answer—no, she is not aware of any contacts—but the answer isn't the problem; the question is the problem.

"No," she says. "He—no, that can't be."

"Afraid it is," Hamilton says.

"Can you please get to the point?" Jonah says.

Hamilton says, "Mr. Peters was buying illegally grown marijuana from Bledsoe and reselling it in his shop."

"Oh, holy bullshit," Jonah says.

"That's ridiculous," Carey says, more because she doesn't want to believe it than that she can't.

"Mr. Peters has admitted as much to us," Hamilton says. "Our preliminary inquiries indicate that Bledsoe may have had similar relationships with other legal dealers in the region. And, as you may or may not know, Bledsoe is—or was—affiliated with a dangerous criminal in Detroit."

"Who may have had him killed."

"Your husband insists he didn't know he was doing business with Bledsoe. Everything was done by phone and text and anonymous drops involving piggy banks."

"Piggy banks? This is beyond silly."

"Mr. Peters says he was not aware precisely whom he was dealing with until very recently."

It hits Carey then that her husband may be responsible, however indirectly, for her son's disappearance. "I want to see him."

"What about Dulcinea Pérez?" Hamilton says. "Know her?"

Carey thinks of Dulcy's wide-set eyes, the stretchy V-neck sweater accentuating her cleavage. "She's a lazy do-nothing who couldn't get to work on time. Pete was supposed to fire her yesterday."

"Ah," Hamilton says. "Do you happen to know if Pérez was aware that she was about to be canned?"

"How would I? Why does it matter?"

"We think she works for the same Detroit dealer Bledsoe did, probably sent here to keep an eye on your husband." Hamilton waits a beat. "She also may have had communications with your son."

"No way. She came to the house once, and Danny probably saw her at the shop a couple of times, but that's all."

"Mr. Peters told us he would regularly send Pérez to check on Danny if he was busy at the shop. Usually late afternoons."

"So," Jonah says, "she could have seen the inside of the house, gotten an idea of Danny's routine?"

"He was taken in late afternoon."

When Pete was at the damn bar, Carey thinks. "So what are you saying? This person in Detroit took Danny? Or his guys did? Or that Dulcy bitch did?" She feels tears starting to come, pinches them back. "We're fucked. Danny's . . . oh my God."

Radovich comes around the desk, lays a gentle hand on Carey's shoulder. "We don't know that," he tells her. "We are looking for Pérez. The Detroit police are also on the case." He nods at Will. "Can you please go find Malone?"

As Will slips past her, Carey feels Jonah touch the small of her back. She feels woozy, closes her eyes against the sudden spinning of the room. She tries to picture herself on the beach deck with Danny on a bright afternoon, glasses of lemonade sweating on the arms of the adirondack chairs. She and Danny would be debating, yet again, his favorite poem. And he would tell her that the palm in the opening line, the one Carey mistook for a hand instead of the tree it was, "is forever out of reach."

She always heard his declaration as defeatist, as if Danny had given up on whatever dreams swirled in his mind. It crushed her. Now his observation strikes her as realistic, mature, even liberating. Danny wasn't saying people couldn't have what they yearned for. He was saying that the yearning would never cease, no matter what was gained or gathered. It was enough to embrace the yearning, then let it go. She wishes she'd listened harder.

"Carey?" It's the chief. "Do you happen to know where Danny's laptop was purchased?"

She thinks for a second. "Pete got it online, I think. Before we moved here for good. It was kind of a bribe."

"When was that? A year ago?"

"A little longer."

Radovich turns to Hamilton. "Will says the one in our possession seems newer."

Will comes back into the office, followed by another man. A thread of scar curls from the man's left cheekbone to his mouth. Carey thinks she has seen this face before.

"Dispatch is hunting Malone down," Will says. "No luck yet."

"Agent Locke," Radovich says.

Carey feels her shoulder blades contract around her spine.

"Locke?" Hamilton says. The look on her face is not approving. "We weren't aware you were assigned to this case."

Without so much as a glance at Carey, Locke holds up a small clear plastic bag half filled with a powdery white substance. "We found this in the tire well in the trunk of Jeffrey Bledsoe's car." Then he addresses Hamilton. "Missed you in Schoolcraft, Agent. Not polite to leave your riders behind, you know. Reflects poorly on the bureau."

Locke finally turns to Carey. His sepia-tinted glasses are crooked at an angle. "Special Agent Allen Locke," he says, moving the baggie closer to her. "Do you recognize this, Ms. Peters?"

"How do you know who I am?"

"I assumed. Sorry if I offended."

Fuck you, Carey thinks.

"Do you happen to know what this is?"

Carey wishes she didn't. She takes a breath. She sees Danny asleep on the leather sofa, the Cubs on the tube, Paddle snuggled into his supine body, the dog holding his head upright, eyes still open, watching over his slumbering friend.

"It looks like Paddle's ashes. Danny's dog. We had to put him down. Danny kept some of his ashes in his wallet."

Then Carey sees those jaws again, the ones on her phone.

"Could be cocaine in there, for all we know," Hamilton says. "Can we get it analyzed pronto?"

"We will," Radovich says. "But we probably should assume it's evidence that Danny was, well, I think you follow."

Locke nods. "Agent Hamilton is right. It could be something else. It could be a ruse, planted by someone who knew about the ashes."

"On it," Will says, taking the baggie from Locke and leaving the office. Jonah wraps an arm around his sister.

"Thank you, Chief," Locke says. "If nobody minds, I would like to speak with Ms. Peters in private for a moment."

"For what?" Hamilton says.

"For a moment," he says, looking at Carey. "Please."

She glares at Locke, refusing to flinch, instead lying: "I don't know you, Agent."

Locke nods and says, "All right," slipping a sheet of paper from inside his sport jacket. "I need to ask you about someone."

Pressman, she thinks.

"He calls himself Quartz," Locke says.

230

That throws her. How would Locke know about Quartz? How would anybody, unless they had followed her to Valparaiso?

"Like the many-faceted stone. Are you familiar with that name?"

She feels Jonah and everyone else looking at her. The longer she hesitates, the more suspicious they'll be.

"Quartz is not his real name, Ms. Peters. But it's what he told you, isn't it?"

Locke steps closer. "Carey?"

"What does this have to do with my son?"

"Good question," Hamilton says.

Locke unfolds the paper in his hand and holds it up in front of Carey. It's a printout of the Jeremiah email from Danny's laptop. "Mr. Northwood kindly provided this."

"No," Carey says, "I kindly provided the police with that. And there's nothing about any Quartz in there."

"But there is this." Locke reads aloud: "'Maybe hit up randy boss-man.' I believe Randall Pressman is the head of the company where you work, is he not?"

"He is."

"And how well do you know him?"

"He's my boss." She stops herself from adding, "That's all."

"Do you have any idea why Jeremiah would refer to him in that way? The 'randy bossman'? Small *r*?"

Even with her brother at her side, Carey couldn't feel more alone. This man, Locke, is the one who's been harassing her with texts about her Valentine's Day tryst, demanding the documents she spirited out of Pressman's computers. Stalling, Carey says, "What does this have to do with anything?"

Locke withdraws the printout, backs away, looks around at the others. "Quartz works for Pressman. Off the books, as it were." He turns back to Carey. "But you already knew that, didn't you?"

Radovich speaks up. "Agent Locke, what does this have to—"

"I'll bet you've spoken with him, haven't you, Carey? Is that where you disappeared to today?"

He might be bluffing. But of course he's correct. *Fuck it*, she thinks. "I've made mistakes in my life, Agent Locke. Now's not the time to judge."

"Nobody's judging. I just don't want you to make decisions based on the assumption that Quartz is going to help you find your son. That would be a tragic mistake."

"Locke, would you care to fill the rest of us in on this Quartz?" Hamilton says. "Sounds like we ought to be looking for him."

Locke pushes his glasses up on his nose and addresses not Hamilton but Chief Radovich. "I'm not at liberty to say much, but Quartz—which is not his real name—is a fugitive from the law. He used to work for the federal government, and he compromised this country's security in serious ways."

"A spook."

"Yes. He does similar work for Pressman. Again, off the books."

"It's an anagram." Will bursts back into the office, waving his phone. "The Twitter guy's an anagram."

"One second, Will," the chief says.

Locke goes on. "Quartz may also have been in contact with Jeffrey Bledsoe."

He's just guessing, Carey thinks. But it's giving her a queasy feeling. She knows Quartz hacked into Bledsoe's laptop, which the police confiscated from the apartment in Schoolcraft. Maybe Locke knows it too.

"Have you considered the possibility," he asks Carey, "that your employer may be involved in this matter?"

I'm considering it now, she thinks, even if she suspects Locke is gunning not for the kidnapper but for Pressman. But if Pressman is involved, then he must know—and Quartz must know—where Danny is.

She's confused. Maybe, she thinks, she should tell them everything, from Valentine's Day to the blackmail. But what good would it do? Locke seems to know anyway. And if she reveals the blackmail, she could wind up in custody. She doesn't want to be sitting in a jail cell when Danny is found.

Or.

Carey doesn't know whom to trust. Radovich is clueless, Malone has vanished, she doesn't know the others. She hasn't heard from Quartz, with two and a half hours to her six o'clock deadline.

"For all I know, you took my son, Locke."

"Please," he says. "I'm not trying to upset you. But if you know where Quartz is, you should tell us."

"I'll keep that in mind."

"Look," Will speaks up. "I figured out this Jeremiah's phone number. And this Twitter handle, @drewthenobody, deciphers as 'the drowned boy,' like the kid in that story from 1945."

"Whose name also happens to be Jeremiah," Locke says.

"So we need to track this Twitter guy too," Hamilton says.

"And that number that's been texting Carey—5373642445? If you substitute letters for the keypad numbers, you get Jeremiah 45."

"Jesus," Hamilton says. "Chief, better get all this stuff to the Detroit cops. See if they can find a connection to Vend." Then she glances at Locke, reluctant. "The Quartz stuff too."

But they have no idea really, Carey thinks. Whoever this fucked-up individual is, he's smarter than all of them, leaving little trails of digital crumbs that might lead to Danny or not. She slips Jonah's grasp and shoves past Locke to the door.

Mom. Pete. What are you doing?

"Good luck," Carey says. "Jonah and I are going to see our mother now, because it's looking like we're going to need a lot of money." She reaches toward Will. "My phone, please."

"No way," Hamilton says. "We need that phone. You shouldn't have been allowed to keep it or your laptop. We'll also need any passcodes."

"I need the phone if this Jeremiah or Danny or Quartz or whoever it is tries to contact me."

"We'll pass on any messages. Meanwhile, get yourself a substitute. It doesn't look like this guy has any trouble finding you. Will?"

Will hesitates, looks to the chief, who nods for him to give the phone to Hamilton.

"What about Bledsoe?" Carey says. "Did you find anything on his phone?"

"Some, uh, unsavory texts between him and Ms. Delacroix from last night," Will says. "And this afternoon, one to his grandmother in Tampa and one to someone in the Detroit area we have yet to identify."

"We also have your husband's phone, Carey," the chief says. "We'll probably be releasing him soon."

"Fantastic."

"Ms. Peters," Locke says. He offers her a business card. She takes it without thinking. "Please think twice about trusting Quartz."

"I don't know what you're talking about, but it sounds like he could find my son before any of you do. Do not lose those ashes."

———

"Who is this Quartz person, Carey? Was he who you went to see in Indiana?"

"Don't worry about it," she tells Jonah. They're on the sidewalk outside Darlington's, the phone-and-computer store on Lily that used to be a TV-and-radio shop. Carey leans against an empty, rust-fringed *Bleak Harbor Light* vending machine near the door, focused on one of the two burner phones she just bought—one for her, one for Pete—for $49.95 each at Darlington's.

"Carey? Is that where you went?"

"Like Locke said," she says without looking up from the phone. "He works for Pressman. He finds things. He's damn good at it. Better than them."

"Did you tell—"

"Hold on, just hold on a goddamn—" She stops herself, squeezes her eyes shut, puts the phone facedown on a knee, looks up at her brother. "I'm sorry."

"It's OK. I'm just—I don't know what's going on."

"I don't mean to be such a bitch."

"I know. But, Carey."

They had left the police station through a rear door to avoid the reporters and cameras waiting out front, then squirmed shoulder-to-elbow through the sweat-slickened throngs of festivalgoers crawling along the sidewalks, the wings of their idiotic dragonfly hats flapping, their Nucci's go-cups sticky with vodka and cranberry juice. Most had come from else-where, but Carey could feel local eyes on her as she passed. *There's the witch who let her poor retarded son get kidnapped*, she imagined them thinking. *Fuck them*, she thought. *Every single fucking one.*

She comes up off the vending machine. "I know," she says. "Focus. I texted Malone with this phone number and emailed it to Spitler."

"What about the chief?"

"Fuck the chief."

She doesn't tell Jonah that she also sent a text to the number Quartz had given her, informing him of the new ransom amount.

"OK, but—"

"Where's your car?"

"This way."

They start down Lily toward Violet, the heart of the festival. As they walk, Jonah puts his arm around her and pulls her in close against the sideways glances. Lily is crammed with people tramping down the fake cobblestone. The beer-tent music blares. A voice on a megaphone says it's time for the blueberry-pie-eating contest. Carey keeps working her new phone. When she and Jonah reach the corner at Violet, she stops and breaks free of her brother.

"Shit," she says.

"What?"

"I'm just—maybe it's this phone."

"What is it?"

People bump and jostle them as they pass. Carey's punching numbers and letters on the phone keypad, trying to access the bank account she and Pete keep. "This isn't right," she says. "I know this password."

"What password?"

"This one."

She's squinting into the phone. She hasn't heard from Quartz and wants to see if Pressman has sent the money yet. She's worried that he won't, that he's just stringing her along, hoping the cops will do his work for him. And now the damn password won't work.

"Pete must have—shit."

Maybe Pete changed the password. Maybe because Oly helped out. She'd love to know, but Pete's sitting in jail, and she's not going back there, not while Locke is still inside. "He should have told me. And now here's an email from Spitler. He says we can see Mother at four thirty."

An email appears. A series of letters and numbers fills the To field. "What the hell?" Carey says, and clicks on it. "Oh Jesus. Oh God, Jonah, what the fuck."

"Now what?"

She pushes the phone up into Jonah's face:

wasting time with poh-lice? u want to find danny boy—or not find him—at bottom of the lake w me?

"Holy God," Jonah says.

Again Carey sees Bledsoe's limp body on the floor, the blood, the dark men, the empty room, the empty faces of the cops.

"This motherfucker," she says. "This—this—this motherfucking fucker."

Carey closes her eyes and squeezes the phone in both hands, wanting to crush it into a silvery powder, knowing people must be looking at her, thinking she's out of her mind. She takes a breath, eases her grip, and gazes upward, looking for something that makes even the smallest bit of sense. What she sees is an inflatable plastic dragonfly fluttering in the breeze over the building that houses Pete's pot shop. And then, in her mind, she sees again the sketch she saw that morning in Danny's bedroom, how vacant the insect's eyes looked as its jaws crushed its prey.

She turns to Jonah. "Where is my son?" she whispers. Then raises her voice. "Where is my son?" She could cry if she wasn't so angry. "Come on. Let's go crawl to the bitch."

36

Pete sits on a concrete slab. He looks down at his feet. He's wearing flip-flops. How the hell, he thinks, could he be wearing flip-flops on a day like this?

He stands and climbs onto the jail cell bed. On his tiptoes he's tall enough to see through the sliver of window carved into the wall. Through the silver wire crosshatched into the glass, he watches a Ferris wheel arcing through the sky over Bleak Harbor. The lights along the wheel spokes twinkle. He can't hear the fake calliope or the children squealing.

Reporters bristling with notebooks and TV cameras had bludgeoned him with questions as sheriff's deputies escorted him, handcuffed, into the police station. That was when he heard that Bledsoe was dead and Danny remained missing.

"Where were you when your son got taken?" he had heard a reporter ask. "Were you really in a bar?" Pete wanted to stop and tell them he was doing what he could, he really loved Danny, but the officers shoved him on. "Can you tell us whether you'll pay the ransom?" "What did you expect, bringing a business like that here?" "Do you think Serenity Bleak will help you?"

The Ferris wheel slows to a stop, hovering in Pete's field of vision, the early-evening sun throwing shadow trapezoids across the faces of the woman and the boy in the seat at one o'clock. The boy is kicking his legs, his head on a swivel, while the woman—his mother? his aunt?—frowns over the phone in her hands. Pete wants to call out to her, tell her everything he now knows.

In the interview room, he'd held nothing back from the chief and the FBI agent, Hamilton. He almost vomited when Hamilton told him, her eyes black bullets of barely disguised anger, about Dulcy Pérez and the hoodlum she worked for and how she might have been sent to keep tabs on Pete.

When they finished with him and ushered him down the hallway, the chief's hand a pincer inside his elbow, he was relieved to have unloaded his secrets, but as Radovich stuffed him in the cell and walked out, clanging the door shut without a word or a look of reassurance, he was frightened to think he was potentially connected to Danny's abduction. Even though he knew he'd had nothing to do with it. At least not intentionally.

He sat down and pondered the gray floor and feebly reminded himself that he'd gotten Oly to come through, and maybe that would save Danny.

The Ferris wheel starts up again. The boy and the woman cycle out of Pete's world. He's grateful for the hypnotic circling of the painted spokes, the swaying of the chairs. It's only a block away, but it seems as distant as the day Pete calls to mind.

———

He had met Carey on Chicago's Navy Pier after 5:00 p.m. It was a Tuesday in August, the sky gauzed with humidity, Lake Michigan a griddle sheen at the far end of the pier.

He was glad to see her sipping a margarita through a straw stuck in a red cup. She was standing at the outdoor bar at Harry Caray's in a summer dress that made him think of sunflowers. She didn't smile when she first spied him, so Pete started waving and clapping and mugging, and she began to smile around her straw, her eyes asking if he was nuts. When he leaned in for a kiss, she let him have a cheek. Grinning, though. Not disappointed at his lateness, just coy. Good.

"You're gonna want more than that," he said, "after you hear about my day."

She set her cup down. "Where have you been? You're sweating."

"I was running. Had a couple of beers with Oly."

"Beers with the boss?"

"Hell, yes. I had a day, girl."

"A day?"

"A great big fucking day."

"How big?"

"Guess."

She canted her head to the right, hair draping an eye. *God*, Pete thought. "Beat your record?" she said.

"Oh yeah."

"Three fifty?"

Pete jerked a thumb upward. "Higher."

"Four hundred?"

Carey picked her cup back up. "Four fifty?"

"Four hundred seventy-three thousand dollars."

Her big eyes went bigger. Pete felt himself swoon. He didn't care about the money, most of which would go to the O'Nallys; he just wanted to make Carey proud.

He knew he'd gotten lucky. A government report had suggested plains flooding would shrink the fall harvest. Corn prices zoomed up, soybeans followed, and Pete spied a trader on the edge of the pit who looked ready to off himself. The poor guy was sitting on a bunch of bets that prices would fall. Pete gladly took his business. It was especially gratifying because Pete had lost more than a hundred grand the day before. He hadn't mentioned that to Carey.

"Woo-hoo!" she said, high-fiving her boyfriend. "Not bad for a cow tipper from Wisconsin." She signaled the barmaid for another margarita. "I guess you can have one drink."

"Sorry I'm a little, uh, sloppy." He grinned and backed up a step, peering down the promenade. "Celebrate on the Ferris wheel?"

She squinted. "What about our drinks?"

"We'll take them for the line."

"Really? The Ferris wheel?"

"Yeah." Pete winked. "I heard things can get hot up there. Closer to the sun, you know."

"They can, huh? Oops—damn. Excuse me." Her phone was ringing on the bar. She grabbed it. "It's Kimi."

Pete's margarita arrived while Carey talked to the girlfriend who was babysitting her son. He took a sip, watching her face darken.

"All right," she said. "I'll be home for dinner."

"Everything OK?" Pete said.

"Nope." She dropped her phone on the bar. "He dumped all his pills again."

"The expensive ones?"

"They're all expensive. Only seven, but he knows what he's doing."

Pete offered her a hand. "It's going to be all right. Come on."

"We can't have dinner out."

"No worries. We'll eat with Danny."

The Ferris wheel line was short. Pete insisted they wait for cab number 11, partly for Carey's November 11 birthday, more because he saw no one in the cabs above or below it.

They sat on a plastic bench the color of a clown nose, facing the lake stretching beyond the pier and the locks along the skyline to the south, the skyscrapers backlit orange by the sun. A Stones' song floated up from the bar below, something about a kiss. Pete rested a long leg on the facing bench and took Carey's left leg and hooked it over his knee. As they rose from the platform, he slid his hand inside her dress.

"Pete."

She squirmed as he spread his fingers along the inside of her thigh. She almost pushed him away, but then she didn't. He bent to her neck as his forefinger slipped beneath her panties. "Goddamn it," she whispered.

He kissed her. Her tongue was silky with lime. "You're so beautiful," he said, and she gasped as he slid his fingers into her.

As they crested the arc, he drew his face away and said, "Look. Look at it, Carey. Everything is so beautiful," and he started to laugh. "It's ours. It's all ours. See the families playing Putt-Putt down there? It's all ours." He leaned back into the porcelain curve of her neck. "God, baby," he said. She was unzipping him. "I love you."

They were laughing as the cab descended to the ground, Pete hurrying to zip his jeans. "Uh-oh," he said. Two security guards in yellow-and-black vests were waiting.

"Pete, I have to get home to Danny," Carey said.

The people waiting in line were wearing goofy smiles, craning their necks to see. "I got this," Pete said. As he stepped off the ride, he shrugged at the guards. "I'd say I was sorry, but, you know."

Then he turned back to Carey. "You love me too?"

She smiled. "Sure."

———

"You can go for now."

The voice startles Pete from his reverie. The bittersweet thrill leaches away. Standing in the doorway is the young man he met that morning in his yard with Officer Malone. Pete wants to tell him he didn't mean for any of this to happen.

"I'm sorry. Any news on Danny?"

"Afraid not. Better get out of here before Chief changes his mind."

37

The woman in front of Malone turns and walks away, shaking her head. Malone steps up to the counter.

"Hello, Kris," she says.

Krissy Oliver is the pharmacist on duty at Strawman Drug. She's in a white smock with her name stitched in pink over the left breast, batting keys at a coffee-stained desktop computer and tugging the blonde hair out of her eyes. She looks perplexed to the point of annoyance.

Malone has to wonder if she's faking the distraction. Krissy can't want to see Malone any more than Malone wants to see her. Every six weeks or so, when Malone has to pick up one of her antidepression prescriptions, she calls ahead to make sure one of the other pharmacists is on duty.

"Oh," Krissy says. "Katya."

A lanyard marked with little red hearts and the words *LOVE LOVE LOVE* swings as she turns to Malone. The ID badge dangling at the lanyard's end has to be at least a year old, because it shows Krissy in the hairstyle she wore when she was sleeping with Malone's ex.

"Busy day?"

"Lately—oh, no, not again. Excuse me, sorry."

She turns and goes through a door marked **EMPLOYEES ONLY**.

Malone waits. Will had called her while she drove back from the murder scene in Schoolcraft to tell her Pete Peters was in custody.

Malone could believe that he wasn't aware he'd been dealing with Bledsoe, or that he didn't know that Dulcinea Pérez—an obvious plant—was connected to the dealer in Detroit. But she didn't believe Peters could harm Danny or intentionally put his stepson in harm's way. It wasn't that Peters was innocent. He was not innocent. But he was too defeated—best word she could think of—to be guilty. He was a loser, not a criminal.

Malone is a loser too, standing there in her cop's uniform, hat literally in hand, waiting on the woman who fucked the loser she had married, who had fathered her beautiful Louisa. Willowy Krissy Oliver, with the pouty mouth and exquisite teeth, was the "k" in the texts she'd found on his phone.

Malone has come to Strawman Drug on a hunch. If she's right, she might be able to find Danny. Otherwise, she doesn't know what to try. Maybe they can lure the abductor out with money.

Krissy returns and goes to the computer, taps a few keys. "I'm sorry, Katya. I'm afraid I might have to disappoint you like I did Mrs. Derdzinski and about—"

"I'm not here for a prescription."

"—a hundred other people. Our computer system caught some bug. It keeps sending these emails saying refills are ready when it's not time yet. At least for the people I know, and I know a lot."

"I'm not here for a prescription."

Krissy finally looks up. "How can I help you then?"

"You've heard about the Peters boy. Danny?"

"The kidnapping? I thought they—you—I thought you found the kidnapper. Isn't he dead?"

"We're not sure he had Danny."

"I'm so sorry. How is Carey holding up?"

"You know Carey?"

"I know of her."

"Is she the one who picks up Danny's prescriptions?"

"I'm sorry. I really can't divulge that. Privacy rules."

"Wherever Danny is, he doesn't have his meds."

"He doesn't?"

"No, and that's not good. Do you happen to know Danny's stepdad, Pete Peters?"

"I know who he is."

"Does he come in for Danny's prescriptions?"

Krissy tries to arrange her face into something stern. "Really, I just can't talk about that."

"You don't want to help find this boy, Krissy?"

"My hands are tied."

"I could get them untied with a warrant," Malone says, knowing she probably couldn't. "But by then Danny Peters might be dead."

"I can have you speak with—"

"Did you hear me?" Malone wishes she didn't have to say what she says next. "Do you really want another child's blood on your hands?"

The tears that appear in Krissy's eyes are angry. *Tough*, Malone thinks. *I won't ask you, Krissy Oliver, if you gave him permission to steal Louisa. You weren't driving the car I chased off the road into a tree. But I won't let you off the hook with Danny.*

"You know that's not fair," Krissy says.

"Can't help that. But you can help Danny."

Krissy wipes at an eye, glances over her shoulder. Malone sees the security camera pointing at them. Krissy hits some keys, waits, reads. "Danny's father was in here sixteen—I mean eighteen days ago to pick up prescriptions. He signed for them."

"His stepdad. How many prescriptions?"

"Three."

Malone takes out her notebook, where she had copied the numbers of the prescriptions off the vials at the police department. She tears out the page and hands it to Krissy.

"These?"

Krissy holds the paper up to the computer screen. Malone follows her eyes. "Yes."

"How long were they for?"

"Four weeks' worth."

"Were they automatic refills?"

"No, these are from Dr. Ringel. But they came with two automatic refills."

"Four weeks out and then eight weeks out?"

"Yes. All right?"

"Any activity since those were picked up?"

"There shouldn't be."

"Just check, please."

Krissy folds her arms across her smock. "I'm really not comfortable with this."

"You're already doing it. Any more activity?"

Krissy unfolds her arms, sighs, leans in to the monitor. "Hmm," she says. "Three more this week."

"Pickups? When?"

"Wednesday."

"What time?"

"Two forty-seven p.m."

"Same drugs?"

"Yes."

"Wouldn't your system have seen that and stopped it?"

"Normally, yes. But like I said, we've had this glitch. The computer suddenly thinks everybody's prescriptions are up for refills."

"Was it Peters who signed on Wednesday?"

Krissy clicks her mouse. "Yes, but . . ." She's shaking her head. "Here." She glances toward the front door while rotating the monitor so Malone can see. The signature reads "Pete Peters."

"I doubt he would've signed 'Pete,'" Malone says. "His real name is Andrew." She'd seen it on his driver's license that morning at his home. "And that handwriting looks girly. Were you here when these were picked up?"

"I was off. Lucia was here."

Krissy swivels the screen back, hits more keys, returns the monitor to Malone. "This is how Peters signed eighteen days ago. It's kind of hard to read, but that doesn't say *Pete* Peters."

"Would Lucia have let someone who wasn't actually Peters sign for a prescription? Someone with girly handwriting?"

"She's part-time. If it gets really busy, sometimes things fall through the cracks. Or if she knew the person and trusted her. I don't know."

"She speaks Spanish?"

"Yes."

An electronic jangle signals that the front door has opened. Malone turns to see a silver-haired woman walking toward her, leaning every other step on a cane. Malone looks back at Krissy. "What about video? That should show who signed."

"Unfortunately, that computer glitch killed our video too."

Pretty damn convenient, Malone thinks. "All right, then I'll need this Lucia's full name and contact information."

Krissy's eyes are darting between the approaching woman and Malone. "Please, I can't put her in that position."

"She put *you* in this position."

"Still—"

"I could give old man Strawman a call. I'm sure he'll be interested to know the whole story."

"Katya, please." Krissy averts her eyes, puts on a smile. "Sheila, how are you today?"

"Good afternoon, dear. Hello, Officer."

Malone nods at the woman. "Mrs. Dorset."

The woman says, "Have you found that poor youngster yet?"

Krissy slides a sticky note across the counter. Malone takes it while telling Mrs. Dorset, "Not yet, but we're hopeful."

"I'm praying for all of you."

"Thank you very much." She nods at Krissy. "If you think of anything else . . ."

———

Malone steps onto the sidewalk, oblivious to the crowd rivering past, the tourists streaming down Lily in their emerald-speckle dragonfly tees, the curly-headed girl crying over the scoop of chocolate chip ice cream melting at her feet, the AC/DC blaring from down the street. She stretches a hand out in front of her and starts to trot, bumping people as she goes, saying, "Police. Please. Let me through. Police."

She adds up what she thinks she knows: Danny gets snatched, but three vials of drugs remain behind, leaving the police to think the abductor neglected them. But three days ago, a woman pretending to be Pete Peters signed for refill prescriptions. Presumably, those are with Danny now, wherever he is. And there just happens to have been a computer glitch that helped the woman pick up the drugs.

Could the woman have been Bledsoe's girlfriend, Petunia? Malone doubts it. Bledsoe wasn't bright enough to have thought this through.

Could the woman have been picking up the prescriptions for Carey? Danny would have what he needed in captivity while she and Pete—or maybe Carey was acting on her own—distracted police with Bledsoe and the Detroit drug dealer, all part of a grand and lucrative deception. Serenity Meredith Maas Bleak would part with an ample enough sliver of her fortune. There would be a tearful reunion with Danny, the nonexistent kidnapper now supposedly vanished. The happy family would sorrowfully declare that they could no longer bear to stay in Bleak Harbor. Pete would dump his business, Carey would quit her job, and they would be gone.

But there's a problem with this scenario: Carey would have signed her own name. Or, if insurance required her husband's signature, she would have known to sign with her husband's proper name, Andrew.

There's one other possibility. It's one Malone has secretly hoped would not pan out. It makes her a little sick to her stomach. A little angry too. She's almost back to the station but calls anyway.

"Will," she says, out of breath.

"Katya. Where have you been?"

"We absolutely must find that Pérez woman. Now."

38

Carey's breath catches at the reek of cigarettes. "Good God," she says, turning to Roland Spitler, who just led her and Jonah into her mother's sitting room. "When's the last time you fumigated?"

"Please make yourselves comfortable," Spitler says.

Carey and Jonah waited downstairs for their 4:30 p.m. appointment for more than thirty minutes. Spitler said Serenity was just waking up from her afternoon nap and he didn't want to disturb her.

Now they're waiting again. Spitler is wearing his usual seersucker suit with a pink silk bow tie. Pink is everywhere at the Bleak Mansion, from the towering turrets to the polo shirts worn by the security guards at the compound's gated entrance. It wasn't always so. Serenity had had everything redone in pink a few years before, while Jack was on one of his extended trips. When Carey and Pete had moved into their cottage across the bay, the adirondack chairs on the deck happened to be pink; of course Carey immediately repainted them forest green.

"Where is Mother?" Carey says.

Spitler consults a digital tablet he'd brought as they ascended to the room, tapping on it to unlock doors along the way. Carey doesn't recall security being this tight when she visited last, but that was before Mother announced her "gift."

"I will be bringing her in shortly," Spitler says. "First, a couple of ground rules."

"Ground rules?"

"Your mother is not well. She can give you twenty minutes."

"No."

"Also, direct requests for money are not appropriate."

"Roland, we're not here to catch up on things," Jonah says. "We're here for money so we can get Danny back safe."

Except for a powdering of gray at his temples, Spitler looks exactly as he did when Carey was a little girl: short and slender, with a slight stoop, as if his body had been designed for subservience. Though Spitler was never subservient to anyone but Serenity, who had dismissed all of her husband's assistants and lawyers within twenty-four hours of his death.

"Please curtail the language when your mother is here. As you know in your capacity as mayor, Mr. Jonah, most of Miss Serenity's estate is currently in escrow."

"Shut up, Roland," Carey says. "Get Mother out here, or we'll go find her ourselves."

———

Carey and Jonah had come up the private road to the mansion, two lanes striped with pink lines repainted each year the week before Memorial Day. Pink plastic reflecting poles planted along both shoulders marked each tenth of a mile, forty-seven of them from the start of Mansion Way at the edge of Bleak Harbor to the mansion itself.

The drive needn't have been that long. As a gull flew, Serenity's estate was barely a mile from downtown. Once, long ago, there had been a road that curled directly around the southwesterly bend in the bay before climbing an incline to the house. Townspeople would drive and bike and walk up the road to picnic in the undulating dunes and swaying grass surrounding the mansion, spreading blankets on the sand. Sometimes Violet Bleak, Carey's great-grandmother, would stroll among the picnickers handing out caramel cubes and papery strips of candy buttons as if it were Halloween.

James Bleak, bastard son of Violet, husband to Catherine, grandfather to Jonah and Carey, had put an end to all of that. First he'd ordered the direct road blocked off in the late 1940s. He had stationed a security guard at a temporary barricade visible to puzzled tourists sunning on the downtown beaches. James himself had designed the road Carey and Jonah had just ascended.

James Bleak's lawyers had worked quietly in the background, filing papers that effectively partitioned the family property as a separate legal entity with its own zip code, protected by its own security force and fire department, as if it were a foreign country. Some citizens had organized a mild protest, but the officials elected with the help of Bleak dollars acquiesced to James's machinations on the condition that the family continue to pay an annual stipend to each of the surrounding municipalities.

Carey had never known the old road. But she had come to know and, for a time, love the new one on summer rides with her mother. After breakfast, three or four days a week, they would climb on their bikes—a sky-blue boys' Schwinn Typhoon for Carey, a crimson Hollywood for Serenity—and glide down the smooth asphalt switchbacks into town, hardly ever touching their pedals, laughing as they gathered speed, the pines rushing past in their peripheral vision. When the road flattened before curving onto Blossom Street, they'd both stand and pedal furiously in a race to the stop sign at Lily. Serenity made sure to come in first often enough that Carey wouldn't think she'd let her daughter win the other times.

They would park their Schwinns in front of the cake shop and sit at one of the sidewalk tables with coffee for Serenity and sweet tea for Carey. And they would talk. Sometimes till lunch. They would talk about the colors of that morning's sunrise, about Carey's future as a backstroke champion, about the boys who had begun to ogle her on the beach, about the books they were reading and movies they'd watched, about going to Chicago or Detroit to shop when Daddy took Jonah fishing in Canada.

One summer, their conversations revolved around the vacation they were supposed to take with Jonah and Daddy to Europe in August. Carey was eleven. Serenity attached a wicker basket to her handlebars to tote the travel guides she'd bought for London and Paris, Prague and Barcelona, Rome and Florence. They spread the guides on the little circular table, pretending they were at a café on the water in Nice, and discussed the cities one by one as Carey made a list of sights they had to see.

By the Fourth of July, the list was six pages long. One morning at breakfast, Carey showed it to her father. He glanced at the first two pages, smiled, and handed it back to her. "That is quite a list," he said. "Did your mother help you with that?" As he spoke, he gave Serenity a sideways look that Carey didn't understand. She turned to her mother, who, without looking at her husband, said, "We'll talk about it."

The four of them were supposed to leave for London on August 2. But Carey's father said he had too much business to attend to in London, so he would go over first, and they would join him a week later. The trip was postponed a second time, for similar reasons, then a third, before Jonah and Carey had to start school.

They never went. Carey threw her six-page list on a fire she and Jonah built on the beach one night. Her father stayed in Europe for many weeks. He sent postcards and gifts—an emerald necklace for Carey, a rugby shirt for Jonah—and spoke with their mother on Monday nights on the phone.

A few Mondays, Carey sneaked into the hallway outside her parents' bedroom to eavesdrop. Her mother spoke in hushed tones. Carey couldn't make out most of what she said. But one night Serenity raised her voice enough—in anger or fright, Carey couldn't be sure—that her words became briefly clear: "Then just stay there . . . never come home . . . no . . . no, bullshit, New York is not London, you're lying, Jack . . . just stay—don't ever come back."

Tuesday morning at breakfast, Carey asked her mother whether—not when, but whether—her father would be coming home. Serenity raised her eyes from the grapefruit half she had blanketed with sugar.

"Young lady," she said. "Have you been spying?"

Serenity's face gave Carey a start. She hadn't really noticed before, but her eyes were so bagged that their pools of blue were barely visible slits between her eyelids.

"Is Daddy coming home?"

Serenity stabbed a spoon into her grapefruit. Spitler moved in behind, placed a hand lightly on her shoulder. "Soon," Serenity said.

"How soon?"

"Who cares?" Jonah said, jamming a rolled-up slice of toast with peanut butter into his mouth. "I don't care if the fucker never comes back."

"Language, Jonah."

"Fuck Dad."

Carey felt her eyes welling. She looked from Jonah to Spitler to her mother. "What's going on?"

Serenity rose from her chair and without saying a word walked to the kitchen elevator, hitting the button for four. Spitler collected her dishes. "Time for school," he said.

Her father did return. It was late October. He moved immediately into a guest bedroom in the turret opposite the master. Serenity now spent hours every day locked in her bedroom. Spitler began ascending there several times a day, delivering glasses of what appeared to be iced tea. Carey and Jonah spoke with their mother at meals, if at all.

The Schwinns rusted in the garage.

———

Carey and Jonah sit next to each other in two straight-back chairs facing a slightly raised platform. In the middle of the platform sits a chair of snow-white satin in a wingback frame of gold flake.

The room is circular, like the turret in which it sits, the creamy-pinkish walls rising two stories into a dome ringed with arched windows. Long ago the room was a chapel where Violet Bleak, Carey and Jonah's great-grandmother, had prayed each morning.

Jack Bleak had it converted a year after Jonah was born. The lone remnant of the chapel is the outline of a crucifix that once hung on a wall. Painters over the years tried repeatedly to obliterate the shadow, without success.

Their father had used the room to meet vendors, customers, legislators, lobbyists. Carey imagines them sitting where she and Jonah wait, supplicants with hands folded on briefcases in their laps.

She feels as hapless as they must have.

Jonah is twisting in his chair, looking around the room. "You think anybody still uses the tunnels?"

Beneath the mansion are three concrete-walled tunnels. One leads to the mansion's private marina, one to the downtown bay shore, one to a boathouse secreted on the lakeshore a mile south. They were designed as security measures but had functioned mostly as means for Jack Bleak to spirit women into and out of the mansion.

Carey doesn't reply. She's staring at her hands.

"You look a little pale," Jonah says.

She reaches for his hand, squeezes it. "Thank you for being a good uncle to Danny."

He offers a weak smile. "You know, I plan to destroy him in backgammon this weekend."

"What about this escrow thing?"

"We asked Serenity's lawyers to put some of her estate in escrow as proof in good faith that she wasn't just messing with us. We have yet to see evidence that this account actually exists. Her two hundred lawyers keep telling us about it, though."

"How much money does she have?"

"Who knows? I've read three hundred, four hundred million. Spitler probably knows."

"Hell, Jack knows."

"Oh yeah." Jonah nods toward the wall behind the throne-like chair. "How about that, huh?"

Hanging there is a framed *Light* page. The banner headline reads:

City Father Bleak Dead of Heart Attack

A photograph of Jack Bleak as a younger man occupies a two-column space on the left side of the page. He's smiling in that beguiling way that left you wondering later whether he was laughing with or at you. Carey can see Danny in her father's arching eyebrows and cheekbones. She can see her son, too, in the inscrutable smile. She has told Jonah before that the resemblance unsettles her.

"Dashing," she says. "That's what the paper always called him."

"Dashing from woman to woman in city after city."

"He was a successful businessman—don't forget that."

"How could I forget that?" Jonah snorts. A door on the wall behind the platform opens. "Oh, there she is."

Serenity appears in a wheelchair being pushed by Spitler. She doesn't look up from the paperback she's reading as Spitler rolls her across the platform and locks the wheelchair in place next to the gilt-framed wingback.

Serenity raises a forefinger, still reading. Spitler steps away. Serenity turns a page.

"Mother," Carey says.

Serenity's hair, gray-turning-white, is swept into a bun secured with a pink-on-silver ribbon. Her book is open on an afghan striped in pink and gray on her lap. A tall glass, about half full, is seated in her left armrest. She sets her bookmark and looks up.

"How is Daniel?"

"Danny has been kidnapped, Mother."

"That I am aware of, dear. But I thought the police were close to finding him." Serenity turns to Spitler. "Mr. Spitler, were those church bells I heard all afternoon, or was that my imagination? Do they have Mass during the festival?"

"I'm sorry, Miss Serenity. Perhaps they were testing—"

"Damn it, Serenity." Jonah is hitched forward in his chair, elbows to knees. "We need your help."

His mother lifts her glass, sips. "And what of this article on the computer? Who would dredge up such trash?"

Carey and Jonah exchange looks. "The kidnapper calls himself Jeremiah," she says. "Like the boy who drowned in that story."

"Jack's older brother," Jonah says.

"He didn't like to speak of it," Serenity says.

"I'll bet."

"Miss Serenity," Spitler says, "I called the publisher's office. They had the article removed."

Serenity is staring at her daughter. "Don't be so hasty to judge," she says. "Did you know that your father kept a picture of his brother in his wallet?"

"No."

"He was buried with it."

"Didn't know."

"Now you do." She turns to Spitler. "Whoever put that newspaper story there chooses to disgrace our family in front of all of these strangers traipsing around our town."

"Yes, ma'am."

"I'd quite prefer that the situation with Daniel not become a national scandal."

Serenity's chest is heaving now, the exertion of two long sentences apparently exhausting. She starts to set her glass in its holder, reconsiders, and takes another swallow before addressing Carey again. "You look fraught, young lady."

"Maybe I am."

"You were always a fraught child. I expect you'd be fraught if you won the lottery."

Jonah interrupts. "Christ, Mother. What about Danny?"

"Language, Jonah."

"Oh, fuck that."

"Please," Carey says.

Serenity looks at her, gives her head a barely discernible shake. "Danny," she says. "He never liked me much, did he?"

"Or you him."

"Didn't you have one of those tests before you had him? We didn't have those tests when you and your brother came out."

"What tests, Mother?"

"Genetic tests. So you can, you know, avoid an unnecessary situation."

"I know you won't understand this, Mother, but Danny is the most necessary thing in my life."

Serenity pauses, searching Carey's face. "Granted," she says, "I was an awful mother. Terrible. You're no June Cleaver either, dear."

"What is that supposed to mean?"

"Oh, now," Serenity says, reaching again for her glass, "don't go putting words in my mouth. Don't think I believe the rumors. Roland keeps me informed on what's going around town. Those people are fools; you and I both know it. With nothing better to do than run their neighbors down. You wouldn't harm Daniel, no matter how difficult he gets."

"No, I wouldn't."

Serenity continues as if Carey never spoke. "It's not your style, dear. Better to simply, you know, abandon him—am I right? Abandon whatever isn't convenient to your life. Like your premed major? Or law school? Or your little bleeding-heart adventure in Detroit?"

Jonah stands. "I've had enough of this bullshit."

"I've done my best, Mother."

"Please sit, Mr. Jonah."

"Is our time up yet, Roland? What about Danny?"

"Thank you, Mr. Jonah."

He sits.

A wan smile appears on Serenity's lips, fading as quickly as it came. "Of course, that is the perfect alibi: 'I did my best.' Well, I did my best, dear, with no help from your worthless father, and as you know, it wasn't very good. I am well aware that it wasn't very good. Are you?"

Carey feels as if a sheath of unbreakable glass has materialized around her, and she is trapped inside it with her mother. Ten seconds pass that could be an hour. Serenity waits, smug frown frozen on her face. Carey imagines herself slamming the glass with the heel of her hand, cracks spidering out, speckled with her blood.

She tries to calm herself before speaking. "Are you going to let your only grandson die?"

Serenity smooths the afghan over her knees. She begins to rock back and forth, tapping her fingertips on her thighs. Without lifting her head, she says, "I am a dying woman."

Jonah starts to say something. Serenity stops him. "No." She turns in her wheelchair, cranes her neck at the framed *Light* page, gazes at it, turns back to her children.

"I should have left him. I should have left him a hundred times. I made excuses for him. I should have taken every penny and walked away. Or not taken every penny, just . . ."

She doesn't finish.

The words tear at Carey, not because of Jack or the newspaper sale or even her mother, but because of her, Carey. She had made the same devil's bargain when she said yes to Pete. All she could think of then was how she would provide for her blessed, yearning, troubled young son. Pete had provided, she had provided, but she had failed to find Danny the things she wanted most for him, things he needed most: friends, a school, a place in the wider world beyond the deck, the dock, and the boat. *Who is it?* he had asked her, speaking of himself. *Who is it?*

"You should have left him long before that," Carey says, knowing she could be speaking to herself.

"I should have—that's true. But I was afraid."

"Afraid of what?" Jonah says.

"Afraid of being poor. Afraid of being alone."

Carey thinks she sees tears in Serenity's eyes. She hasn't seen her mother cry in a long time, maybe not since Serenity's father's funeral, and even then, not much. Crying wasn't her way of coping. Instead she sucked her sadness and humiliation and fury into herself and, eventually, into her daily drinking regimen. She was well into that by the time Danny was born. She had never gotten to know her grandson.

That was Carey's fault too. It's something she's known for years but has never wanted to acknowledge. She had decided long ago, before Danny was even old enough to speak, that if her mother and father wouldn't accept her son as he was, then they wouldn't have a grandson at all. Jack and Serenity didn't seem to care.

Part of Carey wishes she could continue this don't-make-the-same-mistake-I-made conversation, find some middle ground. But there's no time for wistful epiphanies. She turns to Jonah, says, "I need that picture of Danny I sent you." He hands her his phone.

She stands, steps onto the platform, and approaches Serenity. "Miss Carey," Spitler says, stepping up behind her.

Carey holds the phone up in front of Serenity's face. She avoids looking at it, averting her gaze to her daughter instead.

"What is this, dear?"

"It's your grandson. Look."

Serenity's eyes focus on the screen. "Those are just feet."

"Danny's feet."

"Why doesn't he get up?"

Carey doesn't answer. She just pushes the phone closer to Serenity's face. Her mother recoils, leaning back into her chair as far as she can. "All right, take it away," she says. "That's enough."

Carey withdraws the phone and reaches across her mother's lap for her glass. She raises it to her lips and swallows the contents. It's mostly vodka, some sort of juice, maybe lemon. Her teeth crunch shrunken ice cubes. Then she raises the cup over her head and hurls it at the framed newspaper page on the wall. It clatters to the floor, a thin drip of backwash trickling down the wall.

"I'm not a dying woman, Mother," she says. "I need your help."

Serenity's lower lip is trembling.

"We're leaving now. Jonah."

Spitler walks them to the door. "Mr. Spitler," Serenity calls out, and they all stop and turn, seeing she has pushed her wheelchair to the edge of the platform. "Give them what they need."

"Of course, Miss Serenity."

———

Carey looks at her phone as the three of them descend the marble stairs. It's 5:58. Less than six hours till the ransom is due. She has two missed calls from Malone. Not a word from Quartz. In the front vestibule at the bottom of the stairs, she turns to Spitler. "What do you need from us? A bank account number?"

He tugs at his bow tie, looks at each of them. "I'm afraid it's not quite that simple, Miss Carey."

"Meaning?" Jonah says.

"Miss Serenity is not altogether aware—not aware at all—of how her finances work, especially as regards her new obligations."

"You heard her, Roland."

"Yes, but I cannot wave a magic wand and secure the funds that quickly. I need more time."

"Don't tell me it's because of those imaginary escrows."

Spitler gives them each a look as if to say, *Yes, it is.* Carey steps in close to him, lowers her voice.

"Don't you give a damn about my son, Roland? Are you just going to let him die?"

"I care very much about Danny."

"You heard my mother."

He bows his head. "I must attend to Miss Serenity. I will keep you apprised."

39

Dulcy Pérez crouches in a copse of birches twenty yards up the slope from Boz's Bayfront Bar and Grill.

Every few seconds, she looks at her phone, shielding its glow with a cupped hand. With each passing car, she squeezes herself into a ball against the ground.

Michele Higgins watches her from behind an oak across the bayside road. Pérez appears to be waiting for something, some cue to proceed with whatever she's about to do. The clinking of glass, the cackle of laughter roll up the hill from Boz's. Michele hears mostly the hammering in her chest.

Her instincts had been correct. Her pal Lengel's instructions on where to locate Pérez were on target. Michele had found her at a two-story, beige-brick apartment building in Watervliet.

The license plate on the sole vehicle parked behind the building, a black Ford Escape, was from Ohio. A rental, Michele thought. Probably charged to a credit card linked to one of Vend's shell companies.

Michele had parked down the street and walked back to the building. She was almost there when the Escape pulled out in front of her and swung into the street. She'd waited until the Escape was a few blocks away, then trotted back to her own car and followed. Soon the two vehicles were approaching Bleak Harbor from the north, skirting the bay.

Pérez's brake lights had flashed as she approached the Peters cottage. Michele had hit her own brakes, keeping her distance. She noticed the mailbox in front of the vacant house next to Danny's: **HELLIKER**.

A few more houses down, Pérez, without signaling, swerved up a sandy two-track and into the woods across the road from Boz's.

Michele drove past while keeping an eye on the side-view mirror, hoping Pérez hadn't noticed her following. When she saw the lights blink out on the Escape, Michele hit the gas, sped around a curve, then spun a U-turn and parked on the shoulder beyond the bend, where Pérez couldn't see her.

She grabbed her phone and a notebook and scrambled up into the woods for a place to hide. As she scuttled sideways along the hill, she saw Pérez run across the road toward Boz's and take up her crouch in the birches.

Where she still is.

She pictures Pérez nuzzling Danny Peters's milk-white neck, trying to imagine why Pérez would want sex with a teenager, let alone this teenager, and whether it was merely coincidental to the events of the past twenty-four hours.

Probably not, she decides.

———

Michele encountered Danny once in person. It was a few months back, before the night he ran away, before Carey Peters railed at Michele for writing about that night.

She had been perusing the zucchinis and squash at Sawyer's Farm Market when the boy appeared at her side. His narrow face was animated by bright-green eyes and framed by auburn curls that touched his shoulders. For a second she thought he might be a beautiful girl. She felt him next to her, giving her a once-over. She turned to him. His eyes locked on to hers.

"Why are you here?" he said.

It startled Michele. She had no idea who the boy was. "Looking for dinner," she said. "How about you?"

The boy's eyes wandered across the produce tables and past Michele, then back to the zucchinis and finally to her again. "You put those police officers in jail," he said.

"Excuse me?"

"At the *Detroit Free Press*. You were an exceptional journalist."

She chuckled.

"You were," he insisted, as if she shouldn't be surprised at all that he knew about her past.

"'Were'? Thank you, I guess. Who are you?"

"Always an excellent question," he said. She thought he was going to offer a handshake. Instead he stuffed his right hand into a pocket of his cargo shorts. He had something in his other hand. An orange.

"Danny," he said. "I live here."

"I see. You apparently know who I am."

"Yes." He opened the hand holding the orange and regarded it, as if he were surprised to find it there. "Do you know Wallace Stevens?"

"I don't think so. Does he live here too?"

"I thought you were a writer."

Who is this kid? Michele thought. Then it came to her. "Oh, that Wallace Stevens." The boy was staring away from her across the store again. "I read him in college."

"Poems."

"Yes, poems."

"Did you have a favorite?"

"Hmm. I can't say I really remember."

"Of course not. People only read him in college. Then they stop."

"Sorry about that."

"Not your fault. So why are you here?"

"I told you. Getting dinner."

"No," Danny said as Michele heard a man's voice calling the boy's name from the next aisle. "You don't really know."

He set the orange in the zucchini bin and walked away. On a whim, Michele took out her phone and googled *Wallace Stevens* and *orange*. It took her to a poem, "Sunday Morning," with a line about a late breakfast of oranges and coffee.

Michele looked up. Danny was gone. She thought, for no particular reason, that it would be easy to underestimate that kid. She didn't see him again until she began spying on him from afar through the window at the *Light*.

———

Now Pérez rises from her crouch in the birches. She's short, probably shorter than Danny, certainly thicker. She takes a step outside of her shadow cage, hesitates, then steps back inside, squats again. Michele imagines she can hear Pérez's heavy breathing. She must be afraid. She's doing something she isn't really ready to do.

On the deck that fronts the beach at Boz's bar, a white-haired guy with a belly sagging over his apron—Michele figures it must be Boz himself—limps around collecting pint glasses and bottles, lowering umbrellas at the tables. He goes inside the bar. The deck is empty.

Why are you here? Danny asked Michele that day at the market. As if Michele never asked herself the same question, as if she had no idea. She knows she ran from Detroit in shame and anger after the security guard walked her out of the *Free Press* building with her packing box of photographs and old press passes. She knows she found a hiding place in Bleak Harbor. She knows she doesn't belong. She knows this when she lies alone on her futon at night with the sheet and blanket scattered to the floor, hoping the sweat beading along her arms and legs is from the summer heat and not the stirrings of menopause.

I am here, at this moment, to find you, Danny Peters, she thinks, almost saying it out loud. *You are my last assignment. Then I'm getting the hell out of Bleak Harbor forever.*

A few more minutes pass. Michele is considering whether to edge nearer when Pérez scurries down to the rear wall of Boz's, where she dips her head and moves beneath the windows along the side of the building. Michele slips down her hill and crosses the empty road.

Pérez is on all fours now, creeping along the sand next to the outer deck. She stops at the far end of the deck, looks down the beach both ways, then crawls to the covered boat at the dock. Michele sidesteps down the bank into the trees where Pérez hid before. She stops and watches as Pérez unwinds the rope tethering the bow of the boat to the dock, then slides into the water along the starboard side, her wrist flicking upward as she undoes snaps on the tarpaulin.

No way, Michele thinks.

At the stern, Pérez undoes another rope, unsnaps another snap, and hoists herself onto the gunwale, the soaked lower half of her body disappearing beneath the tarp.

The bow of the boat swings away from the dock. Michele listens for the outboard to start as she crab walks through the sand closer to the shoreline. From there she can just barely see the water churning at the stern. The boat is now a good hundred yards from shore.

Pérez is stealing the goddamn boat.

What the hell for? Why would Vend have her steal a boat? Too public, too obvious, too easily traced.

The boat putters away, trailing almost no wake, Pérez staying low as she steers it into the channel to the big lake.

She's either working for Vend or against him; Michele can't tell which. It reminds her of what she thought that day in the market, that it would be easy to underestimate Danny Peters. And then she thinks, with a certainty that surprises her: *Pérez knows. She knows where Danny is.*

Michele spins around and crawls past the deck and back up the hill. She stops in the birch stand where Pérez had hidden and takes out her phone. She dials the Bleak Harbor Police, then kills the call and stands watching the boat recede, considering, deciding, then dials the cops again.

40

"So that Dulcy bitch was in our home?"

Carey and Pete sit elbows to knees on the balcony outside Jonah's fourth-floor condo, the festival cacophony floating around them. Indoors is a swelter. A blown fuse has killed the air-conditioning throughout the building.

Jonah made them sandwiches they barely touched; then they slept, fitfully, for an hour or so. Carey and Pete haven't spoken since she finished a short call with Malone twenty minutes ago. Pete asked about the call, and Carey had chosen not to say anything. Until now.

Pete looks up. "Is that what Malone told you?"

"Was Dulcy in our house or not?"

"She just looked in on Danny once in a—"

"She works for a drug dealer, Pete. A real fucking bad drug dealer."

"I didn't—"

"Stop."

"—know."

"Just stop lying."

"I swear, Carey, I did not know. Do you really think I would've done business with that guy if I had known?"

"Did you send Dulcy to pick up Danny's prescriptions?"

"What are you talking about?"

"Malone told me a Hispanic woman picked up Danny's prescriptions two days ago. Twenty-four hours before he was taken."

"How do you know it was Dulcy?"

"I just told you the police think it was."

"No, you didn't; you said—"

"Stop with the bullshit, Pete. You lied about Bledsoe, you lied—"

"I never saw him. I didn't know. I fucked up, all right? I'm sorry. I'm—Jesus—I wouldn't have done it if I knew."

"No, you chose not to know."

Pete looks away. She can tell he's about to say something he only partly believes. Then he says it: "Maybe I was feeling a little too much pressure to make the thing work."

Carey wants to grab him by the collar of his baggy T-shirt and fling him over the balcony railing. "You're not putting this on me. You made the decision to up and leave Chicago and pursue this stupidity. And now you've put Danny's life in danger."

"Calm down."

"Fuck you."

"Carey. Why would Dulcy get Danny's prescriptions? Huh? Malone's just guessing. All they've got is guesses. This whole Bledsoe thing could be just a sideshow to what's really going on. A coincidence."

"Sure it is," Carey says, but in her head she hears Locke again: *Have you considered the possibility that your employer may be involved in this matter?*

The thought's been trying to wriggle its way out of the back of her mind ever since. Maybe the men who killed Bledsoe don't work for the dealer in Detroit but for Randall Pressman. She recalls the catalytic converter thieves who were unlucky enough to encounter Pressman's men.

It had been Quartz who found them. *My hunting dog*, Pressman had called him. What if Quartz really was the criminal Locke said he was? Quartz, the scrawny dweeb with all the pockets, had compromised national security? Seriously?

She gets to her feet, goes to the balcony railing. Quartz still hasn't responded to her texts. His 6:00 p.m. deadline came and went more than two hours ago. She hasn't had any calls or emails from Spitler either.

What is she supposed to do?

She thinks of Quartz again and digs in her back pocket for the card Locke gave her. She warned Quartz before. He must not have taken her seriously. His mistake. Carey takes Locke's card, copies his cell number into her phone, writes him a text:

C peters here . . . quartz last seen mexican restaurant across from Valpo courthouse

Then she texts Quartz:

locke here, deadline up. goodbye

She lowers her phone and peers through the dark skeleton of the festival Ferris wheel half a block away, lifts her view to the bars along the beach, the misty glow of the phony streetlamps, then beyond to the bay and the haphazard silhouettes of the masts, the stray blinking cruisers and speedboats anchored there, their sloshed occupants making the last feeble noises of the festival's first day.

"Carey?" Pete says behind her.

She locates their house on the far shore. The yellow do-not-cross tape scissors the deck and front windows into jagged shards.

She pictures herself and Danny and Pete sitting on the deck on this very night, watching the festival fireworks. Danny liked the fireworks best when the explosions were spaced far apart. He would leave the deck and walk out to the end of the dock and try to count each of the starburst strands falling into the water. The fury of the finale brought cheers from the festivalgoers but frustrated Carey's beautiful son.

The question is out of her mouth before she knows she's asking: "Why the perch?"

"What?" Pete says.

"Why does Danny love the perch so much?"

"He's never really said. I always figured it's because they seem so gentle and, I don't know, helpless?"

"He loves the dragonflies too, and they don't seem helpless."

The glass door on the balcony slides open. Carey's and Pete's heads both snap around to Jonah. "Sorry, nothing new," he says. "But I was thinking maybe we should head back to the police station."

"A few more minutes," Carey says.

"Any instructions from the kidnapper yet?"

She shakes her head no. Jonah goes back inside. Pete leans on his knees again, drops his head into his hands. He is the handsomest man who ever loved Carey. She turns back to the town, wipes sweat from the skin along her collarbone, squints into the Ferris wheel.

———

On the Ferris wheel that night in Chicago, the air tasted of fried shrimp and mustard.

As Carey clambered into the red cab, number 11, with Pete, she was trying not to think of the expensive pills Danny had flushed down the toilet and how she would try, probably in vain, to talk the pharmacist into replacing them for nothing.

Pete was giddy and a little drunk after his best day ever on the trading floor. He had made almost half a million dollars for O'Nally Bros., an amount her parents would sneer at but that she could see, hard as she tried not to, as a kind of salvation for her and Danny. OK, so Pete didn't get the whole half a million. But even a fraction of it would go a long way toward paying for her son's needs.

She felt Pete's tongue wet on her neck, the tip just beneath her ear, his long slender fingers gliding along the inside of her thigh. She opened her eyes, saw the skyline swoop down beneath them as they rose, told him *no*, not meaning it, as he took her hand and pressed it against his firm crotch, gasped as his three fingers slid into her, Pete whispering into her ear, "You're so beautiful," Carey letting go of her son for a delicious second, then another, then one more.

Pete started to laugh. Carey wanted to laugh with him, but she was struggling to catch her breath.

"Everything is so beautiful," he said. "Look at it. It's ours."

She had him unzipped before they began the descent, and she was coming as they slid past the apex of the circle, her heart pounding, coming again, opening her eyes, seeing the lake stretching into the distance, a shimmer of green and then blue disappearing into the sky. Somewhere out there was Bleak Harbor, as safely distant and invisible as China.

She truly and sincerely liked Pete Peters. She liked his nickname, obvious as it was. She liked how he got out of bed before her alarm went off and took Danny down the street for coffee and turnovers. She liked the way he jabbered about his day on the trading floor over a glass of wine until Danny appeared at the dinner table, and he just shut it off, never brought it up again, as if it didn't matter as much as being there with her and Danny. She liked how he teased Jonah about Danny kicking his butt in backgammon. She liked how he taught Danny to fish at Diversey Harbor. She liked how he told her everything would be all right after Danny threw one of his fits.

Carey wanted to love Pete Peters. Truly and sincerely, she did. And she thought maybe she would, with enough time.

She was glad to be with him on the Ferris wheel. She had known then that it would never get better than that afternoon. She had known she should have ended it then, or that night, or the next morning. She had known it as they stepped off the ride and saw the waiting security guards, had known it as she took the taxi to collect Danny from Kimi's place, had known when Pete showed up at her apartment giggling after three hours at the precinct.

She had known it the next morning when she was trying to decide whether to return his emails. She had known it when he asked her three days later to marry him. Did it matter whether Carey loved him? She loved Danny, he loved Danny, and he could take care of Danny, and her.

Until he couldn't.

———

Everything is rushing back at Carey now as she stares through the black bones of the Ferris wheel, sluicing through her heart, rattling up her spine, tumbling into her head: everything she and Pete did and failed to do, every choice they made or didn't, every foolish, selfish, shortsighted decision that has trapped them on her brother's balcony above Bleak Harbor on this muggy, endless night.

She had told herself over and over she was doing it all for Danny. Only for him. She conjures a vision of his face, so calm and certain as he told her that the palm in his favorite poem "is forever out of reach."

Forever.

How ridiculous she was, she reminds herself now, to think that the palm was a hand she could grasp instead of a tree with a bird perched in its wind-rustled fronds, a bird that could fly away at any instant.

She turns and looks at Pete. He's too tall for the folding chair he's in, looks like he might tip it over. His head is in his hands. He might be dozing. The sandals she kicked off earlier are askew beneath his chair. For a second, she considers telling him she slept with her boss. Telling him it was just the once, and the once was horrible. Imagines Pete looking up, face pleading. At this point, he might even apologize. She thinks to reach out and touch him but can't bring herself to do it.

Then he actually says it. "I'm sorry."

Carey almost laughs. "Sorry for what?"

"I'm sorry I brought you back here."

"What difference does that make now?"

"Can I ask you something?"

Carey waits.

"Who do you think would be better off without the other?" Pete says. "On their own again?"

"What do you mean?"

"You know what I mean. You or me? Who?"

"Who cares?"

Pete's chuckle is sour. "Right. So now what?"

"Now what *what*?"

"Now what with our son?"

Our son, Carey thinks, knowing Pete loves Danny almost as much as she does. "What choice do we have? We pay this guy; we get Danny back."

"And then?"

"I don't know."

"Well. I'm thinking I love Danny, and I don't want to be without him. I'm thinking you and I gotta rethink things. Everything."

"Like how?"

"Maybe we can, you know, go back. Rewind."

"Go back to Chicago?"

"Yeah."

She looks at the balcony's concrete floor, unable to say this directly to Pete: "I guess we have to try."

"We'll just pay this jag-off. All that matters is we get Danny back."

"OK."

"You hear anything from Spitler?"

She shakes her head. "Not yet. Thank God for Oly."

"But we still need another two million? Before midnight?"

"Maybe Mother really will help."

"That reminds me," Pete says, pulling out the burner Carey had bought him. "I think Oly might have called me right before they put me in the cell."

The door bangs open. "Chief called," Jonah says. "They got Pérez. She stole a boat."

"A boat?"

"Trying to get away?"

"The Coast Guard grabbed her."

"Omigod, does she have Danny?"

"Don't know. We should get over there. Pete? You hearing this?"

Pete is leaning out over the balcony railing with a finger in one ear and his phone on the other, shaking his head.

"This makes no fucking sense," he says.

"Chief sounded pretty excited, Carey," Jonah said.

"Let's go. Come on, Pete. You can call him later."

"No, wait—listen to this. I couldn't get into my cell phone voice mail, but old-school Oly left a message at my office too."

He puts the phone on speaker and holds it up for them to hear: "Andrew," Oly's disembodied voice says. "I guess this is your answering machine. Son, what are you doing wiring me the money back? I wanted you to—unless—did something happen? Did you find your Daniel? I haven't heard anything on the news. If you can, call my secretary, Wanda—you know her. She'll find me. God bless."

"Wire the money back? What's he talking about?"

"Gimme a second."

"Do it on the way to the station."

"It's the ransom, Carey. Hold on a damn second."

He's punching keys, starting over, punching more. "This browser sucks," he says. He stops and waits, then stares into the phone, eyes widening as he brings it closer to his face. "No. Carey, what's our password again?"

"I thought you changed it."

"No. What is it?"

"*MommylovesDANNY*. Lowercase *mommyloves*, all-uppercase *Danny*."

Pete types, his face aglow in the phone light. "Not working. I'm gonna try 'Forgot Password.'"

"Did you type it in right? Here, give it to me."

Pete twists away. "I can't type if you're making me move. Security question. 'What's your favorite pet?' Paddle?"

"Yes."

"Our money's in here, Jeremiah's blood money." Pete types and waits, the changing light flickering on his skin. "OK, I changed the password to *carey11PETE11* for now. *Pete* all caps."

They wait.

"This can't be right."

"What?"

"Goddamn banks."

"Pete, come on," Jonah says.

"Fuck. The money. It's gone. It's fucking gone."

"What money?"

"Oly's money. Five-point-one million fucking dollars. It's not there."

"What do you mean it's—"

"It's gone. It was there before, I told you. What is happening?"

"Are you in the right account?"

"Yes I'm—fuck. I checked it earlier. It was all there."

"How much?"

Carey grabs the phone from Pete.

"Five million plus."

"It says two thousand three hundred fifty and eighty-one cents. Is that what was in here before Oly transferred his money?"

"No. We had like five grand."

"So what happened?"

Carey feels her phone vibrate. Another text.

"Maybe Oly changed his mind? I don't know."

"He said *you* sent him back the money, Pete." She looks at her phone. "Why would Oly leave two thousand three hundred whatever bucks behind?"

A text appears on Carey's phone. From Quartz. She opens it:

D found. meet rt 23 and s bay no cops no locke

She almost drops the phone. She looks up at Jonah. "Malone," she lies. "Let's get out of here."

Carey thinks fast as she follows Pete and Jonah out of the condo and into the elevator. She's wishing she could take back that text she sent Locke.

The elevator opens into a ground floor garage, where Jonah's Camry is parked. Pete's getting into the seat behind Jonah when Carey pulls up short. "My car's on the street," she says. "I don't want it getting towed because of the festival. We might need it."

"It's not going to get towed."

"I'll go with you," Pete says from inside the car. But Carey's already trotting, then running away, waving him off.

"No, go. I'm right behind you."

She doesn't know why, but as she gets into her car she has a fleeting feeling that she's never going to see Pete again. It makes her sad; then it's gone.

41

The text from Carey Bleak Peters shoots a needle of fright through Quartz:

> locke here, deadline up. goodbye

Locke hasn't been this close to Quartz since DC. And then, actually, it was Quartz who got close to Locke. The agent was speaking on a panel at an internet security conference at the National Press Club. Quartz sat near the back of the meeting room in a tattered winter coat he'd bought for $8.50 at an army surplus store. He wore a fake beard and tinted glasses beneath a Baltimore Orioles cap. When the session ended, Quartz crept behind Locke and his fellow panelists as they posed for a group photo. The next day, Quartz posted the picture of him photobombing Locke on Locke's LinkedIn page. He sent a link to the page to a *Washington Post* reporter. Then he fled DC for good.

That was four years ago. Now Quartz wishes he hadn't met Carey at the restaurant beneath his apartment. At least, he reassures himself, he hadn't let on that he was staying upstairs. Still, he'd been lazy. And cocky. To be fair, he was unaware then that Bledsoe had screwed up. And out of selfish curiosity, he'd wanted an up-close look at the woman Pressman had fucked and seemed bent on fucking over.

Quartz knows he should probably disappear now. The $2 million Pressman sent for the kid's ransom is parked in an account Quartz created for a shell company at a bank in Nevada. From there it will zigzag among other phantom accounts he has at other banks in other cities before it winds up safely overseas. Those transfers will never be traced—not to Pressman, certainly not to Quartz.

He could find work again. There are plenty of self-obsessed rich bastards who need a wraith like Quartz, the kind who can find almost anything almost anywhere and has no qualms about calling in men paid to punish the fools who dare to steal a self-obsessed rich bastard's things. Like those dunces who hijacked that Pressman semitrailer supposedly filled with catalytic converters—actually, Chinese carfentanil—and tried to make Canada via North Dakota.

Or Quartz could simply use the ransom cash to go totally dark, hide in some faraway place. He could hope that Locke—an FBI veteran of twenty-three years, not the hapless job-hopping bureaucrat Quartz had invented for Carey's sake—would give up after a few more years. Quartz would have to change his identity again, maybe have some more surgery. He could do it if he had to. Eventually he would be free to live his life as he saw fit.

He hopes.

He knows all of this, knows that Locke might at this very moment be on his way to Valparaiso. But Quartz stays at his table above the restaurant, bent over his devices, rattling his keyboards, chewing his nails. The blood has come. A strip of black electrical tape is twisted around the tip of Quartz's left forefinger. His ring finger is next. He pictures Locke pushing his speed on I-94, imagines the agent creeping down the hallway outside his apartment door.

But he stays. He hasn't left his kitchen table except to piss since leaving Carey at the restaurant downstairs. Because he's onto something he's having trouble believing.

———

He had spent a fruitless hour scouring the innards of Danny's hard drive. There were glittery close-up photos of dragonflies alight on dock pilings, slow-motion videos of dragonflies devouring mosquitoes. Word files filled with musings on a Wallace Stevens poem whose meaning escaped Quartz, PDFs from environmental websites about the spawning tendencies of yellow perch. And a drawing, presumably in the boy's hand, of a dachshund that appeared to be sleeping, or dead.

There were also photographs of Danny's mother. Quartz skimmed them quickly, then went back after noticing that they all seemed to have been taken without her being aware.

She was standing at the end of a dock, backlit by sunset, head bowed, arms enfolding her shoulders. She was on one knee in sand, smiling as she scratched the belly of the dachshund. She was leaning on a balcony railing in evening shadow, one hand holding a phone to an ear, the other covering her eyes. She was curled into a quilt in a chair on a balcony with a distant view of Chicago's silhouetted skyline.

Looking at the pictures, Quartz wondered if Carey knew that, whatever his mental state, her son loved her. Loved her a lot. It reminded Quartz of his last memory of his own mother, the fragrance of hairspray blanketing him as she bundled him into a minivan he'd never been in before. She'd taken him away to Valparaiso, where his grandparents had raised him. Locke undoubtedly knew that, undoubtedly had checked it out before, undoubtedly assumed that Quartz would never hide in such an obvious place.

Quartz thinks of his grandparents' twin gravestones at the Graceland Cemetery off State Road 2. He liked to go there once a week, around dawn, when their names, Patricia and Norbert, seemed to glow in the early sun. He realizes that he's probably been there for the last time.

Sitting at his kitchen table, he has plundered the emails and social media accounts of every individual and institution that he can imagine could be involved directly or indirectly in the taking of Danny Peters: Carey; stepfather Pete; the boy's now-dead father, Bledsoe; Mayor

Jonah; the *Light* reporter, Higgins; Officer Malone; Chief Radovich; an employee of Pete's named Dulcinea Pérez; the bartender Boz Flanagan. Some Detroit drug lord has surfaced here and there. The sleuthing hasn't been difficult because even police officers and coke dealers are ridiculously trusting of the online world.

Serenity Bleak apparently had no internet presence. Quartz succeeded in hacking the email of a man named Roland Spitler who spoke on her behalf on the rare occasion that she deigned to address the commoners of Bleak Harbor. Spitler's email account was barren, as if he deleted everything on a daily basis. It made Quartz wonder what he had to hide.

Wherever he went, Quartz kept stumbling over the digital footprints of another hacker. Each time Quartz squirmed through some back door in the computers that made these people's lives whole, he saw that the hacker already had been there. And not just minutes or hours before, but days before, even weeks. Whoever it was had been rooting around in servers like a raccoon in a garbage dump. And he—or maybe she?—wasn't just excavating but was manipulating, perpetrating. He'd been inside the computers at Pete Peters's sorry pot shop and invaded the porous servers of the *Light*, where he appeared to have posted the article of the 1945 drowning of the "eccentric" young Jeremiah Bleak.

This hacker had, in various guises, conversed with Carey and Pete and Bledsoe. He'd posted a gruesome video of Bledsoe's demise to Facebook, Tumblr, and Twitter. He'd prowled the servers at Bleak County on several occasions, accessing, for reasons unclear to Quartz, property tax records. For the hell of it, Quartz wormed his way into the servers at two local banks. He couldn't be sure, but it looked as if the hacker had penetrated one account at Bleak County Bank & Trust.

He or she had also been at play on Twitter under the handle @ drewthenobody, an account Quartz discovered was registered to one Morton Needelman. The name was strangely familiar. Quartz had flipped back to the 1945 story that popped up on the *Light* website.

And there was Morton Needelman, the Bleak County prosecutor who had declared the drowning of Jeremiah Bleak accidental. Quartz was still laughing when he noticed the date atop the *Light* page. "Holy shit," he said. The date was May 18, 1945. The boy, Jeremiah, had drowned seventeen days earlier. On May 1. The original ransom demand had been $5.145 million. As in 5/1/45.

———

Now an icon starts blinking yellow in the lower-right corner of Quartz's laptop screen. He shifts his mouse, clicks on the icon.

"Show me, T. rex," he says.

When he was Danny's age, Quartz obsessed over dinosaurs and an ancient world dominated not by women and men but by mind-less meat-eating beasts who didn't waste a second of their short lives pretending they were anything but predators. He enrolled in Purdue University to become a paleontologist. Organic chemistry put an end to that. Video games nurtured his only intimate relationship, with computers.

In his ensuing fourteen years at the National Security Agency, Quartz thought of his work prowling in other people's digital lives as that of a paleontologist who could discern the size and shape of a forty-five-ton brachiosaur from a smattering of bones weighing no more than the chisels and awls used to dislodge them from prehistoric rock. It helped him rationalize the consequences of what he did for a living, which more and more he came to consider amoral.

When that hollow logic no longer helped him sleep, Quartz sought out a *POLITICO* reporter he mistakenly thought he could trust and gave her a thumb drive filled with classified files suggesting how his employer routinely spied on law-abiding American citizens. For her stories on the NSA's intrusions into private lives, she won a promo-tion and some prizes that Quartz assumed nobody but journalists cared about. By then, Quartz had changed his name and his looks and was discreetly hiring himself out to men like Pressman. "The bitch for the rich," Quartz told his mirror reflection each morning. At least most of the people he hurt in his new incarnation deserved it.

His phone pulses on the table. Quartz glances at it, sees it's Pressman again, ignores it again. A rectangle opens on his screen.

Quartz leans forward, squinting. "Aha," he says.

On a hunch, Quartz had ventured into the computers at the Bleak Harbor Police Department. Soon he had the make, model, and serial number of Danny's laptop. He'd spent fifteen minutes concocting a program he named "T. rex" that would search FedEx, UPS, and the postal service for that serial number. It took almost two hours to produce the date, time, place, and credit card attached to the purchase of the laptop Carey had given the cops—Danny's Lenovo ThinkPad X.

It had been ordered April 11 from a website called SalesAblaze. Two days later it appeared in a mailbox at a UPS store on Lily Street in Bleak Harbor. The price of $1,299.63 plus tax and shipping was charged to an American Express credit card held by the City of Bleak Harbor, specifically Jonah E. Bleak, mayor.

Quartz leans back into his computer, fingers hopping across the keyboard as he follows the hacker's trail into Jonah Bleak's city Amex account. "Come on, come on," Quartz says, urging speed on the computer. He bites the electrical tape off of his left forefinger. The mayor's most recent statement appears on his screen.

The card has been busy buying things for the past week: Two Champion portable power generators. A wireless router. Half a dozen disposable phones. A thirty-seven-inch-tall Vornado tower fan. A $499 pair of night-vision binoculars. A police scanner. Two goose-down pillows. A box of chocolate brownie Clif Bars. A case of Gatorade. And a small library of security software, the essential tools of a digital B-and-E artist: Spy Argus96, Metasploits, John the Ripper, Nmap, HellRazer666, CataLyst, MrKleen.

Impressive, Quartz thinks. Even he hasn't tried Spy Argus96.

He can't tell where the software wound up. But the generator, router, and other items were delivered to an apartment in Watervliet, not far from Bleak Harbor. Quartz finds a rental website that lists the building, calls the phone number, gets a recording in Spanish, then English. He hangs up and flips back to the Amex statement to see if he missed anything. On his third try, he sees that something new has appeared in the pending transactions column:

Nardella's Pizza. $12.31.

It makes Quartz laugh again. "Are you kidding me? A pizza? Dude, you are the man."

He googles the pizzeria on Haroldson Road, a mile north of Bleak Harbor, and punches the phone number into a disposable. A boy answers in a pubescent squawk.

"Nardella's. Can I help you?"

"Yeah, hey, sorry, didn't get my pizza."

"Pardon?"

"My pizza. It should be here by now."

"Oh. Uh, can you hold a second?"

The phone goes to a country song. Quartz considers what he'll say if the kid asks his name.

The kid comes back on. "When did you order, sir?"

"At least an hour ago."

"Name?"

"Jonah."

"Joe?"

"No. Jo-nah."

"Got it, Jo-nah. I don't have that here."

"No?"

"Nope."

Quartz has a notion that actually makes him a little giddy. "Oh, yeah, my brother ordered. Jeremiah."

285

"OK," the kid says.

Fucking A, Quartz thinks.

"We have it being delivered at 7:43. Cheese with ham and pineapple. Left it on the front porch, as requested. Have you looked?"

"Yep. Nothing there."

"Yeah, we really don't like just leaving things, but . . . lemme just confirm, you're at 39874 South Bay Drive?"

Quartz pumps the address into the Google slot. A map pops up on his laptop.

"Sir?"

Quartz kills the call. He sits still for a second, staring at the map on the screen, light-headed at what he believes he has found. He fits a Bluetooth device into an ear and dials Pressman, who answers in the middle of the first ring.

"Why aren't you answering my calls?"

"Been busy working for you."

"Any luck on the kid?"

"Maybe."

"Time is running out."

No, Quartz thinks, *it really isn't.* But no sense letting Pressman know what he knows until he knows for sure.

"I'm getting calls from the Bleak Harbor Police," Pressman says.

"You haven't spoken with them, have you?"

"Hell, no. Why are they calling me?"

Quartz relishes the idea of Pressman having to answer other people's questions without getting paid in cash or sex or obsequiousness. "It's probably just routine," he says. "Although Agent Locke is in Bleak Harbor. Did I mention that?"

"Fuck me. Fuck. We're back at square fucking one. This was a stupid fucking plan, Quartz."

"Relax. As long as the kid comes back alive, you're fine. They're not going to bust you for screwing his mom. You get your two million back, and Locke has no case."

The phone goes silent. Quartz hears the squeak of Pressman's chair. He pictures him turning, as he often does when things aren't going his way, to look at the sole photograph on the wall, of a man holding a giant wrench. Pressman's father, Harold T. Pressman.

Quartz conjures a picture of a much younger Randall, home from Bloomington on spring break, going frantically from room to room in his father's bungalow in Hammond, finally, reluctantly, resignedly, going to the garage out back. The young man hearing the hum of the car engine as he lifts the garage door, coughing against the fumes.

Twenty years old and suddenly alone. Blaming not his feeble, embittered drunk of a father, Quartz now realizes, but the rich family in Michigan who had sold his father's plant and left Harold Pressman jobless, broke, and wallowing in Seagram's. Pressman had told Quartz about it late one night when he'd had a few too many Macallans himself.

When did that plant close? Quartz thinks. *What was the date?*

"Who's got the kid?" Pressman says.

"Hang on," Quartz says. "Gonna mute."

He's googling. He can't immediately bring to mind the Japanese company that bought Harold T. Pressman's steel mill. Matsuyama. Mayeda. Murakami. Something with an *M*. And then, there it is. Matsunaka. The company that bought the mill that Joseph Estes Bleak built in 1887 was sold by his great-grandson, Jonathan Estes "Jack" Bleak, on July 3, 1988.

Quartz unmutes his phone. "Back," he says.

"Where is the fucking kid?" Pressman says.

"His name is Danny."

"I don't give a flying fuck. Where is he?"

As Pressman continues to yell, Quartz works his mouse and keyboard, trying to find the hacker's jump box, the computer from which he's launching his attacks. It probably won't reveal much, but it's worth checking for clues to the hacker's identity.

"Maybe we wouldn't be in this position," Quartz says, "if you didn't have to bang every woman on your payroll."

"Excuse me?"

"I mean, really, why this Carey chick? I'll admit she's pretty hot. But she's married with a kid. Do you ever—"

"Do you think I can't find you, Quartz? Do you imagine that you're the only finder on my payroll?"

A site is loading on the laptop screen. "Listen, Randall. This afternoon, Carey was told the ransom is now seven-point-three-eight-eight million dollars."

"So I'm supposed to give her more money? Give me a fucking break."

"Doesn't that number strike you as odd? Seven-point-three-eight-eight million?"

"Get to the point, Quartz."

"It happens to correspond to the exact date that Bleak Holdings sold its steel mill to Matsunaka. The mill that employed your dad."

It takes a moment for this to register with Pressman. "Bullshit," he finally says. "Coincidence."

"That's the thing about this guy. He picks numbers that have some weird significance to him. There's a pattern. He's serious, Randall."

"I don't give a shit."

"But the authorities might give a shit. If things go sideways somehow, they might see something in that number. Like maybe motive."

Pressman goes quiet again. Quartz walks into his bedroom. The bed is made but rumpled because he rarely bothers to get under the covers.

"No," Pressman says. "I wouldn't do that."

"You wouldn't take revenge on the Bleaks?"

"No, I would not. Not for that."

"Please."

"It was just business. I wouldn't—this has nothing to do with that."

Quartz doesn't find that convincing. He slides the nightstand drawer open and removes the .22-caliber Luger. He holds the gun in both hands, pointing it away and down by the butt. Engraved into the grip are his grandfather's initials.

"Quartz, are you listening?"

"I'm sorry, Randall. What did you say?"

Quartz had taken the pistol from a locked cabinet in his grandfather's house two days after the old man died. Quartz hadn't any idea how to pick an actual lock. He finally used a hammer on the cabinet glass. He took the .22, a box of bullets, and a pair of handcuffs his grandfather had used as an MP in Korea. He signed up for shooting lessons. Turned out he wasn't bad at hitting targets. He started bringing his bull's-eyes home and pushpinning them to the kitchen wall.

"You heard me," Pressman is saying, his voice back to its usual tone of a man who knows he will get what he wants. "Jesus, Quartz. I don't even know your first name."

Quartz sits back down at his laptop. "You never cared."

"I care now."

The queue of files in the hacker's jump box—Jeremiah's jump box—is on the laptop screen.

"No point in telling you now, Randall. Best for both of us if we remain anonymous, don't you think?"

The names of Jeremiah's dozens of jump-box files are not words Quartz knows. They remind him of high school biology. He copies one at random—*pachydiplax*—then punches up Wikipedia and searches the word. *Pachydiplax longipennis* is the scientific name for the blue dasher, a dragonfly common to the United States.

"You think you're pretty damn smart, don't you, Quartz?"

He chooses another file name, *libellula*, and searches that. Another common dragonfly.

"Quartz, do you hear me?"

He gets out of the chair and goes to the window facing the street, peeks through the blinds. A Valparaiso police car is parked across the street, idling.

Time to go, Quartz thinks. *Back way.*

"I hear you, Randall."

"What are we gonna do here?"

"Well, you know what they say."

"What's that?"

"All's well that ends."

Quartz tosses the burner phone on the table. He looks at his watch. At this time of night, he can make Bleak Harbor in an hour, an hour fifteen. He briefly considers that he will miss those fish tacos downstairs. He picks the phone back up and types a text to Carey Bleak:

D found. meet rt 23 and s bay no cops no locke

Quartz takes his backpack into the bedroom and tosses in two pairs of underwear and socks, an extra pair of sneakers, some CVS sunglasses, his grandfather's handcuffs. He makes sure the Luger is at the top of the pile.

He returns to the kitchen and unplugs the laptop before stuffing it into the backpack, telling it, grinning, "You didn't count on me, did you, Jeremiah? Or, sorry—Danny."

42

Danny watches.

Across the bay, his mother and stepfather are silhouettes against the setting sun on the balcony of his uncle Jonah's condo.

They keep their distance.

Carey and Pete are autistics of a sort, albeit supposedly functioning ones. It's not pain that fills them at this particular moment but fear. They are afraid of the choices they have made and how those choices could now lead to the unbearable.

Danny lowers his night-vision binoculars and steps back from the gable vent in the attic of the Helliker place.

A sole pair of headlights gleams on South Bay Drive, approaching from downtown Bleak Harbor. Danny follows them from his dark hiding place. They bend one way and disappear behind trees, bend another and reemerge, winding past Boz's bar.

Danny has tried not to worry about the vehicles that have driven past since he left one of his green high-tops in a clump of grass near the bay road, crawled through the broken boards in the security fence, and climbed into his secret shelter the day before. The snapping turtle that surprised him in the weeds on the Helliker side of the fence met with the sharp, fatal end of a rock.

He watched with mild amusement as his long-gone father, Jeffrey Bledsoe, skulked around his parents' cottage, looking for him. He watched him move around the house, peeking into windows, looking over his shoulder, finally giving up and going to his car on the bay road shoulder and pulling away. *Milkshakes*, he thinks. He was supposedly going with his father for milkshakes.

He heard Carey and Pete searching downstairs that night until he triggered the alarms. He'd sent Pete a text from the phony 537 number—alarmed?—and later watched his stepfather lope down the beach toward his shop, where he would see on his pathetically unguarded computer the selfie Danny had taken of himself duct-taped into the chair, one green shoe missing, a smudge of charcoal on one cheek meant to look like a bruise.

Pete: *lukkytrayd72*. Profession, birthday, password. He didn't change it even after trayd upon trayd went unlucky.

Early the next morning, Danny pressed an ear to the floor as the fat guy who had come with the lady police officer walked around the ground floor, coughing and gagging, obviously allergic to the mildew in the walls and what furniture was left behind.

Later, Danny listened to the volunteer searchers giving the Helliker house a once-over. He heard a woman tell someone else she thought the kidnapping was a scam. "I don't trust these Bleaks," she sneered. "That Carey woman is probably trying to shake her mother down for money. They hate each other, you know." Her partner said, "You seen that movie *Fargo*?"

Danny allowed himself a grin at that.

He watched the cars and SUVs and pickups that slowed as they passed the house next door, his home since his parents had dragged him here from Chicago. What did the gawkers hope to see beyond the police tape?

They reminded him of a black-and-white photograph that had appeared on the front page of the *Bleak Harbor Light* in 1945. Men in Sunday suits and women in dresses were crowding the beaches to gape at the search-and-rescue boats out looking for Jeremiah.

They never did see Jeremiah.

And they would never see Danny.

Joseph Estes Bleak had come to Michigan from Boston in 1868. He had created a family and a town. He would have recognized neither today, either in structure or soul. He and Eudora Marie Randolph Bleak had had Blossom. Then had come Lily and, much later, Violet.

Typhoid had taken Blossom. A horse had flung Lily to her death. Violet had left the convent to care for her mother after her father died. It was 1902. Four years later, she had had a son, James Estes Bleak, out of wedlock.

James had married a woman named Polley. They had had two children, Jeremiah Estes, and five years later, Jonathan Estes, whom they called Jack. Both had been in the sloop with their father on Lake Michigan that day in 1945. It had been unseasonably warm and humid for May. The clouds had sunk lower and heavier as the afternoon had worn on.

Sitting alone at the microfilm machine at the Joseph E. Bleak Public Library, reading about what happened to Jeremiah, Danny always wondered if the clouds should have been a warning. James Estes Bleak was an expert sailor who competed each year in the Port Huron-to-Mackinac race, so he must have known the weather would be dangerous. Yet he still had gone out on the day Jeremiah would die.

Danny would try to visualize the storm clouds stacking up on the horizon. He'd imagine Jeremiah reaching out to sweep them away. As Danny himself would have. He'd imagine what happened on that dark afternoon, and it would become as true to Danny as if he'd read it, word for word, on the old *Light* page.

Jeremiah and Jack, fifteen and ten, wore life jackets. Jeremiah had refused to buckle his. He called it a straitjacket. He had glimpsed strait-jackets in the hospital where his parents took him to see his special doctor. His father usually did not wear a life jacket on the sloop. Today, though, he did.

Danny would wonder if Jeremiah had noticed.

The storm boiled up from the north. A wave swamped the deck as the boat bottomed in a swell and keeled starboard. The mast snapped in two. The boat capsized. James Bleak and his sons bobbed orange in the water. They clung to the hull. Jeremiah's jacket dangled from an arm. "Jer," brother Jack called out. "Your jacket. Fix your jacket."

Jeremiah heard. He knew about his straitjacket. He saw his father's hand reaching across the hull. He looked up. The sky was a roil of smoke and feather, swaying to and fro. Jeremiah asked himself if that could be heaven. Or so Danny would imagine in the library, the vinegar tang of the microfilm in his nostrils.

Young Jeremiah's father and brother were yelling. Jeremiah reached for his father's hand. It was slick with the lake. Jeremiah turned toward Jack. "Hang on, Jer." Jack was draped over the bow end of the hull. Spray obliterated his face. He saw his brother trying to stretch an arm toward him. His father turned to Jack and screamed, "Hold on with both arms." But Jeremiah felt his hand slipping. Young Jack couldn't hold him. And his father merely watched.

"Your jacket," Jeremiah's father yelled. "What did I tell you?"

"My jacket," the boy gurgled. His father watched as Jeremiah slid off the boat slowly enough to look up one last time at the welcoming sky.

In Danny's mind, that's how it had been. Something terrible. No accident.

James Bleak "almost drowned as he heroically tried to save his son," the *Light* lied. Danny printed a copy of the page and sneaked the roll of microfilm out of the library. That was the day he told Zelda that she was a very beautiful woman. He had wanted her to know because he didn't think he'd ever see her again.

Danny unraveled the film from the microfilm roll and burned it on the beach as horseflies swooped through the coiling smoke. The Bleaks had abandoned their "eccentric" boy just as they would their timber mill and steel plant, just as they would abandon the town that was named after their family by isolating themselves on their wedge of land. Danny was sure that if Pete and Carey would abandon Paddle, then eventually they would abandon him. Like young Jeremiah, like the helpless perch, he was drowning too.

—

The headlights pass. Danny hangs back in the darkness. He reaches for the half-eaten slice of pizza in the box on the floor, the pieces of shattered chair resting nearby.

The pizza is cheese with ham and pineapple. Barely more than a day in the attic, and already Danny is sick of Clif Bars. The delivery boy left the pie on the Hellikers' front stoop. Danny counted to three hundred before snaking an arm through the front door to retrieve it. Risky, he knew.

It has all been risky since the day after Mother and Pete killed Paddle. They could have saved Danny's dog. It would have cost them $2,350.81. Danny saw the veterinarian's to-the-penny estimate in an email on Pete's laptop.

There is nothing we can do, son.

Pete's new casting rod (February, $439.77) + Carey's shoes (March, $228.14) + dinner at Carmine's (January, $321.00) + the security fence (April, $1,897.96) = Paddle gone.

Danny sees the dachshund wobbling along the shoreline in his final days. He knew the sand felt cool and soft on his sore pads.

Good boy, Paddle-daddle. Good boy.

That's when Danny put his plan into place. He would save his mother from Pressman, whose emails and texts he had read with disgust. He would save Pete from himself.

And Danny would save himself.

Now Pete and Carey have their $2,350.81. He left it in their account when he emptied it of all the other money that afternoon and returned Oly's to Oly.

Everyone must pay for their sins.

Gotta pay, in Bledsoe's imagined lingo.

Danny washes down the last of the cold pizza with a swallow of Gatorade. He has to crouch a little beneath the trusses to tip the bottle up over his head. Staying low, he moves to the folding table.

The table holds a small electric fan, his laptop, a box of kitchen matches, and three disposable phones. A police scanner rests atop the box of Clif Bars. Beneath the table, a generator powers the laptop, Danny's main source of light. Next to the generator stands a one-gallon can of gasoline he took from his parents' garage.

Danny leans his face toward the battery-powered fan. The tepid air blows across his cheeks and forehead. By now Dulcinea has dropped her own disposable into the lake. He heard the dispatches on the scanner. She is in custody.

Not optimal, Danny thinks. He quiets the apprehension pinging in his head by assuring himself that Dulcinea will tell the police nothing. One million of the dollars he would soon be snatching would guarantee her silence.

She had come to Danny on many afternoons. She said she liked him, then was falling in love with him. Danny knew she pitied him. He knew he would never find love. Pity would always come first. Even his parents pity him. They forget he's almost sixteen years old. They forget he's smart. Smarter than they are. Now they will know.

Dulcinea became integral to his plan. She used what she'd learned at coding school to help him infiltrate the digital lives of his family and the others who figured in his plan. He promised Dulcinea an escape from the people who enslaved her, in the form of $100,000. And she relieved him of his virginity, riding him as in his head he recited a verse from his favorite Stevens poem over and over to the accelerating rhythm, without feeling, without meaning.

The dragonfly is without feeling. Its exquisite senses of hearing and direction enable it to deduce precisely where its ignorant prey will be when the dragonfly is ready to strike and crush and mash and digest while veering immediately toward its next target.

Now, as Danny sits before his laptop, he lets the song his mother made up float through his head:

Pretty pretty dragonflies . . .

Danny has had the laptop since moving to Bleak Harbor a year ago. The police have in their possession another one that he bought a few weeks ago with his uncle Jonah's city credit card. Danny filled that computer with what the police and his parents expect to see, frivolous evidence of his various interests, what they and his doctors refer to as "obsessions," and he copied the same things to his external hard drive.

Danny sent the text Thursday night with the picture of the empty chair holding the roll of duct tape. He had photoshopped the images of the angry rottweilers, Daisey and Hoho—pictures and names he'd found in a Google search—and sent the phony audio of them drooling over his green sneaker.

He planted the glitch in the Strawman Pharmacy computers (password: *StrawFrm220lily*) that allowed Dulcinea to pick up an extra cache of his meds so he could leave his others behind. He rang the bells again and again at Saint Wenceslaus through the church's computer and shut down the generators that powered the festival rides. He made the tavern sound system blare that awful Eagles song Dulcy liked. He bounced that $5 million gift back to Oleson O'Nally. He taunted his mother's lecherous boss with the second ransom number that matched the date of the steel-plant sale. He even went to the trouble of telling the post office to send his uncle's credit card statements to Dulcinea's Watervliet address so Jonah wouldn't see them and notice any odd purchases.

Sometimes it was fun.

Danny had become Morton Needelman, owner of Twitter handle @ drewthenobody. He had posted on the *Light* site (password: *lightNOOZ*) the 1945 article about Jeremiah's death, with the headline that called his distant cousin "eccentric." The label pasted on Danny—autistic—hadn't yet become fashionable in the 1940s.

Danny sent the email to himself from Bledsoe's computer (password: *Jbl33dsoe*) that Carey saw Friday morning: *Y not, Danny boy?* He planted the spyware on Carey's phone that traced her to Valparaiso. He typed 5373642445 is a landline # into a text to his panicked mother.

He read the reckless emails between Bledsoe and Petunia Delacroix that funneled him into her Facebook account, where he posted the photo of her in a yellow bikini. He accessed the webcam on Bledsoe's laptop that recorded his father's demise.

The sudden appearance of the two men in Bledsoe's apartment had taken Danny aback. They had not been part of his plan. He'd had to remind himself that no scheme would play out perfectly, that there would be unexpected glitches. Even the dragonfly missed his quarry on rare occasions. This development, though unexpected, wasn't entirely unwelcome. Bledsoe had long ago chosen his perilous path. Danny's mother, and Pete, were finally free of him.

But now, on the laptop aglow in the attic gloom, there is something else he didn't expect.

Earlier Danny had noticed that someone or something from the outside appeared to be looking in. Someone or something that might actually know what to do, and how. There were digital fingerprints in Danny's jump box. Someone or something had looked at his files. Danny had hoped it was merely some anonymous hacker who had blindly stumbled in, maybe even a misdirected bot.

But his laptop makes a sound Danny has never heard before, a sharp retort like what he imagines a gunshot sounds like. An image materializes on the screen. Danny hits the "Esc" button to kill it, clicks his mouse, but it continues to take shape. It is a hand holding something he cannot yet make out.

He looks over his shoulder at the vent where he was standing a few minutes before. Diffuse light is bleeding in. Another vehicle on the bay road. Danny stays in his seat, watching the light brighten, then fade to dark. He imagines a clacking keyboard, chasing him. He closes his eyes, tries to slow his heartbeat. It can't be Pressman, not the police, not Locke. None is smart enough.

He looks back at the screen. A man's right hand displays a pistol in the palm. The hand is moon white, the pistol midnight black. The grip is engraved with letters of dull silver:

N A G

Danny whispers them to himself, reaches for his mouse. Before he can touch it, the screen goes dark. Danny's hand hovers over the mouse. The screen slowly turns the color of blood. A thin white line of words appears at the middle. Danny leans in a little, sees it:

hereSheis

Taunting Danny as Danny had Pete with *hereheis* on the computer in his office.

Danny lowers his hand and left-clicks. The words vanish. He knows what comes next. The red bleeds away. A shape begins to form at the bottom of the gray. Danny clicks again and bends his head to the screen. The image unfolds, two feet at the bottom of the screen, duct-taped to the legs of a chair. Danny watches the rest.

Mommy.

He picks up his phone. A noise, scratchy, barely audible, begins to emanate from the laptop. A song. Danny stands, leans an ear in.

Desperado, he hears.

He reaches under the table, drags out the can of gasoline. He taps a key on his phone.

"Bleak residence."

"Mr. Spitler," Danny says.

A pause, then, "I thought you weren't going to call."

"I'm going to need your help."

43

"I will handle this, Locke."

Hamilton steps pointedly in front of Locke, blocking the corridor two cell doors from where Dulcinea Pérez waits behind bars.

"I'll just be a fly on the wall, Agent," Locke says.

"Why are you here anyway?" She angles her head in a way that suggests she's not inclined to believe whatever he says. "Chicago didn't say anything about Indy working this."

"I don't work for Chicago."

"Excuse me," Malone says. She heard the exchange as she stepped into the hallway, her hand clutching Pete Peters's elbow. He had arrived a few minutes ago with Jonah Bleak but no Carey Peters. They said Carey was right behind them. But she isn't responding to calls or texts. Peters and Jonah swear they have no idea where she is.

Hamilton and Locke turn to Malone. "Hamilton and Chief are on the phone to Chicago now about Pressman. Let's go see Pérez," she says. "Mr. Peters has a few things to say to her."

"Pressman?" Pete says. "What about him?"

"Quiet, sir," Locke says. "You're in a lot of trouble."

"I told you I did not know that—"

"Just shut up."

"We really don't need a clusterfuck in there," Hamilton says. "Pérez will know we're grasping."

"I'll be a polite observer, agent," Locke says. "I'm not interested in headlines or book deals."

"Seriously? I heard you were a jag-off."

"This is my jail," Malone says, tugging Peters past them. "We have less than two hours. Both of you. Now."

———

Pérez slumps over her knees on the concrete bed, wrapped in a gray wool blanket. Her black hair still glistens with damp.

Hamilton takes a spot facing her. Locke backs up against a wall. Pete steps into the cell with Malone, who says, "I brought a friend."

Pérez looks up, sees Pete, swallows hard, looks back down.

"Dulcy," Pete says, his voice cracking. "We need your help with Danny."

The Coast Guard had picked her up in Lake Michigan off the beach at Van Buren State Park. She was close enough to shore, as if she had planned to tie up there, that she had tried to make a swim for it. Malone and Radovich had confronted her in the interview room. They told Pérez they'd seen communications between her and Danny, told her a witness had put her in Danny's bedroom, told her they could charge her with statutory rape.

She had stared at the table, hands folded in her lap, shaking her head no to each question, even about her name and address. She had no cell phone to inspect, probably lost it in the lake. Her soggy driver's license put her last address on Bagley Street in Detroit.

Now Malone nudges Pete closer to Pérez. "Dulcy," he says, "if you know where Danny is—"

"She knows," Hamilton says.

"—you need to tell us. He may be in danger."

Pérez says something, barely a whisper.

"What was that?" Malone says.

Pérez says it again, a little louder: "El niño va a estar bien."

Hamilton and Malone both look at Peters.

"She's always doing that with the Spanish," he says, then turns back to Pérez. "Dulcy. Goddamn it, I thought you liked Danny. Do you want him to get hurt?"

Hamilton squats down at Pérez's level.

"Dulcinea," she says. "You don't want to be an accessory to kidnapping. It's a federal felony. You could spend a lot of years in prison, with no parole or breaks for good behavior. Your boss's friends will have all those years to reward your disloyalty."

Pérez is shaking her head no again. "El niño va a estar bien."

Hamilton rises from her crouch. "You give me no choice, Dulcy. I'm going to take you out of here and into federal custody."

No, you're not, Malone thinks, but holds her tongue, looks over at Locke. He steps over, sits on the slab next to Pérez, and asks, "¿Alguna vez has oído hablar de un hombre llamado Quartz?"

"No. Es un nombre muy extraño."

"Agent Locke," Hamilton says. "We are trying to find a boy. Tell us what she's saying."

Locke ignores her and asks Pérez, "Nunca se ha oído hablar de Quartz?"

She shakes her head harder.

Locke looks up at Pete. "What about you? The name Quartz ring any bells?"

"Mr. Peters?"

Pete rubs his goose neck. "No," he says, then lowers himself to a knee in front of Pérez. "Dulcy, you don't want to end up in prison, do you? Isn't that why you came here in the first place, to get away from all that? Isn't that what you told me when you asked for a job?"

"Oh, she's not going to prison," Malone says. "Think about that for a second, Dulcinea. Excuse me."

Malone hurries down the corridor to where she's out of earshot. She returns the call she got earlier from Michele Higgins.

"Higgins."

"It's Malone."

"Did you find her?"

"Yes. Thanks for the tip. I know you didn't have to do that."

"What about Danny Peters?"

"So far, Pérez isn't talking. I need the name of Vend's lawyer."

"He has a lot of lawyers."

"How about one Pérez might recognize?"

"Hang on. I'll text it."

Malone waits.

"Done."

"Thank you."

"You gonna find the Peters boy?"

"I hope so."

———

As the cell door clicks shut behind her, Malone sees Locke and Hamilton having a whispered conversation against the back wall. They stop and separate, neither looking pleased.

Peters is sitting next to Pérez. His eyes are red. A snapshot rests on Pérez's knee. Malone sees it's a picture of a boy sitting on a balcony, a city skyline in the background. Maybe, finally, Peters has done something right.

"Dulcy," Malone says. "We're out of time."

Pérez looks up. She's been crying too. Malone says, "We have videotape of you picking up Danny's prescription on Tuesday."

"No," Pérez says. "You don't."

"Ah, now you speak English. Great. So you'll understand this. I was just returning a call from an attorney in Detroit." She waggles her phone in Pérez's face. "Henry Stokes. You know Mr. Stokes? He represents your old boss, Jarek Vend."

"Officer Malone, can we have a word?" It's Hamilton, with an incredulous look on her face. Behind her, Locke wears a faint, knowing smile.

"Not right now," Malone says, then addresses Pérez again. "Mr. Vend is concerned about you, Dulcinea. He doesn't want you in jail. Mr. Stokes called from Battle Creek, so he should be here soon."

"No."

"Yes. We will release you into his custody, and he can take it from there. I'm sure he and Mr. Vend will take very good care of you."

Pérez picks up the snapshot. She looks at Pete. He puts a hand on her shoulder.

"No más," she says.

"No más," Pete repeats.

"Danny is a good boy."

"What does that mean?" Malone says.

Pérez holds herself as she rocks back and forth. "He's in the house," she says.

Malone leans closer to her. "What house?"

Pérez nods at Pete. "Next door. Boarded up."

Pete sits up straight. "No way. We checked it."

"What is she talking about?" Hamilton says.

"Go ahead, Dulcy," Malone says.

It takes her a couple of minutes. As she speaks, Pete keeps saying, "Oh my God," again and again, louder and louder, while Malone thinks of the morning before, she and Will and Peters standing on the dewy lawn next to the supposedly abandoned house where Danny, poor Danny, poor autistic Danny, was probably watching them, maybe laughing to himself, the little bastard.

Malone turns and bolts the cell, rushing down the corridor. *The kid's going to pay*, she's thinking. *His mother, too, if she's in on it. Where the hell is she, anyway?*

She stops at the door to the main room, closes her eyes, steadying herself, her head spinning dizzily again as it did that afternoon she saw blessed, lovely, fragile Louisa's tiny body crushed between the pickup truck and the tree. Her cheating husband, who'd lost control of the car as Malone had given chase on those twisting two-lane roads, was unconscious behind the wheel, secured by a seat belt. Malone bent over her dead daughter, shrieking with grief that would calcify into permanent, irredeemable guilt.

"Malone." She feels Locke behind her. "You OK?"

She takes a breath, tells herself, *Do your job, Katya.*

"I'm fine."

The door opens. Radovich is standing there. "Did she give it up?" he says.

"It's the kid," Malone says. "It was him the whole time."

"What do you mean?"

"He bamboozled us."

"He frigging kidnapped himself?"

"Danny fucking Peters is in the boarded-up place next to his parents' house."

"The Helliker place? No way. We just sent fire there."

"Fire? Why?"

"That place'll be burned to the ground in ten minutes."

44

When Quartz undoes her blindfold, the first thing Carey thinks is that she has been here before.

The walls are corrugated steel, the floor concrete, the peaked ceiling high above her, the air sickly sweet with diesel. There isn't much light. She thinks she can see a stack of old tires standing in a corner. She's sitting in a metal folding chair. Duct tape fixes her ankles to the chair legs. Her wrists are handcuffed behind her. Two feet away, a phone faces her atop a tripod.

She hears the blurt of another phone's text alert, recognizes it as the burner she bought. She starts to recall what Quartz told her about Danny in the car when he appears in front of her, brandishing the phone.

"Text," he says, reading her the number. "Password?"

It comes to her. She's in a Pressman Logistics truck depot, seven or eight miles east of Bleak Harbor, one in a network that stretches from Spokane to the Twin Cities to Chicago and across Michigan to the East Coast and Canada. She came here once to pick up a package for Pressman. She had wondered why he hadn't had it delivered directly to his office, but never inquired about it.

"Undo my legs," she tells Quartz.

"The password, now, if you want to live to see your freaky genius of a son."

She had considered slapping the pistol from Quartz's hand when he had surprised her at their rendezvous on Route 23. But she knew from her time dealing with Detroit druggies that guns went off. She let Quartz lash her hands and feet with the plastic ties. He hid her car in some bushes on a dirt turnout.

"I'm losing circulation."

"Why do you have a disposable phone anyway?"

"Cops took my phone," she says.

"And who's this text from?"

"Sounds like Roland Spitler," she says. "My mother's personal assistant."

"Why would he be texting you at this hour?"

He would never be texting me, Carey thinks. Roland Spitler, pushing seventy, does not text. He calls. Sometimes he emails. He does not text. "You can find out when you undo my legs."

There was no kidnapper, Quartz told her, grinning over the front seat of his car. Danny had been hiding in the Helliker place since the day before. Watching. Eavesdropping. Manipulating. Torturing his mother and stepfather. "He ordered a pizza," Quartz said, laughing out loud. "A goddamn pizza with pineapple."

Her son. Her Danny.

"You and your hubby had no idea, huh? Right."

Carey remembers looking up at the nailed-shut attic with Pete the night before, the flaking paint, the parched odor of abandonment. Was Danny peering down at her through a crack in the ceiling? Laughing at her? Or cursing her? Was he playing, or was he punishing?

Her anger wants out. It wants to flow from her like smoking lava, to surge and burst from her veins. But where to send it? She should be angry at Quartz, at Pete, at her mother, at her late father. She should be angry at herself for not knowing what she did not know, what she should have known. She should be screaming and banging her head against the chairback, kicking her feet free, snapping her wrists from the tape, tearing Quartz to pieces. Instead she's telling herself to breathe, stay calm, listen, get away, get to Danny.

And she's thinking that Roland Spitler does not text, would not text, that's not Spitler on her phone. That's someone else.

Quartz collects the other phone from the tripod, his pale cheekbones aglow in the shadows. He puts that phone in one of his pockets and says, "I sent some nice pictures to our friend Jeremiah. A.k.a. Danny."

"What exactly do you want?"

"I want what your son wants, Carey. What he's been trying to get. I might even give you some of the money, if Danny plays."

"What are you talking about?"

"I think he'll play. Password?"

Carey thinks Danny will, too, though maybe not the way Quartz intends. She gives Quartz the password, watches him punch it in, sees his eyebrows pop up as he reads.

"So," he says, "this is a shakedown. Nice."

"What does it say?"

He leans into Carey, gloating, shaking the phone in her face. She can smell sweat, though, and it isn't hers.

"It says you have a husband with a money-losing pot shop and a nasty dealer breathing down his neck. And you, you're not going to see a cent of your daddy's money. So you get your mommy to pony up the ransom, and you bolt town. You cut in Roland, who might be the only one who can get at her money anyway—am I right? The old lady gets hurt, but so what; she's on her deathbed. And meantime, you job your fuck buddy Pressman for a few million more. Nice."

"You're delusional, Quartz."

"Call me cynical—that's how I see it. But here's what it actually says." He seems pleased with himself. "Something about a gold bird. How obvious can you get?"

It's obvious, all right, Carey thinks, *but not to you.*

"I'll bet your brother's in on it too. He's probably just as pissed off at Serenity for screwing him out of his inheritance."

"Probably."

"Danny boy is a smart kid. He just didn't figure on a smarter one showing up."

He's typing. Carey says, "What are you telling him?"

Quartz shows her:

what now?

"You know," he says, "I could blow your plan out of the water."

"But then there's Locke."

"Locke. Fuck him."

"Undo my feet, Quartz."

"What do you know about Locke, really?"

"I know he wants you." She's bluffing, a little. Guessing. "He doesn't really care about Pressman, does he? Pressman's just a way to get at you."

She hears the muffled ring of a phone. The one Quartz put in his pocket. "Quiet," he says. Carey can't tell whether he means her or the ringing. "Unknown caller," he says, then puts the phone to his ear. "Hello, Danny."

"Danny," Carey shouts, straining forward in the chair. "Honey, call the police—it'll be all right."

"Or do you prefer Jeremiah? I hope you liked those pictures."

Quartz cups the phone close and turns away. Carey hears him say, "My name is Quartz," but she can't make out what else he's saying.

She cranes forward again and shouts, "Let me talk to him. Quartz. Let me talk to my son."

He swivels back toward Carey, listening with his eyes closed, his other hand on the back of his neck. "We want the same thing, Danny," he says. "No, I can't—" A pause. Quartz's eyes open. "I—Daniel." Another pause, then he lowers the phone from his ear and stares at it, looking surprised, even embarrassed. He drops the phone to his side.

"He's telling you what you're going to do, isn't he?" Carey says. "Danny can be pushy."

Quartz shakes his head. "We'll see about that."

"You're no longer in charge, Quartz."

Carey recalls the hot afternoon on the sidewalk outside the Mexican place. Jeremiah—Danny—texted her then. He knew where she was. Or at least where her phone was.

"Danny knew I went to Valparaiso, Quartz," she says. "He tracked my phone."

"He can't track your burner, even if he knows the number."

"You can take a chance on that, Quartz," she says, bluffing. "But I'm telling you he knows where we are. Why don't you just let me go, and you can get out before Locke and the cops show up? Danny's probably telling them this minute."

Quartz is shaking his head. "No, he's not. That would mess up his plan." The phone beeps. He looks at it, holds it up for Carey. "What does this mean?"

The text says, proceed to the wedge of space.

It takes Carey a second. But it fits with the gold bird, from the poem. "The mansion," she says. "My mother's place."

"It's called 'the wedge of space'?"

"It's a joke."

"A joke? Your son wants us to go there."

"Why would he want that?"

"Maybe he's cutting me in on your not-so-little scam."

"I guess we should go then."

"I'm a sitting duck there, and you know it."

"Actually, no. Real cops haven't been allowed near the mansion in years. They won't even know you're there."

Quartz stares at the floor, considering.

"Tell me, Quartz," Carey says. "If you're so good with computers, why don't you just hack into Pressman's bank accounts? He has way more money than Serenity."

"Maybe I don't want to die."

"Good luck with that. Maybe Danny's the smarter kid here, huh?"

Quartz steps over and leans his face close to Carey's. Again she smells his sweat. He's afraid of something. He says, "Did I not find your son?"

"I don't know. Could be he found you."

Quartz steps back, reaches into one of his pockets, and produces the pistol. "Now we're all in this together. See?" Then he stows the gun, digs in another pocket, shows Carey a box-cutting knife.

"What the fuck?" she says.

"Relax. You're still going to get your money, and you're still going to screw your boss over. Isn't that what you wanted?"

"I want my son back."

"Right." Quartz squats and takes the box cutter to the duct tape on Carey's ankles. "You're going to take me to the wedge of space."

45

Michele Higgins tastes soot on the back of her tongue. The heat stings her cheeks and knuckles and nostrils. She has watched houses burn before while waiting for the smoldering corpses to be hauled out. She wishes she wasn't so accustomed to it.

"Malone," she says.

The officer is crouched on the lawn of the Helliker place, shielding her face with a hand as she squints at the flaming bones of the house. The firefighters appear to have kept it from spreading to the Peters cottage next door. Next to her a man Michele doesn't recognize stands holding a kerchief over his nose. He's wearing those clunky black shoes that detectives wear. Maybe FBI.

The second floor of the house has collapsed into the first, which convulses with coal-black billows and intermittent plumes of flame. Serpents of smoke slither up the surface of the security fence alongside the house. Silver spews of fire-truck water arc through the camera lights. The TV trucks rolled up a few minutes after Michele arrived, male anchors crouching into side-view mirrors to shape their gelled hair.

"Malone," Michele says again, louder, as she steps closer, waving her phone. "You need to see this."

The man turns and motions Michele away with his kerchief. "Police scene. You'll have to move back."

"Who are you?" Michele says.

"Move back now, please."

Malone turns and touches the man's elbow. "It's all right," she says. "Agent Locke, this is Michele Higgins, with the local paper. She helped us with Pérez."

"I'm sorry, Katya. I don't think we need—"

"Are you looking for someone named Quartz? Or something like that?" Michele says. Locke's face changes. "If so, you need to listen to this."

"Let me see," Malone says.

"Officer, can you tell us what's going on?" The voice comes from behind Michele's shoulder. She turns to see a TV reporter and a put-out-looking cameraman standing next to her.

"Move back to the road now," Malone tells them.

The reporter, a tall redhead named Portia something, says, "What about her? She shouldn't get—"

"Move now, or you're going to jail."

Portia gives Michele a look as she and her cameraman retreat. Michele doesn't care.

"What do you have there?" Locke says.

Michele taps her phone and waits for the *Light* mobile app to display the front page. Locke reaches for the phone; Michele yanks it away. "Hold on," she says. "Here."

She punches a headline that reads, "Festival Weathers Minor Glitches for Opening Day Success," and hands the phone to Malone. The headline gives way to a miniature video screen. A tiny dot at the bottom of the screen begins to slide to the right along a timing bar.

"I don't see anything," Malone says.

"It's audio. Listen."

An oscillating schematic in the middle of the screen comes to life with the echo of a man's voice:

Hello, Danny. Or do you prefer Jeremiah?

And then:

My name is Quartz.

A woman's voice in the background:

Let me talk to my son.

Michele watches Malone and Locke listen. She has listened to the two-minute-eight-second recording half a dozen times since it appeared in her email an hour ago.

A man who calls himself Quartz is speaking with what sounds like a boy, apparently over a phone. Quartz wants something and seems to think he has leverage. The boy, who doesn't seem at all fazed, hangs up on him.

"That's Danny Peters," Malone says.

"Play it again," Locke says.

"Wait," Michele says. "Danny's coming on again."

After a short silence, Danny's voice returns, clearer now, as if he's speaking directly into a recording device. "The festival is on," he says. "The dragonfly lives."

"What does that mean?"

The schematic melts away. A silhouette materializes in pale gray against a black background. As the gray gradually brightens to pink, Michele sees the shape she saw each morning hovering over downtown Bleak Harbor as she parked in front of the *Light*.

"Looks like the Bleak Mansion, doesn't it?" she says.

"What are you saying? Danny is there? Why aren't you there if you think he is?"

"Maybe I went. Maybe the gates were locked and the house was dark, so I gave up and went looking for you."

The screen goes blank again. Malone looks at Locke, then back at Michele. "Danny put that there?"

"Yeah. Like he put that old story on the page today."

"Like he fooled us with his meds," Malone says. "The kid's just been toying with us."

"Quartz too, it appears," Locke says. "The young man is not to be toyed with."

"That was Quartz's voice?" Malone asks Locke. "You sure?"

"I'm sure."

"Who is this Quartz?" Michele says.

Malone is on her phone ordering a roadblock on the road to the Bleak Mansion. Locke says, "Not his real name. He's wanted by the FBI on separate matters."

"And you're FBI?"

"I am." Locke nods past Michele. "And so is she."

Michele looks left and sees a woman trotting toward them.

"Let's get out of here, Malone," Locke says.

"I want to ride with you," Michele says.

"Not happening," Malone says. "But do us a favor. See this woman coming up the road with Chief? She's an FBI agent, and she's a bitch. Occupy her for a minute. You'll be the first reporter I call when I know what's what." She grabs Locke by the arm. "Let's get to the house."

———

Michele watches Malone gun the cruiser past the approaching FBI agent, who's waving her arms at them and yelling while the chief watches.

"Agent?" Michele says, waving a notebook at her. "Can I ask a few questions?"

Hamilton points back at Malone's cruiser receding around the bend. "Where are they going?"

"No clue."

"Get out of my way."

The clamor of the firefighters comes back to Michele as she walks around the TV trucks toward her car. She hears the crash of the cascading water, the boom and crack of the fire.

For some reason, she doubts Danny is at Serenity Meredith Maas Bleak's mansion. She doubts he's even in Bleak Harbor. She pictures again the lithe boy in her binoculars, swatting at the air from the end of his dock, so alone and so—no, not helpless, not helpless at all.

Hearing a TV reporter calling out for her, Michele walks faster. She feels everything falling away behind her—the dying house, the taped-off one next door, the cops and firefighters, the Peters family, the boy, the bay, Bleak Harbor.

Maybe Danny is safe now. Maybe he is in danger. He may be brilliant, he may be deranged, but he's responsible now for whatever happens to him.

Inside her car she takes her phone back out and calls up her email. The screen fills with the email with the link to the audio posted on the *Light* website. "You should look at this" was all the unknown sender had written.

Beneath that was a separate email that had been forwarded from Carey Peters's email at Pressman Logistics to her personal Gmail account and apparently purloined by whomever had sent it to Michele. Attached to it were eight PDFs. Michele had opened three. They appeared to be copies of bills of lading from Pressman Logistics. There were references to catalytic converters, lists of some large dollar figures, and stamps etched with what looked like Asian characters.

Michele doesn't know what it all means, but she plans to find out. Whatever it is, she figures it probably isn't good for the billionaire Pressman. But it might be good for what remains of her career.

As she pulls off the shoulder, she takes a last look at the Helliker place in her rearview mirror. It's almost gone. She steers toward town, slowing at the fork where the two-lane veers south toward the interstate and Chicago. She imagines that repairman, the Grasshopper, probably sipping from a Solo cup in the beer tent at this very moment, waiting for her. She smiles.

A canopy of trees shrouds the road to Bleak Harbor in darkness. Michele starts to take the right, then swerves left and punches the accelerator hard toward the freeway and Chicago.

46

The surface of the bay flashes and throbs with the glittery reflections of the festival rides. Beyond the town, security lamps bathe the Bleak Mansion turrets in a pinkish glow.

"My grandmother is in that tower," Danny says, pointing. "She is sedated, asleep. I locked her door so she can't get out and nobody can get in. The rest will be in the turret on the opposite side."

"Serenity's a little nuts, isn't she?" Boz says.

"Are you still holding a grudge about her interfering with your liquor license?"

"How do you—never mind."

"Actually, Mr. Flanagan, she is brilliant, in her way."

Danny sits at a high top at Boz's Bayfront Bar and Grill, Boz standing at his shoulder, both of them peering across the bay through the one window on which the blinds aren't drawn. Lifesaver rings festooned with the USS *Boz* and other fake boat names hang from the knotty pine paneling above their heads.

A laptop is open on the table in front of Danny. It's the one he took with him to the Helliker attic. The screen presents a checkerboard of static black-and-white images:

Two high-ceilinged corridors leading from opposite directions to a downward staircase. A wingback chair set on a platform in a circular room. A kitchen with an empty fireplace. A dock extending from a boathouse on the Lake Michigan shore. A brick plaza sloping down to twin iron gates. An upward swoop in a two-lane road. Another gate crossing that road, blocked by police cars, lights flashing, officers pacing.

"You're in her security system?" Boz says.

Danny doesn't reply.

"I suppose you spent some time in that place."

"I can count the times on one hand."

"She is your grandmother, right?"

Danny recalls one of his earliest memories. He was sitting on the floor in a room with ceilings that stretched far over his head. A man the adults referred to as Mr. Spitler crouched before him, offering a spatula. There were no real toys at the mansion; spatulas and whisks were the main entertainments. "Grandma?" Danny said to the man, who shook his head. "Grandma is tired," the man said. "She is very tired."

"Technically," Danny tells Boz, "she is my grandmother. But she is too inebriated and too wounded and too alone to be much of anything to anyone. Unfortunately."

"Like I said, nuts—whoa, what the hell's that?"

Danny clicks on one of the image boxes. It expands to fill the screen. Two shadows inch along the boathouse deck, each with an arm extended frontward.

"Those guys got guns," Boz says.

"My mother's boss sent them."

"Sent them for what?"

"For someone he no longer needs."

"This was supposed to go down without any trouble."

"There will be no trouble for you, Mr. Flanagan."

"I thought that damn fire was gonna burn down this whole side of the lake."

"You will have your money. You can go wherever you like. You can buy yourself a nice new boat."

Boz points at the screen. "They don't look like good guys."

"They are not my concern or yours." This is partly an untruth, but Danny can't have Boz losing faith at this juncture. "My mother should be gone by the time they do anything."

"How did they even know to go there?"

Danny taps a finger on one of the three disposable phones resting next to his laptop. "My mother's boss knows."

"You told him?"

Yes, Danny thinks, *but Pressman has no idea.* Nor does he suspect how badly this will go for him. Danny doesn't tell Boz any of this, instead asking, "What did you do with the title?"

"The title?"

"The title to the boat."

"Ah, right. I put it in the name of my asshole ex-sergeant."

"And where is he?"

"Retired in northern Minnesota, last I heard."

"So by the time the police locate the title, then locate him, you will be long gone."

"Let's hope. Shitbags, kid."

"Everything is under control. You should get yourself a drink."

"Good idea."

"Could I please have a Coke too? Without a cherry, thanks."

Danny closes his eyes and listens as Boz walks away, his bottle-shaped body and bullet-shot leg syncopating the rhythm of his steps.

———

"What happened to your leg?"

Danny posed the question to Boz Flanagan on a May afternoon. They were standing on the beach deck outside Boz's bar. The sky was dull with prickly gray mist. Danny had taken to stopping at Boz's on afternoons when Pete was peddling pot and his mother was away. Now he intended to persuade the white-haired man to participate in his birthday plan.

Boz looked down at his leg self-consciously. "Why?" he said, looking back up with a grin. "Does it show?"

"You walk funny."

Danny knew he could say this without offending. His condition gave him a tacit license to say almost anything to people who might in fact be offended but would be too filled with pity to respond with anything but that.

"All barkeeps walk funny, son."

"Pete said someone shot you with a gun."

"Uh-huh. You want to come in where it's dry?"

Danny had gone inside and taken a stool at a high-top table along the windows facing the beach. He noticed the Bleak Mansion across the stirred-up bay, framed in one of the knotty pine rectangles. Behind him a mop leaned against the bar into an aluminum bucket. Danny smelled soap and old beer. He scanned the back of the bar, three TVs hung around a pair of ceramic starfish. One TV was tuned without sound to *Jeopardy!*

Boz brought him a glass of 7UP with crushed ice and a maraschino cherry. He set a plastic sport bottle on the high top and sat across from Danny.

"So what did your old man tell you?"

Danny plucked the cherry from the glass and dangled it in front of his face before setting it on the table. "He said you were off duty. You intervened in a fight at a bar."

"Something like that," Boz said. "That's pretty much it."

"Actually, no."

"No?"

"Pete didn't tell me. He didn't know. I know."

"You know what, kid?"

"I know you were undercover, not off duty. I know about the man you shot in the back." Danny patted the back of his left shoulder. "I know about the department investigation. I know you didn't really need or want to retire. I know your superiors didn't back you up."

Boz had been a cop for too long to show surprise. But the grin he offered Danny then wasn't its usual shape. "That's some juicy stuff, kid. You make that up all by yourself?"

As Boz spoke, he tapped the bottom of his cup on the tabletop.

"I can print out the file and bring it to you."

"What file?"

"Your file. Robert John Flanagan Jr., CPD02-126674D."

Boz took a drink, then swished his cup around, trying to look undisturbed. "How could some kid get a file?"

"Computer. It's not that hard if you know what you're doing."

"Shitbags," he said. "Gonna get a refill."

Boz went behind the bar. Danny looked across the bay. The mist shrouded the mansion's pink turrets. Danny imagined his grandmother sitting at one of the windows, looking across the water at him without knowing it.

Boz came back with his cup. "Computers, huh? That one of your, like, you know, things?"

Danny knew he meant obsessions. "Computers are useful," he said. "I like dragonflies better."

They sat in silence for a moment, Boz staring at his hands folded around his cup. Then he looked up and said, "That guy was a gang-banger, you know."

"OK."

"They paid that scumbag's family ten times what they paid me when they kicked me out the door."

"Yes."

"And, by the way, he wasn't 'running away,'" Boz said, curling his forefingers to signify quotation marks. "He was chasing another guy he was going to shoot through the fucking head."

"I did not see that in the file."

"Ha, fuck no, you didn't. They're not that stupid."

"No."

"So." Boz pointed a finger at Danny. "Now you know it all."

"I can help you, Mr. Flanagan."

"Too late for that, kid."

"You hate this place, and you want to get out, go spend your days fishing somewhere sunny."

"That wouldn't suck."

"I can help."

"You know what, Danny? You are full of surprises."

"For someone like me."

"For—yeah, exactly. You said it."

Danny got out of his chair. He said, "Be sure to look at your bank account first thing in the morning. You will see a deposit for three hundred ninety-eight dollars and eighty-two cents from this afternoon."

"What are you talking about?"

"It's actually a transfer, executed"—Danny looked at the time on his phone—"one hour and nine minutes ago, from the Chicago Police Pension Fund."

"Kid."

"Computers."

"You can't be serious."

Danny picked up the cherry, put it in a pocket. "Thanks," he said. "I better get going before Pete gets here."

"You're going to get me in trouble."

"Nobody will be able to trace it until you're long gone." Danny had the door to the deck open, the breeze damp on his cheek. "I told you I want to help you."

"What does that mean? How?"

The door slapped shut behind him. Danny heard it squeak open as he stepped onto the beach.

"Danny," Boz called out. "What was that number again?"

Danny smiled. "Three-nine-eight-dot-eight-two."

"My address here?"

"We will talk."

———

Danny hears Boz clumping back to the table as he clicks into the grid on his laptop screen, maximizes another image box. It shows a small table set up in the circular room. Spitler has adjusted the security camera as Danny had instructed.

On the table stands a desktop computer, wires winding away from it across the floor. Spitler crosses in front of the table, then stops and gestures as Danny's mother and a scrawny man with a hand in one of his many jacket pockets move into the view, their backs to Danny.

"That's your mom, ain't it?" Boz says.

"Please do not transfer the bar over to Pete for a few weeks. Wait for this to run its course."

"I didn't like turning him in, kid."

"This place will be perfect for him." Danny almost smiles at the thought. "And I couldn't just leave him nothing."

"What's your mother going to think?"

"She has nothing to do with Pete."

Boz looks confused. "Don't you want to get them back together?"

"They were never apart."

Danny clicks his mouse, and the matrix of images reappears. He sees an apparent commotion involving Pete, Uncle Jonah, and some police officers at the entrance to the mansion road. Pete is pointing up the road and shouting at a cop who's trying to calm him.

In another square, Danny sees the two dark men inching down a second-floor corridor. He will manipulate door locks to direct them where he wants them when he wants them there. In another square, he sees the police officer, Malone, who'd come to his parents' house that morning after he disappeared. She's scaling one of the twin gates at the mansion entrance with a boost from a man wearing a jacket and slacks, no uniform.

Danny hits a combination of keys. The gate slowly opens. Malone climbs down.

"I assume you think this is about love," Danny tells Boz as he manipulates his mouse to zoom in on the face of the man with Malone. "Like all of this is going to make my parents realize how much they really love each other?"

"What's wrong with that, kid?"

"Nothing is about love."

"Nothing but money, eh? That's it?"

Danny zooms out from the man's face and punches a name into Google. It pops up on the LinkedIn page Danny had seen two weeks before: Allen P. Locke, special agent, FBI, Indianapolis. George Washington University.

Danny doesn't understand why this man would be here. But it doesn't matter now. *Calm*, Danny thinks. He picks up a phone and hits a single number followed by the pound sign. On the laptop, he sees Roland Spitler touch a finger to his left ear.

"Mr. Spitler."

Serenity Bleak's aide turns away from the others. "Yes."

"This function is going to be a bit bigger than we expected."

Spitler's words come in a harsh whisper. "Who is this man? Did you send this man here?"

"Quartz is going to help us."

"He has a gun, Daniel. This was not part of the bargain."

"He will not affect your cut."

"That has nothing to do with it. He kidnapped your mother and brought her here."

"She belongs there. You need to proceed with the plan, Mr. Spitler."

"We are in danger."

"I am prepared for everything. Remember, on my signal, direct my mother, get her out of there."

Spitler lets out a long breath. "Daniel."

"Or you can wait around and take your chances. I do not see them working in your favor."

Danny puts the phone down. Boz is rapping his cup on the table again. "Kid, what the hell you got me into?"

"Have you checked the account I set up for you?"

"Yeah, saw it." He gulps from his cup. "A hundred large. Jesus."

"With more to come. Just do your job, Mr. Flanagan, and everything will be all right."

"Someone's gonna catch me. You should have left me the speedboat."

"You will be better off in the fishing boat. No one will suspect anything. I programmed the locations into your phone."

"You got focus, kid. Pete had a word for it. Brain-blindness?"

"Mind-blindness," Danny says.

"Doesn't sound so good."

"Most people have blindness, period."

Boz points at the laptop screen. "Who's that guy?"

"It doesn't matter."

Danny looks out the window at the mansion. Today he will be sixteen years old. Danny has never cared much for birthdays, the song as inane as a revolving door, the pointless gifts, all the pretending that a particular day had more meaning than another. Although his uncle Jonah did give him the Wallace Stevens collection for his twelfth birthday—he was glad of that. Sometimes he wished he could remain one age forever. It would simplify things. It wouldn't even matter what age it was. Eighty-seven, sixty-four, forty-two, twenty-eight. Just one, all the time. Fifteen, sixteen. Any one.

But the moment of his birthday—his birthdate—was useful in his current endeavor. He had known it would engage his mother's emotions. He had known it would make the ruse believable, had known Pete would go for it, the police would go for it, everybody he needed to believe would believe. And they did.

His plan is going as he had plotted it in his head. Except for Dulcy's arrest; she was supposed to collect Danny's mother in Boz's speedboat. Dulcy: her eyes glittering onyx marbles until she closed them hard and leaned back and away from him, gasping, begging him in words he did not understand.

Danny will not see her again.

Then there are the dark men. And Malone and Locke. Danny had anticipated there would be complications. He was prepared to deal with them. *Mother will be fine*, he tells himself, steadying his breathing, instructing his heartbeat to slow. He had not expected a complication quite like Quartz, though Quartz could actually be useful.

"Quartz," Danny tells Boz, "is me."

"Meaning what? He's autistic?"

He feels Boz's breath on his neck, sees the fear on his face reflected in the laptop screen. He says, "I am not autism."

"Uh-huh. Kid, you got two bad guys with guns in the same house as your mom and grandma. What are you gonna do?"

Danny refocuses on the computer screen. "This is not your concern, Mr. Flanagan. You should get going."

Boz is looking around, rubbing his arms, more nervous by the second. "What about the storm?"

"That doesn't hit until midafternoon. You'll be safe by then. Your money will be safe."

"That's what it's about, huh?"

"On the other hand, if you renege on me, the money will evaporate, and the police will know all about you within one minute."

"I can't believe a damn kid is threatening me."

"You wanted out of Bleak Harbor. You wanted to sell your bar. It is sold. You are leaving. So leave."

Danny moves his mouse, and the gate that opened for Malone and the man with her swings shut. They're now crouched in the shadows of the mansion's enormous front vestibule, a spiral staircase before them. Danny has trapped the two dark men on a different stairway between the second and third floors.

Danny punches up Malone's cell number on his phone. After seeing her in his parents' yard, he'd copied her number from a supposedly private directory in the city computer system. He sends her a text:

house mine. follow me

He watches Malone squint into her phone before she shows the text to the man, who nods in apparent recognition. They both look around as if the texter might suddenly materialize out of the shadows. Danny texts again:

elevator in kitchen behind stairway. go. 4

Malone reads it, starts typing, shows the man. A text appears on Danny's phone:

Who are you?

Danny smiles as he texts:

jeremiah

He watches Malone and the man step alongside the staircase and vanish into the shadows behind it.

Danny adjusts the small video cam attached to the top of his laptop screen so that it points up at his face. He needs to focus. He needs Boz gone.

"Why aren't you up there, kid?"

"I am where I always am. Go now."

"What if I need to contact you?"

"You won't. Leave now. My mother will be waiting."

Danny watches Boz walk outside past the spot where he used to set out a bowl of water for Paddle.

He climbs into his fishing boat and yanks the cord on the outboard motor, once, twice, before it splutters to life. The boat chugs away toward the channel, Boz looking around anxiously as he vanishes in the gloom.

Danny checks the time: 10:54. Fifty-two minutes to go.

47

Carey gasps.

"Danny, my God, Danny."

Danny's face fills the desktop screen on the table where Spitler sits, his eyes peering downward, curls falling along his ears, the bruise on his cheek gone.

Carey leans over Spitler's shoulder as if she could gather her son out of the screen into her arms. "Danny, can you hear me?" she says. "Are you all right?"

"I can hear you." His voice issues from speakers on the desktop. "I am perfectly fine."

The background behind Danny is a blur of chalky white that Carey doesn't recognize, something shaped like a star beyond his left ear. "Where are you?" she says. "I thought you were coming here."

"Everything is going to be fine if we move quickly. Mr. Spitler?"

"Yes."

"Mr. Quartz, are you ready? Mother, you need to stand aside."

———

The kid's not here.

A hot flush of foolishness washes over Quartz. Danny is not here, in this room, in this house. Quartz looks around, his neck muscles taut and cracking as he turns. He shouldn't be in this room, in this town, with these people. He should be gone. He should be in his car racing the back roads up Michigan's little finger, across the big bridge and around the peninsula to Sault Sainte Marie.

Quartz really hadn't wanted all that much. Just enough to escape to somewhere warm and bright and green and far away. Somewhere nobody could find him—not Locke, not Pressman, not anyone. After two years, he'd had enough of running, had enough of serving vile masters like Pressman. He would be perfect alone.

Now there's a text on his phone. From Pressman:

U are dead Q

Quartz could have escaped with the $2 million in ransom. But then there was Jeremiah, there was Danny, the brilliant boy with the brilliant plan, the plan so impossible and diabolical that it was truly beautiful to someone like Quartz, who was, he had thought, not all that different from the boy.

But Danny is not here. He's an image on a computer screen, averting his eyes.

"Where are you, Danny?"

"I am where I belong, Mr. Spitler."

The room isn't quite dark, the window shades drawn. The smell of stale cigarette smoke is choking. Quartz doesn't like the decisions he's made in the last hour. He looks over at Carey, watches her watching him. She's breathing hard. He takes out his pistol.

"Put it away, Quartz," she says.

She punched him hard in the chest when they got out of the car at the iron gates outside. He had let her. Now he's wondering if she knew that her son would not be here.

"Where is he?" he says. "You lied to me."

"No." She turns to the screen. "Danny?"

"We have work to do, Mr. Quartz. And we don't have much time. It is in your interest to cooperate."

"You know, I could walk out of here now."

"No, you couldn't. Mr. Spitler, please let Mr. Quartz take your chair, and stand by. We are going to move some money around."

Spitler stands. Quartz sits and stares into the screen, into Danny's face. The boy's eyes are fixed downward. He's busy with something. *This kid*, he thinks. *What if the spooks at NSA knew about him?* Quartz hitches his chair forward, sets a hand on the mouse. *Maybe they will someday.*

———

Danny watches Quartz's eyes dart about. He knows the feeling. Every few seconds, he feels his hamstrings quivering against the chair seat. *Calm*, he tells himself.

On the checkerboard screen, the dark men, their faces shrouded in hoods, glide down a third-floor corridor to a door Danny has locked. He holds his breath as one of them slams a shoulder into the door, to no apparent effect. The other points his handgun at the doorknob, but the first one touches his arm, shaking his head.

Danny had not expected that someone might shoot out the locks.

Malone and Locke are in the elevator. Danny told them to go to 4 but then stopped it between 2 and 3. She texted him a moment ago: get us out now more police coming. She's talking on her phone now, and Locke looks like he's trying to jimmy the elevator doors. Danny hits some keys. Malone and Locke back away as the elevator rises to 3 and stops. Danny releases the doors and texts Malone:

follow corridor to stairway.

He cannot let them get to the turret room before the job is done. Same for the dark men.

Danny has never been in the turret. Spitler had provided him with a hand-drawn map indicating the location of the hidden wall panel that opens to a staircase spiraling down to the tunnels that once facilitated Jack Bleak's trysts. Danny uses his mouse to swivel a camera, scanning the room until he sees the spot that Spitler marked on his map.

He looks up from his laptop toward town. Between the shadow shapes of buildings, he sees the flash of police vehicles and ambulances speeding toward the mansion road. He hears the church bells clanging. He closes his eyes and thinks of Jeremiah flailing in the churning lake, the burn and resignation in his lungs as the water rushed in to devour him. He imagines the docile silver perch spinning and rising as they passed Jeremiah, both going to their deaths.

An overhead camera in the turret room captures his mother's face. Weariness pinches her eyes, sags her cheeks. Danny knows the look too well. He has seen it as she waits in doctors' offices, as she walks into the house after another three days in Chicago, as she sets her phone aside after an abortive conversation with her mother, as she listens to Pete expostulate after his fifth beer about expanding his marijuana business, as she toils on her laptop while the eleven o'clock news plays on the great-room TV, as she leans on a deck railing with a gin-and-tonic tumbler, staring at a sunset, dreading the next morning.

Danny has seen enough.

Soon this will all be over, he thinks. *Soon you will be saved. We will all be saved.*

———

Frozen behind Spitler and Quartz, Carey watches the downcast eyes of the boy on the computer screen. She doesn't know him. Not this boy, with his face bent to his mysterious task, issuing his blunt orders to Quartz.

But Danny knows her. Or at least knows her in ways Carey never would have wanted. He has prowled inside her email, her phone, her texts, her online explorations of new places to live. He knows about her fantasy of escaping from Pete and her revenge plot against Pressman.

She steps backward to a window and eases the shade over an inch. Downtown Bleak Harbor is ablaze now with the lights of what seems like a hundred police cars. Blockades are set up at both intersections leading to the interstate. Clusters of townspeople and tourists line the mansion road up to the point where the police have obstructed it. Carey sees Jonah and Pete standing in the road, looking helpless.

She lets the shade go. There will be no escaping. For anyone. Even Danny. He can't have gone far. The police will find him. And then what? Interrogations? Charges? A trial? Danny walking with a lawyer through a phalanx of shouting citizens and reporters? His face on TV screens and front pages of newspapers? She would have thought a few days ago that any of that would be too much for her Danny. But now, she has no idea.

An image appears, unbidden, in her mind. Danny is sitting at a table with her and Pete on a Saturday morning at the Palace Grill near their Chicago condo. The owner, a large, smiling man named George, is telling Pete a groaner of a joke. George always stopped at their table to say hello, and Danny liked him enough that he broke his daily CoCo Wheats routine to have blueberry pancakes and sausage. On this morning, while Pete laughs at George's joke, Carey reaches across the table and touches her son's free hand. He doesn't stop eating, doesn't even look up from his plate, but he doesn't pull his hand away—he lets Carey take it in her fingers and squeeze.

If only, she thinks now, *we could just go back and—*

"We have four accounts to access."

It's Danny voice, behind her, louder than before. Quartz must have turned up the speaker volume. Carey lets the shade go and walks back to the table, positioning herself just behind Quartz, where she can keep watch on the doors at either end of the room.

"Mr. Spitler has installed the correct links and software you will need," Danny is saying. "I have the passcodes. Mr. Spitler will provide his thumbprint."

"Really?" Quartz says.

"My grandmother signed over her power of attorney five months ago. The accounts held quite a bit more money then, didn't they, Mr. Spitler?"

"Roland," Carey says. "You stole from my mother?"

If Spitler regrets this, he doesn't show it. "Forgive me, Miss Carey," he says, "but I don't recall you or your brother ever being around to mop up her vomit."

"Mr. Quartz, do you see the icon in the top-right corner of your screen?"

"BCBT? Bleak County Bank & Trust?" Quartz says, recalling how the mystery hacker—Danny—invaded the bank's servers.

"Click on it, please."

"Why?"

"Proceed, Mr. Quartz. Our visitors will be arriving very soon."

"Danny, hurry," Carey says.

Quartz clicks on the icon, and a window filled with a list of twelve-digit numbers materializes. "We're going to access all of these?"

"No, just the first, the fourth, the tenth, and the thirteenth."

"Because?"

"Because I said so, Mr. Quartz."

Quartz clicks on the first number. "It wants a thumbprint," he says.

"Mr. Spitler."

Spitler leans over and presses his left thumb onto a small biometric pad. The computer screen fills with columns of numbers blinking in green on black.

"Damn," Quartz says. "One hundred eighteen million? And there was more?"

"There is more. Deploy the software."

"This isn't going to work," Quartz says. "The bank's gonna notice if you start moving big sums of cash around."

"I have accounted for that," Danny says.

"Really? OK. So mine is here?"

"Your share? Do not worry. You will get yours, Mr. Quartz."

Quartz sits back from the table. "How much?"

"How much do you get? Let me think." Danny pauses. "One million, one hundred eleven thousand. Deploy, please."

"Why that number?"

Carey leans forward and slaps Quartz across the back of his head, shouting, "Do what he says, goddamn it." Quartz comes halfway out of his chair, but Spitler grabs him by a jacket pocket and shoves him back down.

"I don't have to fucking do this," Quartz says.

"Look at this, Mr. Quartz." Danny's face disappears from the screen and is replaced by a view from a camera of two dark men edging along a corridor wall. "Do they look familiar?"

"My God," Carey says. "They're in the house? Now?"

"Near the guest rooms in the south turret," Spitler says. "One floor below us."

"Fuck me."

"That is a perceptive analysis, Mr. Quartz," Danny says as he switches the image off. "I suggest you proceed if you want to leave that room alive."

48

"Now what?"

Malone and Locke crouch in darkness, weapons out, heads swiveling, at the top of the stairway to the fourth floor. A series of texts signed *jeremiah* guided them here. Malone suspects the corridor extending to her right leads to the turret they saw from the ground with the two dimly lit windows.

"The kid say anything else?" Locke says.

Past Locke through the windows on the front of the mansion, Malone sees fire trucks blinking at the Helliker ruins. "Goddamn it," she says.

"What?"

"He better be here."

"The boy? Where else would he be?"

"I don't—never mind." Malone peers into the corridor blackness, looking for a door. "Gonna call Chief."

"For what?"

She ignores Locke, dials Radovich. "We're on the top floor," she tells him. "It's dead quiet, no sign of anyone."

"You shouldn't have gone up yourself, Katya."

"Well, we're here now." Her phone beeps. "Hang on," she says, clicking on the new text from Jeremiah:

two men armed and dangerous in the house

She raises the phone briefly so Locke can read it, sees the glow of the text reflected in the lenses of his askew spectacles. "That's not good," he says.

Malone returns to Radovich. "Just got a new text from the kid. He says some bad guys are here somewhere."

"This is why—never mind. Just stay where you are then. I got backup coming, along with the FBI guys."

"Ten-four."

Another text beeps in.

"Just stay there, Malone. Hear me?"

She hangs up and reads the new text. "The kid says the door we want is down this hallway to the right. Chief said to wait."

"I don't like this."

"What?"

Locke is looking up and down the corridor, checking the ceiling, glancing back down the stairs. "Gonna wager those are the guys who killed Bledsoe," he says. "They don't work for a drug dealer. They work for Pressman."

"How do you know?"

"I know." Locke cranes his neck to squint around her at the corridor. "Setting aside their identical outfits, just make the connections: Quartz, who works for Pressman, all of a sudden has Carey Peters. I'm thinking Bledsoe was supposed to grab the boy, but he screwed it up."

"And you don't want those guys to get to Quartz before you, do you?" Malone takes a step back, reassessing Locke. "You don't give a shit about Danny or his mom. You're not here for them. You're here for Quartz."

Malone knew it before but didn't want to believe it. In her mind she sees her ex's lying face again, its smirk of willful ignorance, the wandering eye she once thought sexy.

"We're in this together, Katya. If you're right and the kid's not here, then he might be OK, but we've gotta get his mom out."

"You know, Locke, I can't explain why fucked-up people do the fucked-up things they do."

He gives her a sideways what-the-hell-does-that-mean look as he moves into the hallway and crosses to the far wall.

"You coming or not?"

"I'm here for the boy, Locke—got it?"

She turns then and bolts down the dark hallway, raising one leg high as if to kick in the door.

49

Danny watches Malone assault the door, sees her stumble backward, almost topple over.

He sucks a breath through his teeth and looks away from the laptop screen. He makes himself imagine Paddle asleep in his lap at the end of the dock, the dachshund's ear silky between his forefinger and thumb. Sometimes Paddle would snore, and then Danny knew the dog was happy. Danny was happy too.

Calm. Every ninety-third target evades the dragonfly, he reminds himself. *Only by luck: A sudden gust. Another blind, stupid bug disrupting the vector. And only every ninety-third.*

Calm.

He spent the last day and a half preparing for this, breathing mildew and seagull-poop fumes in the muggy rot of the Helliker attic, his fingers pink with cracking, wishing he had thought to order some Vaseline Intensive Care lotion, wishing he had had just a little more time, wishing Paddle would come trotting down the beach, ears flapping, snout swaying like a metronome over the sand.

Paddle never came, of course.

That drizzly spring afternoon on which Danny and Dulcinea had stumbled onto Spitler's ham-handed manipulations of Serenity's funds was one of the few happy moments Danny could recall from the days of Paddle's final sufferings. Dulcinea had wriggled out of her jeans and sat smiling on the edge of Danny's bed, beckoning him. "OK," Danny had said. "I guess that would be all right."

And it was.

Once Danny had hatched his plan and blackmailed—or, alternatively, incentivized—Spitler into cooperating, he could have simply used Spitler's credit card to buy the stand-in laptop and the extra prescription meds. But it was so much more amusing to tap into the City of Bleak Harbor's budget just as the bureaucrats and elected buffoons were plotting how to squander Serenity's gift.

Working overnight in the Helliker attic, Danny used his laptop and a batch of code improvised by Dulcinea to create a daisy chain of automatic bank transfers that would propel digital cash from account to account, each account accepting a fraction of the fortune that Serenity Meredith Maas Bleak had inherited and that her faithful servant Roland Spitler had tried, at least in part, to appropriate for himself. Danny scheduled the transfers, each different by a few cents, so that they would be staggered over the course of several weeks, preventing anyone from noticing how the four accounts he'd selected were slowly being drained. When the operation was complete, each account—he would leave Serenity plenty in the other accounts—would be left with a balance of $5,145, to match the date of the drowning of Jeremiah Estes Bleak.

Danny wishes he could sit in Quartz's chair to watch up close the shrinking sums flitting from one account to the next to the next like so many dragonflies darting from one unsuspecting mosquito to a hapless moth to an ignorant, fluttering butterfly. But he is where he belongs, at a distance. He had needed Mr. Spitler's thumbprint. Having the able Mr. Quartz to work the keyboard was fortuitous, although he might soon have to confront the ruthless men his employer had dispatched.

Quartz is nearly finished emptying the third of the four accounts when Danny switches back to the checkerboard screen on his laptop and sees that one of the squares—the one where he last saw the two men—has gone blank. Either the camera malfunctioned or the men found it and shot it out.

Danny hadn't expected that either.

The entire face of the mansion blinks with cop lights. Danny will turn sixteen in eighteen minutes. He should be done and gone by then. He hopes.

He checks on Malone and Locke again. Locke is rearing back to take his own shot at the door to the turret. The two men appear in another view in the hallway leading to the room from the opposite side.

"No," Danny says. "Stop."

His view of the men goes black. He hears a muffled explosion. The three heads in the turret room snap around. Another blast sounds, and the door to the left of the table where Quartz sits buckles inward, the knob bursting away in a spray of wood and metal splinters.

"Stop what?" Quartz says. "What the fuck?"

Danny holds his right palm up to the videocam. "Mr. Spitler, now," he shouts. "Mommy, it is within reach. It is within reach."

———

Malone crashes into the room behind Locke and dives to the floor, shouting, "Police, everyone down, police," as she hears the dull spatter of gunfire through silencers. She sees a man in a suit grab Carey Peters by the shoulders and haul her down and another man sitting at a table reaching frantically into a pocket and saying, "What the fuck what the fuck what the fuck?"

The lights go out; the room goes dark. Bullets thwap the wall and shatter windows behind Malone. She's shimmying along the floor, smelling old cigarette smoke and fear, when a single ceiling light flashes on across the room, shining on two men covered in black but for a thin slit exposing the widening whites of their eyes. Malone shoots one in the left collarbone. He screams and flails backward against the wall while his partner ducks out of the light.

"Police, drop your guns now," Malone is yelling. Her eyes have begun to adjust to the dark. She's looking around as fast as she can, looking for the other shooter, but mainly for the boy, for Danny Peters, when a knee cracks the back of her head. It's Locke, crab walking past her to the man at the table, who's now on the floor, fumbling with his jacket. Locke karate chops something out of the man's hands.

Quartz, she thinks. Locke grabs him by his collar and starts dragging him back toward Malone. She sees a shape sliding along the wall behind them and squeezes off two shots in that direction, yelling, "Locke, gun behind you." He doesn't seem to see or hear her—he's just hauling his man back to the door where they entered the room. "Locke, what are you doing?" she shouts again. A wall sconce blinks on over the head of one of the masked men dropping to a knee and extending his pistol toward her. *Danny*, she thinks as she twists around to fire, *where is goddamn Danny?*

———

Quartz sees the two strangers in black scurry into the room just as everything goes dark. Picturing their masked faces as a pair of black-and-orange bull's-eyes, he reaches into a pocket for his Luger, but it's the wrong pocket, no gun there; he reaches into another pocket, but he can't get his hand on the gun butt, maybe because he's shaking so hard, telling himself, "Fuck fuck fuck." Without the earplugs he wore on the range, he can't hear anything for the exploding guns and the cold silence of the intruders.

A bullet tears through the computer monitor in front of Quartz. "Oh God, oh God," he cries out, feeling bits of plastic and glass cut into his face. He falls to the floor, and just as he gets his Luger out, something hard smacks his hand, and the gun goes spinning away across the floor. Then he feels a hand rough against his ear, his jacket collar tighten around his neck. He's being pulled away.

Without even looking, Quartz knows it's Locke who has him in his grip. Locke is saving him from these men Pressman sent to kill him.

And while he's still scared shitless, he feels a certain relief. For all his years of running, Quartz, wanted by the FBI for half a dozen different crimes of espionage, would rather be taken by this clumsy, desperate agent than shot to death because of a boy who outsmarted him.

But then Locke stumbles, drops to a knee, loosens his grip. Quartz lifts his head and sees a police officer lying a few feet away, blasting as she yells, "What the fuck are you doing?" Locke is struggling to right himself when he lurches forward onto his face. "Hit," he gasps. Just beyond him, Quartz now sees Spitler stuffing Carey into a doorway Quartz hadn't noticed before. He rises to his hands and knees and begins to crawl away from Locke, bullets whizzing over him as he calls out, "Take me. Please."

———

It is within reach.

Carey sees Danny's palm on the screen. She hears the alien passion in his cry. She understands. She lets Spitler take her by the shoulders. "Miss Carey, follow me. Now."

They stoop low and move past Serenity's gold-flake chair across the platform to the wall beneath the framed *Light* page blaring the news of Jack Bleak's death. Behind her she hears two rapid gunshots, then another, then a male shriek of pain, a clatter and thud. She knows she should be afraid. Spitler's face is a rictus of fear. But Carey feels an odd, welcoming calm, as if she is bulletproof, as if she is untouchable, immortal. She understands now what Danny was telling her a moment ago:

It is within reach.

Spitler reaches up and thumps the wall with his fist three times fast, pauses, looks around, sweating, breathing hard, whacks the wall again twice. A door swings open into the wall. "Here," Spitler says, pulling Carey into a cramped, dark space smelling of must.

"Now, Miss Carey," Spitler says, but she turns back to the room, sees Quartz crawling toward her. "Take me," he's saying. "Please." Locke is behind him, struggling to raise himself from the floor, holding the back of his left leg. "I found your son," Quartz is saying.

She reaches out and takes his hand, hears Locke groan, "No." He's on an elbow, the heel of one of Quartz's shoes in his other hand. "You are aiding and . . ." His voice trails off. He collapses. Carey pulls Quartz away.

"Do not move," Malone says. She's lying on her side beyond Locke with her gun pointed in Carey's direction. "Stay where you are." Their eyes meet. Carey sees that Malone is in pain and for a fleeting instant wishes she didn't have to disappoint the officer. But she knows now that she will finally be with Danny, only Danny, always Danny, forever.

There's another gunshot from the other masked man. A chandelier smashes on the floor next to Malone, and she rolls out of the way. "I'm sorry," Carey says. Spitler pulls the door shut, slams two deadlocks into place, and takes Carey hard by her wrist.

"Hurry."

They move a few steps in one direction, Quartz following, the floor uneven with screwheads and warped boards. They swerve right, then left, and a light snaps on, a bare bulb overhead spilling a glow the color of puke down a wooden stairway corkscrewing into blackness. Carey hears Malone yelling after them, "We'll find you, Carey. We will find you."

Spitler stops—"Wait one second"—takes out a disposable phone, hits a few buttons. His hands are shaking. "Damn it, damn it," he says, hitting more buttons. "All right. Let's go. Hold on to me, go go go."

———

Officers in blue and brown, a few not in uniform, rush the mansion from every side. Danny undoes all the locks. On the laptop he hears

Malone's shouts, the splutter and bang of the guns, the thuds and screams.

The masked men might be dead. Locke and Malone have been shot. Danny's mother and Spitler are escaping. Quartz might be with them. That wasn't part of the plan. Nothing Danny can do about it.

With a ripple of keystrokes, he sends a neutron bomb of software to the computer in the turret, erasing all the steps that he and Quartz just took.

Then Danny picks up a phone, texts Boz: on their way

Boz replies: 10-4

Danny gets off his chair, steadies himself with two hands on the table's edge, takes some deep breaths. It's over. Quartz got to only three of the four accounts. That will do. Everyone will get paid: his mother, Dulcinea, Boz.

And the others Danny has in mind.

He walks outside, keeping his eyes on the mansion. Boaters have pulled up there to ogle the goings-on from the bay.

Danny crosses Boz's deck, the sand in front of it, then steps up to the dock. At the end of the dock, he takes a wallet from his back pocket and digs out a folded-up plastic baggie. Danny unfolds the baggie and shakes it.

Paddle's ashes float away.

Danny stands for a moment watching the white flecks disappear on the water. He wishes he hadn't had to have Dulcinea plant the other ashes in Bledsoe's trunk, but he'd wanted the ruse to be authentic.

He drops the baggie on the dock. Then he stares across the bay to the turret where his grandmother sleeps in a drugged haze. He closes his eyes, imagines the big lake beyond, stretching all the way to Chicago.

"Goodbye," he says.

He walks back into Boz's, gathers up his laptop and phones, and goes through the bar into the kitchen, where he stops, reconsidering.

He returns to the bar, finds an order pad and a ballpoint pen, tears a page out of the pad, and writes:

Pete,

I would not call it Pete's if I were you.

Good fishing. Go Cubs.

Danny

He folds the note over once and secures it beneath a bottle of vodka, then moves past the men's room through the kitchen to the screen door facing the bay road. He glances around, making sure no one is near before he walks to the SUV parked in the gravel driveway. A single key is in the ignition, where Boz left it. Danny climbs in and turns it. The dashboard clock lights up: 11:46. He's sixteen. He latches his safety belt and pulls out onto the bay road, heading north, away from Bleak Harbor.

LATER

50

"Locke."

Malone reaches out with her good arm to touch him, draws it back. He's on his back in a hospital bed, his left leg suspended over the bed, wrapped in bandage. He's been in a drugged stupor for three days.

"Locke. I know you're awake."

His eyes open, slowly focus. He gives Malone a once-over, inclines his head at the sling on her left shoulder. "What happened to you?"

"Shot through the arm. Pretty clean. Like on TV."

"What happened?"

"You don't remember?"

He stares at his leg. "We were in that room. There was shooting. Some screaming. I don't really know."

"You got shot in the butt."

"Hurts."

"Yep. Tough. I mean, it's good you're not dead. But tough."

Locke nods at that. He looks at the empty tray next to his bed, as if he might find something there. "Your head OK?"

"You probably don't remember that either."

"Remember what?"

"You kicked me."

"No, I didn't."

"Yes, you did. In your hurry to get Quartz."

Locke doesn't say anything.

"You really screwed with me, Locke. You better hope I forget."

This doesn't seem to register. Locke says, "Quartz got away."

"Yep," Malone says. "Your fellow agents are looking for him, but so far, they've got nothing. Just deserts, in my opinion. Had you done your job—"

"Excuse me, Officer, but—" Something, maybe pain, stops him, contorting his face.

Malone doesn't care.

"Excuse me, Agent Locke," she says, "but I was on my own in a shit fight with two assholes, and you were basically AWOL. And you haven't even asked about Danny Peters."

He's still catching his breath. "What assholes?"

"Just stop, Locke."

"They shot me. Where are they?"

"One's in ICU; the other's in the morgue."

"Good."

"You still haven't asked about the boy."

Locke shakes his head. "He's not the dangerous one. Quartz is the dangerous one. I told you."

"No. You told me shit."

"I told you, Quartz—"

"Really, Locke? Really?" Malone thinks about rapping a knuckle on his leg, decides no. "Danny Peters is gone. Nobody has a clue where he is. His mom and pop are lawyered up, not saying a word, probably because they don't have a clue either."

"Don't you wonder, though?"

"Wonder whether they were in on this somehow?" Malone recalls Carey Bleak Peters disappearing into that door in the wall. "The thought has crossed my mind. But as for evidence? We have nothing. We have a plastic baggie with the residue of a dead dog's ashes. We have some drawings of dragonflies and a bunch of computers and phones full of jack shit. Although there's some evidence that Carey may have been trying to blackmail her boss. Not that it really matters now."

"Hah," Locke says. The chuckle makes him grimace. "No shit."

"No shit what?"

Locke coughs, shifts himself in the bedding, coughs again. "She and Pressman had a little Valentine's Day date."

"Really?"

"Yes, ma'am. You don't want to mess with that woman. She went after him, stole a bunch of documents that could've gotten her boss in a lot of trouble. I'd have liked to get her to give me those."

"So you could squeeze Pressman for Quartz."

Locke shrugs.

"How the hell did you know all this anyway?" Malone says.

Locke leans his head back into his pillow, closes his eyes. "I don't know for sure, but I got a couple of emails out of nowhere."

"Of course. The boy."

"The boy."

"Damn. That kid." Through the window beyond Locke's bed Malone sees the festival Ferris wheel, partially disassembled. "How the hell did he invade all these people's private places without getting noticed?"

"Are you kidding?" Locke says. "You got Fortune 500 companies with people crawling around in their stuff for months, and they don't notice. These people are good, Malone."

"They're bad, Locke."

"Well, bad but good. What the boy did isn't all that big a deal, really."

"So far as we know," Malone says. "But fuck that kid. It's on you now to find him, Locke."

Locke shakes his head. "Officer," he says. "You don't know anything about me."

"You're right about that." Malone cradles her bad arm with her other. "Don't take this personally, Agent, but I hope our paths never cross again." She starts to leave, then stops and turns back to Locke. "On second thought," she says, "do take it personally."

———

Malone steers her car with one arm past the cemetery gates.

The road curves into a shallow rise. She parks at the crest and steps outside. Lake Michigan glistens in the sunny distance. The grave is a few steps away, beneath an oak. Malone kneels before the headstone lying flush with the trimmed grass:

Louisa Josephine Brecher

She starts to whisper her customary prayers—an Our Father, a Hail Mary, a Glory Be—but stops in the middle of the first at "Forgive us our trespasses as we forgive—"

She leans down and lays her hands flat on her daughter's headstone. A sob escapes her, then another. "LouLou," she says, barely a whisper. She hears the gentle surf washing up on the shore below. How Louisa loved to swim in the big lake.

"LouLou. Honey. Please forgive me. I've done—I'm doing—my best. Please, please forgive me."

51

Carey's phone is ringing again. She sees the number, turns the phone facedown on the café table.

"Hi."

She looks up. "Jonah," she says, accepting his over-the-shoulder hug. "Glad you came."

He nods at the phone. "Pete again?"

"Yeah. I don't want to talk to him just yet."

Jonah sits. "You heard about the bar."

"How the hell did that happen?"

"Who knows? Boz just up and disappears, and Pete suddenly owns a bar. The cops are all over it."

Carey says, "Just what Pete needs, huh? A liquor license. You gonna order something?"

"In a minute. I don't think I've ever been in a place that sells bikes *and* coffee."

"Very hipster."

"Give Bleak Harbor two years, we'll have one too."

"I'm sure."

"What is this neighborhood again? Lakeshore?"

"Lakeview. Even though you can't really see the lake."

"How long will you stay?"

"I got it online till the end of the month. Then we'll see."

"But you're glad to be back in Chicago."

Carey sighs and sips her tea. Jonah reaches across the table for her free hand. "You haven't heard from Danny?"

She pushes something across the table. Jonah picks it up. "A cherry stem?" he says.

"I found it stuck in his laptop last week. I don't know why; I just kept it."

"OK."

"He sent me a text this morning. He says he's all right."

"That's good. He hasn't called?"

"He keeps saying he will when the time is right. Whenever that is."

"Can't the police trace the texts?"

"Fuck the police."

Jonah lets that sit there for a few seconds, then says, "You've got to come back, Carey."

"Does anyone know you're here?"

"No."

"Nobody followed you?"

"The Bleak Harbor Police?"

"What about Hamilton?"

"Hamilton. As soon as the national media started calling it a fiasco, she disappeared. Reminds me, I did see the chief last night at a budget meeting. He said to tell you they're on it twenty-four seven."

"Well, now, that is a relief."

Carey pushes her teacup to the side and reaches into the purse hanging on the back of her chair. She pulls out another phone, looks to see if she missed anything. She didn't. "His texts come on these disposables," she says. "He FedExed me a box of them."

"No way."

"He thought of everything, Jonah."

"Was there a postmark?"

"Yeah." She chuckles sourly. "Hingham, Massachusetts."

"Hingham?"

"Think."

"Shit. The patriarch?"

"The esteemed birthplace of the esteemed Joseph Estes Bleak, founder of Bleak Harbor."

"You don't think he's really in Massachusetts, do you?"

Carey shakes her head. "I wish I knew. Speaking of the Bleaks, how is Serenity?"

"Hard to say. She hasn't returned my calls. I spoke briefly with one of her lawyers. There's apparently some problem with her finances. He wasn't too specific."

Carey's real phone starts ringing again. Jonah stands and says, "I'm gonna get a coffee. Want anything?"

"I'm good."

She turns the phone back over. The area code is 616. Probably not Pete. She answers. "Hello?"

"Mrs. Peters?"

She doesn't recognize the voice. It sounds like an older man's. "This is Carey Peters."

"I'm terribly sorry to bother you, Mrs. Peters."

"Carey, please. Who is this?"

"Carey, of course. My name is Brian Doyle. I teach literature at Kalamazoo College. In Michigan."

Carey turns to see Jonah waiting in line between two young women with baby strollers. "And?"

"Well, it's this. I happen to know your son a little, in a sort of side-long way, and I just wanted to call to say I'm so sorry—"

"Excuse me? You know Danny?"

"I do, I mean, not well, a little. We corresponded via email."

Carey sits upright, pressing the phone against her ear. "Do you know where he is? Have you heard from him?"

"No, no, I don't. I wish—no. I haven't heard from Daniel for at least a few weeks."

"Why didn't you come forward—I'm sorry, what was your name again?"

"Call me Doyle. I did try to call you last week, just after Danny was kidnap—that is, disappeared. There was no answer. Maybe I should have left a message."

Everything crashes over Carey again, as it does whenever her phone rings, she walks past a TV, she walks the beach on Lake Michigan. Danny tricked her, tricked Pete, tricked them all. But more than anything, Danny is gone, and she has no idea where.

"Carey?" Doyle says. "Are you there?"

"Yes," she says, swiping a damp cheek. "Why were you emailing with Danny? Forgive me, but it's weird."

"I understand. Please rest assured there was nothing untoward about it. Danny actually reached out to me. He is—"

"He reached out?"

"—such a smart and wonderful boy, Carey. Honestly, I had no idea until I saw the newspaper stories that he was autistic."

Autistics can be as smart and wonderful as anyone, Carey thinks, but she says, "Why did he contact you?"

Jonah sits across from Carey with a latte in a foam cup. He mouths, "Danny?"

Carey shakes him off.

"As I said, I teach literature," Doyle says. "Mostly poetry, and especially the poetry of Wallace Stevens."

"Danny emailed you about Wallace Stevens?"

Jonah leans in closer.

"Yes, several months ago. Daniel has such an enthusiasm for Stevens's poetry, and—"

"Danny. Nobody calls him Daniel."

"Oh, apologies. He never corrected me."

Carey looks at Jonah, seeking comfort. "Go on. Wallace Stevens. How did Danny even find you?"

"Google, I assume. One of my essays comes up quite prominently in searches for Stevens. I'm sure you knew of Daniel—Danny's appreciation of Stevens's verse."

"Yes. I did. But you said 'poems,' plural, not singular."

"Why, yes. He was especially fond of 'Sunday Morning.' Also 'The Man with the Blue Guitar.'"

Carey struggles to remember the name of the poem that had ice cream in it. She feels her heart breaking. "I see."

"For such a young man, your son has an unusually profound understanding of Stevens's work, if a little personal. But that's how we all read poetry, isn't it? The best poets don't have a fixed meaning in mind, they leave spaces for the readers' imagination. And Danny had quite—well, you know."

"Can you excuse me a moment?"

She presses the phone against her chest. She closes her eyes. She's remembering the text that Jeremiah sent her as she was driving back from Valparaiso. That actually came from Danny:

u quit on people its in yr blood.

"Carey?" Jonah says.

She shakes her head, gets back on the phone. "I'm sorry, Mr. Doyle, but I'm afraid I'm going to have to report this to the police. Please don't call me again. Goodbye."

"Who was that?" Jonah says.

"No one."

Carey tells herself she will not cry. She sets her phone down, picks up the disposable in both hands, and breaks it in half with a sharp crack. "What are you doing?" Jonah says. She unloops her purse from the chairback and stands.

"Sorry," she says.

"Sorry for what?"

"The palm."

"The palm?"

"The palm. The palm is a fucking tree," she says. "And it really is forever out of reach."

52

"I've been learning about snails."

"Snails?"

"The lake here is shaped like a snail."

"The lake where?"

"Snails can just crawl into their shell and hide for a while."

"Are there dragonflies?"

"Yes. Big ones."

"Where are you, honey?"

"Where are you, Mother?"

"Chicago. I have an appointment tomorrow with the police."

"You did nothing wrong."

"They want to talk about you."

"So I will not put you in the position of having to lie."

"What about your meds? You must need more."

"I am fine."

"I miss you."

"I have been avoiding the internet, but I did hear that your former boss is encountering some legal trouble."

"That reporter did a number on him in the *Trib*. I guess she got hold of some documents. You wouldn't know anything about that, would you, Danny?"

"She is an exceptional journalist."

"Uh-huh. I can't say I mind that Pressman is finally getting his."

"And Gordon Michael Baron got away."

"Who?"

"You know him as Quartz."

"That's his real name?"

"Nobody knows where he is, do they?"

"Just like you."

"Has he tried to contact you?"

"No. The last I saw of him, he was running into the woods off the beach where Boz picked Spitler and me up."

"I suppose he is the one who took over my Twitter account."

"Your what?"

"At drewthenobody."

"That was you?"

"That was Jeremiah. Now it is Quartz. So he is out there."

"Does that frighten you?"

"Not too much. Gordon Michael Baron liked me. What about the FBI agent?"

"Which one?"

"The one who was harassing you. Mr. Locke."

"One of Pressman's guys shot him in the mansion. I heard he woke up in the hospital screaming for Quartz."

"It really is a connected world."

"Excuse me?"

"You will see."

"When? Where are you? I won't tell anyone."

"Soon enough. I have to go now."

"No, Danny, wait. I have so much I—wait. Why in the world would you give Quartz that money?"

"He did not get any money."

"When we were up in the house, you said he was getting one million, one hundred, whatever it was."

"Yes. I lied. Apologies."

"Why that amount, though?

"Think, Mother. Eleven eleven."

"My birthday?"

"Obviously. Sometime in the near future, you will receive notification of a new bank account in your name. I would not tell the police about it just yet."

"Danny."

"What of Mr. Spitler?"

"Unemployed and spending a lot of time with lawyers."

"But he has not been charged with any crime?"

"I don't think the cops understand what happened, Danny. Do you?"

"I have to go."

"Not before you tell me why."

"Why what?"

"Why you did this. Why you kidnapped yourself and put me and Pete and everyone else through all this."

"Why did you kill Paddle?"

"Paddle? That is not fair."

"Why did they kill young Jeremiah?"

"This is ridiculous. You did all this because a dog died? Because somebody drowned half a century ago?"

"Why did they close the mills? Why did they abandon everybody who made that town what it was?"

"Danny. I never would abandon you. Never."

"It all could have been much worse."

"Never in a million years."

"But look: You will be OK. Pete will be OK."

"I will not be OK until I see you again, safe and sound."

"You will. In the meantime, you can let Pete go."

"He is still my husband. And your stepfather."

"That is not what this is about, Mother."

"What?"

"Did you think I was trying to get you two to be happy together? Would everything be all right if that was why I did what I did?"

"It's not all right."

"Correct. I have to go now. I have work to do."

"Honey."

"Remember: 'They flit about the sunny sky like flowers that can fly.'"

"Danny."

"I have a plan. I love you, Mommy."

"Danny, please—"

53

Feds Investigating Mysterious Bank Deposits

"Free Money" May Be Linked to Autistic Boy's Disappearance

By Michele Higgins of the *Chicago Tribune*

Federal bank and law enforcement authorities are investigating the sudden appearance of large, identical sums of money in the bank accounts of hundreds of residents of Bleak Harbor, Mich.

Deposits of $59,666.67 began mysteriously popping up in Bleak Harbor, Bleak Township and Bleak County checking accounts last week, said a federal official who spoke on the condition of anonymity. "Looks like free money to me," said Bleak Harbor mayor Jonah Bleak. He confirmed that he had received one of the deposits but declined to comment further.

Bleak Harbor is a popular summer retreat for Chicagoans. The deposits originated from bank accounts in Illinois and at least 13 other states. Officials were still getting reports of additional deposits late yesterday.

The common thread appears to be that recipients identified thus far all have lived in the Bleak Harbor area for at least 20 years, authorities said. Longtime local librarian Zelda Loiselle called it "a godsend for a single mom like me, with four kids." She said she had no idea who might have sent it.

Coincidentally or not, at least some recipients are former employees of Bleak Steelworks, which was sold decades ago to a Japanese conglomerate that later closed the factory in northwestern Indiana.

"I couldn't believe it," said Russell Brenner, 72 years old, of Saugatuck. He lost his job and pension in the sale. "It sure ain't all what I lost, but I'll take it."

Law enforcement sources said they're looking into whether the cash movements are related to the disappearance six weeks ago of 16-year-old Daniel Bleak Peters, sole grandchild of Serenity Meredith Maas Bleak, heiress to the Bleak fortune. The boy is believed to have faked his own

LOG IN OR SUBSCRIBE

ACKNOWLEDGMENTS

Thanks first to the readers of my earlier books for bugging me about the next one. I hope you liked it. Another one is coming soon. No, really, it is. Promise.

This book would have remained unseen in my laptop if it weren't for my agent, Meg Ruley (who obviously belongs with me, Gruley). My heartfelt gratitude to Meg, Amy Tannenbaum, Jessica Errera, and all their helpful colleagues at the Jane Rotrosen Agency. And thanks to Bob Dugoni for the introduction.

Liz Pearsons at Thomas & Mercer grew up in southwestern Michigan not far from my fictional town. She insists, however, that that wasn't the only thing that attracted her to the tale. I'm forever grateful to her and to Gracie Doyle, Alison Dasho, Sarah Shaw, and all the T&M folks for giving Danny, and me, a chance.

Caitlin Alexander made Danny's story better in countless ways. Headstrong writers are prone to recoil at editors who fill the margins with questions like, "Why do you say this here when you said the opposite four pages ago?" Caitlin delivered her incisive queries with gentle affection and made the rewriting invigorating and fun.

For their generous advice on hacking and hackers, thanks to my Bloomberg colleague Michael Riley; Tod Beardsley (who happens to look like Quartz) and Jen Ellis of Rapid7; Trey Ford of Salesforce.com; and my brilliantly geeky son-in-law, Andy Stoutenburgh. For cop stuff, thanks again to my sister, Kimi Crova, and my dear hockey pal, Detective John

Campbell of the Chicago Police Department. My sister-in-law Laura Nitsos helped with Spanish translations, and my old *Detroit News* colleague Bob Roach gave me some personal insight into autism. Any screwups with this material are mine and mine alone.

I had to be kicked in the ass a few times to make this book happen. Marcus Sakey embraced this duty with gusto over occasional boozy lunches, as did Jonathan Eig, Ali biographer extraordinaire. Thanks to those who read drafts and offered suggestions and encouragement: Joe Barrett; Tom Bonnel; John Brecher; Jim Casurella; Michael Harvey; Julie Jargon; David Kocieniewski; my beautiful daughter Danielle and her ex-trader hubby, Billy Leinemann (no, he's not in the medical marijuana business); Javier Ramirez; Sean Sherman; and especially Erin Malone Borba. I'm also grateful to the kind folks at Chicago's finest coffee shops—Heritage General Store, Nohea Café, and Osmium Coffee Bar—where I wrote big chunks of this book.

Nothing is possible without my family, the heart of which is my wife, Pam, who endures my bouts of insecurity and self-doubt with just enough impatience to make me think she's right—I probably ought to keep writing.

And so I will. Thank you for reading.

ABOUT THE AUTHOR

Photo © 2014 Graham Morrison, Bloomberg News

Bryan Gruley is the award-winning author of the Starvation Lake trilogy of novels. He is also a lifelong journalist who is proud to have shared in the Pulitzer Prize awarded to the staff of the *Wall Street Journal* for their coverage of the September 11 terrorist attacks. Gruley lives in Chicago with his wife, Pam. You can learn more by visiting his website at www.bryangruley.com.

BARBERSHOPS, BIBLES, AND BET

BARBERSHOPS, BIBLES, AND BET

EVERYDAY TALK AND BLACK
POLITICAL THOUGHT

Melissa Victoria Harris-Lacewell

PRINCETON UNIVERSITY PRESS   PRINCETON AND OXFORD

Library of Congress Cataloging-in-Publication Data

Harris-Lacewell, Melissa, 1973–
Barbershops, bibles, and BET : everyday talk and Black political
thought / Melissa Harris-Lacewell.
p.   cm.
Includes bibliographical references (p.   ) and index.
ISBN 0-691-11405-6 (cl. : alk. paper)
1. African Americans — Politics and government.   2. African
Americans — Intellectual life.   3. African Americans — Attitudes.
4. Conversation analysis — United States.   5. United States — Politics
and government — 1989–   6. Black nationalism — United States.
7. Feminism — United States.   8. Conservatism — United States.
9. United States — Race relations — Political aspects.   I. Title.

E185.615.H295 2004
320.5′089′96073 — dc22

2003055452

British Library Cataloging-in-Publication Data is available

This book has been composed in Sabon

Printed on acid-free paper. ∞

pup.princeton.edu

Printed in the United States of America

1   3   5   7   9   10   8   6   4   2

To Parker

Contents

Tables

Figures

Acknowledgments

THOSE OF US who were children and adolescents in the 1980s have been labeled in a variety of ways. We were just a little behind the age cohort known as the "me" generation and a little before the group now called "generation dot com." Soda companies targeted us as the "Pepsi generation" and most settled on calling us "generation X." But I have always thought of myself as part of the "Cosby" generation. I was one of the thousands of African American youth who learned that Thursday night was a sacred night for television. That was the night when it seemed that everyone tuned into NBC at eight o'clock. For me, the "Cosby" generation's only real divisions were associated with whether you identified most strongly with Denise, Vanessa, Rudy, or Theo. *Cosby* was unique because it quietly challenged racism simply by normalizing the Huxtables' blackness. "It present[ed] in microcosm the importance of black unity — between genders and generations — without any sloganizing about the necessity of holding together for survival in a hostile environment" (Downing 70). It mattered to be part of the "Cosby" generation. It normalized blackness and made me, as a child, feel proud and confident in my black womanhood.

I got this same feeling again in college when my girlfriends and I founded the Nia House. We were thirteen black women on a white college campus who were tired of the racism we experienced in the residence halls. Together we formed our own residence and named it the Nia House. (Nia means purpose in the East African language Kiswahili. Nia is one of the seven principles celebrated in the African American winter holiday, Kwanzaa.) My pride in this place came from realizing that we had done more than flee a bad situation. We had created a refuge, a haven for other black students who were also tired of wearing the mask. In the Nia House we could all be ourselves. We disagreed, we argued, we fought, but we did so within a cocoon of racial safety. In the Nia House we talked about ourselves and about each other. We talked about sex and parties. We talked about religion and life. And we spent a lot of time talking about blackness and politics. "Da House," as it came to be known on campus, was a place where many black students talked with one another about how to survive in the racially hostile environment of our university. We sympathized and strategized and, in so doing, we defined and processed what it meant to be black.

It was being a "Cosby" kid and Nia House woman that led me to my research agenda about how and what black people think about the public world. I am thankful to all my childhood and college friends with whom I shared those early experiences.

I am deeply indebted to a family and community that have supported and nurtured me throughout the preparation of this book. A work of this size is never the result of an individual effort, but is the product of collective intellectual engagement and sacrifice. Thank you, John Brehm, for believing in this work when it was nothing more than an ill-formed dissertation idea, and for your continuing support, guidance, and friendship over the years. Thank you to John Aldrich, who was the first person who made me believe it was possible to do political science and still be true to myself. Thanks also to Karen Stenner, who has been a friend, confidant, and teacher. I owe a special debt to Michael Dawson for inspiring me before we even met, and for being such a dear friend and intellectual companion since we have known one another. I am thankful to Cathy Cohen for her faith in me, for her guidance and humor, and for finally reading those chapters! Thank you to Lisa Weeden, Jacob Levy, Patchen Markell, and Dan Drezner for being my junior colleagues and partners in crime. I am grateful to Dr. Maya Angelou, whose spiritual and financial support made graduate study possible for me. A broad community of scholars have read and commented on the work, supported me in the madness of preparing it, and given me invaluable resources and support. Special thanks are owed to Lee Baker, Wahneema Lubiano, Jarvis Hall, Carlton Wilson, Mazella Hall, Todd Shaw, Rob Brown, Andrea Simpson, Lester Spence, and Shayla Nunnally.

I am grateful to the organizations that have financially supported this research. Karla Holloway and her team at the African and African American Studies Department at Duke University provided valuable financial resources toward the collection of empirical data. The social science division and the Center for the Study of Race, Politics and Culture at the University of Chicago generously provided funding for the research in chapter 5. I am indebted to a terrific team of student researchers: Ashley Nall, for her transcription work, and Quincy T. Mills, for his irreplaceable assistance with the barbershop chapter. Thank you so much to Bethany Albertson for basically running my entire life! I also must thank the students at North Carolina Central University and Kennedy-King College, Reverend Kenney and the members of Orange Grove Missionary Baptist Church, and the men of Truth and Soul who volunteered their time and passion to make my research possible.

A special thanks is owed to my sisters, Rolisa, Dana, and Elizabeth, for keeping me laughing. Thank you to my nieces, Catherine, Christina, Claudia, and Elisse, and to my nephew, Mac, for helping me keep it all in perspective. Thank you to my dad for being my first academic role model. Thank you to my mother for reading, transcribing, editing, watching the baby, and caring so deeply. Thank you to Deidre for providing loving care for my daughter so that I could work and feel a little less guilty. Thank you to my best friend and spiritual sister Blair, without whose intellectual and emotional support everything would be impossible. You are Zuzu's petals!

Introduction

Knowledge is from the very beginning a co-operative process of group life, in which everyone unfolds his knowledge within the framework of a common fate, a common activity, and the overcoming of common difficulties (in which, however, each has a different share).
—Karl Mannheim, 1936

ZENO NAMED his mule Toussaint L'Overture to honor the great Haitian revolutionary. A married father of three and a former marine, Zeno now makes his living driving a mule-drawn carriage for the tourists in New Orleans's French Quarter. It's a job that rewards funny, informative characters who use rhymes, songs, and humor to cajole tourists to ride. Even among this animated lot, Zeno is a personality. He is working on a bachelor's degree from the University of New Orleans and fancies himself a serious historian with a particular commitment to the stories and perspectives of black people, so he reserves a special tour for his African American patrons, one he describes as a "unique Afrocentric tour of the historic Vieux Carre."

Zeno's tour not only takes riders all over historic New Orleans, it takes them all over the map ideologically. He starts the tour with a stop in Integrationism. He visits the graveyard where the famous nineteenth-century Integrationist litigant Homere Plessy is buried. Ernest "Dutch" Morial, the first black mayor of New Orleans, is also buried here. Although Zeno speaks proudly about how Dutch's arrogance and stubbornness were just what the city needed in a black man, he suggests that Dutch's son, Marc, a recent mayor of New Orleans, will be remembered as the better leader because, unlike his father, his political maneuvers have gained the loyalty of a cross-racial coalition in the city council. Riders start to get comfortable, assuming they can read Zeno's politics. He appears to be a classic Integrationist, holding up the heroes of civil rights litigation and electoral politics.

But it would be bad idea to get comfortable in Zeno's buggy. As he lurches across a busy intersection coming from the cemetery, he crosses into Nationalist rhetoric. Zeno reveals his deep suspicions about whites and their involvement in black life and culture. As he drives the mule past the Funky Booty nightclub, he complains that it is owned by a white man who stole the name from a black nightclub in black Storyville. "It is just another example of white people's theft of black people's culture." As he points out the Louis Armstrong Park on the left, he complains that jazz music in New Orleans has become an inauthentic commodity sold to whites. When Zeno fails to come to a complete stop at the traffic light, a white officer in a patrol car pulls up beside and jokingly threatens him with a ticket. As the cruiser pulls off, Zeno hisses his contempt for the police. "They always harass people for no good reason. Don't deal with real problems. I mean damn, the sound of a police siren is a universal signal for fresh donuts." He peppers this part of the tour with critiques of violent and oppressive whites. He tells of a white woman, "just like Martha Stewart," who tortured and murdered black slaves, her barbarous acts entirely unnoticed by the community until a fire in her attic revealed the broken bodies of dozens of black men and women. This, he suggests, is just how whites treat African Americans today.

Just as Zeno really gets worked up into a Nationalist fervor; Toussaint gets agitated by something in the street. The mule stops abruptly and starts backing up. Zeno tries to guide the mule, but his riders are in for a scary few moments, and they clutch the sides of the buggy and hold on as the tour takes a new direction, now coming around by the Mississippi River. Zeno's language, like his mule, has also taken a turn, this time into Conservative sentiment. Talking proudly about the many notable black men who hail from New Orleans, he starts praising the New Orleans native who played an aggressive, black Republican car salesman in the Spike Lee film *Get on the Bus*. In that role, the black men on the bus eject the character when he repeats: "Niggers are lazy." Zeno argues that "the brotha was right, so what if he said 'niggas, niggas, niggas,' I mean black people need to do more for themselves and not complain so much about what the white man is doing." The statement is stunning to riders after listening to nearly an hour of Zeno's complaints about whites' mistreatments of blacks. At the end of his tour, Zeno encourages his customers to eat at the restaurant where his wife works because it is black-owned, and "we don't need to be givin' the white folks all our money." He makes it seem a racial duty to tip him and then to patronize his wife's restaurant. Riders emerge from his long, twisting ride with a sense of both physical and ideological whiplash.

Margaret is a pleasant, round-faced, light-skinned woman. A schoolteacher who has never been married and has no children of her own, she has lived in Durham, North Carolina, and attended Orange Grove Missionary Baptist Church her entire life. When she speaks of Orange Grove, it is with great respect and ferocious loyalty. She remembers the Orange Grove of her youth as a small, family-centered place where the congregation spent as much time visiting in the parking lot after services as they did worshipping in the pews during church. Margaret speaks of Ms. Sophie Lee, an older black woman who sat in the front pew watching Margaret and her friends when they were children singing in the youth choir. Ms. Sophie Lee would watch the kids. Whoever fell asleep or acted badly knew they would be called to task later that week when Ms. Sophie Lee paid a visit to their parents. But for Margaret, Ms. Sophie Lee and the long after-church discussions are wistful, almost bittersweet memories.

Now when she thinks of Orange Grove, she describes a church that is so large and dominated by new faces that she feels like a visitor even though she has been a member for thirty-two years. Although she says that "sometimes I don't feel like I am at home anymore," she just as quickly affirms that she would never leave Orange Grove because "it is my home church." And although she is nostalgic about the little, family-centered church she remembers, she is excited about how her Orange Grove has evolved. She describes a place where people are drawn to services by the powerful and relevant messages of an energetic, young minister. Her pride is tangible when she speaks of Reverend Kenney and how he has led Orange Grove into an activist role in Durham's African American community. She mentions the minister's weekly column in the local paper and the active participation of church leaders and members in the antiviolence marches in Durham's black community. She talks of how proud she is to tell people that she attends Orange Grove, because everyone knows the church for all it does in the city. Margaret mourns the loss of community among the church membership, but she celebrates the church's increased connection to the larger community.

Louise is a wiry, thin, brown-skinned woman. She has been attending Orange Grove for only six months. Her first contact was not with the church, but rather with the minister, Reverend Kenney. The Reverend lives on Louise's block, and when she began to have marital troubles, he offered her and her husband free counseling, even though they were not members of the church. Unlike Margaret, she has no particular loyalty to Orange Grove as an institution and is instead bonded to the church because of her respect and gratitude for Reverend Kenney. Louise takes particular interest in the way that Reverend Kenney and Orange Grove are connected to Durham's black community. She describes Kenney as "a fighter for the underserved, the underprivileged, just the kind of people that Jesus catered to and served." She explains that his stances are often unpopular and "put him in the line of fire." She says that his willingness to stand firmly on his beliefs encourages her when she faces difficult challenges in her own life.

Hajj is the owner of Truth and Soul: Black Stars, a barbershop on Chicago's Southside. He says of his shop, "in this barbershop you hear all kinds of shit," and he is by far the ringleader of the shit talkers. He renamed himself Hajj when he became a Muslim and explains that his given name "wasn't mine to begin with. I had to shed my slave name." Hajj believes, "Your name is everything. If I told you Cho Ping was coming to get a haircut today, you would automatically think a Chinese man was coming to the shop. Your name means everything, it tells people who you are. Let me give you an example. Let's say you had a spotted cow in your barn and I lived next door with a spotted cow as well and both looking identical. Say one day you left your gate open and your cow wandered in my barn. And you came over and said, 'You got my cow.' How would you know which one is yours? . . . By the brand. That cow will have your initials branded on him. So, no matter where your cow roams, you will always be able to identify him." Black people in Hajj's estimation continue to carry the brand of white racists through their "slave names."

He criticizes important black intellectuals for failing to see the oppression inherent in a slave name. "How can Alex Haley, after doing all of that research, find out that he comes from the Kente people and keep the Haley name?" He talks about meeting Alex Haley at an award banquet for Haley and John Hope Franklin at the downtown Hilton hotel. "A friend of mine worked for *Ebony* and gave me a couple of tickets. When I got the chance, I went to their table, shook their hands and said hello. I asked him why he kept the name Haley after doing all that research and he said, 'You know it's political man.' Politics my ass. And John Hope Franklin, what black man you know named *John Hope*?"

When Zeno picks up black passengers, his mule-drawn carriage is transformed into an unexpected space. Although he owns neither the mule nor the buggy, he uses them as a place to express his beliefs about what is good and bad about black people. He constructs a narrative of a particular black history, which emphasizes the power and accomplishments of African American men in his city, he offers analysis of the current problems facing black people, and he suggests solutions for them. In his willingness to expresses several, seemingly contradictory, political attitudes within the space of a single hour, Zeno is emblematic of the intersections and textures in black political thought that defy neat categorization.

Margaret and Louise look to the examples of Orange Grove's membership and leadership to help them make sense of the complex and often hostile society in which they find themselves. Long before Hillary Clinton spoke of a village's responsibility to young people, Ms. Sophie

Lee taught Margaret that raising black children should be a shared, communal responsibility. When Louise must deal with the racist and demeaning behavior of white co-workers, she draws strength from Reverend Kenney's battle with Durham's white power structure over the rights of Durham's black citizens. She is able to survive her own troubles when she thinks of her embattled minister. These are not solely moral lessons. These are political lessons that help to shape the way that Margaret and Louise define problems and propose solutions in the political world.

Hajj sees his shop as more than a place to cut hair. It is a place where black people talk about everything from the political to the raunchy. It is a place where he can inject his own brand of truth and soul into his neighborhood. Hajj pushes brothers to think about the meanings of the things they say. No idle comment is left unexamined. In Truth and Soul there is a politics to hanging out.

At the turn of the century DuBois described black life as an existence that occurred behind a veil. He understood that when white Americans forcibly separated themselves from blacks, they lowered a dark shroud between the races that allowed a certain covert reality for African Americans to operate beyond the reach of whites. A veil is opaque but not impenetrable. While African Americans have operated in a world that is institutionally and culturally distinct, others have always been able to detect movement on the other side of the veil. There is a distinct, if not entirely separate, African American public sphere that operates among African Americans, and it continues to influence the political lives, thoughts, and attitudes of those who interact there.

Insufficient empirical attention has been paid to the continuing significance of the black counterpublic in the political lives of African Americans. Not only have historical circumstances created different forms of discourse for black people, but the complex reality of living in a society where one's daily communication is stratified and separated by race has serious political consequences for African Americans. The black counterpublic (the life that exists behind the veil) is both a reaction to exclusionary policies of white institutions and an assertion of the value of intragroup interaction that is neither observed nor policed. This book is about the effects of interaction in these counterpublic spaces and how they contribute to the reproduction of black ideology.

This book investigates how this distinct black life contributes to the development of political thought among African Americans. By focusing on the development of political worldviews among African Americans, it contributes important insights about the nature of ideology. It examines how black people use their interactions with one another in the black counterpublic to develop collective understandings of their political interests. These understandings constitute ideological stances, which both tie black people to an African American intellectual tradition and inform contemporary strategic thinking about the political and social world. This work intervenes in current notions of ideology by demonstrating that black people construct personal worldviews by borrowing from multiple ideological traditions in ways that are complex and often surprising. It is not only an empirical study intended to provide an accurate depiction of contemporary black thought, it is also a theoretical contribution that forces a reevaluation of social scientific understandings of ideology, its reproduction in marginalized communities, and its influence on individual social and political attitudes.

Two critical arguments frame this book. First, there are four political ideologies that constitute the framework of contemporary black political thought: black Nationalism, black Feminism, black Conservatism, and Liberal Integrationism.* These ideologies emerge from an African American intellectual tradition, and clusters of these four worldviews continue to organize individual political and racial attitudes among blacks. These ideologies help African Americans to understand persistent social and economic inequality, to identify the significance of race in that inequality, and to devise strategies for overcoming that inequality. By asserting the value of ideology as a meaningful way of understanding the political attitudes of ordinary African Americans, this text centers itself in a contemporary stream of research in political science, interested in reexamining ideology.

Second, the book offers a theory of black political thought, which states that African Americans use everyday talk to jointly develop understandings of their collective political interests. By entering spaces of everyday black talk, the book grapples in a unique way with contemporary black culture from the Baptist church, to *Essence* magazine, to hip-hop music. It returns political agency to ordinary people by privileging the voices of regular black men and women whose discussions contrib-

---

* Throughout the text, capitalization on the ideologies is used to designate specifically African American versions of these ideologies. Each of the ideological traditions discussed in this text emerges from a black intellectual history and is rooted in the experiences, traditions, and scholarship of that history. However, each is also tied to larger intellectual and political trajectories. Nationalism, feminism, conservatism, and integrationism have variants among many peoples in different times and spaces. This text is not centrally concerned with engaging the extensive literatures on these related ideological traditions. For example, although there is some reference to the research on nationalism, there is no specific attempt to locate black Nationalism within scholarship on nationalisms. Therefore, capitalization of the ideological terms is used in order to maintain both clarity and specificity with regard to the central arguments made in the book and to distinguish arguments made in reference to African American ideologies from claims about related traditions.

ute to the extraordinary process of ideology building. The text listens in on black college students talking about the Million Man March and welfare. It asks Southern, black Baptists about homosexuality and the church. And it eavesdrops on black men in a barbershop early on Saturday morning.

Because these settings are free from the discursive restrictions of the racial mask that African Americans must don when they venture beyond the veil, the counterpublic affords African Americans the opportunity to exchange interpretations of the truth; to understand the complexity of the political world; to link their individual experiences to group narratives; to identify friends and foes; to define desirable outcomes to public problems; and to devise strategies for achieving those outcomes, all through everyday talk. In short, this black counterpublic makes available the resources necessary for building the social language and individual knowledge structure that is political ideology.

This text seeks to understand men and women like Zeno, Hajj, Margaret, and Louise by investigating the ways that their interactions with other African Americans contribute to their beliefs and attitudes about the political world. The chapters that follow first present a theory linking everyday talk to black political beliefs and situate this theory in existing literatures on ideology, resistance, and public opinion. The text then presents a series of empirical chapters designed to offer evidence that African Americans do in fact use spaces such as barbershops and churches to express and explore important issues of power, inequality, race, gender, and politics, and to demonstrate that these discussions are linked to identifiable patterns of public opinion that can be understood as ideologies. This text will use ethnographic, statistical, and experimental evidence to trace contemporary African American political thought and its connection to everyday talk. Together, these empirical pieces demonstrate the existence of identifiable ideologies in contemporary mass opinion; provide some evidence of the causal linkage between conversations among African Americans and the expression of ideological attitudes; and flesh out the content of these conversations through careful observational work. Finally, the book offers evidence that the ideological work done by ordinary men and women actually constrains the content and style of ideological appeals made by political elites. Ultimately the text both revives the concept of ideology as a useful construct for understanding the political attitudes of ordinary men and women and demonstrates that a substantial portion of the work of ideological development occurs through processes of adult socialization in the African American counterpublic.

BARBERSHOPS, BIBLES, AND BET

CHAPTER ONE

Everyday Talk and Ideology

Say it loud: "I'm Black and I'm proud."
— James Brown, 1968

Instead of a closing-ranks mentality, a prophetic framework
encourages a coalition strategy with those deeply committed to
antiracist struggle.
— Cornel West, 1993

They have journeyed through the pothole-ridden road of liberal
promises and found it ends in a frustrating dead end.
— Black and Right, 1997

Whoever walked behind anyone to freedom? If we can't go hand
in hand I don't want to go.
— Hazel Scott, 1974

BLACK PEOPLE come together to worship; organize around communal problems; sit together to cut and style one another's hair; pass news about each other through oral and written networks; and use music, style, and humor to communicate with each other. Along with the intimacies of family and the responsibilities of work, these are the everyday spaces of black people's lives. Yet, with the exception of the church, these everyday contexts of black interactions have largely escaped the notice of social scientists studying the politics of black communities. To more fully appreciate the political thought and action of African Americans, it is imperative to understand that these interactions are more than social. They are the spaces where African Americans jointly develop understandings of their collective interests and create strategies to navigate the complex political world. These strategies are best understood as ideologies, tied to a black intellectual tradition and alive in contemporary African American public opinion. The study of everyday talk in spaces of ordinary black life provides a framework for understanding what African Americans think and the mechanisms of how black people develop political attitudes.

If we are to understand the genesis and development of political thought among African Americans it is important, but insufficient, to study the fully articulated ideological utterances of black elites. It is important, but insufficient, to map the extraordinary instances of mass-based social movements. It is important, but insufficient, to apply, without revision, models of American public opinion primarily designed to investigate the attitudes of white Americans. It is important, but insufficient, to study the influence of family and childhood socialization on individual attitudes. Understanding African American political attitudes requires an analysis of seemingly mundane interactions and ordinary circumstances of daily black life, because it is in these circumstances that African Americans often do the surprising and critical work of constructing meaningful political worldviews. Through worship, discussion, music, laughter, and news, African Americans construct meaning from the ordinary. Therefore, one important element in understanding how black people interpret and make sense of the political world is to listen in on their everyday talk.

That discourse is central to the work of politics is an old notion. Critical theorists, largely within their work on the public sphere, have argued for the essential role of citizen conversation in cultivating democratic attitudes and action (Tocqueville 1835; Arendt 1958; Habermas 1962; Eagleton 1985; Herbst 1994; Putnam 2000). Mansbridge (1999) locates the everyday talk of citizens at the center of the deliberative political system. She calls attention to this system of interactions that anchors democratic processes and argues that everyday talk is as important as formal deliberation to producing creative and just governance. Engaging in either purely expressive or more goal-directed conversations in protected spaces allows citizens to identify conflicts, better understand their interests, and learn whether or not their interests contribute to a common good.

Gamson empirically demonstrates the significance of ordinary citizen interaction and argues that the study of American public opinion is plagued by a serious deficiency in its failure to account for these interactions. Referencing the collective knowledge of decades of public opinion scholarship, Gamson notes, "We do understand a lot about the end product—the content of opinions they [the American public] express. But on how they get there, on what the issues mean to people, and how they reach their conclusions, we are still groping" (1992, xi). For Gamson, political talk supplies the answers to these unsolved puzzles of public opinion. Listening to people talk about politics, he argues, "allow[s] us to observe the natural vocabulary with which people formulate meaning about issues" (192), and thus to explore the ways that citizens are able to make sense of political issues about which they appear to have little information. Sociologist Nina Eliaoph argues that neither the theoretical contributions of critical theorists nor the empirical work of social scientists have gone far enough in studying the politics of citizen talk because "none of these works have analyzed actual political conversations as they unfold in real time, within existing groups, circulating across a range of everyday life spaces" (1996, 263).

This book makes progress toward the goal of better understanding how ordinary deliberative processes contribute to the work of democratic politics. Using the specific case of African Americans and employing a number of social scientific methods of inquiry, it offers both a theoretical and empirical exploration of ordinary black people's political attitudes and the processes that contribute to their development. This study both identifies several unique patterns of public opinion among African Americans that can be understood as expressions of black political ideology and uses an analysis of black organizations, public spaces, and information networks to suggest the ways that African Americans (re)produce these ideologies when they interact with one another. Ordinary spaces of everyday talk among African Americans serve as forums for dialogue that contribute both to the development of individual ideological dispositions and to the revisions of ideologies across time. A study of ideology formation through this talk demonstrates that engaging in black community dialogue is a distinct process that affects ideology separately from the impact of socioeconomic or demographic variables and shows that black political thought can be understood more fully through an analysis of the ways that African Americans use conversation to engage in ideological construction.

AFRICAN AMERICAN COUNTERPUBLIC

There is no better place to begin an empirical study of the relevance of everyday talk to American politics than among African Americans. Studies of black political participation have demonstrated the historic and continued importance of a communal approach to political life among African Americans (Campbell et al. 1960; Dawson 1994; Tate 1993). African American cultural and political life is shaped by a reliance on and respect for oral communication (Henry 1990; Levine 1977). Because black politics is traditionally marked by communalism and orality, the "search for black ideology must begin with the oral tradition" (Henry 1990, 7). It must begin with the study of the conversatin', shit talkin', gab fest, rap sessions, where black people are just kickin' it on the set. Such a study is situated squarely within the concerns raised by James Scott (1985, 1990) and Robin Kelley (1994) about the ways that subjugated members of society resist hegemony.

Scott (1990) locates resistance to political, cultural, and ideological hegemony among the daily acts of the relatively powerless. While the social movements literature tells us about what happens in extraordinary circumstances when marginalized members of society directly confront oppressive forces,[1] Scott's contribution is to allow us to glimpse how normal circumstances contribute to hidden modes of resistance. Scott juxtaposes public and hidden transcripts and encourages close observation of the acts, language, and symbols of the hidden narratives acted out offstage. The study of the everyday allows entry into the world where the "ordinary weapons of powerless groups" are forged. The study of African Americans interacting with one another apart from whites is in the spirit of Scott's concerns with how the subjugated develop distinct political realities that often counter the hegemonic narratives of the powerful.

Robin Kelley takes up this project in *Race Rebels*, where he explicitly links Scott's theory of the hidden transcript to daily acts of African American resistance in the Jim Crow South and contemporary urban spaces. Kelley delineates black working-class resistance of both white domination and black middle-class cultural norms. Articulating why the everyday illuminates the politics of African Americans, Kelley firmly rejects "the tendency to dichotomize people's lives, to assume that clear-cut 'political' motivations exist separately from issues of economic well being, safety, pleasure, cultural expression, sexuality, freedom of mobility, and other facets of daily life. Politics is not separate from lived experience or the imaginary world of what is possible; to the contrary, politics is about these things" (1994, 10).

Both Scott and Kelley offer an important reconceptualization of the behavior of subjugated populations and of politics. Foot dragging, sabotage, and dissembling can be understood as weapons of resistance used by those without access to conventional forms of power and influence, rather than seen as pathological behavior by lesser members of the polity. Politics can be found hidden in the zoot suits, rap lyrics, and broken milkshake machines of the black working class. While this text is not primarily interested in *acts* of resistance per se, it is interested in discourse that occurs as part of creating the hidden transcript.

In black public spaces, in black organizations, and through black information networks, African Americans enter into dialogue with one another. Much of what they discuss is task-specific, personal, or frivolous. Church members plan choir rehearsal. Friends share stories about their families. Neighbors gossip. Sports fans argue about what team will win on Friday night. But alongside these kinds of conversations is an everyday talk that helps black people to develop collective definitions of their political interests. Embedded within conversations that are not always overtly political is language that seeks to understand American inequality, to define the importance of race in creating inequality, to determine the role of whites in perpetuating inequality, and to devise strategies for advancing the interests of self and group. It often does so through the use of personal anecdote, urban legend, and tall tales, but the work of this everyday talk is serious. By uncovering how ideology is developed by black people talking to one another in their daily lives, we can better describe, analyze, and predict variation in African American political thought.[2]

Scholars have long been interested in determining the ways that political culture is created and transmitted in identifiable communities. Habermas's (1984) theory of the bourgeois public sphere, where men engage in creating the politics of our "lifeworld," has been particularly influential in shaping contemporary discourse on the role of deliberation in the development of political worldviews. Both feminist and black studies scholars have critiqued his formulation of the public sphere as inappropriate for the study of marginalized publics. Feminist scholar Nancy Fraser critiques Habermas for idealizing the liberal public sphere because of his failure to account for competing public spheres, or counterpublics, that are not liberal, bourgeois, or male. "Virtually from the beginning, counterpublics contested the exclusionary norms of the bourgeois public, elaborating alternative styles of political behavior and alternative norms of public speech" (Fraser 1989, 116). For Fraser, the assumptions of deliberation that underlie Habermas' conception of a single public sphere are exclusionary and masculinist. Stratified societies are better served by a plurality of competing publics than a single deliberative arena governed by the discursive norms of the powerful. These subaltern counterpublics are "parallel discursive arenas where members of subordinated social groups invent and circulate counterdiscourses to formulate oppositional interpretations of their identities, interests, and needs" (1989, 123).

Scholars of African American politics have also leveled critiques of the exclusionary Habermas formulation. These scholars have sought to define the African American counterpublic as a "sphere of critical practice and visionary politics, in which intellectuals can join with the energies of the street, the school, the church, and the city to constitute a challenge to the exclusionary violence of much public space in the United States" (Black Public Sphere Collective 1995). For scholars of black politics, Habermas's formulation does not adequately account for the ways that inequality alters discursive relations between citizens, nor does it speak to the ways that the relatively powerless are excluded from the idealized bourgeois space. "The bourgeois public sphere has a historically specific provenance and development; it cannot be simply mapped onto contemporary African American lifeworlds" (Holt 1995, 326).

Scholars of black history, society, and politics have offered broader visions of the black counterpublic as an oppositional space composed of relatively autonomous spaces of civic life and culture.

It is incorrect to conceive of the black counterpublic as historically static or as ideologically cohesive at any given historical moment. The churches, political organizations, news outlets, fraternal clubs, mutual aid societies, barbershops, juke joints, and labor unions that constitute the black counterpublic are internally contested spaces. Identities of gender, class, color, sexuality, and privilege crosscut the terrain of a racially homogenous public sphere. Fraser reminds us that even oppositional counterpublics are not always virtuous, "even those with democratic and egalitarian intentions are not always above practicing their own modes of informal exclusion and marginalization" (1989, 124). In pursuit of racial goals, black counterpublics have often sought to suppress the internal differences of gender, class, and sexual identity that mark blackness (Cohen 1999). Jane Mansbridge (1999) warns that deliberative processes can transform the "I" into "we" through an often invisible assertion of control by the more powerful members of the group. The African American counterpublic is vulnerable to such exclusionary practices. Thus the African American counterpublic itself spawns subaltern, oppositional publics organized around gender, class, color, and sexual identity. The existence of these multiple layers complicates the task of talking about a single black counterpublic just as the existence of a black counterpublic challenges the notion of a single public sphere.

The black counterpublic is historically contingent, with different elements of the sphere emerging as relevant in distinct moments. The black press in the years before the Civil War (Hutton 1992); the clubs of middle-class black women at the turn of the century (Higginbotham 1993); the church meeting halls of the civil rights movement (Morris 1984); and the hip-hop of the late 1990s (Kelley 1994) all constitute aspects of the black public sphere that have taken on relatively greater significance as sites of political discussion in black communities at different points in American history. Although historically contingent and internally contested, it is still meaningful to speak of a black public sphere. Michael Dawson reminds us that "the black counterpublic sphere is the product of both the historically imposed separation of blacks from whites throughout most of American history and the embracing of the concept of black autonomy as both an institutional principle and an ideological orientation" (2001, 27). Within this counterpublic, African Americans produce hidden transcripts, not with a single, unchanging voice, but with many that are all distinctly shaped by the position of blackness in American society.

The promise of a unique and insurgent black politics is at stake in the contest over the contours of the black counterpublic. The hidden transcript is a collective enterprise that must be created within a public sphere that operates beneath the surveillance of dominant classes. "For that to occur, the subordinate group must carve out for itself social spaces insulated from control and surveillance from above. If we are to understand the process by which resistance is developed and codified, the analysis of the creation of these offstage social spaces becomes a vital task" (Scott 1994, 118). But, in 1994, political scientist Michael Dawson questioned whether a counterpublic still existed among African Americans in the nineties. Dawson asserts that "a black public sphere does not exist in contemporary America, if by that we mean a set of institutions, communication networks, and practices which facilitate debate of causes and remedies to the current combination of political setbacks and economic devastation facing major segments of the Black community" (1995, 201). If this pessimistic assertion is correct, then the prospects for a unique black politics forged through collective racial deliberation are bleak.

The current text takes issue with the notion that the black counterpublic was nonexistent in the 1990s. Even today, there are contemporary social sites carved out by African Americans in which African Americans create hidden transcripts by exploring ideological alternatives to dominant white discourses. These gathering places provide space for black people to engage in everyday talk. In the most contemporary formulation of the black counterpublic there are three areas of particular interest: black organizations, black public spaces, and black information networks.[3]

The proliferation of voluntary, formal organizations in the black community is a testament to the centrality of organizations to the black counterpublic. By the close of the civil rights movement, African Americans had established 35 national black political organizations with 3 million members, 112 predominately black colleges and universities, 37 national black professional organizations, 17 national women's organizations, and 36 national fraternal organizations (Yearwood 1978). More importantly, African Americans have engineered and sustained a counterpublic through the creation of separate, indigenous, race-based institutions at the local and community level. These local organizations serve political, social, economic, and spiritual functions. Often a single organization serves several of these purposes simultaneously. Organizations have traditionally served as crucial sources of collective political, educational, and economic advancement for African Americans. They also serve as sites for dialogue, discussion, and dissension within the community. They are the vehicles for black political leaders to persuade and mobilize the community and the forum where people communicate with leaders by granting or withdrawing support. Many black organizations whose primary purpose is not political in fact serve important political functions in the black community.

The church is widely acknowledged as the single most important political organization among African Americans (Lincoln and Mamiya 1990; Wilcox and Gomez 1990; Higginbotham 1993; Smith 1994). It is the oldest indigenous black institution, and it is historically and currently significant in developing African American political culture and encouraging African American political participation (Chong 1991; McAdam, 1982; Dawson 1994; Tate 1993; Holden 1973; Henry 1990; Morris 1984). But churches are not political organizations. Their sacred and spiritual functions, not their political ones, are the primary purpose of their existence. However, the historic and contemporary centrality of the black church has extended into social, political, and economic realms. Interaction in the church is particularly relevant for shaping black political ideology because the church offers individuals the opportunity to come together and discuss how to manage the complexities and rigors of life. The church is in the advice-giving business. The content of the spiritual advice it gives can shape the political perspective of those who receive it. Previous research shows that the black church fosters the networks, skills, mobilization, and contact opportunities necessary to nurture political action (McAdam 1982, Morris 1984) and contributes to the psychological resources, such as self esteem and internal efficacy, that encourage black churchgoers to engage with politics (Harris 1999; Calhoun-Brown 1996; Ellison 1993).

Black public spaces are at the heart of the black counterpublic. It is in public spaces where the potential of the black counterpublic is manifest. Public spaces are those forums where African Americans believe themselves to be exclusively in the company of other African Americans. These spaces are generally marked by a constant physical space that has regularly changing "memberships." Black public spaces are unique because African Americans come together in these arenas *because* of their blackness in a way that can, but does not necessarily, happen in other counterpublic arenas. In organizations individuals come together because of the particular mission of the organization. For example, one attends a black church both to worship God and to be with other black people. But in public spaces blackness can be a sufficient condition for membership. When black students sit together in the cafeteria, it is not because they all like each other, or because they are necessarily making a cliché stance on black unity. The conscious and voluntary creation of separate black cafeteria tables is an example of students finding that race is a sufficient condition for togetherness. There is no established definition of what constitutes the boundaries of black public space. However, there is one type of space that would fall within any definition: barbershops and beauty salons. Black-owned and supported barbershops and beauty salons are public spaces because the shops are definite and semipermanent physical spaces even though the people who occupy the space change regularly.

Barbershops and beauty salons have both a mythic and an actual relevance among African Americans. Drake and Cayton remarked in *Black Metropolis*, "If colored undertakers have a virtual monopoly in burying the Negro dead, the colored barber and beautician have an even more exclusive monopoly in beautifying the living" (1945, 460). Barbershops are the archetype of the black public space, consisting of a relatively permanent physical space, but with constantly changing memberships. Barbers and hairstylists still constitute the overwhelming majority of entrepreneurs in the African American community. There is an informal hierarchy of the stylists and regular customers, but there is no official organization or membership. The boundaries to these spaces are permeable and unfixed, meaning that the composition and characteristics of the space are constantly shifting. The one constant is that black people in these spaces believe themselves to be free to talk to one another beyond the gaze of racial others. Usually financially autonomous, sole proprietorships, black barbershops and salons operate beyond the fiscal control and below the radar of whites.[4]

African Americans also make contact with one another outside of formal organizations or public spaces. African American popular culture, black literature, movies, and music as well as black news media are means through which African Americans engage with one another in a kind of everyday talk. These media convey information about black people, create interpretations of black experiences in America, reinforce shared cultural norms and actions among African Americans, and produce representations of black life. African Americans share the larger American popular culture and media but also have access to predominately and uniquely black information sources.[5] African American music, movies, television, newspapers, and magazines give voice to many different elements of black American life, sometimes in ways that are controversial, problematic, subjective, or distressing.

Race is a social construct that adjusts through time and space, and American blackness is constantly subject to redefinition both within and outside the group. Popular culture is one of the ways that African Americans engage in the creation of a definition of blackness.[6] Black popular culture in the form of music, media, and entertainment communicates what is "acceptable and authentic" in terms of fashion, speech patterns, personal style, and personal behavior.[7] Similarly, these information sources communicate what political ideas are considered "acceptable and authentic." In their mammoth study of Chicago's Bronzeville community in the early twentieth century Drake and Cayton explained that as a black newspaper, "The *Defender*, like all other Negro weeklies, has the dual function of reporting news and stimulating race solidarity" (1945, 411). Then and now, the black media maintains an African American readership, viewership, or clientele by carving out a role as a racial institution.

> The Chicago *Defender* is typical of America's three hundred Negro weeklies in tone and format. Some may be more or less belligerent or sensational, but all conceive of themselves as "Race papers." Despite the fact that these papers are businesses, they like to define their role as did Fernand Barnett in the Eighties: "The *Conservator* is a creature born of our enthusiastic desire to benefit our people rather than any motive of self-aggrandizement or pecuniary profit." Bronzeville people know that this is only a half-truth, but they do not expect the Negro press to be Simon-pure; they merely expect it to be interesting and to put up a fight while it tries to make money." (1945, 412)

It is difficult to provide explicit boundaries for the definition of black media. Black media certainly includes newspapers, magazines, and radio stations that are owned by African Americans and marketed to a predominantly black audience, but it also includes books and novels by black authors and radio stations that are not owned by, but are staffed by and promoted to African Americans. To the extent that African Americans perceive a media source (television show, radio station, novel, magazine, movie, or Internet website) to be something that "belongs" to black people, it can be considered a black media space. Although impossible to quantify, to the extent that there is a broad sense among blacks that "this is *our* show," it is a part of everyday black talk. When African Americans perceive a media source as a medium for expression of racial humor, information, entertainment, or values, then it is proper to understand that source as part of black media. Actual fiscal ownership is less important than a sense of psychic ownership in defining a media source as a part of the black counterpublic.

Jordan's historiography of the role of the black press in World War I describes black newspapers as occupying "a parallel public sphere, not fully a part of the mainstream of public opinion and debate that links society and state but a separate arena where African Americans have worked out among themselves alternatives to the dominant culture's views of their identities and interests" (2001, 4). This description situates the black press squarely at the center of the black counterpublic during the war years. The contemporary independent black press is substantially weaker than the one Jordan chronicles. But if we expand our understanding of the black press to include publications like *Essence*, *Ebony*, *Jet*; Internet sites like Black Voices; cable television stations like BET., popular black novels like those by E. Lynn Harris, and nonfiction self-help texts like those by Iylana Vanzant, then it is still possible to identify a parallel public sphere where African Americans are doing the work of identity and interest formation.

The black counterpublic is not solely or even primarily constituted as a political realm. African Americans do not necessarily enter into racialized discourse for the explicit purpose of developing public, participatory strategies. There are aspects of the counterpublics that are formed for these purposes. For example, civil rights organizations have as their main organizing purpose the articulation of black public interests and agitation for political, economic, and social rights, but much of the black counterpublic is a response to exclusion from high politics of traditional participation (voting, office seeking, political organizing). These spaces exist as an assertion of African American uniqueness in cultural, artistic, epistemological, and spiritual frames. Everyday black talk asserts a need for a separate black sphere that nurtures multiple facets of African American intellect and spirit.

IDEOLOGICAL DEVELOPMENT THROUGH EVERYDAY TALK

Think of an African American woman who comes to her Bible study class on Wednesday evening after leaving her office job. She sits down in the pew and starts chatting with other group members as they wait for the minister to arrive. She shares several stories illustrating how verbally abusive and condescending her white male supervisor has acted toward her this week. Upon hearing the stories, one man shakes his head in disgust, calls the supervisor a Godless racist, says that African American cannot trust whites, especially those in positions of direct authority over blacks, and suggests that the woman sabotage the supervisor on one of the work assignments with which he has recently overburdened her. Another woman, listening to the narrative, brands the brother's response as un-Christian and advises the woman that it is her responsibility to complete her job tasks to the best of her ability regardless of the discomfort she may experience in this situation. She argues that God will fight the battle for his people as long as they are living by the right moral standards. By the time the minister arrives, the three congregants are engaged in a heated discussion about whether, as Christians, black people should confront racist whites. This exchange may seem to be about private and theological matters, but debating strategies of resistance or acquiescence in the private sphere of employment is relevant for deciding when to employ these tactics in the political world. By discussing the relationship of God to black people and their struggle with whites, these Bible study participants are expressing judgments of deep political relevance. And potentially they are helping one another form answers to questions that are central to the development of political ideology.

The theory of everyday talk posits that although none of the individuals engaging in the conversation will be instantly convinced by the arguments of others, all will be affected by their participation in this conversation. Each person who has shared in this interaction will adjust his or her political attitudes to the extent that she or he is convinced by the various arguments being made. It is possible that if this kind of discussion occurred regularly in the Bible study class, and if the advice of the class had a consistent ideological bent, then the individuals who regularly meet in this space are likely to develop similar approaches to addressing discriminatory circumstances.

Everyday talk may operate in this way, allowing African Americans to use their interactions in the counterpublic to construct hidden transcripts. One way to understand this process is the production and reproduction of political ideologies. The term political ideology is a contentious one in the study of American politics from at least two perspectives. First, there is a strong tradition within political theory that connotes ideology negatively as the fictions of ruling elites used to deceive the masses of their true interests (Horkheimer 1972; Rorty 1994; Arendt 1958). Second, a related but distinct tradition in empirical public opinion research argues that mass publics are largely incapable of the sophisticated reasoning necessary to define attitudes as ideological (Converse 1964; Kinder 1983; Zaller 1992).

Ideology is contested terrain among critical political theorists, particularly those working in a Marxist tradition. For these scholars, ideology is a largely pejorative term used to describe the deceptive illusions that do the oppressive work of promoting false consciousness, masking class interests and social cleavages, and usurping the potential for democratic debate (Arendt 1958; Horkheimer 1972; Habermas 1989). Ideology represents illusory rationalizations for inequality and injustice. It is maligned for its deceptive disconnection from the material world, its false essentializing influence in the face of historical contingencies, and its mystifying effect on the relatively powerless. Reviewing the Marxist approach to ideology, Eagleton asserts that ideology is understood in this tradition as a "set of discursive strategies for legitimating a dominant power, . . . a coherent bloc of ideas, which effectively secures the power of a governing group" (1994, 8). There are at least two strands of

Marxist critique of ideology: on the one hand is the notion that ideologies, as systems of ideas, are themselves internally false or deceiving, but on the other hand, and more central to Marx's own concern in early writings, is the notion that ideologues, by functioning in the realm of ideas, ignore the concrete world of material conditions. By this argument, the system of ideas itself may be unobjectionable, but it is superfluous to the work of real politics. Arendt's critique of ideology is among the most scathing. In her estimation, all ideologies contain totalitarian elements. Totalitarian movements are often necessary to bring these characteristics into fruition, but the seeds of domination are inherent in all ideological projects. "The real nature of all ideologies was revealed only in the role that the ideology plays in the apparatus of totalitarian domination" (1958, 470).

Viewed from this scholarly tradition, it is difficult to imagine why one would evoke ideology to describe political attitudes created as part of the resistant hidden transcripts of subordinate peoples such as contemporary African Americans. To the extent that ideology conjures images of hegemonic domination, it is hard to appreciate the desirability of ideology as a descriptor for the work of everyday black talk. However, Dawson rightly asserts that the Marxist tradition in the study of ideology cannot fully account for the complicated ways that ideology operates among African Americans. "A common feature of all these critiques of ideology is their assertion that a single, universal ideology dominates society. Many scholars critique Habermas' treatment of the public sphere on the grounds that he assume a single bourgeois sphere, it is equally incorrect to assume that a single ideology operates within societies that have heterogeneous populations and multiple public spheres" (2001, 50).

Once we allow that the African American counterpublic is operating beyond the reach of powerful whites, we must allow for the possibility that the ideological work being done in that counterpublic is distinct from the hegemonic work of elite discourse.[8] Certainly, there are individual African Americans whose political attitudes reflect an embrace of hegemonic elements of American ideology such as meritocracy, individualism, and uncritical patriotism. But ideological projects within black discourse specifically counter these notions. Reclaiming ideology as a way of understanding contemporary black political attitudes is not so much grounded in the work of critical theorists on the left as it is responsive to the elitist literature of empirical, public opinion researchers who, in a parallel tradition, have wrested ideology from ordinary citizens.

At the root of this tradition is Converse's study of mass belief systems, which demonstrated that the American electorate fails to hold meaningful beliefs on many fundamental political questions. Converse avoided the term ideology but defined belief systems as "a configuration of ideas and attitudes in which the elements are bound together by some form of constraint or functional interdependence" (1964, 207). Constraint, for Converse, is the predicative capacity of one belief in the system with respect to other beliefs in the system. An individual demonstrated constraint if a conservative perspective on social security was predicative of a conservative position on federal aid to education and if a change in one belief forced reevaluation of other beliefs in the system. His empirical evidence suggested that mass belief systems lacked the constraint, stability, and range he associated with ideological thinking and showed that individuals professed agreement with multiple, contradictory positions; professed different and often opposing attitudes over time; and failed to apply general political concepts to specific, concrete instances. His research mounted a serious challenge to earlier assumptions about the nature of public opinion.

Scholars wondered what were the implications for democracy if average men and women are guided by no identifiable ideological dispositions. Such findings call into question the capacity of ordinary citizens to make democratic decisions. Political psychologists have attempted to revive ordinary citizens by suggesting that individuals process large amounts of information and make difficult political decisions by using heuristics, schemas, and other rational cognitive tools (Popkin 1994; Conover and Feldman 1981; Feldman 1988, Lau and Sears 1986, Dawson 1994). Citizens may not have complete recall of political figures or events, but they are remarkably capable of creating order and meaning both in low-information and information-saturated environments. This research renewed faith in the ability of citizens to handle the complexities of democratic participation, but little contemporary work has attempted to revive the notion of ideology per se as a way of describing the political worldviews of ordinary African Americans.

The recent work of Michael Dawson is an exception. Dawson critiques both Converse and his later proponent Don Kinder as having proscribed an overly narrow and elitist definition of ideology that "is removed both from the considerations of social groups and from other aspects of everyday life. . . . This is an extraordinarily elitist and misguided view of the connection between ideology and politics. . . . Converse and Kinder's vision of ideology is so abstract that it is removed from the field of politics" (2001, 62).

Dawson goes on to criticize Zaller's *The Nature and Origins of Mass Opinion*. Perhaps the most influential contemporary work on American public opinion, Zaller's is a deductive model accounting for how individuals respond to survey questions. Zaller proposes a "Receive-Accept-Sample" or RAS model composed of four axioms: reception, resistance, accessibility, and response, and he accounts for elements of ambivalence and unevenness in public opinion. His model tells a story that explains inconsistencies in the constraint and stability of mass opinion by delineating the role of political awareness in connecting ordinary citizens with elite discourse. While these are significant contributions, Zaller's theories further remove ideology from the everyday. For Zaller, ideology is only "a mechanism by which ordinary citizens make contact with specialists who are knowledgeable on controversial issues and who share citizen predispositions" (1992, 327). Thus, ideology is removed from its historical context and is, by definition, outside the capacity of ordinary men and women. Borrowing the language of Dawson's critique, "the rupture between social and political theory on the one hand, and empirical research on the other is complete. . . . Conservative economic policy is what conservative economists say it is, and conservative foreign policy becomes what conservative foreign policy experts say it is" (Dawson 2001, 63) While formally rejecting the notion of elite manipulation, Zaller continues to locate ideology exclusively within the ranks of specialists who set the terms of discourse. Common men and women are able only to sample from these elite discourses; there is no reproduction or revision of ideology on the ground. For many public opinion researchers of the second half of the twentieth century, the capacity to reason ideologically rests solely with elites.[9] This is a strikingly different conception of ideology from that which emerges from an investigation of the everyday, which asserts the value of uncovering ideology in the messier attitudes of ordinary citizens.[10]

RESTORING IDEOLOGY

Borrowing from literatures in social psychology, public opinion, and discourse studies, ideology in this text is understood as public discourse that is rooted in the life and thoughts of ordinary men and women. Ideology is both a cognitive structure that exists in the minds of individuals and a social construct that binds individuals to social groups. For individuals, ideology is an organized system of beliefs, values, and attitudes (Rokeach 1968). Beliefs are those aspects of thought that individuals associate with deeply held convictions about truth. To say someone believes something is to suggest that they hold that particular piece of information to be true. Beliefs are the "cognitive components that make up our understanding of the way things are" (Glynn et al. 1999, 104). Values are an expression of how things ought to be. Like beliefs, values are rooted in deeply embedded notions of truth. Values can be either terminal ends or instrumental means (Rokeach 1973). Some are articulated and reinforced by family during childhood; created and disseminated by religious teachings and morality systems; and presented as ideals specific to the society, nation, cultural, or racial group.

Ideology is composed of attitudes, which are individual orientations toward objects and are recognizable as personal choices rather than absolutes (Glynn et al. 1999). Public opinion scholars measure and predict mass attitudes toward candidates, parties, policies, and issues. Pollsters predict the outcome of elections based on the expressed attitudes of registered voters in the months and weeks preceding the election. Social scientists describe the continuing or decreasing relevance of racial animosity by exploring the attitudes of whites toward African Americans and Latinos. Representatives gauge the mood of their constituents by asking for their attitudes toward economic and social issues. Although attitudes are the most directly observable and measurable element of political thought, they are derived from systems of beliefs and values, which guide their development and expression. Together, beliefs, values, and attitudes create a *knowledge structure*. The particular order that these beliefs, values, and attitudes take is the framework for individual ideology.

Ideology can be understood in its social form as a language because, like language, ideology is a social construction created and accessed by individuals. As Mannheim's early study of ideology asserts, "only in a quite limited sense does an individual create out of himself the mode of speech and thought that we attribute to him. He speaks the language of his group; he thinks in the manner in which his group thinks" (1936, 5). In this way, ideologies are like natural language. Languages such as English, Chinese, or Kiswahili are also systems that are essentially social and shared by the members of a group—the speakers of those languages. But that does not keep the members of such a speech community from using the language individually (van Dijk 1998). Scott's understanding of the hidden transcript is also illuminated by the language metaphor. "The hidden transcript has no reality as pure thought; it exists only to the extent that it is practiced, articulated, enacted, disseminated within these offstage social sites . . . not unlike the way in which a distinctive dialect develops. A dialect develops as a group of speakers mixes frequently with one another and rarely with others. Their speech patterns gradually diverge from those of the parent language" (1990, 119, 135). So too, does a distinct ideological language develop among "speakers" in the black counterpublic.

Like language, ideology gives group members a way of communicating by beginning with a set of critical, shared assumptions that govern interaction. These assumptions are not explicitly discussed; instead they structure the way that group members talk to one another. Additionally, ideology is like language because individual use and expression of both ideology and language are subject to wide variation and even contradictory or wrong usage. Just as we recognize both the distinct Boston accent and the Southern drawl as individual expressions of American English, we also should be willing to accept that individual political attitudes can have a distinct accent and still be guided by an ideological construct. Just as individual grammar can be wrong by the official standards of the English language and still be recognizable as English (and not Chinese or Kiswahili), so too can some individual expressions of political attitudes be "wrong" by the standards of the ideology and still be recognizable as part of that ideological language.

Socially, ideology is composed of a set of problems and the solutions to those problems. Socially, what ideology *is* is closely related to what ideology *does*. Ideology poses a set of dilemmas, provides the answers to those questions, and simultaneously constructs an interpretative narrative of the world and of the group. Scholars of political ideology have offered a number of possibilities for the question and answer structure of ideology. Lane (1962) states that political ideology deals with the questions of who will be the rulers, how will the rulers be selected, and by what principles will they govern. Hinich and Munger (1996) assert that ideology answers what is good, who gets what, and who rules. Van Dijk (1998) writes that ideology answers who are we, what do we do, why do we do this, what are our values, what is our social position, and what are our resources. With specific application to black political ideology, Dawson (2001) argues that ideology responds to the questions who or what is the enemy, who are friends, what is America like, what is the nature of whites, and what strategies with regard to whites are necessary or desirable.

Throughout this text, black political ideology is understood as serving six related functions: interpreting truth, reducing complexity, linking individual experiences to group narratives, identifying friends and foes, defining what is desirable, and providing a range of possible strategies for achieving desired outcomes.

Ideology is an interpreter of truth. Ideology is what groups believe and claim to know. For the social group, the truths created by ideology are its core ideas, not its specific policy prescriptions. Ideological adherents may diverge on a number of specific opinions, but they must agree on the basic truths of the ideology.[11] In the process of asserting and maintaining truth, ideology also reduces complexity. Socially, ideology functions similarly to how schemas work for individual thinkers. Ideology reduces complexity by working as a perceptual screen. The a priori truth assumptions of ideology give individual adherents a way to filter information in the political world. In this way, ideology is a social decision rule that provides a road map for navigating the political world.

Ideology also gives meaning to ambiguous personal and historical circumstances. Ideology provides a lens through which individuals give political meaning to occurrences in their lives. Just as individuals are linked to their social group through a shared language, so too are they linked to an ideological group by a shared interpretation of personal experience. Individual lives are filled with a number of unambiguous circumstances; things that people know are good or bad. Other life experiences are less clearly endowed with social meaning. How these experiences are understood is largely a result of ideological position.

Further, ideology proscribes rules for membership in the group, thereby defining who is in and who is out. By identifying friends and foes, ideology provides answers to the questions who are we and what do we stand for? Friends and enemies are then defined with respect to this self-definition and goal statement. Ideology not only provides a statement of the problems facing a social group; it also suggests a vision for the future. Ideology defines what is desirable for the social group. The definition of desirable outcomes is central to popular understandings of ideology. When the average American speaks about liberals or conservatives, he or she means people who either do or do not envision government involvement in a range of policy areas as desirable. But definition of "the good" is only a part (albeit an important part) of what ideology does. Defining the good is an extension of the basic truths that ideology rests on and is intimately linked to the conceptions of friends and foes. We want to be with our friends and triumph over or at least be separate from our enemies, and we want the truth to be reflected in our daily lives. Defining the desirable is also part of how ideology functions to reduce complexity. By determining which outcomes are good and which are bad, ideology helps adherents to better understand the political world by defining actions, people, and policies with respect to the ideologically defined good.

Finally, ideology offers a range of possible strategies for achieving desired outcomes. Not only do ideologies provide a definition of the good and a vision for the future; they offer some prescriptions for achieving it. Each ideology offers a range of possibilities. There is no single strategy for achieving each desired goal. Ideologies offer adherents a variety of strategies for achieving desired goals. In addition to narrowly defined political approaches, many of these strategies are reflected in the way that individuals live their daily lives. Ideology not only shows up in people's electoral and policy decisions, it also can be evidenced in the schools where they send their children, the places where they buy their cars, and even the way they style their hair. Because ideology is grounded in core beliefs, it has an extensive impact on people's daily lives.

Ideology for the individual is an organized set of values, beliefs, and attitudes; for the social group, ideology is language. For both the individual and the group, ideology interprets truth, reduces complexity, links individual experiences to group narratives, identifies friends and foes, defines what is desirable, and provides a range of possible strategies for achieving desired outcomes. Because it acts as a language that provides these answers to individuals and groups, ideology can be understood as a narrative. Ideology is the story we tell ourselves and others about how the world works. The narrative encompasses historical events, personal experiences and collective realities. This narrative then directs interpretation of the political world and structures expressions of political attitudes.

AFRICAN AMERICAN POLITICAL IDEOLOGY

If ideology functions as a social narrative that interprets problems and offers solutions, it is reasonable to understand African American political attitudes as resulting from a limited number of identifiable black political ideologies. Building on the definition that ideology interprets truth, reduces complexity, links individual experiences to group narratives, identifies friends and foes, defines what is desirable, and provides a range of possible strategies for achieving desired outcomes, there are four continua relevant for understanding black political ideology. These dimensions assert that black ideology must be understood beyond a traditional left-right continuum. African American ideology cannot be easily constrained in a state-in vs. state-out dichotomy or an accommodation vs. militancy dichotomy that marks some traditional ways of approaching the study of black political thought. Existing in multiple dimensions, black ideology takes on several interrelated tasks:

1. It helps individuals determine what it means to be black in the American political system. This can range from an attitude that race is a relevant characteristic but not one that hampers life chances to the belief that race is an immutable characteristic that overdetermines life chances. It attempts to understand the extent to which blackness constrains life chances. Black Conservatism and Nationalism are on the extremes of this scale, with Liberal Integrationism and Feminism staking out positions in between these extremes.[12]

2. It helps individuals identify the relative political significance of race compared to other personal characteristics. Ideological approaches to this

question range from a belief that race is only one of several characteristics that are of political importance — for example, Feminism at one end of the continuum asserting that gender, class, sexual orientation, age, and ability are as important as race in determining position in American society — to a belief that race is the most important, relevant political characteristic. Nationalism sits at this end of the scale, asserting, in its most extreme manifestations, that all internal divisions within the black community must be subordinated so that African Americans can concentrate political and economic struggles on behalf of racial interests alone.

3. It helps individuals determine the extent to which blacks should "solve their own problems" or look to the system for assistance. At one end of this scale is Conservatism, advocating the idea that African Americans must be entirely self-sufficient, and demanding no official recognition of or redress for any historical or contemporary inequalities stemming from racial discrimination. At the other end is Liberal Integrationism's attitude that African Americans have a morally and historically justified obligation to seek specific, race-based or race-targeted benefits from the American system. Between these extremes, Nationalism and Feminism contain varying degrees of advocacy of the extent to which blacks should make demands on the American political, legal, and economic system.

4. It helps individuals determine the required degree of tactical separation from whites necessary for successful advancement of group interests. At one end is the belief that maximum integration of African Americans into the American society is the most desirable outcome of reducing black inequality. Conservatism and Liberal Integrationism share space near this pole, with both traditions perceiving whites as appropriate political partners for African Americans who are interested in achieving personal and public success. At the other end of the continuum is the belief that African Americans must achieve complete social, political, and economic independence from whites. At its most extreme, this end of the continuum can include a Nationalist belief that African Americans can achieve an equal society only in a nation state that does not include white citizens.

Each of the four ideologies occupies space at different points along these continua by offering various responses to these four racial dilemmas. There is no single dimension along which one might array these ideological approaches. At times it is Nationalism and Feminism at the poles, while at other times Liberal Integrationism and Conservatism take up the extreme positions. By identifying solutions to these four dilemmas, black political ideology functions as a social narrative that explains the sources of black inequality, justifies action of behalf of the group, provides strategies for addressing black inequality, and provides a vision of a different future. By addressing these questions, black ideologies allow African Americans to understand persistent social and economic inequality, to identify the significance of race in that inequality, to determine the role of whites in perpetuating or eliminating that inequality, and to devise strategies for overcoming that inequality. As social narratives, black political ideologies justify themselves as methods of addressing racial inequality in America.

Individuals then make use of these ideological traditions by sampling from the menu of available belief patterns. No individual African American, not even from the political elite, is likely to fit perfectly and neatly within any of these categories, but each individual thinker is likely to have a central ideological tendency that is moderated by elements of other ideological dispositions. In the empirical chapters that follow, we will meet a Baptist minister who is an Integrationist and a Feminist with touches of Nationalism. We will listen in on a Nationalist owner of a barbershop who makes occasional use of Conservative ideological arguments. We will hear how mostly Conservative students from a community college temper their own Conservatism with elements of Nationalist thought when discussing welfare reform, and how mostly Nationalist students from a historically black university are able to move toward Feminist critiques of the Million Man March. Finally, we will see how even black public figures like Colin Powell and Kweisi Mfume can be classified within a single ideological tradition while still displaying strong elements of competing political worldviews.

This sampling of ideological choices by individual thinkers has led to a rich ideological diversity within the tradition of African American political thought. Michael Dawson's *Black Visions* is the most important, comprehensive, contemporary text on black political ideology. It maps constellations of belief among African American mass publics across the twentieth century and provides careful and textured descriptions of the ideologies that reveal their nuance and complexity. It is important to understand the ways that the empirical study that follows intersects with and departs from the work in *Black Visions*. Both texts are engaged with reclaiming ideology as a useful framework for understanding black political thought. Both texts understand ordinary African Americans as central actors in the reproduction of these ideologies, and both are interested in understanding black political attitudes as heterogeneous and complex. However, there are some important differences in the emphasis and content.

First, *Black Visions*, by its title and content, reflects a deep engagement with the historical roots of black political thought. Dawson's project is, in part, to draw together a fragmented intellectual history and to link that history to current strands in public opinion. Thus *Black Visions* is intent on presenting a historically textured description of each ideological project that reflects its changing emphases and proponents over the course of the twentieth century. Alternatively, this text can only nod to those historical complexities and will paint each ideological position with broader strokes. The ideological traditions this text addresses are necessarily less fine grained with respect to their history. In some ways this book takes up where *Black Visions* leaves off, by directing attention to the most contemporary manifestations of these traditions and their reproduction in ordinary black discursive spaces. Dawson convincingly argues for the historical relevance and complexity of black political ideologies. He also offers initial evidence for their persistence in black public opinion. This text martials a broad range of empirical strategies to uncover the ways that contemporary black ideology is created through processes of everyday black talk.

Other important differences in focus distinguish these projects. Dawson is centrally concerned with the effect of structural issues such as poverty and racism on the genesis of black ideological traditions; this study takes these structures as a given and asks about the unique contribution of discourse within these structures. Dawson's story is mostly about organizers, activists, and thinkers; this narrative is about more ordinary citizens.[13] Dawson's story is historical; this one is contemporary. In many ways this text assumes the work done by Dawson. It is neither feasible nor desirable to retell the history of black ideology in this volume, but it is important to note that this text grounds its assumptions in the historical contingencies and internal heterogeneity that Dawson explicitly outlines.

Dawson's constellation of black ideologies includes six historically rooted traditions of black thought: black Marxist, black Nationalist, black Feminist, black Conservative, Activist Egalitarian, and Disillusioned Liberal ideologies. Here the framework for black political thought is constructed from four distinct African American political ideologies: black Nationalism, Conservatism, Feminism, and Liberal Integrationism. Black Marxism is not under investigation because of the contemporary focus of this inquiry. Dawson acknowledges that black Marxism coheres poorly in contemporary black opinion and is only marginally responsible for shaping and directing African American political attitudes in the nineties. Dawson's Radical Egalitarianism is defined very closely to this text's Liberal Integrationist ideology.[14] These four ideologies are not meant to be an exhaustive or exclusive formulation of black ideologies, but each has important historical traditions and particular contemporary significance to African Americans. Each has its own complex history that leads to diversity within each of the ideological approaches.[15]

Common Sense

Research in black public opinion has done the important work of asserting that African Americans are engaged members of the political system, not apolitical, uninvolved participants at the margins. In particular this research has pointed to the unique historical and cultural factors that contribute to a black politics that is distinguishable from white political traditions in the United States (Marable 1995, 1995b; Morris 1975; Walton 1985; Henry 1990). Unfortunately, the emphasis of much of this scholarly work on a unique black politics has obscured the heterogeneity within this black politics. Whether it's Levine's (1977) assertions of a single black cultural tradition or Dawson's (1994) description of a single heuristic for black political decision making, these scholars have often inadequately captured the ways that politics is a contested terrain within blackness. More recent work, most notably Cohen's *Boundaries of Blackness* (1999), challenges these notions of a unitary black politics and draws attention to the cross-cutting identities and communities within African American politics.

African American political thought can be understood as simultaneously heterogeneous and bound by important commonalities. Black Nationalism, Feminism, Conservatism, and Liberal Integrationism each represent distinct approaches to politics, but all are indigenous ideologies in that they are located in the black American experience. Each of these ideologies is part of a unique black politics because each is rooted in a notion of *black common sense*. Defined by Lubiano as "ideology lived and articulated in everyday understanding of the world and one's place in it" (1998, 232), by my definition, black common sense is the idea among African Americans that blackness is a meaningful political category. Rootedness in black common sense sets black political ideologies apart from political ideologies more generally. Adherents to a black common sense tradition perceive blackness as identifiable, persistent over time, and relevant to making personal life decisions. Political attitudes informed by black common sense are held by African Americans who consider the statement "I am a black person" to have political, not just personal, meaning.

Blackness is an insufficient condition for inclusion in a black ideological tradition. Instead, black ideology rests on a fundamental, underlying attitude shared by many, but not all, African Americans. It is the implicit notion of "we-ness" that defines black common sense. Zora Neale Hurston's autobiography *Dust Tracks on a Road* includes a chapter titled "My People! My People!" As an anthropologist, Hurston was an intent observer of human behavior, and particularly of the lives of African Americans. For Hurston, "My people! my people!" is sometimes a cry of disgust, at times of pride, at times of shame, but always, it is a cry of recognition. The feeling "My people! my people!" conveys the essence of black common sense. Hurston writes, "Our lives are so diversified, internal attitudes so varied, appearances and capabilities so different, that there is no possible classification so catholic that it will cover us all, except My people! My people!" (1942, 189). Thus, black common sense is not an inability or unwillingness to recognize or cope with diversity among African Americans; it is an assertion that even within this diversity, there is a sense both of belonging and of ownership that links African Americans in a way that defies clear articulation.

Common sense here employs multiple definitions of common. Common sense is common not only in the sense of "ordinary" but also in the sense of "shared." Arendt's discussion of loneliness is useful here. Arendt claims that totalitarianism exists by generating terror and that terror is created through the production of human loneliness. Loneliness locks human beings in isolation and hampers social intercourse. For Arendt this loneliness is the antithesis of common sense, by which she means shared sensual experience. "Only because we have common sense, that is only because not one man, but men in the plural inhabit the earth can we trust our immediate sensual experience" (1958, 476). By logical extension, nurturing commonality of sensual experience counteracts loneliness, reduces the power of terror, and resists totalitarianism. Although not anticipated by Arendt herself, one way to understand the black counterpublic is as a set of spaces used for the purpose of building this shared sensory experience, or common sense.[16] Philosopher Charles Mills (1998) reminds us that in the face of anthropological and scientific evidence that race is neither essential nor biologically real, the persistence of race as a significant social category for African Americans is baffling to many liberal theorists. Shared sensory experiences, reinforced though participation in the counterpublic, account for part of the answer.[17] Common sense is both the act of and product of shared racial experiences.

This notion of black common sense is closely related to the familiar social psychological concept of group identification. Scholars Tajfel and Turner established that group identification is both a cognitive awareness of belonging to an identifiable group and a normative evaluation that group membership is meaningful (Tajfel 1982; Tajfel and Turner 1979). Self-awareness of membership and affective attachment to the group is the traditional psychological model of group identification (Gurin, Miller, and Gurin 1980; Conover 1984). This designation of black common sense is informed by the idea of group identification because it argues that ascriptive membership in the black race is not necessarily an indication of a sense of attachment to the race. Black common sense, like group identification, indicates a psychological tie to the group that is distinct from, yet precipitated by, a biological or cultural attachment.

Common sense, while an important step to understanding black ideology, is only a point of departure. Common sense does not lead to only one set of ideological conclusions. Black common sense informs adherents: "I am black and you are black, and that matters." Ideology explains how and why it matters that we are both black. The Integrationist might believe "I am black and you are black and this matters because we were once subjected to the same set of discriminatory laws that make our present situation more difficult." The Nationalist may believe "I am black and you are black and this matters because it means I have a responsibility for protecting you and you owe the same to me." Thus, black common sense structures African American political thought while still leaving space for variation in political approaches.

Contemporary Black Nationalism

Twentieth-century black Nationalism has its foundations in the theories and organizing efforts of Marcus Garvey.[18] Garveyism, promoted through the Universal Negro Improvement Association (UNIA), was the largest mass-based movement of African Americans in the twentieth century, eclipsing even the modern civil rights movement. By 1920 the UNIA had hundreds of chapters worldwide; hosted elaborate international conventions; operated the Black Star Line, the first black-owned steamship company; and published *Negro World*, a controversial weekly that frequently critiqued the National Association for the Advancement of Colored People (NAACP). Garveyism identified the international and historical bases of black subjugation and declared the right and necessity of black separation from oppressive polities by developing separate political representation, cultural icons, and economic institutions.[19] Few contemporary black Nationalisms share Garvey's fully articulated internationalism and separatism, but all are rooted in an insistence on some form of cultural, social, economic, and political autonomy for African Americans.

It is more accurate to speak of black Nationalisms than a single Nationalism. These approaches differ strategically but share common assumptions about the nature of race in America. Garvey asserted that blacks required a separate state, but many midtwentieth-century Nationalisms looked to a kind of racial self-determination within the American state. Growing out of black demands for full citizenship rights articulated by African Americans midcentury, black Nationalists from organizations such as the Student Nonviolent Coordinating Committee (SNCC) and the Black Panthers advocated the development of distinct, black-controlled centers of politics, economics, and culture as the central strategy for addressing black inequality. In 1966 the SNCC produced a position paper on black power asserting that SNCC should be "black-staffed, black-controlled and black-financed. . . . If we continue to rely upon white financial support we will find ourselves entwined in the tentacles of the white power complex that controls this country" (SNCC 1966). The position paper reflects a common suspicion among Nationalists that alignment with outsiders, particularly whites, compromises the integrity of black struggles (Pinkney 1976; Henderson 1978; Lincoln 1961).[20]

Pinkney identifies at least four manifestations of black Nationalism: cultural, educational, religious, and revolutionary.[21] Dawson adds a fifth, community Nationalism, which employs both economic and electoral strategies and is articulated through a language of self-determination and racial pride. Although different in emphasis and taking on significance at various points in the past century, Nationalism has some consistent elements, including an emphasis on the immutable and unique relevance of race, a perception of whites as actively resisting black equality, and an insistence on African American self-reliance through the creation of separate institutions. Nationalists tend to privilege race over other identities, such as gender, class, and sexual identity. "Black nationalist theoretical vision of black liberation continues to be based on the contention that understanding the plight of blacks and achieving black salvation must be based on taking race and racial oppression as the central feature of modern world history" (Dawson 2001, 86). It is these common threads that identify it as an ideological approach.

Contemporary Liberal Integrationism

Liberal Integrationists want a society in which African Americans enjoy the political, economic, and social freedoms and rights of other citizens. They locate the source of black inequality in corrupt institutions but believe that individuals can have good intentions and that cross-racial alliances are both possible and necessary. Integrationist thought accepts that liberal democratic tenets of representative democracy, liberalism, and capitalism are the most appropriate ways to order American society. Integrationists suggest that the American system works in theory; the problem is that, in practice, it only works for privileged members of society. Integrationism is an ideology that seeks to access that privilege for African Americans. Further, it argues that the most effective way to pursue the interest of blacks is to link black interests to those of the larger American society.

Liberal Integrationism must be understood within the context of American liberalism.[22] Although closely aligned with the liberal tradition in American political thought, black Liberal Integrationism contains inherent critiques of the American system. Among the most important divergences in these traditions are Liberal Integrationism's greater emphasis on equality, the notion of collective rather than individual rights, and the reliance on a strong central state.

Liberty and equality are benchmarks of the American creed, but within white public opinion liberty is often professed as the most important. This pattern is reversed among African Americans, who tend to rank equality as the guiding principle of political action (Rokeach 1968). This trajectory within African American thought emphasizes not only equality of opportunity, but also a strong notion of equality of outcome. Schuman, Steeth, and Bobo (1997) demonstrate that even when whites and blacks are supportive of general notions of equal opportunity, black Americans are consistently more likely than whites to support specific policies designed to create equality of outcome. Black Liberal Integrationism is not about taking on a junior partnership in American democracy, it is about full and equal participation in the polity. Martin Luther King, Jr., whose philosophies are more often understood as theories of freedom, understood that for African Americans freedom was possible only under conditions of material equality. "When millions of people have been cheated for centuries, restitution is a costly process. Inferior education, poor housing, unemployment, inadequate health care — each is a bitter component of the oppression that has been our heritage" (1983).

Not only are black Liberal Integrationists attentive to equality as a guiding political principle, they also perceive the state as the best tool for achieving this goal. In his classic text on black politics, Hanes Walton asserts, "The struggle of black people in America has been one of seeking to bring the federal government to their side. In fact, the basic thrust of blacks in the American political system has been one of having their rights defined by law" (1972, 31). Dawson concurs, writing, "Since the end of World War II, the economic status of African Americans has been powerfully linked to the economic policies of the federal government" (1994, 44). Since Reconstruction, black political and economic fortunes have been tied to the strength of the federal government, and contemporary Liberal Integrationism continues to focus on government strategies for ensuring black progress. Electoral participation, federal litigation, pressure for state-based economic redevelopment, and support for race-targeted government programs are the hallmarks of Liberal Integrationist strategy. The contemporary civil rights movement was largely initiated within a Liberal Integrationist ideological framework.

Finally, Liberal Integrationism is less individualistic than traditional American liberalism. Harold Cruse asserts that African Americans shun notions of individual meritocracy because they recognize that "this dilemma rests on the fact that America, which idealizes the rights of the individual above everything else, is in reality, a nation dominated by the social power of groups, classes, in-group and cliques" (1984, 7). African American Liberal Integrationism has generally framed its discourse as an agitation for the rights of African Americans as a group.[23] Citing the historic, categorical exclusion of blacks as a race, they claim that redress can come only through similarly collective-oriented strategies and policies. Although King is now often painted as an individualist by citing the "content of their character" line from his "I Have a Dream" speech, he was in fact deeply attuned to the collective realities of black life. Not only did he seek to employ mass-based strategies for change, he was aware that race in America was a collective experience. "Being a Negro in America is not a comfortable experience, it means being a part of the company of the bruised, the battered, the scarred, and the defeated. . . . It means the ache and anguish of living in so many situations where hopes unborn have died" (1967).

Liberal Integrationism is an internally heterogeneous and contingent ideology. It is an ideological tradition that encompasses aspects of the political philosophy of Frederick Douglass, Martin Luther King, Jr., Ralph Bunche, and W.E.B. DuBois, among many other thinkers. Although contingent and contested, it remains an identifiable and coherent ideology linked to and critical of traditional American liberalism.

Contemporary Black Conservatism

Black Conservatives locate the source of black inequality in the behavioral or attitudinal pathologies of African Americans and stress the significance of moral and personal rather than racial characteristics to explain unequal life circumstances. They stress self-reliance, hope for a colorless society, and shun government assistance.[24] Core concepts of black Conservatism include an appeal to self-help, an attack on the state as an overly intrusive institution that retards societal progress, and a belief that the free market is nondiscriminatory. Black Conservatives stress that political strategies are inferior to strategies of economic development for addressing the problems of blacks in America. Conservatism includes a rejection of policy strategies that diminish the honor of African Americans by allowing a perception of undeserved benefits for blacks (i.e., affirmative action). Black Conservatism is rooted in a history of racial uplift, a belief that African Americans must fortify their moral and economic strength in order to compete in the American meritocracy (Dawson 1995; Washington 1969; Hamblin 1996; Williams 1996; Loury 1990).

Twentieth-century black Conservatism is grounded in the work of Booker T. Washington. His accommodationist philosophy found institutional expression in the Tuskegee method of industrial education, designed to instill work ethic and manual skills in post-Reconstruction blacks with the promise of making African Americans profitable and pliable members of society (Washington 1895). Many contemporary black Conservatives trace their ideological roots to the emphases on thrift, industriousness, and moral character that are infused in Washington's writings.

Many Conservatives are willing to acknowledge that there is a history of racial discrimination in the United States, but most argue that the external factors of black inequality have been largely addressed and that in contemporary America, black pathology is the true perpetrator of inequality. Conservative Mike Green captures the spirit of this aspect of black Conservatism in an analysis of the relationship among the federal government, black behavior, and the contemporary state of African American communities.

The notion that we are still victims of slavery is a ploy designed to influence us and apologetic whites to support liberal causes such as expanded government. It's a bogus claim. Our ancestors recovered quickly from the despair of slavery. Communities were built, businesses were started and colleges were constructed by freed slaves and their immediate descendants. In 1964, when Southern Democrats lost their fight against the Civil Rights Act, blacks progressed at a phenomenal rate. Albeit poor, we were moving in the right direction. . . . What sent the black out-of-wedlock birth rate soaring into the stratosphere? In 1965, liberals began introducing hundreds of government programs creating a massive welfare state now in dire need of reform. The dirty secret is that, under the guise of government assistance, those wishing to suck from the federal cash nipple must remove the male provider from a household or find their cash cut off. As a result, black illegitimacy skyrocketed. Between 1965 and 1975, the implementation of these programs more than doubled in the black community. No other factor in the history of black Americans has produced such devastation in such a short time. Out-of-wedlock births and fatherless homes go hand-in-hand. Women are sometimes ill-equipped to raise boys, and rampant crime originates from these uncontrollable boys without fathers who grow into ignorant and dangerous men. The cycle of violence escalates with each new generation of black bastards. Should black America assume some responsibility for this mess? You bet.[25]

In black communities, black Conservatism is often critiqued as an alien ideology, and Conservatives are maligned as "Uncle Toms," but it is important to remember that black Conservatism is a part of the indigenous intellectual tradition within black America. Conservatism may not enjoy a substantial popular following, but it is an ideological tradition with deep roots in African American history. Because Conservatives are often caricatured, it is easy to forget that Conservatism, like other black ideologies, is a contested space. Dawson (2001) points to the diversity in approaches between Conservative black economists, arguing that Glen Loury is atypical among Conservative leaders in his analysis of the continuing legacy of racism operating in the lives of African Americans and his belief that the government bears some responsibility for African American inequality. Economist Thomas Sowell is on the other extreme of this spectrum, arguing that, even historically, racism is not a significant explanatory variable in black life chances. In an introduction to a volume on contemporary black Conservatism, editors Stan Farnya, Brad Stetson, and Joseph Conti emphasize the heterogeneity and continuities of black Conservative thought. "There is no single ideology 'black conservatism.' Conservative African Americans speak in many different voices, hold a variety of sometimes divergent opinions and ideas. But they are all characterized by the sanguiness about the American prospect and humanist—as opposed to race-centered—consciousness that leads them to manifest social, political, and economic concerns that are not tinged with the hue of racial victimization which is so pervasive in the discourse of conventional black advocates" (1997, xiv).

Contemporary Black Feminism

Black Feminism is an ideology rooted in recognition of the unique intersections of race, class, and gender faced by African Americans. Black Feminism focuses on the intersection between race and gender and seeks gender equality within the African American community as well as racial equality within the American state. It is concerned with resisting both patriarchy and racism. While Feminists are often willing to form coalitions with black men on questions of racial justice and with non-black women on gendered issues, they resist the racism and classism of the white women's movement and reject the sexist element of black liberation discourse and activism (Collins 1991; Hull, Bell, and Smith 1982; hooks 1992).

Black Feminism as a fully articulated ideology is built on the realities of African American women in the middle of the twentieth century who were engaged in resistant political action. Black women confronted patriarchal domination by men in the black liberation movement and the paternalist racism in the women's movement. Black women found that their political agenda was sacrificed on the altar of "unity." Black Feminism as an ideology derives from an attempt to address real material circumstances, to create a way to understand how race, gender, class, and sexuality intersect in black people's lives to create unique forms of political, economic, and social oppression. Feminism has emerged as a critical theory employed in academic work and as a political ideology engaged in the work of political mobilization.

Black Feminism is not an essentialized identity that automatically accrues to black women: "Being a biological female does not mean that one's ideas are automatically Feminist. Self-conscious struggle is needed" (Collins 1991, 27). Nor is black Feminism simply an articulation of white feminist thought by black women. It is a unique intellectual contribution to the understanding of relations of power, domination, and resistance. Black Feminism marks its contemporary roots in the 1977 Combahee River Collective "Black Feminist Statement." Staking out a place for unique black women's politics, this group of activist African American women wrote: "We are actively committed to struggling against racial, sexual, heterosexual, and class oppression and see as our particular task the development of integrated analysis and practice based upon the fact that major systems of oppression are interlocking. The synthesis of these oppressions creates the condition of our lives. As Black women we see Black feminism as the logical political movement to combat the manifold and simultaneous oppressions that all women of color face" (Combahee River Collective 1977). The Collective's statement reflects many of the central tenets of black Feminist ideology: a blurring of identity politics, an unwillingness to ignore either race or sex in pursuit of political goals, an insistence on insurgent political action aimed at liberation of broad categories of people, and a centering of marginalized persons within political movements. Kimberle Crenshaw argues that only an intersectional approach to political action can adequately address the multiple sources of domination that face black women.

An intersectional framework suggests the ways in which political and representational practices relating to race and gender interrelate. This is relevant because the separate rhetorical strategies that characterize antiracist and feminist politics frequently intersect in ways that create new dilemmas

for women of color. For example, political imperatives are frequently constructed from the perspectives of those who are dominant within either the
race or gender categories in which women of color are situated, namely
white women or men of color. These priorities are grounded in efforts to
address only racism or sexism — as those issues are understood by the dominant voices within these communities. Political strategies that challenge
only certain subordinating practices while maintaining existing hierarchies
not only marginalize those who are subject to multiple systems of subordination, but also often result in oppositionalizing race and gender discourses. (1997)

Black Feminism both stakes out a new intellectual ground and maps a
unique political strategy. It would be incorrect to understand Feminism
as an entirely unified political approach. Like all intellectual traditions
within black thought, Feminism is contested terrain. Patricia Hill Collins's *Black Feminist Thought* (1991) is a central text in the Feminist
tradition, but its insistence on "presenting feminist thought as overly
coherent" has drawn criticism from more recent scholars of the Feminist tradition who are intent on exploring the contradictions and tensions in contemporary black Feminist thought (White 2001). Some
scholars in this tradition reject the term Feminism in favor of Womanism.[26] Black Feminisms are variously attentive to issues of class, religion, private/public dichotomies, interracial alliance, and sexual identity.[27] Although these contestations are critical for understanding the
nuance of black Feminism, it is also clear that all Feminism is "concerned by the negative impact that interactions between categories
of identity, such as sexuality, race, class, and gender, have on black
women's lives" (White 2001, 80).

These four ideologies represent important alternate political worldviews available to African Americans through the process of everyday
talk. The ideology-as-language metaphor instructs us that these ideologies exist in pure form only in ideal types. Individual Nationalists,
Feminists, Conservatives, and Integrationists will express a broad range
of attitudes within these political worldviews. For most adherents, individual political ideology is some combination of elements from these
four ideologies. Comprehending black political ideology is a complicated process of both knowing the central building blocks of black
thought patterns and understanding how these ideologies work in combination with one another. An important way to grasp black political
ideology is to study everyday black talk.

There are a number of a priori conditions that influence the kind of
community dialogue an individual will engage in and the type of space
she or he will use to engage other African Americans. These conditions

include class, gender, age and religiosity. For example, black men often consume different public spaces from those occupied by black women. Only those who attend church are exposed to church-centered spaces. Poorer African Americans are less likely to have opportunities to interact in organization-based spaces. While African Americans are guided by these characteristics and preferences when making choices about where to spend their time and energy, these preferences are not the whole story of political attitudes. Within each of these spaces, African Americans discuss issues of personal and public concern. As they do so, they express opinions about what it means to be black in America, how important blackness is as a personal characteristic, the extent to which blacks should make demands on the American system, and the extent to which whites are friends or foes in the struggles of African Americans.

INTRODUCTION TO FINDINGS

The remainder of this project uses multiple methods of academic inquiry to provide evidence to test the everyday talk theory of black ideology advanced above. It begins with a case study of a Southern, black Baptist church; moves to a statistical analysis of national survey data and experimental data; and follows with an ethnography of an urban barbershop and a textual analysis of the writings of several black public figures.

Chapter 2 presents findings from a case study of a black, Baptist church in Durham, North Carolina. Evidence gathered from interviews with church membership, content analysis of the minister's writing and speaking, and participant-observer experiences shows how a black organization self-consciously presents its ideological messages to its members. This case study explores how members receive and process elite messages, how they use them to build individual political worldviews, how they understand and express their political and religious ideologies, and how they use these ideologies to make sense of the world.

Chapter 3 builds on the argument that there are identifiable political ideologies operating as social and individual knowledge structures among African Americans. This chapter makes a case that ideology exists among black Americans and that individual worldviews are derived from combinations of the four ideologies. Using survey data from the 1993–1994 National Black Politics Study, it provides evidence for the existence of ideology among African Americans and specifies the ways that everyday talk influences ideological development. Using statistical analysis of this national data, the chapter provides measures of ideologies, for the core beliefs that contribute to their development, and for elements of the black counterpublic. It demonstrates that these ideologies exist in the black population and gives a sense of their distribution among African Americans. It further shows that membership in black organizations, participation in politicized black churches, and exposure to black media sources are important sources of discourse that African Americans use to inform their political and racial attitudes.

The book then turns to an analysis of two experimental studies in chapter 4. The 1998 North Carolina Central University Political Attitudes Study and the 2001 Kennedy-King College African American Attitudes Study both offer evidence that some political attitudes are encouraged and others are policed within African American dialogue. The studies focus on receptivity to Feminist and Conservative sentiments in a variety of settings and specify the ways that these often unpopular ideologies find space in the everyday talk of African Americans.

Chapter 5 is a participant-observer ethnography of a black-owned barbershop in Southside Chicago. Co-authored with Quincy T. Mills, who spent several months hanging out with the men of Truth and Soul, the barbershop study demonstrates the rich political content of African Americans talking with and for themselves. The ethnographic work adds nuance and texture to the understanding of the ways individuals use racial and political reasoning in their daily lives.

In the final empirical chapter, textual analysis demonstrates how representatives of four black ideologies use claims of racial authenticity to gain adherents among African Americans. Bell hooks and the black Feminist criticism of the 1995 Million Man March; Colin Powell and the Conservative appeal of the 1996 presidential race; Kweisi Mfume and the battle to integrate network television; and Tom Joyner and the fight to save Tavis Smiley serve as examples of how ideological elites use claims of authenticity to gain credibility among black masses. These cases show how black elites tap into African American messianic beliefs; assert themselves as part of the defiance tradition; make claims of morality; and use appeals to the American promise. This chapter inspects the use of each of these cultural elements in the narratives of black public figures and demonstrates how elites are constrained by the expectations of everyday talk.

The concluding chapter draws together the findings from the statistical evidence, experimental research, and ethnographic studies into a coherent whole. It discusses the unique contributions of this book to the studies of political ideology and African American political thought. This chapter also traces the emergence of everyday black talk as a matter of public notice in popular culture in 2002 during the controversy surrounding the movie *Barbershop*.

CHAPTER TWO

Ideology in Action: The Promise of Orange Grove

> I promise to be the Christian that God has made me to be. I can
> do all things through Christ, which strengthens me. This little light
> of mine, I'm going to let it shine.
> — OGMBC Congregation, every Sunday

REVEREND KENNEY said "she." He was preaching about the Holy Spirit
and he said "she." Despite the male-centered traditions of the black
Baptist Church, which soundly reject the notion that God in any form
could be a woman, Reverend Kenney had in fact referred to the Holy
Spirit as feminine. No one in the congregation seemed ruffled or upset.
Everyone was still at rapt attention, taking sermon notes and punctuating Reverend Kenney's sentences with "Amen." Everytime I thought the
minister had pushed the congregation as far as they would go, he went
a little further. I scribbled his comment down on the program and returned my attention to the sermon. There are many things that make
Orange Grove Missionary Baptist Church exceptional, and Reverend
Kenney's little feminist theological outburst is only one of them.

The study of African American religiosity and political behavior has
largely centered on the question, does Christianity encourage or dis-
courage political activism among African Americans? Lincoln and Mamiya's (1990) review of the literature on black churches reveals several
models that dominate scholarly understandings of the church's relationship to black politics. The assimilation model argues that the church
hampers ethnic assimilation into the American state and criticizes black
religion as anti-intellectual and authoritarian. Writing in this tradition,
Frazier critiques the black church, writing, "The petty tyrants in the
Negro churches have their counterparts in practically all other Negro
organizations. As a consequence, Negroes have had little education in
democratic processes. Moreover, the Negro church has and Negro religion have cast a shadow over the entire intellectual life of Negroes and
have been responsible for the so-called backwardness of American Negroes" (1963, 90). Isolation model scholars such as Orum (1966) and

Silberman (1964) argue that the church is isolated from civic affairs, lower class, and other-worldly in focus. Urban researchers Drake and Cayton (1945) characterize the church as a compensatory institution that allows the masses to flirt with the power, control, and acclaim that is unavailable in daily life. Assimilation, isolation, and compensatory models are all part of what political scientist Fred Harris calls opiate models because each argues that the church discourages political action through an other-worldly focus on divine restitution in the afterlife. "Opiate theorists argue that religion works as a means of social control offering African Americans a way to cope with personal and societal difficulties and undermining their willingness to actively challenge racial inequalities" (1999, 5). Scholars in this tradition include Gary Marx (1967), Gunnar Myrdal (1944), E. Franklin Frazier (1963), and Adolph Reed (1986).

Alternatively, there are researchers who claim that the black church acts as an inspiration for political action by galvanizing black people to work toward political righteousness. Important contributors on this side of the debate include Genovese (1974), Childs (1980), McAdam (1982), and Morris (1984). This work claims that the black church was crucial in initiating and sustaining the modern civil rights movement. Morris articulates this position: "The black church functioned as the institutional center of the modern civil rights movement. Churches provided the movement with an organized mass base leadership of clergymen; an institutionalized financial base; and meeting places where the masses planned tactics and strategies and collectively committed themselves to the struggle" (1984, 4). Reed (1986) critiques the connection between the church and progressive, racial, social movements as "mythology." But scholars of the black church like Lincoln and Mamiya (1990), and researchers of black political behavior such as Tate (1994), continue to find empirical evidence linking African American churches to the political mobilization of African Americans. Verba, Schlozman, and Brady find that African Americans are more likely to attend churches that both offer opportunities to develop politically relevant skills and are "more politicized, where they are exposed to political stimuli, requests for political participation, and messages from the pulpit about political matters" (1995, 384). Whether for the midcentury civil rights movement or for the 1980s' presidential bids of Jesse Jackson, the black church appears capable of providing organizational resources for black political involvement (Nelsen, Madron, and Yokley 1975; Dawson 1994).

Working in this tradition, Harris takes a multidimensional approach that looks at the many structures and influences within the black protestant tradition and ultimately uncovers both macro and micro resources that support a variety of political activities by African Americans. Macro resources include "indigenous leadership, communication networks, easy availability of mass memberships, and social interaction of political actors" (1999, 28). Micro resources include the psychological and cultural factors that help individuals do the work of politics, including religiously inspired efficacy and oppositional civic culture. Harris's model links internal religiosity to both self-esteem and personal efficacy, which both contribute to political efficacy and activism. "Religion's psychological dimensions could potentially empower individuals with a sense of competence and resilience, inspiring them to believe in their own ability, with the assistance of an acknowledged sacred force, to influence or affect governmental affairs, thus — in some instances — to act politically" (82).

Similarly, Ellison (1993) finds that religious involvement fosters self-esteem and personal empowerment among African Americans through networks, socioemotional support, and tangible aid. He argues that the black church allows African Americans to see themselves through a lens that asserts their inherent uniqueness as individuals and emphasizes spiritual qualities, such as wisdom and morality, over material possessions as a standard for self-evaluation.

Also in this tradition, Calhoun-Brown advances a model that seeks to specify the psychological resources that accrue to African American churchgoers and contribute to political action. Using data from electoral participation in the 1984 and 1988 Jackson campaigns for president, Calhoun-Brown makes an important distinction between political and nonpolitical churches. Reflecting the diversity that exists within the black religious tradition, she finds little evidence supporting a general connection between political sophistication and church attendance, but she does find an important link with political churches. "Politically speaking all African American churches are not created equal. Context is an integral factor in influencing political participation. . . . the direct influence of African American churches in the political arena is significant, it is largely confined to political churches. . . . these political churches have the capacity not only to coordinate tangible and intangible resources needed for political action but to impact the motivations and consciousness of individuals as well" (1996, 946–51).

There is still debate about whether the black church discourages political action by encouraging followers to focus on the rewards of an afterlife, but there is a good deal of empirical evidence that many black churches are able to provide worshippers with the organizational and psychological resources necessary for political action. Lincoln and Mamiya (1990) remind us that the black church is deeply embedded in black culture in general so that the sphere of politics in the African

American community cannot be easily separated from it. They further argue that politics must be broadly defined beyond electoral politics and protest politics to include community organizing and community building. Whether it is through organizational contact or psychological resources, religiosity and church attendance are capable of encouraging a more politically engaged African American electorate.

Sociologist Mary Pattillo conceives of the black church as a cultural training ground. Using an ethnographic study of a Chicago neighborhood, she demonstrates the "power of church rituals as cultural tools for facilitating local organizing and activism among African Americans" (Patillo-McCoy 1998, 767). For Patillo, the church is a place where actors learn cultural norms and styles that are then employed in secular settings. The African American residents of Patillo's Groveland community use prayer, call-and-response interaction, and Christian imagery when coordinating nonreligious activities around issues of youth delinquency and community safety. From this perspective, the black church helps us to understand not only the *what* of participation, but the *how* of social action. "Black church culture constitutes a common language that motivates social action" (768). But even this notion of culture continues to understand the church primarily as a toolbox where individuals receive the psychological resources, contact the collective networks, develop the organizational skills, or learn the cultural language that they can then use in the political world.

The historical work of civil rights scholars and the empirical work of social scientists based on a theoretical framework of the church as an inspiring force in politics have been critical in shaping the inquiry into African American politics and the church. These findings also reflect a bias for thinking of the church as a structure that brings actors into contact with specific kinds of resources (organizational or psychological) that can be used in the political realm. Social scientists have less adequately specified the ways that church allows African Americans to come into contact with *ideas* that then shape the direction of their political thinking. This chapter uses a case study of a single black church as a way to investigate the possibilities for political ideas embedded in church-based everyday talk and to question what happens when the church becomes a place where individuals are challenged in their political thinking by a figure endowed with sacred authority.

A study of the members and leader of Orange Grove Missionary Baptist Church during 1999 provides some insight into how the church can bring black men and women into contact with political ideas that are consequential for the development of political ideology. This chapter presents the narratives of five black women, three black men, and one dynamic minister from a Baptist church in Durham, North Carolina, in

1999.[1] Orange Grove Missionary Baptist Church, which draws its congregants from middle-class black communities in Durham, Raleigh, and Chapel Hill, and from the students of nearby North Carolina Central, University of North Carolina-Chapel Hill, and Duke University, sits on Durham's East End Avenue in a small working-class black community. Like its physical location close to a railroad crossing, the study of Orange Grove provides an opportunity to examine the junctions of black everyday talk, that is, the ways in which the real-life attitudes of black people clash, meld, and interact as people struggle to make sense of their world. Orange Grove Missionary Baptist Church demonstrates how African Americans use the cues and messages of their organizational life to inform their political worldviews, providing a unique opportunity to study the ways in which people engage political ideology, even during Sunday sermon. The chapter presents a cross-section of Orange Grove members who vary in terms of length of membership and involvement in church activities, but all of whom attended Orange Grove services regularly.[2]

Orange Grove overturns many traditional assumptions about church and politics. In many ways, it is a distinctive community with unique, perhaps even exceptional, people. But despite the distinctive character of Orange Grove, the study of this church outlines the complexity of political interaction in black everyday talk. Traditionally, we might expect that a church with an influential and politically vocal minister would be filled with members in full agreement with his beliefs. But the chapter will demonstrate that it is essential to assess black churches as more than bastions of traditionalism, filled with a few male leaders and largely pliant, resilient, and agreeable women followers. Orange Grove reveals the tensions inherent in spaces of black political dialogue, where members, despite their engagement with the church and its minister, may share, reject, contest, or revise the opinions presented in the pulpit.

THE REV

Orange Grove is a physically beautiful church boasting a relatively new sanctuary featuring a high, A-framed ceiling, light oak pews, and soft green carpeting. The pulpit is raised but not ostentatious. The church has a state-of the-art sound system and four choirs to tax its abilities. The balcony is large but still insufficient to hold the overflowing Sunday crowds. Services are held at both 8:00 a.m. and 11:00 a.m. to accommodate the large and growing membership. Sunday services are attended by about five hundred people a week. Even with its size and modernity, Orange Grove still maintains the atmosphere of a smaller house of worship, located literally and figuratively just across the rail-road tracks in a poor, historically black neighborhood known as North-east-Central Durham. Orange Grove's middle-class congregants face poverty and crime-ridden neighborhoods to make it to their oasis of modern worship. Much like Durham's black community, Orange Grove is a growing church, enriched by its long history, bolstered by a strong and socially committed middle class, and battling to address the poverty and violence plaguing local communities.

The main attraction at Orange Grove is Reverend Carl W. Kenney II, or "the Rev," as the congregation affectionately knows him. In the church's visitor information packet, Reverend Kenney is quoted saying, "Many ministers hide behind a façade of strength, while deep down they struggle with their own vulnerability. People need to know that the person who preaches the Word is virtually going through the same issues day after day." Tearing down the traditional façade that separates pastors from members is at the center of Kenney's ministry. He is a highly educated man with academic and professional credentials. Grow-ing up in Missouri, Kenney completed degrees in journalism, religion, and education at the University of Missouri-Columbia. He received a Master of Divinity from Duke Divinity School in Durham, North Caro-lina, and is working on a Doctorate of Ministry from Princeton Univer-sity. He served as a reporter, producer, anchor, and account executive in television and radio in Missouri, Kentucky, and North Carolina and as pastor of two churches in Missouri before taking over Orange Grove in 1989, but this résumé of accomplishments obscures Kenney's real appeal.

The life that Kenney talks about in the pulpit and in his weekly news-paper column in Durham's *Herald-Sun*[3] has almost nothing to do with these academic and professional achievements. He most often talks about the days when he dropped out of his senior year of high school and spent his afternoons getting high in the school parking lot. I have never heard him mention his dissertation on a Sunday morning, but I have often heard him reference his days as a drug dealer and wom-anizer. He talks of dark days when crack cocaine was his only friend and when he thought of women as little more than ornaments in his macho world. It is almost impossible to believe that such a young man (Kenney was forty-eight at the time of the study) has lived such dispa-rate existences. But he assures the congregation, "I was once lower than most of you have ever been, and God's deliverance of me is my best evidence of his ability and willingness to deliver you." For this reason Kenney calls his ministry a "journey toward wholeness."

Kenney's raw personal revelations and the candid style with which he shares his past and present mistakes would be rejected by most Southern black traditionalists. But Kenney weathers storms that Frazier (1963) or Lincoln and Mamiya (1990) would likely have thought impossible. He takes controversial stances on issues of gender and sexuality, such as chastising the black church for its homophobia and opening the church's deacon board to women. And he does things in his personal life that no Baptist minister is supposed to do, such as when he divorced his wife of nineteen years, met and married another woman, and hyphenated his last name after marriage. But Kenney survives it all, buoyed by the enthusiastic support of a fiercely loyal congregation.[4] All of the members I spoke with praised Reverend Kenney for his vibrant "open spirit" and his willingness to reveal that "he hasn't always been a pastor and he doesn't claim to have been." Kenney uses his candidness as a tool to connect with people marginalized by male-centered, apolitical, black church traditionalism. And he uses his pulpit and his pen to send out a radical call to all congregants who will listen.

THE CONGREGATION

Orange Grove is a young congregation. For African Americans who grew up in Southern, Baptist churches dominated by senior citizens, Orange Grove's youth can be almost disconcerting. On July 10, 1999, Orange Grove celebrated Senior Citizens Day. The church's senior members entered the church together and were seated in a place of honor; altogether they occupied only one pew. On the same Sunday the Upward Bound Program was visiting from the University of North Carolina at Chapel Hill. They filled four full rows. The dominant presence of the under-twenty-one crowd, even on a day for older members, is illustrative of the age imbalance at Orange Grove. The "Gospel Youth Explosion" is the church's largest choir. The Singles Ministry, which caters to the twenty- and thirty-something crowd, is the church's most active ministry. And it is much easier to get a seat at Orange Grove in the summer when the college students have all gone home.

Orange Grove's congregation is also very insular. Most members are originally from Durham and the surrounding counties and cities. Many began going to Orange Grove while attending college in the area. This means that many people come to the church already tapped into a community of friends and fellow worshippers. It can be difficult for members who are not already part of this network to break into the workings of the church's social life. Only active, consistent participation in church activities can get an individual through the barriers of preformed familiarities. This is not to suggest that Orange Grove is unfriendly. People smile and greet one another, but much of the friendliness is superficial even though it is sincere. Some members who regularly attend church, but who are not active in church organizations, continue to feel like outsiders for years. My eight informants came to Orange Grove for a number of different reasons.

There Is a Balm in Gilead

Bridgett is thirty, but you might guess she was nineteen from her small frame and friendly eyes. Her youthful appearance makes her own story of coming to Orange Grove surprising. At the time she began attending she had been having a difficult time in her eight-month-old marriage, so her best friend suggested that they attend Orange Grove together. Bridgett remembers that it was on the second Sunday of her attendance "when the violence occurred." On that Sunday her husband became violently angry and beat her. Bridgett fled for her life. She immediately sought counseling and refused to return to the home until he too would seek counseling. Then things really got ugly.

> He was so unhappy that I left and would not come back. He was so outraged that he came to my job and attempted to kidnap me. He didn't get me all the way because the authorities arrived as he was taking me away. It was traumatic and I really needed to heal from it. I turned to Orange Grove. People were praying for me and with me and helping me to understand the Word and healing me. It was just so wonderful for me at that time, because I needed nurturing and I needed support and I needed to regain the mental sense that I didn't need to be with that man.

Bridgett turned to her new church in her time of need, and it was there for her. After divorcing, she was asked by Reverend Kenney to become the co-chair of the Singles Ministry. Together, she and her co-chair Bill turned it into one of the most active ministries in the church. During her activities in the ministry, she met her fiancé and was planning a May wedding when we talked. Bridgett explains, "Because of my experience I am able to minister to other women who continue to come into my midst."

While the church helped Bridgett to end her marriage, it helped Louise to save hers. At fifty-two years old Louise and her husband of twenty-nine years began to have serious marital problems. One of Louise's daughters was a member of Orange Grove, and she encouraged her parents to go to Reverend Kenney for advice. Even though they were not members of the church, Reverend Kenney offered them free counseling. Louise says that "he was very instrumental in helping us through our conflict and I never forgot that. It was a testimony for our family." So Louise became a member of Orange Grove. For Louise, Orange

Grove is "vibrant, very vibrant. It's a young church, and it reaches out to the community. It's a church that speaks to your needs."

Michael found that Orange Grove spoke to his needs when he underwent the most painful experience of his life. Only thirty-two years old, Michael is already a widower. He and his late wife began attending Orange Grove after they saw Reverend Kenney perform the wedding ceremony of a friend. "My wife and I, we were really impressed. It was a great wedding and I like the way that Reverend Kenney performed the ceremony. So we just said that we wanted to go back and hear him speak." They began attending the church in 1994. In 1995 Michael's wife died suddenly and unexpectedly of an undiagnosed case of spinal meningitis. He found that Orange Grove offered him support in his time of grief. Although Michael was not a member, Reverend Kenney displayed genuine concern for him in his time of need, and that concern cemented Michael's relationship to the church. "When I went through it, Reverend Kenney would come up to me after church and say, 'Are you doing alright?' He'd call me, come by, whatever. He knew I wasn't a member. He didn't care. That told me that he was really concerned about my well-being. He would have John call to check on me. John would say, 'Pastor wants me to check on you' and stuff like that. I knew he was thinking about me, I knew that I was in his prayers. That definitely meant a lot."

Michael, Louise, and Bridgett found the balm in Gilead. They discovered that Orange Grove was a place of compassion and healing. They are deeply bonded to the church because it helped them through difficult times in their lives. For them, the church is first and foremost a place of healing. Each found it to be a space of nonjudgmental comfort, a place that rushed to their aid, when they were unable to help themselves. But not everyone came to Orange Grove out of pain and trials. Some were simply searching for a comfortable place to worship.

A Church Home

Margaret, a pleasant, round-faced school teacher, grew up in Orange Grove. She is the only one of the eight members I spoke with who attended the church before Reverend Kenney became pastor. Her loyalty to Orange Grove is rooted in the tradition of her attendance. "This is my home church. I've been here since day one of my life. I don't want to change my membership. This is my home church. My grandparents participated in the church, my mom, my brothers and sisters, and I'm here. Orange Grove is a wonderful church." For Margaret, Orange Grove is home.

For other members, attending Orange Grove was a decision made in search of the "home church" feeling that Margaret has developed. Keith is thirty-three and newlywed. He grew up in eastern North Carolina but came to Durham to attend college at North Carolina Central University. He first came to Orange Grove when a good friend invited him to visit. He felt immediately at home. "It's real positive. I like that it is a real young congregation, a lot of college students and high school students." He's been attending ever since that first visit three years ago and now thinks of Orange Grove as his church. The same is true for Christopher. While in college at NCCU he often heard people in the barbershop talking about Reverend Kenney and about Orange Grove. Although he never attended while in college, this twenty-nine-year-old car salesman had been attending the church with his girlfriend regularly for four months. Echoing the observations made by Keith, he described the church as "a very positive church. It gives you an opportunity to really relax and be comfortable in a church atmosphere around other people who are our age."

Shirley, a thirty-year-old kindergarten teaching assistant, had been attending Orange Grove for six months when we talked. She too had been looking for a church home because she was no longer inspired by the church she attended while growing up. Friends encouraged her to visit Orange Grove, and she's been "hooked ever since." She describes the church as energetic and friendly, and she feels that this has really become her new home: "Hopefully I'll be here until I'm ninety-nine."

Finally, twenty-three-year-old Andrea had also been looking to attend church more regularly. Having just graduated from the University of North Carolina-Chapel Hill, she was feeling guilty for not going to church regularly while in school, so she decided to try Orange Grove on the suggestion of friends. When we talked, she had been coming regularly for only a month, and she was a little unsure about the size and style of Orange Grove. Andrea sought an intimate experience and hated "not being able to know everyone in the church by name or face." Andrea, unlike the other members I spoke with, was still in the process of deciding if Orange Grove could become her new home. But she, like the others, began attending because of friends, and although she wasn't entirely comfortable, she felt good enough about the church to give it a chance.

These eight people represent the "congregation." I talked with each of them at length about their experiences at Orange Grove as well as about their views on a variety of social, political, racial, and religious questions. To help the reader remember them, I have provided a brief chart of their basic personal characteristics (table 2.1).

All of the congregants came to the church looking for something specific. Bridgett, Michael, and Louise each cemented their bonds to Or-

TABLE 2.1
Orange Grove Church Respondents

	Age	Length of Attendance at Time of Interview	Married/Children at Time of Interview	Occupation at Time of Interview
Andrea	23	1 month	Unmarried, no children	Recent college graduate working in the RTP
Shirley	30	6 months	Living with boyfriend, no children	Teaching assistant Kindergarten
Christopher	29	6 months	Unmarried, one daughter	Car salesman
Keith	33	3 years	Married, no children	Graduate student Former high school teacher
Louise	52	1 year	Married, two daughters	Nurse at NCCU
Bridgett	30	4 years	Divorced/engaged, no children	Office assistant
Michael	32	5 years	Widowed, no children	Systems analyst
Margaret	32	32 years	Unmarried, no children	Elementary teacher

ange Grove with the glue of personal tragedies and life challenges. Christopher, Andrea, Keith, and Shirley were all looking for a place to call home. And Margaret, having thought of Orange Grove as home her whole life, was tied indelibly to the church. The deeply personal and mostly idiosyncratic reasons that these men and women offered for why they attend Orange Grove are important for the theory of everyday talk. When pressed to think about why they chose to attend Orange Grove, none of these individuals mentioned the social and political views of the minister or church. This is not to suggest that there is no selection bias. The people who attend Orange Grove are probably ideologically different from those who frequent other area churches even before they attend their first service. But it is important to remember that it is familial traditions, social networks, and pastoral care rather than political action that draws worshippers to Orange Grove. They come for God, for the understanding of God they see reflected in the church leadership, and for the fellowship with God that they experience in a community of believers. The members I spoke with got all of this, and much more than they expected. In addition to the pastoral care they were seeking, these participants were exposed to a prophetic vision that connects social, political, and religious beliefs in a way that is communicated between Reverend Kenney and the church.

ORANGE GROVE AND BLACK IDEOLOGY

Chapter 1 argued that black political ideology functions as a social narrative that attempts to explain African Americans' place in the political world. Black ideologies outline the sources of black inequality, justify action on behalf of the group, provide strategies for addressing black inequality, and present a vision of a different future. The four continua relevant for understanding black political ideology are:

1. Ideology helps individuals determine what it means to be black in the American political system.

2. Ideology helps black individuals identify the relative political significance of race compared with other personal characteristics.

3. Ideology helps individuals determine the extent to which blacks should "solve their own problems" or look to the system for assistance.

4. Ideology helps individuals determine the required degree of tactical separation from whites necessary for successful advancement of group interests.

By framing an analysis of these four aspects of black political thought in a form familiar in the black church—the call and response—this chapter uses the writings of Reverend Kenney and interviews with the Orange Grove congregation to show how real political actors address the fundamental concerns of black ideology. For each dilemma, Reverend Kenney's writings and sermons are used to address each ideological question with a call. The varied attitudes of the congregation offer the response. But just like on Sunday morning, there are times when the response does not meld with the call; instead of punctuating his opinions with "Amen," the members either remain silent to his prodding or flatly disagree with his analysis. Together these nine voices create a dialogue that illuminates how political attitudes function among African Americans, outlining the connections and disjuncture present in everyday black talk.

ON BEING BLACK IN AMERICA

The Call: The truth is, not everything is about race. On the other hand, there are racial implications to just about everything.
—Kenney, *Herald-Sun*, August 30, 1998

For Reverend Kenney, race is a significant barrier in human relationships. Reverend Kenney believes that being black exposes one to mistreatment by political, social, and economic systems that are biased against African Americans. When discussing how racial difference erects a barrier between people who are supposed to be bonded by the common identity of Christianity and American citizenship, Kenney writes, "It's tough talking about race, but we must because our nation will never overcome racism without talking about race. We must expose the hold race still has on the American character. Race remains a badge for privilege and a sign of social stigma. Race is the cancer eating at the soul of America" (*Herald-Sun*, February 1, 1998).

For Reverend Kenney, blackness in America means vulnerability to dangerous and unfair treatment by a system that disrespects the value of African American life. In the spring of 1998 Kenney used his sermons and his *Herald-Sun* column to highlight the injustices that black Americans face in the political and economic system. He asked, "Why are *our people* still plagued with the failure to find wholeness." He drew linkages between the stories of the Israelites bound for the promised land and the history of African Americans. He told those in his congregation that they must remember the blessings of the promised land and that to be blessed they must find their roots. He assured them that "we have a purpose that comes out of a shared historical understanding" and suggested that "we could begin to build a Black Christian Community that is built on the Holy Spirit" (sermon, February 22, 1998).

He spent the rest of the spring using the *Herald-Sun* as a forum for revealing the character of the wilderness that lay between black people and the promised land. He was enraged by the controversial conviction of a local black teenager. The boy was accused of raping an adolescent white girl, and although there was no physical evidence that the girl had been molested or that the boy was connected to her in any way, he was convicted by a jury composed of eleven whites and one African American. Kenny's analysis of the case placed blame squarely on the shoulders of racial prejudice. "The criminal justice system stinks. . . . Taureen was assumed guilty. The jury saw a young Black thug. They had been conditioned to assume his guilt because of what they hear on the news day after day. . . . What they failed to see was a young man struggling to make life work. They failed to see a good kid from a good family. What they saw was yet another nigger being accused of a crime" (*Herald-Sun*, March 15, 1998).

Later that month, Kenney also explained that black, urban youth are open to the attacks of racist corporate strategies. In March he used the pulpit to urge the congregation to boycott Phat Boy beer and the stores that were selling it. He directed the congregation, "If you see it being sold, then call the church office and I will call for a boycott of the store" (sermon, March 15, 1998). Two weeks later he used his *Herald-Sun* column to urge the community to do the same. Calling for a boycott, he explained,

> Phat Boy is going after those inner-city youth who drink malt liquor. The product is packaged with them in mind. Forget the white supremacist who may desire a swig. They can purchase another product. Never mind the stockbroker who may take a hit during the Carolina game. This bud's not for you. The makers of Phat Boy are out to get the boys on the corner with their pants falling off their behinds. . . . The makers of malt liquor have designed a long range plan to keep young Black men drunk. (March 29, 1998)

By June, Reverend Kenney used the firing of a beloved Durham school principal to further highlight how racism continues to restrict the life opportunities of African Americans. After Principal Paylor, an African American woman administrator at Southwest Elementary School, was fired, Kenney argued that her dismissal critically damaged the educational development of black children in Durham. "The board is unable to see how painful that can be to those who witness these moves. What does it say to the countless Black children who desire excellence? It says no matter how successful you may be, you can still get fired in the real world" (*Herald-Sun*, June 21, 1998).

Reverend Kenny's answer to the first dilemma is clear. Being black in America means being vulnerable to a system that continues to attack with multiple weapons of oppression. It means that you can be falsely accused and then convicted of a crime. It means that you can be the target of racist marketing. It means that you can be fired without cause. For Reverend Kenny, blackness is a source of pride. He encourages his congregation to learn and understand the rich legacy of African American life and culture. But he also warns his congregation that race still marks black people in America for subjugation. He encourages constant vigilance and is unafraid to label the public actions of local officials as racist. He believes it to be both his theological and political duty to expose racist actions to harsh scrutiny, to denounce them, and to encourage his followers to resist.

> **The Response:** African Americans are definitely still trying to overcome, dealing with people being prejudiced against us.
> —Bridgett

> **The Response:** I think that the family is our biggest problem—we are disjointed; we have forgotten old-fashioned values.
> —Louise

The response is more varied than the call. Two distinct camps are clear from interviews with the congregation. One group of members describes the biggest problems facing black America in a manner very similar to Kenney. They identify interpersonal and structural racism as a major obstacle in the lives of African Americans. The other group insists that a disintegrating family structure is the root of the black community's troubles. These viewpoints are entirely consistent with membership patterns. The three individuals who identified racism as a continuing problem for blacks have been members for more than a year and have been attending Orange Grove only during Kenney's ministry. The members who locate African American troubles in the family structure have been attending Orange Grove for less than a year.

In response to my question about the biggest problem or challenge facing black America, Michael, a five-year member, responded, "even today it is still racism. It's still stereotypes. I've heard some of my friends say that today some people are afraid of you because of your skin color. Even today that still exists. It's sad, but that's still very strong."

Bridgett, who has been attending Orange Grove for three years, describes economic oppression as black America's biggest challenge.

> Economic depression. Which to me involves some fights to still be recognized as equal in the same type of jobs and education and to be accepted. Another challenge for us is overcoming the drug world. I think that goes along with the economic depression, because it's mostly economics that turns people to the drugs. African Americans are definitely still trying to overcome people being prejudiced against us.

And Keith, a four-year member, describes a combination of unemployment and underemployment as the major challenge facing blacks.

> Economics continues to be a problem. It creates a cycle. If you grow up in a poor house or in an environment where the father is dissatisfied with his choice of employment, though he's tried this and that. You eventually have to come to accept whatever it is that you can do to support your family. But still the frustration can obviously be seen and it can trickle down from him. It can just trickle down through his personality. It's economics. It's oppression.

Keith then goes on to explain that black men are often shut out of education and employment opportunities that could help break this cycle. Keith, Michael, and Bridgett explain the meaning of blackness similarly to Kenney. They identify institutionalized, racial bigotry as a major obstacle to the progress of black Americans. Like Kenney, they express pride, not shame, in being black Americans, but they simultaneously express an awareness of the vulnerability of black people in a system that continues to perpetrate racial injustice. Like their minister, they believe racism is a contemporary, not just historical, menace, and that African American life is still structured by the contours of race.

The newer members of Orange Grove have a different answer to the dilemma of what it means to be black in America. Louise argues, "I think that the family is our biggest problem. We are disjointed. We have forgotten old-fashioned values. The love of family, I don't think is taught anymore." Shirley echoes this sentiment and includes the deleterious influence of hip-hop music as an explanation for why young blacks have lost a sense of respect and morals. "It seems like the younger generation of children are just getting the wrong message. The music, . . . they should just not produce that junk. That junk that they are listening to, the music, guys calling girls 'bitches and hoes.' Girls saying that 'niggers ain't shit.' There is just no respect, so I wish they could just have some sort of role model that delivered more positive music message."

Interestingly, Andrea, who had been attending Orange Grove for only a month, offered a very different perspective on the biggest challenge facing African Americans. She claimed, "health issues are a challenge, like healthy living habits, from how they eat to taking care of themselves overall. My family has this terrible health history. And I am at the point where I am trying to figure out how can I correct some of it. I guess it affects African Americans more. It seems like we have our own specific set of health problems that don't affect other people." For Andrea, being black means being vulnerable to a specific set of health issues. Her mother died of breast cancer and she is concerned that African Americans fail to take care of themselves. Her analysis expresses racial concern, but it is not around an issue with explicit political meaning. For her, health crises are a more individualized problem, one that does not center on issues of power or inequality.

For longer-term members of Orange Grove, blackness means vulnerability to social and economic racism. They, like Reverend Kenney, are concerned about the continuing ability of race to overdetermine the life chances of blacks. For newer members, blackness means being part of a community that faces specific, individual problems like family ethics or family health concerns. There is a distinct split in the membership responses, suggesting that exposure to Reverend Kenney's beliefs and attitudes has an effect on the attitudes of members. Lincoln and Mamiya write, "The Black Church has no challenger as the cultural womb of the Black community. Not only did it give birth to new institutions such as schools, banks, insurance companies, and low income housing, it also provided an academy and an arena for political activities" (1990). In black communities, the church is a critical location for the definition of truth, and as individuals interact with one another and with church leadership, they enter a process that helps them create a worldview central to the construction of a political ideology. Among the most important to black ideology is the question of the meaning of race in the lives of individuals. Orange Grove is a place for learning an answer to this question.

The men and women who enter the church looking for healing, or looking for a home, also find a place that shapes their understanding of race. Reverend Kenney understands his own theology as connected to the tradition of Black Liberation Theology.[5] Black Liberation Theology is rooted in the foundational texts by Albert Cleage (1968), James Cone (1969), and J. Detois Roberts (1974) and is extended in the work of new generation of black male seminarians (Young 1986; Evans 1992; Hopkins 1993, 2001; Spencer 1990; Davis 1990) and womanist theologians (Grant 1989; Cannon 1988, 1995; Weems 1988; Williams 1993). At its core, Black Theology is predicated on the assertion that God has a unique relationship with African Americans. God is not a passive bystander in human history, but rather an active participant in the struggles of oppressed and dispossessed people. In the American context, this means that God is on the side of blacks as they struggle against the social, political, and economic marginalization caused by the legacy and persistence of white American racism.

Reverend Kenney's own writings and teachings reflect a similar understanding of racial struggle as central to Christian work. Members of Orange Grove who have had an opportunity to learn from Kenney and to interact in the church reflect a similar understanding of race and racial struggle. Certainly it is impossible to say that these attitudes result directly from their engagement with Orange Grove. But it is possible that Orange Grove offers these women and men a place to engage in meaningful contact with politically relevant ideas, such as the meaning of blackness in American society. But the story of Orange Grove would not be very interesting if members always simply learned to accept Reverend Kenney's definitions of the political world as they spent time in the church. Orange Grove is a site of contestation around other critical aspects of black ideology.

SIGNIFICANCE OF RACE COMPARED
WITH OTHER CHARACTERISTICS

The Call: Durham is in need of an organization that puts people above issues. What we need is an organization that builds across race, tradition,

and neighborhood. . . . Durham residents need to take this no-prisoners approach. Imagine Blacks, whites, Hispanics, Asian-Americans, Christians, Jews, Muslims, and anyone else interested in a better Durham organizing for the rights of everyone.
— Kenney, *Herald-Sun* December 14, 1997

A second dilemma addressed by black ideology is deciding the significance of race as compared with other personal characteristics. Black ideologies help adherents to determine the extent to which race is only one of several characteristics that are of political importance or the extent to which all divisions of class, gender, and sexuality must be subordinated so that African Americans can concentrate political and economic struggles on behalf of racial interests alone. Ideology requires that adherents identify friends and foes and determine who shares a common stake in the political system.

Reverend Kenney has a very broad and inclusive vision of racial politics. He consistently argues that political struggles must occur across lines of class, gender, and sexual orientation. He articulates and models a vision of black struggle that includes multiracial coalitions, women leaders, and class-sensitive struggle. Kenney uses his *Herald-Sun* column to draw attention to the interlocking issues of poverty and race and to criticize black leaders who fail to account for class when representing racial interests.

> The real issue in Durham is class division. Most people think the city is divided by race. To some extent that is true. Take a closer look and you'll discover the real cause of pain. Who speaks for the poor when the poor are not all Black? We are accustomed to marching and picketing when the issue is about racial difference. People will protest when their brothers and sisters are being denied equal opportunity, but what happens when the enemy is poverty? (September 13, 1998)

Kenney chastises black citizens for their failure to agitate for economic justice. He argues that "poverty is often attributed to something the person refused to do. The person is too lazy to get a job. The person failed to take advantage of the system. No one fights for the poor, because deep down, it is felt they get what they deserve" (September 13, 1998). In this, he challenges the notion that the poor have no fighting spirit and calls upon African Americans to use strategies employed in the fight for racial equality for the purpose of economic equity. He refuses to allow race to trump class and draws attention to the intersections between race and poverty as they conspire to subjugate the people of Durham. His tone is similar in his criticism of Durham's black leadership.

I am surprised that Lavonia Allison, chairwoman of the Durham Committee on the Affairs of Black People, has asked the City council to dissolve a
subcommittee formed to study public-housing issues. The Durham Committee belongs to us all. It is not the Durham Committee on the Affairs
of Rich Black People, or the Durham Committee on the Affairs of Black
Homeowners. The committee was organized to represent the needs of all
Durham's Black citizens.[6] (February 8, 1998)

Kenney offers a strong critique of members of the black middle class
who are willing to let the needs of the poor and dispossessed go unanswered. He refuses to allow black leadership to heed only the voices
of the privileged. By doing so, Kenney argues that black people have
allies outside the race, and enemies within it. By criticizing the Durham
Committee, he implies that not all black people are to be trusted as
political allies. By focusing on the shared interests of the poor, he lays
the foundation for an argument for cross-racial coalitions. Lincoln and
Mamiya argue that "the major challenge facing a predominately mid-
dle- and working class Black Church is whether it can effectively reach
out to the extremely deprived members of the truly disadvantaged"
(1990, 269). Reverend Kenney is addressing this challenge by pressing
an agenda of racial solidarity that challenges his wealthier congregants
to address the needs of their poorer brethren.

The pastor's inclusive political circle also encompasses African Americans with a criminal past. For him, those who are not morally perfect
are also part of the struggle. Kenney encourages the congregation and
his readers to accept their brothers who have struggled with issues of
drug addiction and crime. Kenney uses both the pulpit and the paper to
call on Christians to offer a second chance to black men who are or
have been incarcerated. As part of this mission, Orange Grove has an
active prison ministry, and in February 1998 Kenney gave the leaders of
the prison ministry an opportunity to appeal to church members to
come and minister to what he referred to as "young men between eighteen and twenty-one in the prisons who need role models who are good
Christians." He argued that the prison is a special place of redemptive
power and that God works special miracles for black men in prison.
The minister based his appeal on the notion that "85 percent of those in
our facility at Polk Youth Institution in Butner are *us*," by which he
meant that they are black. In this appeal there was a clear sense that
racial solidarity should extend to include these young men. Reverend
Kenney echoed this message in his column:

A new group of people are coming to be part of the church I pastor. This
group comes with a particular set of issues that the church and society
have failed to address in a meaningful way. A large crowd of Black men

with criminal records have come to the church. They come hoping to change their lives. . . . The church, they've been told, has all the answers. They've been told if they fix their souls then everything else will fall into place. . . . I watched the men cry. I could feel their pain. I remembered when I sold drugs and committed other crimes. I remember how hard it was for me to prove to those who knew me that my life had changed. All I wanted was another chance. That's all that these men want — a chance to prove they are not what they used to be. (July 26, 1998)

Drawing on his own experiences, Reverend Kenney challenges Christians to stand by their faith in redemption. He presents the boys and men who join the community after incarceration as legitimate members of the race and faith. And in drawing attention to their particular struggles for acceptance, he refuses to see black people as a monolith. He recognizes the very real divisions that exist between African Americans, and he calls on his congregation to heal those divisions.

One of the most distinctive elements of Kenney's ministry is his insistence on the fair and equal treatment of gay men and women in the church and in the black community. The active AIDS ministry of Orange Grove has become a vehicle through which Kenney urges black Christians to accept and love, rather than to reject and castigate, their homosexual brethren.

The Black church has been shamefully silent about AIDS. It's silence has led to an epidemic within the Black community. . . . The Black church must get over its homophobia. From the pulpit a Black minister will preach "God made Adam and Eve, not Adam and Steve." At the end of the sermon a gay soloist will rise to sing a song. Sunday after Sunday the pews of Black churches are filled with Black gays and lesbians. The Black church, an institution that has stood for Black liberation, refuses to unlock the arduous chains that bind gays and lesbians. The homophobia of the Black church contradicts the love ethic at the heart of what the Black church believes. The homophobia of the Black church tarnishes its ministry. (March 8, 1998)

This is an unusual position for a black religious leader. In her analysis of the black political struggle around the issue of AIDS, Cohen (1999) demonstrates that African American lesbians and gay men are often categorically excluded from black political struggles. This marginal position is forced on gay blacks by indigenous institutions that are concerned with protecting their image of respectability and legitimacy. The church has been a vicious perpetrator of this forced exclusion. Seen in this light, Kenney's insistence on the inclusion of homosexual church members represents a real attempt to demonstrate that black struggle must be broadly conceived. He refuses to define blackness as sameness. He draws specific attention to how sexual identity cross-cuts race in ways that make it difficult for black gay men and lesbians to find a home in the black church.

Finally, Reverend Kenney makes clear to his congregation that women have a right and a responsibility to assume spiritual and political leadership roles in the African American church and community. Both his words and his actions emphasize that gender equality is a necessary component of leadership. In June he used his column to harshly criticize the Southern Baptist Convention for adopting a declaration that a "woman should submit graciously to her husband." He wrote that "the passing of this amendment is major step backward" (June 14, 1998). Earlier in the year, he used his forum in the paper as an opportunity to praise the hiring of a black, woman police chief.

> The challenge before Chambers are legion. Durham is a tough city. As Durham's first female chief, Chambers will have to contend with the good 'ol boy mentality that can still be found in the department. Despite her record and skills, many will challenge her simply because she's a woman. . . . Sadly Chambers will spend months proving that she can do the job better than any man. . . . Chief Chambers, you make me proud to live in Durham. I'm proud to live in a city that selects a female police chief because she's the best fit. (January, 25 1998)

More influential than these statements is the equitable way that Reverend Kenney shares leadership at Orange Grove. On the same day that his column about Chambers appeared in the *Herald-Sun*, Kenney announced in church that the deacon board would be opened to women. Saying that "we at Orange Grove do not discriminate based on gender," he encouraged church members to nominate whomever they believe is fit to be a deacon. On March 15, 1998, Monica Taylor was initiated as the first woman deacon of Orange Grove Missionary Baptist church. Kenney shares his pulpit each week with several women ministers, including Vanessa Abernathy, who has a ministry aimed specifically at adolescent girls, and Regina Ingraham, whose ministry focuses on women who are survivors of domestic violence. The message at Orange Grove is clear. Men and women are equal partners in the work of a Christian community.

For Reverend Kenney, race is only one characteristic. Class, sexual orientation, previous incarceration, and gender also affect life chances, convey different perspectives, and deserve equal treatment. Kenney has pushed the boundaries of blackness to include many people who are often considered inauthentic or dangerous by other African American leaders. Kenney wants to make Orange Grove a wide circle, capable of embracing a diverse group of people who find themselves bound by their common vulnerability to oppressive institutions.

> **The Response:** I just think that if you want to worship you should worship wherever you want to regardless of your race, or what you look like, or where you come from. I mean this is God's house, this isn't our house.
> — Margaret

> **The Response:** I think that it's important for black men and black women to pursue leadership roles. It's very important for black men, but it's also important for black women.
> — Michael

The congregation members were not as eloquent in their discussions about how race relates to other personal characteristics of political importance, but there are elements of Kenney's perspective that are revealed in the attitudes of the congregation. Margaret and Bridgett both offered articulate statements about the need to be inclusive within a Christian community, and there was unanimous support among the members about the importance of women's leadership in the church and community.

Bridgett is the most deeply embedded church member with whom I spoke. She regularly attends Wednesday Bible study, is a member of several ministries, and is co-chair of the Singles Ministry. Her intimate involvement with the church and her deep respect for Reverend Kenny are reflected in the proximity of her attitudes to the pastor's. She is the only member who mentioned Reverend Kenney's controversial position on homosexuality, and she did so to express her agreement.

> The AIDS ministry is really growing among the Black churches, but it's not very widely accepted, but it's really needed. We are a missionary church and we need to do missionary work in our own community. We can't judge people because of the reason that they have HIV. They go to the church first and there are many churches that turn them away. I know that Orange Grove is known for its work. Not everyone at Orange Grove would agree, but we shouldn't turn away homosexuals. We want everyone to come here and to be saved. Everyone needs love.

Although Bridgett is the only member to specifically include a discussion of gay issues in her discussion, her awareness of the church's official stance reflects that Kenney's inclusive messages do penetrate his congregation. He is not simply allowed to have "outlandish" opinions because he is waltzing before a blind audience. The congregation can see him, and some appear to appreciate his performance. Bridgett does convey that Kenney's position is controversial within the membership. She points out that not everyone at Orange Grove agrees with the minister's inclusiveness. Reverend Kenney's position on homosexuality is in conflict with very long-standing, Southern, religious traditions that many of these members still hold dear. Bridgett's support of her minister, however, demonstrates that there is room for negotiation on these attitudes when a strong advocate pushes for a reconsideration of the doctrine.

Reverend Kenney's inclusiveness has been incorporated in other aspects of the congregation's behavior. In 1998 Orange Grove instituted fourth Sunday as "dress-down Sunday." This policy was started because of a discussion initiated by members in weekly Bible study. It was their suggestion that Kenney make an official policy that on the fourth Sunday of every month members are to wear blue jeans, t-shirts, or any casual outfit. Kenney explained during morning worship that the Bible study group was concerned that some people are excluded from church because they have nothing "appropriate" to wear. The purpose of fourth Sunday is to allow individuals who do not own traditional church attire to come to worship and feel comfortable, rather than feeling odd or singled out. It is an inclusive policy that further reflects the church's commitment to broadly defining the boundaries of the community. Margaret has been encouraged by this policy to be more accepting of people who do not fit traditional images of church members. She told me that before Reverend Kenny took over as pastor she never wore pants to church, but now she wears them regularly.

> If your clothes are dirty, if your sneakers are torn, you haven't taken a bath, whatever, if you want to come to church, come to church, and somehow the word got out. And there were several whites who started to come to church, and they were not well-to-do people. And I just think that if you want to worship you should worship wherever you want to regardless of your race or what you look like, or where you come from. I mean this is God's house, this isn't our house. People are people. God belongs to everybody. Wherever you want to worship that's where you should be welcomed, regardless of what you have on.

Margaret has used the lessons of dress-down Sunday to create a more inclusive social perspective. She includes race, appearance, and class in her analysis. Wearing jeans to church is more than a fashion choice; it is a statement about the willingness of a church to accept people who are unconventional. Margaret has gotten this message. Further, dress-down Sunday was initiated, not by Kenney, but by the members themselves. That members of the Wednesday night Bible study group could institute a lasting change in the church's policy shows the multiple directions of communication flow within Orange Grove. This is not a church where members passively accept the directives of church leadership. Instead, it is a place of dialogue, where members are assured a voice in creating the theology and practices of their church.

Both Bridgett and Margaret say that something other than race is relevant for individuals in the social and political world. They display a recognition that blackness is not a sufficient descriptor for understanding someone's struggles. They, like their minister, have embraced a wider circle of worshippers and, possibly, a wider circle of compatriots in their political life as well.

While there was not significant discussion of class or sexual orientation among the members, there was widespread agreement with respect to the issue of gender equity. Every respondent told me that women should assume leadership positions in the church. Although there was some disagreement among members about women's role in the family, there was unwavering support for women as community and political leaders. Bridgett and Michael offered two of the most articulate statements representative of the congregation's support for women's leadership. Bridgett said,

> I think black men and black women should both be taking leadership roles. It reduces the amount of male chauvinism and egotism, and it reduces the amount that women are looked down upon as if they cannot handle positions of authority. Women's organizations should be run by women and men's should be run by men, but if it is something that incorporates men and women then it should not matter. I can really appreciate that Reverend Kenney allows women to minister here. I have had several people come here and say, oh my goodness, that is so odd. So I think that it's good, it's real good. These women do have a ministry, they know the Word just like the men do, and they are filled with the spirit just like the men.

Echoing these sentiments and offering additional justification for the importance of women in visible roles of national leadership, Michael said,

> I think that it's important for black men and black women to pursue leadership roles. Black girls need someone they can identify with, to say hey, I can grow up to be just like her. I think it's great that we have a woman trying to be a deacon. The church where I grew up, I have never seen a woman deacon. The old way of thinking is that the woman was in the background, the husband was the deacon. She was just the wife of the deacon. But who's to say that she doesn't have good ideas also?

Michael went on to praise the women ministers at Orange Grove.

> You used to hear, "Women are not supposed to preach." But who said God couldn't give them the gift too? Who said that? We can't make that decision. I can't sit up here and say that He did not call you to preach. How do

I know what He said to you? I think it's good too to have women in those leadership roles.

Both Michael and Bridgett are aware that Orange Grove is unique in its acceptance and support for women church leaders. Bridgett has heard others call the practice odd, and Michael is aware that traditionally women belonged in the pew, not the pulpit. "Fewer than five percent of the clergy in historic black denominations are female, . . . the vast majority of them are found in storefront churches or independent churches" (Lincoln and Mamiya 1990, 289). But Bridgett and Michael are proud to be members of a church that defies this sexist tradition. Each is able to articulate religious and social reasons why women should share leadership.

Other members were less enthusiastic about women as equal partners in all realms. Keith and Louise each had more traditional views on women's role in the family. Keith argued that women actually craved male leadership and that black men had simply failed to fulfill their duties. "What I believe is that they [women] would like someone that they can look to for some advice and at the same time just look to who can take control of a situation. So I think that the men need to work on the confidence." Even though he held this chauvinistic view of women's familial leadership, he still enthusiastically supported Orange Grove's female ministers. "I think it's awesome. She's [Regina Ingraham] an inspiration to everybody. I think it's awesome."

Louise was also concerned about women's leadership in the home, saying, "I have often seen devastation in families without men. Men tend to make families more stable, and individuals who come from families with men in them tend to be more well adjusted. On most issues we ought to be taken equally. We ought to be taken as partners, but the family is a special situation." While Louise was concerned about the inadequacies of women as leaders in the home, she felt that women had a right to be church leaders and pointed to her experiences at Orange Grove as the source of that belief. She recounted, "I have no problem with women leaders. It all is a question of how God wants to deal with you. If God calls you to preach and you're a woman, then you ought to. I really like the woman who runs the Sunday school. She is very good. There are male deacons in the class, but there is a lot of give and take and a lot of respect. As long as you are with the Lord and you are doing what God has called you to do, then it is sufficient."

Lincoln and Mamiya accurately captured the traditional gender biases of black churches, arguing that "traditionally in the Black Church, the pulpit has been viewed as 'men's space' and the pew as 'women's place'" (1990, 274). Bettye Collier-Thomas' *Daughters of Thunder* chronicles more than a century of African American women's preaching and notes that "in the critical area of ordination and in the appointment of pastors, the women in the pew have not been willing to challenge publicly the dominant male clergy leaders" (1998, 36). Traditionally, the black church has been emblematic of the way that an oppositional counterpublic can internally reproduce and promote other inequalities. "Although Afro-Christianity has provided the ideological and material resources to resist racial domination, it has also privileged patriarchy. . . . Patriarchy has operated though religious sanctioned rules that exclude women from sharing power and authority with men" (Harris 1999, 157). Analyzing data from the 1994 National Black Politics Study, Harris demonstrates that black women who are active in the church are less likely than lay men to support women ministers, and that those women who are most active in the church are those least likely to support black women's political leadership as well. His results suggest that women who learn that men are the rightful leaders of the church are also more likely to defer to male leadership in the political realm. Calhoun-Brown (1996) shows that attendance at politicized black churches is related to generally more liberal gender attitudes among blacks, but she also finds that these politicized religious settings have no influence on support for female political leadership.

Understood in this context, the unanimous agreement of Orange Grove's membership that women belong in the pulpit is exceptional. The extraordinary clarity with which members responded to questions about women's proper role in the church is evidence of a dialogue of inclusiveness and equality. The women clergy of Orange Grove foster recognition that black women are equal partners in religious leadership. Because Harris finds a connection between the support for women's religious and political leadership, Orange Grove members who welcome and support women's religious authority are likely to support a more equitable political agenda as well. Pattillo (1998) demonstrates how church culture translates into nonreligious settings of social action. She shows how African Americans use the style, form, and content of their sacred lives to map the contours of their secular activism. For the men and women of Orange Grove, church culture includes the equal inclusion of women's voices, ideas, bodies, concerns, and leadership. To the extent that this is translated, these same norms of gender equity may apply in political organizing as well.

BOOTSTRAPS OR GOVERNMENT

The Call: Hit them where it hurts — the purse. We should line up in front of those businesses and warn people. We should tell them that supporting those establishments is hazardous to the community's health.
—Kenney, *Herald-Sun*, March 29, 1998

The Call: The County needs to put more energy into developing a substance abuse plan that works. Failure to do so has put more strain on communities like North-East Central Durham.
— Kenney, *Herald-Sun*, October 4, 1998

A third dimension of black political ideology is the question of the extent to which African Americans should be self-reliant or press America's political systems for assistance in addressing the problems of racial inequality. Reverend Kenney takes a clear stance on this issue. He strongly expresses the need for African Americans to expect and demand legal and political assistance from government. He consistently criticizes local government for its failure to provide economic programs that would increase equality in the city, and he is quick to praise any initiatives by local agencies to create programs that help Durham's underserved, poor black communities.

In May 1998 Reverend Kenney criticized local and national policies that focus on incarceration as the solution to national crime and praised local efforts at economic development as a solution aimed more directly at the root causes of crime.

Reversing the negative trends will require more than tougher laws. We can continue to build bigger prisons to accommodate these young offenders, but sooner or later we must confront the root causes of crime. . . . The reduction of juvenile crime will require a tough look at existing policies. It will also require an honest appraisal of the messages that we adults put out there. . . . we've created a world that teaches young people, especially Blacks and Hispanics to be cool, non-feeling, and mean. We can blame rap music and television but the truth is that we created this mess. (May 24, 1998)

Kenney also proposed that crime must be addressed by controlling means rather than individuals. "We need stiffer gun laws to address the recent rash of shooting rampages at U.S. public schools" (June 21, 1998). By the fall, Kenney had developed a pointed criticism for Durham's local government. He once again indicated that it is the responsibility of government and economic elites to assist in creating solutions to the problems of poor, black communities.

The County needs to put more energy into developing a substance abuse plan that works. Failure to do so has put more strain on communities like North-East Central Durham. . . . The City Council Planning Department needs to place a limit on the number of new houses built in North-East Central Durham. This community is already overpopulated. We can't solve the problem by building more in an already overpopulated area. Instead of building new properties, come up with a plan to remodel those homes that are currently boarded up. . . . Begin constructing a seed plan now. The

Police Department is weeding the community. Soon we will hear of a major drug bust. Pressure will be put on the criminals, and the streets will be cleared for awhile. If we're going to keep it that way, a plan must be constructed to plant in the community things lacking. (October 4, 1998)

While believing that the government is largely responsible for addressing issues of inequality, Kenney simultaneously believes that African Americans have a unique role in the fight. He holds his congregation and other middle-class African Americans to a standard of racial accountability. His philosophy is, "He's not heavy, he's my brother." But while he encourages blacks to be integral in the work of rescuing their community, he de-emphasizes a sense that individuals should be required to pull themselves up by their own bootstraps. Instead, he consistently points to systematic causes for racial inequality and poverty and looks to communal, organizational, and governmental solutions. In addition to encouraging the congregation to become politically involved through voting and boycotting, Reverend Kenney consistently reminds the congregation of the need to volunteer their energies in the black community through economic, social, religious, and political action.

Just before Christmas in 1996, Reverend Kenney chastised the Orange Grove congregation in the Sunday bulletin for the failure to support Quicksilver, a fast food restaurant in Durham's black community. Quicksilver was a project of a black Durham community development corporation. Profits from its sales provided youth with money for scholarships and field trips and created entrepreneurial opportunities.

As a people we have run away from the problem. We have hidden behind our big desk and large homes in the plush section of town. We send our children to the best schools and pay well to assure that they will not be negatively impacted by "those people." We have run so fast and far that we have forgotten that we once belonged to the class of people that we seek to hide from today. . . . It's a sad indictment that we would rather eat at McDonald's, Burger King, Hardees, or Wendy's than to support a project that could help our youth. . . . What difference would it make if everyone here made a trip to Quicksilver this week? We have the resources in this room to save this business from going under! So the next time you decide to criticize the church for what it has not done, think of what you have failed to do. (Notes from the pastor, December 8, 1996)

Kenney repeated this reprimand two years later in his *Herald-Sun* column by offering a progressive understanding about where church leadership should originate: "The truth is the problem is larger than Black ministers. Ministers are a reflection of the people they serve. They can only do as much as the people are willing to do. Our communities are in need not because of worthless leadership from out pulpits, but rather because of shabby leadership from our pews" (March 1, 1998).

A month later, Kenney offered the community a way to banish pew apathy by becoming involved in the Triangle Regional Summit on America's Promise. Again calling for volunteer efforts, he wrote:

> The Triangle Regional Summit on America's Promise will be held April 24–25 at Hillside High School. The summit seeks to develop and implement systems and processes that improve the identification of needs surrounding disadvantaged youth. . . . We need people to develop an ongoing relationship with youth. Black men are needed. Hispanic and Asian men are needed. We need women of all races. Rich and poor people. Preachers and teachers, politicians and homemakers. Everyone is needed. (April 12, 1998)

Kenney's call is clear. Black people have a communal responsibility to one another. Each Sunday when the church lines up to bring its tithes and offerings, Kenney reminds them that God wants your "time, talent, and money." He expects his congregation to lead Durham in fighting for social justice. And he expects this leadership to be directed at pressing the system for its assistance. His sense of black responsibility is not insular and isolated. Rather he supports multiracial coalitions to press the local and national government for solutions to systemic problems. He chastises black people for collective apathy and holds himself to the same high standard. Kenney has chaired the Durham Congregations-in-Action, an interracial, social justice organization of local churches. He is a member of multiple community organizations, writes a weekly column in the city's paper, and is instrumental in organizing boycotts, marches, and vigils in response to local political concerns. This level of community involvement, combined with his active ministerial style, which includes significant personal counseling and support of members, takes a heavy toll on his personal life. He makes these sacrifices willingly, out of a belief that he is linked to a prophetic, activist tradition in the black church. He therefore requires a great deal from his congregants. He fully expects that they, too, will sacrifice to assist one another and other black people, and that they will press the government to address the needs of the disenfranchised.

> The Response: Everyday you've got a choice. You've got a choice to do right or wrong. And you've got to stop being selfish, you can't just think me me me me. You've got to think, OK if I'm going to go over here and do this line of cocaine, who's it going to affect. It's going to affect a lot of people. Not just your sorry little self who wants to do it, but everybody around you. Your children, your nieces, your momma, your grandma, it

affects everybody, everybody is going to be touched by this awful thing. I
think it's the individual.
— Shirley

The Response: Truth be known, some of these companies wouldn't hire
any African Americans if they didn't have to meet a quota.
— Michael

Several trends emerge in the way that Orange Grove members addressed the question of the bootstrap dilemma. First, the congregation is
much more judgmental than Reverend Kenney of individual failures.
They are more likely to suggest that people are faced with choices and
that those who make bad choices should suffer harsh consequences.
This trend was particularly prominent among the members who suggested that disintegration of family values was the biggest challenge
facing African Americans. Shirley talked to me about her older sister,
Keisha, who at twenty-one has three children by different fathers. Because she is strung out on drugs, none of her children are living with
her. Shirley's annoyance with her sister, and with other women in her
situation, was palpable as she talked. Although she told me that both
she and Keisha were victims of abuse at the hands of an alcoholic stepfather, Shirley feels that Keisha's troubles are a result of her own bad
choices and believes that Keisha is solely responsible for ending her own
cycle of destruction.

> Keisha keeps using that as an excuse, we had such a bleak childhood grow-
> ing up. But he only came into our lives around twelve or thirteen. I think
> that is just an excuse to say, I just had a baby so that I could have someone
> to love, who would love me back. I said, "Now you done heard some
> white girl say that and I don't know where you got that junk from." It's
> just an excuse. She started having sex early, and I did too. But I was re-
> sponsible. I got myself on the pill. I did not want children. I was not going
> to let that happen. Somehow I knew that things would slow down and I
> would start taking the steps to becoming a reliable, responsible adult. But
> she never did, she just never did.

Bridgett also placed significant responsibility for problem solving
with the individual. She acknowledges the role of outside forces in creating the black community's struggle with illicit drugs, but she argues
that ultimate responsibility lies with individual choices. She places the
responsibility for overcoming racism in the choices of individuals who
either allow racism to hinder their progress or fight it and choose to
succeed. "We know that drugs are not the right way of life. Whether we
are using it or selling it. It can only bring you down and bring other
down in the process. So even if the white people are allowing it to come

into the country. Even if they are controlling it. They may be the master-minds, but that doesn't mean we have to buy into it."

These members, unlike Kenney, are willing to argue that individuals are ultimately accountable for their successes and failure. Margaret and Louise both believe that parents need to do a better job of monitoring their children and punishing them for bad behavior. Christopher lamented the "stupidity" of black men who commit crimes while still on probation from first offenses. And Michael argued that "if you are going to have this baby, you've got to raise that baby, take care of that baby, teach that baby. Don't just say I can't do anything with them." In these sentiments the congregation displayed a harsher standard of individual responsibility than what appears in the writings and teachings of their minister. For them, the bootstrap philosophy continues to have an important place in addressing black inequality. Black people cannot hope to overcome economic and social ills that plague the community without a shift in the choices made by individuals.

But the congregation is not entirely in disagreement with Kenney's position on this dilemma of black ideology. Two other trends in the members' responses demonstrate their proximity to Kenney. The second major trend in responses is the willingness to blame forces outside of the African American community for the problems that face blacks. Christopher felt that government welfare systems trap individuals in vicious cycles from which it is difficult to escape.

> They are putting people in the situation to get caught. If you know that all these people just live in the projects because of their upbringing. Their mother, being brought up on welfare or other type of government help where they have a say so over where you can live, such as the projects. Those people who want to get out, but can't get out. They set such limits on what you can do. I feel just so they can keep you in that surrounding. Building more prisons instead of building more schools. They should be hiring more teachers instead of police officers.

Keith argued that a subtle, systemic racism restricts black men from reaching their full potential.

> It's sort of oppression or discrimination that continually holds us down. You go to an elementary school and you'll see kids: a black and white kid, both are energetic, both are motivated, both want to learn all that they can, both love their teachers. But as middle school years kick in, then the social aspects of their lives start to change. So even though they start out sort of the same, they start to see inequalities in their lives even at that age. And then the self-esteem starts to dwindle.

Christopher and Keith are representative of the second trend in the congregation's perspective on the bootstrap dilemma. Although they made a more biting critique of individuals, they still acknowledge that systemic forces circumscribe the opportunities and life chances of African Americans. Their narrative is not one of simply blaming black pathology; instead, these church members, like their pastor, continue to place some responsibility on racist social policies.

A few members specifically referred to government and social programs as solutions to these problems. Michael supported racial quotas to lessen the effects of employment discrimination. Christopher argued for increased funding for programs such as Upward Bound that assist African American youth preparing for college. Margaret talked about city programs that could address racial inequality. These members are echoing Kenney's sentiments that social programs are a necessary component of addressing systemic problems.

The chorus of Amens is not unanimous on this dilemma. Members do agree with Kenney that institutionalized racism continues to be a contributing factor in black America's biggest dilemmas, but there is not a clear agreement on who should shoulder the responsibility of solving these problems. Some suggest that blacks should look to organized social and government programs, while others say that individuals have a personal responsibility to succeed despite the obstacles. There is widespread agreement, however, that Kenney is right to expect a role for the black church. All eight members were able to identify some role for the African American church in generating solutions for black community problems. Andrea argued that health issues were the biggest challenge facing African Americans and suggested that the church had a special role to play in addressing that concern. "Even if it's just awareness. A lot of people would listen to our pastor before they would listen to a doctor. So I am sure there are a lot of people that could be reached through the church."

Michael identified racism as a major challenge for black Americans and argued that interracial worship and social action organized through churches could create greater sensitivity and understanding among citizens from different backgrounds. "We need to start integrating some of the churches. We need to have some events that include white churches. I think if they experience that, then they may find that "hey, they're not that bad, they worship the way that we do, or whatever." You're worshipping the same God, who sees no color. I don't see any other forum that can bring people together."

Margaret had a detailed vision of the church's social action. Her perspective is rooted both in her own childhood experiences with the church and in her impressions of Reverend Kenney's ministry.

> The church is here to do something so that outside communities can hear the voices, to let them know that is going on in that community. . . . To

hold vigils like Reverend Kenney has done. . . . There is a lot of stuff that my kids [students in her class] have not been introduced to, in my classroom, in the second grade. They may not have ever been outside of North Carolina. And the church, they can take kids to Raleigh to see the capital or tour museums. I believe the churches need to expose the children to something different than what they see daily. When I was growing up we used to have Vacation Bible School and it wasn't just members of the church, it was for the entire community. Kids loved that.

Kenney's charge is taken seriously by his congregation. They believe that the African American church in general, and Orange Grove in particular, have a specific role to play in addressing community problems. There is some slippage between leader and members on the question of how much individuals should be expected to solve their own problems and how much should be expected of government. Members were harsher critics of other people. Although acknowledging the obstacles faced by many African Americans, members ultimately required individuals to be held accountable for their decisions. Kenney consistently looks to local and national government for assistance in solving the problems he says they have helped to create, but both pastor and congregants wholeheartedly believe that the church must be at the forefront of racial struggle.

FEELINGS AND TACTICS REGARDING WHITES

The Call: Does he understand the difference it makes when white people reach out, in love, to Black children?
—Kenney, *Herald-Sun*, February 22, 1998

The final dimension of black political ideology is an assessment of the nature of white people and an indication of the amount of tactical separation from whites that is required to achieve the desired vision. Addressing this dilemma includes creating a narrative about the historical and contemporary role of whites in perpetuating or alleviating racial animosity. It also includes envisioning a future that is ideally integrated or separate.

Reverend Kenney regularly cautions against worldviews that rely on rigid stereotypes. His message about whites is a complex one. On one hand, he is critical of whites who fail to appreciate the continuing significance of race in American society. He has little patience for those who suggest that "we should move beyond the past, hold hands and sing folk songs" (*Herald-Sun*, January 11, 1998). Instead he encourages whites and blacks to confront the difficult topic of racial difference and inequality. While he was chair of the local church consortium, Durham Congregations-in-Action, the group sponsored a series of community forums and daylong sessions on race relations. Kenney maintains that "the more we talk about it, the more we will understand one another" (*Herald-Sun*, February 1, 1998).

Even as Kenney encourages interracial dialogue, he continues to acknowledge the need for African Americans to be wary of white institutions. This warning about whites was particularly clear in his discussions about Durham's proposal to reduce the size of the city council. Pastor Kenney reminded the congregation about the importance of black turnout in influencing the referendum outcome. He used his column to further explain his perspective.

> Can the Black community trust the Friends of Durham?[7] Can the Black community trust the *Herald-Sun*? What's the real motive behind the proposal [to reduce the size of the city council]? Could it be a conspiracy to reduce Black representation on the council? . . . Can a white man represent a Black woman on welfare? Can he feel the pain and have the same passion as that Black woman when it comes to issues that impact her life? Probably not. . . . Many are afraid of going back to the days of Jim Crow. (August 30, 1998)

Although he encourages caution when dealing with whites, he continues to see white people as a necessary part of his vision for the future. He imagines a beloved community where whites who are committed to racial justice can find a place alongside African Americans. Although he doesn't romanticize "good white people," he does applaud the efforts of sincere racial troubadours. In February, Kenney wrote about his presentation to thirty-five white men at the Saint Andrews Presbyterian Church. At the end of his talk, one white man came to him and talked of his difficulty in connecting with the sixteen-year-old black boy he was mentoring. Reverend Kenney recounted the following story to this white man:

> When I was a senior in high school I dropped out for four weeks. . . . One day I was in my bedroom getting high when I heard a knock at my door. I answered the door to find one of my teachers—a white man. He grabbed me, hugged me tight, and told me he would not let me fail. He took me back to school, talked to me, and loved me as his own son. If it had not been for that white man, I wouldn't have graduated from high school. If it had not been for him, I would not be here today. (February 22, 1998)

Through this narrative he makes room for white people who are sincerely committed to black people. He encourages another white man to continue to reach across the racial divide and suggests that his efforts may be instrumental in saving another African American boy.

Reverend Kenney's attitude about whites is complex because his experiences with them have been varied. He is suspicious of Durham's white political leaders because they have proven to be hostile to the interests of African Americans and poor people. But he still believes in the necessity of multiracial coalitions to address the city's concerns. He believes wholeheartedly in the power of Christian love and desires a community of believers that is built on mutual respect and trust between black and white Christians.

Kenney is unwilling to deny or forgo the cultural uniqueness of black life. For whatever ambiguity Kenney has about whites, he has none about African Americans. He loves black people, black music, black churches, and black culture. His adoration and concern for African American people is tangible in his sermons and his writings. He reflected a yearning for blackness after spending a few weeks in Princeton working on his dissertation.

> Finding folks who look like me in Princeton is not all that easy. Where are the brothers, I asked. Where is the soul food restaurant? The taste of *Dillard's* came to mind. I looked and looked, but couldn't find any down home cooking. Where are the brothers who stand on the corner with the bow tie? Suddenly I missed them. I couldn't find any bean pies. No *Know Book Store* or *Hayti Heritage Center*. No Blues Festival. Forget about Bimbe. You can't find any of that in Princeton. Then I took a look through the local newspaper. I couldn't find any columns written by people who look like me. Where are the opinions of people who stand on the fringes of life? Something was missing in Princeton. Something was wrong. We should celebrate that we are a city that hears the voices of all its citizens. I may not like what some of them say, but I'll take Durham over Princeton any day. (June 28, 1998)

Kenney does not promote racial animosity. He acknowledges the actual and potential contributions of whites in black struggle. Orange Grove even boasts a "Peace and Reconciliation Ministry" organized specifically to promote social action events with white and Latino churches. But Kenney still encourages a cautious relationship with Durham whites, and he remains critical of the continuing racist actions of white-controlled institutions. This balanced opinion about whites is generally reflected in the attitudes of Orange Grove members as well.

> **The Response:** We need to integrate to work with the community, but at the same time hold positions where we still have equal rank. Controlling our own schools and our own political situations. Even then, there would probably be some influence from the outside white community. So I think it's just best to have them integrated but have equal. Have equal rank or equal share.
> — Andrea

Orange Grove's membership generally shares the pastor's views with respect to the nature of whites and the degree of separation required from whites. Orange Grove members were very clear about two things with respect to this final ideological dilemma. First, the members supported a strategic integration with whites. Second, the congregation emphasized their continuing support for the creation and maintenance of black institutions.

I asked the informants whether they believed that African Americans should control the politics, economics, and education in predominately black communities or whether there should be strong ties between white and black areas of the city. The members agree that working with the white community is a realistic, tactical necessity for African Americans. They expressed support for integrated politics, but their support was tempered with caution and reluctance. Michael suggested that programs that could benefit the black community would have a better chance of financial support if they included the participation of whites.

> It's so much more difficult to get the resources when you are trying to do something in the black community that is all black. It's very difficult to get the funds. I think that you still have to keep some type of black leadership, but maybe working with the white community will help you to get some of the things that you need. I think we need to do whatever it takes to get the funding, but don't give all control of the black community over. Because [whites] don't necessarily understand what we are going through.

Christopher also discussed the issue of capital resources in his analysis of the difficulty of starting black businesses.

> [We] as a black community really don't have the backing to put together the strong corporations that white people do. It's just hard as far as building big corporations, in the black community. If you're talking about doing something that has always been done for the white community for hundreds and hundreds of years, it's something new to us, because we are basically just becoming free. I think we would have to first work with the white community in order to start our own.

For both Michael and Christopher, coalition with whites facilitates growth and success in the black community because African Americans traditionally have less access to resources. While each of these men is willing to work closely with whites, they see their decision as strategic rather than resulting from a genuine affection for whites. Andrea expressed similar concerns in her own analysis of the proper relationship between whites and blacks. "We can't live in these small private cities and communities. We must have some sort of integration."

Michael, Christopher and Andrea believe in the necessity of interracial ventures, but they are concerned with the possibility of African Americans becoming junior partners in joint endeavors. They discuss the practicality of combining forces with whites, but each of them emphasizes that only a partnership of true equals is acceptable. They express a belief that the uniqueness of the African American experience requires that blacks continue to have leadership that grows from their own ranks.

The members not only supported a strategic relationship with whites, but some members also echoed Reverend Kenney's concern with building an interracial Christian community. Margaret felt a missionary responsibility to promote interracial cooperation. "In order to get the word out, to spread gospel, it should be a ministry where the black community can talk to the white. Instead of them going on in their own little mission, they need to help us, as one community."

Shirley's discussion of her attitudes toward whites was particularly poignant:

> I don't know if white people talk about love when there is prejudice. I don't know how somebody is going to just hate a whole race of people. I just don't know how you would just hate somebody and still be a Christian. You are supposed to just love everybody. My mom says, "Shirley you just really love everybody." And I say, "I do, I just really try to." I know that sometimes a prejudice thing may come into my mind. But when I'm feeling a little prejudice for a person I automatically just stop and say, I still love that person, no matter how he feels about me. If I'm in a grocery store and I'm feeling that they are not liking me because I'm black, if they are treating me differently, I think, I've still got to love that person. We don't have to put up with any mess, we don't have to be floor mats, but just ask for love and kindness to come into you.

Shirley connects her feelings about whites to a sense of Christian responsibility. She recognizes the historic context and the contemporary ramifications of white racism. But she believes that it is her responsibility to face their animosity with compassion. It is clear from her discussion, however, that Shirley has to actively struggle to repress negative attitudes about the whites whom she encounters.

Louise is less concerned with curbing her negative feelings about whites. Louise believes that there are some good white people, but she rejects the notion that she has a Christian responsibility to embrace the many whites who are not good. "When you see a white person that loves the Lord truly it's so obvious, because you are their equal. But I haven't seen very many." Unlike Shirley, who feels the need to embrace all whites because of a Christian imperative, Louise suggests that most whites are not Christian at all. Her insistence that the majority of whites do not love the Lord is rooted in her belief that those who do love God treat blacks fairly and equally. She interprets racism as an indication that white people are outside of the Christian community. But even Louise is not entirely separatist. She still accepts the notion that some white people are kind and good people, whom she is capable of loving as family.

Overall, Orange Grove's congregation shares suspiciousness about white motives. They generally believe in the need for strategic integration and for the creation of an interracial Christian community, but they approach these notions with wariness rather than optimism. This vigilance about maintaining equal footing in interracial endeavors is reflected in the congregation's continuing support for black economic and academic institutions. Like Reverend Kenney, Orange Grove's members admit a need for integration, but their affection continues to reside in the black community. Just as Kenney's discussion of Princeton made tangible his preference for black life, so too do the responses of Orange Grove's members reflect a continuing desire to be part of the black community.

Margaret believes that "sometimes you need to be around your own race because it balances you. It just gives you a better sense of who you are." Bridgett emphasizes that the black college experience makes African Americans more authentic and grounded.

> I still will be a very strong supporter of black college because of the culture. It's because of learning about your history. It's because of what you learn about the history of that school and other black schools, the town, you can see how black people struggled. And then you learn of course about Greek organizations and religious organizations a lot more than if you went to white schools. And black people who attend black colleges, they continue to be themselves, they're still real, they don't forget where they come from. They might be ambitious and have high plans for where they are going in their life, but they are not phony or fake.

Orange Grove's members expressed support not only for black colleges; they are also enthusiastic supporters of African American entrepreneurship. Andrea views black business ownership as special distinction of success. "A person who can succeed or does succeed in black-owned business, I definitely have a lot more respect. I definitely think that's a measure of success. I am a person who went to a white school and has been working for a white-owned company, but I think that's important that people that can start their own businesses or focus on the black community." Keith argues that black institutions are essential to buffer African Americans from business, economic, and social vulnerability.

I look at corporate America, I look at businesses, and I just see continual downsizing and continual insecurity and I don't want to go through life feeling insecure about things. I feel as though if it's up to me then I'll give it my all and pretty much make it work, I can't guarantee it, but I know if it fails, it'll be a tough life. What we need to do first of all is work together. That's what we need to do. We need to first start with our community. We need to start among ourselves; there is strength in numbers.

The message from leadership and membership is very similar with respect to attitudes toward whites. Both Reverend Kenney and his members view integration as a tactical necessity for African Americans. Recognizing the continuing inequality in resources and influence, they believe that blacks should forge partnerships that assist in advancing black community interests. But Kenney and his congregation remain wary of these partnerships and still believe that blacks require separate institutions to serve as a source of indigenous community strength. Within these strategic calculations, there is a dilemma as these Christians wrestle with the imperatives of their theology. The Orange Grove family is concerned about racial attitudes from a moral as well as a political vantage.

POLITICS AND THE CHURCH

Orange Grove members are able to provide cogent and often passionate responses to each of the four major dimensions that structure black political ideology, but do they believe that political discussion is appropriate in a church setting? Certainly Reverend Kenney is self-consciously political and believes strongly that the black church, and Orange Grove in particular, should be involved in communal and electoral politics. I asked the congregation if they believed that politics and elections were appropriate Sunday morning discussions. The members were overwhelmingly supportive of an overtly political church atmosphere. Bridgett spoke proudly about Orange Grove's involvement in local politics.

The political world is very much a part of Orange Grove. Almost every African American politician in Durham has come to Orange Grove and asked for our support and we have given it. These people have done very well indeed — that's why they know it is a good idea to come here. African Americans want to know what the issues are, and African Americans want to know what their rights are, and they want to know that there is someone out there who is going to protect them, back them up and support their needs.

Michael remembers:

I've heard Reverend Kenney talk about voting. But for the most part for the major elections it didn't affect me, because I was going to vote anyway, but I did vote on the downsizing of the city council. I hadn't planned on voting for that. A couple of times he has had some of the candidates there. I would vote for them, so I would say that may have swayed some of the people I voted for. Yes, because they used to say don't mix politics and the church. But I am saying this is for the well-being of the black community so that's fine. I mean how else are we supposed to know that person. Nobody knows them all, and there is no way to hear them. Sometimes the only way that people are going to hear them is if they come to church.

Keith also believes that his electoral choices have been influenced by his church.

Most of the time Reverend Kenney doesn't really tell you whom to or not to vote for, which is a good thing, but it has opened my eyes about certain things. Like sometimes these bond referendums or other things that I'm not really sure what a yes or a no means. It has opened my eyes to help understand that better, in that way it did. And when a candidate comes to church, that carries some weight. In the end I would look at the total picture too, but yeah that does carry some weight. Particularly if they come during a nonelection year.

Louise believes that disseminating political information is part of a pastor's responsibility.

I have heard Reverend Kenney focus on the importance and the privilege and the right of voting. He don't tell you how to vote, but he does let you know about the issues, and he does emphasize how important it is that you practice your duty as a citizen. I really like for my minister to take a political stance and let us know what is going on in terms of issues. He's down there. He's in it. He's working in it all the time and we're not, so we may not necessarily be aware of what is going on. I appreciate a minister who does not just try to be quiet or stand apart from it, but really gets in there.

The congregation has offered a thunderous Amen to Reverend Kenney's politically focused ministry. The members are able to offer a variety of reasons why electoral politics belong in the church, and they are able to point to times in their own lives when the church's messages affected their own electoral behavior. Both the pastor and the congregation recognize that they are engaged in a political discourse.

CREATING A COMMUNAL NARRATIVE

Together the leader and members of Orange Grove Missionary Baptist Church are engaged in everyday talk that helps them understand what it means when they promise each week to be "the Christian that God has made me to be." As they answer this question, they build political ideology. These interviews are suggestive of one way that political ideology functions as a social narrative that explains the sources of black inequality, justifies action of behalf of the group, provides strategy for addressing black inequality, and provides a vision of a different future.

Reverend Kenney offers a story of black people who are vulnerable to white racism. In particular, he shows that African Americans have been, and continue to be, attacked by biased economic, political, and social systems of oppression. Kenney shows that racial vulnerability is heightened by class, gender, sexual orientation, and previous incarceration. In his narrative these personal characteristics combine with a vicious Southern tradition to create deep and lasting racial inequality. The pastor demands action on behalf of the poor and oppressed. He requires leadership from men and women and encourages openness to multiracial coalitions. He justifies social action as not only a Christian imperative, but also a government responsibility. He derides those who have a narrow view of their social responsibility or simplistic notions of how to solve complex problems. His narrative proposes strategies of communal, organizational, and governmental action. He asks people to change not only their attitudes, but the material circumstances of the marginalized as well.

In making his call, Kenney provides a new vision. He asks his congregation to strive for a world that respects human diversity. He yearns to maintain the dignity and joy in his own cultural traditions, and also to open his life to incorporate the experiences of people who are not like him. When the pastor refers to a "journey toward wholeness," it is not just a voyage of self-healing. He is also referring to a cooperative sojourn. He weeps for a political and religious community that is broken by hate. His is a vision of communal wholeness where differences of race, class, gender, and sexual orientation can be acknowledged without being divisive. Ultimately Kenney is a Feminist and an Integrationist. While he does display elements of cultural and religious Nationalism, he is staunchly anti-Conservative. Because of his self-conscious political identity and his forum in the local newspaper, Kenney has significant opportunity to communicate his political and moral vision to his congregation.

Orange Grove's membership is active in the creation of their communal narrative. They listen to Kenney's call, and they respond with attitudes that are shaped by both their church experiences and their interactions in other parts of their lives. The ideological narrative of the membership is very similar to Kenney's. They too recognize that white racial animosity and institutionalized discrimination play a significant role in creating and perpetuating black inequality. But their narrative differs from Reverend Kenney's because they place more blame on African American individuals. Taking a harsher line on individual accountability, the congregation locates some of black America's problems in the pathological behavior of individuals.

But while the narratives differ somewhat on explaining the source of black inequality, the members agree with their minister on the imperative of social action emanating from the church. Their vision of "the community" is not articulated as broadly as Kenney's, but they are supportive of black women's leadership. There is a hint of their recognition of, and willingness to deal with, the competing interests within the black community. So like their minister they have broad vision of racial struggle and are willing to form strategic alliances across lines of difference.

With Reverend Kenney's help, the membership is constructing a vision of the future. Their vision includes a black community free from drugs and violence. It is a future where communal leadership is shared equally between men and women and where blacks have found a way to exist equally and peacefully with whites. It is more difficult to characterize the ideology of an entire group than of an individual. But the membership is both slightly more Nationalist and somewhat more Conservative than their leader. They are more willing to place blame on individuals and more inclined to reject white people. They display a Feminist perspective, at least with regards to church leadership, and are tentatively Integrationist in their strategies.

Scholars of the black church have argued over whether the black church functions as an opiate that contributes to racial oppression (Johnson 1967; Myrdal 1944; Frazier 1963; Reed 1986) or whether it is an agent of political mobilization and liberation (Cone 1969). This debate is tangential to the larger interest of *how* the church can operate as a site of everyday talk that can cultivate many attitudes. The goal of this chapter was not to categorize the specific ideological messages of Orange Grove's leader or its members per se. Rather, it is to allow a glimpse of how black people use the lessons that they learn in church to make sense of a world outside of the church. In some churches the messages may be Nationalist, in others largely Conservative, or in a rare case like Orange Grove there may be a strong Feminist ideological bent.

Orange Grove provides its members with both organizational and psychological resources for political participation. But it offers something else as well: Orange Grove is a place where congregants encounter ideas about how the world works and how it should work. Reverend Kenney is a willing guide through the complexities of ideological thought. He helps members to sort out the relationships among race, religion, and politics and provides electoral advice, political mobilization, and insightful analysis of current events. His ministry is explicitly politicized, and those who choose to stay in it find themselves engaging both political and spiritual issues. Of course, this means that Orange Grove is not a typical black, Baptist, Southern church, but it represents the potential available in black organizational life. When harnessed to do the work of ideology building, the black church can be an instrument in shaping the political worldviews of African Americans.

In some ways the men and women of Orange Grove are exceptional as well. This study has no way of knowing how many men and women heard Reverend Kenney speak only once and refused to return because of their opposition to his political views. It is impossible to know how many African Americans left before the sermon even started when they saw women in the pulpit at Orange Grove. Those men and women who choose to stay at Orange Grove are those who are willing to be challenged about traditional ways of ordering the church. But it is important to note that these members are entirely ordinary in other ways. When asked about why they attend church, they cite personal and spiritual reasons such as attending with friends or overcoming life crisis. They do not place Reverend Kenney's politics in the foreground of their explanations for their membership. These members are average Durham residents. They tend to be well educated and employed, but they all struggle with the family crises, financial burdens, and personal failings of ordinary citizens. While typical in many meaningful ways, the members of Orange Grove are exceptional in their support for the links between church and politics, their support of women's religious leadership, their analysis of racial discrimination, and their prophetic vision of the church as a vehicle for social change. There is reason to credit their experiences with Orange Grove for these shared political worldviews.

While this case study may succeed in exposing some part of the linkages between political elites and regular people struggling to navigate a complex and hostile world, it is only a gateway into the larger concerns of the text. Still unanswered are the questions of whether ideology actually exists among African Americans, and whether those ideologies are systematically connected to participation in everyday black talk. Perhaps Orange Grove's story is not an example of everyday talk, but only a Zalleresque confrontation of ordinary citizens with elite ideas. There are hints in the Orange Grove case study that political ideology can take shape in a place where ideas are shared, but Orange Grove is an exceptional place with an articulate and engaged leader who sets the ideological agenda for the church. Does political ideology exist among the masses of African Americans? Does everyday talk have political implications in more horizontal spaces? The survey and experimental data of the next two chapters bring evidence to bear on these questions, showing both that ideological formations are present in a national sample of African Americans and that these political worldviews can take shape in the context of everyday talk. The ethnographic research in a black barbershop detailed in chapter 5 provides a glimpse into a less structured setting of everyday talk and shows how, even without the official hierarchy of a church, the exchange of everyday ideas has political meaning in the lives of African Americans.

CHAPTER THREE

Black Talk, Black Thought: Evidence in National Data

When was the last time you were with your friends where the
topic of conversation was what are we doing as a group to make
Black America better? When was the last time you asked yourself,
"What have I done today for the race?"
— Tavis Smiley, 2001

IN THE PRESIDENTIAL election of 1936, African Americans realigned
their partisan affiliation from Republican to Democrat, offering Roose-
velt more than 60 percent of the black vote in cities like Philadelphia,
New York, Pittsburgh, and Cincinnati (Weiss 1983). Democratic partisanship in African American voting has endured and deepened in the
decades since that critical election. The strength and durability of black
Democratic voting affiliation has led many observers of American political behavior to assume that there is no variation to explain in black
public opinion. "The relative homogeneity of black public opinion has
been generally considered one of the few certainties of modern American politics" (Dawson 2001, 44). Overwhelming Democratic partisanship masks the internal contestation within black political thought that
is not discernable through the binary choices available in American elections, making the heterogeneity within black opinion rarely visible.
Black political diversity is unlikely to emerge in electoral contexts; it is
embedded instead in the politics of the black counterpublic. Within the
spaces of internal community interaction, diverse black political attitudes emerge and are given voice. This chapter uses national survey
data to provide initial evidence for the existence of several identifiable
political ideologies among African Americans and demonstrates that
these ideologies are associated with participation in spaces of the black
counterpublic.

MODEL

Figure 3.1 sets out the model estimated in this chapter. Black Nationalism, Conservatism, and Feminism are dependent variables in a system

Forms of Everyday Black Talk						Demographics
Rap · Music Listener	Black Media Exposure	Organizational Member	Church Based Political Discussion	Church Based Political Action	Talking with Family and Friends	Age, Sex, Income, Education, Urban- Dwelling

Core Beliefs					
Black Linked Fate	Women Linked Fate	Black Self- Reliance	Bootstrap Philosophy	Attitude toward Whites	Coalition with Nonwhites

Black Political Ideologies		
Nationalism	Conservatism	Feminism

Figure 3.1. Simplified Form of Estimated Model: Determinants of African American Political Ideology.

of equations.[1] The first half of the model hypothesizes that various forms of everyday talk affect a number of core beliefs held by African Americans. Informal political discussions with friends and family, membership in black organizations, exposure to black media sources, listening to rap music, and engagement in politicized church discussions and activities are believed to affect six core beliefs: attitudes toward whites, belief in a black self-reliance, bootstrap philosophy, sense of linked fate with blacks, linked faith with women, and the willingness to form coalitions with nonblacks. The second half of the model hypothesizes that these core beliefs are the primary building blocks of black ideologies. Specifically, it models combinations of these six core beliefs as contributors to attitude clusters that indicate the identified ideologies.[2]

This model is estimated using data from the 1993–94 National Black Politics Survey (NBPS). The data from the NBPS come from a probability sample of all African American households, yielding 1,206 observations who are African Americans eighteen years old or older. The survey was conducted between November 20, 1993, and February 20, 1994, with a response rate of 65 percent. The survey was administered through the University of Chicago with principal investigators Ronald Brown of Wayne State University and Michael Dawson of the University of Chicago. The NBPS is particularly appropriate for this analysis because the survey was designed intentionally to allow measurement of African American political ideologies. It is a unique national data source for this reason.[3]

MEASURING EVERYDAY TALK

The National Black Politics Survey questioned African Americans about their participation in a number of different elements of the black counterpublic; therefore, the data allow an assessment of several different elements of everyday black talk. Although the survey provides no reasonable measure of participation in black public spaces, such as barbershops and beauty salons, it does ask respondents whether they have discussed political matters with friends and family. There is not much variation in this measure, with 90 percent of the sample reporting having had some political discussion with friends and family. Still, this measure is included to capture some element of informal political conversations.

The survey allows for a better assessment of black media usage. Most respondents to the NBPS are embedded in black popular culture through hip-hop music and black media exposure. Fifty-two percent of respondents reported listening to rap music in the past year. Male, urban, wealthier, and more educated African Americans are more likely to listen to rap, but by far the most important divide is age. Young African Americans are significantly more likely than older blacks to listen to hip-hop.[4] Rap music listening is estimated separately from other forms of black media for a number of reasons. Rap music listening is included as a form of everyday talk to provide an empirical test of the assertion by both scholars and public officials that rap music has an effect on the thoughts and attitudes of African Americans.

Hip-hop music was dismissed as artistically and socially irrelevant in the early 1980s. But after more than twenty years on the American cultural scene, hip-hop music and culture have come to define a generation. As *Time* magazine observed, "Just as F. Scott Fitzgerald lived in the jazz age . . . it could be said that we are living in the age of hip-hop" (*Time*, February 8, 1999). The centrality of hip-hop to youth culture has prompted a growing body of research that attempts to understand both hip-hop as an artistic, social, and political endeavor and how hip-hop affects individuals who are immersed in it (Rose 1994; Dyson 1996; Kelley 1997).

African American music has historically played a critical role in black culture and politics (Sidran 1971; Stuckey 1987; Scott 1990; Henry 1990). Cultural critic and historian Tricia Rose draws linkages between hip-hop and its musical predecessors and argues that hip-hop is the voice of an oppositional black culture that is self-consciously resisting white cultural, social, and political hegemony. "Rap music, like many powerful black cultural forms before it resonates for people from vast and diverse backgrounds. . . . For some, rappers offer symbolic prowess, a sense of black energy and creativity in the face of omnipresent oppressive forces; others listen to rap with an ear toward the hidden voices of the oppressed, hoping to understand America's large, angry, and 'unintelligible' population" (1994, 19). Dyson similarly argues that, "At their best, rappers shape the tortuous twists of urban fate into lyrical elegies. They represent lives swallowed by too little love or opportunity" (1996, 177). Whether rap music constitutes an authentic representation of the lives of urban, African American youth is controversial. Reed (1992) perceives hip-hop as little more than packaged images of blackness to be sold primarily to white consumers. Cashmore (1997) questions our capacity to understand black artistic endeavors without appreciating the constraints imposed on these endeavors by commercial interests. From this view, black culture is an industry, and hip-hop is a contemporary manifestation of historic commodification.

Hip-hop does not need to be an explicitly political artistic form nor an absolutely authentic one to be understood as a relevant form of everyday black talk. Some hip-hop observers argue that hip-hop is potentially a progressive political force. Rose argues that Public Enemy "keeps poor folks alert and prevents them from being lulled into submission by placating and misleading media stories and official truths." (Rose 1994, 99) Dyson writes of these same artists, "PE's work in toto has confronted, and at times embodied, most of the conflicts faced by young blacks over the last decade." (Dyson 1996, 165) Other scholars have warned that elements in hip-hop are dangerously misogynist and homophobic (Ransby and Matthews 1999; Cohen 1994). Even those who believe in the political potential of hip-hop for marginalized urban youth have argued that, "Whereas hip hop has spiritually and financially empowered African-American males it has boxed young women into stereotypes and weakened their sense of worth" (George 1998, 187). Whether seen as a progressive or repressive political force, many scholars of black popular culture perceive hip-hop as socially, culturally, and politically influential in the lives of young people. Rap music listening is included in the model as a separate form of everyday black talk to provide an empirical test for the assertion of rap's influence.

African Americans consume many other forms of black popular culture through various forms of black media. The NBPS asked whether in the past year the respondent had read a novel by a black author (56%);[5] seen a black movie (72%); read a black newspaper (54%); read a black magazine (81%); listened to a black news program on radio (78%); and watched a black TV program on cable (72%). Results indicate that the black media is widely used by African Americans. Well over half of the respondents reported exposure to every form of black media. Younger, wealthier, and more educated African Americans are more likely to be exposed to more forms of African American media than older, poorer, and less educated blacks.[6] African Americans overwhelming choose to consume information and entertainment that contain images of African Americans. Only 2 percent of respondents failed to engage any of these media sources, and nearly three quarters reported having consumed three or more. This reflects a significant overall media usage by African Americans. For example, Nielsen media research reports that African American households in the United States watch more television in primetime, daytime, and late night than all other households across all age groups. But it is notable that within this general use of the media, African Americans are also heavy consumers of African American images, sounds, and stories. Watching television, reading magazines, and listening to rap music are all part of how African Americans engage in a black counterpublic.[7]

African Americans in the NBPS sample also engage the black counterpublic through African American organizations. Seventy percent of respondents report being members of an "organization working to improve the status of black Americans." Women and men are equally likely to report membership, but older, wealthier, and more educated African Americans are more likely to be organization members.[8] In light of the recent research mapping America's declining social capital, it is notable that 70 percent of the sample reports organizational membership. Putnam (2000) chronicles plummeting civic engagement among all racial groups in the second half of the twentieth century. While it is not possible to know the type of organization or to gauge the level of involvement in or commitment to the affiliation from the measure in the NBPS data, the measurement allows a very rough approximation of engagement with some type of African American organization. And this affiliation with an organization is quite high among NBPS respondents. Many individuals may be considering their church membership in response to this question; others may be indicating membership in a national organization such as the NAACP that amounts to little more than a mailing-list membership. Still other respondents may be over-reporting membership because of social desirability effects, the same effects that are responsible for massive over-reporting of voting in most public opinion surveys. Even with these measurement flaws, there is some evidence here of engagement with a black counterpublic through organizations.

The NBPS asks a number of detailed questions about the level of political information and action that respondents encounter in their places of worship. Recent work by both Harris (1999) and Calhoun-Brown (1996) offers empirical evidence that politicized African American churches contribute to both the organizational and psychological resources necessary for political mobilization and action. The previous chapter suggests that a politicized church like Orange Grove has the capacity to affect the political ideas and attitudes of members. Using the measures available in the National Black Politics Survey to model participation in politicized churches allows an empirical assessment of the relationship between politicized churches and African American ideologies.

More than 40 percent of respondents report attending religious services at least once a week and actively participating in committees, special projects, and meetings at church. Women and older people are more likely to be regular and active church attendees. Further, nearly half of respondents report engagement with some form of church-based political discussion. Thirty-four percent reported talking to people about political matters at church; 50 percent heard a clergy member talk about the need for people to become involved in politics; 38 percent heard a political leader speak at church; and 23 percent heard a church official suggest voting for or against certain candidates.

Respondents were somewhat less likely to be engaged in political activity at church than in church-based political discussion, but nearly a quarter reported some involvement with church-based political action. Twenty-three percent helped in a voter registration drive; 25 percent gave people a ride to the polls on election day; 24 percent gave money to a political candidate; 27 percent attended a candidate fund raiser; 23 percent handed out campaign materials; and 42 percent signed a petition supporting a candidate as a part of her regular religious duties in the past two years. For the majority of African Americans, church is not a site of political conversation or action, but a substantial portion of blacks do encounter political ideas and opportunities for involvement in their religious lives.

These two different measures of political church engagement allow an important distinction between the church as a source for political information and the church as a place for political action. Both listening to political information and engaging in political activity should be understood as forms of everyday talk, but they are substantively different. Engaging in political activity requires a higher level of individual commitment of time and resources. Activity is likely to offer more opportunities for face-to-face interaction and political idea exchange than the more hierarchally structured political discussions that flow from clergy to members, but these heirarchally ordered conversations have the benefit of authority contributing to their potential influence on mass attitudes. Both constructs of political discussion and political action are necessary in order to distinguish among the effects of these different forms of everyday talk.

The model estimated in this chapter uses six measures of everyday talk: a dichotomous measure of talking politics with friends and family; a dichotomous measure of rap music listening; a dichotomous measure of organizational membership; and latent constructs indicating black media usage, church-based political discussion, and church-based political action (see table 3.1). All of the latent constructs are reasonably well measured with large and statistically significant coefficients on all indicators. These six types of everyday talk are hypothesized to directly affect a set of core beliefs among African Americans, which in turn are related to specific ideological positions.

CORE BELIEFS

African American political ideology is structured around its response to four key issues. Ideology helps individuals determine what it means to be black in the American political system. Ideology helps individuals identify the relative political significance of race compared with other personal characteristics. Ideology helps individuals determine the extent to which blacks should solve their own problems or look to the system for assistance. Ideology helps individuals determine the required degree of tactical separation from whites necessary for successful advancement of group interests. These central tasks of ideology can be measured in the national data as six core beliefs:

- Black linked fate
- Women linked fate
- Coalition with other nonwhites
- Black self-reliance
- Bootstrap philosophy
- Attitude toward whites

TABLE 3.1
Summary of Measures of Everyday Talk

Construct	Coefficient	S.E.
Talk politics		
Discussed political issues with family and friends	Yes = 1	
Rap music listener		
Listened to rap music	Yes = 1	
Black organization member		
Member of any organization working to improve the status of blacks	Yes = 1	
Black media exposure		
Read a novel by a black author	1.0	
Saw a black movie	1.14	0.11
Read a black newspaper	0.60	0.09
Read a black magazine	0.97	0.09
Listened to a black news program on radio	0.70	0.09
Watched a black TV program on cable	0.78	0.09
Church-based political discussion		
Talked to people about political matters at your church	1.0	
Clergy member talked about the need for people to become involved in politics	1.26	0.10
Political leader spoke at church	1.02	0.08
Church official suggested voting for or against certain candidates	0.75	0.07
Church-based political activity		
Helped in a voter registration drive	1.0	
Gave people a ride to the polls on election day	0.61	0.06
Gave money to a political candidate	1.05	0.07
Attended a candidate fundraiser	1.16	0.08
Handed out campaign materials	0.98	0.07
Signed a petition supporting a candidate	0.86	0.07

Source: 1993–94 National Black Politics Survey
Note: Model is estimated using a covariance structure analysis using maximum likelihood estimation. The package is Statistical Analysis Software (SAS), Procedure CALIS. All coefficients significant at $p \leq .001$

Dawson (1994) has established the centrality of black linked fate to the politics of African Americans. Black linked fate acts as a heuristic through which African Americans use the interests of the race as a shortcut for discerning personal political interests. In this model, black linked fate functions as a measure for the extent to which blackness is perceived as a central characteristic in American politics. Nearly 75 percent of respondents believe that what happens to black people has something to do with what happens to their own life, and nearly half of those believe that it affects their life a lot.

Black political ideology also provides guidance about the relative importance of race compared with other characteristics. A sense of linked fate with women and a willingness to form coalitions with other nonwhites are indicators of a broader vision of political solidarity. The willingness to perceive nonblack women and other communities of color as political partners reflects some notion that race is only one of several relevant political characteristics. Gender and shared minority status may also be important identities. Eighty-seven percent of black women indicated a sense of linked fate with women in general. About 60 percent of black women expressed a sense of linked fate with white women, and 64 percent with nonwhite women. Black men were not questioned about a sense of linked fate with women in general, but 72 percent of black men reported a somewhat or strong sense of linked fate with black women.[9] Forty-seven percent of respondents believe that Latinos, Asian Americans, and other disadvantaged groups are potentially good political allies for blacks.

African American ideology also responds to questions of racial self-reliance and racial separation. Black self-reliance directly addresses the extent to which blacks should solve their own problems or look to the system for assistance. More than 80 percent of respondents believe that black people "should rely on themselves not on others." The wording of the black self-reliance measure indicates that it is probably tapping support for collective, group responsibility. It measures the belief that blacks should rely on other African Americans and not on the government or other groups. But self-reliance is not only a collective strategy. Historically, black political thought has also included more individualist notions of self-reliance. The bootstrap philosophy is the notion of individual self-reliance, such that each person is responsible for his or her own success and failings. In this model, the bootstrap philosophy is measured as agreement with the statement that "government should let each person get ahead on their own." Approximately 33 percent of the NBPS respondents agreed with the bootstrap philosophy of individual self-reliance.

The final dilemma addressed by black political ideology is the degree of tactical separation from whites that is necessary to advance African American interests. At one end of the spectrum, whites may be seen as actively opposing the interests of black advancement and may be viewed as dangerous and deliberatively hostile. At the opposing end of this continuum, whites may be seen as benevolent or benign partners in advancing the interests of African Americans. Still another perspective

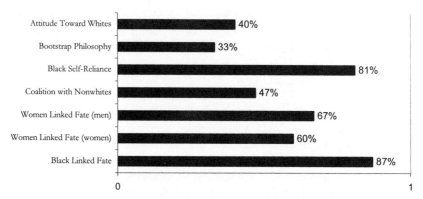

Figure 3.2. Percent of NBPS Sample Supporting Measures of Core Beliefs. *Source*: 1993–94 National Black Politics Survey. Attitude toward whites and women "linked fate" (women) are means of latent variables estimated using a covariance structure analysis using maximum likelihood estimation. The package is Statistical Analysis Software (SAS), Procedure CALIS.

views whites as strategic allies with whom it is sometimes reasonable to form short-term coalitions for political action. In the NBPS data, attitudes toward whites are measured with three indicators: the feeling thermometer toward whites, an equitable support for white elected officials, and a belief that whites are interested in black advancement. The average feeling thermometer toward whites among NBPS respondents is 51, putting it just above a neutral rating. This is substantially lower than the mean feeling thermometer rating for blacks (85), but higher than the mean feeling thermometers for gay men and lesbians (30 each). Less than one-third of respondents believe that white elected officials from black communities represent black interests just as well as black elected officials. Only 18 percent of African Americans believe that whites want to see blacks get a better break, and nearly half believe that whites do not care about blacks one way or another. These attitudes toward whites are part of the core beliefs that structure African American political ideology.

In the model estimated below, these six core beliefs are modeled as intermediary variables between participation in forums of everyday talk and black political ideology. The model hypothesizes that as African Americans talk with their family and friends, listen to rap music, engage the black media, join black organizations, and attend politicized churches, they develop positions on each of the four major functions of political ideology. These functions of ideology are indicated by the core belief system that underlies black political attitudes. These core beliefs are then hypothesized to contribute to each of the political ideologies. Rela-

TABLE 3.2
Summary of Core Belief Measures

Construct	Indicator	Coefficient	S.E.
Black linked fate	What happens to black people affects my life.	4-point scale: High = 1	
Women linked fate (female respondents)	What happens to women affects my life.	1.0	
	What happens to white women affects my life.	0.91	0.03
	What happens to nonwhite women affects my life.	0.95	0.03
Black women linked fate (male respondents)	What happens to black women affects my life.	Yes = 1	
Attitude toward whites	Feeling thermometer toward whites.	1.0	
	Most whites want to see blacks get a better break.	0.85	0.18
	White elected officials can represent black interests.	1.22	0.24
Black self-reliance	Blacks should rely on themselves not on others.	Yes = 1	
Bootstrap philosophy	Government should let each person get ahead on their own.	Yes = 1	
Coalition with nonwhites	Latinos, Asian-Americans, and other disadvantaged groups are potentially good allies.	Yes = 1	

Source: 1993–94 National Black Politics Survey
Note: Model is estimated using a covariance structure analysis using maximum likelihood estimation. The package is Statistical Analysis Software (SAS), Procedure CALIS. All coefficients significant at $p \leq .001$

tive strength of linked fate with blacks and women, support for self-reliance and bootstrap philosophy, attitudes toward whites, and willingness to form political coalitions are hypothesized to be the building blocks of black ideology (table 3.2).

MEASUREMENT OF POLITICAL IDEOLOGY

Most African Americans continue to perceive the United States as a racially unequal society. In 1994 more than half of NBPS respondents felt that African Americans were not fairing well economically as a group. Only 4 percent of NBPS respondents believed that African Americans have achieved racial equality. And nearly 85 percent agreed that American society just has not dealt fairly with black people. Even within this context of general agreement about the inequality of racial life in the United States, there are a number of ideological approaches to the politics of black America. Although they may agree that racial disparities exist, African Americans derive different and often oppositional positions to key questions of black political life. Is inequality the fault of white racism or black pathology? Should inequality be addressed through the creation of autonomous black institutions or through success in the corporate world? What role should black women have in providing leadership to black communities facing racially unequal circumstances? What is the role of the government in ameliorating these inequalities? Heterogeneity in black thought is visible in the existence and distribution of multiple political ideologies. The National Black Politics Survey allows for reasonable measurement of three of the identified ideological traditions within black political thought: Nationalism, Conservatism, and Feminism.[10]

Black Nationalism emphasizes the unique and immutable relevance of race as a political characteristic, perceives whites as actively resisting black equality, and encourages African American self-reliance through fostering the development and support of autonomous black institutions. Nationalism includes a support for cultural, social, economic, and political autonomy. Pinkney (1976) acknowledges the historic heterogeneity of black Nationalist thought in America but argues that there are three consistent indicators of contemporary Nationalist ideology: a notion of racial solidarity, pride in black cultural heritage, and a belief that some degree of autonomy is essential for black progress.

Solidarity is high among African Americans in the national sample. Seventy percent of respondents believed that the movement for black rights has affected them personally. While there is no available measure of pride in black cultural heritage, the feeling thermometer for "blacks" averaged 85. This is the highest average feeling thermometer of any group asked about in the NBPS. In the United States the issue of black autonomy has taken on many variations within modern Nationalist thought, ranging from the cultural projects of Maulana Karenga to the revolutionary efforts of young Malcolm X. At times Nationalist projects have called for the establishment of a separate black nation either within the United States, in the Caribbean, or on the African continent. Among African American respondents to the NBPS there is little support for the most strongly articulated separatist element of Nationalism. While 44 percent of respondents believed that African Americans are more like a nation within a nation than like an ethnic group, only 14 percent of respondents agreed that black people should have their own separate nation. Further, these two indicators do not cohere well with other measures of Nationalism. Nationalism among NBPS respondents is articulated as a support for autonomous black institutions and control over aspects of African American communities.

The Nationalism measure coheres around six indicators of support for the statements that blacks should participate in black only organizations whenever possible; form their own political party; always vote for black candidates when they run; shop in black stores whenever possible; have control over the government in mostly black communities and have control over the economy in mostly black communities. The Black Nationalism factor is reasonably well measured. Coefficients are all robust and all are statistically significant (table 3.3). Black Nationalism, measured as support for autonomous racial institutions and control of black communities, is nearly normally distributed among African Americans. Most respondents are moderately supportive of Nationalist ideas, with a slightly skewed distribution toward higher levels of Nationalism (fig. 3.2).

Conservatism is rooted in a belief that African Americans must fortify their moral and economic strength in order to compete in the American meritocracy. Conservatism critiques the state as an overly intrusive institution that retards societal progress; believes that the free market is nondiscriminatory; and stresses the significance of moral and personal attributes rather than racial characteristics to explain an individual's life position. Conservatism locates the sources of racial inequality in the moral, behavioral, and attitudinal pathologies of African Americans, rather than in racist structures, individuals, or groups. Further, Conservatives elevate economic strategies over political ones for ameliorating negative circumstances in black communities.

Black Conservatism coheres in the national sample around a five-indicator construct. Agreement with the statements that "there has been so much progress over the past several years that special programs for blacks are no longer needed" and that "black people depend too much on government programs" taps the antigovernment aspect of Conservatism. The economic aspects of black Conservatism are indicated in agreement with the statements that "America's big corporations are a powerful source of economic growth that benefits the black community" and that "America's economic system is fair to everyone." Finally, the moral aspect of black Conservatism is indicated in the statement that "poor people don't want to work" and is captured in part by the special programs statement. The factor loadings for this construct are high and all are statistically significant (table 3.3). The distribution of black Conservatism in the sample indicates that it is the least popular of

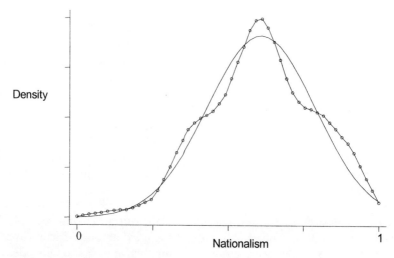

Figure 3.3. Smoothed Black Nationalism Distribution. *Source*: 1993–94 National Black Politics Survey.

the ideologies examined here. The majority of the sample expresses significant disagreement with most indicators used to measure Conservatism. However, there is evidence of a small minority whose political attitudes can be categorized correctly as Conservative.

Black Feminism is an ideology grounded in recognition of the intersection of multiple identities and positions that profoundly affect the lives of individuals and communities. Feminism is concerned with racial, economic, and gender justice and focuses on the inequality that results from intersections of race, gender, class, and sexual identity. Only a small portion of black women in the National Black Politics Survey use the label "feminist" to describe themselves.[11] Thirty-five percent of black women report that they consider themselves to be a feminist, and just over half of those respondents claim to be strong feminists. However, of those who do not use the label feminist to describe themselves, only 6 percent report that they are strongly opposed to feminist ideals. This suggests that the reluctance to use the feminist label may be related to connotations of the label rather than a reflection of the gendered consciousness or political attitudes of African Americans. Self-identification with the label feminist loads poorly on a construct of black Feminism measured as support of gendered equity in leadership and agenda setting. Black women may be unwilling to call themselves feminists, but this does not mean that black men and women are uncommitted to issues of gender equality.

Black Feminism in the national sample coheres around five indicators. All are related to the position of black women in American society and

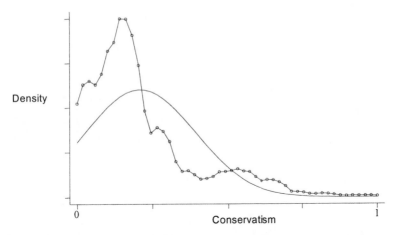

Figure 3.4. Smoothed Black Conservatism Distribution. *Source*: 1993–94 National Black Politics Survey.

in the black community. They are in agreement with the statements that the problems of racism, poverty, and sexual discrimination are all linked and must be addressed by the black community; that black feminist groups help the black community by working to advance the position of black women; that black women should share equally in the political leadership of the black community; that black women have suffered from both sexism within the black community and racism within the women's movement; and that there is a strong tendency in American society to attack and silence strong black women. Each of these indicators is significant with large coefficients (table 3.3). The distribution of black Feminism in the NBPS sample shows it to be clearly more popular than Conservatism, but not nearly as pervasive as Nationalism (fig. 3.5). When disengaged from the feminist label, ideas of equitable gender treatment and shared political leadership enjoy reasonable popularity among ordinary African Americans.

Overall, each of the three ideologies is well measured using indicators available in the national sample, and each is present within contemporary black thought.[12] The analysis below estimates the influence of various forms of everyday black talk as antecedents for these ideological positions.

ESTIMATION OF THE MODEL

The model hypothesizes that interaction in the black counterpublic leads to the development of core beliefs, which then act as the building blocks of the ideologies. The discussion begins with the second half of

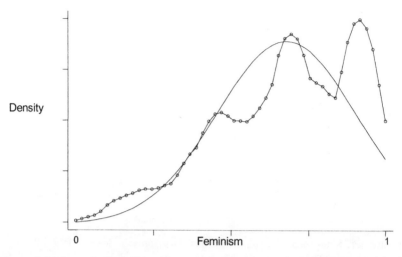

Figure 3.5. Smoothed Black Feminism Distribution. *Source*: 1993–94 National Black Politics Survey.

the model by specifying the relationship between core beliefs and political ideology. The discussion then turns to an analysis of the effects of everyday talk on core beliefs. Overall, results from the model are modest. There are several important relationships indicated in statistically significant relationships between variables, but overall coefficients are small. Still, the analysis is suggestive of the ways that black political ideology is related to participation in the black counterpublic.[13] Results from the second half of the model are presented in table 3.4.

The results indicate that Nationalism rests on four core beliefs: a sense of linked fate with blacks, a negative attitude toward whites, a belief in black self-reliance, and a rejection of the individualized bootstrap philosophy. A sense of linked fate with women and a willingness to form coalition with other nonwhites are not significantly related to Nationalism. The most robust coefficient, by far, is the negative relationship with attitude toward whites. This result suggests that Nationalist support for separate racial institutions is rooted in a basic distrust of white Americans. A sense that African Americans share a common destiny and should rely on themselves are important elements of black Nationalism, but in this model they pale in comparison to the effect of negative racial attitudes. African Americans who distrust or dislike whites are likely to have strong Nationalist tendencies, especially when this dislike is combined with a sense that black people share a common destiny. The results are consistent with the definition of Nationalism provided by Pinkney (1976). Nationalism does seem to be about racial

TABLE 3.3
Summary of African American Ideologies Measures

Constructs	Coefficient	SE
Black Nationalism measure		
Blacks should participate in black only organizations whenever possible.	1.0	
Blacks should form their own political party.	1.19	0.07
Blacks should always vote for black candidates when they run.	0.75	0.09
Black people should shop in black stores whenever possible.	1.3	0.12
Blacks should have control over government in mostly black communities.	1.82	0.15
Blacks should have control over economy in mostly black communities.	1.85	0.15
Black Conservatism measure		
Poor people don't want to work.	1.0	
There has been so much progress over the past several years that special programs for blacks are no longer needed.	0.98	0.30
Black people depend too much on government programs.	1.27	0.34
America's big corporations are a powerful source of economic growth that benefits the black community.	1.92	0.50
America's economic system is fair to everyone.	2.14	0.53
Black Feminism measure		
The problems of racism, poverty, and sexual discrimination are all linked and must be addressed by the black community.	1.0	
Black feminist groups help the black community by working to advance the position of black women.	0.82	0.15
Black women should share equally in the political leadership of the black community.	0.82	0.15
Black women have suffered from both sexism within the black community and racism within the women's movement.	0.51	0.14
There is a strong tendency in American society to attack and silence strong black women.	0.69	0.14

Source: 1993–94 National Black Politics Survey

Note: Model is estimated using a covariance structure analysis using maximum likelihood estimation. The package is Statistical Analysis Software (SAS), Procedure CALIS.
All coefficients significant at $p \leq .01$

TABLE 3.4
Effects of Core Beliefs on Black Ideologies

Construct	Coefficient	SE
Nationalism		
Black linked fate (women)	0.002	0.02
Women linked fate (men)	0.02	0.02
Attitude toward whites	−0.80**	0.16
Black self-reliance	0.12**	0.01
Bootstrap philosophy	−0.03**	0.01
Coalition with nonwhites	−0.002	0.01
Conservatism		
Black linked fate	−0.02*	0.01
Women linked fate (women)	−0.03*	0.02
Women linked fate (men)	−0.01	0.01
Attitude toward ehites	0.42**	0.14
Black self-reliance	0.001	0.01
Bootstrap philosophy	0.03**	0.01
Coalition with nonwhites	0.01	0.01
Feminism		
Black linked fate	0.03*	0.02
Women linked fate (women)	0.11**	0.03
Women linked fate (men)	0.08**	0.03
Attitude toward whites	−0.57**	0.15
Black self-reliance	0.01	0.02
Bootstrap philosophy	−0.02	0.02
Coalition with nonwhites	0.13**	0.02

Source: 1993–94 National Black Politics Survey
Note: Model is estimated using a covariance structure analysis using maximum likelihood estimation. The package is Statistical Analysis Software (SAS), Procedure CALIS.
$*p \le .05$ $**p \le .01$

solidarity and racial autonomy. According to these results, Nationalism is informed by a belief that your fate is linked to the fate of other African Americans. Those who believe blacks should collectively solve their problems without either looking outside the group or relying entirely on individualized efforts are most likely to express a Nationalist ideological position. Most importantly, support for independent black institutions and control of black communities derives from a significant dislike and distrust of whites.

A different constellation of core beliefs fundamentally influences Conservatism in the national sample. Conservatism is the ideology of those who lack a sense of linked fate with blacks or women, those who feel positively toward whites, and those who support individualized solutions to inequality through a bootstrap philosophy. These results are consistent with a priori understandings of this ideological perspective. Race and gender for the Conservative are incidental, personal characteristics, not politically relevant identities that link individual fortunes to collective fates. Lacking a sense of common destiny with other African Americans, or with other women for women respondents, is an indication of the irrelevance of identity politics for Conservatism. Instead of a collective definition of political fortunes, Conservatism rests on an individualized notion of success and a positive affect toward white Americans. Believers in the bootstrap philosophy, Conservatives believe that individuals should go it alone and be allowed to succeed or fail on their own merits. Conservatism is an individualistic ideology that perceives neither race, nor gender, nor disadvantage as attributes that would link individuals to the fate of groups. As with Nationalism, the single largest coefficient is attitudes toward whites. Conservatism is an ideology of those who seek no strategic or affective separation from whites. Instead whites are generally liked and trusted and are regarded as benevolent, or at least neutral, fellow citizens.

Feminism is distinct from both Nationalism and Conservatism in its antecedent core beliefs. Feminism rests on a sense of linked fate with blacks and with women along with a willingness to form cross-racial coalitions. This is consistent with the definition of Feminism as an ideology that expands the boundaries of political communities and that recognizes the intersecting importance of race and gender. Black women who perceive their fate as being linked to other women and black men who see their own lives as tied to the lives of black women are more likely to express agreement with Feminist attitudes. Those who are able to simultaneously understand the ways that blackness links their fate to that of the race and can still appreciate the role that other nonwhites may play in political struggle are more likely to be Feminist. Neither black self-reliance nor the bootstrap philosophy has any statistically significant effect on Feminist thought, but negative attitudes toward whites have a large effect in encouraging Feminism. The most surprising result is the magnitude and direction of this attitude-toward-whites coefficient. After controlling for a sense of gender-based linked fate, distrust of whites is nearly as important to Feminism as it is to Nationalism. This is evidence for the distinctiveness of black Feminism from feminism more generally. Black Feminism does not include an uncritical embrace of white women based on gender solidarity. Quite the opposite, black Feminism is rooted in a sense that whites are neither particularly well liked nor trusted. Feminism gives equal weight to identities based on race, gender, and social disadvantage. The analysis shows that Feminism is indicated by black-linked fate and women-linked fate and includes a significant willingness to form coalitions with others who are disadvantaged. This result is consistent with the definition of black Feminism as an ideology concerned with the triple threat of race, gender, and class.

Ideologies provide narratives of the past, assessments of the present, and visions of the future. Ideology is a way of interpreting public and personal events and a way of negotiating and giving meaning to ambiguous personal and historical circumstances. The data evidence the existence of identifiable sets of ideas that go together and show that these sets of attitudes are consistent with the historical and scholarly definitions of contemporary ideologies: black Nationalism, Conservatism, and Feminism. Further, these sets of attitudes are related quite strongly to a set of identifiable and measurable core beliefs. The way that core beliefs affect ideology is predictable and consistent with the theoretical expectations of what ideology is and how ideology works. Black Nationalism, Conservatism, and Feminism are composed of a number of core beliefs: black linked fate, women linked fate, attitude toward whites, black self-reliance, the bootstrap philosophy, and coalition with other nonwhites. Nationalism is a blend of a sense of linked fate with blacks, a negative attitude toward whites, a belief in a black self-reliance, and a rejection of the bootstrap philosophy. Black Conservatives lack a sense of racial and gender linked fate. They have a positive attitude toward whites and believe in individual initiative through the bootstrap philosophy. Finally, a sense of linked fate with blacks and with women along with a willingness to form coalitions with other nonwhites positively contributes to Feminism, but Feminists are not uncritical coalition builders, as they remain deeply suspicious of whites.

Not only does the model provide evidence for the presence and structure of contemporary black political ideology, it also allows an assessment of the ways that this ideological structure is related to participation in various forms of everyday black talk. The first half of the model posits that the core beliefs that constitute ideology are related to engagement in the black counterpublic through informal political discussions, rap music, black media, organizational membership, and church-based political discussion and action. Estimation of the effects of everyday talk on core beliefs shows that:

- Informal political conversations are positively related to a sense of linked fate with African Americans and women (for female respondents). These conversations are also positively associated with a belief in black self-reliance.
- Rap music is negatively related to attitudes toward whites.

- Black media exposure has large and significant effects on almost all core beliefs. Exposure to black media is positively associated with a sense of black linked fate, women linked fate, a belief in black self-reliance, and a willingness to enter into coalition with nonwhites. Additionally, it is negatively related to attitude toward whites.
- Membership in a black organization is positively associated with a sense of black linked fate and women linked fate, while negatively related to the bootstrap philosophy.
- Church-based political discussion is associated with higher levels of both black linked fate and linked fate with women, and negatively associated with attitudes toward whites.
- Church-based political action has no statistically significant effects on core beliefs after accounting for other aspects of black everyday talk.

INFORMAL CONVERSATIONS

Most respondents to the National Black Politics Survey report having talked with family and friends about political issues. These conversations have meaningful effects on the core belief systems of those who engage in them. For both male and female respondents, political conversations with friends and family reinforce both a sense of black linked fate and a belief in black self-reliance. Further, for women respondents these conversations are associated with a higher level of linked fate with women (table 3.5).

It is surprising to find results associated with these informal political conversations as measured using this dichotomous variable. This measure offers no sense of the substantive content of these conversations, nor does it indicate the intensity or frequency with which respondents engage in them. Yet there are still discernable differences between those who engage in these discussions and those who do not. As they share political ideas and search for answers to political problems, African Americans fortify their sense of connection with others who share their racial and gender identity. They also reinforce their support for autonomous, collective approaches to addressing racial inequality. By strengthening a sense of black linked fate and support for self-reliance, these informal political conversations support Nationalism while mitigating against Conservatism. For black women these discussions undergird the gendered identification that is critical in the development of a Feminist worldview. Although the coefficients are modest, there is some evidence here that even the most informal elements of everyday black talk may have important consequences for the development of black ideology.

TABLE 3.5
Effects of Informal Political Conversations on Core Beliefs

Talking with Family/Friends	Coefficient	SE
Black linked fate	0.08**	0.02
Women linked fate (women)	0.05**	0.01
Women linked fate (men)	0.005	0.02
Attitude toward whites	0.002	0.01
Black self-reliance	0.06*	0.03
Bootstrap philosophy	−0.01	0.03
Coalition with nonwhites	0.02	0.03

Source: 1993–94 National Black Politics Survey
Note: Model is estimated using a covariance structure analysis using maximum likelihood estimation. The package is Statistical Analysis Software (SAS), Procedure CALIS.
*$p \le .05$ **$p \le .001$

BLACK INFORMATION NETWORKS: HIP-HOP AND MEDIA

Both scholars and public figures have expressed a belief that rap music potentially affects its listeners. Public critics like C. Delores Tucker and Tipper Gore have expressed concern about the violent and misogynist elements of hip-hop. Artists like KRS One and Chuck D have argued for the political mobilizing potential of hip-hop. The current data show that being a rap music listener has one consistent effect within the core belief system. Although it does not generate less attachment to women or to African Americans, rap music is associated with a more negative assessment of whites (table 3.6).

This result is interesting for a number of reasons. First, it is noteworthy that rap music can encourage negative feelings toward whites without necessarily increasing a sense of black linked fate. Attitudes toward whites and blacks are separate categories of opinion and not simply opposite ends of a single racial attitude continuum. Rap music can inform listeners that whites are untrustworthy without suggesting that race is the most important commonality between blacks. It may seem unusual that rap does not promote black linked fate. Earlier hip-hop artists such as Public Enemy and X-Clan promoted strong Nationalist messages that stressed the importance of African American unity. But by the time of this national survey in the mid-1990s, rap music lyrics and their racial messages had shifted focus. An increased focus on material and commercial success as well as an emerging rivalry between East Coast and West Coast rap artists began to structure hip-hop music and culture. Rap listeners at the time of this national survey were less likely to receive overt messages encouraging a sense of black linked fate.

TABLE 3.6
Effects of Rap Music on Core Beliefs

Construct	Coefficient	SE
Black linked fate	0.001	0.01
Women linked fate (women)	−0.02	0.02
Women linked fate (men)	0.002	0.02
Attitude toward whites	−0.04**	0.01
Black self-reliance	0.02	0.03
Bootstrap philosophy	0.01	0.03
Coalition with nonwhites	0.03	0.03

Source: 1993–94 National Black Politics Survey

Note: Model is estimated using a covariance structure analysis using maximum likelihood estimation. The package is Statistical Analysis Software (SAS), Procedure CALIS.

$*p \leq .1$ $**p \leq .05$ $***p \leq .01$

It is not surprising that rap music discourages positive racial attitudes toward whites. Many rap lyrics are critical of white police, white politicians, and white cultural styles. This result suggests that rap listening could potentially have significant effects on black ideology. In the second half of the model, it is clear that attitude toward whites is consistently the most important single contributor to ideological positions. Rap's negative relationship to attitude toward whites means it is positively associated with Nationalism and Feminism, and clearly opposed to Conservatism. Through the mechanism of attitude toward whites, rap music has a potentially important effect on African American political ideology.

Exposure to other elements of the black media contribute positively and significantly to five of the six core beliefs. Black media exposure has the largest and most pervasive effects of any of the forms of everyday black talk considered in this analysis. It is strongly positively associated with a sense of black linked fate as well as a sense of linked fate with women for both male and female respondents. Further, exposure to the black media is strongly positively associated with black self-reliance as well as with the willingness to form coalitions with nonwhites. The bootstrap philosophy is unrelated to black media exposure, but the black media is significantly negatively related to attitudes toward whites (table 3.7).

These results are evidence that the black media is an important source of information. In the NBPS, more than half of respondents made use of each of the sources. African Americans are plugged into this counterpublic space, and it has an important influence on their political attitudes. The results are also indicative of the breadth of black media

TABLE 3.7

Effects of Black Media Exposure on Core Beliefs

Construct	Coefficient	SE
Black linked fate	0.54**	0.08
Women linked fate (women)	0.23**	0.05
Women linked fate (men)	0.30**	0.05
Attitude toward whites	−0.20**	0.04
Black self-feliance	0.36**	0.07
Bootstrap philosophy	0.05	0.07
Coalition with nonwhites	0.14*	0.07

Source: 1993–94 National Black Politics Survey

Note: Model is estimated using a covariance structure analysis using maximum likelihood estimation. The package is Statistical Analysis Software (SAS), Procedure CALIS.

$*p \leq .05 **p \leq .01$

sources. Together these media manage to address all of the major building blocks of ideology. No other form of everyday talk has such a wide impact in the estimated model. The construct for black media exposure includes novels, movies, television, newspapers, and magazines. Within these different media there are a variety of messages about race, gender, American identity, and politics. As African Americans consume this media, they build core beliefs that contribute to the development of ideologies. The breadth and importance of the black media is evident in its significant effects on most of the identified core beliefs.

From these estimations, black media has a straightforward negative effect on Conservatism. It decreases positive affect toward whites while increasing black linked fate and support for black self-reliance. Black media exposure also clearly supports a Feminist ideology by encouraging linked fate with blacks and women, encouraging coalition with nonwhites, and discouraging positive attitudes toward whites. Importantly, black media exposure has a statistically significant positive relationship with a sense of women linked fate among black male respondents. Thus, black media exposure may have an important potential for increasing Feminist sensibilities for black men through increasing linked fate with black women. Finally, black media exposure encourages Nationalism through its large effect on black linked fate and black self-reliance and its negative effect on attitude toward whites.

BLACK ORGANIZATIONS: SECULAR AND SACRED

Organizational talk is measured in three ways: membership in an African American organization, engagement in political discussions at

TABLE 3.8
Effects of Membership in a Black Organization on Core Beliefs

Construct	Coefficient	SE
Black linked fate	0.08**	0.03
Women linked fate (women)	0.05**	0.02
Women linked fate (men)	0.02	0.02
Attitude toward whites	−0.01	0.01
Black self-reliance	0.04	0.03
Bootstrap philosophy	−0.10**	0.03
Coalition with nonwhites	−0.03	0.03

Source: 1993–94 National Black Politics Survey
Note: Model is estimated using a covariance structure analysis using maximum likelihood estimation. The package is Statistical Analysis Software (SAS), Procedure CALIS.
*$p \le .05$**$p \le .001$

church, and participation in church-sponsored political activities. Membership in a black organization has several statistically significant relationships with core beliefs. Organizational membership is positively associated with a sense of linked fate with blacks and, for female respondents, a sense of linked fate with women. Like informal conversations with friends and family, organizational membership reinforces connections with those who share relevant political identities. Membership in a black organization is also negatively related to the bootstrap philosophy (table 3.8).

This organizational variable is a blunt instrument. It asks about organizational membership but cannot distinguish between someone who is president of the local sorority chapter and someone who is an NAACP member, but who never attends local meetings and does not follow the business of the national organization. It is an imperfect tool for measuring organizational talk in the sense of active participation in an organization. Still, there are important and consistent effects that are visible in these moderate coefficients. Organizational membership supports both Nationalism and Feminism in its positive relationship with racialized and gendered linked fate. Because organizational membership is also negatively related to the bootstrap philosophy, it clearly counters Conservative ideology.

Data from the NBPS allow a fairly comprehensive analysis of black church talk by providing indicators of both discussion and action in the church. Church-based political discussion has several statistically significant and substantively important effects. Those respondents who report hearing political discussions by clerical and political leaders in the church have a higher sense of linked fate with both blacks and women.

The higher sense of linked fate with women occurs for both male and female respondents. These respondents also express cooler attitudes toward whites. Other than exposure to black media, church-based political discussion has the most wide ranging and substantively significant coefficients in the entire model, suggesting that everyday talk in the black church is a particularly influential form of political dialogue.

Conversely, church-based political activity has no statistically significant effects on the core belief structure once all the other forms of everyday black talk are taken into account. After accounting for informal political discussion, exposure to black media and hip-hop, organizational membership, and engagement with politicized discussions in the black church, there is no discernable independent effect for church-based political action. This suggests that it is the church's role in facilitating everyday talk that makes it an important contributor to the political attitudes of African American men and women (table 3.9).

It is not surprising that church-based political discussion increases black linked fate. When church leaders make political appeals to their congregations and political candidates use churches as a place to gain support, they tend to couch their language as appeals to racial commonality and racial struggle. Many empirical analyses of the black church suggest that the church serves as place to build political consciousness and racial identity among African Americans that can then be used to mobilize African American political action (Calhoun-Brown 1996; Harris 1994; Shingles 1981). This analysis reflects these earlier findings: church-based political discussion bolsters a sense of linked fate with other African Americans.

It is perhaps more surprising that church-based political discussion encourages a sense of linked fate with women, especially for male respondents. Calhoun-Brown (1996) anticipates this result when she demonstrates that attendance at politicized black churches is related to generally more liberal gender attitudes among blacks. However, one might expect that the traditional gender hierarchies in many African American churches might work against black men's sense of connection with black women. This is not the case. When African Americans engage in church-based political discussion, it contributes to a broad sense of connection both to other African Americans and to women in particular. Although the strength of Reverend Kenney's Feminist articulations at Orange Grove are exceptional, this result suggests that they may be in line with some of the content of other political churches. By reinforcing both black linked fate and linked fate with women, church-based political discussion contributes to higher levels of Feminism among respondents.

Negative attitudes toward whites are also associated with church-

TABLE 3.9
Effects of Church-Based Politics on Core Beliefs

Construct	Coefficient	SE
Church-based political discussion		
Black linked fate	0.18**	0.06
Women linked fate (women)	0.14**	0.04
Women linked fate (men)	0.10**	0.04
Attitude toward whites	−0.05*	0.02
Black self-reliance	0.001	0.06
Bootstrap philosophy	0.05	0.06
Coalition with nonwhites	−0.04	0.06
Church-based political action		
Black linked fate	0.06	0.06
Women linked fate (women)	0.03	0.03
Women linked fate (men)	−0.04	0.03
Attitude toward whites	0.03	0.03
Black self-reliance	0.08	0.06
Bootstrap philosophy	0.06	0.06
Coalition with nonwhites	0.07	0.06

Source: 1993–94 National Black Politics Survey

Note: Model is estimated using a covariance structure analysis using maximum likelihood estimation. The package is Statistical Analysis Software (SAS), Procedure CALIS.

*$p \leq .05$ **$p \leq .001$

based political discussion. One might expect that black churches would emphasize Christian identity rather than racial identity by arguing that "we have no race in Christ." Politicized black churches are teaching a different lesson, however. As the church produces everyday black talk around issues of electoral politics and participation, it encourages African Americans to be more critical of whites as partners in the struggle for racial equality.

Perhaps the most surprising result from this section is that church-based political action has no discernable, independent effect on the core belief system. These results question the resource-based understanding of the role of the black church in African American politics. Using the church as a forum to organize rides to the polls, register citizens to vote, and participate in group action may teach African Americans important social and civic skills that they use when participating in politics outside of their religious communities (Brady, Verba, and Schlozman 1995). But this analysis suggests that these actions have little impact on the content of the political attitudes that African Americans hold and express. Instead, it is the content and process of everyday black talk facilitated through official pronouncements, clerical encouragement, and lay conversations that shape the contours of black political thought. When clergy emphasize the importance of political action, when officials address Sunday morning services, and when African Americans incorporate discussions of politics into their worship, they develop a stronger sense of connection with other blacks and with women, and they become more suspicious of whites. These attitudes undergird elements of both Nationalist and Feminist political ideology.

OTHER SIGNIFICANT RELATIONSHIPS

Demographic characteristics of age, sex, income, education, and urban dwelling were also included in the model.[14] These variables are used as controls so that the effect of everyday talk can be estimated separately from the confounding influence of individual-level characteristics. However, several of these variables had statistically significant effects of their own. Younger African Americans are more likely to express negative attitudes toward whites and support cross-racial coalitions. Young women also have higher levels of linked fate with other women. Women also have lower levels of black linked fate and are less likely to support cross-racial coalitions than black men. Income has no statistically significant relationship to black core beliefs, but education is related to greater women linked fate among both men and women and is related to a support for coalition with nonwhites. Finally, city dwellers are significantly more likely to support cross-racial coalitions (table 3.10).

Overall, these results indicate that demographic characteristics are no more responsible for the structure of a black core belief system than elements of everyday talk. There is a generational gap among blacks. Younger blacks are more likely to be Feminist because of their greater sense of women linked fate, more negative attitudes toward whites, and greater support for coalition politics. Education also contributes to Feminism by increasing women linked fate among men and women and by increasing the support for coalitions. Importantly, income has no independent impact on black core beliefs once participation in everyday black talk is accounted for in the model. Countering the expectations of pluralist scholars who might expect wealthier African Americans to differ systematically from poorer blacks, it is participation in forums of the black counterpublic, rather than income, that accounts for the heterogeneity in black political thought. Even if class is measured as education rather than income, it is important to note that it does not have a conservative effect on black public opinion. In the early 1990s increased public attention to vocal black Conservatives led some observers to predict that an ideological class divide would emerge in the black commu-

TABLE 3.10
Other Significant Effects on Core Beliefs

Construct	Age	Female	Income	Education	Urban
Black linked fate	-0.02 (.03)	-0.14 (.03)**	-0.03 (.03)	0.04 (.03)	0.01 (.02)
Women linked fate (women)	-0.05 (.02)*	—	0.02 (.02)	0.05 (.02)*	-0.03 (.02)
Women linked fate (men)	-0.03 (.03)	—	-0.01 (.02)	0.04 (.02)*	0.02 (.02)
Attitude toward whites	0.04 (.01)**	0.005 (.02)	-0.01 (.01)	-0.01 (.01)	-0.01 (.01)
Black self-reliance	0.01 (.03)	-0.02 (.02)	-0.01 (.03)	0.02 (.03)	0.003 (.03)
Bootstrap philosophy	0.003 (.03)	-0.03 (.03)	0.05 (.03)	-0.01 (.03)	-0.03 (.03)
Coalition with nonwhites	-0.11 (.03)**	-0.10 (.03)**	-0.01 (.03)	0.08 (.03)**	0.09 (.03)**

Note: Model is estimated using a covariance structure analysis using maximum likelihood estimation. The package is Statistical Analysis Software (SAS), Procedure CALIS.

$*p \leq .05$ $**p \leq .001$

nity similar to that of immigrant ethnic groups, such that middle- and upper-class blacks would be more Conservative than those of the lower class. This analysis indicates that it is Feminism, not Conservatism, that emerges along class lines in the black community. More educated African Americans are more likely to share a broad vision of political identification along lines of gender and shared minority status. Even accounting for the effect of education, the estimation of this model makes it clear that everyday talk has an explanatory value in understanding black ideological heterogeneity.

SUMMARY

These results are only suggestive. Most of the coefficients are sufficiently modest that it would be inappropriate to make sweeping generalizations about the effects. Also, because this is a single cross-sectional analysis, it is impossible to estimate the durability of these relationships. There are, however, many statistically significant relationships that are consistent with the a priori understanding of these ideologies and the ways that they are reproduced among African Americans. Attitudes toward whites have the strongest and most consistent impact on all three ideologies. The most important factor separating black Nationalists and Feminists from Conservatives is their view on white Americans. While both Nationalism and Feminism derive from some degree of suspicion about whites, Conservatism rests on positive affective and political assessments of whites.

The politics of racial and gendered consciousness as indicated in a sense of linked fate with blacks and women sets Nationalists and Feminists apart from Conservatives. Nationalism derives from a sense of common destiny with African Americans. Feminists share this belief as well as a sense of linked fate with women. Feminists are further distinguished from Nationalists because they view other disadvantaged, non-white groups as appropriate partners in political struggle. Finally, Nationalism and Conservatism differ on the appropriate locus of responsibility. Conservatism is related to an individualistic bootstrap philosophy, whereas Nationalism rests on a more collective notion of black self-reliance.

Importantly, this model offers evidence that these beliefs are associated with everyday black talk. Nationalism is bolstered through informal political discussions, rap music listening, black media exposure, organizational membership, and church-based discussion. These forms of everyday black talk are related to higher levels of black linked fate, support for black self-reliance, and more negative attitudes toward whites. Feminism emerges in informal political discussions, black media exposure, organizational membership, and political discussions in the church, which are all associated with a stronger sense of linked fate with women. Conservative messages find little space of articulation in the spaces of the black counterpublic modeled in this analysis. Perhaps black Conservatism is found in spaces of everyday black talk that are not adequately captured by NBPS data. Together these results provide initial empirical evidence that engaging in black everyday talk in multiple forums of the black counterpublic contributes to the development of political ideologies through the vehicle of a core belief system.

QUESTIONING THE CAUSAL ARROW

The statistical evidence shows that there are discernable patterns of political attitudes in the African American public, and these attitudes are organized in a way that is consistent with the historically meaningful ideologies of Nationalism, Feminism, and Conservatism. Additionally, this analysis confirms that these attitudinal patterns are related to participation in informal conversation, black organizations, and information networks. But this empirical approach is hampered by a significant flaw. There is no way to determine the direction of causality when analyzing a single cross-sectional survey. These data clearly show a relationship between black political ideologies and exposure to black everyday talk. They do not, however, show a causal relationship between the two. Arguably, African Americans choose their interactions based on a priori political convictions. In other words, maybe it is not the church or hip-hop encouraging certain core beliefs, but the core beliefs influencing consumption of the church or hip-hop. Demonstrating causality requires a different approach to the empirical study of the relationship between everyday talk and ideology. The following chapter uses experimental data to provide evidence that everyday black talk is a causal factor in the development of political attitudes among African Americans.

Policing Conservatives, Believing Feminists: Reactions to Unpopular Ideologies in Everyday Black Talk

> But when you get down to the nitty gritty, we are *all* black. We're bound by social conditions, it don't matter how far up the ladder you go, until you can make people realize that your color does not define who you are or what you are. It doesn't matter how far you go, if they don't like you and they see you're black, you will get the same kick in the ass whether you are high yellow or pitch dark.
> — NCCU student, 1998

> I think there a lot of times, too, when we ourselves hold ourselves back, limit ourselves on what we can do, we don't give anyone else a chance to hold us back because we're doing such a good job of it.
> — NCCU student, 1998

THE TWO STATEMENTS above are a glimpse into the diversity of political thought among African Americans. Both statements were made by African American women, of about the same age, who attend the same college. While these two students are similar in many respects, they have very different views of the political world. The first student assesses black inequality in America as a result of continuing racial bigotry. The second places the blame on the shoulders of African Americans. How these two black students came to express such divergent political attitudes is the subject of this chapter.

Much of the research on African American public opinion has been preoccupied with a few well-defined questions: the gap in political attitudes between whites and blacks (Schuman, Steeth, and Bobo 1997); the relative significance of racial or economic indicators in structuring black attitudes (Wilson 1980; Dawson 1994); and the change (or lack of change) in black attitudes over time (Tate 1993). This has been productive scholarship and has significantly deepened our understanding of African American public opinion. It is a research agenda, however, that has not asked many other important questions about black political thought. One such question is about the unique processes that contribute to the development of heterogeneous political attitudes among black Americans. The everyday talk theory of political ideology seeks to fill that gap by offering a testable theory of how black people use processes of intracommunity interaction to develop ideology. This text has made some progress in providing empirical evidence that a set of identifiable, historically relevant political ideologies exists. Further, the data from chapter 3 suggests that these ideologies are correlated with processes of everyday talk in black organizations and information networks.

Early in the training of any good empirical social scientist, one learns the old adage that "correlation does not prove causation." Whenever we observe that two variables are moving together, there are several possibilities that explain the relationship between them. Variable X could be causing change in variable Y, or variable Y could be causing change in variable X, or some third variable could be causing the change in both X and Y. While cross-sectional survey analysis provides a highly generalizable snapshot of political attitudes, it cannot adjudicate between these different claims of causality. Therefore, while data from the 1994 National Black Politics Study (chapter 3) offer evidence of the existence of ideologies among ordinary African Americans, these data cannot demonstrate that everyday talk is a *cause* of heterogeneity in African American thought. This chapter attempts to outline this causal relationship by subjecting the theory of everyday black talk to the rigors of experimental testing.

The main advantage of randomized, controlled laboratory experiments is their ability to allow for causal inferences. The experimental design allows the researcher to create a situation that is identical for all respondents, except for the variables of interest. Therefore any observed differences between the control group and the experimental group can be attributed to the effect of the manipulation by the researcher (Aronson et al. 1998). This does not mean that doing an experiment means that one has determined causality, but the possibility of casual determination is latent in experimental work. Laboratory experimentation has several shortcomings: these experiments are intrusive, they can test only one or two independent variables at a time, and they cannot be generalized beyond the often-limited population from which the sample is drawn. As Kinder and Palfrey rightly argue, "experimentation is by no means a complete remedy, but it can add a badly needed and valuable dimension to the study of politics" (1993, 1). To supplement the survey data and ethnographic research that form the other empirical pillars of this text, this chapter submits evidence from two experimental studies about the causal link between everyday black talk and political ideology.

EXPERIMENTAL STUDIES

The theory of everyday black talk states that the best way to understand variation in African American political thought is to understand the content of ordinary interactions among black people. To the extent that these interactions are infused with social and political content, they assist black people in developing ideological worldviews. With this in mind, the design of the experimental studies is straightforward. If I hypothesize that people form, change, and update their beliefs in the context of political discussions, then I should get black people together to have these discussions and measure any changes in their political beliefs wrought from these interactions. The remainder of this chapter presents evidence from two experiments with precisely that goal. The data for the empirical work of this chapter is drawn from two studies: the 1998 North Carolina Central University (NCCU) Political Attitudes Study[1] and the 2001 Kennedy-King College (KKC) African American Attitudes Study.[2]

Both studies are political psychology experiments designed to investigate how discussions among African Americans about racially and politically significant issues affect the ideological positions of the participants. Specifically, the studies question the ways that black men and women respond to Feminist and Conservative positions within the context of group discussions about the Million Man March (NCCU) and welfare policy (KKC). The NCCU study was conducted between January and April 1998 using 98 student participants at North Carolina Central University.[3] The KKC study was conducted in January 2001 using 130 student participants at Kennedy-King College.[4] The KKC study is not a replication of the NCCU study. It is an extension, designed to test specific hypotheses that emerged from the results of the NCCU study.

The two projects share a number of similar features. Each experiment consisted of three phases: a pretest questionnaire, an experimental manipulation, and a posttest questionnaire. In the 1998 NCCU study, all subjects completed a pretest that measured elements of personality, self-esteem, political predispositions, participation in black organizations, and exposure to African American popular culture. Then subjects were assigned randomly to one of seven groups.[5] The control group simply responded to a second questionnaire designed to measure ideology. All other respondents read a news story about the 1995 Million Man March and 1997 Promise Keepers Rally. Students in the news-only group wrote their reactions to the story and then completed the second survey instrument. Students in the peer discussion group were given twenty minutes

TABLE 4.1
NCCU Political Attitudes Study Experimental Manipulations

Manipulation	News article	Discussion	Hierarchy	Posttest
Control				Completed questionnaire
News-only	News article			Completed questionnaire
Peer discussion	News article	20-minute discussion		Completed questionnaire
Man-led Feminism	News article	20-minute discussion	Male authority	Completed questionnaire
Woman-led Feminism	News article	20-minute discussion	Female authority	Completed questionnaire
Man-led Conservatism	News article	20-minute discussion	Male authority	Completed questionnaire
Woman-led Conservatism	News article	20-minute discussion	Female authority	Completed questionnaire

Note: N = 98. Fourteen subjects were assigned to each of these seven manipulations.

to discuss the news story with other students and were directed to complete the second questionnaire. In the four remaining groups, the respondents were guided in their discussions by someone working for the project. This discussion leader took on one of two different roles using prompts designed to guide the discussion from a specific ideological perspective. Then respondents in each of these groups completed the second questionnaire. All group discussions were audiotaped. In the NCCU project, subjects were exposed to either a black male minister or a black female professor[6] who took on either a Feminist or a Conservative perspective in the discussion of an article on the Million Man March and Promise Keepers Rally (table 4.1).[7]

All of the 98 subjects retained in the analysis are African American. Thirty-five are male and 63 are female. Eight are married and 18 have children. The students range in age from eighteen to forty-three, but 77 percent are eighteen to twenty-one. The subjects mostly identify with the Democratic Party, with 80 percent of them identifying themselves as leaning Democrats or stronger. They perceive themselves as ideologically moderate. Nearly 60 percent ranked themselves as moderate or moderate leaning in a seven-point ideology scale. Eighty-nine percent ranked religion as quite important or very important in their daily lives, but only 30 percent are members of a local church. Nearly half are members of student organizations at NCCU. Although 80 percent attended high school in North Carolina, they were evenly divided into thirds when characterizing the place they went to high school as urban, suburban, or rural. They overwhelmingly ranked the social class of their families as working class (38%) or middle class (45%).

The 2001 KKC study is similar in design. Like the NCCU study, all subjects completed a pretest instrument that measured elements of personality, self-esteem, political predispositions, participation in black organizations, and exposure to African American popular culture. Then subjects were assigned randomly to one of six groups. The control group simply responded to a second questionnaire designed to measure black political attitudes. All other respondents read a news story about welfare policy and the black community. Students in the news-only group wrote their reactions to the story and then completed the second survey instrument. In the four remaining groups, the respondents were guided in their discussions by a trained graduate student working for the project. Respondents in each of these four groups completed the second questionnaire. All group discussions were videotaped. In this study the ideological messages to which respondents were exposed, by either a male or a female group leader, were more nuanced than in the 1998 NCCU study. Subjects received either an Integrationist Feminist, Womanist Feminist, Economic Conservative, or Moral Conservative ideological message (table 4.2).[8]

All of the 130 respondents retained in the analysis are African American. The sample was mostly female (73%), and respondents ranged in age from sixteen to fifty-nine, with an average age of thirty. Twenty percent of respondents are married, and 35 percent have children. Most (57%) are members of a Chicago area church, and about half identify themselves as Protestant. Only 1 percent of respondents identify with the Republican Party. Forty-two percent are strong Democrats; the remaining respondents are more weakly tied to the Democratic Party. The average annual household income of respondents is $24,000, and most identify themselves as middle class. A majority of the respondents (67%) report caring a good deal about politics in this country and 80 percent claim they voted in the 2000 presidential election.[9]

These experiments are designed to test several, but not all possible, elements of the theory of everyday black talk. First and foremost, these studies are looking for a discernable and statistically significant difference in the ideological sentiments expressed by subjects who are exposed to the experimental manipulations as compared with those in the control group. Reading politically important news stories and discussing them with others should prompt respondents to express a different set of opinions from those they would otherwise express in the absence of these interventions.

TABLE 4.2
KKC African American Attitudes Study Experimental Manipulations

Manipulation	News article	Discussion	Hierarchy	Posttest
Control				Completed questionnaire
News-only	News article			Completed questionnaire
Integrationist Feminism	News article	20-minute discussion	Half group–man leader Half group–woman leader	Completed questionnaire
Womanist Feminism	News article	20-minute discussion	Half group–man leader Half group–woman leader	Completed questionnaire
Moral Conservatism	News article	20-minute discussion	Half group–man leader Half group–woman leader	Completed questionnaire
Economic Conservatism	News article	20-minute discussion	Half group–man leader Half group–woman leader	Completed questionnaire

Note: N = 130. Approximately 22 subjects were assigned to each of these manipulations.

More specifically, these studies are designed to test the responses of African Americans when exposed to Feminist and Conservative interpretations of political events.[10] Feminism and Conservatism share the distinction of being "unpopular" ideologies among African Americans. Both Feminism and Conservatism have frequently been accused of being alien ideologies. This is because both contain critiques of black people. Black Feminists point not only to white racism, but also to black sexism, patriarchy, and homophobia as problems facing African Americans. Conservatives argue persistent inequality is as much a result of black pathology as of historical racism. Using unpopular ideologies in the experimental manipulations serves two purposes. First, these ideological perspectives are likely to provoke internal disagreements within the discussion groups. The possibility for heightened dissent should provide more opportunities to observe the heterogeneity within black public opinion. Second, because these are unpopular ideologies, the introduction of them into the group discussions allows us to observe internal mechanisms of authenticity arguments and racial policing. Observing and recording how subjects respond to group leaders and peers who advocate these positions provides insight into how these ideologies penetrate (or fail to penetrate) spaces of everyday black talk.

In addition to testing reactions to the ideological messages, the design of these studies allows an exploration of the effect of ideological messengers. In both the NCCU and the KKC study, each ideological message is presented to some respondents by a male advocate and to other respondents by a female advocate. In the NCCU study, the man was a preacher and the woman a professor. In the KKC study, no professional designation was offered. By varying the gender of the group leader, the study tests the relative effectiveness of different ideological advocates.

Finally, these two studies complement each other because the design of the KKC study is an extension of the NCCU study. In the 1998 NCCU experiment, group leaders advocated a general Feminist or Conservative position in their discussions of the Million Man March. In the 2001 KKC study, Feminism and Conservatism are divided into their more complex, constituent elements. Rather than expressing a general Feminist perspective, group facilitators in the KKC study took on either a specifically Integrationist or Womanist Feminism, either talking about welfare policy as an issue affecting women of all races (Integrationist) or presenting welfare policy as a specific concern of black women (Womanist).[11] In the Conservative groups, the discussion leaders either discussed the economic rationale behind welfare reform (Economic) or argued about the morally degrading aspects of welfare dependency (Moral).[12] Observing and recording subjects' responses to the elements of each of the ideologies allows a further exploration of results from the NCCU study.

MODEL

The hypothesized model for analysis is straightforward. Political ideology is expected to be a result of exposure to the experimental manipulations. Because respondents do not enter the experimental setting as blank slates, and because I am interested in modeling a variety of forums of everyday black talk, I include interaction terms that model the subjects' exposure to black media, hip-hop music, and political information in interaction with the experimental conditions to which they are randomly assigned (equation 4.1).[13] The hypothesized model for the KKC study is also straightforward, but the statistical techniques used for analysis are different. The experimental category is the unit of analysis and is expected to have a direct, causal relationship to the respondent's ideology (equation 4.2).

Equation 4.1: Estimated Equation for 1998 NCCU Study Ideology (Nationalism, Integrationism, Feminism, Conservatism) = *f*:{Experimental Category, Black Media Knowledge, Hip-Hop Knowledge}

Equation 4.2: Estimated Equation for 2001 KKC Study Ideology (Womanist Feminism, Integrationist Feminism, Economic Conservatism, Moral Conservatism) = *f*:{Experimental Category}

MEASUREMENT

I analyzed data from the NCCU study using structural equation modeling with the maximum likelihood estimation technique LISREL. Each of the four political ideologies is constructed as a latent variable using factor analysis. This measurement model specified the latent variables, their observed indicators, and the errors associated with measurement of those indicators. The estimation technique for data from the KKC study is different. These data are analyzed through simple difference of means tests. The four ideologies are not constructed as latent variable factors; instead they are constructed as additive scales (tables 4.3 and 4.4).

In both studies, measures of black media knowledge and hip-hop are constructed as additive scales from responses to matching games on the pretest questionnaire. Subjects in both studies were asked to match famous African American individuals or artists with the names of the magazines, movies, television shows, hip-hop crews, books, or phrases with which they are commonly associated. For example, when Susan Taylor appeared in the left column, the correct match in the right column was *Essence*. When Rah Digga appeared in the left column, the correct match in the right column was Flip Mode Squad. These measures are quite different from measures used for black media and hip-hop knowledge in the 1994 National Black Politics Study. Rather than simply asking respondents to rate usage of black information networks, this measure is able to approximate the level and intensity of exposure by testing reception of basic information available through these networks. For example, in the 2001 KKC study Oprah Winfrey was one of the least recognized figures. Although most of these students know who Oprah Winfrey is, they were unable to match her with Angel Network. Matching the two requires that an individual actually watch the *Oprah Winfrey Show*. These instruments are more sensitive than those available in the national data and should provide a more detailed picture of how black information networks affect ideological development.

The exact measures used in the 2001 KKC study differ from those used in 1998. Because of the fast-changing nature of popular culture, it

TABLE 4.3

Indicators for Measurement of Feminist Ideologies in 1998 NCCU and 2001 KKC Studies

1998 NCCU General Feminism latent variable	2001 KKC Integrationist Feminism additive scale	2001 KKC Womanist Feminism additive scale
Black women should share equally in the political leadership of the black community.	Oftentimes, black women share more in common with women of other races than with black men.	The problems of black men and black women deserve equal attention.
Do you think that what happens to black women in this country will have something to do with what happens in your life?	Women share many of the same issues no matter what color they are.	The problems of racism and sexual discrimination are linked and both must be addressed by the black community.
I am concerned about what happens to women in this country because I know that what happens to them will affect my life.	I am concerned about what happens to white women in this country because I know that what happens to them will affect my life.	Black feminist groups just divide the black community. (opposition coded)
The problems of black men and black women deserve equal attention.		
The problems of racism and sexual discrimination are linked and both must be addressed by the black community.		

was necessary to update the individuals used in the matching game in order to maintain a sense of exposure to the most contemporary elements of black media and hip-hop.

Each of the experimental groups is constructed as a dummy variable. For example, a respondent was either in the Feminism group or not. In analysis of the 1998 NCCU data, the control group is the excluded group. All coefficients must be interpreted with respect to subjects in the

TABLE 4.4

Indicators for Measurement of Conservative Ideologies in 1998 NCCU and 2001 KKC Studies

1998 NCCU General Conservatism latent variable	2001 KKC Economic Conservatism additive scale	2001 KKC Moral Conservatism additive scale
Many African Americans are not trying hard enough; if blacks would only try harder they could be just as well off as whites.	It is more important for black people to focus on economic strength than political power.	Affirmative action makes blacks believe that they don't have to work very hard.
Affirmative action makes blacks believe that they don't have to work very hard.	Most poor people want to work, but there are not enough jobs. (opposition coded)	Hard work and patience will do more for the cause of black equality than demanding things from the government.
Big corporations are unfair to the black community. (opposition coded)	Big corporations are an important source of economic strength for black communities.	Welfare is a major cause of the breakdown of morals and family in the African American community.
Most poor people don't want to work.		
Welfare is a major cause of the breakdown in morals and family in the African American community.		

control group. In analysis of the 2001 KKC data, statistical significance of the difference of means is always predicted with respect to the control group.

RESULTS

There are two big stories from the 1998 NCCU Political Attitudes Study:

- Respondents in groups with a Feminist message displayed significantly higher Feminism scores than the control group. This effect was partic-

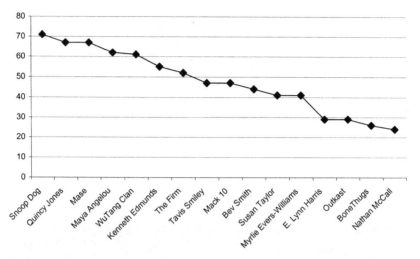

Figure 4.1. Percent of Respondents Who Correctly Matched Popular Figure, 1998 NCCU Political Attitudes Study.

ularly pronounced among those who were exposed to a Feminist message by a male group leader.

- Respondents in groups with a Conservative message displayed slightly less Conservatism than the control group. Among these subjects it made little difference whether a male or female leader presented the Conservative message.

FEMINIST MESSAGE GROUPS

A very clear story emerges from the Feminist message groups in the NCCU study. Subjects in Feminist sessions displayed higher levels of Feminism than control group subjects, and this effect was particularly strong in the male-led Feminist group. On average, subjects in the male-led groups had Feminism scores 23 percentage points higher than the control group. Subjects in female-led Feminist groups demonstrated higher Feminism than control group subjects, but the effect was more modest. For average subjects, the effect was a score 10 percentage points higher on Feminism. In both the man-led and woman-led groups, there were also strong anti-Integrationist effects. For average subjects, exposure to the male-led Feminist groups produced an Integrationism score 17 percentage points lower, and for those in female-led groups the effect was a score 10 percentage points lower than those in the control group (fig. 4.3). It is useful to keep in mind that the ideologies are

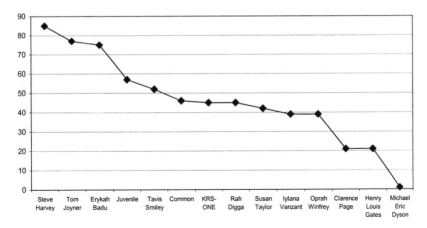

Figure 4.2. Percent of Respondents Who Correctly Matched Popular Figure, 2001 KKC African American Attitudes Study.

scored on a scale from 0 to 1, where 0 represents no agreement with the ideological position and 1 represents complete agreement with the ideology. Therefore, an effect of 23 percentage points indicates a movement of nearly a quarter of the available scale. These are very robust results.

In some ways these results are unsurprising. Social psychological studies of attitude change have consistently shown that subjects update beliefs toward consistency with authority figures, especially if those authority figures are seen as credible. Thus, Feminist messages should increase Feminism when presented by a professor and preacher (Havland and Weiss 1951; Kelman 1958). However, the strength of the effect when the male leader advocates this message is quite striking and requires comment. A male advocate of a Feminist position appears to be more persuasive than a female. Psychological theories and studies on source credibility could provide possible explanations for why this is true. Source credibility is the set of perceptions held by the audience about the competence, believability, and qualifications of the presenter. Perhaps the male leader was more influential because of his maleness or because of his status as a member of the clergy (Cohen 1964; Rosnow and Robinson 1967).[14]

While some studies in persuasion suggest that men are consistently viewed as more authoritative sources than women (Goldberg 1968), this type of source credibility does not explain what is at work in this case. As I will discuss below, the results of the Conservative groups show no distinguishable difference between the effects of the male and female leader on Conservatism. If gender alone explained the greater credibility of the male leader, then he should also be more persuasive with a Conservative message. He is not. This lack of differential influence in the Conservative groups also rules out an explanation based on his status as a minister. Again, if his status as a clergy member was sufficient to explain the differential influence, then it should show up in Conservative groups as well. Instead of a simple story about subjects perceiving the male preacher as more credible than the female teacher, there is a more intricate narrative about the violation of norms and expectations. King, in his work on social influence, states that "Because of extensive experience with many situations that have common attributes, people derive expectation of 'what goes with what.' . . . . A violation of these expectations produces a good deal of psychological confusion and increases one's susceptibility to influence" (1975, 89–90).

For respondents, a male minister openly advocating a strong Feminist position created a violation of norms that made them more open to persuasion.[15] This could happen for two reasons. First, the surprise of hearing a male preacher advocate a Feminist position could increase attentiveness and therefore increase the ability of subjects to receive the message. The novelty of the experience forced subjects to "sit up and take notice." Perhaps students in the female-led group expected a woman professor to take a position that addressed concerns of female equality. The messenger and message go together and therefore do not require a particularly high level of cognitive processing. Students in the male-led group were not expecting to hear a minister take a woman-centered approach, and in their surprise and confusion they became more susceptible to influence.[16]

Second, the violation of norms might have created a particular kind of source credibility. Subjects may perceive the male Feminist as more credible than a female Feminist because the man does not appear to have a personal stake in the position he is advocating. Subjects might reason that if he is not personally benefiting from the position he is advancing, then he must have particularly compelling reasons for his stance. Alternatively, a woman Feminist may simply be perceived as self-serving.

Tapes of group discussions reveal that the male leader is quite persuasive in his advocacy of Feminism, both in his own arguments and in his supportiveness of the Feminist opinions of group members. In the minister's Feminist sessions, the students often began by being supportive of the patriarchal approach of both the Million Man March and the Promise Keepers March, but when the male leader encouraged them to question the exclusion of women, the students quickly expressed more egalitarian views.

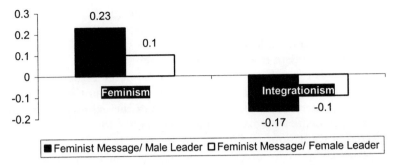

Figure 4.3. Effects of Feminist Message Groups on Respondent Ideology, 1998 NCCU Political Attitudes Study. Unstandardized maximum likelihood estimates for latent variable equations, estimated using LISREL. Coefficients are significant at $p \leq .05$.

Male Leader: Society is not going to progress if we exclude women. So why have these two organizations excluded women? What do you think of the traditional idea that women aren't leaders? Are you saying it is OK?

First Female Student: I know it's not right. I don't agree with it, but that's how it is. The man is normally the head, the leader.

Second Female Student: (*softly*) I don't know about that.

Male Leader: What is it that you don't know about it?

Second Female: I just don't think that man is the real head. Man may bring home the bread, but woman is the one who is really leading that household.

First Female: But when people are on the outside looking in, they don't look at the woman as leading anything. I know she's in the house and she's normally taking care of the house, but the man is normally the one who gets all the credit. I know that's not right and I'm totally against it too, but that's the way society looks at it.

Second Female: Because they're not working together. It should be half and half. It should both of them leading. It shouldn't be just one person shoveling all the dirt and then carrying it too. It should be both of them working together to make it work. You have to do it together if you want it to work.

This exchange is important for seeing how advocacy of the Feminist position by the authority figure served to increase Feminist sentiment. The second female student in this exchange had been very quiet during the first seven minutes of the tape. When she interjects early in this exchange, her voice is barely audible. But because the male authority figure turns to her and supports her position, she has an opportunity to expand on her ideas. By the end of this exchange, her voice is loud and confident and she is disagreeing with the first woman's opinion that men are the natural leaders. The presence of a supportive authority figure allows this student to express her ideas about gender equality. In the absence of this type of support, she may have never verbalized this rationale to her peers. The Feminist authority figure not only provides Feminist arguments himself, he also facilitates the expression of Feminism from students who may not have been bold enough to speak without external validation.

Together these two sources of Feminist argument function as a powerfully convincing message for the more reluctant members of the group. Early in the discussion, the first student explained her support of the Million Man March by saying:

> **First Female Student:** Man is supposed to be head of the household. I feel like they were just trying to get themselves together in order to go to the sisters and lead. Normally men are the leaders. I just think they are trying to get themselves together. I mean how you going to lead someone if you don't have yourself together?

After engaging in several exchanges like the one first highlighted, this student begins to change her opinion. Gradually she becomes more critical of men as the unquestioned leaders of the household and community. As in the exchange reported above, she begins to say that she does not agree with patriarchal standards but suggests that they are an aspect of society that cannot be changed. By the end of the session she offers a bitter criticism of a society that attempts to restrict the potential of women.

> **First Female Student:** That's how it's been from the beginning, but it's the nineties now and things are changing. More and more women are coming up. You see more and more women being leaders. More and more women having their own companies. They're doing their own thing. A lot of people don't like that 'cause they feel that women should be sitting at home with the kids. And a lot of women are getting jobs and they are actually doing something. And a lot of people, they don't like that.

The changing language of this student is indicative of the kinds of attitudinal adjustments that occurred in the male-led Feminist groups. Guided by a purposively Feminist preacher, these students became increasingly critical of the goals of both the Million Man March and the Promise Keepers Rally. They offered increasingly Feminist statements and openly rejected the exclusion of women from roles of political, racial, and religious leadership.

Similar, but less dramatic, changes also took place in the woman-led Feminist groups. The data show that the woman-led Feminist groups produced more modest results than those led by the male preacher, and the content of the discussions reveal some interesting differences in student reaction to the two group leaders.

> **Male Student:** In one of my classes we're talking about Ida B. Wells' anti-lynching movement. We learned that Ida B. Wells gets criticized for her personality, for being aggressive and having male characteristics. She gets criticized. Not to say that her campaign wasn't good or effective, but it goes back to what the white man conceptualizes as society.
>
> **Female Group Leader:** Let's take Ida B. Wells as an example. She was a political activist at the turn of the century. She did a lot to stop lynching in America. What if she had been not invited to a march and her talents and her skills hadn't been incorporated into the many organizations that bloomed out of a march. Are we wasting our resources if we don't incorporate women into a movement? If a wonderful person like an Ida B. Wells made a sandwich instead of going to the rally, we are halving our power and our strength as a community.
>
> **Female Student:** I understand what you're saying, but if you're the type of person and you have leadership qualities and you don't think to improve your community, a march is not going to make you do that faster. I think that she would have done it anyway. The way I'm feeling is that we as women have qualities already, we don't need a march. And I think the march served its purpose in helping men.

In this exchange the male student explained that men need to be leaders because women leaders are often criticized for being too masculine. The female group leader questions the validity of an approach that would exclude a leader as effective as Ida B. Wells based solely on her gender. The most interesting aspect of this exchange is when the female student suggests that only men, not women, need something to help them cultivate their leadership qualities. The response of the female student rejects the notion that both men and women should be groomed for leadership. But she does so in a strange way. She claims that women will rise to the fore even if they are not given the opportunity to participate in political demonstrations. It is a statement that rejects gender equality while still asserting the positive qualities of women. This is a much weaker version of "Feminism" than the expressions of students in the male-led Feminist groups. This contrast can be put into sharp relief by a comparison of statements by two young women. The first is from the man-led Feminist session, the other is from a woman-led Feminist session.

From Male-led Session: Before you try to lead somebody, you have to find out deep down who you are. Before you try to lead somebody else and try to show them the way, you have to find the way yourself. And black men haven't done that yet. They are just trying to take charge and you can't do that.

From Female-led Session: Women are already working hard to support their children, and they are already trying to keep their families together so it wasn't a problem with the women. It's a problem for the men, so they have to get it together.

The first woman offered a statement that based leadership on human rather than gender qualities and that offered a critique of masculinity based on false assumptions of gender-based entitlement. The second woman suggested that women are superior to men in their work and personal ethics but concluded that men had a right and responsibility to organize separately from women in order to regain their own masculine ethics. These statements are generally indicative of the differences between the male-led and female-led Feminist groups and further underline the different quantitative scores of these two manipulations. The male preacher was able to bring the subjects to a stronger and more fully articulated Feminist attitude. Although the woman teacher was equally insightful and capable of arguing a Feminist perspective, the students found the male preacher to be a more compelling Feminist spokesperson.

The peer group experimental condition, which had no assigned advocate of Feminism, also consistently led to higher Feminism scores among the 1998 NCCU participants. Scores on Feminism were higher by eight percentage points in the peer discussion groups than in the control groups. The strength and statistical significance of this result is surprising given that there was no group leader explicitly advocating a Feminist message. The statistical results demonstrating higher Feminism, however, were not a result of discussions that offered Feminist critiques of the patriarchal agendas of the Million Man and Promise Keepers marches. In fact, these criticisms were almost wholly absent from the discussions. Instead, the group discussions reflected a kind of "back-handed Feminist" perspective. Young women participants in the peer sessions emerge as the most vocal and ardent discussion leaders. These young women blame black men for their failure to live up to their traditional masculine responsibilities. They argue that black men face more difficult life conditions and therefore deserve the right to gather in Washington, but in the same breath they cite the failure of these men to do better for themselves and their communities.

Their "Feminist" sentiment emerges as they compare the failings of black men with the achievements of black women. They portray black women as the strength of the African American community. They praise black women for their greater fortitude and achievement. Criticizing black men for their failure to live up to the promises of the Million Man March, two young women argued about the failure of black male students at North Carolina Central University to become involved with campus and community activism.

> **First Female Student:** I think that the Million Man March was a good thing because men talk a good game, but they don't do anything about it really. Most of the women, when they say they are going do something, they just go ahead and do it. I think that when you look at a lot of volunteer and service organizations you mostly see women, you don't see that many men. I just don't think men get involved as a member of the community as they should. If they are going to have a march talking about brotherhood, then they need to start doing other things for the community to keep that spirit alive.

> **Second Female Student:** I agree. I'm a youth coordinator and I work with different kids from the housing projects. It makes you feel sad because out of all those communities, I may have ten girls and then maybe one or two guys. And in some of the communities I work with there's none. So right now I'm trying to see how I can get them included in it. But the problem is they are up there playing basketball but they don't find it important to come to any of the meetings.[17]

This criticism of black men is accompanied by a feeling that black men deserve special attention because of their special problems. The statement by a young woman in a peer discussion setting is particularly telling: "I didn't see the purpose of the Million Woman March. I mean the Million Man March was important because black *men* are the ones who are inferior to everyone else. They are the ones being killed everyday. They are the ones who are killing each other everyday."

This student attributes major social and moral problems to black men, but the discussions of black women's problems were reduced to the need for strong father figures and good men in the family and community. A restoration of the patriarchal order is presented as the only salvation for black communities. These are not the types of sentiments I would have expected from a group that demonstrates an elevated level of Feminism. Two things are at work that provide a more complex picture of how Feminist sentiment finds a place in everyday black talk. First, women emerge as the main leaders in the peer discussion groups. This assertive female presence translated into a willingness to perceive women as appropriate leaders in the black community, which is one aspect of the Feminism measure. Second, these women are expressing reluctant acceptance of a leadership position. They express a yearning for more male leadership but also make clear that they will fulfill those roles in the absence of responsible male partners. The peer discussions demonstrate that elements of support for gender equity and support of black women's leadership find their way into everyday black talk, even in the absence of a specifically Feminist articulation. But the most unpopular aspects of Feminism, specifically the critique of a patriarchal ordering of the black community, are still absent from the sentiments of respondents, unless a vocal Feminist advocate, like the preacher or professor, is present.

Another unpopular aspect of some Feminist discourse is policed in everyday black talk: the Integrationist element. The 1998 NCCU study shows that Feminist discussion groups not only increased Feminism but also decreased Integrationism among respondents (fig. 4.3). In many ways the anti-Integrationist effect is counterintuitive. It is reasonable to expect that Feminism would reinforce Liberal Integrationist ideology based on the belief that black women share political concerns with other women that crosses racial lines. But in both the male-led and female-led groups, Feminism moves in an opposite direction from Integrationism. Rather than acting as reinforcing ideological positions, there is evidence that they are distinct, and perhaps opposing, ideologies.

For the students in the NCCU study, black Feminism does not necessarily indicate a commitment to gender as a cross-cutting political identity. When the students talked about black women, they normally spoke about them in relation to black men. They discussed female roles and rights by referencing women's positions within the African American household and community. They did not discuss solidarity with white or other nonwhite women. There was very little discussion of womanhood as a politically meaningful category across racial lines. Rather, discussion of black women's life positions involved explicit criticism of white power structures seeking to destroy black families. The kind of African American Feminist thought demonstrated throughout this study is more concerned with dynamics within the black community than with gender solidarity across racial boundaries.

Features of the study itself may be responsible for this result. Most important is the centrality of the Million Man March to the group discussions. The most prevalent, available public critique of the march was offered by black Feminists who decried the misogynist and patriarchal tone of the march's leadership and mission (see chapter 5). Thus, the public frame for the march was one that focused most specifically on gender issues within the African American community, rather than cross-racial gender alliances around issues of concern to many women. Still, the strength of the anti-Integrationist and pro-Feminist effects and the language by respondents in Feminist discussion groups of the NCCU study warranted further investigation. Overall, the Feminist sentiments expressed by respondents in the NCCU study were Womanist (concerned with gender equality within the black community) rather than Integrationist (concerned with cross-racial gender alliances). The KKC study was designed in part to subject this conclusion to further experimental research. The KKC study was designed to question if black Feminism is always expressed as concern with black women vis-à-vis black men or if there are instances when black women will support crossracial, gender-based alliances.

To investigate this question, the KKC study exposed subjects to one of two different Feminist messages. The group leader discussed the issue of welfare reform either from a Womanist Feminist viewpoint, emphasizing the particular struggle of black women and encouraging racial solidarity across gender lines, or from an Integrationist Feminist perspective, emphasizing the ways that welfare affects women's lives across racial boundaries (table 4.5).

The quantitative results from the KKC study are modest. A simple comparison of mean scores on both Womanist and Integrationist Feminism as expressed by respondents in these two message groups is presented in figure 4.4. Several features of this test are readily apparent. First, in the control group Integrationist and Womanist sentiments are found in equal measure among KKC respondents. These students are equally likely to agree with both elements of Feminist thought.[18] Further, exposure to either an Integrationist or a Womanist group discussion raises overall levels of Feminism among respondents.[19] Those exposed to Womanist messages are more Feminist overall by 4 percentage points, and those exposed to Integrationist messages are more Feminist overall by 9 percentage points, than students in the control group. These are modest differences, but the direction is consistent and positive in all Feminist message groups.

Of particular interest is the greater influence of an Integrationist message on levels of both Integrationist and Womanist Feminism. When respondents are encouraged to think about welfare as a cross-racial gender issue, they are more likely to express both variations of Feminist thought. Interestingly, exposure to a Womanist perspective does not increase expressions of Womanist Feminism, but it has a modest influence in generating more Integrationist Womanist sentiment among participants (fig. 4.4). What is at the heart of these somewhat conflicting quantitative results is made much clearer when we examine the content of the conversations among respondents that produced these results.

First, exposure to Feminist messages contributed to higher levels of overall Feminism for subjects. Thinking about welfare reform from the

TABLE 4.5

Examples of Prompt Questions Used by Feminist Group Leaders, 2001 KKC African American Attitudes Study

Womanist Feminism	Integrationist Feminism
Is welfare reform a way for government to make sure that black women and children do not have what they need to survive?	Do you think that welfare reform addresses the concerns of women such as child care and job training?
Is welfare reform just a way of attacking welfare black women as "welfare queens"?	Do you think that women of all races (for example, black women, Hispanic women and white women) should get together on the issue of welfare reform?
Do you think that black women should get together to resist welfare reform? Should black men support them in these efforts?	Do you think that welfare reform tries to blame everything on women?
Do you think that welfare reform addresses the concerns of black women such as child care and job training?	Do you think that welfare is a women's issue affecting poor people of many races?

perspective of the women who are affected by this policy debate encourages a stronger sense of gender equity, fairness, and identification among the respondents. Feminist prompts by discussion leaders encouraged lively debate in one Womanist-Feminism group. After being prompted to think about the effect of welfare reform on African American women, two female respondents offered very different perspectives. The first woman offered a comprehensive analysis of the challenges facing black women. She discussed the role of familial responsibilities in obstructing educational opportunities for girls. She analyzed the ways that welfare policy and abortion policy intersect, and she argued for the importance of maintaining a social safety net for women and children. Another woman in the group took a harder line, suggesting that individuals need to be more sexually responsible and financially independent.

> **First woman:** Some girls, their mothers have left them in the house and they have younger brothers and sisters that they have to take care of. They have to drop out of school and take care of what their parents should have done. That's why a lot of people don't have education. It's not all because they don't want to go. You have to look at their background. Maybe they have problems.

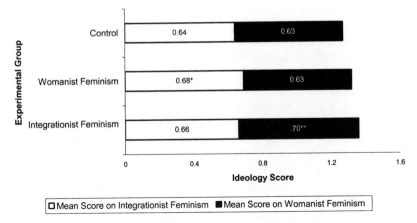

Figure 4.4. Comparison of Mean Scores on Feminism across Experimental Categories, 2001 KKC African American Attitudes Study. Posttreatment mean scores of respondents in each experimental group, measured on a scale of 0–1, where 0 indicates no agreement with the tenets of the ideology and 1 represents full agreement. *denotes significance at $p \leq .10$, **denotes significance at $p \leq .05$ using a test of first difference.

Second Woman: But, people don't just pop up pregnant. If you are going to have sex, you are going to have consequences.

First Woman: No. No. No, this is what I'm saying. They didn't mean to get pregnant. But what if they don't believe in abortion. What if they cut the welfare system and then they cut out abortion. No abortions and then what.

Second Woman: We are not talking about abortions. We are talking about welfare.

First Woman: But if you don't have a job and you are pregnant now. You are eight or nine months pregnant. Now what? You don't have a job, but couldn't get an abortion. What now? What are you going to do? What if the system wasn't there? What you going to do?

Second Woman: Go out and get a job.

First Woman: But who is going to hire you pregnant? Nobody is going to hire you.

The first woman is insistent that women face multiple pressures associated with their role as care providers. She argues that women are not entirely autonomous individuals in these issues; the choices of others and the decisions of policymakers have a profound influence on life chances of women. Although she is prompted to think specifically about black women, her argument is framed in gendered terms that are not necessarily race specific. Although there was debate between these two participants, the other men and women in the group tended to side with the first woman, and to see the second as too punitive and unrealistic in her demands. While there is no single message here, the presence of an articulated position on the multiple policy domains and life circumstances that face women contributed to a higher overall Feminist sentiment among these respondents.

While Feminism overall was expressed at higher levels by all Feminist groups, it is interesting that Intregrationist Feminist prompts are influential, and that they increase both strands of Feminism. To understand these results, it is important to note the indicators used to measure Integrationist Feminism. This ideology is scored as level of agreement with the following statements: oftentimes, black women share more in common with women of other races than with black men; women share many of the same issues no matter what color they are: I am concerned about what happens to white women in this country because I know that what happens to them will affect my life. In many ways, this could be defined as diagnostic Integrationism. In other words, these sentiments reflect a belief that African American women share a set of common problems and concerns with women of other races. Importantly, however, this measure does not include indicators of a strategic Integrationism. There are no indicators of a belief that these shared struggles should lead to coalition strategies for addressing them. Much of the previous thought on Integrationism has assumed a connection between diagnostic and strategic Integrationism: if we see how we suffer from similar circumstances, then we should be more likely to engage in common struggle. The results of this experiment call this common wisdom into question. When introduced to Feminist messages, the men and women of Kennedy-King College are able to see the ways that both black and white women are affected by welfare, but that does not make them more likely to advocate an Integrationist political strategy in response. Exchanges between respondents in several groups illuminate the reasons.

In a Womanist Feminist group, several students responded angrily to their impression that the article was an attack on black women as welfare abusers.

Male Student: The article seems to be about black women on welfare. They didn't directly say it, but you got a sense that they were talking about black people. I felt that was unrealistic, because there are more white people in this nation, therefore, there are more white people on welfare. I think that they should address white women and the issue of whites being on welfare too.

Female Student: I agree. The first thing I was going to bring up is that there are more Caucasians on welfare than there are African Americans.

Second Female Student: The article doesn't say how before African Americans were getting public aid, white people were getting it all the time. There were programs set up for so-called poor white Americans when black people were still struggling to pick cotton.

This exchange is typical of many in the Feminist groups. In another group, one student expresses his distress with the way that the media portrays African Americans. After being asked if welfare reform is an issue that women of all races care about, this man offers an analysis of how the media deceptively portrays blacks.

Male Student: People learn by what is around them. We learn by our surroundings. If all you see are black people going on welfare or in handcuffs, you will get in your mind that they always do this or they are always doing that. Even if you don't know anything about that individual. They always got black people doing this and black people doing that. Just like in the news. Its a lot of stuff going with drugs and white people that you never hear about, but soon as there is a bust on 47th Street they got it all in the news. They are always emphasizing on black people just to make us look bad. But things that white people do like mass murders and stuff like that, we don't hear about that.

Female Student: But if they put white women out there, then white women would start complaining.

Students are expressing an awareness that welfare is not a race issue, but one that affects poor people across racial lines. However, they are also expressing a deep resentment that policymakers and media represent welfare as a black women's issue. Their recognition of the shared use of the welfare system does not lead to expressions of Integrationist strategy. Instead, the students in this group express deepening distrust of whites as they continue to analyze the issue of welfare reform legislation. By the end of their discussion, their conversation has turned to strategies that blacks could use to resist welfare reform. When one student suggests voting, several others use the 2000 elections as an example of black disenfranchisement.

Second Female Student: That's a prime example of this welfare picture. We have some 60,000-odd folks in Florida that did not count for anything. But they tell us that our votes count. But they have already decided for us.

Similar sentiments are reflected by students in another Womanist Feminist message group.

Group Facilitator: So do you think that this affects women of all races?

First Female Student: It's usually whatever race you are, that is what you tend to see. If you are white and you live with white, then you tend to see white. I mean *they* always bring up blacks, they hide the trailer park trash. We are black and we are around blacks, so that's what we see. If we lived in a white community we would know how many white people receive AFDC.

Second Female Student: And how they take advantage of it.

First Female Student: Yeah, and how they take advantage of it.

Again, the respondents in this group are more than willing to acknowledge welfare as a cross-racial issue. They identify welfare dependency and abuse as a problem of black and white neighborhoods. However, they are not expressing a sense of strategic, political solidarity with the white women they have identified. Instead, they express annoyance that white media has obscured the problem of white welfare dependency in an attempt to cast the policy issue as a racial one. When exposed to Feminist messages, the students of the 2001 KKC study are more Integrationist in their definition of political problems, but recognition of a shared a condition does not contribute to a belief that blacks should form political alliances with whites. In fact, quantitative evidence shows that respondents in the Feminist groups have considerably more negative attitude toward whites[20] and experience a modest decline in their agreement with strategic Integrationism (fig. 4.5).[21] Respondents in Womanist Feminist groups have an assessment of whites 14 percentage points lower and respondents in the Integrationist Feminist group have an agreement with aspects of strategic Integrationism 7 percentage points lower.

The relationship between Feminism and Integrationism discovered in the 1998 NCCU study is borne out in many ways in the 2001 KKC study. Although there are clearly policy arenas in which African Americans can be encouraged, through Feminist messages, to provide Integrationist definitions of problems, there continues to be a resistance to Integrationist strategy within a Feminist approach to black politics.

Feminism has a presence in spaces of black conversations about political and social issues. The preacher-led Feminist groups of the NCCU study show that the strongest forms of Feminist articulation arise when there is a credible, authoritative advocate guiding the analysis. But other elements of Feminist thought find their way into everyday black talk even without an explicitly Feminist leader. In the peer discussion groups of the NCCU study, subjects express their respect for black women as capable and committed leaders, but they simultaneously argue that the black community needs more male leadership and claim that the culti-

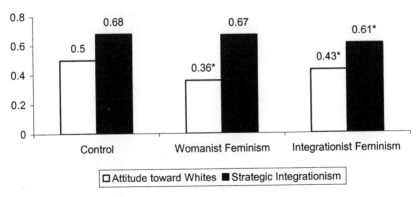

Figure 4.5. Comparison of Mean Scores across Experimental Categories, Attitude toward Whites and Strategic Integrationism, 2001 KKC African American Attitudes Study. Posttreatment mean scores of respondents in each experimental group, measured on a scale of 0–1, where 0 indicates no agreement with the attitude and 1 represents full agreement. *denotes significance at $p \leq .05$ using a test of first difference.

vation of male leadership should be a racial priority. Theirs is not fully articulated Feminism, but it does express seeds of Feminist thought in its notions of women strong and capable leaders.

Both the NCCU and the KKC study results indicate that when Feminism finds a place in black political discussions, it is tempered with a specific concern for black women and not expressed as belief in cross-racial gender alliances. Although African American subjects willingly admit that there are many shared concerns across racial boundaries, the strategies offered for addressing the problems of black women are always in-group strategies. Although there is room in everyday black talk for critiques of black men, patriarchy, and gender inequality, there is little room for understanding gender as a more salient political identity than race. The results of these two studies indicate that strategic Integrationist elements of Feminism are the most unpopular aspects of this ideological position.

CONSERVATIVE MESSAGE GROUPS

Many persuasion studies predict that respondents exposed to any given message will adjust their own views in accord with those of the group leader. The Conservative message groups of the NCCU study produced the opposite result. Both the male- and female-led Conservative groups decreased Conservative sentiment among participants (fig. 4.6). For av-

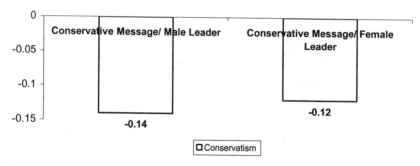

Figure 4.6. Effects of Conservative Message Groups on Respondent Ideology, 1998 NCCU Political Attitudes Study. Unstandardized maximum likelihood estimates for latent variable equations, estimated using LISREL. Coefficients are significant at $p \leq .05$.

erage respondents, exposure to Conservative messages from a male leader led to a score on Conservatism 14 percentage points lower than the control group. For those exposed to a Conservative female leader, Conservative sentiment was 12 percentage points lower.

The same male preacher and female teacher who led the Feminist groups also led the Conservative groups. Why were these individuals persuasive in one setting and not in another? Studies pointing to source credibility are relevant for explaining the differential persuasiveness between male- and female-led groups with the same ideological message, but they are useless for understanding why the same individual failed to persuade with a Conservative message when he or she was so persuasive with a Feminist message.[22] Differences in the audience are not the reason, because random assignment of subjects to treatments assures negligible differences between the Conservative and Feminist group participants. Therefore, it must be the ideological message itself that not only is less persuasive but actually causes a countereffect. Participants exposed to Conservative groups become less Conservative!

The content of the discussions demonstrate how subjects both passively and actively resisted Conservative messages of the group leaders. In the woman-led Conservative groups, participants often used the group leader's Conservative promptings to generate counterarguments. The professor pushed the students toward Conservatism by consistently questioning them about issues of individual responsibility, male hierarchy, and moral duties. In one session, two students bucked the facilitator's traditionally Conservative message and responded with arguments of their own.

Female Leader: Do we think that black men can break down some of the stereotypes that people have about them by atoning and through a political focus on being more responsible?

Female Student: I think that they can, within themselves. But there is still going to be those people who say, "Oh, they're still going to do this, they're still going to do that." No matter what you're doing right, they're still going to think in their minds like, "They can't do it, they can't do it." You might be doing right, but that doesn't mean that others are going to see that.

Male Student: I agree. No matter how much we do right, it is the media that controls it. Like in North Carolina we have one of the most black colleges in one state, but every year they show the number of black people who go to prison. But, they never show all the black universities graduating. There's twice as many black men and women going to college and graduating as there are going to prison. But they never say that.

Here the students resist a message that individuals are responsible for how others perceive them and instead point to larger problems of societal racism. Instead of accepting a Conservative perspective that blacks are pathological and need to atone for their shortcomings, these respondents argue that the negative image of African Americans is a construction of biased media and racist sentiments. Throughout this session, participants continue to emphasize the importance of racial unity and cohesion, while rejecting the notion that blacks are solely responsible for the inequalities affecting them. This resistance of the Conservative message is an indication of why the Conservative groups produce lower overall Conservative scores.

In addition to offering this sort of counterargument, subjects in the woman-led Conservative groups took the facilitator's Conservative prompting and turned them into Nationalist articulations. Conservatism and Nationalism share several important conceptual ideas. Both ideologies focus on the importance of African American self-help,[23] and both have traditionally advocated a male hierarchy. Where these ideologies part ways is in their placement of blame (white racism vs. black pathology) and in their vision of the future (racial separatism vs. racial integration). There is a trend in the woman-led Conservative groups toward finding the intersection between Nationalism and Conservatism and pushing the analysis in a more traditionally Nationalist and less Conservative direction.

For instance, in one group a male student expressed Conservative opinions, but his Conservatism has something of a Nationalist undertone:

Female Leader: So how would we create a political movement that might make people more moral and responsible?

Male Student: You got to pick an issue that is important to them. And then it has to be that people morally cast them out if they don't go. Like if she didn't go (indicating another girl in group), but we all went, then we all wasn't going to talk to her no more if she didn't go. To force her into it. Making her go, making it morally right to go.

This student agrees with the facilitator's Conservative opinion that morality and responsibility are appropriate goals of a political movement, but he is advocating a communal policing system to bring about that moral change. This use of a communal strategy is far more Nationalist than Conservative. The idea that individuals should be held to the moral standards imposed by other black people is a traditionally Nationalist articulation. This respondent's belief that there is a black community, and that it exists in a sufficiently cohesive form to punish and reward the behavior of its constituents, is Nationalist by definition.

The trend toward reinterpreting the facilitator's Conservative prompting as Nationalist is clear in the following exchange.

Female Leader: Do you think that it's more important for black people to rely on themselves personally and to think in the ways of the Million Man March?

Male Student: I definitely do. Like the civil rights movement and how people were constantly doing things. I think that it made us be stronger. A lot of those movements were started on the college campuses. And the college students were the ones who were doing it. Here now at Central, it's not the "in" thing. It's not the "in" thing to stand up and speak out and have a word. You know what I mean. People are more comfortable sitting back and letting things happen. Let things go. I can't knock anyone because I think that I do the same thing. But I do think that we have to do more. We do have to come together more, so that we can have a stronger base, a stronger background, so that we can branch out to the wider community and stuff.

Female Student: I agree. I went to a white high school and coming to a black college, it feels like it was just something that I needed to do, because to see a lot of black people trying to do something for themselves, it like it's important to me.

The group leader hoped to emphasize that black people had been lazy by relying on the government and that they now would be forced by the march to be responsible *individuals*. The students chose to reinterpret that message for themselves and for their peers as a responsibility of African Americans to care for one another. It is this subtle distinction that marks the departure of the communally focused Nationalism from the individually focused Conservatism. Given a bootstrap prompt, these respondents transformed it into a black self-reliance articulation. Given the strength of this trend in these sessions, it is clear why the woman-led Conservative groups had Nationalism scores that were six percentage points higher than among control group respondents.

There were moments in the male-led Conservative groups when exchange between the respondents and leader was rapid and heated. It is in these exchanges where the anti-Conservative effect is clearest. The students willingly and openly argue with the Conservative position that the preacher advances. Unlike the subtle counterarguments offered by those in the woman-led group, these respondents are clearly disagreeing with a number of Conservative prompts. In one exchange, several female students question the pragmatism of thinking in terms of a color-blind ideal.

> **Male Leader:** I don't understand why there are groups anyway. I think that we should be able to operate under the general auspices of the constitution. . . .
>
> **Female Student** (*interrupting*): Without color?
>
> **Male Leader** (*continuing*): Together and be empowered to do the things that are necessary and utilize self-help and overcome our problems.
>
> **Female Student:** But it, it's not like that.
>
> **Second Female Student:** (*Laughter*) . . . that's a utopia. . . . (*Laughter*)
>
> **Female Student:** That's how it should be, but that's not how it is, so you have to do whatever you can to make it better.

In another session, the minister openly attacks Louis Farrakhan and is met with strong disagreement.

> **Male Leader:** So would you describe Louis Farrakhan as a liberal monster, agitator of evil, perpetrator of hell?
>
> **Female Student:** No, I think he's just, for his people, for his own people.
>
> **Male Leader:** Who's his people? Who would you describe as being Farrakhan's own people?
>
> **Female Student:** The black people. That's who he's basically looking out for. I know there was some white men there, but it doesn't seem that he was trying to bring white and black people together. I think that he was trying to teach the black men, uniting black men.

In both of these exchanges we see students offering strong counter arguments to the group leader's Conservative message. When he attempts to offer a vision of a color-blind society, the students remind him that African Americans continue to labor under real inequities that keep this ideal from materializing. When he criticizes Farrakhan, the discussants point out that Farrakhan, while not perfect, is basically concerned with the welfare of African Americans and therefore cannot be seen as entirely worthless or bad. When the group leader tries to praise Clarence Thomas, he is met with similar incredulity.

Male Leader: So Clarence Thomas is truly one for the ages.
(Laughter from a female student)
The things that he does. I mean he is very Conservative. He is very good. Welfare reform. Had a sister on welfare. Didn't bother him.
(Behind group leader you can hear several female students making disagreeing sounds.)
He's Conservative and he's adapted. And this is right.
Female Student: I think that there is something wrong with that.
Male Leader: What? (annoyed)
Female Student: I don't think that . . . I don't know. If you are given the opportunity to benefit and you have the power to help them. I don't see what amount of money or what, what type of respect or you know, or somebody else's view, I don't see how that would prevent me from . . . I . . . I . . . I don't know. It's hard to say. If you have that much power and influence, then it shouldn't be just about *you.*

This student's argument, coupled with the discussion of Farrakhan, offers insight into the reason that these African American students oppose the Conservative messages. In both statements there is a sense that African American leaders must justify their actions as being directed toward the good of the larger black community. The students apply a litmus test to black leadership: if you appear to be using your status and wealth for the advancement of black interests, then you pass. If your actions appear to be entirely self-serving, then you fail. Consistently, the discussants in Conservative groups associated Conservative ideology with the quest for personal rather than communal gain. The following exchange in one of the male-led Conservative groups is quite telling on this point.

Male Leader: Is there a problem with being Conservative, do you think?
Male Student: It depends. On the situation. Like you have to dress up Conservative in order to get a job or into a school. You have to wear a black suit—you can't go up in there with a red suit on. You have to wear Conservative colors. For instance, if I was making an investment or something I would rather someone who is very Conservative handle my finances because a liberal might make a bad investment with my money.
Male Leader: Why is that?

Male Student: Because people who are liberal tend to change things. They're always lookin' for change, yeah. And they may put my money in something risky. In that instance, I'd be looking for someone with a more Conservative view rather than more liberal.

Evident in this passage is the belief that Conservative thought is associated with personal gain—for example, getting a job or making personal investments. For this student, Conservatism has a place in African American lives because it represents the necessary goals of personal achievement and fiscal responsibility. But he demonstrates why it is unacceptable as political thought. His language represents Conservatism as the antithesis of change. Therefore, to the extent that one perceives the political and social situation of African Americans as requiring change, the more one would resist a Conservative political approach.

The findings from these two Conservative groups fill in the outline provided by years of earlier black public opinion research. Scholars have found that black public opinion is made up of a social conservatism and economic/political liberalism (Smith and Seltzer 1992). Researchers have attributed this paradox to greater religiosity and increased likelihood of lower-class status among black Americans. African Americans often self-identify as Conservative and can be described as Conservative in many respects, but still African Americans tend not to act on their social Conservatism when making voting decisions. The language of these discussion sessions reinforces the presence of this dichotomy and shows us why it happens.[24] These discussants imply that political decisions have to be justified by their impact on the community as a whole, focused on making changes in unequal circumstances, and cognizant of continuing racial biases. Conservatism is appropriate only in the personal realm, not the public.

One might predict from the results of the Conservatism groups that the subjects in this study are unwilling to accept Conservative messages in any form. However, results from the news-only group provide evidence that it is possible to prompt Conservative leanings from this population of respondents. When subjects were asked simply to read the news article and record their reactions to it, but not given an opportunity to discuss the article, they actually became more Conservative in response. Subjects in the news-only group had Conservatism scores twelve percentage points higher than subjects in the control group.

The news story on the Million Man and Promise Keepers marches had many Conservative elements, such as the reclamation of masculinity and the reliance on personal morality. In the absence of group discussion, these elements of the story influenced the ideological expressions of students. Written reactions to the news story expressed nearly complete unanimity on the worthiness of the male-centered goals of the rallies. Women subjects in particular expressed concern over the particular status of men. Below are several quotes, all from female students.

I think it is about time that men start realizing and taking on the role they have in society.

I can see where the Million Man March made black men feel good about themselves because day after day they are ridiculed and belittled by women and society at large, and that day of affirmation uplifted their spirits.

The role of men changed and diminished due to the feminist movement. Women felt that they are equal to men and should be able to do everything the men do and that they could put their natural role aside. Women took responsibility away from the men, which in turn allowed them to shirk their responsibilities. Now everyone is suffering—women, men, and children.

Conservatism among these respondents is evident in two forms. First, the students are nearly unanimously supportive of a patriarchal hierarchy in which men fulfill traditionally masculine roles. Almost all of the subjects allude to the failure to fulfill these roles as a source of conflict and pathology in the African American community. Second, the students' Conservative sentiments are insistent that black men rely solely on themselves to fix the problem. No student mentioned the ills of racism or the responsibility of government. Instead their comments reflected a belief that black men are the only ones capable of solving the problems that afflict them.

The Conservatism of the news-only group makes the results of the Conservative message groups more stunning. When exposed to an implicit Conservative message, and when that exposure took place without the benefit of intraracial dialogue, the students became more Conservative. When the same message was made explicit by ideological leaders pressing a Conservative viewpoint, not only did the respondents fail to become more Conservative, they became less Conservative. There is evidence here that Conservatism is policed out of settings of everyday talk, where it is seen as an inappropriate approach to politics. However, the discussion groups also suggest the possibility that some forms of Conservatism might be more palatable than others, at least with respect to issues of personal achievement and success.

Results from the 1998 NCCU study show that respondents who engaged in group discussions always had lower levels of Conservatism than those who simply read the news article or had no exposure at all. This effect was particularly pronounced when students were exposed to

TABLE 4.6

Examples of Prompt Questions Used by Conservative Group Leaders, 2001
KKC African American Attitudes Study

Economic Conservatism	Moral Conservatism
Do you think welfare reform will lead to a much needed tax break for tax payers?	Do you think that welfare reform makes sure that people will go out and find work?
Do you think it is the government's responsibility to use tax money to support individuals who don't work? Are there other, more important, ways to use tax money?	Do you think that welfare conveys a negative image of African Americans?
Do you think welfare is bad for the economic strength of African Americans?	Do you think welfare reform will make people think twice before having babies outside of marriage?

explicitly Conservative authority figures. The 2001 KKC study was designed, in part, to test whether Conservatism is consistently policed in everyday black talk and to question if it makes a difference whether Conservatism is expressed as a moral strategy or an economic strategy.

To parse out the differences in reception of Conservative ideology, the 2001 KKC study exposed subjects to one of two different Conservative messages. The group leader either discussed the issue of welfare reform from a Moral Conservative viewpoint emphasizing the degradation of personal values that results from welfare dependency or discussed the welfare reform article from an Economic Conservative perspective that focused on issues of taxation and financial fairness with respect to welfare expenditures (table 4.6).

The results of the KKC study provide a very different picture of Conservatism and its place in everyday black talk from the results of the NCCU study. In the KKC study, respondents who are exposed to both moral and economic Conservative messages demonstrate higher mean scores on overall Conservatism. When exposed to a moral Conservative message, respondents indicated slightly lower levels of moral Conservatism (−2 points), but they became quite a bit more economically Conservative (+6 points). The largest results of the study can be found in the Economic Conservative message groups. When exposed to this viewpoint, subjects show considerably higher levels of both economic and moral Conservatism. In these groups, subjects had economic Conservatism scores seven points higher and moral Conservatism scores fourteen points higher than the control group (fig. 4.7).

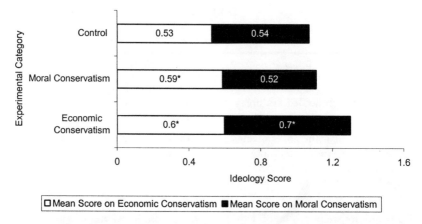

Figure 4.7. Comparison of Mean Scores on Conservatism across Experimental Categories, 2001 KKC African American Attitudes Study. Posttreatment mean scores of respondents in each experimental group. *denotes significance at $p \leq .05$ using a test of first difference.

There is little reaction against explicitly conservative messages in this study. Instead, students articulated very traditional notions of moral Conservatism in their discussion groups. After receiving Conservative prompts, students in Conservative groups argued for a restriction on welfare benefits in order to address abuses and dependency on a system of government provided support. The clarity and strength of their Conservative reasoning is quite stunning, especially when considered in light of the strong anti-Conservative response from the NCCU study.

Moral Conservatism did decline somewhat in groups where subjects were prompted to think specifically about issues of back pathology. Evidence for this mild decline can be found in their conversations. When a group facilitator specifically questioned respondents about black immorality, students offered an argument that incorporated elements of moral Conservatism but tempered this perspective with arguments about historical racism.

> **Group Leader:** Do you think the article was right when it talked about children having children? Do you think that welfare should support women that have two or three babies by different fathers?
>
> **Male Student:** Black women have a situation or circumstance that's unique. When you talk about family values and family stability, we know that as black people we have to set our minds to break the chain. We are still in the process of 160 years of breaking the chain, not only slavery but also trying to define ourselves in an American society. We are

‌up. That's part of the explanation with why some of our
‌ould have two or three kids and not care. We are still fighting
‌thing that's perpetuated by where we have been. However, I'm not
‌oing to excuse the fact of irresponsibility. I mean we still have to promote a level of responsibility in regards to welfare reform. I think that
the stipulations should be okay. You should try to obtain some level of
job training. And I honestly do think that it should be for a specific
amount of time, because what it has done, is created a huge level of
codependence that's actually been passed down in three or four generations in the black community.

This student's argument is indicative of several that occurred as a
result of explicitly moral prompts. While he is willing to argue for individual responsibility, and to set restrictions and stipulations on welfare,
he is unwilling to place the entire blame for welfare abuse and dependency on black people. Instead, this student points to a legacy of slavery
and racism and its continuing effects on African Americans. To him,
these issues, rather than collective racial irresponsibility, are the best
explanation for problems in the welfare system. This exchange, and
others like it, offer some reinforcement of the NCCU study results.
When faced with explicitly moral Conservative messages, subjects reject
them in favor of a more nuanced explanation of African American inequality.

No such complexity emerged in response to economic Conservative
prompts. When encouraged by the group facilitator to think about issues of taxation and economic capacity, students expressed striking critiques of welfare dependence. In one exchange from an Economic Conservatism group, two students offer moral arguments for supporting
welfare reform.

Female Student: It is costing taxpayers money when people are not doing
what they are supposed to be doing. It is like they want free handouts
but, you are not taking care of your responsibilities either. I feel that
nothing in life is for free, you know. I'm speaking from experience. I
have had hard times too, but I also know that I need to get an education
to do better. That's why I am where I'm at right now.

Group Leader: She raised an issue about taxes. Do you think that welfare
reform was needed to give a much needed tax break for taxpayers?

Male Student: No it won't. The government is going to find something else
stupid to spend the money on it in anyway. So I don't think that the
taxpayers are going to get a single penny back. But still, I'm glad that
they decided on welfare reform, because the welfare system as it was
before it had it so that people basically lived off of welfare. There was
no incentive to say get a job or go to school. Generations lived off of

welfare. Generations would just stay there. There was no reason to improve because the government was taking care of them.

In this exchange the first student began with a concern about taxes but swiftly shifted her criticism to those who simply refuse to "do better." She references her own experience with hard times and her ability to overcome them as an indication that others should be able to do the same. The second student dismisses the issue of taxes altogether by claiming that the government will always find something on which to spend money, but he argues that breaking the cycle of intergenerational dependency is a good reason for welfare reform, even if taxpayers will not see any particular economic relief. Respondents made similar arguments throughout the Conservatism sessions. Often referring to either their own experiences with public aid or their firsthand knowledge of those who are part of the welfare system, these subjects argued that there is widespread misuse of and dependency on welfare. Frequently they cited their own attendance at Kennedy-King College as an example of how African Americans can better themselves when they try. In these sessions there were very few moments of dissension with the general tone that welfare reform was good because it forced people to take responsibility for their own lives.

How do we reconcile this result with those of the 1998 NCCU study? The NCCU study suggests that some forms of Conservatism are acceptable articulations within black spaces. When Conservatism was framed as an individualistic, personal strategy for getting a job or making an investment, then it was acceptable. (Recall the discussion of the NCCU student about wearing a Conservative suit to a job interview.) Conservatism was considered unacceptable only when it was framed as a political strategy that would keep black people from collectively enjoying improved life circumstances. In the KKC study, students remain uncomfortable with a group leader who prompts them with arguments about irresponsibility and derogatory racial images. Even among KKC students, there is a modest decline in Conservatism when it is framed in this way. Subjects in the moral Conservative message groups continued to resist an understanding of black inequality that did not account for continuing racial biases and the legacy of historical racism.

Economic Conservatism has a very different effect. Students express greater agreement with economic elements of Conservatism in both message groups, and when presented with economic arguments they add fairly scathing moral critiques of individual black people. This is quite different from the NCCU respondents who shied away from these kinds of arguments. The KKC respondents frame welfare dependency as an individual moral failure. But, like the NCCU students, these respondents are concerned with how these individual failures lead to distressing outcomes for the broader racial group. In their estimation, those who abuse and become dependent on welfare are bringing down the race. The frame of taxpayer versus welfare dependent, offered in the economic message groups, allowed the respondents to take on the mantle of responsible citizen and to see themselves in opposition to the frivolous and lazy welfare recipients. Although many of the KKC students tell stories of their own short-term use of public assistance, they also express pride in having shed their need for external assistance by pursuing educational and employment opportunities. In the moral Conservatism groups, the critiques leveled against welfare recipients are framed as racial pathologies. Because they are black, working class, and sometime users of public aid, the students reject this explicit frame because it includes them in the criticism. The economic frame frees these students to be critical of those who persist in their use or abuse of welfare because it offers them a different position in the story, that of taxpayer and citizen whose own economic strength is undermined by the poor choices of the welfare dependent.[25]

The students in Economic Conservatism groups further expressed concern that welfare dependency contributes to negative images of African Americans. In their estimation, these irresponsible actions are causing African Americans to be seen as inferior people. The exchange below offers evidence of a concern about the negative effect of welfare on black images.

> **Female Student:** Welfare conveys a negative image of African Americans when they let it. The majority of people who are on welfare are not African Americans. But they make it look like we are the only ones on it.
>
> **Male Student:** That is because a lot of black people don't know how to act. White people got more respect about what they do.
>
> **Female Student:** The media projects this image that "this is what all the little homeboys and homegirls in the hood are doing." This is how they get down.

These students resent how the media distorts images of African Americans, but they place part of the blame for that distortion on the black men and women who "don't know how to act." Because most of these students live in black communities, and because many of them have used some form of public assistance in the past, they are angry that those who abuse the system are the major focus of media accounts of race and welfare. They feel that their own stories of self-sufficiency are rarely told. Thus, even their moral Conservatism is infused with a sense of larger, black community purpose. Their distaste is with how individual choices burden working black people or reflect negatively on African Americans as a whole.

Understood in conjunction with the 1998 NCCU results, a story emerges about how the unpopular ideology of black Conservatism finds space in the everyday talk of African Americans. First, the topic of discussion and the participants in it matter. Conservatism was more fully policed in the conversations of twenty-year-old, middle-income, Southern college students talking about the Million Man March than it was in the discussions of thirty-year-old, working-class, urban students talking about welfare. The respondents in the KKC study expressed a great deal of personal knowledge and experience with issues of welfare. When they offered critiques of welfare dependency, they did so from a position of familiarity that made them comfortable with making those moral arguments. But these studies tell us more about Conservatism than simply, "Some people accept it in some circumstances and others don't." There are some consistent reactions to Conservative reasoning present in both the NCCU study and the KKC study.

Explicitly moral Conservative messages, presented without sensitivity to the specificities of racial struggle, are often rejected. Whether presented by a professor, a preacher, or a nonauthoritative facilitator, African American respondents argued against broad, negative categorizations of black behavior. When faced with prompts about individual responsibility, subjects argued for communal responsibility. When faced with prompts about black pathologies, subjects offered historical reasons for the poor decisions made by some black people.

This does not mean that all forms of Conservatism are without support in black discourse. In fact, respondents were willing to offer their own critiques of black behavior, but only when understood in contrast to their own example of black achievement. African American subjects were willing to support Conservative strategies for personal advancement, and to see individual choices as a necessary building block for racial advancement. Respondents are willing to employ Conservative reasoning about self-betterment, individual initiative, and a bootstrap philosophy in their strategies to address racial inequality.

A CLOSER LOOK AT INTERACTIVE EFFECTS

The experimental manipulations of both studies had discernable effects. Students who were exposed to specific ideological messages updated their own political worldviews in comprehensible ways. However, the men and women who participated in the studies were not blank slates. They came to the experimental settings with political and racial views that were affected and shaped by many elements of their lives. These respondents had already spent many years interacting in a variety of other spaces of everyday talk. These earlier experiences influenced the effect that the group interaction had on these individuals. In particular, the extent to which these students were already plugged in to outlets of black information networks affected their experiences in the experimental settings. How prior knowledge of black media and music contributed to the ideological changes caused by the experiment provides a glimpse into how black popular culture functions as everyday talk for African Americans. Further results from the 1998 NCCU Political Attitudes Study illuminate the role of black information networks in the formation of black ideology.

In the tables below, I take a brief look at the interactive effects of black media and hip-hop knowledge on the main ideological message of the discussion. Several trends emerge. First, prior knowledge of black media interacts with the experimental settings to increase the pro-Feminist direction of the Feminist message groups. On average, the male-led group increased Feminism by twenty-three percentage points and the female-led increased it by ten percentage points. This pro-Feminist effect is amplified by knowledge of black media. In each case, moving from the lowest level of black media knowledge to the highest level of black media knowledge interacted with the experimental settings to increase the positive effect on Feminism scores by nearly eleven percentage points. Students who are already well-integrated into black media were more open to the messages and messengers in the discussion group. Second, although the Conservative groups generally decreased Conservative sentiment among group participants, those who came to the group with significant exposure to black media sources actually resisted the anti-Conservative trend. Conservative-group members with the highest level of black media knowledge had Conservatism scores that were only ten percentage points lower, rather than the thirteen percentage points lower scores of average group members.

In the Feminism groups, students with high black media exposure were more likely to accept the Feminist messages from the group leaders. When exposed to Conservative messages, the black media knowledgeable are also more likely to accept the Conservative messages. In the case of black media, being "plugged in" increases the willingness of students to accept the ideological messages of the group leaders. Accustomed to gathering information about black politics from movies, magazines, and television shows presented by black entertainers, these students are more open to learning from their group leaders.

When the impact of hip-hop is considered as an interactive effect in the experimental settings, its effect opposes the effect of black media

TABLE 4.7

Effects of Black Media on Ideology Scores across Experimental Conditions, 1998 NCCU Political Attitudes Study

	Low black media knowledge	Average black media knowledge	High black media knowledge	Difference
Effects on Feminism				
Feminism–male leader	0.18	0.23	0.29	0.11
Feminism–female leader	0.05	0.10	0.15	0.10
Effects on Conservatism				
Conservatism–male leader	−0.15	−0.13	−0.10	0.05
Conservatism–female leader	−0.15	−0.12	−0.09	0.06

Source: 1998 North Carolina Central University Political Attitudes Study

Note: Unstandardized maximum likelihood estimates for latent variable equations, estimated using LISREL. Coefficients for interaction variables are conditional coefficients.

knowledge. Hip-hop knowledge interacts to reduce the pro-Feminist effect of the Feminism groups. And when hip-hop knowledge interacts with the Conservative group settings, it bolsters the anti-Conservative effect. The hip-hop knowledgeable express even less Conservative sentiment than the unknowledgeable, when exposed to a Conservative authority figure. In combination, these results suggest that hip-hop knowledge made subjects more resistant to the group leaders. In both the Feminist and Conservative groups, hip-hop aficionados resisted the ideological messages of the group leaders more than their less knowledgeable colleagues. Just as black media primed students for a greater acceptance of the ideological messages of elites, hip-hop encouraged a rebelliousness against those same leaders.

These results indicate that hip-hop and black media constitute two very different types of space within the black counterpublic. Hip-hop cultivates a respect for resistance in a way that black media does not. Hip-hop is part of a black musical history and tradition that understands itself as resisting the dominant values and paradigms. Therefore, hip-hop listening encourages more resistance to ideological authorities than does black media exposure.

Together these findings suggest an interesting role for black information networks in the development of black ideology. The relevant ques-

TABLE 4.8

Effects of Hip-Hop on Ideology Scores across Experimental Conditions, 1998
NCCU Political Attitudes Study

Experimental group	Low hip-hop knowledge	Average hip-hop knowledge	High hip-hop knowledge	Difference
Effects on Feminism				
Feminism — male leader	0.25	0.23	0.21	0.04
Feminism — female leader	0.12	0.10	0.08	0.04
Effects on Conservatism				
Conservatism — male leader	−0.12	−0.14	−0.14	0.02
Conservatism — female leader	−0.11	−0.12	−0.13	0.02

Source: 1998 North Carolina Central University Political Attitudes Study

Note: Unstandardized maximum likelihood estimates for latent variable equations, estimated using LISREL. Coefficients for interaction variables are conditional coefficients.

tion is not simply what are the messages in the music and the images that black people are exposed to, but how is it that these information networks affect African Americans as they enter other spaces of everyday talk? Rather than fretting over the specific messages present in media and music, we should be involved in uncovering the ways that these information networks contribute to an individual's willingness to accept or critique the variety of political messages he or she encounters. These results are anticipated by Sidran's claim that "the potential of black music to alter social orientations and value structures . . . does not operate at the level of opinions but, rather, alters perceptions and the nature of perceptual information" (1971, 141–44). Black media and hip-hop exposure do not so much dictate a specific set of attitudes as much as they alter perceptions. Therefore, they indirectly affect the development of political ideology by serving as a lens through which other political information is filtered.

CONCLUSION

Group interaction affects African American political attitudes. Variations in ideological expression are visible across different experimental manipulations. These studies have contributed more than a simple "yes" to the question of whether everyday talk affects political attitudes. These studies have revealed patterns in black ideological development that offer a more complete picture of African American thought.

Message matters. African Americans do not accept an ideological perspective simply because they are exposed to it. The process of ideological development is more complex. These subjects bring with them to the political discussion a set of beliefs and attitudes already informed by their prior experience with the political and racial world. They are resistant to messages that offend their fundamental notions of how the world works. In particular, they are resistant when these contradictory messages are made explicit. Therefore, they are willing to accept the Conservative messages when reading the article, but not when discussing it. They are willing to express moral Conservatism, but only when prompted with economic arguments. They are willing to express support for intraracial gender equity, but they remain suspicious of cross-racial gender strategies. Unpopular ideologies are mediated by black common sense. They are not entirely policed out of spaces of everyday talk, but they are tempered by more popular ideologies such as Nationalism.

Experimental results allow me to draw more clearly the causal arrow between everyday talk and ideology by demonstrating that group interaction has a discernable impact on political attitudes. The next chapter leaves the artificial setting of the lab and enters a Chicago barbershop, allowing African Americans to speak for themselves rather than constraining them by survey questions or experimental manipulations. Listening in on the actual talk of ordinary black people presents a fuller vision of how individuals use cues from their interactions to develop political worldviews.

Administration of 1998 NCCU Political Attitudes Study and 2001 KKC African American Attitudes Study

1998 NCCU POLITICAL ATTITUDES STUDY

Subjects for the NCCU Political Attitudes Study were recruited from six history and political science courses at North Carolina Central University. These courses are required classes for graduation and therefore attract students with a wide variety of academic interests. Some go on to become majors in these fields, but most major in other academic departments throughout the university. Two hundred students completed a preliminary questionnaire between January 15 and January 17, 1998. The questionnaire was administered during class time by the principal investigator, with the permission of instructors of the courses. This first questionnaire included measures of partisanship, ideology, and perceptions of parties with respect to African American interests. It also included measures of religiosity and feeling thermometers on social groups and political individuals. Additionally, it included measures of attentiveness to black media sources, exposure to hip-hop, and measures of political knowledge. There are no measures of the four black political ideologies on the pretest instrument. All posttest ideology scores are compared across experimental categories (between subjects design) rather than with pretest vs. posttest measures (within subjects design).

In April 1998, students who completed the first questionnaire were asked to participate in the second half of the project. To encourage participation, instructors granted extra credit to students who participated, and the study advertised a chance to win $150 to all students who completed the second half of the project. One hundred of the original two hundred students returned to complete the second half of the project. Two of the one hundred students were white. They were assigned to the control group and then their questionnaires were discarded and were not used in the analysis. Ninety-eight participants were used in the final experimental results. The second half of the project was conducted outside of regular class time. Participants were not told the purpose of the study. They were told only that the researchers were interested in social and political attitudes of black college students.

When the students arrived for participation in the second half of the project, they were asked to draw a number out of a box. This number corresponded to a particular classroom. In each classroom there was a different experimental condition. This allowed the student participants to be randomly assigned to one of seven groups: control group, reading-only group, peer discussion, male-led Feminism, male-led Conservatism, female-led Feminism, female-led Conservatism.

All subjects, except the control group, were given a news article to read and asked to write a brief record of their feelings about the article. Subjects were asked to read an article taken from the February 1998 issue of *Essence* magazine. The author, Sam Fulwood, discusses his experiences at both the 1995 Million Man March and the 1997 Stand in the Gap rally organized by the Promise Keepers. The subjects in the experiment did not know the source of the article or the name of the author, but the text of the story was exactly as it appeared in the *Essence* article. This article had several important features. First, since 1995 African Americans had publicly expressed a variety of views on the Million Man March. Because there was public debate on this event, there were differing positions on the march widely available to participants, who could feel free to express their own viewpoints without feeling censored by a single acceptable point of view. Second, this article contained elements that would prompt expression of all four ideological viewpoints. Nationalist sentiment could be evoked in support of the Million Man March. Feminist sentiment could be evoked in opposition to both the Million Man March and Promise Keepers Rally. Integrationist feeling could come forward for those who opposed the separatist Million Man March and supported the integrated Promise Keepers Rally. And Conservative arguments could be offered in support of both marches. Therefore, this article provided the ideal vehicle for investigating the ideologies.

After completing the tasks of reading and writing about the article, subjects in the read-only group completed a second questionnaire designed to assess their political attitudes. In the peer discussion group, after independently reading the article the students were given twenty minutes to discuss what they had read with the other students in the room. After the twenty-minute discussion, each student then independently completed the second survey instrument.

The four other groups also involved subjects reading the news article, recording their feelings, and discussing the article for twenty minutes. But in these four groups the subjects were guided in their discussion by an authority figure that purposely encouraged a specific ideological viewpoint. In the Feminism with a male leader group, an African American man who was introduced to them as a minister guided subjects in their discussion. In this group the minister purposely advocated a black

Feminist position. An African American woman who was introduced to them as a professor led another group of students in discussion. She also purposely advocated a Feminist stance. In another variation of the manipulation, the male preacher and female teacher took purposely Conservative positions when leading other groups of students. The decision to act as either a Conservative or Feminist was also made by drawing a number from a box and was therefore randomly assigned.

Blair L. Murphy and Reverend Anthony Rainge served as group leaders in the experiment. Murphy was an advanced history graduate student at Duke University. Rainge was a graduate student in the Divinity School at Duke University. Both were familiar with the purpose of the experiment. Each group leader read the experimental design and understood that the study was testing the connection between group interaction and political attitudes. Rainge and Murphy each read several writings by and about black Feminists and Conservatives. They met as a group on several occasions in the months leading up to the second half of the study. Together the researchers discussed the news article and determined common definitions of a Feminist and Conservative approach to analyzing the article. These discussions acted as a guide for the group leaders as they conducted the group sessions, but the leaders did not follow a set script during the group discussions.

A control group of subjects was simply instructed to complete a second survey instrument. They neither read the article nor engaged in any discussion. None of the students was aware of what was occurring in the other groups. The control group is used in the analysis for comparing each of the experimental manipulations.

2001 KKC AFRICAN AMERICAN ATTITUDES STUDY

The design of the KKC African American Attitudes Study is meant to extend the findings of the 1998 NCCU study. The studies use a similar protocol, but the KKC study is not a replication of the earlier study, so there are several key differences.

Subjects were recruited from six different sociology, psychology, and political science courses at Kennedy-King College. The principal investigator attended each of these classes and explained that the study was interested in the political and social attitudes of black college students. No tests were administered during class; instead, subjects were asked to report the following week at an assigned time for the study. Subjects were paid $10 for participation in the study, and food and soda were provided. One hundred thirty respondents completed a preliminary questionnaire that included measures of personality, self-esteem, political predispositions, participation in black organizations, and exposure to African American popular culture. Like the NCCU study, the KKC study randomly assigned these respondents to one of six experimental manipulations. The control group responded to a second questionnaire designed to measure levels of black ideology.

All other respondents read a news story about welfare policy and the black community. The welfare article was compiled from several different news stories from 1998 to 2000 that dealt specifically with the aftermath welfare reform legislation. The article is credited to a fictional author, Victoria Gray. Half of the subjects received a version that presented arguments in opposition to welfare reform and then support of welfare reform. The other half received a version of the article that began with support of welfare reform and then presented opposition.

Students in the news-only group wrote their reactions to the story and then completed the second survey instrument. They were given twenty minutes to discuss the news story with other students and then directed to complete the second questionnaire. In the four remaining groups, the respondents were guided in their discussions by a trained graduate student working for the project. This group leader used prescripted prompts designed to present the question of welfare from the perspective of either an Integrationist-Feminist, Nationalist-Feminist, Economic-Conservative, or Moral-Conservative. Then respondents in each of these four experimental manipulations completed the second questionnaire. All group discussion sessions were videotaped with the consent of the respondents.

The Kennedy-King College study deconstructs the black Feminist and Conservative message into their meaningful, constituent elements. The NCCU study did not allow a measure of the effects of different forms of the ideologies being presented. Nationalist and Integrationist Feminist sentiments were bundled in presentation, as were Moral and Economic Conservatism. This study allowed observation of how discussion changes when different elements of the ideology are presented.

Appendix 4.2

Estimation for Experimental Studies

Estimation for 1998 NCCU Political Attitudes Study was conducted using Statistical Analysis Software, *SAS*. Coefficients reported in figures 4.3 and 4.6 are derived from a maximum likelihood estimation of a structural equation model using LISREL.

Ideology = *f*: Experimental Category, Black Media Knowledge, Hip-Hop Knowledge

Estimation for 2001 Kennedy King College African American Attitudes Study was conducted using Stata Statistical Software. Numbers reported in figures 4.4, 4.5, and 4.7 are group means. Statistical significance is determined using a t-test of first difference of means.

Ideology = *f*: Experimental Category

Independent Variables: 1998 NCCU Political Attitudes Study

	Measures
Experimental category	Control
Constructed as dummy variables	News-only
Control group is the excluded group in the analysis	Peer discussion Male-Feminism Female-Feminism Male-Conservatism Female-Conservatism
Black Media Knowledge	Susan Taylor
Constructed as dummy variables 1 = correctly identified 0 = incorrectly identified	Tavis Smiley Quincy Jones E. Lynn Harris Kenneth Edmunds
Scale is additive and constrained to unit range	Myrlie Evers-Williams Nathan McCall Maya Angelou Bev Smith

Independent Variables: 1998 NCCU Political Attitudes Study
(*Continued*)

	Measures
Hip-hop knowledge	Mase
	Wu-Tang
Constructed as dummy variables	Snoop Dog
1 = correctly identified	Outkast
0 = incorrectly identified	The Firm
	Mack 10
Scale is additive and constrained to unit range	Bone-Thugs-Harmony

Source: 1998 NCCU Political Attitudes Study.

Independent Variables: 2001 KKC African American Attitudes Study

	Measures
Experimental category	Control
Constructed as dummy variables. Statistical signifi-	News-only
cance is determined in relation to the mean of the	Peer discussion
control group	Womanist-Feminism
	Integrationist-Feminism
	Economic-Conservatism
	Moral-Conservatism

Source: 2001 KKC African American Attitudes Study.

Dependent Variables: 1998 NCCU Political Attitudes Study

Indicator	*Coefficient*	*SE*
Black Feminism		
Black women should share equally in the political leadership of the Black community.	1.00	
Do you think that what happens to Black women in this country will have something to do with what happens in your life?	2.01	0.57
I am concerned about what happens to white women in this country because I know that what happens to them will affect my life.	2.22	0.06
The problems of black men and black women deserve equal attention.	1.52	0.3
The problems of racism and sexual discrimination are linked together and both must be addressed by the black community.	1.51	0.3

Dependent Variables: 1998 NCCU Political Attitudes Study
(*Continued*)

Indicator	Coefficient	SE
Black Conservatism		
Many African Americans are not trying hard enough; if blacks would only try harder, they could be just as well off as whites	1.00	
Affirmative action makes blacks believe that they don't have to work very hard.	1.62	0.37
Big corporations are unfair to the black community.*	0.31	0.23
Most poor people don't want to work.	0.74	0.26
Welfare is a major cause of the breakdown in morals and family in the African American community.	1.05	0.29
Black Nationalism		
Black people share most important things in common.	1.00	
Black people should shop in black stores whenever possible.	1.62	0.33
Blacks are a nation within a nation.	1.18	0.27
Black elected officials can best represent the interests of the black community.	0.79	0.33
Blacks should control the economy in mostly black communities.	1.58	0.32
Blacks should form their own political party.	1.09	0.26
Blacks should participate in black only organizations whenever possible.	1.06	0.26
Liberal Integrationism		
There are many whites who are concerned about the issues facing blacks. Blacks should work on forming alliances with these whites.	1.00	
Whites cannot be trusted as political allies. Blacks should avoid biracial coalitions.	1.04	0.17
One of the most important things about the civil rights movement is that it showed that Blacks and whites can work together in America.	0.73	0.16
It is more important for educated Blacks to own their own business than to reach top positions in corporate America.*	0.69	0.16
Although historically black colleges are important, it is equally important that many of the best black students attend whites colleges as well.	0.69	0.16
I would attend a predominately white college or university.	0.87	0.16
I would join a civic organization that was predominately white, for example the P.T.A.	1.01	0.17

Dependent Variables: 1998 NCCU Political Attitudes Study
(*Continued*)

Indicator	Coefficient	SE
I would join a church that has a white minister and a predominately white congregation.	0.82	0.16

Source: Compiled by M. V. Harris-Lacewell from 1998 NCCU Political Attitudes Study. Each of the dependent variables is estimated as a latent variable in a system of equations. Each indicator was scored on a unit range before estimation, and each latent variable is constrained to a unit range by the first indicator.

*Opposition coded.

Dependent Variables 2001 KKC African American Attitudes Study

Variables	Sample Mean
Integrationist Feminism	
Oftentimes, black women share more in common with women of other races than with black men.	0.64
Women share many of the same issues no matter what color they are.	0.79
I am concerned about what happens to white women in this country because I know that what happens to them will affect my life.	0.54
Womanist Feminism	
The problems of black men and black women deserve equal attention.	0.85
The problems of racism and sexual discrimination are linked together, and both must be addressed by the black community.	0.73
Black feminist groups just divide the black community. (opposition coded)	0.51
Economic Conservatism	
It is more important for black people to focus on economic strength than political power.	0.68
Most poor people want to work, but there are not enough jobs. (opposition coded)	0.68
Big corporations are an important source of economic strength for black communities.	0.66
Moral Conservatism	
Affirmative action makes blacks believe that they don't have work very hard.	0.43
Hard work and patience will do more for the cause of black equality than demanding things from the government.	0.72

Dependent Variables 2001 KKC African American Attitudes Study
(*Continued*)

Variables	Sample Mean
Welfare is a major cause of the breakdown of morals and family in the African American community.	0.63
Attitudes toward whites	
White people want to see blacks get a better break.	0.45
White people want to keep blacks down.	0.66
White people cannot be trusted as political allies.	0.53
Strategic Integrationism	
There are many whites who are concerned about issues facing blacks. Blacks should work on forming alliances with these whites.	0.64
One very important thing about the civil rights movement is that it showed that blacks and whites can work together in America.	0.76
Although historically black colleges are important, it is equally important that many of the best black students attend white colleges.	0.63

Source: Compiled by M. V. Harris-Lacewell from 2001 KKC African American Attitudes Study. Each of the dependent variables is an additive scale. Each indicator was scored on a unit range before estimation, and each scale was constrained to a unit range after addition.

CHAPTER FIVE

Truth and Soul: Black Talk in the Barbershop

Written with Quincy T. Mills

> One of the most satisfying times in my life was going to the barbershop and getting a clear cut fade on Saturday mornings, bonding with other brothers, talking about everything and nothing in particular.
> —Leroy Carter

> The barbershop has none of the religious constraints of the black church. There aren't the academic requirements of the black college. Everyone's welcome in the barbershop and everyone's welcome to speak out.
> —Mark Curnutte, 1999

DAMON HAD JUST finished cutting a customer's hair and was sitting in the chair a few feet away. The shop was quiet and I was sitting near the opened door trying to catch a breeze. "So, have you learned anything yet," Damon asked me, "after a couple of days at the shop, what have you learned so far?" I had been hanging out at Truth and Soul for less than a week, but already I had learned a lot. Listening to the buzzing conversations, I had learned that Hajj was not only the shop's owner but its heart, the animating force that made this place dynamic. Looking at the wall of framed photos, I had learned that in the last few decades most of Chicago Southside's black elite had sat in one of the three barber's chairs in front of me. Watching the customers, I had learned that the men who frequent the shop are looking for much more than a haircut. They come to Truth and Soul because they are welcomed here, not just for the dollars they will spend, because some of them won't spend a dime, but because they are part of a community. Engaging with them, I had learned that they come because they have a story to stretch, a fact to check, or an idea to flesh out. Laughing with them, I had learned that the entertainment here was better than in downtown clubs. I had learned that these men come because "the barbershop is the black man's way station, point of contact, and universal home. Here he always finds a welcome—a friendly audience as he tells his story and a native to give him the word on local doings" (Grier and Cobbs 1968). But that is not what I said to Damon. I told him, "I'm just observing."

To make any assertion about everyday black talk, you must eventually enter the barbershop. The barbershops and beauty parlors, more than the churches, the schools, or the radio, exist as spaces where black people engage each other as peers, where nothing is out of bounds for conversation, and where the serious work of "figuring it out" goes on. This text, too, eventually had to lead back to the barbershop. How to do research in a barbershop as a black woman was complicated. Having spent several years studying Orange Grove Missionary Baptist Church in Durham, North Carolina, I knew how to act as a participant observer, and I knew that in my own body I could never enter the barbershop without fundamentally altering the dynamics of the space I hoped to study. Therefore this chapter is collaborative. It offers research from an urban ethnographic study of Truth and Soul: Black Stars, a barbershop on Chicago's Southside. I have never met many of the men it will discuss. I have only been to Truth and Soul once. The eyes and ears of this operation belong to Quincy T. Mills. Quincy spent a summer gathering field notes and personal impressions of Truth and Soul. His research, and my interpretations of it, are the core of this chapter.[1] Beyond this paragraph, the first person singular is reserved for my interpretation of Quincy's voice as he retells his experiences with the men of Truth and Soul, where he spent the entire summer of 2000 hanging out with the barbers, regulars, customers, and characters.

This chapter asserts that through eavesdropping and hanging out we can uncover hidden relationships. The study asks: how do informal interactions among African Americans in barbershops inform the political worldviews of those who participate? How do black barbershops function as sites of transmission of political information and ideas? In addition to providing an empirical answer to these questions, the study is a glimpse into the politics of ordinary interactions and everyday talk among African Americans. Using the field notes, impressions, and discussions acquired during a three-month study of Truth and Soul, we hope to add the final narrative to the story of black ideological development.

This chapter first will situate the case study by providing a brief history of black barbering to illustrate an ongoing relevance and centrality of barbers and their shops in African American communities. It then presents an argument for the specific position of black hair and hair care within the social, cultural, and political traditions of black America. The chapter concludes by presenting evidence gathered in the ethnographic study of a single black barbershop on Chicago's Southside in the summer of 2000.

A BRIEF HISTORY OF BLACK BARBERING

From slavery to freedom, barbers and hairstylists have constituted the overwhelming majority of entrepreneurs in the African American community.[2] In antebellum America, black men labored and held a monopoly in the barbering profession that primarily served wealthy whites, often prominent businessmen and politicians. Many black barbers served only white customers, and others owned separate shops for blacks and whites.[3] The small capital investment in a barbershop attracted many black entrepreneurs. Their monopoly and white customer exclusivity were due to the stigma of personal service occupations as "nigger work" that required servility and deference. As Berlin argues, "The servile nature of the job [barbering] drove away white competitors, while it encouraged the patronage of white customers who felt they should be served by blacks" (Berlin 1974, 235–36; Walker 1998, 107).

Black barbershop proprietors who catered to a white clientele were among the most prosperous black business enterprises in antebellum America. This placed barbers among the occupational elite in the black class structure. Many slaves involved in barbering used their renumeration to purchase their own, or other family members', freedom. Many free blacks who accumulated wealth invested in real and chattel property (Walker 1998). In 1860, among Southern black realty owners with $20,000 worth of property, 10 percent were barbers (Schweninger 1990). William Johnson of Mississippi, known as the "Barber of Natchez," owned three barbershops between 1835 and 1851 and a plantation on which he employed both free black and white laborers. At his death in 1851 he was worth $25,000 (Davis and Hogan 1954; Walker 1998, 108). The most successful Northern black barbers owned exclusive shops, either as separate establishments in the urban white business districts or in exclusive hotels.[4] Both as slaves and as free men, black barbers used both monopoly and a white consumer base to their advantage. Their profession provided them with power, prestige, and status in the black community.

These men did not use this status and wealth solely for individual gain. African American barbers often used their earnings to actively engage in uplift activities. William Watson, a Cincinnati barber and former slave, purchased freedom for his mother and siblings and invested in building black churches. Barbers Lewis Woodson and John Vashon co-founded Wilberforce, the first all-black university (Watson 1998). Even when African American barbers were serving primarily white clientele, their fortunes and status were frequently reinvested in black communities, a reality that made them a center of black life in the nineteenth century.

In the mid- to late 1880s, German and Italian immigrants competed with black barbers and eventually usurped their white customers, driving them out of the downtown business districts into separate black economies. The decline of black barbers, waiters, and other businesses that catered to a predominately white clientele was a trend in all Northern cities in the late nineteenth and early twentieth centuries (Greene and Woodson 1930). DuBois noted in the 1890s in his study of Philadelphia that "the Negro barber is rapidly losing ground in this city" (1899, 115–16, 119). In 1909, George Edmund Haynes (1913, 125, 128–29) noted a similar trend in New York, where only seven of fifty barbershops served a white clientele. Cities with smaller black populations and less industrialization did not experience this trend as rapidly. In 1870, 43 percent of Cleveland's barbers were black, compared to 18 percent in 1890. By 1910, less than one in ten barbers in the city was black, and they primarily served black customers.[5] In his 1901 autobiography *The Story of My Life and Work*, Booker T. Washington noted:

> Twenty years ago every large and paying barbershop over the country was in the hands of black men, today in all the large cities you cannot find a single large or first class barber shop operated by colored men. The black men had had a monopoly of that industry, but had gone on from day to day in the same old monotonous way, without improving anything about the industry. As a result the white man has taken it up, put brains into it, watched all the fine points, improved and progressed until his shop today was not known as a barbershop, but as a tonsorial parlor. (Washington 1986)

During this period, a white barber in Durham, North Carolina, admitted that he met "a great deal of competition from the Negro Barbers. It was difficult to change the habits of whites who had grown accustomed to particular black barbers. We found it impossible to get them to change to our shops. However poor white men who moved into Durham from the country much preferred our services to that of a Negro, and especially a Negro who was more or less wealthy" (Weaver 1987, 353). In some states, such as New York and Ohio, white barbers organized in racially exclusive labor unions, particularly the Journeyman Barber's International Union of America founded in 1887.[6] Without the patronage of whites, personal service occupations, such as barbers and waiters, became less prestigious during this racial shift in consumer base (Kusmer 1976). More importantly, Reconstruction provided new economic opportunities for African Americans. Undertaking, banking, and insurance endeavors supplanted barbering, and by 1870 barbers constituted only 1.7 percent (down from a high of nearly 10 percent) of the black economic elite (Byrd and Tharps 2001).

The black barbering profession started as a service industry to whites, but it was transformed in the twentieth century into a black public space. By the turn of the century, black barbering began to take on the contours of the contemporary profession. African American migration to urban centers generated a new market for black barbers. Many black newspapers were nationally distributed and sold in black barbershops. Blacks purchased the *Chicago Defender*, for example, from the local barbershop and often discussed its contents. This everyday practice was particularly important when Southern blacks were deliberating the move north during the Great Migration. In Southern barbershops, blacks discussed the *Defender's* portrayal of Northern employment opportunities and life in the city, read letters from relatives and friends in the North, and listened to labor agents recruiting for Northern industry. Between fall 1916 and January 1917, Robert Horton, a barbershop proprietor in Hattiesburg, Mississippi, convinced nearly forty men and women to migrate with him to Chicago. After his arrival, "he opened the Hattiesburg Barbershop, which became a gathering place for migrants from Hattiesburg, Mississippi and its environs" (Grossman 1989, 95).

The relative profitability of individual proprietors never again reached antebellum levels. Those who became wealthy from black hair in the twentieth century were those who packaged and marketed products for the commercial industry. But the status of barbers and barbershops took on new dimensions as their clientele shifted to an African American base. The urban working class and the growing black middle class increasingly became the clientele of African American barbers, and black barbers increasingly opened shops serving these customers. By 1920, the Chicago Blue Book directory of black businesses in the city, listed 211 barbers and 108 beauty salons (Byrd and Tharps 2001, 83). African Americans increasingly demanded black hair care products as they continued to face the styling challenges of black hair in a country where very few products or services were directed toward their specific needs. Savvy entrepreneurs soon learned that profits would now come from specializing in the care and upkeep of black hair.[7] It was during this time that the black hair care industry generated the first black women millionaires, as Madame C. J. Walker and Annie Malone packaged and marketed commercial hair care products and services (Bundles 2001).

Black barbers became exclusive specialists in black men's hair. World

War I politics of respectability dictated short, conservative styles for black men. The Depression hit black barbers hard, but they rebounded by World War II as they became specialists of the flamboyant conk sported by zoot suiters of the urban North. In the 1960s barbers marketed Afro blowouts and precision trims to keep up with a changing black aesthetic. In the 1980s they became experts of the Gheri Curl and mastered the high top fade. As they turned their focus to the styling needs of black communities, barbershops emerged as a central gathering place for African American men. Although by the end of the twentieth century much of the retail of black hair care products was taken over by the white cosmetic industry, African Americans continued to dominate the barbering aspect of the black hair care business.

BARBERSHOPS AND EVERYDAY BLACK TALK

What is all this discussion of hair and the hair care industry doing in a book about the politics of African American talk? It appears here because skin color and "kinky hair" are so intertwined that it is hard to separate the two when examining the forces that shape black people's lives (Morrow 1973; Banks 2000). During the twentieth century, anthropologists, psychologists, and sociologists regularly debated the various cultural and social meanings of hair (Freud 1922; Berg 1952; Leach 1958; Hallpike 1972). In the past fifty years, scholars of African American history and life have paid increased attention to the relevance of black hair. Morrow's (1973) *400 Years without a Comb* is a history of black hairstyling practices. Koena Mercer (1990), Bruce Tyler (1990), Nowlie Rooks (1996), Robin D. G. Kelley (1997), Maxine Craig (1997), and Ingrid Banks (2000) have chronicled the sociopolitical relevance of African American hairstyle choices such as the conk, the Afro, the fade, the curl, braids, and locks. These authors have effectively argued that "black hair and hairstyling practices can never escape political readings" (Banks 2000).

This chapter is not primarily interested in the politics of black hair per se, but it is concerned with documenting how a space that is presumably about cutting hair operates as a political space through its facilitation of meaningful everyday black talk. To do this we want to demonstrate two points. First, hair and hair care is a racial marker that identifies blackness and distinguishes black life experience. Black hair has its own vocabulary and rituals that are integral to everyday black talk. Second, black hair rituals contribute to the notion of a common African American experience. This notion of commonality allows barbershops and beauty salons to function as racialized public spaces with the potential to contribute to the development of black politics. "Hair is never a straightforward biological 'fact' because it is almost always groomed, prepared, cut, concealed and generally 'worked upon' by human hands. Such practices socialize hair, making it a medium of significant 'statements' about self and society and the codes of value that bind them, or don't" (Mercer 1990).

The idea of a black hair vocabulary is familiar for many African Americans. Whether it is memories of a searing hot comb on freshly greased hair, do rags knotted tightly into place, the burn of relaxers, or the search for the perfect afro pick, black folks know that much of what they take for granted about their hair is completely unknown to most whites.

> Although academics and laypeople alike might doubt the assertion that a culture specific to Black hair exists, the truth is self-evident. . . . From day one, Black children are indoctrinated into the intricate culture of hair. Vocabulary words like *grease*, *kitchen*, and *touch-up* are ones a Black child hears at a very early age and needs to learn in order to fully participate in the Black hair lifestyle. Phrases like *nappy-headed*, *tender-headed*, and *turn back* aren't so much taught as they are absorbed in the growing lexicon of a young Black mind. (Byrd and Tharps 2001, 135)

This common language and ritual are central to the transmission of an African American hair culture. A volume edited by Juliette Harris and Pamela Johnson (2001) offers a "comb-bending collection of stories" by African American men and women who reflect on uncovering the social meaning of their blackness as they learned about their hair.

Annabelle Baker, a retired nurse, recalls that childhood hair rituals were fraught with social significance.

> In my early childhood, Grandma would section my hair into neat square parts, grease my scalp with Excellenta pomade, and plait the hair. . . . The *number* of plaits Grandma gave me held social significance. The fewer the braid the greater the social event I was being readied for. Multiple plaits were for casual times like sleeping or staying around the house. Three plaits—one on top and two side by side below, were for school or church. On really special occasions, like Easter, I wore no plaits at all. At those times, my hair would be straightened with a hot comb and the ends turned up with a curling iron. (Harris and Johnson 2001)

Harvard Professor Henry Louis Gates remembers the smell when his mother was heating a hot comb on the gas stove to press hair for friends and neighbors. Gates recalls, "I liked what that smell meant for the shape of my day" (Gates 1997). Feminist scholar bell hooks remembers that doing hair was a time of intimate social connection for black people.

Hair pressing was a ritual for black women's culture — of intimacy. It was an elusive moment when black women (even those who did not know one another well) might meet at home or in the beauty parlor to talk with one another, to listen to the talk. It was as important a world as that of the male barbershop — mysterious, secret. It was a world where the images constructed as barriers between one's self and the world were briefly let go, before they were made again." (Harris and Johnson 2001, 111)

Perhaps the most important hair-related rite of passage for young black boys is the first haircut. The first haircut is frequently heralded as a marker indicating the boy's initiation into grownup black male culture. It is a ritual that many black men maintain through decades of Saturday mornings. Author Melvin Murphy remembers:

Going to the barbershop every other Saturday morning was a ritual. . . . It was my turn to get my head mauled. It was time to get my ears scraped. It was time to get the most sensitive part of my body touched by the clippers that sounded like a swarm of bees. I hated it when the barber trimmed the back of my neck. . . . As I grew up, going in and out of Black barbershops, I began to notice many unique and fascinating social affinities, such as male bonding. (Murphy 1998, 24–28)

Racialized hair language makes hairstyling practices an in-group activity. Black barbershops and beauty salons are chosen communities. When black people come together to cut and style one another's hair, it is a coming together that affirms and comforts. Having to explain to someone the basics of your daily hygiene and personal style is degrading and debilitating.[8] Black barbers and stylists free their clients of that need to explain. Barbershops are a place where black men can retreat into a racialized and gendered world where they are not the "other." Recounting the experience of African American men on a white college campus, one student recalls that when black men are looking for a community, they look for the barbershop.

The Black students at Columbia University say that looking for a barbershop gives them a way to get to know the historic, culturally rich neighborhoods of Harlem and Washington Heights that border their upper Manhattan campus. "Freshman year the guys at school were so excited when they realized they'd be able to get their hair cut at the same barbershop as Malcolm X." (Byrd and Tharps 2001, 147)

Barbershops function as a reassertion of essentialized racial identity. The social construction of race has been a primary focus of race scholars for the past decade. Social scientists, and those in the humanities, have worked successfully to deconstruct the notion of race as an enduring, biologically determined, and essential category. Instead these scholars have pointed to the sociocultural, historical specificity of racial categories and identities. But in the midst of this, African Americans have continued to operate the one recession-proof industry in the black community: black hair care. Barbershops and beauty salons bring people together, not because of shared history per se, but because of fundamental differences in hair texture, necessary products, and services. Black hair care remains the one service that black people provide almost exclusively to other African Americans. This sort of essentialized racial space makes blackness a sufficient condition for membership in a way that can, but does not necessarily, happen in other arenas. In organizations, for example, individuals come together because of the particular mission of the organization. When one attends a black church it is both to worship God and to be with other black people. In schools, educational attainment is the primary goal. With media and hip-hop, entertainment is the motivating factor bringing people together. But in the public space of the barbershop, blackness is both the necessary and sufficient condition for membership.

Barbershops offer a unique and largely unstudied space for uncovering everyday black talk. This text enters the black barbershop in hopes of discovering patterns of belief and discourse that are obscured in other spaces.

HANGING AT TRUTH AND SOUL

In the typical black barbershop, business is always slow, except on Friday afternoons and Saturdays. Slow business and slack activity are not to be equated; however, the barbershop has its "regulars" who only occasionally support the business financially.
— Trudier Harris, 1979

Hajj has small eyes and a broad, distinctive nose.[9] His hair is peppered with gray, his belly protrudes from his slight frame, and his forehead is etched with lines from laughing, worrying, and living. He isn't tall, but he is a presence. Hajj owns Truth and Soul, a three-chair barbershop that has served Chicagoans for more than thirty-one years. Hajj's father, mother, two sisters, two aunts, two uncles, and three cousins all owned barbershops in Chicago. His father and mother migrated to Chicago from Mississippi and Arkansas, respectively. Together his parents owned the Elegant Barber Shop in Chicago's Westside. After Hajj graduated from a Westside Chicago high school in 1960, his father offered to enroll him in barber college.[10] Hajj somewhat reluctantly entered McCoy's Barber College in 1961. He remembers, "I was there during the cuttin' sessions, but I always ditched the theory sessions." After graduating from McCoy's, Hajj's parent's did not immediately allow him to work in their shop. Instead they encouraged him to find employment on his own. Hajj apprenticed in two shops, and after the owner of the second gambled Hajj's wages on the horses, Hajj's father finally allowed him to take over the Westside business.

Elegant remained a crucial part of the Westside neighborhood under Hajj's leadership, but in 1970 Russell Roberto, the Italian owner of Southeast Barbershop, was looking to sell his shop. Hajj decided to buy. Roberto was looking to sell because of the changing racial demographics of the Southside neighborhood. It was changing from primarily white ethnic to African American. After Hajj acquired the shop, the Italian and Russian barbers who worked for Roberto failed to abruptly leave as Hajj had expected. As Hajj recalls, "they stayed around two or three months to let them [white customers] know where they were going. The white customers thought I was the shoeshine boy or porter. I told the two barbers, 'whatever they ask that I am, *tell em'* that's what I am and get their money.'"

Hajj found himself in a dilemma in the racially shifting neighborhood. As whites discovered the ownership was black, they no longer wanted to patronize the shop. But many African Americans still believed the shop to be white-owned. So Hajj began a campaign to inform the new black residents that the barbershop was black-owned. First he changed the name of the shop to Truth and Soul, but there were white business owners in the neighborhood who included the word "soul" or some other racial code word to give the impression their businesses were black-owned. Hajj added "Black Stars" to the name and included a door sign with a black man with two raised fists emerging out of the African continent. He also advertised by standing in front of his shop in his white barbering smock to catch the eye of passing black residents. Many of his customers and friends from the Westside shop would also visit him so that others would see the growing African American presence.

His most successful racial advertisement is emblematic of both Hajj's personality and the character of Truth and Soul. In 1970, Soul Train presented a show at the High Chaparral, a few miles from Truth and Soul, featuring Bobby Womack, the Intruders, and Eddie Kendricks, from the original Temptations. Hajj suggested to a friend that he wanted to get Kendricks in the shop, but his friend responded with disbelief. Hajj was confident. "Man, I got the gift of gab." Hajj was able to convince Kendricks to stop by the shop and get his hair cut. Kendricks agreed on the condition that Hajj not tell anyone. But Hajj knew that Kendricks's presence would be a tremendous asset for his young business. When the "big, black Cadillac drove up," Hajj went through the back door and let the guys on the street know that Kendricks was coming. A crowd formed. From then on, Truth and Soul was an established spot for black folks in the neighborhood. Over the years, the shop has also been visited by a wide array of black celebrities, entertainers, and politicians. Billy D. Williams, Curtis Mayfield, and Mahalia Jackson have all been Truth and Soul visitors. Hajj's "gift of gab" convinced Kendricks to visit the shop, and it is this gift that remains the central characteristic that places him at the center of Truth and Soul.

In the summer of 2000, Hajj had three barbers working with him in the shop. His son Damon is a partner in the shop. He has Hajj's smile and his coloring, but Damon is taller and leaner than his dad. Sherman is a big guy. Tall, heavy set, light skinned, with tattooed forearms, Sherman is an imposing figure. Then there is G, the youngest of the barbers, who wears his hair braided straight back in cornrows. He sports gold jewelry, a goatee, and urban streetwear. These four men and their regulars make up the core of the shop.

While Hajj is the most colorful, there is a rowdy standard cast of characters at Truth and Soul. The three other barbers, Damon, Sherman, and G, regularly engage Hajj on matters of sex, politics, money, and religion. Willie is a regular customer, as is Fred. Over the course of the summer, different personalities and voices took center stage. Sometimes it was Sherman engaging in raunchy, male bravado. At times it was Fred annoying Sherman with his insistence that he knows everything and everybody. Damon always has plenty to say about what is wrong with the black family, and suggestions for how to fix it. G is a young, quiet guy whose main preoccupation was the fine sistas passing by outside the shop. In the months spent at Truth and Soul, the shop was visited by black community leaders, policemen, working guys, and wealthy men, by gay men and straight, by women and by school kids. In those months they talked about a wide range of topics. There were discussions of the relationships between black men and women. They talked about white power structures and the relationship of African Americans to the state and to capitalism. They critiqued black leaders, discussed the political power of the black church, argued about reparations, and cheered on African American Olympic athletes.

I would sit for hours watching whatever sports, music videos, or talk shows that were playing on the little TV near the old-fashioned 7-Up machine. Usually I sat in the chairs by the door, with my back against the concrete wall. Dozens of framed photos of black celebrities, athletes, politicians signed to Hajj were hanging over my head. There are photos of Hajj with Martin Luther King, Jr., Julian Bond, and Jerome Bennet. There are photos of Jesse Jackson, Whitney Houston, Eddie Kendricks, Chicago rapper Common, and Blues artist Bobby Blue Bland. From this seat, I faced the three turquoise vinyl barber chairs and the wood paneled wall with more photos and long, flat mirrors. A barber's pole is painted on the floor-to-ceiling plate-glass window in the front of the shop and, in block letters, TRUTH AND SOUL: BLACK STARS. Over the front door is a painted red, black, and green flag with a black man bursting forth from the center of Africa, arms raised in triumph. The shop is on the end of a row of storefronts, next to a parking lot.

I spent the summer in the chair, watching the guys come and go, listening to them talk. Truth and Soul has no official closing time; they just keep going until they are done. So I would usually hang out in the shop from early afternoon until eight or so in the evening, taking a break to catch a bite at the vegetarian, soul food restaurant down the block, and to record my notes from the afternoon into a tape recorder or on a mini note pad. I never taped or took notes while sitting in the shop. Whenever I took a run for beer or to pick up some food, I would record everything I had heard. The barbers knew that I was doing work to learn what goes on in black barbershops, but many of the customers just assumed I was hanging out.

There is more to tell from those summer months than a single chapter or even a single book can accommodate. There was an energy and intensity to many of the exchanges that was palpable. But there was very little order. Unlike conversation in the black church, structured by the tradition of call and response, or the black college, ordered by the academic hierarchy, the barbershop is unruly. Guys shout over each other to make points. Conversations start in one place, circle around, double back, and end abruptly. My notes reflected the rambling nature of the interactions, and there is a real danger that imposing order on the conversations inauthenticates them. To really feel the shop, to experience it, as I did, it might be better to allow the stories to unfold just as they did during the summer: with missing places, cracks, and fallacies. But we are most concerned with demonstrating that, even within this seeming chaos there are discernable themes that reflect the work of ideology building. These themes emerge in many surprising ways throughout the course of the summer.

From the first chapter, this text has maintained that African American political ideology serves four interconnected functions:

1. Ideology helps individuals determine what it means to be black in the American political system.

2. Ideology helps individuals identify the relative political significance of race compared to other personal characteristics.

3. Ideology helps individuals determine the extent to which blacks should "solve their own problems" or look to the system for assistance.

4. Ideology helps black individuals determine the required degree of tactical separation from whites necessary for successful advancement of group interests.

Truth and Soul. *Credit*: Bridgett R. McCullough

Hajj posing in front of his shop, Truth and Soul.
Credit: Bridgett R. McCullough

Damon (foreground), Sherman (seated), and Hajj.
Credit: Bridgett R. McCullough

These four thematic functions shape the structure of our narrative of Truth and Soul. For each of the four aspects, we draw on representative conversations and interactions that implicitly and explicitly address the central dilemmas of political ideology. While it is impossible to use ethnographic evidence of this kind to prove that the hypothesized mechanisms between everyday talk and political thought are operating, it is possible to suggest the richness and complexity with which these issues emerge in the daily conversations of ordinary people.

ON THE MEANING OF BLACKNESS IN AMERICA

Since the barbershop is one of the few places where African-American men gather and do not feel threatened as black men, they communicate openly on social and political issues.
—Melvin Murphy, 1998

As the men of Truth and Soul talked with each other over the course of the summer, they regularly addressed the dilemma of being black in America. Their definitions of blackness, of black people, and of the position of black people in U.S. society were often revealed in surprising conversations. The jokes they told, their analysis of sporting events, and the spin they put on current events all reflected the multiple, complex meanings of black racial identity.

Sometimes the message about American blackness was an affirmation of African Americans as especially resilient. These affirmations reflected a belief that the unique, historical struggles of black people have created in them a stronger character than other groups. The conversation around a Friday afternoon tennis match is indicative of this position. The television in the shop was tuned to sports. In early September everyone gathered to watch Venus Williams play Martina Hingis. Hingis was stickin' it to Venus in their match that day. She was up 5–3 in the last set and one game away from victory. Hajj was cutting Michael's hair.

From the chair Michael announced, "No way she can come back, this match is over!"

Hajj had a different take on Venus's chances. "Man, don't worry, she knows what pressure is! When Ali fought Foreman, he told the media he would dance all over George. Well when he got in the fight, he stood still, against the ropes, with his guards up to tire him out. Everyone thought Ali was gonna lose because Foreman was whippin' him. But Ali said, 'Don't worry, I know what I'm doin.' See, Ali's a champion. He didn't get there doing nothing. Just like Venus, she's a champion. She knows how to handle pressure. Plus, she knows how to handle pressure more than those other girls, 'cause she's black. Being black, livin' in Compton, and achieving the status she has, is pressure enough. I ain't worried about her, she'll win."

"Man, what are the odds that she can come back. No way. No way," challenged Michael.

Hajj's customer was pragmatic: the odds were certainly against Venus as she had to win four straight games to move on to the championship match. But for Hajj, this was not just a case of athletic prowess or gaming odds, this match was a question of racial endurance. Hajj stood by his "faith in the race" approach and maintained Venus's ability to win. Venus indeed fought her way back and won. Hajj, of course gave the shop a serious "I told you so" coda once the match was concluded.

Hajj racialized Venus's victory. He was not just making an argument about superior athletic ability on her part, he was making a claim that the struggles she faces as an African American make her especially well suited to addressing the challenges of competition. He draws on the narrative of Ali, not just because it is an important moment in sports history, but because Ali marks a particular place of racial pride and challenge to racial subordination.[11] The disagreement between Hajj and Michael is not just about who better understands the odds of victory in athletic competition, it is about who better understands the mettle of black people, who believes in the ability to triumph, who has access to the historical narrative that makes Venus's victory a surety even in the face of long-shot odds. By claiming the position of *race man,* Hajj assures that Venus's victory will not stand as a marker of her personal athletic ability but will be a testament to the inevitable triumph of the race.

There was no single, hegemonic view of black people expressed by everyone in the shop. The portrayal of black folks depended largely on who was talking. One young brother, Samej, spent a hot August Friday arguing that the black man was the original man and all other races descend from the black man. Although an older cat named Ed was a major critic of this view, Samej stuck to his guns and answered all of Ed's challenges with an adamant assertion of black superiority. Over the course of the summer, no one else made such a highly essentialist claim to black superiority. Hajj's view of Venus's victory is contextual. She can beat Hingis because she is better acquainted with struggle. For Samej, African American superiority derives from a biological fact of being the origin of all human life.

Sometimes the language about race was more complex. On a Friday afternoon in early September the traffic was slow. There were only five or six of us hanging around the shop, so Hajj decided to tell us all a joke.

A bunch of people were on a plane and the plane was going down because of too much weight. After tossing off the baggage, the flight attendant said some of the passengers will have to volunteer to jump off the plane to save the lives of others. After no one volunteered, the flight attendant said, "Without being discriminatory, I'm going to call the name of your culture or race in alphabetical order, and I just ask that your group get off the plane to save the lives of others on the plane, and you will surely be blessed." She began, "Afro-American." No one got up. She said, "Alright, black people." Again, no one got up. She then said, "Well, Colored people." Still no one got up. A little girl turned to her mother and said, "Mommy, hasn't she called us already." The mom looked at her daughter and proclaimed, "Baby, today we're niggas!"

All the guys in the shop cracked up.

Although this seems to be little more than a bad racial joke, Hajj's story highlights several aspects of his racial philosophy. First, the joke illustrates the many different names that black people have been called and have called themselves in America. Self-naming is an important element in Hajj's own racial philosophy. Born Tommy Williams, Hajj changed his name, believing that Tommy was a slave name that obscured his true heritage. Hajj is particularly critical of African Americans who claim to be progressive and still "hold on to the slave name."[12] For Hajj, what a man calls himself has deep meaning for how he sees himself. Hajj's joke plays on the almost dizzying array of labels that have been ascribed to African Americans, and in doing so it reveals the absurdity of having no stable name by which to call oneself.

His story also reflects the black cultural trope of the trickster. In his joke the black mother turns the derogatory language "nigger" to her own use. Like Brer Rabbit, who begs not to be thrown back into the briar patch, when that is precisely where he wants to be, this mother appropriates the language of "nigger" to save herself and her child.[13] Levine argues for the centrality of the trickster figure in African American culture and consciousness. "Antebellum slaves manifested a central feature of their consciousness graphically and dramatically though the medium of the trickster tales featuring the victories of weak things over the strong" (1977, 83). These trickster stories of black slaves were much more than whimsical tales of talking animals or magical occurrence. They were "a means by which psyhic relief from arbitrary authority could be secured, symbolic assaults upon the powerful could be wage, and important lessons about authority relationships could be imparted" (105–6). Hajj's joke serves these same purposes. The mother and daughter seem to be caught in an impossible position. The flight attendant is calling them over and over again using different labels. But the mother is smarter, craftier, and the joke suggests that she can outwit the danger of this arbitrary authority and come through safely on the other side. The joke uses the familiar trickster to suggest that African Americans do have a way of resisting racist power.

While the trickster narrative suggests a powerful position for African Americans, Hajj's joke also reflects the tenuous position of blacks in white America. The flight attendant is clearly trying to get the black people off the plane. Using whatever name she can think of, the idea is clear, let's sacrifice black lives in order to save the more valuable people on the plane. Unspoken in the joke is the reality that, even as "niggers," the mother and daughter are alphabetically prior to whites. White comes so late in the alphabet they are the only safe cultural group on the flight. Nearly everyone else (for example, Hispanics, Latinos) will be sacrificed before whites are called. While the mother and daughter appear to be tricksters, they still occupy dangerous terrain. There is a sense that black folks have some power—they have outsmarted the attempt to throw them off the plane—but it is a fleeting kind of power and one that does not make them safe in the long run.

At times, Hajj more explicitly articulated the precarious position of blacks in America. During the months leading up to the 2000 presidential election, the men often mentioned the tight race between Al Gore and George W. Bush. One afternoon Damon bet his customer Maury $50 that Al Gore would win the election.

Maury took the bet, arguing, "This country is still very racist and very Anglo. They ain't gonna let Gore win because of Lieberman."

Damon shot back, "You can't underestimate the economic and political power of the tight-knit Jewish community."

Just as this exchange was about to heat up, Hajj interjected, "You better hope Gore wins. Everybody knows that if Bush wins, we going back to slavery."

Hajj's pronouncement went unchallenged. It was as if someone had just popped a balloon. No one responded. No one even continued to talk about the election. Hajj had tapped into a deep fear of racial vulnerability under a Republican administration. Hajj's comment suggested that, like the mother and daughter on the plane, blacks lack security within the American state. In both the brief exchange of humor and the election bet, there are layers of understanding about race, blackness, and U.S. society.

One of the most heated conversations about the nature of black people and their position in American society went down on an August evening. Hajj wanted to make the point that black people pose a threat to white power. He evidenced the fact that the prison population is majority black because "they fear you." He claimed there is no other group of people more likely to constitute a threat to the preferred social order of American racial hierarchy. "We [African Americans] are a threat to the status quo."

Sherman and one of the regulars, Fred, were against this view. They argued that blacks are not a threat. Instead they claimed that whites didn't spend much time or energy thinking about blacks. Sherman argued, "Do you think white folk are thinking about yo' dumb ass. You think they care what you do?"

Fred echoed Sherman, "Man, these brothas are standin' on the corner all day. They ain't no threat." Fred and Sherman argued that blacks posed no real danger to the social and political power of whites.

As Sherman and Fred argued with Hajj, their voices got louder and louder. Then Fred asserted, "These brothas on the corner are dumb."

That really got Hajj heated. Screaming at the top of his lungs, Hajj yelled, "Now, how you gonna say some shit like that? Weren't you on the corner when you were a kid? That's what I mean. So, how you gonna say that niggas that stand on the corner are dumb? I know some of the smartest brothas are on the corner. I was on the corner when I was young, you were on the corner too."

By this point Hajj was heated, loud, and argumentative, pointing his finger and interrupting Fred and Sherman. Hajj had turned off his listening and set his volume on high. Eventually Sherman chastised him, saying, "Man would you stop yellin! See a conversation is when everyone has an equal say!"

Like the airplane joke, this exchange operates on many levels. These black men use the barbershop not only as a place to get their hair cut, but also as a space where they can talk about important issues with one another. Sherman is angry when he feels that Hajj is trying to dominate the conversation. He asserts the right of reasonable men to disagree with one another and wants Hajj to respect the multiple viewpoints being offered. This exchange is one of many over the course of the summer that demonstrates that all black folks are not of a single mind. Public opinion researchers often mistake overwhelming Democratic partisanship among African Americans as an indication of ideological homogeneity. The summer of 2000 was a presidential election season. The men of Truth and Soul consistently reinforced the importance of voting, and of voting Democratic. But this electoral sameness did not translate into substantive agreement on many political issues. When Sherman tells Hajj to stop yelling and to engage in a real conversation, he is asserting the value of black men holding and exchanging contradictory viewpoints

Further, this exchange demonstrates that these conversations are imbued with both analysis of the state of American race relations and with strategic discussions of how to address inequality. Sherman, Hajj, and Fred are questioning power, the meaning of power, and the nature of American racial hierarchy. For Hajj, whites are actively threatened by the possibility of African American social and economic equality, and therefore they implement specific institutions, such as prisons, to keep black people from reaching their full potential. For Sherman, white power is maintained through institutionalized neglect. He does not perceive whites as actively working to subjugate blacks; instead, he sees them as privileged because they can afford to be unconcerned with people who are lower in the social hierarchy.

These men are not only arguing about the limits and possibilities within the boundaries of American racism; they are also questioning if African Americans have enough power to mount a serious challenge to the racial status quo. They are asking, who are the allies in this struggle? Do the brothers on the corner have anything to offer? For Fred, these men are powerless, disfranchised, ignorant. For Hajj, they represent untapped potential. Hajj sees the corner men as smart but misguided. He uses his own "up from the corner" narrative to express his belief that these men represent potential allies in the fight for racial equality.

Several ideological lessons are embedded in the shop talk about race. The men of Truth and Soul unanimously agree that race matters. Blackness is a powerful indicator of an individual's social and political position. Racial inequality makes black people more vulnerable to either the neglect or the malice of powerful whites. These men recognize the resources that African Americans have for resisting oppression. Racial struggle makes Venus more competitive, and it makes the mother on the plane more cunning. For Hajj, there are untapped resources of black intellect waiting on the street corners. While the men of Truth and Soul shared no single vision of blackness their conversations did reflect a black common sense that led them to agree that race remains a central concern in the lives of black people. They did not always agree on the ways that race articulates itself in the lives of individuals and communities, but they found common ground in elevating race as the single most important characteristic of individuals. They made broad generalizations about the nature of black people and the nature of white people. Their stories, jokes, and conversations usually assumed an adversarial, or at least distant, relationship between the races. Their conversations further revealed that these men tended to diminish the importance gender, class, sexual orientation, and other cross cutting identities in their understandings of black people and black struggle.

THE RELATIVE IMPORTANCE OF RACE COMPARED TO OTHER CHARACTERISTICS: GENDER, CLASS, SEXUALITY

The Black barbershop . . . is an environment that can bolster egos and be supportive as well as a place where phony men can be destroyed or at least highly shamed, from participation in verbal contests and other contests of skill. It is a retreat, a haven, an escape from nagging wives and the cares of the world. It is a place where men can be men.
—Trudier Harris, 1979

One of the central assertions of this text is that African Americans are not a monolith. There are multiple, crosscutting identities within blackness. Gender, class, and sexuality are among the most important of these intraracial differences. A central function of political ideology is to understand the relative significance of these characteristics in African Americans' relationship to each other, other groups, and the state. The men of Truth and Soul often took up these questions in their conversations and in doing so generated answers to a central ideological dilemma.

On the Question of Black Women

Black women were a frequent topic of conversation among the Truth and Soul men. Much of what these men said about black women is peppered with criticism, misogyny, stereotypes, and a notion of black women as adversaries rather than partners in the racial struggle. As I walked into the shop one day in July, the television was tuned to the music videos on BET. The computer-animated character, Cita, was introducing videos. She is a neck-popping, eye-rolling animation who reinforces many negative stereotypes of black women. This cartoon character uses ebonics, wears short skirts, and is loud and annoying. As she was doing her thing, Damon and Sherman made clear that they wouldn't want to "come home to that woman." Randall agreed, saying, "I'd stay at the bar. I'd call home and see if she's there . . . if so, 'give me another, bartender.'" Although they disapproved of this negative characterization of black women, a similar picture of black women as overpowering, uncontrollable, and problematic emerged in many of the shop conversations.

During my first week at the shop, Damon offered to give me his analysis of the problems facing black America.

"Women these days don't know how to cook and the family structure ain't how it used to be. A big part of the reason that the family structure is messed up is because women don't cook anymore. There are no more family meals together and the family doesn't communicate as a family anymore. Instead, the women are out working and many times makin' more money than the man."

Sherman huffed, "I don't give a shit about that, I can cook!"

In these early weeks Damon was still checking me out, so he asked me what I thought. I responded, "My future wife doesn't have to cook all the time, sometimes I'll cook, sometimes she'll cook. I could give a shit if my wife makes more money than me, because I know I'm gonna be bringing in a nice income. It would be different if I was sitting on my ass while my wife was bringing in all the dough. She'll do her thing and I'll do mine and together we'll manage the family."

Jeff, a young brother in his mid-twenties, was having G cut his hair. Jeff responded to my comment by complaining, "Nowadays women think they know everything. They don't understand their roles. You gotta find a woman who knows a bit less than you and mold her."

I replied, "Mold her! I ain't got time to mold nobody. She better be able to stand on her own. I'm not lookin for a child, I'm lookin for a wife!"

Unwavering, he came back, "Why would you want someone who

knows the game better than you? You gotta be able to teach her some-thing, if you ain't got nothing to teach her, then it ain't gonna work."

Damon chimed in to reiterate his point by saying the male and female roles in the black family were ill defined.

But Sherman suggested, "Things have changed and you gotta learn to change with them."

To refute Sherman, Damon said, "Look at these Arab women and these Indian women. Go ask the Arab down the street what his wife does and he'll tell you she takes care of the home. Their family structure has managed to stay intact over the years. It's the black family that has fallen apart."

This conversation was indicative of many that occurred during the summer and captures many of the central themes surrounding the rela-tionships of black men and women. Damon is taking a position that provides for a very narrow role for women within the family and home. For Damon the root cause of continuing African American inequality is a black family pathology rooted in a dominating black woman. He ar-ticulates the concern that black women who hold tightly to notions of independence, and who are more concerned with their own wages than with preparing family meals are the source of moral breakdown and instability. Damon refuses to see changing family structures as a sign of progress and instead points to other cultures as a way of asserting that traditional gender roles can survive in contemporary society.[14]

Sherman and I argued that black men and the black community are best served by relationships where African American women are equal partners in finances, home care, and intimacy. Damon and Jeff were arguing that black women should put the needs of the race first. And they were defining the needs of the race in a narrow, patriarchal man-ner. Sherman and I defined the racial good more broadly and supported women's right to pursue personal ambitions historically denied them. Damon and Jeff's is a stance that Michele Wallace (1978) would have described as Black Macho. Frances Beale and other black women of SNCC's Black Women's Liberation Committee would recognize in Damon's argument language reminiscent of Stokely Carmichael's asser-tion that the position of women in the movement was prone.

Damon's position reflects a long tradition in both Nationalist and Integrationist thought. This tradition asserts that women should not press concerns about gender equality within the context of racial strug-gle in order to preserve a unified racial front, not distract from the critical issues facing the race, support black men in their struggle for manhood against emasculating white racism, and provide the necessary "backbone" for the movement by performing domestic tasks.[15] "Many believed that women should step back and take a supportive nonpolitical role in the Black struggle or strengthen the family and become breeders to provide an army for the revolution" (Anderson-Bricker 1999). Damon offers the same analysis of gender within the African American community. His views of black women and the family are not simply personal ideas, they are linked to an older activist discourse on black women's contributions to racial struggle.

Damon was not the only Truth and Soul man to take this view. The brothers in the shop often complained that black women did not support black men, and they frequently questioned whether women of other races would make better partners. A middle-aged regular named Ed felt that black women were too critical of black men.

"Black women only want a man who already has something, but white women will see the potential in you," he asserted, and then he asked me if I dated white women.

"No," I responded.

"Oh, you one of those righteous brothas."

"No, I just prefer black women."

"You'll find out," Ed insisted, "you ain't gonna find a black woman who is interested in the shit you doin'. After awhile, she gonna want you to get out there and work, forget that school shit."

I told him that the women I have dated have been very supportive of my educational pursuits.

Ed replied, "Well, you're the exception. That's rare, uncommon. White women, on the other hand, see the potential in their men and support them."

"So you only date white women?" I questioned.

"Yeah, I am divorced from a black woman. We have five kids. I'll tell you what, I'm gonna give you my business card and if your pride doesn't get in the way, call me if you need some advice."

When he offered the business card, I realized that Ed was not just shooting the breeze. He was attempting to influence my thinking on this matter. He was confident that my African American girlfriend would eventually turn on me and that I would find myself in need of his advice. His attempt to change my thinking is evidence of the ways that the shop operated as a discursive space interested in affecting the worldviews of those who participated in it. Although he was attempting to convince me of the virtues of interracial dating, Ed still referred to my dating exclusivity as "righteousness." His tone and word choice conveyed that by choosing to engage black women in intimate relationships, I attained a righteous stature. He thought I was foolish and would soon learn that black women were too much trouble, but he also indicated a certain respect for black intimacy.[16]

The opinion that black women are adversaries in the racial struggle is underscored by narrowly defined masculinity that emerged in the conversations. One of the most important, recurring themes in the everyday talk of Truth and Soul was the question of black manhood. The men in the shop often leveled critiques against African American women for attempting to overpower or control black men. Hajj suggested that black women and black preachers were in cahoots in supporting the white establishment. He argued that black women make black men go to church and make them put money in the basket. And this money, in turn, is deposited in white banks. And preachers use their congregation's money to obtain their own power and influence.

Hajj challenged a married customer, saying, "If she says, 'come on let's go to church', you goin. Men need to be heads of their households. They shouldn't let women tell them what to do."

Like Damon, Jeff, and Ed, Hajj holds a narrow view of black manhood. Primarily manhood is predicated on an individual man's ability to be an entirely autonomous unit, free from the responsibility of consulting anyone, and especially a woman, on the course of his actions. The ability to resist the influence of women and remain the sole decision maker in the home and family is the marker of selfhood, manhood, control, and worthiness. This is a deeply Conservative position, and one that sometimes created friction with other men in the shop who had a less rigid perspective.

One afternoon Gregg, one of Sherman's customers, commented that he had shared Hajj and Damon's views with his wife. He said with a grin, "Man, my wife said I can't come to the shop anymore. I told her what ya'll said, that I'm suppose to be wearin' the pants."

Hajj looked at Gregg like he was crazy and responded with disbelief, "Man, you told her that. You ain't suppose to take that home. That's suppose to stay here in the shop."

For all their bravado, it was pretty clear that the patriarchal and sexist worldviews the men expressed were supposed to remain within the shop. By talking with his wife, the customer went against the confidence of this black male public space. Much of the discourse in the barbershop becomes "barbershop talk," which "stays in the shop." Truth and Soul is a space where African American men work to assert their masculinity by gaining a respect of other men rooted in a specific gendered ideology. The barbers and customers inflate truths and realities in order to portray an image that is admirable and enviable. They say things like, "I wear the pants in the family and my woman does whatever I say." The other men are aware that this is more bravado than truth, but they go along with the stories because they provide similar stories of their own.

There are many things that this kind of boasting represents. On the one hand, it gives working-class men who lack many of the material trappings associated with successful "manhood" a way of establishing the legitimacy of their masculinity. By bragging of their ability to assert and maintain control over black women, these men declare that they are not just a race problem to be solved by others. They are agents of their own lives. But there is also something melancholy about this boasting. Hajj's reaction to Gregg — "Man why'd you take that home" — tells us that these brothers are not being entirely honest with themselves or each other. They are saying things to one another that don't hold up in the harsh light of scrutiny beyond the shop. They are asserting a veneer of strength and invincibility that is far from their daily realities. Because manhood is at stake, these men are unable to share the deeper vulnerabilities that surely touch their lives.

On the surface, most of the discussions about black women appear narrowly sexist. And they are. The strongest personalities in the shop consistently argued that black women need to be more subservient and less demanding. Although they were talking almost exclusively about the private sphere, they probably would have advocated a similar supportive role for black women in the public realm. In this way their views reflect a long and enduring belief that the establishment of patriarchy within black families will cure the ills of racial inequality. Like Martin King, Eldridge Cleaver, and Louis Farrakhan, many of the men of Truth and Soul sought to address the problems of African Americans by silencing the voices of black women.

But there were complexities in this position as well. Ed's reference to righteousness and Hajj's incredulity about taking the shop talk home suggest that these men may see their bravado as extending no further than the walls of the shop. Although they push, criticize, and crack on brothers who are failing to be men in their narrowly defined way, and while some of them date nonblack women hoping to find a more traditional gender dynamic, there is sometimes a reluctance to impose the barbershop manhood standards on real relationships. Also, there are dissenting voices in the shop — men who talk about how black women are allies and supporters of black men. These voices are not as loud and outrageous as the more sexist ones, but they are present.

Overall, the shop is a space that narrowly defines black manhood and is suspicious of black women. In influencing ideological development, it is a space that elevates race and attempts to hide, subjugate, or squelch the cross-cutting identities inside of blackness. This impulse is reinforced by notions of otherness imposed on gay black men within the space.

Boundaries of Sexual Identity

Eric was one of the regulars in the shop. It was clear from their words and actions that the barbers and many customers assume that Eric is gay, but Eric never came out to me. The barbers' and customers' reactions to Eric reveal the position of gay men in this black male public space and show the racial boundaries that the men of Truth and Soul drew. I was talking with Eric one day about his education plans when Stan Willis came in for a haircut. Willis is the attorney who represented a gay black man who was sexually abused by police on Chicago's Westside. Hajj had recently read an article about the case and announced to the other guys in the shop that Willis was "representing that gay guy." When Eric heard this, he turned his attention away from me and toward Willis. He asked Willis questions about the case and about its status in the courts. He also offered his own stories of witnessing police brutality.

The case Willis was working on is the kind of story that Hajj and the fellas normally would have been all over. It had all the elements they love: a wronged black man, legal drama, and police misconduct. But Eric was the only one engaging Willis. Hajj's statement that "he's representing that gay guy" speaks volumes. Normally Hajj would have referred to him as "the brother" or used his name. Referring to the victim as "that gay guy" implicitly diminished the relevance of the trial and its outcome for the other men in the shop. Eric's responsiveness to and interest in the story further exacerbated this. Damon, Hajj, Sherman, and G often ignore Eric and act annoyed by his mannerisms and voice. They tolerate his presence but do not engage with him when he brings up issues. Their body language usually reflects a lack of interest in having a true dialogue with him. Once, during one of Eric's long narratives about places he'd seen and plans for his future travel, one of them whispered to me, "He's a little fruity."[17]

Eric's position within the shop helps us to understand how these men viewed the relative significance of sexual orientation within blackness. Eric's presence complicates the black male solidarity of the barbershop. He is a regular at the shop, a frequent participant in conversations, but he is also marginalized. His identity is shrouded in suspicion and innuendo. I cannot be certain that Eric is gay. I am certain that the reactions of the barbers and customers to him is based on their belief that he is gay, but there was no confirmation of his sexual identity in the months I spent at the shop. If he is gay, then Eric is not in the same position as the other men in the shop. For him it remains a place where he is the other. The straight brothers can remove their masks when they walk through the door, but his remains in place. If he is not gay, then Eric is still being drawn outside the boundaries of blackness because his demeanor and speech are beyond the narrow definitions of masculinity constructed by the men of Truth and Soul. Either way, it is clear that his experience of the shop and the shop talk is marked by his assumed difference from the barbers and other customers.

Eric's experience of being silenced as an agenda setter within the shop reflects an assumption that the issues and concerns of homosexual black men are less relevant than those of straight men. Often, when Eric would initiate conversations, the men would turn away, ignore him, or patronize him for a short while only to move quickly to other topics. Without an ability to set the topic for conversations, Eric was left in a compromised position within Truth and Soul. His position is indicative of the broader failure of the African American community to recognize the specific concerns of gays and lesbians as legitimate items for the black agenda. This failure is documented most convincingly in Cohen's (1999) text on the failure of traditional black political organizations to respond to the AIDS crisis in the black community. By accepting the notion that HIV/AIDS was a gay issue, and therefore not a race issue, traditional sites of African American political organizing remained silent while the disease wreaked havoc in black communities. Churches and civil rights organizations silenced AIDS activists just as the men of Truth and Soul silence Eric.

Class Divisions

Truth and Soul is an essentialized space where blackness is narrowly defined and concerns of gender and sexual orientation are seen as potentially divisive agendas that should be subordinated to heterosexual, male-centered, racial goals. Interestingly, class almost never emerged as an issue. Although this was a space where wealthy men, working-class guys, and poor folks all entered, there was almost no discussion of class differences or dynamics.

Once, during a discussion on slavery and reparations, Hajj did mention that "blacks in the suburbs don't wanna talk about no black shit, they don't wanna talk about slavery." I perked up when I heard this because it was my first indication that Hajj might harbor some class antagonisms. But none of the other men took up his comment, and soon the conversation took a different turn. On another occasion, a regular named Jasper came walking into the shop with a kind of intensity that indicated he had a story to tell. His pants, sweatshirt, and work boots were stained with paint. He headed to a spot by Hajj's chair where he could have the attention of the entire shop. Jasper wanted to tell the story of how someone in power tried to get over on him and more importantly to share how he handled it.

"Man, let me tell you what happened. I almost got 'got.'" He continued, "I just came from a job, paintin' this church, right. Spent about five, six hours doin' this. So, come the end of the day, I'm looking to get paid. And the bossman, he says, 'Jasper the job ain't finished and I can't pay you right now. We got a couple doors to paint.'"

Damon chimed in and asked, "Did you know that before startin' the job?"

Jasper replied, "Naw, that wasn't a part of it."

Damon asked another question, "Could those doors had been painted tonight?"

Jasper said, "Naw, they're big doors. About three of em'." Jasper continued, "So, bossman goes, 'Can you come back on Monday?' So, I goes, 'Naw, I ain't got no money to get back Monday.' So, after telling him I couldn't come in on Monday 'cause I didn't have no money, he reached in his pocket and pulled out a stack of hundred dollar bills and peeled off a hundred for me. He always claimin' he broke. Can you believe that! Wanted me to wait until Monday to get paid, for work I already did. So, I told him I wasn't go'n come, 'cause I ain't have no money. He changed his tune real quick then."

Then Bobby asked what we had all been thinking, "He white?"

Jasper responded, "Naw, he's a brother. One of those *educated* brothers."

I held my breath, expecting that they would use this opportunity to talk about the class differences among African Americans. An "educated" brother attempted to cheat a working man out of his hard-earned pay. He had behaved in a way that made the rest of us assume he was a dishonest white man. In standing up to him and asserting his right to be paid, Jasper had resisted and prevailed against unfair labor practices, and he had done it against a middle-class black man. This turned out not to be a story of white exploitation of black labor, but of class divisions within the black community. But for Jasper his boss's race was almost irrelevant. He didn't start the story with a sense of moral outrage or racial indignation for having been treated this way by another black man. The guys listening to him did not probe further or offer particular criticisms of the boss. Jasper is a regular, and when he referred to his boss as an *educated* brother, he was speaking in an established context. Maybe these men have already established that middle-class blacks are not likely to behave with an appropriate sense of racial solidarity. Their lack of surprise at the boss's race may indicate a kind of unspoken class division.

The most explicit statement about racial desertion by the middle class came from Willie on a Friday afternoon in July. Willie was sitting near me in the chairs along the wall and fell into one of his thirty-minute monologues. The central theme of his talk was the ways that the middle class had abandoned African American communities during the process of integration.

"Before integration, you had black people living in the same neighborhood. You had Lou Rawls down the street, you had professional athletes on the next block, the businessmen and so forth. The kids had black people to look up to. Once integration came, then all the black folk who had money moved out."

Willie's narrative identifies monied African Americans as blameworthy for allowing integration to instigate divisive class relationships among African Americans. He points to the absence of a middle-class presence in urban neighborhoods as a problem of racial disloyalty. His statement, like Jasper's story, suggests that the men of Truth and Soul believe that middle-class African Americans should subordinate their economic interests for the greater good of the race. Willie's statements, like Jasper's story, did not evoke much further conversation in the shop. In their regular attempts to define the problems of and solutions for African Americans, the issue of class differences never became a central theme. This silence can be interpreted in different ways. Their silence may suggest their belief that class is an irrelevant characteristic, that black men face the same challenges and defeats no matter what their economic standing. This reading of their silence on class is consistent with their beliefs that gender and sexual orientation are relatively less important than race for African Americans. But their silence may also convey a lower set of expectations for wealthier African Americans, an assumption that working men represent the authentic black experience and that the educated brothers are less predictable because they are less authentic. Truth and Soul is not an exclusive domain of working-class men. Lawyers, teachers, and college students were as frequently present as day laborers. The men who were aware of my own doctoral studies were always supportive and interested in my work. The shifting class composition of the shop and the support for my own academic goals make the former a more compelling explanation. Class simply never emerged as an important analytic category for the men as they worked to confront racial inequality.

The shop talk regularly and strongly reinforced the primacy of race as a personal characteristic. Gender, sexual orientation, and class were all seen as identities with less legitimate claim to an individual's identity. The men of Truth and Soul maintain an essentialist, biological notion of race. When watching golfing events, they always claimed Tiger Woods

Hajj and longtime Truth and Soul customer. *Credit*: Bridgett R. McCullough

as one of their own, ignoring his own, more complicated racial self-identification. One evening when the guys were talking about Halle Berry, Gill suggested, "Halle Berry got her a brother. I thought she would go white, cause she's half white." But Hajj asserted, "You can't tell she's half white, she looks black. Those people who wanna say they half white, give 'em the KKK test and see if they can join." For Hajj, and the men in the shop, blackness is an absolute. It is an essential identity, and it has more claim than any other characteristic on the politics of individuals.

SELF-HELP OR GOVERNMENT ASSISTANCE

Talk about some hard times. That was the beginning of the Great Depression. Nobody had much money. But Uncle Jed kept going around to his customers cutting their hair, even though they couldn't pay him. His customers shared with him whatever they had — a hot meal, fresh eggs, vegetables from the garden. And when they were able to pay again, they did.
— *Uncle Jed's Barbershop*, a children's storybook

One of the important functions of African American ideology is how it addresses the extent to which blacks should make demands on the American political, legal, and economic system. At one end of this continuum is a belief that African Americans must be entirely self-sufficient, demanding no official recognition of or redress for any historical or contemporary inequalities stemming from racial discrimination. At the other end of the continuum is the attitude that African Americans have a morally and historically justified obligation to seek specific, race-based or race-targeted benefits from the American system. There is a bias in barbershops on this question. Most black-owned barbershops are sole proprietorships or partnerships. The black men who own them are the largest single category of entrepreneurs among African Americans. It is likely that these men will see economic self-help as essential to any strategy for addressing racial inequality. Margaret King Mitchell's (1993) award-winning children's book *Uncle Jed's Barbershop* tells the story of an African American girl, Sarah Jean, living in the South before World War II. Her great uncle Jedediah Johnson is the only black barber in the county. He has no shop but travels to his customers' homes. Uncle Jed dreams of owning his own shop and saves conscientiously, but he suffers setbacks when he has to pay for an emergency operation for Sarah Jean and later loses his savings when the banks fail during the Great Depression. But by faithfully serving his black customers, and by saving his money, he is finally able to realize the dream of opening his own shop on his seventy-ninth birthday. Along the way to his dream, Uncle Jed is able to help others in his family and community. Jed never turned to the government for relief, and because they could rely on him, neither did Sarah Jean's family (Mitchell 1993). His story, while fiction, reflects a common model of black entrepreneurship. Barbering as a single proprietor with low startup cost offers the realistic possibility of self-employment to black men who are frequently subjected to exploitative labor relations. We might expect to find that barbers are strongly supportive of a self-help strategy to addressing racial challenges. There is an element of this in the conversations of *Truth and Soul*, but there is also an insistence on the responsibilities of the government to address racial grievances.

Bill and Wes are in their fifties. One afternoon they were talking with Hajj about the failure of the black church to develop a coherent strategy for black economic development.

Bill argued, "The black churches in the Chicago metropolitan area deposit $1 million a week in *white-owned* banks."

"That's because black banks are nothing but glorified currency exchanges," offered Wes.

Hajj responded, "That may be true, but we have to support our own. No one else is going to look out for the best interests of blacks. The chamber of commerce around here doesn't really care about helping the businesses sustain the neighborhood. If they really cared, they would set up a fund to help businesses when they need it. They'll come ask you for your dues to be a member [of the chamber], but then that's it. And if something happens and you gotta move out, they are nowhere to be found. They are there when you move in, but not when you leave. They right there to greet the next one [business owner] when they move in and ask for that guy's dues money."

"I hear you, but man I hate it when I'm in line and the cashier is runnin' her mouth about her personal business," Wes countered. "When I am at Seaway I am in line forever, but the white banks have you in and out."[18]

"Yeah, that is just unprofessional. It is one thing to talk to customers and be nice, but all that personal business has no place when you are supposed to be working," Bill agreed.

Then Wes suggested that black banks are crooked. "And they are not really helping out black folks anyway. Seaway had a partnership with HUD. HUD gave them $800 million in home loans to be given to poor people to help buy houses. But Seaway didn't give out not one loan. The federal government had to get involved and told them to either distribute loans or hand over the money."

Bill, Wes, and Hajj are interrogating the notion of self-help as a racial uplift strategy. They begin by being angry with black churches for depositing black wealth in white banks. They are laying claim to the million dollars that African Americans contribute each week to their churches, and arguing that it should be put to use in the community, rather than being exported to white institutions. The conversation also reflects a deep suspicion of black institutions. Arguing that they are unprofessional and untrustworthy, Wes suggests that African American banks may not be a better vehicle of black economic development. In fact, Wes ends by arguing that the federal government is more interested than black banks in contributing to the growth of the neighborhood.

As is true of many barbershop conversations, the truth of these claims went entirely unchallenged. Do black churches really collect a million dollars a week in Chicago? Do all of them deposit with white banks?

Does Seaway actually have a partnership with HUD? Were they really guilty of failing to make low-income homeownership loans? The veracity of these claims is less important than the spirit of the conclusions the men draw on the basis of them. For Wes, community self-help, at least through black-owned banks, is not a panacea for the economic woes of African Americans.

Hajj's strategic vision included a blend of government responsibility and communal tactics. Hajj often talked about reparations. The details of his reparations claims were fuzzy, but he clearly believed that black people were owed a debt by the United States, and he sometimes suggested that reparation payments were already beginning.

"Quincy," Hajj asked me, "have you heard about the $5,000 they are paying blacks born in 1928 or before? If you have a relative that fits this criteria, then you just have to fill out a form and you'll get a check and it's for slavery."

"Naw man, this is a new one by me!" I responded "Who's paying the money?"

"I don't know, Mar told me about it." Turning from me, he called to a big guy in another chair. "Hey Mar, what's up with that money they giving out to black people for slavery?"

"Yeah, that's right, the Treasury Department is giving the $5,000 away. I got the form in the mail," Mar confirmed

I was honestly concerned that someone might be trying to scam these guys, so I said, "I've never heard of this and I'm kinda skeptical. Something like this would be big news. Reparations has been a national debate lately, and if this repayment were true, I think it would be all over the news. You should check it out before sending that form in, cause I'm sure you gotta provide your social security number and other personal stuff."

Mar looked concerned, "Yeah, cause why was I the only one that got the letter."

I said, "Yeah, you're right. Why didn't I get one?"

Hajj continued, "You know they calculated how much money each black person would get if we were paid reparations and it came out to be $5.63." I wanted to ask him who calculated this and how they arrived at the figure, but Hajj was on a roll. He went on, "Now, everybody was saying, 'what the hell I'm gonna do with $5.63, that'll barely get me a pack of cigarettes.' You see how people think. Now if all the black people in this neighborhood took their $5.63 and put it together, we could buy everything in this neighborhood. If every black person put their money together, we could buy half the world."

Others in the shop were less convinced about the ability and willingness of African Americans to pursue collective strategies. When Hajj talked of pooling the reparations money, Gill laughed, "The funny thing is, we won't do that."

Hajj argued, "Man, the Black Panther Party had breakfast programs and all that shit. Don't tell me we can't come together."

Gill responded, "I'm not saying we can't do it. We've done it in the past. But we *won't* do it."

Hajj went on, "In the sixties white folk didn't know what to do. You had SNCC, CORE, NAACP, Martin, Malcolm, Muhammad. They didn't know where to look. There is no reason we can't do the same thing now."

I don't think Hajj ever quite believed Mar's claim that he simply needed to request his $5,000 and a check would be cut. Hajj knows that I study black history, and by drawing me into the conversation he was checking Mar's story. But Hajj's vision for black empowerment welcomes the idea of reparations. Hajj sees potential in a miniscule five-dollar reparation. His strategy does not require that African Americans shun government assistance. In fact, he supports the notion that black people deserve financial remuneration from the government for the sins of slavery, Jim Crow, and contemporary racism. Once a young customer remarked, "You know they would pour tar on a black person and put feathers on him and torch him. Ain't that some shit?" Hajj's response was, "That's why we need reparations." Hajj does not believe the government will be generous. He expects meager payment for black suffering, but he also believes that African Americans can use collective strategies to make something small far more powerful. By pooling resources and developing collective strategies, Hajj conceives of a role for self-help even in the context of government involvement. Laying claim to a history of black organizing, Hajj argues that power for African Americans is derived from strong leaders, common goals, organizational capacity, and economic collectivity.

While the men debated the value of self-help strategies and the possibility of racial reparations, there was universal agreement on the importance of voting. Even faced with the less than ideal choice between Al Gore and George W. Bush, the men of Truth and Soul encouraged each other, and especially the younger men, to vote in November. Fred would often ask the younger guys how old they were and then ask them if they were registered to vote. One nineteen-year-old told Fred he was not registered and did not care much about the election.

Fred let him have it. "Don't you know that if Bush wins, all hell's gonna break loose. You ain't gonna be able to walk down the street. People gonna be getting executed left and right. *You better care.*"

Jointly the men of Truth and Soul strike a balance between advocating self-help and government-focused strategies. They see voting as a necessary counter to the potential racial evils perpetrated by government. Rather than arguing that blacks should avoid government involvement altogether, they encourage young men to become voters in order to protect their basic rights and freedoms. These men are not particularly optimistic about government's relationship with African Americans. They are suspicious that many in government wish them ill. Hajj, in particular, continues to see a critical role for racial self-determination. Hajj remains convinced that black people need to "get together" and to "pool resources" in order to address the goals of the race. He is never entirely clear on what these racial goals are, but he wholeheartedly believes that they are identifiable, common to most black people, and achievable through sacrifice and unity. It is a Nationalist vision of blackness that is reinforced through the barbershop talk. Through sharing their stories and "facts," the men generate narratives that emphasize common interests and communal strategies.

TACTICAL SEPARATION FROM WHITES

I was fifteen years old when I began to hate people. I hated the white men who killed Emmett Till and I hated the other whites who were responsible for the countless murders Mrs. Rice had told me about and those I vaguely remembered from childhood. But I also hated Negroes. I hated them for not standing up and doing something about the murders.
—Ann Moody, 1968

The survey data and experimental evidence of earlier chapters clearly demonstrate that attitudes toward whites are a critical factor in African American ideology. Black ideology is not solely concerned with understanding white people, but African Americans do advocate differing strategies for dealing with whites, and those strategies are among the central elements that contribute to ideological diversity. The men of Truth and Soul rarely spoke about whites in particular. In most conversations, whites were placed in the context of their dynamic and complicated relationships with blacks, and the idea that whites are adversarial to black interests was largely assumed. In only a few cases did whites and whiteness emerge as a central topic of conversations. The men of Truth and Soul generally saw whites as outsiders and labeled them not only as different from African Americans, but also as hostile to black interests. At their most virulent, the men sometimes theorized about how to punish, circumvent, or even eradicate white men; but most often, their strategies for dealing with racism were focused on changing the behavior of blacks rather than seeking to change whites.

The men of Truth and Soul distinguished between white men and white women in their discussion of the race. Several of the most vocal participants in shop discussions advocated interracial dating as an appropriate response for dealing with troublesome black women. There were men in the shop staunchly opposed to dating white women, but there were many who expressed anger and resentment toward white men but still perceived white women as acceptable romantic partners. Fred offered the most vivid example of this position. I had been in the shop for several months when Fred pronounced a theory on how to eradicate whites.

"Now, I know you gonna laugh, but hear me out. The best way to wipe out the white race is through their women. If every black man impregnated every white woman, three, four generations down the line, the race would get darker and darker. You see, instead of attacking them with guns, we can get 'em with our dicks, nonviolence. There is nothing white men could do about it."

Fred's "nonviolent" racial strategy is startling. He offers a deeply essentialized notion of race as biological. By his estimation, miscegenation offers a panacea for racism because it turns white people into black people by mixing their genetic material. He fails to account for any historical, cultural, or social meaning for blackness and instead equates race and skin color. Further, his solution casts white men as the enemy, provides no role for black women, and makes white women a passive ally in the struggle for black racial interests. Fred's suggestion seems outrageous, but it was presented with sincerity. And while the specifics of this approach were never articulated by any of the other men, the general stance that white men and black women are adversarial to black male interests was expressed by many guys throughout the summer, as was the notion that race is a biological truth rather than a social construction. A clear example of the latter was Kevin's discussion of a classroom writing assignment.

Kevin is a college student. He is light skinned with reddish hair that he wears braided in a zig-zag design. One afternoon he told us about an assignment he had to do for his creative writing class.

"Hey Hajj, check out this question we had for our creative writing class. If you died and went to Heaven, when you got there God said that it really wasn't your time to go. But He also said the only way He would send you back was in white skin. You could still have your same personality, you would still be yourself, but you would just be in white skin. Would you go back?"

But before Hajj could answer, Kevin responded to his own hypothetical question. "If I could still be who I am, man I'd come back in a hurry. I sure don't wanna die!"

The shop exploded in laughter.

Fred's biological notion of race is mirrored in Kevin's question and response. He does not question the assumption that one could "still be yourself" in white skin. This is a stunning blindness. Kevin is clear that he would rather be white than be dead. But his willingness to accept whiteness as a precondition for reincarnation rests on the assumption that he can maintain his personality and selfhood beneath the white skin. Fred believes that brown skin can eradicate whiteness. Kevin believes that one can become white skinned without losing the personality developed over a lifetime lived black. On the surface the claims may seem contradictory, but both are rooted in a notion of blackness and whiteness as biological, oppositional forces.

For the men of Truth and Soul, whites, particularly white men, create obstacles that black Americans have to overcome. But when the guys talked about white racism and white institutions as problems facing black America, they often cited specific black pathologies as contributing to racial inequality. Although deeply critical of whites and keenly aware of contemporary racism, they were rarely willing to blame whites exclusively for the problems facing African Americans. An important example of this evenhandedness emerges in the way that some of the men talked about the police. Public opinion research on attitudes toward various American social and political institutions has demonstrated a large and persistent gap between whites and blacks on levels of trust in the police. Significant portions of African Americans perceive police as little more than a racist gang, inciting violence in, rather than serving and protecting, black communities. It is imprecise to equate beliefs about the police with beliefs about whites generally, but it is not naïve to draw some inferences about attitudes toward whites from expressed attitudes about police. Even within the context of the deeply strained historical and contemporary relationship between Chicago police and Chicago's black residents, the men resisted blanket condemnation of police actions.

Jasheed, a brash nineteen-year-old, was in the shop on a Thursday evening complaining to Damon and Fred of being harassed by the police. "Man, you should see how many tickets I've gotten in the past few months. The police just fucks with black men."

So Fred asked him, "Did you have the seat leaning way back and the music loud as hell?"

"Yeah," the kid answered.

"Well there." Fred went on, " I don't allow my son to drive his truck like that; he is just asking for trouble."[19]

By questioning Jasheed about his behavior, Fred implies that police racism may not be the only cause of the excessive ticketing. He is turning the blame away from the actions of hostile whites and focusing on the issue of black behavior. Fred implicates Jasheed's behavior rather than police bias in his narrative. The discourse on the police was further balanced by the presence of Gene, an African American police officer who is a regular customer. One evening he came in after having not been in the shop for a long time. Everyone spoke to him, and Hajj asked him where he'd been.

"I've been on the low end."[20] The officer went on, "Man, they need me down there. When I stop them, I usually talk to them. They look at me like I'm crazy. They say, 'You new, you ain't from 'round here.' They're shocked 'cause I ain't throwin' them against the wall. They say, 'the other cops usually kickin' our ass, you talk to us.' They don't get that too much. Ain't nobody talkin' to them about God or responsibility or anything."

Gene was a welcomed member of Truth and Soul. He was not in the shop as frequently as many other regulars, but he was an identifiable member of the community, and his status as a police officer did not alienate him from this black public space. But Gene's discussion of his policing involves a racialized perspective. When Gene speaks of being needed on the low end, he is referring to the need for a black police presence. He implies that white officers do little more than harass the African American residents, but as a black man, he is concerned with the welfare of the young men he is policing. The white officers kick their ass, but he talks with them. Importantly, Gene talks with these young brothers about God and responsibility, presumably the same solutions that Fred was offering Jasheed as the answer to his constant run-ins with the police. This does not mean that the men of Truth and Soul were unconcerned with white racism, racial profiling, or police brutality, but it does mean that they also placed an onus of responsibility on black men for addressing these problems by changing their own actions. Fred believes that Jasheed should sit up straighter in the car, and Gene believes that if the people he is policing would be more responsible, then each would have fewer negative encounters with white police. This insistence on a role for black pathology in the perpetration of racist action mediates the generally negative attitudes toward white men expressed at Truth and Soul.

More than any particular conversation or set of interactions, the men's attitude toward whites was illustrated in an oft-repeated action that both Sherman and Hajj practice. Often, when a white peddler was on the street heading toward the shop to sell his wares, either Sherman or Hajj would stand up, close the shop door, and lock it. Often the white man would stand at the door, yelling through the window, "Can I come in and just show you guys a few things." But the men in the shop would simply ignore him until he went away. Hajj once remarked on this practice.

"Look, I know that if a brother was going to sell something in a white store, the owner would just say, 'Get your shuffling black ass outta here.' I got no reason to treat *them* any different. I can't go in no white store and sell shit, so why should I let them in here to sell stuff."

Hajj's practice of locking white men out of the shop is a powerful statement about his attitude toward whites and an assertion of the nature of Truth and Soul. We began this chapter with a claim that barbershops function as essentialized racial spaces because blackness is both a necessary and sufficient condition for membership. Truth and Soul is a carefully policed space. Old and young, workers and lawyers, married and single, boisterous and reserved, conservative and progressive black men are all welcome at Truth and Soul. Even black women accompanied their partners or children to the shop, but Hajj and Sherman physically bar white salesmen. In the estimation of these men, whites may not be responsible for all the woes of the black community. It may be acceptable for brothers to date white women. But it is not acceptable for white men to enter Truth and Soul. This shop is a protected racial space; it is solely for the use of black men who are using it as a safe space where they can develop answers to important social and political questions without interference or observation by whites. By locking the door, Hajj and Sherman assert the importance of protecting their space.[21]

LESSONS OF TRUTH AND SOUL

Truth and Soul is the end of the empirical journey into the development of black political ideology through processes of everyday talk. This study, more than any other, posed a serious challenge to the ethics of this research. The respondents in both the survey and experimental research are protected by anonymity. The men and women of Orange Grove are concealed by pseudonyms, and, because they were interviewed, they could choose to reveal only what they wanted to be told to others. But the men of Truth and Soul granted us a more intimate access. Although the customers are protected by changed names, they have allowed a glimpse into their everyday talk that few people could ever gain access to, and we are deeply committed to presenting these men as honestly and fairly as we can.[22]

Presenting honest and accurate ethnographic narrative is more complex than simply accurately quoting and citing. It requires a self-consciousness about the processes through which the evidence was collected and the ways that we affected the space we were studying. Our first attempt at ethnographic study of a black barbershop failed. Quincy began his first study at Smitty's. Smitty's had all the attributes that led us to believe it would be a productive space to study black talk. It is an established barbershop on the city's Southside. It has a backroom that operates as a gathering place for a group of regulars who come to play cards. When we first identified Smitty's as a possible site for study, we were certain that these daily gatherings in the backroom would give rise to the kinds of conversations we were interested in studying. After several months in the shop it became clear that these conversations were not a part of the ethos of Smitty's. The men who gathered in the backroom talked to each other. But as they played cards, they mostly talked about cards. Not even with our broadest definitions could we uncover a politics of everyday talk in this space.

This experience did not disprove the theory of everyday talk, but it did add an important dimension to the understanding of how everyday black talk operates. Smitty's had all the features that would seem to contribute to political discussion, but it did not function as a meaningful discourse space because it did not have a center. Truth and Soul works as a political space for the same reasons Orange Grove Missionary Baptist Church works. Hajj, like Reverend Kenney, is a political entrepreneur, not in the narrow, self-interested sense of using the customers or congregants to advance their own interests, but in the sense that these men take racial, social, and political questions seriously and use the space over which they have influence to encourage meaningful discourse. The experience at Smitty's led us to believe that in the absence of this kind of entrepreneurship, the relevance of public spaces for ideological development remains latent.

Truth and Soul not only taught us about where everyday talk is likely to occur, it also taught us something about different elements of everyday black talk. Broadly, there were three kinds of conversations that occurred at Truth and Soul during the study: (1) common talk, which consisted mostly of casual interactions between the men, such as when two people who had not seen each other for a while spent time catching up with one another; (2) conjured conversations, which were a direct artifact of the research presence in the shop (there were a handful of conversations or topics that were conjured by Hajj or Damon to create some "good information" for the study; we are confident that these conversations were a small percentage of the overall talk we observed and were largely restricted to the early weeks before Quincy became a regular feature of the shop); and (3) authentic everyday talk, which are conversations that would have occurred between the men regardless of the presence of an outsider, and which contained politically or socially relevant features. This type of talk made up a very large portion of the conversations at Truth and Soul, but a far more miniscule aspect of talk in Smitty's. The relative balance between these three kinds of talk in any given public space is dictated by the physical features and personalities that are found in the space.

In Truth and Soul, authentic everyday talk has real political meaning. Kelley writes that "the political history of oppressed people cannot be understood without reference to infrapolitics, for these daily acts have a cumulative effect on power relations" (1994, 8). Kelley defines politics not by how the black working class participates in politics, but by why they participate and their motivations and subsequent strategies. Truth and Soul is a black public space where black men, through everyday discourse, shape and reshape their political attitudes and worldviews. Everyday talk is critical in their claim to respectability and manhood. Collective discourse is how they teach and learn. In this process of learning, those engaging in this barbershop discourse come to understand their identity and how they are situated in the complex world around them. Through everyday talk, black men at Truth and Soul are able to use racial and political meaning and develop ideology in collective discourse. They gain respectability through their "truths" as expressed through lived experiences. The space is instrumental in the daily upkeep of their "soul," which becomes made and remade in their experiences at the shop.

It is not a one-way or unitary learning, but a challenged space. Hajj is a strong personality. He often instigates conversations and sets the agenda for the dialogue, but he is consistently challenged by other men in the shop. Barbershops are safe racial spaces, but they are ideologically contested terrain. Black political ideologies allow African Americans to understand persistent social and economic inequality, to identify the significance of race in that inequality, to determine the role of whites in perpetuating or eliminating that inequality, and to devise strategies for overcoming that inequality. As social narratives, black political ideologies justify themselves as methods of addressing racial inequality in America. In these barbershop conversations, Hajj and his customers are constructing a social narrative about black equality developing strategies for achieving racial goals.

About 7:00 on a mid-September evening, the shop was winding down after a long and intense day. Chris, a guy in his mid-twenties, and Joe, a guy in his mid-fifties, were sitting around talking about jobs. Chris had been in the shop a number of times to get his hair cut. He is married with two small children and works on the stock exchange. Joe is a manual laborer and had only been in the shop twice during my time there. I was sitting in Hajj's chair, while Hajj was sitting in the waiting chairs closest to me. The two guys were sitting at the other end of the row, near the television As they talked, Hajj looked up at me and said, "Man, it's late. I'm all talked out. I'm tired of talkin shit, I ain't gettin in' this." He would glance over at the two gentlemen, then at me, slouching in the chair with his face resting on his hand. They talked on.

CHAPTER SIX

Speaking to, Speaking for, Speaking with: Black Ideological Elites

Ideology designates a rich "system of representations," worked up in specific material practices, which helps form individuals into social subjects. . . . It is not a set of narrowly "political" ideas but a fundamental framework of assumptions that defines the parameters of the real and the self.
—James Kavanagh, 1990

LIKE LANE'S *Political Ideology*, this book is about the political attitudes of the common person. It is not primarily a history of black political ideologies, nor an exploration of elite discourse. It is about how men and women use their everyday lives to inform their politics. But linking the ideas and dialogue of ordinary folks to the discourse of public figures is a useful way to illuminate the politics of everyday talk. This linkage is the task of this chapter. It examines the contours of the four ideologies by providing examples of black public figures in the late twentieth century who can be classified in each ideological tradition. Specifically this chapter looks at bell hooks and the black Feminist criticism of the 1995 Million Man March; Colin Powell and the 1996 presidential race; Kweisi Mfume and the battle to integrate network television; and Tom Joyner and the fight to save Tavis Smiley. These four examples offer a foundation for thinking about the complexities of black ideology. Categorizing each illuminates how contentious and permeable the ideological boundaries are and emphasizes the complexities of political discourse.

Mansbridge has rightly noted that within the field of political science, the label "political" has a certain legitimating power for objects of study (Mansbridge 1999). To the extent that this book claims that politics can be found in the daily interactions of ordinary African Americans, it elevates this talk as a field of serious inquiry normally reserved for elite discourse. Traditionally political scientists have tried to prove or disprove the existence of mass ideologies based on how closely mass attitudes adhere to the patterns of elites (Converse 1964). This chapter "flips the script." Rather than justifying the politicalness of mass ideology by the standards of elites, it uses examples of real public figures to demonstrate the ways that the expectations and understandings of ordinary African Americans constrain the public ideological appeals of elites.

Black ideological elites perceive themselves as competitors in a marketplace of ideas, and they attempt to sell their ideological product to African American masses by making authenticity claims. Adherents to forms of Nationalism, Liberal Integrationism, Conservatism, and Feminism use specific elements of black political culture to argue that it is their ideology that best represents the truth of black thought and experience. These claims are made to legitimate a specific racial agenda on American social, political, and economic institutions. The empirical work of the book is centrally concerned with mapping everyday talk among black masses. But the study of political attitudes is crucially informed by the activities of political and ideological elites who frame debates, offer alternatives, and try to sell political projects to the masses. More importantly, patterns of black elite discourse reveal the ways that mass cultural expectations shape and constrain the appeals of ideologues.

AUTHENTICITY AND THE MARKETPLACE OF IDEAS

Black political culture is central to the project of African American political ideology. In their quest to connect with black masses, ideological elites have historically used messianic beliefs, defiance traditions, moralism, and appeals to the American promise. These four aspects of ideological narratives continue to structure the appeals of Nationalists, Liberal Integrationists, Conservatives, and Feminists. African American public figures are able to claim authentic racial leadership to the extent that they convincingly employ these cultural arguments.

Authenticity is a marketing strategy as these ideologies compete in a marketplace of ideas. Hoping to attract potential consumers, elites package their ideological products in the wrappings of black political culture. Understanding ideology in this way is a shift in the dominant view on the relationship between masses and elites. Social scientists have generally asserted that elites are the keepers of ideology and masses can choose only from the menu provided to them (Converse 1964, Zaller 1992). While I acknowledge the important role of political entrepreneurs interested in attracting ideological consumers, I am also interested in the question of who is buying and the ways that the common sense of ordinary African Americans shapes the rhetoric of black public figures.

The first chapter discussed black common sense as "ideology lived and articulated in everyday understanding of the world and one's place in it" (Lubiano 1998, 232). Black common sense is informed by a combination of personal, familial, academic, religious, and media experiences. When African American masses encounter ideological messages, these messages are mediated by black common sense. We can gain a better understanding of how elites are speaking to, for, and with black people when we understand the elements of black common sense to which they appeal.

Everyday black talk is the mechanism black masses use for discerning the authenticity of elite narratives. As ideologies are competing in the marketplace of ideas, their success is largely dependent on their ability to penetrate spaces of black talk. Elites' messages are successful if they can direct the dialogue of African American masses and incorporate their ideological views into common sense.

Messianic language, defiance, morality, and appeals to the American promise are all central elements of a distinct black politics. These cultural tropes connect African Americans across many barriers. African American academic, activist, and political elites attempt to claim authenticity by constructing narratives of black history that position their ideological claims at the center of the black experience. Using messianic claims, images of defiance, morality arguments, and appeals to the American promise, they enter a complicated dialogue. Black elites have the task of simultaneously speaking to, speaking for, and speaking with black masses. They are speaking to black people to when they attempt to win adherents and frame the solutions to the black dilemma. They are speaking for black people when they are under the gaze of white power structures that attempt to understand and predict "what the Negro wants" from the appeals of leaders. And they are speaking with black people in an intricate, reciprocal cultural reproduction of ideas.

ELEMENTS OF BLACK POLITICAL CULTURE

The *messianic tradition* is based on a belief in the redemptive power of suffering. The messianic role can be understood as an avenging angel come to set things right in an immoral world, or it can be constructed as a sacrificial lamb, offered to help the rest of the world repent of their sin. America as a whole has a messianic myth, believing itself to be a redeemer nation with a specific mission of uplift for the world. Within that context, black Americans often perceive themselves as having a specific role in helping America meet the moral duty to which it has been called. The inequities faced by African Americans constantly force the country into the difficult task of introspection. The injustice of slavery pricked the moral conscience of a nation whose founding documents assert the inherent equality of humankind. Jim Crow segregation highlighted the hypocrisy of America's battle for freedom and democracy abroad.

The messianic belief endows black political thought with the idea that African Americans have a special mission among God's people. Suffering, oppression, and inequality are given specific meaning. Endurance of those miseries is seen as an honorable duty (Moses 1982; Henry 1990). African Americans can, therefore, understand their collective suffering as part of God's plan for America's democratic mission in the world. Black messianic belief is not only about redemptive suffering; it is also about belief in deliverance from God that will come in the form of a messiah figure (Holden 1973).

One of the best modern examples of the black messianic belief that God will deliver black people by sending a savior is Ossie Davis's eulogy of Malcolm X:

> Did you know Brother Malcolm? Did you ever touch him, or have him smile at you? Did you ever really listen to him? Did he ever do a mean thing? Was he ever himself associated with violence or any public disturbance? For if you did you would know him. And if you know him you would know why we must honor him: Malcolm was our manhood, our living black manhood! This was his meaning to his people. And, in honoring him, we honor the best in ourselves. . . . And we will know him for what he was and is — a Prince — our own black shining Prince! — who didn't hesitate to die because he loved us so. (Malcom X 1965, 454)

Davis's words could very well be the words of any of Christ's disciples at Calvary. Davis asks if you have ever touched the hem of his garment and reminds listeners that Malcolm died because he loved us so. Davis is purposely drawing this analogy between Christ and the slain Muslim, not because he actually believed Malcolm to have been a savior, but because he knows that this story will resonate with an African American audience. It touches a deep cultural chord that is rooted in a hope for deliverance.

Also central to black political culture is a *tradition of defiance*. The tradition of defiance is manifest in African American cultural expressions of admiration for individuals who resist following the rules of the system. In particular, trickster stories and the figure of the "bad nigger" are examples of black cultural respect for the defiant figure that refuses to bow to white authority. Holden (1973) emphasizes that a spirit of defiant heroism is central to black understandings of the concepts of suffering and endurance. He points to David Walker's *Appeal*, the poetry of Claude McKay, and the hymns of James Weldon Johnson as examples of the latent spirit of defiant heroism apparent throughout black culture. He argues that it is this defiance that allows African Americans to retain a sense of selfhood (or specifically in Holden's argument a sense of *manhood*) in the face of constant subordination and dehumanization in the American system.

Scholars of black political culture have regularly noted the bad man as a recurring icon in African American culture. Levine marks the emergence of this tradition in the stories of Stagolee that first surfaced in 1895 in the Mississippi Delta. Stagolee was portrayed as a murderous bully, a bandit who remained arrogant even when captured and punished (Levine 1977). The black bad man has reemerged throughout black history. Nat Turner, Shaft, and Tupac Shakur have filled this role. The "bad nigger" is about the power of the powerless. Black bad men are cathartic because they represent a kind of direct resistance that is not realistically available to most African Americans. These bandits provide a vicarious means through which a community of dislocated, subordinated people can free themselves from the strictures of a repressive society.[1]

A third element of black political culture is a *moralistic approach to politics*. African American politics is imbued with a spiritually informed belief that people ought to do what is right. Black moralism asserts that political activity must be justified by something greater than self-interest. Leaders and individuals are expected to justify their action with appeals to the fundamental rightness of action, and this often takes the form of appeals to biblical scripture. African American political leaders of all ideological persuasions have claimed moral basis for their political beliefs and have attempted to win supporters by using the language of righteousness. Contemporary studies of black public opinion reveal the continuing strength of religiosity among African Americans and the continuing influence of religious beliefs on political attitudes. Arguing the morality of a strategy functions as a means to claim authenticity.

Morality has been central to shaping the secular culture of African Americans. "Religion is the heart of culture because it raises the core values of that culture to ultimate levels and legitimates them. . . . The core values of black culture like freedom, justice, equality, an African heritage, and racial parity at all levels of human intercourse are raised to ultimate levels and legitimated by the black sacred cosmos" (Lincoln and Mamiya 1990, 7). Moralism, often defined in the language of the sacred, functions in black political culture as a source of legitimacy for political claims. Religious justifications for political stances strike a chord with black audiences because religious morality is a central aspect of African American political culture.

Black political culture also has a tradition of justifying demands for racial advancement by *appeals to the American promise*. African Americans have consistently employed the language of founding documents and principles of the United States to frame the content of their dissent. There are several ways that African Americans have made appeals to the American promise. African Americans have used the Declaration of Independence and Constitution as means of drawing attention to the condition of blacks in America. In the fight against segregation, blacks claimed citizenship rights based on citizenship duties, particularly the payment of taxes and military duty, and at times have expressed a belief in the fairness of colorblind institutional processes.

Black Americans have also asserted their political interests by arguing that while blacks performed the duties of American citizens, they failed to receive the rights of American citizens. These arguments are made most forcefully pertaining to labor, taxation, and military duty. African Americans have claimed ownership of American wealth and capital because building the country was made possible by the uncompensated labor of black slaves.[2] African Americans have asserted their right to public services such as schools and welfare because black citizens have historically paid taxes while receiving inferior government services and protections (Kluger 1975). Military duty by African Americans has been another way that blacks have asserted their right to share in the American promise. In the first half of the twentieth century there was an upsurge in black activism in the wake of valiant black service in international wars (McPherson 1968; Chafe 1995). African American soldiers returning to second-class citizenship after having risked their lives in military duty for America served as a stark example of the black condition. African American service and causalities in the Vietnam War stoked the fires of the Black Power movement that regularly called attention to the hypocrisy of African Americans performing citizenship duties without receiving the rights and privileges of citizenship.

There are also aspects of the black appeal to the American promise that assert a faith in the fairness of certain processes of law, government, or the economy. Much of the 1960s' civil rights movement was centered on a faith in the power of the vote. If blacks could vote, it was reasoned, then they would have equal access to the halls of power and decision-making. The NAACP legal strategy for battling Jim Crow is grounded in an explicit belief that, through changing laws, citizens, leaders, and private enterprises would adhere to the rulings of U.S. courts. Economic uplift strategies convey a belief that the market is race-blind. The belief that these processes are free of racial prejudice is another variation of the black political cultural theme of appealing to the American promise.

The remainder of this chapter considers several contemporary African

American political figures. Telling a small part of the story of each of these African American ideological elites illustrates the centrality of black cultural tropes in making autheniticity claims in order to gain adherents among black masses.

FEMINISM: BELL HOOKS AND THE FEMINIST RESPONSE
TO THE 1995 MILLION MAN MARCH

In 1995 bell hooks published a treatise on American racism titled *Killing Rage*. In it she expressed concern that "the contemporary feminist movement has had little positive impact on black life in the United States. There has not been any mass-based effort to do education for critical consciousness in black communities so that black folks would engage the politics of feminism" (1995, 62). That same year, Nation of Islam leader Minister Louis Farrakhan called for a million black men to gather in Washington, D.C., for a day of atonement and reconciliation, for a Million Man March. This march, and the nation's fascination with it, offered an opportunity for Feminists to engage in precisely the kind of mass appeal that hooks suggested was lacking from Feminist ideology. The coincident timing of the publication of *Killing Rage* with the call for the march meant that hooks was on a book tour just as the nation was gaining interest in the march. Hooks's voice became an integral part of the Feminist response to Farrakhan's call.

The 1990s offered several distinct moments when black Feminism had an opportunity to make specific demands on African American mass ideological loyalty. In 1991 the Clarence Thomas Senate nomination hearings generated a public spectacle surrounding Anita Hill. Women's rights advocates publicly rushed to define Hill's experience of sexual harassment within feminist terms of gender exploitation. But it was Clarence Thomas who won the racial authenticity claim, when he decried the hearings as a high-tech lynching. His public approval ratings among African Americans shot up from 54 percent to nearly 80 percent immediately following the lynching plea (Crenshaw in Morrison 1992). Hill had no parallel, easily available, racial trope to place her experiences within the history of the degradation of black women's bodies.

In fact, the unwavering support of white feminists for Hill likely hampered black Feminists' ability to intervene effectively in the black talk around the hearings. Feminist historian Christine Stansell observed that white feminists were largely silent when Thomas used his Conservative, patriarchal rhetoric to batter his welfare-dependent sister. But "Anita Hill was, in contrast, instantly recognizable to us [white feminists] — as a subject with whom we might empathize" (Stansell in Morrison 1992,

263). This public adoption of Hill by white feminists along with Thomas's strategic invocation of racial tropes allowed him to cast Hill in the role of "black-woman-as-the-traitor-to-the-race" (Painter in Morrison 1992). While the unity of purpose among black and white feminists around the Thomas-Hill hearings was heartening for those concerned with women's equality, it compromised the ability of black Feminists to use authenticity images to make a claim on black mass ideology.[3]

Then, in early 1992, Mike Tyson was convicted of raping teenage beauty pageant contestant Desiree Washington. His denial of the charge, the subsequent trial, and the public discourse surrounding Washington's culpability for agreeing to accompany Tyson to the hotel room was another blow to mass Feminist discourse. Again, black Feminist voices did not seem to stand a chance against the powerful racial imagery of a black man facing the criminal justice system. As the O. J. Simpson trial several years later would reinforce, the history of legal bigotry played out in America's courts is a powerful cultural signal for African Americans. Tyson was convicted, but it did not play in black communities as a triumph of the courts rushing to the aid of a wronged black woman. Tyson, not Washington, was the sympathetic focus of everyday black talk. Feminists found it difficult to make convincing authenticity claims during both Thomas and Tyson.[4]

Hooks argues that these events focused the attention of the public on the reality of sexism as a problem in black life, but she argues that Feminists failed to use these opportunities to "actively share feminist thinking and practice with other black people . . . creating spaces within black life where feminism might gain consideration" (1995, 63). The 1995 Million Man March offered a welcomed opportunity for a public Feminist discourse. Farrakhan was not in a defensive position vis-à-vis white legal authority. He also was not a traditional black leader coming out of the civil rights movement vanguard. He was open to criticism on a number of cultural grounds within black America. For example, many black church leaders around the country opposed the march because Farrakhan is Muslim. And unlike with the Thomas-Hill hearings, black Feminists would not have to compete with white feminists for discursive space. White feminists did not engage in a critique of a black men's march, even if it reasserted patriarchal, heterosexist norms. African Americans were talking and arguing about the march. Farrakhan and the march were open to critique, and black Feminists were the ones most able to level it. It was a real opportunity for a black Feminist discourse to penetrate everyday black talk.

In the weeks leading up to the march and the months following it, black Feminist critiques came from several different sources. A group of notable black women (and some men), such as activist and author Angela Davis, then editor-in-chief of *Ms. Magazine* Marcia Gillespie, founder of the *Coalition of 100 Black Women* Jewell Jackson McCabe, and author and professor Paula Giddings, formed the African American Agenda 2000. In the last days before the march they called a news conference to release a public statement opposing the march. It read in part:

> No march, movement, or agenda that defines manhood in the narrowest terms and seeks to make women lesser partners in this quest for equality can be considered a positive step. Therefore, we cannot support this march. . . . Justice cannot be achieved with a march that excludes Black women's oppression. Justice cannot be served by countering a distorted racist view of Black manhood with a narrowly sexist and homophobic vision of men standing "a degree above women. (African American Agenda 2000)

Their public critique of the march in clearly Feminist terms seems an answer to hooks's criticism. Using language like equality and justice to frame their discussion, they draw on deeply held values within black political culture. They make clear that the establishment of patriarchy is not a liberation strategy and argue that while they agree with the "frustration and anger we all feel about the push to dismantle hard-fought civil rights laws," they staunchly oppose a sexist and exclusionary approach to racial inequality. These Feminists are appealing to black people. This was not a statement written solely to engage other academics and activists, it was a clear insertion into the everyday talk of black people making up their minds about whether they would support or attend the march. These Feminists were speaking to, for, and with black folks. Challenging the right of Farrakhan to ascend as the "new black leader," Feminists had to speak *for* all the black people excluded by the narrow Nationalism of the march. Concerned with the message of the march, they had to speak *to* black people about the dangers of a sexist political agenda. And concerned with developing alternate participatory strategies, they had to speak *with* black people about a Feminist vision of liberation.

Bell hooks's was an important voice in the public discussion surrounding the march. As a prolific, popular, and widely accessible Feminist scholar, hooks was in a powerful position to influence black public opinion about the march.[5] Like the Agenda, she acknowledged that "black men have been wounded and hurt by racism" but opposed the idea that "the way they're going to heal themselves is by embracing patriarchy" (hooks 1995). Her critique, and that of the African American Agenda 2000, used elements of black political culture to make subtle authenticity claims.

Authenticity claims are an integral part of the black Feminist project. Messianic imagery is used when making the claim that black women need Feminists to help them develop a more complete political consciousness. Black Feminists, at times, represent themselves as deliverers by arguing that, as Feminists, they can help black women to throw off the false consciousness of identifying only with one's race and help them discover gender consciousness as well. One example of this tradition comes from Collins (1991). Collins explains that many African American women have learned to cope with the dual causes of their inequality in America, but that "being a biological female does not mean that one's ideas are automatically Feminist. Self-conscious struggle is needed" (27). She goes on to say that only black Feminist intellectuals can lead women into that self-conscious struggle. She writes "Black women intellectuals are central to the production of Black Feminist thought because we alone can create the group autonomy that must precede effective coalitions with other groups" (35).

A messianic claim resonates in hooks's opposition to the march. She argues that the march offers the wrong messiahs. It is an argument that she advances on two fronts. First, she warns African Americans to be careful of foisting Farrakhan, Chavis, and their patriarchal baggage to the head of black struggle, "I am not one of the people who is convinced that you can separate the message from the messenger. I don't think there was one messenger in relationship to this march; there were many. But all of the messengers, to me, had an underlying value system that I felt I had to oppose." She further warns against the deliverance claims of the march. She registers her disturbance that black men were being asked to prove their responsibility through getting jobs: "What if there are no jobs out there." She critiques the march's assumption that to heal the wounds of black inequality, black men need only the volition to be stronger patriarchs. Hooks complicates the march's narrative when she assets that "mass black male unemployment or underemployment is necessary for the maintenance of our current economic system, . . . there will never be a day when all black men who want to can work and provide for families" (1995, 66).

Instead she roots herself, and her Feminist approach, in a familial, religious, and racial tradition that locates redemption in education. "I mean, I grew up in that grand era of civil rights where people really emphasized if you want to fight for freedom, you're going to have to learn to read and write. I'm where I am today because of reading and writing and learning how to think critically, and that positive affirmation was given to me by my family, my church." Her approach engages the march not only on its exclusion of women, but on its misplaced goals for black men. She offers an analysis of the structural barriers facing these men who went to Washington seeking atonement. Why atone for unemployment if there are real structural barriers to black male employment? Instead, she suggests remembering a black liberation tradition rooted in the importance of education. It is an argument likely to resonate with African American cultural understandings and to give strength to the authenticity of her Feminist argument.

Feminist opposition to the march also relied on a spirit of defiance to authenticate their claims. In presenting her opposition, hooks described the march as conservative, fascist, narrow, antiwelfare, promilitaristic, proimperialistic and a forceful attempt to control other people. Thomas and Tyson may have been able to call on images of black male victimization at the hands of the criminal justice system, but hooks does not yield the racial ground this time. She constructs the Feminist stance as the defiant one, arguing that as a black Feminist she does not "have any trouble with men marching without me. They can march every single day of the week. It's what they are marching for that matters." Thus, it isn't her brothas she is attacking, instead she is resisting hegemonic assumptions about the rightful role of men. She uses the language *conservative, fascist,* and *controlling* to evoke African American appreciation for defiance. She is using Feminist ideology to access the legacy of resistance in black political culture.[6] The Feminists of the African American Agenda 2000 also paint Feminists as the truest defiants. They argue that "we need to repudiate the Far Right's claim that we, rather than racism, are the cause of our problems, not echo their rhetoric" (African American Agenda 2000). By evoking and equating the efforts of the march with the Far Right, Feminists employ an important racial strategy. The Far Right, conservatives, and fascists are widely accepted as antithetical to African American political and economic interests. By opposing those elements of the march, Feminists access authentic racial defiance.

The clearest authenticity claim of Feminists opposed to the Million Man March is the uniquely Feminist version of an appeal to the American promise. Black Nationalism and Liberal Integrationism both use appeals to the American promise to make claims for racial equality based on citizenship duties performed by African Americans on behalf of the country. Elites from both perspectives argue that blacks have a right to share in the privileges of American citizenship because they have met their responsibilities as citizens. Feminism makes a parallel argument with respect to the duties and privileges of citizenship in the Black Nation. Rather than appealing directly to the promise of America, Feminists appeal to the promise of the black liberation struggle. By demonstrating that black women have served faithfully in the African American struggle for equality, Feminists lay claim to the right to be seen as authentic members of the community. Just as Integrationists argue that blacks should be seen as authentic American citizens because they pay taxes and serve in the military, Feminists argue that they must be seen as authentic *race women* because they have paid their dues to the black community.

Michelle Wallace's *Black Macho and the Myth of the Superwoman* (1978), Frances Beale's "Double Jeopardy" (1970), The Combahee River Collective's "Black Feminist Statement" (1977), and Toni Cade's "On the Issue of Roles" (1970) are groundbreaking manifestos by black Feminists that illustrate this appeal. Each of these women was personally involved with the civil rights and black power movements, but all found that they were not offered equal citizenship rights within these movements. Wallace critiques the male-dominated civil rights and misogynist black power movements. She remarks that "it took me three years to fully understand that Stokely was serious when he said my position in the movement was 'prone'" (Wallace in Guy-Sheftall 1995, 221). Beale was a founding member of SNCC's Black Women's Liberation Committee and she argued that "we need our whole army out there dealing with the enemy, not half the army. . . . Black women sitting at home and reading bedtime stories to their children are just not going to make it" (1970, 3). The Combahee River Collective argued that their Feminist ideology resulted from "our experience and disillusionment within these [Black] liberation movements" (Hull et al. 1982, 14). Together these works represent an appeal to equality based on a recognition of services rendered. Black Feminists demonstrate that women fought alongside (not behind) black men throughout African American history, but they were consistently relegated to a second-class status within the African American community.

Feminism, like the other ideologies, accesses the cultural tradition of appealing to the American promise on the basis of exchanging citizenship rights for duties performed, but it does so by making these claims on black liberation movements. By creating a narrative that reclaims the contributions of women (many of whom were explicitly Feminist) to the struggles of African Americans, Feminists lay claim to their inheritance of authenticity. If Martin Luther King, Jr., and Huey Newton are to be remembered as black heroes, then Septima Clark and Kathleen Cleaver must be remembered as black sheroes. If men can demonstrate their "realness" by their active involvement in black struggles for equality, black women who struggled with them deserve the same badge of racial authenticity. By creating a narrative that specifically addresses the contributions of black women, Feminists make use of this element of black culture as an appeal to authenticity.

This kind of Feminist appeal is central to the opposition to the Million Man March. The Feminists of the African American Agenda 2000 remind black folks that black women have always been integral to black struggle, and they argue that the march's exclusion of women is regressive and counterproductive. Instead, they offer a vision of an inclusive racial battle fought on many fronts.

> For more than 400 years African American women and men have stood shoulder to shoulder united in our struggle for justice. . . . the organizers of this march tell us that now is the time for men to step forward and women to step back. . . . we, the organizers of African American Agenda 2000 raise the call for men and women to come together and create an inclusive, well-organized social and political movement to combat racism, sexism, and homophobia and to transform the lives and conditions of our community. (African American Agenda 2000, in Birbaum and Taylor 1997)

Calling on a history of black women's activism on behalf of the race, the Agenda Feminists do not allow themselves to be cast as racial traitors, instead they insist that gender equality is the only truly successful organizing strategy. Just as black soldiers returning from international war resisted the hypocrisy of the nation's Jim Crow laws, black Feminists, still nursing fresh wounds of racial battle, refuse to be silent in the face of the march's gender segregation. Hooks says that she would be willing to support an all-male march if "these men had been marching for black self determination from a standpoint that included gender justice, I would really believe that we were going to see a tremendous change in race relations in America" (1995).

The Million Man March was hugely popular. Hundreds of thousands, maybe even the desired million, of black men (and more than a few women) attended the event. Black women such as Maya Angelou and Rosa Parks spoke to the crowd that day. The men who attended universally reported positive, affirming experiences that made them feel closer to other black men. But the success of the march did not represent a failure of the Feminist insertion into everyday black talk. Quite the opposite: black Feminists were able to level effective critiques that drew attention to the misogynist elements of the event. In some ways the Million Woman March in Philadelphia a year later was a representation of Feminist success in influencing the way that the Million Man March was received and understood among black masses.

But for Feminists the attempt to seriously engage with and on behalf of black masses is a difficult process fraught with the historical legacy of black perceptions of Feminism as an alien ideology. As the controversy around the march swelled, hooks's *Killing Rage* hit bookstores. In it hooks laments that "those of us who advocate feminist politics must continually counter representations of our reality that depict us as race traitors" (1995, 79). She rightly points to the legacy of Nationalist insistence that black women be silenced in order to redeem the race. Black Feminists are in a more precarious position than either Nationalists or Liberal Integrationists as they attempt to engage the everyday talk of African Americans. Both Nationalists and Integrationists are able to levy their attacks outside of the race. Nationalists point to virulent, enduring white racism and Integrationists to historically unfair white structures and institutions. Both perspectives are freed from having to critique black folks themselves. When Nationalists criticize "Uncle Toms," "black fags," or "uppity women," they paint them as outside the boundaries of blackness, as inauthentic.

Feminists have a more difficult critique. Not only do they point to white racist, sexist, and class-biased attitudes and institutions as the sources of racial inequality. They also must fundamentally question the behaviors and attitudes of many black people. Feminists have a strong critique of white male sexism and of white feminist racism, but they also point to the misogyny, homophobia, and classism of black people. The object of their criticism is not only "the man" but also "the people." This position makes authenticity claims more difficult for black Feminists because their ideological message requires that black folks take a hard look at the internal politics of the black community. Because of interlocking systems of oppression of race, class, gender, and sexual orientation, black Feminism is often regarded as dangerous and divisive in black liberation movements.

Feminists often express dismay that black people regard Feminism as an alien and disruptive force in the struggle for liberation. Collins (1991) explains that Feminism is problematic because dominant groups have a vested interest in suppressing it. Dubey (1994) describes the alienation of black women novelists who brought a gendered perspective to the nationalist aesthetic. The pioneering Feminists of the Combahee River Collective stress that "the reaction of black men to feminism has been notoriously negative. They are of course, even more threatened than black women that black feminists might organize around our own need. Accusations that black feminism divides the black struggle are powerful deterrents to the growth of an autonomous black women's movement" (Guy-Sheftall 1995, 237).

Maybe this is why not all black Feminists opposed the Million Man March. Most notably absent from the public opposition to the march was Alice Walker. The release of the film version of her novel *The Color Purple* generated significant controversy among African Americans about the appropriateness of the male images presented in the movie. Was it OK to present black men as abusive, cruel, and misogynist? The resounding answer from black women was yes. African American women widely supported Walker's right to present the painful realities of black women's lives even if it meant generating negative public images of black men.

Yet Walker did not offer a critique of the march. Instead, she reported in her 1997 book *Anything We Loved Can Be Saved* that she had her television repaired just so she could watch the television coverage of the march from beginning to end. She remembers making her usual bowl of oatmeal and camping in front of the TV, "still cozy in my jimmies" (1997, 109). She describes elements of the march as courageous, brilliant, radiant, and compassionate. She writes that Farrakhan's numerology was intriguing and Chavis's presence was heartwarming. She was struck by the beauty of the men and the thrill of their collective voices, and remembers that "I did not feel left out at all" (109).

Walker is a vocal black Feminist whose artistic and political work has been centered around the resistance of violent, abusive, oppressive male power. She has seen and reported the devastation wrought on black women's lives when patriarchy is unchecked. Yet she offers no critique of the march. She does not even hint at the possibility of problematic images or messages embedded in the march. Maybe this is only comprehensible within the context of the difficult and exhausting work it is for black Feminists to be seen as authentic. Walker refers to herself in the march essay as "someone who has been thrown out of 'the black community' several times in my life" (1997, 110). Maybe she chooses not to risk expulsion this time; it is easier to curl up in her jammies, eat her oatmeal, focus on the pageantry, and ignore the problematic elements of the march. As Michelle Wallace, who publicly criticized the march, explained, "My first, self-protective impulse was to ignore it" (1996). Given that this is the context that black Feminists like the Agenda and bell hooks faced when they criticized the march, it is truly notable that Feminist ideological messages did influence the everyday black talk surrounding the march.

CONSERVATISM

Colin Powell began his address to the 1996 Republican National Convention, "My fellow Americans, my fellow Republicans!" At the latter phrase the convention hall broke into wild applause. The uncertainty of Powell's partisanship had been dispelled. His stance was clear, he was a Republican, and the vastly white, conservative convention floor loved him for it. In the months leading up to this address, the media commented extensively on the historic importance of a black man being embraced by conservative whites as a potential president. But few discussed the even more striking fact that this black Republican enjoyed significant popularity among African Americans. In 1995, of those blacks who had an opinion, 90 percent viewed Powell favorably (CBS News/ New York Times Poll October 1995). And better than 90 percent hoped he would run for president (ABC Poll September 1995). This support is remarkable given that nearly all of the African American vote has gone to the Democratic presidential candidate since the middle of the twentieth century.

Powell publicly aligned himself with the unpopular Republican Party. He openly acknowledged his almost filial relationship with Ronald Reagan, a president whose economic and social policies were anathema to African Americans. He campaigned for Bob Dole in 1996. He supports the death penalty. Why was Colin Powell so popular among African Americans in 1996? The answer is complex, but it lies in part in Powell's skillful use of elements of black culture that generate understated, but very powerful, racial authenticity claims that allow him to appeal to black common sense.

When I first started talking to colleagues about my plans to use Colin Powell in my study of black Conservatism, several scholars of public opinion told me, "Colin Powell is not a black Conservative!" This criticism came in one of two forms. One colleague argued that Powell's support for affirmative action and his prochoice stance meant that he was more liberal than many African Americans. Another colleague claimed that Powell was certainly a conservative but that he was a conservative black not a black Conservative; in other words, he is not tied to the tradition of indigenous Conservatism within the black community. In his account of Powell, Henry Louis Gates captures the spirit of these criticisms, writing, "Everything clear? Sort of liberal, kind of conservative. Clearly black, not *too* black" (1997, 98). It is this internal disagreement about who Powell is that makes him such an interesting figure. Why is there confusion among black academics, activists, and the general population about who Powell is and what political tradition he represents?[7]

Some immediate answers come to mind. Perhaps it is Powell's West Indian heritage.[8] Both of his parents immigrated to the United States as young people, and Powell certainly speaks proudly about his Jamaican heritage. But Powell himself is not an immigrant. He was born in Harlem and raised in the South Bronx. He is a black American. Perhaps it is his years as a solider. As a high-ranking military official, Powell remained silent on most issues of domestic policy and towed the line of his commanders-in-chief. But, by late 1995, when Powell had become a civilian public figure, he freely shared his views on affirmative action, gun control, foreign policy, and the death penalty. He had written a best-selling autobiography and appeared in countless television and print interviews. There was a lot of information available on Powell.

I think the disagreement over Powell is fueled by a deeply ideological consideration. For many black leaders and folks, black Conservatives are supposed to be the bad guys, and Powell does not seem to fit the bill. African American Conservatives have regularly complained that they are perceived as racial outsiders. Supreme Court Justice Clarence Thomas argues that he has suffered rejection by liberal blacks who show a "cult mentality and childish obedience" to the politics of the left and by white conservatives who fail to fully accept his conservatism because of his race.[9] Thomas claims that he has met with castigation and ridicule by the left and indifference from the right. He concludes that these attacks constitute a "conspiracy between opposing ideologies to deny political and ideological choices to black American." (Faryna, Stetson, and Conti 1997, 11). Thomas's sentiments are echoed by Kathleen Bravo, who bemoans being told that she "looks like a Democrat," and by Stuart DeVeaux, who claims to have overcome peer pressure and discovered Conservative thought that enabled him to "envision a new destiny for black Americans" (ibid., 28). These Conservatives situate their experiences as redemptive suffering. Brad Stetson, Conservative talk show host in Los Angeles, writes, "To be attacked because I think that racism is not public enemy number one, to me that is a badge of honor because it shows that I am saying something that is true" (ibid., 158). Black Conservatives perceive themselves as restricted and censored by traditional African American institutions and organizations. They are frustrated that their ideas will be silenced by a hegemonic black leadership that is not committed to offering ideological choices to African Americans.

My colleagues suspect Powell is not a black Conservative because he does not fit in this category. Unlike Clarence Thomas, Thomas Sowell, Shelby Steele, or Ward Connerly, Powell has not been broadly accused of "Uncle Tomism."[10] While his continuing support for affirmative action makes him qualitatively different from these other black Conservatives, we should not divorce Colin Powell from this tradition of black political thought, whose indigenous origins in the black community are most famously located in Booker T. Washington. It does a disservice both to our understanding of Powell and to our understanding of black Conservatism broadly. By my reading, Powell is a Conservative, and his Conservatism places him squarely within the tradition of indigenous African American thought. Powell is simply more successful than most Conservatives at using claims of authenticity to remain connected to African Americans. Careful analysis shows both that other black Conservatives have attempted to gain a black constituency through authenticity claims and that Powell, while more successful than other Conservatives, still enjoys considerably less success than proponents of other ideological stances.

By 1996 Powell had two important instances of speaking to, for, and with black people: his autobiography, *My American Journey*, and his 1996 speech to the Republican National Convention. When I first picked up Powell's autobiography, I was immediately struck by the image on the cover. I was astounded at the striking physical resemblance between the cover photo of Powell and the famous photo of Booker T. Washington. I am certainly not making an essentialist argument that Conservatism is naturally associated with a particular phenotype. But it is interesting that Powell chose this cover photo. It seems more than coincidence that Powell cultivates an expression and posture mimicking the great black Conservative thinker of the previous century.[11] It is indicative of the subtle ways that Powell lays claim to an authentic black heritage.

Powell is a black Conservative. He keeps several home offices. One is a formal, receiving office where he keeps framed portraits of presidents Reagan, Bush, and Clinton and friendly, candid shots of himself and his wife, Alma, with the Reagans at White House events. Downstairs, Powell maintains a less public office that is decorated with the memorabilia of black military history (Gates 1997). Gates comments, "If the office upstairs is the Fourth of July, this one is Black History Month" (73). Powell's is not a DuBoisian double consciousness. He is not at war within himself. Rather, he comfortably links his pride, heritage, and identity to both Americanness and blackness. Importantly, it is the American identity that receives top, public billing. His blackness is carefully preserved in the basement. Consistent with the black Conservative tradition, Powell is fundamentally concerned about the direction and future of African Americans, but his concern has the specific goal of reaching fully, unhyphenated American identity.

Powell's autobiographical narrative and political addresses make use of the messianic tradition, defiance claims, moralism, and appeals to the American promise. Powell's autobiography begins with a harrowing story. He and Alma are visiting Jamaica just after the end of the Gulf War. Eager to impress the Caribbean-born American general, the Jamaican soldiers convinced the Powells to accept a ride in a Jamaican helicopter. During the brief flight, the helo's transmission seizes and the pilots have to perform an emergency landing. Powell reflects on these scary moments and remembers, "The irony of the moment did not escape me. What had been the land of my folks' birth had nearly become the site of their son's death" (1995, 5). Why would this have been ironic? Most people die in the same country where their parents were born, and most career soldiers have faced the possibility of dying in foreign lands. The idea of dying in Jamaica was ironic for Powell because he had come *up from Jamaica*. Like Booker T. Washington, whose

determined, hard work allowed him to rise *up from slavery*, Powell has
been redeemed by the immigrant dreams of his parents and by his stead-
fast dedication to the American army. Powell's opening narrative is a
story of salvation: not only salvation from the immediate danger of the
helicopter crash, but salvation from being like that Jamaican helicopter—second rate and bound for destruction. Like Christ, who rises from
death to sit at the right hand of God, Powell rises from the Caribbean
to sit at the right hand of the president, leading the most powerful
Army in the world.

Like other black Conservatives, Powell uses this messianic imagery to
connect with African American cultural traditions. He is like Clarence
Thomas, who laments that as a black Conservative there is "No Room
at the Inn,"[12] drawing a parallel between the persecution of Christ and
the persecution experienced by black Conservatives. He is like Lee
Walker, a Chicago black Conservative who portrays Booker T. Washington as a black Conservative messiah: "The next time that you are in
New York City, visit the great Riverside Church in upper Manhattan.
To the right side of Christ hanging high over the altar are three statues.
They are General Samuel Armstrong, the founder of Hampton University, Abraham Lincoln, and Booker T. Washington" (Walker 1997, 30).
Washington, we are reminded, sits at the right hand of Christ. The use
of messianic images by black Conservatives demonstrates that they are
not divorced from or unconcerned with black culture. Instead their
claims fit very much within a traditional black ideological and cultural
framework.

Use of the defiance claims is also prevalent in Conservative appeals.
Conti and Stetson refer to black Conservatives as "black dissidents who
eschew race consciousness and group identity" (Faryna, Stetson, and
Conti 1997, 66). The very use of the term black dissident suggests that
they are not eschewing black consciousness. They are making use of it.
They know that part of the black American political culture is a respect
for the defiant loner willing to break the rules. By labeling themselves,
black dissidents Conservatives make use of this cultural tradition of defiance. Although often labeled as accommodationist Uncle Toms, Conservatives paint themselves as "bad niggers" to the extent that they defy
both black and white expectations and categorizations. It is the strategy
Clarence Thomas used in his denouncement of his Senate confirmation
hearings as a high-tech lynching. Knowing that lynching had traditionally been used to punish defiance and to terrorize potentially defiant
African Americans, Thomas accessed African American cultural understandings in order to build credibility among blacks. By calling himself
a victim of lynching, he rallied the support of those who did not agree
with his politics but for whom the imagery of lynching was powerful.

Powell also describes being shunned by liberal blacks. Near the end of his autobiography, he writes of accompanying the American delegation to the 1994 South African presidential inauguration of Nelson Mandela. His traveling companions included such important black political figures as Jesse Jackson, Carol Moseley Braun, Charles Rangel, Ron Dellums, and Kweisi Mfume. Powell recognizes that these black elites were proud of his career successes, but his impression was that "my fellow passengers would have preferred me to have succeeded under different auspices. In the eyes of this group, I was a product of those trickle-down conservative Republicans Reagan and Bush" (1995, 580). But Powell defies them by proving the authenticity of his blackness: not by offering more progressive political views, but by singing a doo-wop version of "In the Still of the Night" with Dellums and Mfume, by playing cards with Rangel, Dinkins, and Epsy, and by reporting, "Never play cards with three brothers from New York" (ibid). I don't mean to question the genuine camaraderie of that night, but Powell is using the story to emphasize that he is a "real brotha." He tells the reader that although he defies the politics of these popular black leaders, he, like them, is an authentic contributor to black politics.

Powell fits neatly within the black Conservative tradition in his use of morality appeals. Conservatism is distinguished most clearly from other black ideologies by its concern with black pathology. It is the failure of black people's own morality rather than systematic racism that should be blamed for continuing black inequality. Black Conservatives use a narrative of black pathology to make moralistic claims. Conservatives Joseph Brown, Diann Cameron, Joseph Broadnus, Jesse Peterson, Ken Hamblin, Shelby Steele, and others regularly discuss what they call a moral crisis in the African American community that is illustrated by out-of-wedlock births, black crime, homosexuality, and abortion. They claim that these issues represent a pattern of black pathology that is far more determinative of inequality than are historical or contemporary forms of racism. Conservatives stress that strength of moral character is the best indicator of personal success and that the decline of the African American family is the central cause of persistent black inequality in America. These moralistic claims justify Conservative opposition to social welfare programs, by arguing that AFDC, food stamps, and subsidized housing encourage the sloth and idleness associated with black pathology. The absence of these programs is alternatively portrayed as the route to industriousness and thrift. This is the Protestant work ethic in black face, justified by appeals to a higher moral ground. Powell's critique of African Americans is not as harsh and direct as those of Thomas Sowell, Ward Connerly, or Armstrong Williams, but there is a strong appeal to the morality of traditional families as a solution of the nation's ills.

In 1996 Powell told the country that he was raised on the philosophy that "we might be black and treated as second-class citizens, but stick with it, because in America, justice will eventually triumph and the powerful, searing promise of the founding fathers will come true." He went on to tell the crowd that his immigrant parents instilled a particular work ethic and morality. "They found work that enabled them to raise a family. Work that allowed them to come home every Friday night with the fruits of their labor, a decent wage that brought some sustenance and, more importantly, dignity to our home." And he claimed the rightness of Republican partisanship by an appeal to morality. "Our vision, first and foremost, rests on values. Values because values are the conscience of a society. Values which must be lived, not preached. Children learn values by watching their parents in their homes." He locates dignity in a Protestant work ethic of daily labor and parental example. It is a basic morality appeal like that of other black elites. These Conservative arguments function as authenticity claims because Protestant Christianity is influential in African American culture. The Conservative language about right and wrong, sin and punishment, choices and consequences resonates with African Americans by tapping into the cultural tradition of moralism.

Powell's appeal goes further. At the 1996 convention he was speaking to a predominately white audience. Aware of the gaze of these powerful spectators, Powell spoke about the dignity of his home and the example of his parents. But the autobiography allows Powell to connect more directly with black folk, and his narrative about his home is slightly different. The house of which Powell is so proud was purchased with the winnings of a $25 bet his father put on the numbers. His American dream has a distinctly black flavor. Little Colin not only learned hard work and dedication from his father, he also learned a little about how black people make their own luck. His American story is in part the story of a father who bought his house with money "the numbers runner delivered in brown paper bags" (1995, 29).

Powell is a Conservative tapping into claims of morality and righteousness. His discourse includes speaking to black people about the values by which they should live. It includes speaking for black people by reminding whites of the moral strength of black families that helped build the American dream. And it includes speaking with black people with culturally familiar narratives. Powell could have omitted the story of the financing of his family's home. But he kept the story of numbers, luck, and gambling, in part, because it lays claim to the authenticity of his blackness.

Powell's personal and rhetorical appeal is largely rooted in the American promise. For most black Conservatives, the appeal to the American promise is articulated as a faith in the free market. From the very inception of an articulated Conservatism, it is economic success that Conservatives have offered as the panacea for black inequality. Booker T. Washington's advocacy of the Hampton-Tuskegee model of education is a reflection of his belief that in the free market African Americans can find not only success, but fairness as well. He writes in *Up from Slavery*, "My experience is that there is something in human nature which always makes an individual recognize and reward merit, no matter under what colour of skin merit is found. . . . the individual who can do something that the world wants done will, in the end, make his way regardless of his race" (1986, 155). Powell made a similar assertion in his 1996 convention speech, arguing that "we Republicans believe that the good jobs needed to sustain families come from a faster growing economy where the free enterprise system is unleashed to create wealth — wealth which produces more good jobs". This emphasis on the racial justice of the free market may not immediately appear to be a claim to racial authenticity. But appealing to aspects of the American promise is a deeply ingrained black political practice.

Powell used the platform in 1996 not only to justify Conservatism with an appeal to the justice of the free market but to make a more overt appeal to African Americans in his version of the Republican Party in American racial history: "Yet our diversity has sadly, throughout our history, been the source of discrimination. Discrimination that we, as guardians of the American dream must rip out branch and root. It is our party, the party of Lincoln, that must always stand for equal rights and fair opportunity for all. . . . Let the party of Lincoln be in the forefront." Twice Powell uses the phrase "the party of Lincoln." This is an authenticity claim for the benefit of African Americans. The Republican Party is certainly no longer the party of Lincoln. The whites on the convention floor, whom he was addressing, are there because it is the party of Reagan. But when he invokes the party of Lincoln he is invoking a time when black people nearly unanimously linked their political fate to the Republican Party. Powell is appealing to a black tradition of Republican partisanship, one that is historically rooted in a time when black folks had real optimism in the American promise.

Openly Conservative elites are generally unpopular among African Americans. They are often accused of being overly concerned with the opinions and reactions of whites. But black Conservatives are also deeply concerned with black talk. They compete with Nationalist, Integrationist, and Feminists elites for the hearts and souls of black people. Washington's Tuskeege machine, Armstrong Williams's weekly appearances on BET, and Colin Powell's convention speeches are not only about speaking to and for, but also about speaking with black people.

The public appeals of Conservatives are deeply influenced by the expectations of ordinary black people and are structured by authenticity claims rooted in black political culture.

And black common sense acts as a check on their authenticity claims. The early 1990s' television show "In Living Color" placed a common-sensical check on the Conservative defiance claim in a skit about Clarence Thomas. In the skit Thomas is portrayed stepping and fetching for the white Court members in the chamber room. Then one of the white justices informs Thomas that his position as a justice is a lifetime appointment. Thomas, realizing that he has perfect job security, kicks off his shoes, puts his feet up on the table, and begins to speak in black vernacular. In this skit, "Living Color" was expressing the hope of black Americans that Thomas would turn out to be a trickster who had spent all those years fooling whites until he got into a position of power. They hoped that he would truly turn out to be part of the black defiance tradition.

But the defiance claim is a poor fit with black Conservatives because they are defying the wrong group from a black cultural perspective. African American defiance traditions are rooted in resistance of white America. Black Conservatives claim to be resisting black hegemony. The language of defiance and resistance is employed because it resonates with black tradition, but black common sense shows it to be a thin claim. As the "Living Color" skit demonstrates, African Americans receive the authenticity messages of black elites, but they are able to mediate those claims through their own common sense. Thomas was able to temporally shield himself in the cloak of authenticity by evoking the language of defiance, but ultimately he was uncovered by the masses.

Powell is far more effective than Thomas in his appeals. His softer policy positions and the absence of a harsh criticism of black people make him a surprisingly popular Conservative. But his popularity should not be overstated. In 1995 most black men and women wanted to see Powell run for president, but the majority (63%) reported they were likely to vote for Clinton over Powell (CBS News/*New York Times* October 1995). This cannot be read as a strategic voting consideration, that is, blacks would vote for Clinton because he is more likely to win. In fact, twice as many blacks would vote for Powell as an independent presidential candidate than as a Republican, even though no candidate from a third party has ever won the presidency. And even when faced with the choice of an independent Powell, a majority of blacks would choose a Clinton-Gore ticket (CBS News/*New York Times* October 1995). There is good reason to believe that the hesitancy surrounding Powell is in fact related to his Conservatism. Of blacks who once supported Powell and then changed their mind, the most cited reasons for their change of heart was Powell's alignment with the Republicans or his being too conservative. Only a third of blacks felt that Powell's presidency would be good for American race relations; 20 percent actually believed it would be bad for race in America (CBS News/*New York Times* October 1995). These data suggest that for all his racial authenticity appeals, blacks still see Powell as a Conservative, and his Conservatism makes them wary. "The Republicans hoped to dampen the outrage of African-Americans with jobs for black elites and Booker T. Washington-type access to uncritical African-American leaders. But folk won't be fooled so easily" (Ransby and Harris 2001, 17).

LIBERAL INTEGRATIONISM

At the turn of the twenty-first century, the nation's most enduring civil rights organization took on a series of new challenges. In October 1998 NAACP President Kweisi Mfume and eighteen others were arrested for protesting the Supreme Court's failure to hire minority law clerks.[14] Mfume argued that the protest was done to "underscore how strongly and passionately we feel about the whole issue of equal justice under the law for all people" (*Jet*, October 26, 1998). In July 1999 the NAACP, under the leadership of Mfume, launched a campaign against four major television networks in response to a fall television lineup that excluded minority characters in leading roles. Mfume used the NAACP's annual convention to announce that the organization would send "a strong, clear signal that the frontier of television must reflect the multi-ethnic landscape of today's modern American society" (NAACP presidential address, July 12, 1999). Within the year the NAACP took on the South Carolina government, demanding that the Confederate flag be taken down from the statehouse. In January 2000 nearly 50,000 people marched on the South Carolina capitol where Mfume argued, "We are determined to bring that flag down. It represents one of the most reprehensible aspects of American history" (*Jet*, February 7, 2000).

Why these battles? Why at this moment? These campaigns share a number of common elements. Each is Integrationist in its goals. Each demands inclusion in the American landscape: access to the halls of power, representation in the images of popular culture, and recognition of historical value. Each has as its goal an identifiable, measurable unit of success: more black clerks, more black characters, the flag coming down. Each is directed at areas of black commonality. None asks middle-income blacks to sacrifice for poorer blacks, black men to consider the specific needs of black women, or heterosexual blacks to account for the goals of gay African Americans. Instead, each fight focuses on broadly accepted racial symbols of inclusion. Unlike the legal and political struggles that marked the historical greatness of the NAACP, each of these new agenda items is a symbolic battle with little power to fundamentally alter the life circumstances of most black people. Journalist Deroy Murdock (2000) roundly criticized the NAACP for these symbolic fights, arguing:

> The NAACP and the civil-rights establishment desperately need a priorities transplant. Mfume and company resemble a family fighting over the remote control as their house burns down. While they promote employment for black thespians . . . average black Americans have plunged from the radar of these so-called "black leaders." . . . The NAACP . . . should zoom in on the needs of run-of-the-mill black Americans. If they were to do so, it would hardly matter if Ross Geller on *Friends* started dating a black paleontologist.

There is room to critique the strategies and focus of the NAACP at the turn of this most recent century. However, the agenda is strategic within a marketplace of ideas operating through everyday talk and makes sense when we have a deeper appreciation of Kweisi Mfume's own project of Liberal Integrationist authenticity politics. Mfume's 1996 autobiography and the 1999 fight with the television networks demonstrate the ways that considerations of everyday black talk affect the approaches and appeals of African American ideological elites.

When Kweisi Mfume was voted president of the NAACP in 1996 it was with the hopes that he could return the organization to its historical credibility and relevance (Haywood 1997; Zoroya 1996). After several years of scandal involving sexual harassment, hush-money for Executive Director Benjamin Chavis, and financial mismanagement by Board Chairman William Gibson, the NAACP looked to Mfume for energetic, new leadership. By most accounts, Mfume has been equal to the task and has brought new vigor to the floundering organization. Mfume had all the official credentials necessary for the job. He won his first election to the Baltimore City Council in 1979. He was elected to the House of Representatives from Maryland's 7th District in 1986, and he served as chairman of the Congressional Black Caucus from 1992 through 1994. He was a popular, well-respected member of the Democratic Party. But Mfume's leadership approach and the measure of success he has enjoyed are as much a result of his awareness of everyday black talk as of his formal officeholding.

In the same year he was named NAACP president, Mfume published a best-selling autobiography: *No Free Ride: From the Mean Streets to the Mainstream* (Mfume with Stodghill 1996). The text, in both structure and content, functions as an authenticity claim for Mfume as he took on the mantle of the NAACP presidency. The text also provides clues to the reasons for the choices he made for the organization's agenda in his early years as president.

There are many parallels betweens Mfume's personal narrative and the *Autobiography of Malcolm X* (Malcolm X 1965). Like Malcolm, Mfume was born under another name, Frizzell Gray. Like Malcolm, he endured an impoverished and segregated childhood, where his mother served as the central, stabilizing influence of strength. Malcolm's mother is wrested from her adolescent son by madness. Cancer claims Mfume's mother. After a long illness, she collapses and dies in his arms when he is merely sixteen years old (Mfume with Stodghill 1996). Mfume, like the slain Nationalist leader, had a deeply troubled adolescence wrought with petty criminality and sexual misconduct. He becomes a gun-toting numbers runner, dice shooter, and trash talker. Between May 1968 and January 1970 he fathered five sons with four different women. Then, like Malcolm X, Mfume ultimately experiences redemptive change, takes a new name, and goes into the service of his people.[15] Unlike the religious, Nationalist, organizational leader Malcolm X, Mfume becomes an elected official with a distinctly Integrationist political agenda. However, by laying claim to the redemption narrative, Mfume accesses an element of the messianic tradition of black political culture. His youthful degradation earns him more, rather than less, credibility with African American audiences because it reflects familiar themes of everyday black talk.

Mfume remembers his first congressional race against an African American Republican, the Reverend Crosse. During the campaign Crosse attempts to make Mfume's out-of-wedlock parenting a character issue. Mfume writes, "Now I was angry as hell. My youthful errors were not the major issue of the campaign. . . . I had worked hard in both heart and deed to become a person whose life reflected the highest possibilities of change and redemption" (1996, 270–71). Mfume reminds readers that while he is not boastful about the irresponsible behavior that brought his sons into being, he is proud of them and rejects any attempt to make them or their lives seem shameful. He argues that the shape of his years since their births are the true measure of his character because those years reflect his serious belief in redemption and second chances.

It is an interpretation that seems widely shared by his peers and constituents. Remembering his supporters in the early campaign, Mfume writes, "Crosse's charges produced outrage, especially among women voters, who felt they were off the mark. . . . they rallied on my behalf, saying they knew too many men who didn't support their children and that they resented a candidate making false attacks on someone who did" (1996, 273). Nearly a decade after Mfume's constituents demonstrated unwavering loyalty, NAACP Chairman Julian Bond would comment, "If Mfume had done nothing more than father those children, that's just irresponsible and it's to be condemned. That Mfume assumed responsibility for his sons as a young adult is both redemptive and commendable. Forgiveness and second chances are part of the black experience" (Zoroya 1996).[16] Using the autobiography to reveal his foibles and his ultimate moral triumph taps into the messianic impulses in black political culture in a way that conveys additional authenticity to Mfume's political claims, making him part of a tradition of leadership that is tied to the black experience.

Mfume is conscious of the need to reveal and bolster his authenticity. In the preface to his autobiography, he remembers an encounter between himself as a congressman and a young street gang in a tough Baltimore neighborhood. As he is talking with the young brothers, Mfume wonders, "How could I make them realize that I didn't represent that part of the Establishment, that my life, too, is rooted in the same pain and frustration that bonds them together" (1996, 3). The autobiography is exactly that project. It is the attempt to explain that although he is part of the mainstream, he is a defiant, authentic, outsider-within, who is deeply rooted in blackness and therefore qualified to lead from experience.

Mfume further makes use of elements of black political culture when he employs defiance narratives as a way of gaining credibility with African Americans. By 1972 Mfume had taken a new name and turned his life in a different direction. He completed his GED and went to community college,[17] where he became a student activist, making a name for himself through his outrageous, public acts of defiance: "When we weren't challenging, defying, or serving notice on the administration, we were prodding our fellow students into action" (1996, 195). Mfume then spent thirteen years in radio and gained popularity through his unflinching assessments of black politics and culture during his radio call-in show, "Ebony Reflections." "I didn't believe that real power lay in how much legislation you got passed. I felt that the real potential power lay in the hands of black disc jockeys as de facto leaders who could communicate political ideas creatively and compellingly over the airwaves" (197). Although he was in constant trouble with the station owner for failing to play more music, Mfume earned a reputation for being a "tell-it-like-it-is" brother.

Mfume continued to add to this reputation for defiance in his first foray into electoral politics. To gain a seat on the city council, Mfume had to unseat a formidable, established incumbent, Emerson "Doc" Julian. In a brash act of youthful defiance, Mfume walked into a council meeting, past security guards, and with TV cameras rolling sat in Julian's unoccupied council seat and declared, "I'm here. This is my seat and I'm here to claim it for the people. I can't wait until Election Day because Emerson Julian is through! All power to the people! . . . There will not be politics as usual in this city anymore" (227).[18] The stunt earned him a reputation as a "bad nigger." After taking office he maintained an image of defiance: "While I wasn't very effective during my first few years on the Council, my constituents cheered me on as the lone renegade" (253). Mfume continued to cultivate his defiant image even in the leadership of Congress.

> Ascending to the chairmanship at the same time Bill Clinton was inaugurated, Mfume allowed the president no honeymoon and refused to let a Democratic administration take the black vote for granted. Mfume publicly complained that too few blacks were named to administration posts. He refused token Oval Office meetings and photo-ops with the president, insisting upon a substantive agenda to tackle urban problems. He even led a caucus boycott of the White House Conference on Africa because he said the administration did not really consider the continent a foreign-policy priority. (Sobieraj 1995)

In many ways the defiant image is a difficult one for contemporary Liberal Integrationist elites to use convincingly. Liberal Integrationists often demand inclusion in the system rather than refuse to engage it altogether. Mfume is aware of this difficulty when he bemoans being seen by the street kids as a member of the establishment. His own electoral success among African American voters is based, in part, on a continued ability to demonstrate that he is willing to defy powerful people and institutions on their behalf. But it is a delicate balance for Mfume. He writes, "part of my learning process in the City Council was discovering how to deliver for the people in my district. . . . Change takes place when you develop the skills of diplomacy and negotiation. This means understanding that you must often take one step back in order to take two steps forward. That's the true art of political compromise" (259). Mfume and other Integrationists are stuck between the need to appeal to the black cultural respect for defiance as a means of maintaining authenticity and the need to work within narrowly proscribed rules to deliver measurable results.

Mfume accomplishes this by selling Liberal Integrationist goals as defiance. One masterful example of this occurs early in the autobiography. Still a little boy, Frizzell (Mfume) is locked in constant battle with an abusive stepfather. Mfume recalls that as a child he had a phobia of small spaces. One afternoon while he is playing innocently with a cardboard box, his stepfather traps him in the box, kicking and punching the sides of it, in an attempt to terrorize the young boy. "I couldn't break out, no matter how hard I pushed. . . . I started screaming and banging on the lid of the box in hopes that someone might hear me" (22). Eventually, Mfume decides to deal with the torture by becoming motionless and by realizing that "I was a boy and it was a box. That was all." When the he stops fussing, his father becomes enraged and tries to get him out of the box. "He kicked the box a couple of times and tipped it on its side, still, I refused to obey him. Even at that age I reasoned that the best way to defeat my environment was to become part of it. I had become one with the box, and I was beyond the fear created by my father's hoarse shouts" (23). At first blush this may appear to be a story of struggle between son and father, but it is also a metaphor for his political ideology. As a boy he learns to defy the power of his father by becoming one with the box. As an elected official he defies white racism by becoming one with the system. Mfume remembers being disgusted with his Democratic colleagues after the party lost control of the House and Senate in the 1994 midterm elections. "The Democratic leadership was walking around in a daze, wearing a kind of stunned and already-beaten expression after the elections" (79). But Mfume calls on the legacy of African American struggle to explain why he and other minority members of Congress were able to continue fighting despite the apparent defeat.

> For those of us who were black and Hispanic members, being in the minority was par for the course. In the eyes of many that was all we'd ever been. As skilled warhorses accustomed to operating from that position we knew how to seize the time and use whatever leverage was available. . . . After redefining the issues, our next move would have to be to attack and fight like hell. We had to conduct legislative guerrilla warfare. It meant challenging the Republicans at every little turn, and getting up in their faces if necessary. (79)

Through his personal narrative and his political action, Mfume creates an Integrationist authenticity claim that blends both a tradition of defiance and a strategy of working within the system. This is a tricky balance and one that he achieves through attention to important elements of everyday black talk.

In accessing both messianic and defiance traditions in his appeals, Mfume is also careful in his incorporation of appeals to the American promise. Traditionally Liberal Integrationists make frequent and central use of appeals to the American promise. Liberal Integrationist appeals to the American promise have taken two major forms. First, Integrationists have justified access to white schools, businesses, and associations based on the performance of citizenship duties by African Americans. Second, Integrationists have used strategies that make use of traditional American political and judicial institutions. These strategies demonstrate a basic faith in the ability of American institutions to function fairly.

Integrationists have pointed out the injustice of asking African Americans to pay taxes for services they do not receive[19] and asking blacks to fight in wars when their own freedom is not secure.[20] Liberal Integrationists also appeal to the American promise by using judicial and political strategies to press for black interests. The decades of judicial work by the NAACP legal defense fund and the century of agitation for electoral rights demonstrate the Integrationist belief that the American legal and political systems can be an emancipatory tool for African Americans. These strategies are part of the Liberal Integrationist authenticity project in that they tap into a cultural tradition in black politics that uses the American promise as a way of structuring black political demands.

In recalling his segregated childhood, Mfume remembers the centrality of the American promise, even for poor blacks. "The truth is that black people have been no less committed to achieving the American Dream than any other group in this nation — even if it was a dream that could only be fulfilled in 'our' part of town" (1996, 54). But Mfume is careful about his use of this language. He does not want his story to be mistaken for a Conservative "up from" narrative. Rather, he argues that the American Dream is a worthy one, but that African Americans are systemically shut out of the avenues necessary for realizing the nation's promise. In remembering his segregated childhood, he recalls, "Many people in Turners Station and on Division Street lived there not because they wanted to, but because they were trapped there, victims of circumstances far beyond their control and powerless to do anything about it" (108). Again he strikes a careful balance. Mfume is able to use the language of the American promise as a familiar way of structuring black political claims, but he remains committed to an Integrationist vision that requires agitation in order to make the dream accessible to all African Americans.

Through his stories of redemption and defiance and his appeals to the American promise, Mfume's autobiographical narrative reveals an attempt to gain access to everyday black talk through the use of common racial authenticity claims. Understanding Mfume through this lens is helpful in understanding why the NAACP took on the four major television networks in 1999. In important ways, television images are only symbolic. The actors, producers, and writers who would directly benefit from a more inclusive television lineup are a very small and distinct group of black people. Further, there is no indication that black political power or social equality is derived from the presence of black faces on television. Television images of African Americans historically have been, at worst, blatantly racist and, at best, deeply problematic. Even during the wildly popular primetime reign of *The Cosby Show* and *Different World*, the Reagan and Bush administrations were making deep and painful cuts in federal programs that benefit black and urban communities. There is certainly not a direct correlation between the abundance of black media images and a flourishing black community.[21] But the battle to integrate network television makes sense in light of Mfume's own understanding of the politics of authenticity as reflected in his autobiography.

Battles over popular entertainment are not entirely new to the NAACP. In one of its earliest public actions, the NAACP organized national protests against the 1915 silent film *Birth of a Nation*, and in 1939 the NAACP secured the Lincoln Memorial for the performance of Marian Anderson when the Daughters of the Revolution banned the acclaimed soprano from their Constitution Hall. Thus, in his insistence that blacks and other racial minorities be routinely portrayed on network television, Mfume borrows from an older NAACP tradition that asserts the value of black images in media, but why in 1999, and why with such fervor? An absence of minorities in front of and behind the camera was not a new development, and the resources the NAACP devoted to this battle where significant. There are several reasons. First, this battle, along with the Supreme Court clerks and South Carolina flag issues, firmly refocused the ideological message of the NAACP toward Liberal Integrationism. Second, the television battle gave the struggling organization a visible, measurable, comprehensible goal that resonated with a broad cross-section of African Americans. Finally, the fight to integrate the networks allowed Mfume to access authenticity tropes of redemption, defiance, and appeals of American promise.

Mfume first announced the seriousness of the NAACP's campaign to integrate the fall television shows to the audience of *BET TONIGHT with Tavis Smiley* (July 21, 1999). Mfume told Smiley that the NAACP had purchased 100 shares of stock in ABC, CBS, Fox, and NBC so that they could be present at the network board meetings. By August 1999 the NAACP was locked in a full-scale battle, charging the Big Four with a "virtual whitewash." Mfume threatened the networks and advertisers with a sweeps-week boycott and possible government intervention (Scholsser 1999; *Television Digest*, January 31, 2000). In these tactics and rhetoric, Mfume pulled the NAACP back to a decidedly Liberal Integrationist agenda. His focus was not on demanding additional airtime, programming, or advertising dollars for Black Entertainment Television or for developing funding strategies for upstart black cable networks. Rather, the NAACP focused on inclusion in the visual images of the American landscape, behind and before the cameras at major networks. The goal was increased participation in a predominately white arena, not the creation or support of a separate black locus of entertainment. By pulling the reigns on an Integrationist message, Mfume rectified an earlier drift toward more Nationalist rhetoric that occurred under Benjamin Chavis. Mfume was brought in to save the organization, and part of that salvation meant returning to an Integrationist ideological agenda. The network battle allowed Mfume to do just that.

The television fight also had the distinct advantage of offering measurable, attainable, and widely comprehensible goals. After taking leadership of the NAACP in 1996, Mfume offered a five-point agenda to revitalize the organization: (1) civil rights enforcement, (2) voter empowerment, (3) educational excellence, (4) economic empowerment, and (5) youth recruitment. It is an ambitious set of goals that reflect the historical character of the NAACP, but it is also a complex and long-term agenda that requires nuanced policy initiatives and sophisticated political bargaining. Unlike the right to vote or the desegregation of lunch counters, economic empowerment and educational excellence are largely intangible goals. The television network battle offered the NAACP a concrete and specific agenda item. Success could be claimed if more black faces appeared on television screens. The solution would be visible and comprehensible even to average observers. As an astute politician, Mfume recognized the value of being able to claim victory. The television fight would offer the rebuilding NAACP an extensive arena to air a concrete victory and to attract additional support.

Finally, the television network battle allowed Mfume to continue to use elements of black political culture as authenticity claims for the African American public. Much of Mfume's rhetoric was centered in unwavering defiance of powerful executives and appeals to basic notions of American diversity and fairness. In the early stages of the fight, Mfume mercilessly blasted the networks for their failure to create a multiracial fall lineup: "this glaring omission is an outrage and a shameful display by network executives who are either clueless, careless, or both" (*Television Digest*, July 19, 1999). The strength and tone of his language made it clear that he and the NAACP would accept nothing less than a full and immediate redress of the grievances presented. Mfume threatened boycotts, lawsuits, and possibly government intervention to bring the networks in line. This publicly defiant position was a far harder line than he drew in the private, ongoing negotiations with television executives.[22] But it served the purpose of creating a defiant image for the national organization for mass consumption while still allowing Mfume room to negotiate with the networks more privately.

Mfume's rhetoric not only emphasized a defiance tradition in black politics, it also used appeals to notions of American fairness and representation to frame the argument. Mfume was clear that the question of visual images was intimately linked to democratic representation. "We've got to show the world that we're not a segregated, racist society" (*Television Digest*, January 10, 2000). He claimed that television is America's face to the world, and that an all-white face both misrepresented the reality of the nation's multiethnic character and conveyed negative connotations of racism and segregation. This tactic reflects a long history of using the international gaze to press for domestic racial equality. In times of war and conflict, African Americans have used international pressures to hold America's feet to the fire of her egalitarian promises. Mfume is employing the same tactic in this case, and in so doing he connects with a black political tradition.

Finally, Mfume's strategy with respect to the network battle leaves room for the possibility of redemption. In the narrative he constructs, the NAACP is the defiant hero, prepared to seek the American dream for black people against a hostile white power source. But Mfume also is careful to leave room for the networks to redeem themselves. He remains open to the second chances. In January 2000, NBC and ABC announced "unprecedented agreements that were a result of the browbeating that took place over the last six months" (*Television Digest*, January 10, 2000). Fox and CBS followed suit within the month. The NAACP and the coalition of minority groups it represented were able to extract seemingly historic concessions from these powerful media outlets.[23] Mfume did not crow over his accomplishments, and while he promised that the NAACP would remain a watchdog, he also allowed the networks to bask in the appreciation for their willingness to negotiate. Mfume called the agreement the result of a growing trust between the two sides and boasted that the agreement "is a good initial first step and a genesis of a partnership" (*Television Digest*, January 10, 2000). His graciousness reflected a willingness to allow the networks a second chance and opportunity to redeem themselves. The redemption narrative that served him well as an authenticity claim in the autobiography and his own electoral trials was also a useful tactic in this battle.

The presence or absence of African Americans in network television is not the single most pressing issue facing African Americans in the twenty-first century. Many observers do not even rank it as a priority. But pursuing greater black representation in television made sense for Mfume's NAACP. It contributed to the rebuilding effort through its comprehensible and measurable goals. It realigned the organization with a firmly Integrationist ideological agenda, and it allowed Mfume to use authenticity claims that he successfully employed in his autobiography in the political struggle. It was an opportunity to speak for, to, and with black people in a way that reinserted the NAACP into everyday black talk.

NATIONALISM

The *Tom Joyner Morning Show* is funny. Not crack-a-smile funny, not laugh-a-little funny; it is double-over, laugh-until-your-eyes-water, laugh-until-you-feel-sick-to-your-stomach, nothing-is-sacred funny. And there is music. Good music. Just as you catch your breath from laughing, you crank up the volume and start singing along with funk, soul, and R&B hits from the seventies, eighties, and early nineties. It's the music you know all the words to, the music that reminds you of summertime when you were 21 and fine. "*She's a brick . . . HOOOOOUSE, she's mighty, mighty, just lettin' it all hang out.*" Or remember this one, "*REASONS, the reasons that we hear. The reasons that we fear, our feelings a-won't disappear.*" You can't help grooving, even to the show's opening tag line: "*Oh, oh, oh! It's the Tom Joyner Morning Show.*" And Joyner is fascinating because interwoven with the music and the laughs is serious social commentary. Joyner is not just spinning the hits and cracking the jokes, he is organizing people, practicing socially conscious economics, and taking on white power structures. His syndicated morning show is the single most recognizable forum of everyday black talk in black America today.

Tom Joyner was born in Alabama and graduated from Tuskegee Institute with a degree in sociology in 1968. At Tuskegee he served as an announcer for the university radio station, a job Joyner describes as cafeteria DJ because "while the meals were being served my job was to play music and make announcements" (Williams 1998, 134). Like many of his contemporaries, Joyner spent much of his college years involved in student-led civil rights protests in the South. "These were the protest years. I mean, we protested every weekend for something, mostly voter registration but that was like the thing to do. 'Hey man, what you going to do today? It's Saturday, I'm going down here to protest' (134). Joyner got his first off-campus radio gig by way of one such protest. He and other students were picketing the local radio station for its failure to play black music. The station responded by offering Joyner his own show. It was a job he was not paid to do, but he did get to play his own music on Saturday afternoons (Williams 1998). After working at radio stations in Montgomery, Memphis, and St. Louis, Joyner headed for Chicago in the late 1970s, where he worked for a station owned by black entrepreneur, John H. Johnson, the publisher of *Jet* and *Ebony* (Carter 1997). Joyner believes this relationship to have been tremendously influential on his career and his sense of social responsibility. He eventually left Chicago for Dallas where he hosted the number one rated morning show in the city and was recognized with numerous awards for his radio work. But it was in 1985 that Joyner came to national attention. Chicago radio station WGCI hoped to lure Joyner from Dallas and offered him the afternoon radio show. Dallas countered, offering him a good salary to stick with their morning show. Joyner accepted both offers and spent the next eight years doing the unprecedented. He hosted number one rated shows in two cities, 1,600 miles apart (Sims 1999). "For eight years, I worked in Dallas in the mornings and in Chicago in the afternoons. I woke up at 3 a.m., was on the air at 5:30, off at 9, hauled off to the airport, plane left at 9:30, got to Chicago around noon, went to the gym, played racquetball, took a catnap, woke up, and was on the air at 2. I was off at 6, hauled off to the airport, caught a 6:30 flight and was back home at 9" (Carter 1997)

The stunt earned him the nickname "fly jock" and the reputation of being "the haaaardest working man in radio." In 1994 Joyner turned in his frequent flyer miles for syndication under the auspices of ABC Radio. The *Tom Joyner Morning Show* became the first nationally syndicated radio program hosted and produced by an African American. And in 1998 Joyner was the first African American to be inducted into the Radio Hall of Fame (*Jet*, November 9, 1998). Since 1994 Joyner and his cast of characters have been broadcasting weekdays from Dallas, 6–11 a.m. central time. Today the syndicated morning show comes into seven million black homes in more than one hundred cities, like Chicago, New York, Atlantic City, Baton Rouge, Youngstown, and Raleigh.[24]

Joyner's crew sound as if they are all in the same booth, but in fact most of the show's co-hosts and regular guests broadcast from ABC affiliates across the country. Comedian J. Anthony Brown broadcasts from South Carolina; the show's serious newswoman Sybil Wilkes is in Los Angeles daily; outrageous psychic Ms. Dupree is often in New Orleans; Tavis Smiley usually broadcasts from Los Angeles but sometimes is on the East Coast; and on any given day it is impossible to tell where Melvin, D. White Man, or Myra Jay are. The show's ability to seamlessly blend music, comedy, characters, and commentary is a technological marvel — not only because the co-hosts are broadcasting from all over the country, but because the technology is invisible to listeners. The show feels down-home, more like a local show on a shoestring budget than a multimillion dollar national enterprise. When Joyner went into syndication some observers believed the show could not be successful on urban radio, which has always been fiercely local in its programming. "How could Joyner broadcast from a Dallas studio without making audiences feel as if they were tuned into network television? He has silenced his critics by interspersing hometown news, weather, and sports through the show. . . . many listeners sincerely believe Joyner broadcasts from their respective cities" (Sims 1999, 40).

It is almost impossible to capture the spirit and energy of the show. It is something that you really must listen to for yourself. One of the central elements of the show is the serial comedy soap opera *It's Your World*. The Joyner show website says that "unlike other soap operas, most of the characters in 'It's Your World' are African-American and financially well off (that's what makes it a comedy)." Joyner's show revolves around its musical offerings, but the comedy and commentary come in liberal doses. Every show, J. Anthony Brown gives us a joke of the day.

> Golfer comes in the house. He's tired. He's beat.
> Wife says, "What happened to you?"
> He's says "It's the worst day of golf ever. I'm out on the golf course, ninth hole and my partner, Henry, drops dead."
> Wife says, "Oh, that's awful."
> "You damn right it's awful. For the rest of the day it's hit the ball, drag Henry, hit the ball, drag Henry, hit the ball, drag Henry." (TJMS, June 11, 2001)

Each week outrageous psychic Ms. Dupree gives listeners three things to count to get their lucky numbers for the week. "Count the number of cars you see driving around this week with those little spare tires" (June 6, 2001); count the number of speakers in your house that you are using as a table" (April 23, 2001). J. Anthony Brown regularly "murders a hit," changing the words to a popular song to create a hilarious parody. To the beat of Destiny's Child's popular Charlie's Angel anthem "Independent Woman," he sings, "If you're a daddy who lost his Caddy, throw your hands up at me. All you homies with alimony, throw your hands up at me. If you get drama from your baby mama, throw your hands up at me." Melvin's love line, billed as a cross between Liberace and Dear Abby, offers romantic advice from a gay black man to listeners hoping to make sense of their romantic entanglements.

> Caller: Melvin, I need a man. I am a full-figured black woman.
> Melvin: Well how full is your figure? We need to know what we are talking about.
> Caller: 300.

Melvin: Well do you have any medical problems that cause this?

Caller: Yes . . . I can't push away from the table.

Tom: Look you need to go the Caribbean.

Melvin: That's true.

Myra: Girl you are 300 pounds, have you tried just snatching a man? Get you one that is about 175 and just snatch him up. (TJMS, April 20, 2001)

Myra Jay offers weekly advice to single moms.

> Since this is the college graduation season, I'd like to congratulate the single moms as well as their children. Because as soon as they flip that tassel over when they get their diploma, we hear the freedom bell ring. I know how it is when you get to the commencement ceremony. They expect us to be all sophisticated and dignified. Bump that single moms, this is your day too. In fact, you should wear a cap and gown to the graduation! When your child's name is called, I'm telling you single moms, you need to jump as high as you can, do the cha cha slide, tell Big Mama to do the Running Man, high five the people across the aisle, and do a breast bump with another mom. And if anyone has ever told you your child won't graduate until the cows come home . . . bring a cow bell and ring it to the beat of Pomp and Circumstance. (TJMS May 21, 2001)

Some of the show's funniest moments come from the cast's unscripted banter with one another and with a sample of the more than three hundred daily callers to 1-800-Joyner-1 who call in for the daily "Express Yourself" question.

For all Joyner's professional success, the musical and comic popularity of the show is not what makes it worthy of inclusion in this text. Joyner is here because the *Tom Joyner Morning Show* is the best contemporary illustration of the operation of a marketplace of political ideas among African Americans. Quietly, beneath the radar of most average white people, Tom Joyner has eclipsed the NAACP, the Urban League, and the black church as the primary mobilizing agent of national social action among African Americans.[25] "The *Tom Joyner Show* is the single most important mass media connection to the African-American community. When you are trying to get the word out about anything, this is one of the best ways to do it" (Georgia State Representative Vernon Jones to *Atlanta Journal and Constitution*, December 1, 1999).

Even an occasional listener will notice the show's racialized, social justice message. Every Tuesday and Thursday, Joyner welcomes Tavis Smiley to provide a commentary on the current state of black America. Smiley, who spent five years as the host of *BET Tonight*, as a kind of Larry King of Black Entertainment Television, informs African Americans of critical social, political, and economic issues facing black America. He encouraged black Mississippians to turn out for the vote on the flag, gave regular updates when Reverend Al Sharpton was imprisoned for civil disobedience, called for a moratorium on the death penalty and a change in mandatory sentencing laws, and spoke on the evils of racial profiling. Sybil Wilkes also functions as a straight-woman in the midst of the Joyner show hilarity. Her news reports are often sobering reminders of the effects of poverty, drugs, and crime in urban communities. Joyner's social activism is also readily apparent in his successful promotion of the Tom Joyner Foundation, which has used corporate sponsorship and the $10 and $20 donations of listeners to contribute millions of dollars to students at historically black colleges and universities. Joyner is explicit about the larger goals of his entertaining show. "Our format simply is that we want to get people to listen. If we can get people to listen, then we can try to get people to make a change in our community. If we can get people to listen, we can empower people. And if I've got you laughing, I've got you listening" (August 24, 2000).

Joyner's message is not simply one of social action and racial uplift, it is a specific ideological message. Joyner's show, his message, and his organizing efforts are illustrative of a contemporary Nationalist political ideology. Close observation of Joyner and his agenda over the past decade indicates two clear patterns. First, Joyner is a Nationalist—one whose basic social and political organizing principle is that black is good, black people are valuable, and black people should devote time and resources to ensuring quality of life for other black people. Second, Joyner is successful in his organizing because his show functions as a daily authenticity claim. The *Tom Joyner Morning Show* is the cultural wrapping that makes Tom Joyner Nationalism a powerful organizing force for many black people.

Those who are familiar with Joyner may be hesitant to accept my categorization of him as a Nationalist. There are aspects of Joyner that seem entirely at odds with traditional, narrow definitions of Nationalism. For example, Joyner is fundamentally concerned with increasing participation of black Americans in the electoral process. He registers voters at his monthly live, on-location shows, and listeners can even register online at tomjoyner.com[26] or by calling Joyner at 866-YES-VOTE. His concern with mainstream political participation could be interpreted as outside a strict Nationalist tradition.[27] However, history is replete with examples of Nationalist organizations that also promoted black political participation. The Black Panther Party ran candidates for elected office. Farrakhan encouraged Million Man March participants to register to vote. Complete removal from participation in the state is not requisite for Nationalist ideology.

Joyner's Nationalism may also be in dispute because of his far-reaching partnerships with powerful white corporations. Joyner has partnerships with ABC Broadcasting, K-Mart, McDonald's, Oldsmobile, Exxon-Mobil, Southwest Airlines, and many others. His connection to these sources of white wealth and power may seem to place him outside traditional Nationalism. But it is important to look at Joyner's own attitude toward these partnerships. He fancies himself a kind of modern, black Robin Hood, using corporate wealth to bail struggling black college students out of debt, to reward single moms for their dedication, to acknowledge the accomplishments of black fathers, and to bring black history education to African American children.[28] Joyner may not publicly use the word Nationalist to describe himself, but his understanding of himself and his professional mission is Nationalist. He is uninterested in developing a crossover audience or in expanding his base of listeners to include a more racially diverse audience. "Look, my show is targeted, unashamedly to the black community. That's who we entertain and that's who we try to empower. I don't try to be anything other than that. And we don't go after the mainstream crossover audience. We talk about things black people talk about when they're at home or at work or just hanging out, that's the top thing we do" (Barrs 2000). Joyner even believes, as only a Nationalist could, that "the black community in this country is very small because we share so many things in common. The show plays the same in every community that we serve" (Simon 2000). Understanding Joyner as a part of a tradition of black Nationalist thinkers and activists not only broadens and clarifies the comprehension of this complex ideology, it also allows a better understanding of Joyner as an activist.

Joyner's Nationalism explains his choice of protest targets. He has black folks listening and laughing, and he has used this to get them writing, calling, and e-mailing in fully modern displays of technologically assisted social action. In 1997 Joyner expressed his outrage at Fox television network's decision to cancel the popular black sitcom *Living Single* and the urban drama *New York Undercover*. "They had decided to shelve the No. 1 and No. 2 shows in black America without any regard to black people" (Carter 1997). At Joyner's direction, listeners sent more than 7,500 letters and faxes to Fox Vice President Tom Tyer. In response, Fox reinstated *Living Single*, stating that "Joyner reinforced to us the community support for *Living Single* among African-Americans" (ibid.). Fox President Peter Roth appeared on Joyner's program to express regret for the "misunderstanding." *Living Single* did not last past the season, but listeners perceived the show's temporary return as a victory, and Joyner's confidence in his power to mobilize his listeners grew as a result.

Later in 1997 Joyner learned of a planned auction of slave memorabilia at Christie's in New York. "They were going to auction off slave memorabilia, as if slavery is memorable. I heard they had this policy of not auctioning off anything from the Holocaust, and felt that wasn't right because slavery was a holocaust too" (Harris 1999). After listeners flooded the auction house with calls, Christie's decided to donate the items to a museum.

The next year Joyner caught wind of a racist memo being circulated at Katz Media Group. The memo from Katz executives discouraged its sales force from doing business with black radio. Joyner read the memo on his morning show and criticized the memo as "pure institutionalized racism." Again giving out the phone number, fax, and e-mail address of top-level Katz executives led to a flood of correspondence from listeners. Eventually a Katz representative came on the show, issued an apology, and agreed to hire more black salespeople, double its billings for black radio stations, and recruit from black colleges (Harris 1999). Another victory.

In 1999 Joyner combined forces with then *BET Tonight* host Tavis Smiley to launch a national campaign against CompUSA, charging that the largest U.S. computer retailer failed to sufficiently advertise in the black community. Thousands of listeners sent receipts from items they had purchased at CompUSA in a demonstration of the power of black computer purchasing. After a ten-week campaign that included an attempt by ABC Radio to pressure Joyner to cease and desist or be taken off the air, James Halpin, the CompUSA chief executive, appeared on the morning show, apologized to customers, and promised to hire a black-owned advertising agency (Ahrens 1999). Halpin further agreed to offer a 10 percent discount to all protesters who had submitted CompUSA receipts during the campaign. Of this victory Joyner said, "We made CompUSA an example to show other companies like CompUSA that they should advertise with Black consumers" (*Jet*, November 8, 1999).

Some observers have even credited Joyner for the extraordinary popularity of Al Gore among black voters in the 2000 elections.

> Joyner may well have been responsible for more new-voter registrations among blacks during the past election cycle—and perhaps even for more turnout—than any other individual. Leading up to the election, . . . [Joyner] often offered reasons why Gore "had" to be the choice of black voters interested in their own survival. On Election Day, this enthusiastic black support did not come as a result of Jesse Jackson and the NAACP. The outpouring of support for an uninspiring candidate resulted, to some degree, from Joyner's urgent appeals on America's urban radio stations. (Morris 2000)

Joyner's organizing success over the past five years is astounding. Most of the people who respond to his calls for action have never met, nor will ever meet, Joyner. He lacks the ability to make face-to-face Sunday morning appeals as ministers do from their pulpits, trading on their own intimacy with the congregation and the authority derived from their religious stature. He lacks the decades of organizational community ties and historical successes of traditional civil rights organizations like the NAACP. Yet at a moment's notice he is able to move to action thousands of African Americans who never see him or each other. If he says the issue is important, that black folks need to move on it, then it is important, and black folks move on it. Why this success? Because there is nobody keepin' it as real as Joyner. Nationalists are the ideological group most likely to make explicit, unabashed claims to authenticity. More than any of the other black political worldviews, Nationalism professes itself as the one true way for African Americans. From its earliest manifestations in the 1770s to its organizational heyday in the 1960s, Nationalism has presented itself as the defender of realness. Joyner's show functions in this tradition.

On a daily basis Tom Joyner acts as a kind of cultural groundskeeper for African Americans. For example, the daily express yourself questions regularly encourages listeners to share their memories of "back in da day." What was the name of the street that had all the black businesses back in the day? (June 25, 2001) Back in the day, which one of your friends had the finest brother or sister? (June 12, 2001) Back in the day, who was the really mean teacher in school? (June 11, 2001) It's funny, but it is more than funny. These memories serve to reinforce and re-create racial historical memory through an oral culture of story sharing. By providing the forum for these narratives, Joyner underscores his own authenticity as someone who participated in this back-in-the-day black life. The show further operates as an authenticity claim through its use of racial inside jokes. Joyner and his colleagues make daily references to what we think, what we feel, what we remember, what we like to do, and how we are different than white folks. By assuming homogeneity of preferences and commonness of experience, Joyner and his cast construct guidelines for authentic blackness.

Joyner is a messianic figure and a defiant hero. He serves and leads. His foundation literally rescues black students who are struggling financially to make it through college. Every Tuesday, Wednesday, and Thursday, Joyner reinforces the idea that suffering will eventually be rewarded. On Tuesdays black men who have served their families and communities are given accolades, praise, and gifts. On Thursdays black mothers who often have suffered deprivation in order to provide for their children are recognized. Every Wednesday Joyner grants a "Christmas Wish" to worthy individuals and organizations. Each time Joyner serves as a conduit for financial assistance to black people, he cements the loyalty of listeners. This is not to suggest that his community service is manipulative or ungenuine. It is only to say that by sharing wealth he accesses a black cultural authenticity claim by being a sacrificial deliverer. He is not using his success and popularity solely to become rich. He is assuring that his listeners and their communities are also benefiting.

Joyner's authenticity is further reinforced by his defiance. When Joyner and Tavis Smiley took on CompUSA for their failure to target black consumers, his syndication company ABC Radio threaten to pull the plug on the show if Joyner continued to go after CompUSA. But instead of backing down, Joyner and Smiley went after ABC and told listeners that the network had threatened to shut them down for exercising their right to free speech (Ahrens 1999). ABC never pulled the show. This kind of defiance contributes to Joyner's authenticity among African Americans. Nationalist leaders have regularly laid claim to authentic leadership by their willingness to defy white America. In 1960 Malcolm X stated, "We want to get behind leaders who will fight for us. . . . We do not want leaders who are handpicked by the white man. We want brave leaders" (Bracey, Meier, and Rudwick 1970, 416). Joyner's willingness to imperil his own job and to suffer because of his defiance is part of what allows him to call to action other African Americans.

Since 1994 Joyner has successfully made use of traditional authenticity claims to develop a Nationalist agenda that has successfully pressured white corporations and government to take seriously the concerns of African Americans. But in 2001 Joyner took on an opponent that generated a dilemma for his Nationalist strategy. In March of that year he reported on his morning show that Black Entertainment Television was terminating the contract of his friend and morning show commentator Tavis Smiley, host of the popular *BET Tonight*. Originally a half-hour show that was expanded to an hour-long format, *BET Tonight* was a core component in BET's substantive news programming. Smiley had earned a reputation among viewers and Joyner show listeners for being a straight shooter, deeply committed to addressing the political, social, and economic concerns of African Americans. The previous fall (September 2000), Smiley had partnered with Joyner and the NAACP to successfully host the Black Agenda 2000, a two-day symposium that brought together some of the nation's most powerful black political players to generate an electoral strategy and issue platform (PR Newswire, September 9, 2000).[29] The day after the firing, Smiley reported on Joyner's show:

> I learned that BET and its new owner Viacom had faxed a letter to my agent informing us that they would not be exercising their option to extend

my contract for the engagement period when it expires on September 6, 2001. Translation: The End. . . . They say you shouldn't take these things personally. But for me it is personal. I launched, have hosted, and executive produced with the show since its inception. All along I have tried to maintain the integrity and credibility of out advocacy on BET against some pretty incredible odds. (TJMS, March 21, 2001)

Smiley indicated that although he was advised to resign immediately, he would continue to serve as the show's host until September out of loyalty to his production team and his viewers.

Smiley's dismissal came as a shock to him and to viewers. There seemed to be no precipitating incident leading to the dismissal. And Smiley was contacted by a four-sentence fax rather than by a personal phone call. But Joyner made clear what he believed to be the cause of the firing: that BET's new white owners, Viacom, were attempting to silence the voice of one of black America's strongest advocates. In 2000 BET's African American founder and owner, Robert L. Johnson, sold the network to a white parent company, Viacom. "When Johnson sold the company, many were convinced that the heart and soul of BET followed. The umbilical cord to the Black community had been broken, many suspected that under Viacom's direction BET would become little more than a Black MTV" (Cooper 2001). Joyner represented the Smiley firing as an insidious attempt by a white media company to restrict the viewing choices of African Americans. So in the style that has made him effective, Joyner gave out the name, address, fax, and phone number of Viacom Chairman Mel Karmazin. And black folks responded. African Americans flooded both BET and Viacom with thousands of phone calls, e-mails, and faxes. In response, BET terminated Smiley immediately, not allowing him to return to the air to finish out his contract until September.

The protests intensified. Harvard Professor Cornel West led a protest and news conference outside of the BET headquarters in Washington, D.C. Demonstrators marched in Los Angeles when Karmazin addressed the Hollywood Radio and Television Society (*Jet*, March 2001). African Americans took to the phone lines and Internet to express their outrage.

It was just announced on the *Tom Joyner Morning Show* that Tavis Smiley's *BET Tonight* has just been cancelled by the new owners of BET, Viacom. I am very upset about this. The one show on BET that has substance and encourages Black America is no longer going to be on. What do you guys think?

This is one of the most disrespectful acts by a television media outlet. Bob Johnson is a man who has told us time and time again it was never about being socially correct for our community. It was about making money. Well I see he sold us out. He will never justify why he and Viacom refuse to renew the contract on Tavis Smiley.

I think there comes a time where we quit begging for crumbs off the white mans table. And since Viacom bought BET out, it is the white man's table now.

See? That's what I mean. Tavis got too deep for these white folks. Not only that, his show had one of the highest ratings on BET. Now, this is the white man's way of censoring him. White folks are trying to keep us in "line." I bet had Tavis rapped about black bitches and hoes, he'd still be on that channel. I say we boycott the hell out BET for good! (All from Blackvoices.com, March 21, 2001)

It is readily apparent from these early responses that Joyner's assessment of the Smiley firing became the dominant frame immediately. This was a case of a powerful white company silencing the voice of a black man. And as long as this was the frame, it was a perfect fit for Joyner's Nationalist ideological activism. The Smiley firing, like the cases of Fox, Christie's, Katz, and CompUSA, could be seen as a clear racial showdown in which Joyner would harness black public opinion to resist powerful, white, racist decision makers. But on March 26, BET founder Bob Johnson changed the whole game when he made a television appearance during the regular *BET Tonight* hour. During this appearance he took full responsibility for the decision to fire Tavis Smiley. Several times over the course of the hour he reiterated that he, not Karmazin, had made the decision to terminate Smiley. "People can rest. There is no campaign on the part of Viacom to control or influence BET programming."

In shifting the responsibility to himself, a black man, Johnson created a crisis for the Nationalist Joyner. From the day that Joyner announced BET's decision, his show had become the clearinghouse of information about the developing drama between BET/Viacom and Smiley. Joyner allowed his show to operate as a forum for Smiley to stay connected to supporters, and Joyner was using his trademark organizing to bring pressure on Viacom. Everything changed after March 26. The next morning Smiley responded to Johnson's appearance by saying, in part, "Let me be clear: I will not, Tom will not, we will not be participants in some public spectacle for the enjoyment and entertainment of Viacom or anyone else. This will not be Black radio vs. Black television. This is not Tavis and Tom vs. Bob Johnson. We are not Holyfield, he is not Tyson, and Mel Karmazin is no Don King" (TJMS, March 27, 2001). Joyner had always made clear that he refused to engage in public intraracial battles. He explicitly believes it necessary to "keep white companies on their toes" (Joyner to *Atlanta Journal and Constitution*, December 1, 1999). But when asked about black-owned companies and politicians, Joyner responded, "No, I don't criticize them. Any problem I have with a black person, I deal with personally. We need to settle whatever problems we have each other behind closed doors and come out united" (Harris 1999). Informed by this Nationalist rule that disallows public black-on-black battles, Joyner was suddenly hamstrung in his fight against BET. No longer able to point exclusively to the white parent company Viacom, Joyner was stuck with dealing with an intransigent black man.

Many disbelieved Johnson's narrative about Viacom's innocence. Many continued to think that Johnson was only a puppet, but by inserting himself between Joyner and Viacom, Johnson effectively ended Joyner's campaign to save Tavis. But why? If firing Tavis was wrong, then it was wrong no matter who did it. If Karmazin could be accused of attempting to silence a progressive black voice, then why couldn't Johnson be accused of the same? Why not make this a battle against BET? Why not use this moment to call for a full-scale boycott of BET until substantive programming changes were made? Why not demand less booty videos and more social commentary? Why not keep the heat on at a moment when people seemed poised and prepared for action? The only answer seems to be a reluctance to engage in this way with another African American. The answer springs from an ideological commitment to keep the community's dirty laundry under wraps and to never allow black in-fighting to become spectacle.

Joyner continued to attempt to exert private influence over Johnson. He spoke and met with him several times over the course of the next few weeks, culminating in a final meeting that included Joyner, Johnson, and Karmazin—a meeting Joyner described as unfruitful and disappointing. Joyner reported that "Bob thinks everything is fine at BET. He likes the way BET is programmed. Just as simple as that . . . it was pretty sad" (TJMS, April 26, 2001). Although Joyner continued to pursue this quiet strategy, he was unsuccessful. Joyner's power comes from his ability to move the public. It is derived from his credibility with millions of men and women who look to him for an agenda of action. By making it clear that "I refuse to fight with a black man publicly" (ibid.), he abdicated his arena of power, the public. Ultimately, Smiley landed on his feet, ending up with commentary positions on *Primetime* and *Good Morning America*, and his own talk show on National Public Radio. But the Smiley episode revealed a serious chink in Joyner's armor.

Joyner's popularity and his daily authenticity claims make him a powerful agent of potential social change among African Americans. The appeal of his approach and his ideological message resonate with millions. But his Nationalist ideology creates a sensitivity to racial unity and solidarity that hinders his ability to challenge the enemies within. As long as he remains unwilling to harness black opinion for self-critical mobilization, his range of targets will be narrowed. Certainly, there are plenty of battles to fight, even with an exclusive focus on white targets, but it seems a shame that his insight and influence may go unused in the important battles that African Americans must sometimes wage within the race.

COMMON SENSE AS MEDIATION IN THE MARKETPLACE

African American ideological elites are constrained by the rules of everyday black talk. Messianic narratives, defiance claims, moralism, and appeals to the American promise have traditionally structured African American political culture. Those who hope to compete in the marketplace of ideas must employ some or all of these elements of black political culture in order to make credible authenticity claims for racial leadership. But how effective are these claims in building a constituency? Is authenticity a successful marketing strategy for ideological elites? Elites package their ideological products in the wrappings of black political culture, hoping to attract potential consumers. Who is buying?

African Americans enter into conversation with one another in black public spaces, in black organizations, and through black information networks. As they interact with one another they develop collective definitions of political interests. It is these interactions that help build black common sense and that give African Americans the opportunity to determine the credibility of elite authenticity claims. These ideologies are competing in the marketplace of ideas, and their success is largely dependent on the ability of these ideologies to penetrate spaces of black dialogue. Elites messages are successful if they can direct the dialogue of African American masses and incorporate their ideological views into black common sense.

CHAPTER SEVEN

Everyday Black Talk at the Turn
of the Twenty-first Century

> While it is fashionable to point out that black thinking has
> evolved and is no longer monolithic, the fact remains that it never
> has been. Vehement disagreement over goals and tactics has
> marked the black struggle.
> —Steven Holmes, October 2002

IN THE FALL of 2002 the politics of everyday black talk came crashing into public consciousness. At the national level the controversy over the movie *Barbershop* revealed the centrality of everyday black talk to African American politics and offered a national audience a front row seat on the internal contestations in African American thought. Harry Belafonte's public criticism of Colin Powell highlighted the diversity in black ideological approaches, questioned the limits of Powell's Conservative appeal, and reasserted the prevalence of cultural tropes in the ideological battle for black mass opinion. At a more local level, Reverend Kenney was ousted from Orange Grove Missionary Baptist Church in Durham, North Carolina. His departure amidst a tangle of sexual politics suggested the constraints on ideological expression in the black counterpublic. These events are a kind of pop culture epilogue to the scholarly arguments of this text. These events capture in real time the ways that ideological heterogeneity is (re)produced in spaces of everyday black talk, and they suggest questions for future academic inquiry in this area.

THE *BARBERSHOP* MOVIE

In the fall of 2002 MGM released the African American-written, directed, and produced movie *Barbershop*. *Barbershop* was filmed on Chicago's Southside with a cast of popular black entertainers. It details one day in the lives of a struggling shop owner and an eclectic cast of barbers and customers. Like the men of Truth and Soul, the men and women in the movie use the shop as a place for rivalry, irreverence, learning, and hilarity. The filmmakers, two Chicago natives,[1] set out to depict the centrality of barbershops to the everyday lives of ordinary

African Americans. Its content underscores the relevance of public spaces to the development of everyday black talk and the expression of black political heterogeneity. Its message, to borrow the film's language, is that "the barbershop is the place where a black man means something — a cornerstone of the neighborhood, our country club."

At its debut many African American observers commented on the film's authentic portrayal of the barbershop as a space of black racial discourse protected from the gaze of whites. "Two young filmmakers have given us a movie that celebrates our everyday lives. These are the lives that are lived away from the downtown office buildings and in the neighborhood spots where black folks gather" (Mitchell, September 2002). "It's where a lot of guys come to commune. They discuss everything from women to war, sports to politics and back to women again. They laugh, vent, listen to rap music, air their problems and find out what is happening on the street" (Mitchell, October 2002) "Being a barber gives me an opportunity to instill knowledge, inspire and encourage young men to stay focused" (England, *Los Angeles Times*, October 5, 2002). The movie struck a cord of familiarity with black audiences. It made explicit what many African Americans had known all along: the barbershop is about much more than getting a haircut.

Black audiences were so enticed by the idea of portraying this slice of African American life in film that in its first two weeks *Barbershop* was the number one movie in the country. It grossed nearly twenty-one million dollars its opening weekend, a figure that is commensurate with the *total* gross of other, similar, contemporary African American films like *Love and Basketball*, *Kingdom Come*, and *The Best Man*.[2] Its success prompted a flurry of journalistic accounts about the ways that barbershops operate as gathering places in black communities. The *Chicago Sun-Times* reported on how black Chicago barbershops operate as community forums. "The film depicts men playing checkers, selling their wares, discussing politics or women, giving the movie its large does of reality. Such real-life scenes have occurred in many South Side shops where strong debates have raged" (Lenoir, *Chicago Sun-Times*, September 8, 2002). Other papers reported that barbershops are "anchors of mostly black neighborhoods, places where black men can be themselves" (*St. Petersburg Times*, October 4, 2002) and argued that "the appeal of Barbershop is that it shows how black people talk among themselves when white folks aren't listening" (*The Guardian*, October 4, 2002).

Controversy exploded two weeks into the movie's successful run. The reverends Al Sharpton and Jesse Jackson publicly denounced the film and called for a boycott in response to remarks made by one of the characters. Sharpton and Jackson found it objectionable when an older barber, Eddie, leveled critiques against several civil rights leaders. In the movie Eddie argues that "black people need to tell the truth. . . . Rosa Parks ain't no hero. She jess set her tired ass down." He further admonishes Martin Luther King, Jr., for his womanizing, and he ultimately is goaded into saying "F--- Jesse Jackson!" Although the other characters vehemently disagree with his assessment of these African American icons, Eddie asserts his right to express himself. "Is this a barbershop? Is this a barbershop? If we can't talk straight in a barbershop, then where can we talk straight?" Jackson and Sharpton disagreed. They threatened a boycott of the film and demanded that MGM remove the objectionable scenes from future video release.

Newspapers, radio, and television reported the controversy immediately. Op-ed columns were bursting, and experts weighed in on the debate. The response was largely one-sided. Almost no one publicly agreed with Jackson and Sharpton's analysis.[3] Some accused the men of simply having had their feelings hurt by Eddie's brash remarks. "The Reverend Jesse Jackson and Reverend Al Sharpton should get out more — Anyone who takes himself so seriously could use a good laugh" (Editorial, *Los Angeles Times*, September 26, 2002).

Others blamed a generational divide for Jackson and Sharpton's response to the comedy. "It's also significant that the jokes about King and Parks appear in a movie that stars rappers and is geared to the hip-hop generation. King and Parks don't mean the same thing to folks who came of age in the 1980s and 90s" (Seymour 2002). "This is where the generations divide. Young viewers can't see what all the fuss is about, while some of Jackson's generation can't stand to hear their icons put down" (Patterson 2002). "Barbershop was written, produced and directed by a younger generation of black folks who feel the freedom to laugh out loud — and in public — about the stuff we black folks laugh about at home, in church kitchens and, yes, in barbershops" (Shipp 2002).

Other commentators discussed the truths that underpinned the harsh remarks. "Much of what the Comedian's character says about Parks, albeit in a tasteless manner, is true. Indeed, she wasn't the first African American in the Alabama capital to refuse to relinquish her seat to segregation. For quite some time the leaders in the community had been searching for a model citizen willing to get arrested and they finally decided that Parks fit the bill" (Pearson 2002). "Is Eddie harsh when he calls King 'a ho'? Yes, but even when King's infidelity is discussed more delicately and with scholarly authority drama inevitably ensues" (Dyson 2002). "The jokes in the film work because they pick up all of this ambivalence surrounding King and Parks. They unite the audience in an acknowledgement that King and Parks were and are heroes, yes, but not without flaws" (Seymour 2002).

Although MGM executives apologized for offending Jackson and Sharpton, they refused to pull the scenes from the film or to edit them from future video release. The studio also announced plans for a sequel. Then, to add yet another layer of complexity, an organization representing black barbers filed suit against Jackson and Sharpton, claiming that their actions had "created a negative public sentiment about the profession, resulting in a loss of business" (Associated Press, October 30, 2002).[4]

It is beyond the scope of this project to analyze the quality of the movie or to argue whether the filmmakers had a right to challenge sacred civil rights icons. Rather, I want to think about how the film and the controversy surrounding it are a moment when many of the elements of the theory of everyday black talk and the empirical evidence of this text meet. A black public space, the barbershop, is represented in a black media source, an African American-produced, directed, and written film. The film ignites a firestorm of controversy by leaders of black organizations (who also happen to be ministers!), who claim that certain aspects of everyday black talk are inappropriate when represented in film. Then a group of organized laborers accuse the old-guard civil rights leadership of being inauthentic. The movie, its content, and its controversy brought into stark relief the centrality of political discussion and dissent within the lives of ordinary African Americans. In this moment, the role of public spaces, media, organizations, and authenticity claims were all exposed as the internal dissension of black political thought took center stage. In many ways this series of events crystallizes the theory of everyday talk. The *Barbershop* movie and the controversy it brings is centered on two central arguments of this book: (1) ordinary black people hold a diverse set of political worldviews, and (2) everyday talk in forums of the black counterpublic serves as the mechanism through which these political attitudes are reproduced.

Further, the *Barbershop* controversy pushes us to redirect academic inquiry of black politics to include an investigation of the ordinary spaces and interactions in people's lives. Whatever its flaws, this movie resonated with many African Americans because it reflected a shared cultural understanding of the role of everyday places and seemingly unexceptional people in the creation of black politics. Many reacted negatively to Sharpton and Jackson because to silence "Eddie" would be to deny a truth of black political life: that black people disagree, and that public spaces are critical to black social and political life. The current scholarship in black public opinion rarely grapples with these issues.

Jesse Jackson's 1984 and 1988 presidential bids were at the center of many volumes of earlier scholarship in African American politics in the early 1990s (Tate 1991, 1993; Marable 1995; Reed 1986). Jackson's campaigns were historic, and they marked the culmination of the shift in mainstream black politics from the protest activities of the excluded to the electoral tactics of full citizens. But this research agenda also contributed to certain scholarly blindnesses. Jackson is a member of the political elite. He is an Integrationist committed to strategies of civil disobedience, electoral mobilization, and the politics of pressure and influence. Much of the existing black politics literature is similarly oriented. The *Barbershop* controversy demonstrated that Jackson is now marginal to many elements of black cultural and political life. Echoing many who disagreed with the Jackson/Sharpton critique of *Barbershop*, Earl Hutchinson (2002) wrote,

> The biggest gripe many blacks have about some black leaders is that they give to themselves the sole right to speak exclusively on behalf of all blacks. . . . Whites are profoundly conditioned to believe that all blacks, think, act, and sway to the same racial beat. . . . Barbershop is more than a comedic, slice-of-black-life film, it spotlights the historic role that barbershops in black communities have traditionally played in allowing working people to vent, swap gossip and information, keep abreast of social and political issues, and express their own special brand of in-group humor. There is no need to apologize for that.

Many African Americans rushed to defend the authenticity of the film and articulated the right of black people to disagree, to question sacred icons, and to portray realities of black life in film. These reactions suggest that a new agenda in black politics scholarship should focus on uncovering the content and meaning of those daily interactions and the diversity of opinions expressed there. This text is one step in that direction.

As we embark on this new agenda, it is clear that we must broadly define "the political" and expect to find it in unusual places. Commenting on the *Barbershop* controversy, author Michael Eric Dyson (2002) noted, "Politics are at work at all time, sometimes in ways we can spot and at other times in ways we can barely discern. When it comes to black folk, films take on added weight. They bear what James Baldwin called 'the burden of representation.' A film is never just a film. It is seen as a political statement or a social document." Elections, protests, campaigns: these are the participatory strategies that have been mapped and analyzed within the empirical literature on political participation. Less is known about the informal deliberations of citizens in the conduct of their ordinary lives. Mapping the future of black politics requires that we investigate the spaces of black life where African Americans cull meaning from daily interactions.

Although this text has begun the work of drawing a connection between everyday talk and ideology, many questions are left for future research. Why do people find themselves tapped into particular kinds of black counterpublic spaces while others are shut out of them? Poor, urban African Americans often live isolated lives in communities that lack organizational infrastructure. Young black men are tapped into hip-hop. Many read the *Source,* buy Jay-Z, and tune in to urban radio. Older black women are likely to be churchgoers. Many respect their ministers, pray regularly, and turn to their religious communities for guidance. Black gay men and lesbians are often silenced in the church, rendered invisible in the mainstream black media, and marginalized in traditional public spaces. Many are tapped into alternative black counterpublics where racial identity is cross-cut by sexual identity. Before we can have a complete understanding of everyday talk and black political thought, we must investigate the ways that class, age, gender, sexual orientation, and other identities structure access to the black counterpublic. A new agenda for the study of black public opinion could take up this task.

There is a danger that in broadening our understanding of the political and looking outside the boundaries of traditional definitions of the political we can be distracted from understanding politics as the substance that affects the material lives of African Americans. Jackson and Sharpton were criticized for precisely this failure. While Dyson is right to point to the ways that film representations of blackness and black people are inherently political in the U.S. context, it is also true that the fall of 2002 presented many other kinds of political challenges to black communities, most of which received considerably less media attention with respect to their specific impact on African Americans. In the fall of 2002 the country was facing a critical election. Although they lost the American presidency in 2000, Democrats were poised to retake the House and secure a solid majority in the Senate. A Democratic majority in the Congress would have propelled several senior African American legislators to positions of significant influence. In the fall of 2002 the national economy was slumping, having never fully recovered from the post–September 11 downturn of the previous year. African Americans were facing the loss of economic gains made in the previous decade. War with Iraq was imminent. Two African Americans, Colin Powell and Condoleeza Rice, were in key decision-making positions. Rather than appearing as political agents at the forefront of these issues, the press focused on the *Barbershop* controversy. Several observers questioned if this meant that black politics was off-track, misdirected, and obsolete. "The debate over *Barbershop* has deflected attention away from a more threatening problem for millions of African Americans. Last week the Census Bureau reported some disturbing economic news. The median household income of black families fell for the second straight year after rising in all but one of the previous eight years" (Wickham 2002).

While we look for politics in surprising places, it is important to question the efficacy of the black counterpublic in dealing with the structures of economic, political, and social inequality that continue to shape the life chances of black men and women in the United States. Our research must bring empirical evidence to bear on the questions: can everyday talk work as an agent of mobilization? How does the heterogeneity of black public opinion translate into participatory strategies for African Americans? These are the questions that emerge as we set this text in the context of the *Barbershop* movie controversy.

COLIN POWELL AND HARRY BELAFONTE

Other events in 2002 provided opportunities to contextualize the claims made in this book. While the *Barbershop* controversy had African Americans talking about the acceptable limits of public speech by black people about black people, singer and political activist Harry Belafonte publicly denounced Secretary of State Colin Powell as a "House Negro." In a radio interview on station KFMB in San Diego, Belafonte stated, "In the days of slavery there were those slaves who lived on the plantation and those slaves who lived in the house. You got the privilege of living in the house if you served the master. Colin Powell is committed to come into the house of the master, when Colin Powell dares to suggest something other than what the master wants to hear, he will be turned back out to pasture" (reported in *New York Times*, October 10, 2002). Belafonte's critique of Powell's seeming capitulation to President Bush's call for military action against Iraq was couched in racial language meant to discredit him with African American masses.

Powell's explosive popularity from the mid-1990s had dimmed little among a national audience by 2000. However, many African Americans remained ambivalent about Powell, simultaneously feeling proud of his accomplishments and concerned with his political affiliations. Still, in 2000 he remained a generally well-liked and warmly regarded public figure.[5] But by 2002 Powell was more open to racial criticism. He became secretary of state under President George W. Bush. By joining the Bush administration, Powell eroded some of his mass black support. Many African Americans perceived Bush's ascendancy to the presidency as a fraudulent one, wrought on the backs of disenfranchised black Floridians. Bush's reputation as an indiscriminate enforcer of the death penalty while governor of Texas and his conservative policy stances made him one of the least popular presidents in American history among African Americans. "Ninety-two percent of African Americans believe that the president does not represent their interests, with full a fifth believing he is actively opposed to their interests" (Dawson 2001, 324). When Powell accepted a position in the Bush administration, it set the stage for Belafonte's criticism in the fall of 2002.

On its face, there is little that is exceptional about a liberal black public figure criticizing a conservative one. But the language and symbols that Belafonte employed and with which Powell countered are illustrative of the arguments made in chapter 6. Belafonte did not simply state disagreement with Powell's policy positions or even his general political orientation. Belafonte used a well-known, black cultural symbol to question Powell's racial authenticity. Belafonte's critique attempts to strip Powell of any legitimate claim to the defiance tradition in black political culture. The house Negro/fieldhand dichotomy is a frequently employed racial symbol for the ways that powerful whites have divided and conquered African Americans by co-opting selected members of the group through an appeal to individual, material self-interest. No house Negro could be trusted by other blacks because he was too psychologically and economically aligned with powerful whites.[6] Powell had largely eschewed these types of criticisms earlier in his career by maintaining a staunchly nonpartisan public stance. Even in the context of his Republican partisan affiliation, Powell had maintained a sense of personal and policy independence. His allegiance to the Bush administration compromised that position. When Belafonte employed the house Negro metaphor, he tapped into black political culture by asserting the value of independent defiance and arguing that Powell was incapable of such defiance because of his alliance with Bush. It is a rhetorical device meant to expose Powell as a fraudulent trickster.

Powell's response displayed his own comfort with and capacity to employ black cultural tropes. Somewhat beneath the radar, Powell chose to use his own authenticity arguments, engaging Belafonte in a kind of public game of the dozens.[7] Officially Powell stated on *Larry King Live*: "If Harry had wanted to attack my politics, that was fine. If he wanted to attack a particular position I hold, that was fine. But to use a slave reference, I think is unfortunate and is a throwback to another time and another place. I wish Harry had thought twice about using it." On the surface this statement is an unexceptional and predictable response. But there is a challenge embedded in it. Twice Powell referred to Belafonte as "Harry." Although Belafonte had used the secretary's first and last

name in his own interview, Powell chooses to use the familiar and di-
minutive first name only. This rhetorical device has meaning in black
cultural contexts. It suggests that Powell found Belafonte nonthreaten-
ing and largely humorous. Further, by the social rules of the Jim Crow
South, African American men were often demeaned by whites who used
only first names to refer to adult men, while demanding that black men
use titles when addressing whites, even white children. It was a device
used to assert and maintain power relations between the races. Powell
deploys this same device in his casual use of the name "Harry."

Further, while Powell's public statement on *Larry King* was carefully
measured, Powell leaked a more personal attack through other sources.
Powell and Belafonte share a Caribbean heritage, and Powell used press
leaks to question Belafonte's authentic Caribbean identity. The *New
York Times* reported, "Mr. Belafonte and Secretary Powell are both of
Jamaican descent, and Mr. Powell is a huge fan of calypso music. Secretary Powell has often assured associates that Mr. Belafonte's calypso-
style nightclub performances are not the *real thing*" (*New York Times*,
October 10, 2002, emphasis mine). Powell went straight to the heart of
Belafonte's artistic authenticity and in doing so undermined Belafonte's
authority to judge racial authenticity.

For some observers, the Powell-Belafonte exchange was surreal, even
absurd. Here was Belafonte, a seventy-five-year-old, light-skinned Jamaican, who is married to a white woman, accusing Powell, a sixty-six-
year-old, light-skinned Jamaican, who is married to a black woman, of
being racially inauthentic. Powell offers a "yo mama" response by criticizing Belafonte's music as inauthentic. "I'm no fan of the administration Powell serves. But he is no more a racial traitor for that service
than Belafonte was for divorcing a black woman to marry a white one
back in 1957" (Pitts 2002). African American public figures are often
accused of Uncle Tomism for aligning with policy agendas considered
antithetical to black interests—for example, Ward Connerly and Clarence Thomas endure this critique often. Similarly, those in interracial
romantic unions are often suspected of divided racial loyalties. The Powell-Belafonte exchange involves these multiple layers of complexity: skin
color, ethnic identity, and personal, artistic, and political authenticity.

The episode further illustrates the ways that African American public
figures employ elements of black popular culture as they compete in a
marketplace of ideas. Belafonte first challenges Powell's ability to function as a defiant hero. Powell minimizes Belafonte and responds with a
racially recognizable dozens insult. Belafonte refused to back away from
his criticism and later added a moralism claim by stating that Powell's
involvement with Bush was immoral. "When you are actively a part of
oppression, then you are a moral problem" (Lawrence 2002). The inter-

play between these two public figures further reveals the central argument of the previous chapter: black common sense, as expressed in black cultural tropes, shapes the public appeals of African American ideological elites.

REVEREND KENNEY AND THE SPLIT WITH ORANGE GROVE

Although it did not make national news, another event in the fall of 2002 offers an additional epilogue to this text. In September 2002 Reverend Carl Kenney was removed as pastor of Orange Grove Missionary Baptist Church. Each August Reverend Kenney takes a three-week leave from his pastoral responsibilities at Orange Grove. When he returned from his leave in 2002 he received a phone call from the Deacon board. He was told that before he could return to the pulpit he would have to come before the church leadership and answer for a number of incidents that had occurred over the previous twelve months.[8] Reverend Kenney remembers the meeting as a five-hour ordeal where he was called to task on a range of personal and theological issues. Within forty-eight hours of the meeting the church leaders called a forum of the congregation. Without a majority of the church membership present, and in a controversial vote separated by only a handful of ballots, Reverend Kenney was dismissed as pastor. He never returned to the Orange Grove pulpit. "They didn't let me say goodbye to my family," Kenney lamented when he told me the story of his dismissal. "I just wish I had been given an opportunity to preach one last time, so I could have said goodbye."

Reverend Kenney's dismissal is informative about the ideological constraints that continue to shape black religious life in the South, but it is also a story of the surprising success of extraordinary ideological appeals in the context of African American everyday talk. I ultimately ended up with two different sources for the story of Reverend Kenney's break with Orange Grove—his own and the one that emerged in the tales of Imperial Barbershop in Durham, North Carolina.[9] The stories that emerge from the two sources are vastly different, but each surrounds a tangle of sexual politics, personal choice, and theology.

Imperial Barbershop is popular among North Carolina Central students. It is located near campus, and many students and alumni frequent it. Orange Grove is also popular with NCCU students and alumni. Thus, many Orange Grove congregants get their hair cut at Imperial. Before he began growing dreadlocks in the summer of 2001, Reverend Kenney also got his hair cut at Imperial. In the weeks following Kenney's departure, Imperial was site of significant conversation and speculation about the Orange Grove vote.

The rumors can be grouped in three categories. Some speculated that Kenney was dismissed because of financial transgressions. One story suggested that he had a $500 monthly cellular phone bill in the church's name. Another claimed that he purchased a Cadillac in the church's name and failed to make the monthly payments. A second set of rumors swirled around sexual misconduct. Reverend Kenney divorced his second wife in the summer of 2001. Some Imperial customers told stories of Kenney dating several different women and of his being less than discreet. The third storyline that emerged at Imperial was an assessment of Reverend Kenney as too controversial. "Man, you know they were out to get him." "Did you know that he listened to DMX? No minister should be listening to DMX!" "It's all that stuff he was doing to bring in the young people. You know church folks don't go for that." This narrative focused on Kenney's relaxed style, which led some Imperial customers to critique him as insufficiently ministerial. That the men of Imperial debated and speculated about Kenney's departure is evidence that the politics of Orange Grove extended beyond the walls of its sanctuary. This exceptional minister had also penetrated everyday black talk in the public spaces of Durham's black barbershops. As the men tried to make sense out of the separation between this high-profile church and its popular minister, money, sex, and controversy emerged as the likely explanations.

Reverend Kenney's side of the story debunks the specifics of the Imperial narrative but maintains the centrality of sexuality and controversy. Reverend Kenney did indeed divorce a second time. His first divorce was precipitated by his wife's extramarital affair. Although some in the church felt that a divorce should cost Reverend Kenney his pulpit, a majority of the congregation and leadership felt that the reasons for the separation were justified. He endured. Reverend Kenney reports that he felt a great deal of pressure to remarry. As a young, single, minister he felt that rumors would fly if he attempted to date, so he quickly remarried in the summer of 1999. As a sign of his Feminist sensibilities, Reverend Kenney hyphenated his last name and became Daniels-Kenney during his brief second marriage. By the summer of 2001 Reverend Kenney had separated from his second wife. "I should never have married," Reverend Kenney told me. "We were strangers, but I just felt so much pressure." Although he did not immediately lose his pulpit, the second divorce did irreparable damage to Reverend Kenney's reputation with many clergy and laypersons at Orange Grove.

In the shadow of the second divorce, two other "sexual scandals" occurred. First, Reverend Kenney undertook an explicit campaign to tackle the issue of homophobia in the black church. Dedicating a series in his *Herald-Sun* column to the issue, Reverend Kenney called black Christians to task for their bigotry, loathing, and hypocrisy regarding homosexuality. In response, the church leadership requested that Reverend Kenney remove the name "Orange Grove Missionary Baptist Church" from his byline in the paper. He refused. In a second major battle with the church leadership, Reverend Kenney ordained to the ministry a woman who was unmarried and pregnant. "I prayed about it a lot," he told me. "It weighed on my soul. But here was the deciding factor for me. The father of this baby, he was also a minister, and he was ordained just a few months before her. Why should the woman have to bear shame and punishment alone just because we can see her condition when the man can hide? I just had to do it." Reverend Kenney told me that in the meeting with the church clergy he repented for the personal sins. "The divorce. That is a legitimate problem. I was in a very bad place, but I can understand why that was unacceptable." While he was willing to repent for the personal failings he refused to back away from the theological concerns. "I would not apologize for my stance on homosexuality. And I would not apologize for the ordination. Those things were right." In Reverend Kenney's estimation, it was his stand on the sexual politics of homosexuality and extramarital child rearing that led to his ousting.

In important ways, the men of Imperial Barbershop were right. Reverend Kenney left Orange Grove because of sex and controversy.[10] For all its exceptionalism, Orange Grove is still a Southern, black, Baptist church. Womanist theologian Kelly Brown Douglas (1999) argues that black Christianity, warped by its contact with white Western ideals, is infused with both rampant homophobia and the perception of sexuality as sinful. She argues that exploitation of black sexuality is integral to white racial hegemony, and claims that sexuality has become maligned and silenced in African American Christianity as a result. Reflecting this tradition, many of the church leaders found Kenney's actions around various aspects of sexuality unacceptable. These voices prevailed.

Is Reverend Kenney's removal from Orange Grove troubling for the theory of everyday black talk? I think not. First, Kenney's popularity persisted beyond his Orange Grove tenure. Two hundred black men and women followed Kenney to establish a new church, Compassion Ministries of Durham. Aware of his divorces, knowing his stance on homosexuality, informed of his ordination decision, hundreds of black men and women chose to set up a new church under new rules. Douglas asserts that "the Black church and community have a theological mandate to engage in a Black sexual discourse of resistance whenever possible" (1999, 130). Reverend Kenney's separation from Orange Grove was moment of such possibility. With an explicit mandate to engage in this kind of sexual and racial resistance, Kenney remains an important part of Durham's religious and political landscape, leading a new church and continuing his weekly columns.

Kenney's epilogue is instructive about the contours of everyday black talk. The experimental work in chapter 4 offered evidence that certain ideological positions are policed in particular venues of the black counterpublic. Reverend Kenney's largely Feminist ideology had always been an uneasy fit for a Southern, black, Baptist church. Trading on his charisma, commitment to community, and ministerial status, Reverend Kenney did the exceptional work of inserting this unlikely ideological mix into the everyday talk of Durham church folks. But there are real consequences for those who step too far outside the boundaries of acceptable ideological expression within venues of the black counterpublic. The producers of *Barbershop* learned this lesson when they took the private conversations of black public spaces and recreated them in a media source. Jackson and Sharpton have no interest in policing weekend conversations in barbershops all across the country. Their concern was with the media depiction of these controversial leadership critiques. As they brought the language of one counterpublic space into another, the creators of *Barbershop* met the resistance of traditional leaders. When Reverend Kenney chose to profess unpopular ideological positions in a traditional black counterpublic space, he lost his job.

This does not mean that Kenney failed. As controversial as his positions were, he still amassed an enormous following. His new ministry was established within weeks of his departure from Orange Grove. Not everyone followed Kenney. Many chose to stay at Orange Grove or to seek new churches, but Kenney's influence on hundreds of African Americans is clear. They left the comfort of their modern, beautiful, well-resourced church and began meeting in the basement of a local mall as they awaited a new home for their church. I believe that this fierce loyalty reflects more than personal preference for Kenney — it reflects a commitment to his theology and ideology forged through shared everyday black talk.

MAPPING BLACK POLITICAL ATTITUDES

In the end, there is no proof that everyday black talk is the central mechanism of ideological development among African Americans. The empirical evidence is suggestive. Distinct patterns of political thought that can be understood as ideologies do appear in the national survey data. When subjected to experimental manipulation, conversations among

African Americans do influence the political attitudes black people express. At least some black churches and barbershops operate as sites of ideological discourse. Black public figures from divergent ideological positions do employ similar cultural tropes in their appeals to African American masses. But still, there are rival explanations for understanding the shape of black public opinion.

Further investigation into childhood socialization processes can surely illuminate the ideological choices of black adults. Critical exogenous shocks on the international and national stage such as war, terrorism, economic shifts, and political scandal undoubtedly influence black public opinion. Perhaps understanding public opinion lies in places that are entirely unfamiliar to political scientists. An intriguing study published in the *Journal of Personal and Social Psychology* in 2001 suggested that political attitudes may be genetic. Studying nearly four hundred pairs of twins, Canadian researchers found that some political attitudes are heritable, and that those attitudes that are heritable are psychologically "stronger" than less heritable attitudes (Olson et al. 2001). I am not yet ready to concede the study of political attitudes to the biologists, but the twin study indicates that the universe of possible influences on attitudes is broad and still largely uncharted.

One might also ask if the claim of diversity in black public opinion can be sustained in light of the overwhelming support of the Democratic Party in black voting behavior. African Americans vote now, as they have for more than half a century, in a nearly monolithic Democratic block. Ideological diversity seems to map onto electoral homogeneity. Some may wonder if better than 90 percent of the African American vote is going to go to the Democratic candidate in everything from municipal to presidential elections, then what is the value of pointing to heterogeneity in black thought? I believe that it is likely that electoral homogeneity is a result of particular institutional constraints in the U.S. system. It is a first-past-the-post, single-member district, two-party system with a truncated left. In this system, the rush to grab the median voter leaves little opportunity for candidates or platforms reflecting more nuanced ideological positions. Lani Guinier has theorized on the ways that different voting rules and institutions would likely uncover more electoral heterogeneity among Americans.

Even with its limitations, the evidence in this text is suggestive that ordinary African Americans, in the context of their everyday talk with one another, reproduce complex patterns of political belief. Manning Marable observes that "the central theme of black American history has been the constant struggle to overcome the barriers of race and the reality of unequal racial identities between black and white. . . . These collective experiences of discrimination, and this memory of resistance and oppression, have given rise to several overlapping group strategies or critical perspectives within the African-American community, which have as their objective the ultimate empowerment of black people" (1995, 216). With respect to this observation, the lessons of this text are clear. If we are to discern the contours of black public opinion in the new century, we must listen to the talk of ordinary men and women. It is in that talk that a unique black politics is born.

Notes

Chapter One

1. The social movements literature is rich with theory of how ordinary citizens become central actors in the process of social change through mass-based action. The classical model of social movements treats social movements as a response to the structural strains in society that disrupt individual psyches. Once psychological disturbance reaches a given threshold, a social movement emerges. These writers predicted social movements in mass societies marked by alienation and anxiety (Laumann and Segal 1971; Lenski 1956; Smelser 1962). This classical model was heavily critiqued for its characterization of social movements as managing psychological tensions and its perception of social movement participants as psychologically abnormal. Alternatively, the resource mobilization model understands social movements, not as a form of irrational behavior but rather as a tactical response to closed political systems. This view argues that the level of strain is an insufficient explanation for social movement emergence and instead points to the relevance of the availability of resources (McCarthy and Zald 1973, 1977; Jenkins and Perrow 1977). The resource mobilization model was critiqued for its emphasis on movement leadership and failure to fully acknowledge the capacities and resources of the mass base. Building on the strengths of both the classical and resource mobilization models, Aldon Morris (1984) offered the indigenous perspective theory as a way of understanding the American civil rights movement. This theory holds that mass protest is a product of the organizing efforts of activists functioning through a well-developed indigenous base. Doug McAdam's study of the civil rights movement (1982) draws upon the earlier work of Piven and Cloward (1977) and introduces a political process model emphasizing the political rather than psychological elements of social movements. Dennis Chong (1991) used the theories of rational choice and collective action to argue that the civil rights movement is like an iterated prisoner's dilemma where reputational concerns, mutual obligations and commitments, as well as other-regarding interests, and social incentives explain organizing success. All of these theories ultimately predict and explain extraordinary circumstances of citizen involvement and not the ordinary politics that concern this text. A study of the politics embedded in the everyday argues for the relevance of ordinary citizens outside of these kinds of historical moments. By focusing on contemporary African American discourse and attitudes, this text offers evidence that even without voter registration drives or armed resistance, there is politics among African Americans.

2. The emphasis on the black counterpublic should be seen as a supplement to, rather than an alternative for, more traditional models of political socialization that focus on childhood and adolescent processes of political attitude development. Among the most important contributions of the political socialization

literature, whose intellectual roots can be traced to Hyman's 1959 *Political Socialization,* is the demonstration that political ideas and orientations begin to take form in early childhood. Early studies with African American children demonstrated that black children were less efficacious in general, more negative toward political figures who were generally viewed as adversarial to racial interests, and more positive to figures generally perceived as racially friendly (Abramson 1977; Sears 1973; Lyons 1970). In this early literature the family and the school are considered the primary agents of socialization. The primacy principle guiding much of the early socialization work acknowledged that socialization occurs over the course of the lifecycle but maintained that fundamental political orientations were firmly established during childhood (Dawson and Prewitt 1969; Dennis 1968; Greenstein 1965). But, by the late 1970s the primacy principle came under increasing scrutiny as socialization scholars argued for a more central role for adult processes (Searing, Wright, and Rabinowitz 1976). Undoubtedly childhood socialization plays an important role in establishing political orientations and attitudes, but this text will attempt to establish that processes of ideological development continue well into adulthood. Interaction in the black counterpublic is an important element of understanding mature political viewpoints.

3. The following chapters offer more complete discussions of each element of the contemporary black counterpublic.

4. A more complete discussion of the significance of black barbershops can be found in chapter 5.

5. Some relevant sources on African Americans and the white media include Bogle (2001, 1990); Dates and Barlow (1993); MacDonald (1992); Torress (1998); Sook (1999).

6. The mass media has been the battleground for a war of images. It is, in part, through the black media that African Americans develop alternative images of blackness and the ideologies that are associated with these images. "The mass media function as the producers and transmitters of ideologies because the rituals and myths they reproduce for public consumption 'explain, instruct, and justify practices and institutions . . . linking symbols, formulas, plot and characters in a pattern that is conventional, appealing and gratifying' (Dates and Barlow 1993, 4).

7. An example is the small but growing body of research on the effects of rap music on individual social and political attitudes. Took and Weiss (1994) studied the effects of heavy metal and rap music on adolescent turmoil. Their findings suggest that the apparent link between rap listening and school problems, sexual activity, drug use, and arrests is actually an artifact of gender. Johnson et al. (1995), in an experiment using African American adolescents, demonstrated that exposure to nonviolent rap videos tended to increase acceptance of sexual violence. This effect was particularly strong among black girls, who were significantly more accepting of sexual violence after viewing the videos. An ethnographic study by McLean finds:

Music seems to provide these adolescents, who are both consumers and critics, with a way of thinking about their gender roles and contradictions and their ideas of constructing sexual expression. . . . The adolescents in this study are not blindly assimilating meaning and messages presented in musical recordings. . . . They have distinct points of view and are not reticent in articulating them. Most are quite savvy as to the multiple textual meanings in various genres, particularly rap, and at times brought their personal experiences and a critical eye to bear on their interpretations. (McLean 1997)

8. In chapter 2 of *Black Visions*, Michael Dawson carefully engages the study of political ideology among critical theorists and stakes out a distinct agenda for those interested in the study of political ideology among African Americans. He cogently argues that the history of political thought and action among African Americans directly challenges the notion that ideology is the exclusive domain of the ruling classes. He writes, "Black ideologues decisively demonstrate that ideologies can be produced by the opposition, loyal or not, and not just by a ruling race, clique, or class. Black ideologies are almost always highly critical of both the hegemonic American liberal world view of any given period and the actual functioning of the American state and the place of blacks in civil society" (Dawson 2001, 53).

9. Interestingly, this critique coincides with a critical expansion of the American electorate in the middle of the twentieth century. The late 1950s, 1960s, and 1970s in the United States were marked by the emergence of massive participation in social movements among American blacks, women, and youth. The civil rights, feminist, and antiwar movements, along with the legislation resulting from these movements, meant that the American electorate looked very different in 1975 from what it looked like in 1950. It is interesting that the denigration of the mass public as unsophisticated and uniformed could coexist with these political realities that suggested ordinary people were deeply engaged with their government.

10. This analysis is not meant to suggest that only scholars of African American politics have critiqued the elitist strain of ideological research. Indeed, many important texts in the study of American political development have argued that ideology rests with ordinary people. See, for example, Huntington (1981); Foner (1980); Smith (1997).

11. It is the truth claims inherent in ideological projects that tend to make Marxist critical theorists nervous. Arendt (1958, 468) argues that it is the tendency of ideology to "explain everything and every occurrence by deducing it from a single premise" that makes ideologies inherently totalitarian. The truth claims characteristic of black Nationalist thought have often been the object of a similar criticism within the African American intellectual tradition. The point here is not to evaluate the veracity, or even desirability, of this sort of ideological epistemology, but rather to argue that such claims are part of what distinguish systems of thought from idiosyncratic attitude sets.

12. Throughout the text, capitalization on the ideologies is used to designate specifically African American versions of these ideologies which have more general meaning. For example, Nationalism is capitalized to distinguish it from nationalisms which have historical and political meaning in other contexts. The

same convention is used for Feminism, Conservatism, and Liberal Integrationism.

13. Dawson's public opinion data are certainly about mass attitudes, but the bulk of *Black Visions* is spent in a historical account of more elite actors in black politics.

14. Dawson and I disagree on the categorization of Disillusioned Liberalism as a political ideology. In my assessment, disillusionment is an affective state that may overlay any ideological disposition, but that is not linked to liberalism per se. I see no evidence that Disillusioned Liberalism, even as defined by Dawson, addresses the central questions that animate black politics as the other articulated ideological positions do. Dawson's description and empirical measurement seem closer to nihilism, which again is not the exclusive domain of liberalism but may emerge from disaffection within any of the ideological traditions.

15. For the purposes of this inquiry, the ideologies will be painted with broad strokes, and much of the nuance will necessarily be lost. I encourage readers to consult Dawson's *Black Visions* for a more comprehensive historical analysis.

16. The idea of terror also has specific historical significance for African Americans. The maintenance of the racial hierarchy in the Jim Crow South relied heavily on the terrorism of lynching. Lynching was never just about individual acts of vigilantism but was always conducted within a larger framework of racial domination. Lynching created psychological and physical terror for generations of African Americans living in the repressive system of American apartheid. Yet the spirit of resistance remained alive among black Southerners, frequently emerging in the twentieth century as guerrilla skirmishes as white racism and ultimately culminating in the civil rights movement. This resistance to terrorism was nurtured by countering loneliness and isolation through the black counterpublic. In churches, schools, newspapers, and both covert and open political organizations, African Americans carved out space that resisted terror. Some important texts on lynching include Dray (2001); Wells-Barnett, (1969); Duster (1970); MacLean (1994).

17. Bodily appearance, ancestry, self-awareness of ancestry, public awareness of ancestry, culture, and subjective identification are the other elements Mills suggests contribute to the construction of racial identity.

18. Black Nationalism predates the twentieth century. Some useful texts illuminating earlier Nationalist traditions include Geiss (1974), (1969); Redkey (1969); Stuckey (1987).

19. Some important sources on Marcus Garvey include Cronon (1955); Martin (1976); Vincent (1971).

20. This Nationalist position is a historical shift in SNCC's position, which began as self-consciously Integrationist. For more on the history of the Student Nonviolent Coordinating Committee, see Carson (1981).

21. According to Pinkney, "within the context of black nationalism, cultural nationalism assumes that people of African descent share a way of life, or culture, which is fundamentally different from that of Europeans and other non-Africans" (1976, 127). The Nation of Islam is probably the best example of institutionalized cultural Nationalism. C. Eric Lincoln captures the spirit of the

Nation's cultural Nationalism: "black nationalism is a way of life. It is an implicit rejection of the symbols of that culture, balanced by an exaggerated and undiluted pride in black culture . . . Black nationalism addresses itself not to an existent state, but to a state of mind" (1961). Other important sources on the Nation of Islam include Essien-Udom (1962); Muhammad (1965).

Educational Nationalism included a push for curricular reform at primary, secondary, and collegiate levels. Whether focused on the creation of separate academic institutions for black youngsters or manifested as creation of black studies departments on white college campuses, educational Nationalism was an important element in asserting the centrality of educational practices to the black liberation struggle. In 1968 the International Conference on Black Power's Report of the Workshop on Education called for the development of "specific strategies for physically taking over schools and classrooms, disrupting racist learning, whenever the situation demands." Reprinted in Van Deburg (1997).

Black liberation theology is central to the religious Nationalist project. More on black liberation theology can be found in Cone (1969); Cleage (1969); Lincoln and Mamiya (1990).

Major figures in the revolutionary Nationalist tradition include the African Blood Brotherhood, Malcolm X, and the Black Panthers. Citations include Briggs, (1997); Newton (1973); Malcolm X (1965). Dawson (2001) characterizes this tradition as those who "viewed the project of national liberation as one which demands relentless struggle against the structures of white supremacy within the United States."

22. In chapter 6 of *Black Visions*, Dawson carefully explores the "occasionally tortured relationship between black liberalism and the American liberal tradition" from Frederick Douglass to Martin Luther King, Jr. I offer only a hint of that discussion here.

23. In constructing a sociology of black churches, Lincoln and Mamiya stress the communal approach to political thought that marks the African Americans experience. "For African Americans freedom has always been communal in nature. . . . In America, black people have seldom been perceived or treated as individuals, they have usually been dealt with as 'representatives' of their 'race,' an external projection. Hence, the communal sense of freedom has an internal African rootage curiously reinforced by hostile social convention" (1990, 5).

24. Aid to Families with Dependent Children (AFDC) is a frequent target of vehement Conservative criticism. The argument against welfare tends to be couched in terms of the attempt to protect the integrity of black families. Syndicated columnist Ken Hamblin captures the spirit of this critique: "Welfare makes it impossible to provide cognitive stimulation and emotional support to children. . . . The human brain was designed with an inherent thirst for knowledge, experience and information, but I'm convinced we deaden that brain activity when we have a guarantee of survival tied to a welfare check" (1999, 22).

25. This quote is taken from a position paper that is part of Project 21, an initiative of the National Center for Public Policy Research. The project's goal is to promote the views of young African American Conservatives interested in influencing public policy.

26. The term Womanism was coined by Alice Walker in *In Search of Our*

Mother's Gardens. Walker links the term Womanism with a Southern, black tradition of labeling outrageous and willful girl children as "womanish." Womanism reflects a respect for the courage inherent in "womanish" behavior. Walker's claim that "womanist is to feminist as purple to lavender" (1983, xii) has led some to believe that Walker's formulation was arguing for a superiority of Womanism over Feminism, a claim she has denied. This text uses the term "Womanism" in chapter 4 to distinguish a more Nationalist-oriented black Feminist viewpoint. That is a Feminism that largely rejects gender-based interracial alliances in favor of a focus on women's equality vis-à-vis black men within racial struggles.

27. The possible bibliography of black Feminism is considerable, but some canonical sources and important new texts include Collins (1990); Bambara (1970); Cannon (1995); Moraga and Anzalgdua (1981); hooks (1981); Hull, Scott, and Smith (1982); James and Busia (1993); Davis (1981); Giddings (1984); Walker (1983).

Chapter Two

1. In 1962 Robert Lane offered the voices of fifteen "Eastport" men to capture "why the American common man believes what he does." Lane can prove no causal relationships, his informants were not a representative sample of American citizens, and he can offer no hard scientific evidence for the conclusions he draws from his interviews, but his work is widely accepted as one of the most important on the topic of political ideology. In this chapter I hope to capture a little of what Lane offered the discipline more than forty years ago.

2. I selected eight individuals from a group of more than one hundred people who responded to an insert I placed in the church bulletin on Sunday, January 17, 1999. The bulletin said that a member of the Orange Grove family was doing research on African American church membership and asked if they would be willing to talk with me about their experiences at Orange Grove. I randomly selected ten individuals from the hundred respondents and called each of them to set up interviews. I did an enormous amount of followup calling but ultimately ended up with eight of the ten. None of them was compensated for participation, but each agreed to spend about an hour talking with me about general social issues and about their feelings and experiences at the church. I scheduled interviews at their convenience and taped the conversations with their knowledge and with the agreement that their names would be changed in any publications. In addition to speaking with these eight church members, I also undertook two years of participant–observer analysis of the church, taking weekly notes on sermons and church activities, participating in a number of church-based activities, and extensively studying the written statements of Orange Grove's pastor.

3. The *Herald-Sun* is more than one hundred years old. Its daily circulation exceeds 54,000, and its Sunday circulation exceeds 64,000. Reverend Kenney began writing a weekly Sunday column in 1997.

4. Ultimately Kenney did not survive at Orange Grove Missionary Baptist Church. In the late summer of 2002, in a close and controversial vote, Reverend

Kenney lost his position as pastor there. Within two weeks, more than two hundred loyal followers formed Compassion Ministries of Durham under Kenney's leadership. A full discussion of the rupture between Kenney and Orange Grove is taken up in the concluding chapter.

5. Kenney claims neither to be a Black Theology scholar nor to be fully in line with all the tenets of this tradition, but he does assert a connection to this tradition.

6. The Durham Committee on the Affairs of Black People was founded in 1935 by leaders of the black business community. It began as a middle-class intermediary institution, but in the 1960s the civil rights movement pushed the organization to focus more fully on issues of housing, welfare, and racial inequality. Today it functions as a pseudo-political party. Durham has nonpartisan local elections, and the committee spends much of its time endorsing and monitoring local elected officials.

7. Friends of Durham is a citizens group, which in Durham's nonpartisan politics represents conservative politics. In addition to being conservative, Friends of Durham is also thought of as the "white" citizens group and is most often in political opposition to the "liberal" Committee on the Affairs of Black People. The two groups have been embroiled in nasty racial politics concerning school districts, desegregation, and school board representation since 1994.

Chapter Three

1. Liberal Integrationism is not included in the analysis in this chapter. This chapter uses data from the 1993–94 National Black Politics Survey (NBPS). There is no reasonably coherent measure of Liberal Integrationism available in these data that fits a priori definitions of the ideological position. I tested several different constructs that included indicators about the importance of political rights, beliefs in American institutions, and the relevance of coalitions. I discovered that there was not a set of indicators in the NBPS that appropriately matched my a priori definitions of the central attitudes of Liberal Integrationism. Therefore, this analysis will focus on only three of the four identified ideologies. I will return to Liberal Integrationism in the following chapters, which deal with data from the experimental research. The experimental studies included measures that more adequately tap the Liberal Integrationist ideology.

2. The model is estimated using a maximum likelihood estimation technique, structural equation modeling. This technique uses a measurement model that specifies latent variables, their observed indicators and the errors associated with the measurement of those indicators. Political ideology is not directly measurable. If surveys simply asked people to rate their own Nationalism, Conservatism, or Feminism, the measure would say more about public responses to certain labels than it would about people's deeply held political views. Therefore ideological measures must be constructed from the responses to a series of attitude questions. The first part of the structural equation is a confirmatory factor analysis. The factor analytic model is based on the assumption that observable variables (in this case the responses to survey questions) are generated by unobserved, or latent, variables (in this case ideology). The factor model is a mea-

surement model that specifies how groups of observable attitudes are linked to underlying, unobserved ideologies. This factor analysis is especially useful because it accounts for the error associated with estimating unobservable phenomena from measurable responses. It does this by modeling the covariance between the latent factors in the system of equations. This makes it possible to explain the covariance among survey responses in terms of their relationship to underlying black political ideologies.

3. NBPS respondents range in age from eighteen to eighty-eight, with forty-three being the average age. Sixty-five percent of NBPS respondents are women, and 72 percent are self-identified Democrats. They report a high voter turnout, with 80 percent of them claiming to have voted in the last election. Seventy-seven report that religion is important in their daily lives. They are generally well educated, with 86 percent having completed at least a high school diploma. Fifty-six percent are big-city dwellers.

4. These results are from first differences from simple cross-tabulations of those who report listening to rap music. These results are entirely consistent with those reported by Dawson (2001). Using a test of first differences, gender, age, and education are all statistically significant at $p < .001$. Income and urbanicity are significant at $p < .05$ (1993–94 NBPS).

5. Percentage indicates those who answered yes.

6. These findings derive from a simple OLS regression where the dependent variable is an additive scale of these six indicators of black media usage and is modeled as a function of gender age, income, education, and urban dwelling. The coefficient for age, coded in years, is $-.004$ (.0004 SE) and is significant at $p < .001$. The coefficient for income is .02 (.003 SE) and is significant at $p < .001$. The coefficient for education is .01(.002 SE) and is significant at $p < .05$. The coefficients for gender and urban dwelling are non-significant (1993–94 National Black Politics Survey). Estimates are derived from an OLS regression using STATA.

7. Unfortunately the NBPS does not gauge how frequently individuals are exposed to each of these media sources or how much attention they pay to them. Each indicator is a simple yes/no dichotomous variable measuring usage in the past year.

8. These results are from first differences from simple cross-tabulations of those who report being a member of an organization working to improve the status of blacks. Using a test of first difference age is significant at $p < .05$. Income and education are each significant at $p < .001$ (1993–94 National Black Politics Survey).

9. In the full model, a sense of linked fate with black women is substituted for the general measure of women's linked fate for the male portion of the sample that was not given the women-linked-fate battery.

10. Because I am using the NBPS data in this analysis, I do not include Liberal Integrationism measures. In *Black Visions* (2001), Dawson uses NBPS data to measure Radical Egalitarianism, the ideology whose definition most closely matches my definition of Liberal Integrationism. It is measured as the opposite of Conservatism, such that disagreement with items used to measure Conservatism are coded as indicators of Radical Egalitarianism. I am uncomfortable with

this measurement strategy for Liberal Integrationism. Conservatism and Liberal Integrationism are not theorized to be mirror reflections of one another, and therefore the measures should not reflect this assumption. I choose instead to investigate only three of the four ideologies here.

11. Male respondents to the NBPS were not asked whether they self-identified as feminists.

12. Each ideology is measured on a scale from 0 to 1 such that 0 represents no agreement with the various indicators used to construct the ideology and 1 represents full agreement with all indicators. This unit range simplifies interpretation of coefficients in the next section. Each coefficient can be read as a percentage of the ideological scale. For example coefficient of .02 would indicate a two-percentage-point increase in a given ideology as a result of a unit change in the independent variable.

13. The CALIS procedure used to estimate the model offers several measures to assess the fit of the model. The overall Goodness of Fit Index (GFI) for the overall model is .89. The Root Mean Square Residual (RMR) is .07. And the Pr > Chi-Square is < .0001.

14. Age is measured in years as the respondents reported age at time of the survey. Sex is a dichotomous variable coded so that female = 1. Income is measured as self-reported income in one of six income categories ranging from 0 to 70,000 +. Education is measured as reported highest grade completed. Urban dwelling is a dichotomous variable so that those who live in large cities receive a 1.

Chapter Four

1. Funding for the 1998 NCCU Political Attitudes Study was provided by a graduate research grant from the African and African-American Studies Department at Duke University.

2. Funding for the 2001 KKC African American Attitudes Study was provided by a social science division research grant from the University of Chicago.

3. North Carolina Central University is a historically and predominately black, four-year university in Durham, North Carolina. It is a state school with a population of approximately three thousand undergraduate students. Approximately 80 percent of NCCU students are residents of North Carolina.

4. Kennedy-King College is a predominately black, two-year community college in Chicago, Illinois. It is one of the city colleges of Chicago, founded in 1935 as Woodrow Wilson Junior College. In 1965 the name was changed to Kennedy-King College in honor of Robert F. Kennedy and Martin Luther King, Jr.

5. Random assignment is necessary to maintain the comparative advantage of experimental work in making causal inferences. Random assignment allows the researcher to be relatively certain that unobserved differences in participants (personalities, backgrounds, etc.) are evenly distributed across experimental conditions. Therefore differences observed in different settings are a result of the manipulations introduced in that setting and not preexisting, confounding variables (Aronson et al. 1998; Kinder and Palfrey 1993).

6. The minister was actually a graduate student in Duke University Divinity School, and the professor was actually a graduate student in history at Duke University. Both were unknown to the subjects and were presented as simply a "minister" and a "professor." No institutional affiliations were offered.

7. See appendix 4.1 for a complete description of the experimental protocol.

8. See appendix 4.1 for a complete description of the experimental protocol.

9. As can be seen from the demographic characteristics of both the NCCU and KKC samples, North Carolina Central University and Kennedy-King College provided some distinct advantages as sites of experimental research. Unlike many college campuses, where the bulk of social psychology experiments are conducted, both NCCU and KKC have nontraditional student populations. NCCU subjects ranged in age from eighteen to forty-three, and the average age of a KKC respondent was thirty. In both samples many respondents were married, were parents, or were employed full- or part-time beyond the campus. This does not solve the problem of external validity of the samples, but it does allow the researcher to have more confidence in the robustness of the results.

10. This text hypothesizes that there are four relevant political ideologies operating in contemporary black thought: Nationalism, Liberal Integrationism, Feminism, and Conservatism. Ideally an experimental study might test interventions with each of these perspectives. But experiments, like all empirical studies, are constrained by the practical limitations of available resources. When faced with realistic tradeoffs, the Feminist and Conservative perspectives are chosen for the reasons outlined in the text above.

11. I use the term "Womanist Feminism" to describe a Feminist ideology that is more concerned with the position of black women vis-à-vis black men in the struggle for racial liberation than with the building of cross-racial gender alliances. By this I mean a specific concern with the intersection of gender and race and not a recognition of gender as the primary political identity. Womanism is a term first coined by Alice Walker, who describes a Womanist as someone "committed to the survival and wholeness of entire people, male and female."

12. The language used by group leaders to prompt these perspectives and the measurement of the various ideologies in both studies will be discussed in more detail below.

13. These terms are not included for purposes of control. Such statistical controls are unnecessary in analysis of a randomized, laboratory experiment. They are included to test the interaction effects of prior levels of information and knowledge with the messages encountered in the experimental settings.

14. Kelman (1958) introduced the notion that source credibility is tied to three specific factors: credibility, attractiveness, and power. Credibility has been further studied with respect to expertise and trustworthiness (Heesacker, Petty, and Cacioppo 1983). To the extent that men are perceived as more expert and powerful and ministers as particularly trustworthy, the group leader's gender and position could be explanations for his greater persuasiveness.

15. For most who are familiar with the history of the Black Southern Baptist tradition, it probably requires no comment that a Feminist minister constitutes a violation of expectations. But for those less familiar with this religious tradition, it is important to note that an explicitly Feminist stance is traditionally very

unusual for black Baptist ministers. Lincoln and Mamiya's book *The Black Church in the African American Experience* is a particularly good reference for understanding this tradition.

16. Arguably, the most influential contemporary research on attitude change in social psychology is Petty and Cacioppo's (1981) Elaboration Likelihood Model. The ELM provides comprehensive, organizing principles for understanding the effectiveness of persuasion. The model argues that there are central and peripheral routes to attitude change. Central routes require more cognitive processing and are capable of leading to more durable change, but they are activated only when subjects are motivated and able to process new information. The surprise of hearing a minister take a Feminist position may have induced more motivation to process and thus led to more central routes of persuasion.

17. Self-reported data gathered in this experiment found that this student's impressions are not accurate. According to this study, men were slightly more likely than women to be members of campus organizations: 49% of men who participated in the study were members of one or more student organizations at NCCU, whereas 42% of women who took part in the study were organization members. Also, the type of organization in which they participated was not significantly different by gender. These statistics suggest that men are as likely to be involved at NCCU as women are. This student is generalizing from her own experience, but the picture she paints does not appear to be entirely accurate. However, the other women in the group agree with her, and no males dispute her.

18. These two viewpoints are also positively correlated. $r = .77$.

19. There is no actual or statistically significant difference in the effects of a male group leader versus a female group leader in the ideological scores of respondents in the KKC study. Therefore, experimental categories are collapsed across message and not divided by messenger. This may seem a surprising result given the disparity of the effects of a male Feminist messenger in the NCCU study. The design of the KKC study accounts for this difference. In the NCCU study, group leaders are presented as authority figures—a preacher and a professor. In the group discussions, the leaders stood as the respondents sat, and the discussions were ordered in a hierarchal manner. In the KKC study, the group leaders were presented more as facilitators than as authoritative figures. They were introduced as "assistants working for the project" rather than given a role that would have any authoritative meaning beyond the experimental settings. They sat in a circle along with the respondents during the discussions, and they attempted to avoid hierarchy in the discussions. The differences in design are meaningful for changing the effect of the messenger on the reception of the ideological message. In the NCCU study, characteristics of the group leader influenced how the message was received by subjects. No such effect occurs in the KKC study. This was done purposely because the goals of the KKC study were to focus on more nuanced messages rather than on the differential impact of message source. The lack of effect of the group leader's sex means the experiment was successful in this element of its design.

20. Attitude toward whites is an additive scale (0 to 1) measured as level of agreement with the following indicators: (1) white people want to see blacks get

a better break; (2) white people want to keep blacks down (opposition coded); (3) white people cannot be trusted as political allies (opposition coded).

21. Strategic Integrationism is an additive scale (0 to1) measured as level of agreement with the following indicators: (1) there are many whites who are concerned about issues facing blacks. Blacks should work on forming alliances with these whites; (2) one very important thing about the civil rights movement is that it showed that blacks and whites can work together in America; (3) although historically black colleges are important, it is equally important that many of the best black students attend white colleges.

22. There is one aspect of source credibility that must be considered relevant when analyzing these groups. Neither the male preacher nor the female teacher who led the groups is a "real-life" black Conservative. When designing the study, I hoped to keep experimental conditions as similar as possible in all manipulations and therefore chose to use the same facilitators in both the Feminism and the Conservatism sessions. Neither of the group leaders is a self-identified Feminist or Conservative. But, after listening to the tapes, I found that each was generally more convincing as a Feminist than as a Conservative. The personal, political leanings of each is more aligned with a black Feminist ideology than with that of black Conservatives. To the extent that these facilitators were working harder to act Conservative, they were less convincing when promoting a Conservative viewpoint. In this way, source credibility may affect the outcome of the results in this group. I am convinced that this disparity is minimal. Part of my ability to see the difference is my firsthand knowledge of the facilitators' political views and my ability to hear all the sessions in comparison with one another. Subjects exposed to the experiment were not privy to any of this information and therefore may not have been affected by it.

23. Chapter 3 demonstrated the statistical relationship between Nationalism and black self-reliance, and Conservatism and the bootstrap philosophy. Although the self-reliance measure is a more collective notion than the bootstrap philosophy, both are focused on elements of self-help within the race.

24. I generally disagree with characterizing this pattern in black public opinion as a dichotomy or paradox because it comes from trying to fit black public opinion along a narrow "left-right" continuum. One of the larger purposes of my research is to demonstrate that this traditional paradigm is insufficient for capturing the unique shadings of African American political thought. By offering four different configurations of black political ideology, I hope to conceptualize black thought in a multidimensional rather than two-dimensional space. But even with these reservations, I think that it is important to address this "paradox" because it is central to much of the research on black public opinion.

25. Alternatively, this idea of fairness in relation to paying taxes to support the welfare system led some students to suggest that individuals have a right to make use of welfare. One female subject in an Economic Conservatism group expressed this idea in a story about her mother considering going back to school. Because of the loss of income involved with going to school full time, the mother would have to accept some public assistance. Her mother has never been on public assistance and is resistant. But the daughter reports that she told her mother, "I had to let her know. You might not have been on public aid, but

you should use it now because look at all the years I've paid for public aid because I am a taxpayer. So don't look at it as being a negative. You look at it as what you get because I am a taxpayer."

Chapter Five

1. Quincy Mills provided the eyes and ears of the ethnography. All of the empirical evidence presented in this chapter is from notes that Quincy took during the course of the study. The bulk of the analysis is mine. Quincy and I discussed the context and spirit of the conversations as well as the characters and personalities of the participants. These impressions contribute to the work of analyzing these conversations. We jokingly called our research efforts "ethnography by proxy." Although the chapter is written in first person in Quincy's voice, I am the author of the chapter.

2. According to the U.S. Bureau of the Census in 1890, there were 17,480 black barbers. See Harmon, Lindsay, and Woodson (1929, 12). During the National Negro Business League Convention in 1900, it was reported that "the business in which colored men are more generally engaged as proprietors than any other in the United States is that of barbering and hairdressing. In 1890 there were 17,480 colored barbers; probably 5,000 of these were proprietors" "Proceedings of the National Negro Business League" 1900, 18; Spear 1967, 30–31. In *The Philadelphia Negro* (1899) DuBois listed twenty-three black barbershops in 1896 in Philadelphia's seventh ward. According to Gerber (1976), by 1910 there were 85, 109, and 124 black barbers in Columbus, Cleveland, and Cincinnati, respectively. Drake and Cayton (1945) listed "The Ten Most Numerous Types of Negro-Owned Businesses in Chicago: 1938." Barbershops ranked third, with 207 enterprises, behind beauty salons, 287, and groceries, 257.

3. In October 1838, a black man shared a disturbing experience he encountered at a New York barbershop with the *Colored American* newspaper. The newspaper published his complaint, which read in part, "I went out to get my hair cut and my beard taken off, and for this purpose I called at the shop of Mr. . . , a colored barber, and sir, he would not touch my face with the handle of his razor, nor my head with the back of his shears! When I entered Mr. . . .'s shop, he had just finished shaving a white man. I asked him as politely as I could, if I could get my beard shaved off. He turned his eye with a slavish and fearful look toward the white man, and groaned out, 'no sir, we don't shave colored people.'" Although the informant continued to reprove black barbers who practiced this discrimination, he did not identify the barber and identified himself only as "Long Island Scribe." The *Colored American's* response appeared below the anonymous customer's letter. The paper explained that black barbers were "delicately situated" without the "same independence that white men" enjoyed and "we should feel more lenity towards them." The paper's answer to this dilemma was to practice "a measure of policy and forbearance" and "when traveling, whether the barber be a white or colored man, make it a rule to shave ourselves . . . [then] we are always politely served with a good razor, box, and towel, without any hesitancy" (*Colored American*, October 20,

1838, New York). Blacks in other cities also expressed their frustration against black barbers. In 1848, at the National Convention of Colored Freemen in Cleveland, black men spoke out against black barbers for opting to shave white men over black men. See the *North Star*, September 29, 1848.

4. Little financial evidence is available among black barbers to substantiate their financial "success." However, the business records of William Johnson, the Barber of Natchez, provide insight on the amount of wealth they were able to accumulate.

5. Walker (1998); Kusmer (1976, 76). The percentage of black barbers declined in the South from 60.4 percent in 1890 to 49.4 in 1900. See also Stone (1980, 523). He suggests that white barbershops were more efficient (168). Also see Proceedings of the National Negro Business League (1900, 113); Spear (1967, 111–12).

6. The Journeyman Barber's International Union of America founded in 1887. The Barber's Union had a strong presence in Ohio and introduced a barber bill in 1902 to exert influence over the barber trade. For a discussion of the Barber's Union, see Hall (1936).

7. In 1947 Rose Morgan and Olivia Clark founded Rose Meta House of Beauty, Inc., and purchased a vacant five-story mansion in Harlem. In 1950 Rose Meta House of Beauty grossed $3 million with three beauty shops and 300 employees in New York. Morgan also marketed cosmetics and haircare products. By 1955 they had established a chain of beauty shops in major American cities and various countries. Rose Meta House of Beauty became the largest black beauty salon in the United States. Their business philosophy was: Our market is women of color everywhere who are tired of trying to adapt their needs to cosmetics designed for white skins" (Walker 1998, 473–74).

8. In *Hair Story*, Byrd and Tharps retell the stories of African American men and women who have found their hair care to be a great divide between themselves and white America. They recount:

Cora Branson entered Mount Holyoke College in South Hadley, Massachusetts, in 1989. Fed up with traveling two and a half hours to Boston every six to eight weeks to have her relaxer touched up, she went to a salon at the local mall and asked if they knew how to work with Black hair, specifically using chemicals. "This White man said he knew what he was doing, " says Branson, "so I let him. Right away I knew it was a mistake, but he had already starting putting the relaxer on so I let him continue. He took almost half my hair out. I was angry and in pain. I just left the salon with my hair wet. (2001, 146)

9. By consent of the informants, all names used for the barbers and the shop are true and accurate. All names and some identifying characteristics of customers have been changed.

10. Black men learned the barber trade by apprenticing under black barbers. Formal training was not available because barber colleges were exclusively for white people. However, in 1934 Henry Morgan founded the Tyler Barber College in Texas, the first black barber college in the United States, with three chairs in the back of a barbershop. Between 1937 and 1949, Morgan established bar-

ber colleges in Houston, Dallas, Little Rock, Chicago, Memphis, and New York. In 1949, according to the *Beautician Journal and Guide*, Tyler Barber Colleges across the country graduated 14,000 men and women (Dawson 2001, 391).

11. Muhammad Ali's 1974 comeback fight against George Foreman for the world heavyweight boxing championship was billed as "The Rumble in the Jungle." Although this was a bout between two black men, the fight took on racial meaning, as Ali billed himself as a man of the people and cast Foreman as an Uncle Tom. When an aging Muhammad Ali beat the odds by knocking down a much younger and far stronger George Foreman in the heat in Zaire, he not only sealed his position as "The Greatest" heavyweight of all time, he also reasserted himself as a true man of the race. In his youth, Hajj was himself a boxer, and he often speaks of Ali as the greatest boxer of all time. When he draws the analogy between Venus Williams and Ali, he is doing so with full knowledge of the historical, racial importance of his argument.

12. When Hajj met Alex Haley, he challenged Haley for keeping his name after learning that he was descended from the Kente people. Hajj found Haley's response to his challenge entirely unsatisfactory. See introduction for the full story.

13. Levine summarizes this famous story from Joel Chandler Harris's collection of slave tales in *Uncle Remus: His Songs and Sayings* (1880):

> In its simplest form the slaves' animal trickster tale was a cleanly delineated story free of ambiguity. The strong assault the weak, who fight back with any weapons they have. The animals in these tales have almost instinctive understanding of each other's habits and foibles. Knowing Rabbit's curiosity, Wolf constructs a tar-baby and leaves it by the side of the road. At first fascinated by this stranger and then progressively infuriated at its refusal to respond to his friendly salutations, Rabbit strikes at it with his hands, kicks it with his feet, butts it with his head, and becomes thoroughly enmeshed. In the end however, it is Rabbit whose understanding of his adversary proves to be more profound. Realizing that Wolf will do exactly what he thinks his victim least desires, Rabbit convinces him that of all the ways to die the one he is most afraid of is being thrown into the briar patch, which of course is exactly what Wolf promptly does, allowing Rabbit to escape. (Levine 1977, 106)

14. At this time Damon was engaged in an interethnic relationship. Throughout the summer, Damon talked about a woman he fell in love with while traveling in Brazil. Although his girlfriend spoke little English, Damon was enthusiastic about the intensity of the relationship. Later that summer he brought her to Chicago. They have since married and had children. When she first arrived in Chicago, he brought her to the shop. Some of the customers were curious about how they communicated given that she spoke little English. Damon's response was "words are highly overrated."

15. For closer attention to narratives of this kind, see Carson (1981); King (1987); Marable (1982); Wallace (1978); Brown (1992); Birbaum and Taylor (2000).

16. A few weeks after this conversation, I discovered that Sherman lives in

my building. As I was leaving I saw him in the parking lot. Later that day I went to the shop. As I walked in, Sherman looked at me and said, "Damon, guess who lives in my building and who I saw walking in with a white girl? Quincy!" Damon, as well as the other four or five men (young and old) waiting, gave a chuckle and a look of "Oh, word!" Damon said, "So, you was creepin wit a white girl, huh?" He grinned but never broke stride in cutting his customer's hair. Damon knew Sherman had created a story, but others really didn't know if it were true or not. My response was, "Come on man. The lies, the lies, the rumors, the lies." This friendly challenge to my "righteousness" suggests that I was wearing a mask. It suggests that at the barbershop I portrayed a veneer of "blackness" that broke down if I thought no one was watching. It was Sherman's way of conveying both a familiarity with me, because he could tease me, and a challenge to me to be honest about the self I was presenting in the shop.

17. Hajj once told me a story about a mother and her son who had come in for a haircut. As they were waiting, the child was crying and fussing. To quiet the boy, the mother offered him her purse. The boy became content playing with the purse. Hajj then recalled, "I said, 'don't give him that purse, you'll make a sissy out of him!'" I suppose the men of Truth and Soul think that Eric was "scarred" by a similar childhood incident.

18. Seaway National Bank of Chicago was founded in 1965 by a consortium of Chicago black businesses on the city's Southside. Continental Illinois National Bank and Trust Company assisted these businessowners with meeting the requirements for a national bank charter. The black officials of the bank heralded Seaway as "the most important financial breakthrough in interracial cooperation ever achieved here!" The first chair and vice chair of the Board, Moses J. Proffitt and Ernest T. Collins, were black, while three of seven Board members and the president were white. In 1973 Richard Linyard became the bank's first black president and CEO. In the early 1980s, Harold Washington, Chicago's first black mayor, deposited the municipal funds in Seaway. Since its inception, Seaway has been among the leading black banks in the nation. "Seaway National Bank 25th: Building on the Past for the Future, 1965–1990," Seaway Bancshares, Inc., 1965–1990; Walker (1999).

19. The Sunday after this conversation I was at the African Fest in Washington Park. I saw Jasheed in the custody of two policeman. I just shook my head; I guess they are still just messing with him.

20. The low end is considered the area between 22nd and 47th, State and Cottage Grove.

21. This desire by the men of Truth and Soul to protect their space from inspection by whites poses a serious ethical dilemma for us as researchers. Hajj, Sherman, Damon, and G consented to being observed and even photographed. They understood that we were writing a book for publication. But we still wrestled with the reality that by telling their stories we are also exposing these men to precisely the observation against which they locked their doors that summer. Scientific inquiry did not seem to us a sufficient justification for laying bare the souls of men in this protected space. Ultimately, we justify using these stories of Truth and Soul men by our belief that we do more good than harm by excavating the content of everyday talk.

22. As an observer at Truth and Soul, I often felt a kind of double consciousness. I needed to maintain my objectivity in the name of research, to remain a fly on the wall, to just listen, remember, and record. I needed to observe more than participate, so as not to shape the study in my image. But I was also just another black man. I sat with them, watched TV with them, drank beer with them. Just like these black men, I grew up on the Southside of Chicago. During the study, I have seen many of my high school classmates walking or driving down 87th Street or getting a haircut at Truth and Soul. After catching up on old times, they would look at my head full of locks and question, "Yo, Q, what are you doing in the barbershop?" I'd tell them I am in school working on graduate studies, writing about black people's lives. Always they would give me a pound, his fist stacked on top of mine, then my fist stacked on top of his fist, an expression to show agreement, approval, and in this context, pride. I was constantly aware that I could very well be one of the men I was observing.

Chapter Six

1. Malcolm X also serves as an illustration of this aspect of black political culture. In an instructive piece on the "Political and Social Relevancy of Malcolm X", Davis and Davenport argue that Malcolm provides a means of defiance for African Americans who are angry and frustrated with the political system. "The promotion of Malcolm X becomes essentially a 'a kind of voodoo doll — something to shake at white people and say, 'I'm not happy here. I'm not satisfied yet'" (1997, 561). Malcolm X is an important figure for understanding black culture precisely because he fits both messianic beliefs and the defiance tradition.

2. Reparations claims for American slavery are often framed in the language of wages due for services rendered. For a fuller treatment of historical and contemporary reparations claims, see Robinson (2000).

3. Black Feminism has often been characterized as a foreign belief system imported by white women to divide black men and women and distract African American women from the racial struggle. Alliances with white feminist activists can often exacerbate this notion of an "alien ideology" and compromise the ability of Feminists to make authenticity claims. For one interesting treatment of the problem of anti-Feminism in Nationalist and Afrocentric political movements, see White (1990).

4. Black women are in a precarious situation in relation to sexual violence because, as Crenshaw notes, "the primary beneficiaries of politics supported by feminists and others concerned about rape tend to be white women; the primary beneficiaries of the Black community's concern over racism and rape, Black men" (1991, 1270). In fact, Crenshaw notes that "Black women were among Tyson's staunchest supporters and Washington's harshest critics" (1275). Feminists are faced with an uphill task when battling this historical legacy of devaluing black women's bodies.

5. Hooks is arguably one of the most recognizable black Feminist figures. Between 1981 and 2000 she authored fifteen books, and many of them spent time on the best-seller list.

6. The book that hooks was promoting at this time, *Killing Rage*, opens with a strong defiance trope. She begins the text by talking about a racial incident on an airplane that makes her angry enough to want to murder the white man seated next to her. At first shocked by the depth of her own rage, hooks links her anger to a history of angry African American defiance. Importantly, she attaches herself to Malcolm X's "passionate ethical commitment to justice" (1995, 13). By connecting herself with Malcolm and with rage, hooks lays claim to an authentic black tradition of defiance.

7. Gates points to the differing positions among African American leadership on the question of Colin Powell. He reports the Kweisi Mfume was prepared in 1996 to throw the full weight of the NAACP behind Powell if he chose to make a run for the presidency, but Jesse Jackson remained deeply skeptical, calling Powell "a black capable of being a conduit for racist policies" (1997, 85). African Americans were also largely confused about who Powell is. In 1995 a full third of blacks interviewed in an October CBS News–*New York Times* poll reported that they did not have enough information about Powell to make a judgment about whether they liked him.

8. Sociologist Mary Waters argues that West Indian immigrants "display certain psychological and cultural reactions to American society that are closer to those of other voluntary immigrants than to African Americans" (1999, 141). This ethnic uniqueness may lead some to suggest that Powell is not part of an indigenous black American ideological tradition. Interestingly, this charge is rarely leveled against other black ideological elites from the West Indies, most notable Marcus Garvey and Louis Farrakhan. The radical discourse of Garvey and Farrakhan seems to obscure their ethnic heritage. I think it unfair to label a Conservative Jamaican as inauthentic and leave Nationalists unquestioned. Powell, like Garvey and Farrakhan, is rightly understood as a part of black American political discourse.

9. In a 1998 address to the National Bar Association, an organization representing African American attorneys and judges, Thomas sarcastically laments the idea that his Conservatism is not an authentic black ideology. "With respect to my following, or, more accurately, being led by other members of the Court, that is silly, but expected since I could not possibly think for myself. And what else could possibly be the explanation when I fail to follow the jurisprudential, ideological, intellectual, if not anti-intellectual, prescription assigned to blacks. Since thinking beyond this prescription is presumptively beyond my abilities, obviously someone must be putting these strange ideas into my mind and my opinions" (Thomas to NBA July 29, 1998).

10. In 2002 Harry Belafonte called Colin Powell a "House Negro." I take up this event at greater length in the concluding chapter.

11. I am not the first to comment on this physical resemblance. Gates also remarks that "Powell bears an uncanny resemblance to the Wizard of Tuskegee. It's the same haircut, of course, but also the same sort of face — light skinned and blunt featured" (1997, 77).

12. "No Room at the Inn: Loneliness and the Black Conservative" is the title of a book chapter by Clarence Thomas in Faryna, Stetson, and Conti (1997).

13. Justice Clarence Thomas is quite explicit in demanding that he is as much a part of an authentic black cultural heritage as more liberal leaders. When addressing the National Bar Association in 1998, Thomas argued his own authenticity. "Those of us who came from the rural South were different from the blacks who came from the large northern cities, such as Philadelphia and New York. We were all black. But that similarity did not mask the richness of our differences. Indeed, one of the advantages of growing up in a black neighborhood was that we were richly blessed with the ability to see the individuality of each black person with all its fullness and complexity. We saw those differences at school, at home, at church, and *definitely at the barbershop on Saturday morning*" [emphasis added] (Thomas to NBA, July 29, 1998).

14. Only one out of the thirty-four law clerks hired that fall was a minority (a Hispanic). And since 1972 less than 2 percent of the 428 clerks selected by the justices have been African American (*Jet*, October 26, 1998).

15. Mfume traces his conversion from street thug to racial activist to a mystical experience that occurs while shooting dice on a corner with a group of guys. Mfume recounts, "Despite all the noise around me, I was slowly being engulfed in an eerie, all enveloping stillness that seemed to be swallowing up Hankins Corner" (1996, 173). In a mystical, religious vision, Mfume's deceased mother appears to him and conveys to him a sense of both unconditional love and painful disapproval for his current life choices. "I quickly realized that I had to change and that I had already been profoundly changed. God had given me a second chance that night. He dripped my insides out and shaken me to the core. I knew I'd never, ever go back to the life I'd been leading" (1996, 176).

16. A similar forgiveness for out-of-wedlock parenting was granted to Reverend Jesse Jackson in 2001 when the *National Enquirer* revealed that he had fathered a child with a professional colleague. Jackson's active financial and emotional role in the child's life since birth softened the blow of the revelation, and Jackson continued to enjoy high levels of popularity among African Americans.

17. Mfume went on to complete a B.A. degree from Morgan State University (1976) and a Master's in Liberal Arts from Johns Hopkins University (1984).

18. Two months later, Julian died of a heart attack and Mfume found himself in an open seat race against a large field of contenders. He won the tight election, after four recounts, by only three votes. This experience probably made him more sensitive to, and supportive of, Al Gore's recount predicament in the 2000 presidential elections. Mfume's NAACP led the way in demanding Florida recounts and alleging serious civil rights violations in Florida voting procedures during the 2000 election.

19. In postwar Clarendon County, South Carolina, as well as in many cities and counties across the South, African Americans paid income and property taxes and yet their children had inferior schools and had no bus to ride to school. When taxpaying citizens in Clarendon managed to raise enough money from parental donations to purchase their own bus, the county refused to pay even for the gas to run it. (Kluger 1975). In 1954 plaintiffs from Clarendon joined with four other cases to argue *Brown v. Board of Education of Topeka*

Kansas. At the root of this case is the reality that taxpayers did not receive the services for which they paid. The Integrationist NACCP framed its demand as an appeal to the idea of American citizenship under the Fourteenth Amendment.

20. For example, during World War II Integrationists used wartime rhetoric to push for civil rights legislation. Black leaders like Walter White pointed to the absurdity of using segregated armed forces to battle fascism. DuBois condemned fascism and racism as two permeations of the same idea (Banks 1996). John Hope Franklin often tells the story of how his willingness to contribute his intellectual skills to the war effort was rejected by the Navy Department. He writes, "The United States however much it was devoted to protecting the freedoms of Europeans, had no respect for me, no interest in my well-being, and not even a desire to use my services" (1990, 577).

21. To state the symbolic nature of television images is not to say that they are entirely without power. Phillip Harper argues that "the televisual representation of black people has for so long served as a focus of debate that it is seen as having effects that extend beyond the domain of signs as such and into the realm of African Americans' material well-being, which comprises, among other factors, the social relations through which black people's status in this country is conditioned" (Torres 1998, 82). To the extent that the fantasy world of television provides a vision for what is imaginable in the real world, one can argue for the material importance of black representation in television to the life circumstances of actual black people.

22. For example, Mfume ultimately postponed a November sweeps-week boycott in order to continue private negotiations. The networks reached an agreement with the NAACP and other minority groups soon after this concession (Consoli 1999).

23. The agreement included the establishment of a policy to seek and hire people of color as directors for the 2000–2001 season; additional funding for more writing staff on every second-year show in order to generate diversity; a more diverse staff of network pages; an increase in the amount of products and services purchased from minority-owned business by 100 percent within eighteen months; an additional twenty-five minority positions; additional in-house minority lawyers; and active recruitment of minorities for freelance writing jobs (*Jet*, January 24, 2000; *Television Digest*, January 10, 2000).

24. Joyner lags behind many local urban DJs for the youngest audience, but "Joyner is a pied piper among middle class, middle age, middle of the road listeners who are most likely to vote" (Harris 1999). Joyner is on early in the morning. The men and women who listen to him are up early dressing for work, commuting in traffic, and tuning in while they have coffee at their desk. For the most part they are not teenagers and hip-hoppers, they are the black people who remember what life was like "back in the day."

25. In a study conducted by the author (the 2001 KKC African American Attitudes Study), Joyner was the second most recognized figure among African American respondents. His recognizablity among these respondents outstripped that of Oprah Winfrey and Jesse Jackson, Jr., by more than 50 percentage points. The full results of this study were discussed in chapter 4.

26. The show's website is sophisticated. Listeners can log on and listen to the

day's show on their computer using a live or time-delayed stream. Listeners can also access audio archives for months of the show's main attractions, such as It's Your Word, The Smiley Report, or Jokes of the Day. So even if you miss it, you can always catch up with the show on the weekends, or at your desk in the afternoon. The site also links visitors to the foundation and to the sites of many of the corporate sponsors.

27. Joyner developed a friendly, ongoing relationship with President Bill Clinton during his tenure. Clinton appeared on the Joyner show at least three times (September 26, 1997, November 2, 1998, November 2, 2000). Clinton calls himself a big Joyner fan and allowed Joyner a one-on-one interview in the Oval Office. Joyner also accompanied the president to Roger Clinton's wedding and led the president and first lady down a Soul Train dance line during a state dinner (Jones 1995). This genuine friendliness with the white president may seem to disqualify Joyner as a Nationalist, but Joyner worked around this interracial friendship by characterizing Clinton as "the first black president," a label that the president enjoyed repeating.

28. Each Thursday a "Thursday Morning Mom" is chosen from hundreds of letters and faxes sent to the show. These moms are honored for their hard work and dedication to their children with a $2,000 prize made possible by K-Mart. Every Tuesday a "Real Man, Real Father" is chosen from hundreds of listeners' letters. The man is honored with a $1,000 donation provided by Oldsmobile. Each month the Tom Joyner Foundation selects a specific historically black college as the benefactor of funds raised during that month. The money is sent directly to the school and the students. Every cent of each donation made to the Tom Joyner Foundation goes to the students. In 2001 the Ronald McDonald House Charities provided a fifty cent match for every dollar up to $333,000. McDonald's also partnered with Joyner and Harvard Professor Henry Louis Gates to offer "Little-Known Black History Facts" booklets for $1.29 with a food purchase in August and September 2000. Little-known black history facts is a daily item on the Joyner show. These booklets were also made available with a comprehensive teacher's curriculum guide to public senior high schools. Every Wednesday is Christmas on the show. Each week a wish is granted for anything from new carpeting for a church to cots for a daycare center to a wedding for a deserving couple who otherwise would not have a ceremony. The funds for this are provided by Southwest Airlines.

29. Full coverage of the Black Agenda 2000 appeared on C-Span rather than BET. Some observers believed that Smiley's leadership of this event was the impetus for BET's decision to fire him.

Chapter Seven

1. *Barbershop* was produced by George Tillman Jr. and Robert Titel. Both men are young African Americans who graduated from Chicago's Columbia College. They previously produced the successful African American cast film *Soul Food*, which was later adapted as a television series on the Showtime network.

2. Not everyone liked the film. Some observers critiqued the stereotypical

portrayals of blacks that infuse the plot and subplot. "If 'Barbershop' is to be avoided, it should be for reasons that appear to have eluded Sharpton. . . . What's troubling is the film's wealth of Amos n Andy type buffoonery and its treatment of the only African American barber who is educated and articulate as though he isn't 'truly black'" (Pearson 2002).

3. An online poll at BlackAmericaWeb.com asked whether the "offensive" scene should be removed. Out of 4,000 respondents, only 14 percent felt that the filmmakers had crossed the line by mocking historic African American figures (Freeman 2002).

4. The Associated Press reported, "The suit was filed Monday by the National Association of Cosmetologists. It accuses Jackson and Sharpton of intentional infliction of emotional distress, fraud, and negligence stemming from their demands for apologies from MGM" (October 30, 2002).

5. In a public opinion survey of 831 African Americans conducted before the presidential election in the fall of 2000, the mean feeling thermometer for Colin Powell was nearly 70. Although not as high as Jesse Jackson's mean score of 79, Powell's average far exceeded Louis Farrakhan (mean = 54) and Al Sharpton (mean = 56). (2000 Knowledge Networks Survey conducted by Lawrence Bobo, Harvard University, and Michael Dawson, University of Chicago).

6. Malcolm X frequently employed the House Slave analogy in his critique of Integrationist black leaders. He reported in his 1965 autobiography that most African American leaders failed to maintain sufficient autonomy from white power sources that was necessary to provide real leadership to black communities. "Today's Uncle Tom doesn't wear a handkerchief on his head. This modern twentieth-century Uncle Thomas now often wears a top hat. . . . He's the personification of culture and refinement. . . . This twentieth-century Uncle Thomas is a *professional* Negro . . . by that I mean his profession is being a Negro for the white man" (Malcom X 1965, 243).

7. "The Dozens is an Afro-American contest game in which two contestants, in the presence of a spurring audience of peers, try to best each other in casting aspersions on each other or each other's relatives" (Chimezie 1976, 401). For more analysis on the dozens, its origins, practices, and social meanings, see Dollard (1939); Abrahams (1970); Lefever (1981); Smitherman (1977).

8. I met with Reverend Kenney a few weeks after his break with Orange Grove. He told me the story from his perspective. I attempted to speak with several members of the Orange Grove leadership, but I was unable to find a willing respondent from the Orange Grove side. I cannot judge the absolute veracity of this narrative. This is an accurate reflection of Kenney's impressions.

9. A colleague still living in Durham, North Carolina, acted as a participant observer by listening in on conversations at Imperial in the weeks immediately following Kenney's separation from Orange Grove.

10. Reverend Kenney laughed when I asked him about the cell phone and the car. He reported, "I just got a cell phone and I drive a Mitsubishi, and it is in my name."

Bibliography

AAMES Exchange: The Quarterly Newsletter for the African American Male Empowerment Summit. 2001. Volume 1.

ABC News. 1995. Colin Powell Poll. ICPSR 6676. September.

Abel, Elizabeth, Barbara Christian, and Helene Moglen, editors. 1997. *Female Subjects in Black and White: Race, Psychoanalysis, Feminism.* Berkeley: University of California Press.

Abrahams, Roger. 1970. *Deep Down in the Jungle.* Chicago: University of Chicago Press.

Abramson, Paul R. 1977. *The Political Socialization of Black Americans: A Critical Evaluation of Research on Efficacy and Trust.* New York: Free Press.

Adams, Rebecca G. 1998. "Inciting Sociological Thought by Studying the Deadhead Community: Engaging Publics in Dialogue." *Social Forces* 77, 1.

Adler, Patricia A., Peter Adler, and Anrea Fontana. 1987. "Everyday Life Sociology." *Annual Review of Sociology* Volume 13.

African American Agenda 2000. *Civil Rights since 1787: A Reader on the Black Struggle.* Edited by Jonathan Birbaum, and Clarence Taylor. New York: New York University Press.

Agar, Michael. 1986. *Speaking of Ethnography.* Beverly Hills: Sage Publications.

Ahrens, Frank. 1999. "Tom Joyner's Consuming Passion; Radio Host Pushed for Ads Directed at Blacks." *The Washington Post.* October 20, C1.

Allen, Richard, Robert Brown, and Michael Dawson. 1989. "The Schema-Based Approach to Modeling African-American Racial Belief System." *American Political Science Review* 83, 2.

Anderson, Barbara A., Brian D. Silver, Paul R. Abramson. 1988. "The Effects of the Race of the Interviewer on Measures of Electoral Participation by Blacks in SRC National Election Studies." *Public Opinion Quarterly* 53, 53–83.

Anderson, Barry F. 1966. *The Psychology Experiment: An Introduction to the Scientific Method.* Belmont: Wadsworth Publishing.

Anderson, James D. 1988. *The Education of Blacks in the South, 1860–1835.* Chapel Hill: University of North Carolina Press.

Anderson-Bricker, Kristin. 1999. "'Triple Jeopardy': Black Women and the Growth of Feminist Consciousness in SNCC, 1964–1975." In *Still Lifting, Still Climbing: African American Women's Contemporary Activism.* Edited by Kimberly Springer. New York: New York University Press.

Andrews, Frank. 1984. "Construct Validity and Error Components of Survey Measures: A Structural Modeling Approach." *Public Opinion Quarterly* 48, 409–42.

Arendt, Hannah. 1958. *The Human Condition.* Chicago: University of Chicago Press

———. 1966 (1951). *The Origins of Totalitarianism.* New York: Harcourt, Brace & World.

Aronson, Elliot, Timothy D. Wilson, and Marilynn Brewer. 1998. "Experimentation in Social Psychology." In *The Handbook of Social Psychology*, 4th edition. Edited by Daniel Gilbert, Susan Fiske, and Gardner Lindzey. Boston: McGraw-Hill.

Austin, Regina. 1994. "An Honest Living: Street Vendors, Municipal Regulation, and the Black Public Sphere." *Yale Law Journal* 103, 8.

Axelrod, Robert. 1973. "Schema Theory and Information Processing Model of Perception and Cognition." *The American Political Science Review* 67, 4.

Bagozzi, Richard P., and Youjae Yi. 1989. "On the Use of Structural Equation Models in Experimental Designs." *Journal of Marketing Research* 26, 3.

Baker, Houston A. 1993. *Black Studies, Rap and the Academy*. Chicago: University of Chicago Press.

Bambara, Toni Cade. 1970. *The Black Woman: An Anthology*. New York: Signet.

Banks, Ingrid. 2000. *Hair Matters: Beauty, Power and Black Women's Consciousness*. New York: New York University Press.

Banks, William. 1996. *Black Intellectuals*. New York: W. W. Norton.

"'Barbershop' Remarks Bring Lawsuit." 2002. *New York Times*. November 3.

Barker, Lucius J., and Jessie J. McCorry, Jr. 1976. *Black Americans and the Political System*. Cambridge: Winthrop Publishers.

Barnhart, Aaron. 2000. "Getting Ready for a 'Party with a Purpose'; KC Radio Listeners to Welcome DJ Tom Joyner's Morning Show." *The Kansas City Star*. February 10, A1.

Barrs, Jennifer. 2000. "The Fly Jock." *The Tampa Tribune*. May 3, Baylife 1.

Beale, Francis. 1995 (1970). "Double Jeopardy: To Be Black and Female." In *Words of Fire: An Anthology of African-American Feminist Thought*. Edited by Beverly Guy-Sheftall. New York: The New Press.

Beckwith, Karen. 1986. *American Women and Political Participation: The Impacts of Work, Generation, and Feminism*. Westport: Greenwood Press.

Beisecker, Thomas D., and Donn W. Parson, editors. 1972. *The Process of Social Influence: Readings in Persuasion*. New Jersey: Prentice-Hall.

Berg, Charles. 1951. *The Unconscious Significance of Hair*. London: George Allen and Unwin.

Berger, Charles R. and Michael Burgoon, editors. 1995. *Communication and Social Influence Processes*. East Lansing: Michigan State University Press.

Berger, Roger A. 1997. "The Black Dick: Race, Sexuality, and Discourse in the L.A. Novels of Walter Mosley." *African American Review* 31, 2.

Berlin, Ira. 1974. *Slaves without Masters: The Free Negro in the Antebellum South*. New York: Pantheon Books.

Berman, Marshall. 1972. *The Politics of Authenticity: Radical Individualism and the Emergence of Modern Society*. New York: Atheneum.

———. 1993. "Close to the Edge: Reflections on Rap." *Tikkun* 8, 2.

Bettinghaus, Erwin Paul. 1968. *Persuasive Communication*. New York: Holt, Rinehart, and Winston.

Birbaum, Jonathan, and Clarence Taylor, editors. 2000. *Civil Rights since 1787: A Reader on the Black Struggle*. New York: New York University Press.

Black Agenda. 2000. (Radio special on African-American participation in upcoming election.) *Jet*. October 9.

Black Public Sphere Collective, editors. 1995. *The Black Public Sphere: A Public Culture Book*. Chicago: University of Chicago Press.

Bobo, Lawrence, and Frank Gilliam. 1990. "Race, Sociopolitical Participation and Black Empowerment." *American Political Science Review* 84, 2.

Bogle, Donald. 1990. *Toons, Coons, Mulatoes, Mammies, and Bucks: An Interpretative History of Blacks in American Films*. New York: Continuum Publishing.

———. 2001. *Prime Time Blues: African Americans on Network Television*. New York: Farrar, Straus and Giroux.

Bookman, Ann, and Sandra Morgen, editors. 1988. *Women and the Politics of Empowerment*. Philadelphia: Temple University Press.

Borger, Gloria. 1993. "Up from the Street Corner." *U.S. News & World Report*. August 9.

Boston, Thomas D. 1985. "Racial Inequality and Class Stratification: A Contribution to a Critique of Black Conservatism." *Review of Radical Political Economics* 17, 3.

Bracey, John H., August Meier, and Elliott Rudwick, editors. 1970. *Black Nationalism in America*. New York: Bobbs-Merrill.

Brady, Henry, Sidney Verba, and Kay Lehman Scholzman. 1995. "Beyond SES: A Resource Model of Political Participation." *The American Political Science Review* 89, 2.

Branch, Taylor. 1988. *Parting the Waters: America in the King Years*. New York: Simon & Schuster.

Braxton, Edward. 1998. "The View from the Barbershop: The Church and African American Culture." *America*. February 14.

Briggs, Cyril. 1997. "The African Blood Brotherhood in Van Deburg." In *Modern Black Nationalism: From Marcus Garvey to Louis Farrakhan*. Edited by William L. Van Deburg. New York: New York University Press.

Brink, William, and Louis Harris. 1967. *Black and White: A Study of U.S. Racial Attitudes Today*. New York: Simon and Schuster.

Brodesser, Claude. 2000. "NAACP Seeks the Birth of a Diverse Hollywood." *Variety*. February 7.

Brodkin, Karen. 1996. "Race, Gender, and Virtue in Civic Discourse." *Ms.*

Brown, C. Stone. 1999. "Kweisi Mfume." *Crisis*, 106, 5 (September/October).

Brown, Elaine. 1992. *A Taste of Power: A Black Woman's Story*. New York: Anchor Books.

Brown, Linda M. 1998. "The Donation Station." *Black Issues in Higher Education*. October 29.

Brown, Ronald, and Monica Wolford. 1994. "Religious Resources: African-American Political Action." *National Political Science Review*. Volume 4.

Bundles, A'Lelia. 2001. *On Her Own Ground: The Life and Times of Madam C. J. Walker*. New York: Scribner's.

Burger, Mary W., and Arthur C. Littleton, editors. 1971. *Black Viewpoints*. New York: New American Library.

Butler, John S. 1991. *Entrepreneurship and Self-Help among Black Americans: A Reconsideration of Race and Economics*. Albany: State University of New York Press.

"BV My Turn Comments on BET Firing Tavis Smiley." 2001. Blackvoices.com.

Byrd, Ayana, and Lori Tharps. 2001. *Hair Story: Untangling the Roots of Black Hair in America*. New York: St. Martin's Press.

Cade, Toni. 1970. "On the Issue of Roles." In *The Black Woman: An Anthology*. Edited by Toni Cade. New York: New American Library.

Calhoun-Brown, Alison. 1996. "African-American Churches and Political Mobilization: The Psychological Impact of Organizational Resources." *Journal of Politics* 58, 4.

Campbell, Angus, Philip E. Converse, Warren E. Miller, and Donald E. Stokes. 1960. *The American Voter*. Chicago: University of Chicago Press.

Cannon, Katie. 1988. *Black Womanist Ethics*. Atlanta: Scholars Press.

———. 1995. *Katie's Canon: Womanism and the Soul of the Black Community*. New York: Continuum.

Carlisle, Rodney. 1975. *The Roots of Black Nationalism*. New York: Kennikat.

Carmichael, Stokely, and Charles Hamilton. 1967. *Black Power: The Politics of Liberation*. New York: Random House.

Carmines, Edward G., and James A. Stimson. 1989. *Issues Evolution: Race and the Transformation of American Politics*. Princeton: Princeton University Press.

Carroll, Susan. 1984. "Women Candidates and Support for Feminist Concern: The Closet Feminist Syndrome." *The Western Political Quarterly* 37, 2.

Carson, Clayborne. 1981. *In Struggle: SNCC and the Black Awakening of the 1960s*. Cambridge: Harvard University Press.

Carter, Kevin L. 1997. "'Fly Jock' Culls Cultural Conscience on Air." *The Tampa Tribune*. December 7, Baylife, 2.

Cashmore, Ellis. 1997. *The Black Culture Industry*. New York: Routledge.

CBS News/*New York Times* Monthly Poll #1. August 1995. ICPSR 2349.

———. October 1995. ICPSR 6700.

———. February 2000. ICPSR 2924.

Ceglowski, Deborah. 1997. "That's a Good Story, but Is It Really Research?" *Qualitative Research* 3, 2.

Chafe, William. 1995. *The Unfinished Journey: American Since World War II*. 3d edition. New York: Oxford University Press.

Childs, John Brown. 1980. *The Political Black Minister: A Study in Afro-American Politics and Religion*. Boston: G. K. Hall.

Chimezie, Amuzie. 1976. "The Dozens: An African-Heritage Theory." *Journal of Black Studies* 6, 4.

Chong, Dennis. 1991. *Collective Action and the Civil Rights Movement*. Chicago: University of Chicago Press.

Churchill, Richard. 2001. "Southwest Airlines Powering a Sales Liftoff. (Southwest Airlines Co. Advertising Targets African-Americans.)" *Brandweek*. April 2.

Clarke, Stuart Alan. 1995. "Black Politics on the Apollo's Stage: The Return of the Handkerchief Heads." In *Critical Explorations in Social and Spatial The-*

ory. Edited by Helen Liggett and David Perry. Thousand Oaks: Sage Publications.

Cleage, Albert. 1969. *The Black Messiah: The Religious Roots of Black Power.* New York: Sheed and Ward.

Cohen, Arthur R. 1964. *Attitude Change and Social Influence.* New York: Basic Books.

Cohen, Cathy J. 1994. "Contested Identities: Black Lesbians and Gay Identities and the Black Community's Response to AIDS." *Ms.*

———. 1999. *The Boundaries of Blackness: AIDS and the Breakdown of Black Politics.* Chicago: University of Chicago Press.

Collier, David. 1995. "Translating Quantitative Methods for Qualitative Researchers: The Case of Selection Bias." *American Political Science Review* 89, 2.

Collier-Thomas, Bettye. 1998. *Daughters of Thunder: Black Women Preachers and Their Sermons, 1850–1979.* San Francisco: Jossey-Bass.

Collins, Patricia Hill. 1991. *Black Feminist Thought: Knowledge, Consciousness, and the Politics of Empowerment.* New York: Routledge.

———. 1998. *Fighting Words: Black Women and The Search for Justice.* Minneapolis: University of Minnesota Press.

Combahee River Collective. 1977. "A Black Feminist Statement." In *Feminist Frameworks: Alternative Accounts of the Relations between Men and Women.* Edited by Alison Jagger, and Paula Rothenberg. New York: McGraw Hill.

"Comic Salve for Thin Skins." 2002. *Los Angeles Times.* September 26, part 2, 14.

"CompUSA to Hire Black Ad Agency after Tom Joyner Radio Show Protest Campaign." 1999. *Jet.* November 8, 20–22.

Cone, James. 1969. *Black Theology and Black Power.* New York: Seabury Press.

Conover, Pamela. 1984. "The Influence of Group Identification on Political Perception and Evaluation." *Journal of Politics.* Volume 46.

Conover, Pamela, and Stanley Feldman. 1981. "The Origins and Meaning of Liberal Conservative Self Identifications." *American Journal of Political Science.* Volume 25.

Consoli, John. 1999. "Good Posture." *Brandweek.* November 15.

Converse, Philip E. 1964. "The Nature of Mass Belief Systems in Mass Publics." In *Ideology and Discontent.* Edited by D. Apter. New York: Free Press.

Cook, Thomas D. and Donald T. Campbell. 1979. *Quasi-Experimentation: Design and Analysis Issues for Field Settings.* Boston: Houghton Mifflin.

Cooper, Barry. 2001. "Column: Who Fired Tavis Smiley?" Blackvoices.com. Accessed August 3, 2003.

Costner, Hubert L. 1969. "Theory, Deduction, and Rules of Correspondence." *American Journal of Sociology* 75.

Craig, Maxine. 1997. *Hair: Sex, Society, and Symbolism.* New York: Stein and Day.

Crenshaw, Kimberle Williams. 1991. "Mapping the Margins: Intersectionality, Identity Politics, and Violence against Women of Color." *Stanford Law Review.* Volume 43.

————. 1997. "Beyond Racism and Misogyny: Black Feminism and 2 Live Crew." In *Women Transforming Politics: An Alernative Reader*. Edited by Cathy J. Cohen, Kathleen B. Jones, and Joan C. Tronto. New York: NewYork University Press.

Cripps, Thomas. 1977. *Slow Fade to Black: The Negro in American Film, 1900–1942*. New York: Oxford University Press.

Cronon, David. 1955. *Black Moses: The Story of Marcus Garvey and the Universal Negro Improvement Association*. Madison: University of Wisconsin Press.

Cross, Theodore and Robert Bruce Slater. 1994. "Higher Education and the New Political Arithmetic at the Congressional Black Caucus." *Journal of Blacks in Higher Education* 0, 5 (Autumn).

Cruse, Harold. 1984. *The Crisis of the Negro Intellectual*. New York: Quill.

Cunnigen, Donald. 1993. "Malcolm X's Influence on the Black Nationalist Movement of Southern Black College Students." *Journal of Black Studies*. Volume 17.

Cunningham, Kitty. 1993. "Mfume's rise." *Congressional Quarterly Weekly Report* 51, 27 (July).

Curnutte, Mark. 1999. "Barbershop a Haven for Black Men: True Feelings Flow at Jerome Goodwin's Place in Woodlawn." *The Cincinnati Enquirer*. January 11.

Dates, Jeanette L., and William Barlow, editors. 1993. *Split Image: African Americans in the Mass Media Second Edition*. Washington, DC: Howard University Press.

Davis, Angela. 1981. *Women, Race and Class*. New York: Random House.

Davis, Darren. 1997a. "The Direction of Race of Interviewer Effects among African Americans: Donning the Black Mask." *American Journal of Political Science*. Volume 41.

————. 1997b. "Nonrandom Measurement Error and Race of Interviewer Effects among African-Americans." *Public Opinion Quarterly* 61, 1.

Davis, Darren, and Christian Davenport. 1997. "The Political and Social Relevancy of Malcolm X: The Stability of African Americans Political Attitudes." *Journal of Politics* 59, 2 (May).

Davis, Edwin, and William Hogan. 1954. *The Barber of Natchez*. Baton Rouge: Louisiana State University Press.

Davis, Kimberly. 2000. "The New NAACP Turns Up the Heat." *Ebony* 55, 6 (April).

Davis, Kortright. 1990. *Emancipation Still Comin': Explorations in Caribbean Perspective*. Maryknoll, NY: Orbis Books.

Davis, Theodore James, Jr. 1986. "Changing Values and the Politics of the Black Middle Class." *Dissertation Abstracts International* 46, 10.

Dawson, Michael C. 1994. *Behind the Mule: Race and Class in African-American Politics*. Princeton: Princeton University Press.

————. 1995. "A Black Counterpublic?: Economic Earthquakes, Racial Agenda(s), and Black Politics." In *The Black Public Sphere: A Public Culture Book*. Edited by The Black Public Sphere Collective. Chicago: University of Chicago Press.

———. 2001. *Black Visions: The Roots of Contemporary African-American Political Ideologies*. Chicago: University of Chicago Press.

Dawson, Nancy. 1999. "Hair Care Products Industry." In *Encyclopedia of African American Business History*. Edited by Juliet E. K. Walker. Westport, CT: Greenwood Press.

Dawson, Richard E., and Kenneth Prewitt. 1969. *Political Socialization: An Analytic Study*. Boston: Little, Brown.

Dennis, Jack. 1968. "Major Problems of Political Socialization Research." *Midwest Journal of Political Science*. Volume 12.

Denton, Robert E., Jr., and Gary C. Woodward. 1985. *Political Communication in America*. New York: Praeger.

Denzin, Norman. 1997. *Interpretive Ethnography: Ethnographic Practices for the 21st Century*. Thousand Oaks: Sage Publications.

De-uriarte, Mercedes. 1996. "One Press, Divided Nation." *Peace Review* 8, 1.

Dollard, John. 1939. "The Dozens: Dialect of Insult." *The American Image* 1, 3–25.

Douglas, Kelly Brown. 1999. *Sexuality and the Black Church: A Womanist Perspective*. Maryknoll, NY: Orbis Books.

Downing, John D. H. 1988. "The Cosby Show and American Racial Discourse." In *Discourse and Discrimination*. Edited by Geneva Smitherman-Donaldson and Teun A. van Dijk. Detroit: Wayne State University Press.

Drake, St. Clair, and Horace R. Cayton. 1945. *Black Metropolis: A Study of Negro Life in a Northern City*. New York: Harper & Row.

Draper, Theodore. 1969. *The Rediscovery of Black Nationalism*. New York: Viking Press.

Dray, Phillip. 2002. *At the Hands of Persons Unknown: The Lynching of Black America*. New York: Random House.

Dubey, Madhu. 1994. *Black Women Novelists and the Nationalist Aesthetic*. Bloomington: Indiana University Press.

DuBois, W.E.B. 1903. *Souls of Black Folk*. New York: Penguin Books.

———. 1970 (1899). *The Philadelphia Negro: A Social Study*. New York: Schocken Books.

Duncan, Garrett A. 1996. "Space, Place and the Problematic of Race: Black Adolescent Discourse as Mediated Action." *The Journal of Negro Education* 65, 2.

Duster, Alfreda, editor. 1970. *Crusade for Justice: The Autobiography of Ida B. Wells*. Chicago: University of Chicago Press.

Dutton, Susanne E., Jefferson A. Singer, and Ann S. Devlin. 1998. "Racial Identity of Children in Integrated, Predominately White, and Black Schools." *The Journal of Social Psychology* 138, 1.

Dworkin, Rosalind J. 1979. "Ideology Formation: A Linear Structural Model of the Influences on Feminist Ideology." *Sociological Quarterly* 20, 3.

Dyson, Michael Eric. 1996. *Between God and Gangsta Rap*. New York: Oxford University Press.

———. 2002. "Speaking Freely in the Barbershop." *New York Times*. September 27, A31.

Eagleton, Terry. 1985 (1976). *Criticism and Ideology: A Study in Marxist Literary Theory*. London: Verso.

————, editor. 1994. *Ideology*. London: Longman.

Edelson, Max. 1992. "Where to Find the Hot Issues of 2020: Political Values Nurtured in College as Determinants of Future Political Issues." *American Demographics* 14, 9.

Eisner, Elliot. 1997. "The New Frontier in Qualitative Research Methodology." *Qualitative Inquiry* 3, 3.

Eliasoph, Nina. 1996. "Making a Fragile Public: A Talk-Centered Study of Citizenship and Power." *Sociological Theory* 14, 3.

Ellison, Christopher G. 1993. "Religious Involvement and Self-Perception among Black Americans." *Social Forces* 71, 4.

Elton, William. 1950. "Playing the Dozens." *American Speech* 25, 2.

England, Charles. "Real Barbershops Are Less Cutting." *Los Angeles Times*. October 5, B25.

Essien-Udom, Essien Udusen. 1962. *Black Nationalism: A Search for Identity in America*. Chicago: University of Chicago Press.

Evans, James H., Jr. 1992. *We Have Been Believers: An African American Systemic Theology*. Minneapolis: Fortress Press.

Eysenck, Hans J., and Glenn D. Wilson. 1978. *The Psychological Basis of Ideology*. Baltimore: University Park Press.

Fagin, Joe R. 1992. "The Continuing Significance of Racism: Discrimination against Black Students in White Colleges." *Journal of Black Studies* 22, 4.

Faryna, Stan, Brad Stetson, and Joseph G. Conti, editors. 1997. *Black and Right: The Bold New Voice of Black Conservatives in America*. Westport, CT: Praeger.

Feldman, Stanley. 1988. "Structure and Consistency in Public Opinion: The Role of Core Beliefs and Values." *American Journal of Political Science* 32, 2.

Fleming, Jacqueline. 1984. *Blacks in College*. San Francisco: Jossey-Bass.

Foner, Eric. 1980. *Politics and Ideology in the Age of the Civil War*. Oxford: Oxford University Press.

Forman, Murray. 1994. "Movin' Closer to an Independent Funk: Black Feminist Theory, Standpoint, and Women in Rap." *Women's Studies* 23, 1.

Fornek, Scott, and Curtis Lawrence. 2001. "Scholars Pick Top Five Black Leaders." *Chicago Sun-Times*. January 28, 10.

France, K. 1992. "Women with Attitudes." *Working Woman* 17, 1.

Franklin, John Hope. 1990 (1956). *From Slavery to Freedom: A History of African Americans*, Sixth Edition. New York: McGraw-Hill.

Fraser, Nancy. 1989. "Rethinking the Public Sphere: A Contribution to the Critique of Actually Existing Democracy." In *Habermas and the Public Sphere*. Edited by Craig Calhoun. Cambridge: MIT Press.

Frazier, E. Franklin. 1963. *The Negro Church in America*. New York: Schocken Books.

Fredrickson, George M. 1995. *Black Liberation: A Comparative History of Black Ideologies in the United States and South Africa*. New York: Oxford University Press.

Freeman, Greg. 2002. "Black Leaders Critical of 'Barbershop' Need a Little Off the Top." *St. Louis Post-Dispatch*. September 29, D4.

Freud, Sigmund. 1922. "Medusa's Hair." In *Collected Papers*. London: Hogarth Press and the Institute of Psychoanalysis.

Fried, C. 1996. "Bad Rap for Rap: Bias in Reactions to Music Lyrics." *Journal of Applied Psychology* 26, 23.

Fulenwider, Claire. 1980. *Feminism in American Politics: A Study of Ideological Influence.* New York: Praeger.

———. 1981. "Feminist Ideology and Political Attitudes and Participation among White and Minority Women." *Western Political Quarterly* 34, 1.

Fultz, Michael. 1995. "The Morning Cometh: African American Periodicals, Education, and the Black Middle Class, 1900–1930." *The Journal of Negro History* 80, 3.

Gaines, Kevin. 1996. *Uplifting the Race: Black Leadership, Politics and Culture in the Twentieth Century.* Chapel Hill: University of North Carolina Press.

Gamson, William A. 1992. *Talking Politics.* New York: Cambridge University Press.

Gates, Henry Louis. 1997. *Thirteen Ways of Looking at a Black Man.* New York: Random House.

Geiss, Imanuel. 1974. *The Pan-African Movement: A History of Pan-Africanism in American, Europe, and Africa.* New York: Africana.

Genovese, Eugene D. 1974. *Roll, Jordan, Roll.* New York: Vintage Books.

George, Nelson. 1998. *Hip Hop America.* New York: Penguin Books.

Gerber, David A. 1976. *Black Ohio and the Color Line.* Urbana: University of Illinois Press.

Giddings, Paula. 1984. *When and Where I Enter: The Impact of Black Women on Race and Sex in America.* New York: William Morrow.

———. 1988. *In Search of Sisterhood: Delta Sigma Theta and the Challenge of the Black Sorority Movement.* New York: Quill.

Gladney, Marvin. 1995. "The Black Arts Movement and Hip-Hop." *African American Review* 29, 2.

Glynn, Carroll, et. al. 1999. *Public Opinion.* Boulder: Westview Press.

Goldberg, Philip. 1968. "Are Women Prejudiced Against Women?" *Transaction.* Volume 5.

Golden-Biddle, Karen, and Karen Locke. 1997. *Composing Qualitative Research.* Thousand Oaks: Sage.

Goodwin, Marjorie. 1990. *He-Said-She-Said Talk as Social Organization among Black Children.* Bloomington: Indiana University Press.

Gordon, Dexter. 1998. "Humor in African American Discourse: Speaking of Oppression." *Journal of Black Studies* 29, 2.

"Government Minority Role Possible." *Television Digest.* January 31, 2000.

Graber, Dorris. 1984. *Processing the News: How People Tame the Information Tide.* New York: Longman.

Grant, Jacquelyn. 1989. *White Women's Christ and Black Women's Jesus.* Atlanta: Scholars Press.

Greene, Leonard. 1995. "Powell Attracts Blacks for the Hope He Embodies" *The Boston Herald.* September 22.

Greene, Lorenzo, and Carter G. Woodson. 1930. *The Negro Wage Earner.* New York: Russell and Russell.

Greenstein, Fred I. 1965. *Children and Politics.* New Haven: Yale University Press.

Grier, William H., and Price M Cobbs. 1968. *Black Rage*. New York: Basic Books.

Grossman, James R. 1989. *Land of Hope: Chicago, Black Southerners, and the Great Migration*. Chicago: University of Chicago Press.

Gubrium, Jaber. 1988. *Analyzing Field Reality*. Beverly Hills: Sage Publications.

Gurin, Patricia, Arthur Miller, and Gerald Gurin. 1980. "Stratum Identification and Consciousness." *Social Psychology Quarterly.* Volume 43.

Guy-Sheftall, Beverly, editor. 1995. *Words of Fire: An Anthology of African-American Feminist Thought*. New York: The New Press.

Habermas, Jürgen. 1962. *The Structural Transformation of the Public Sphere: An Inquiry into a Category of Bourgeois Society*. Translated by Thomas Burger. Cambridge: MIT Press.

———. 1984. *The Theory of Communicative Action*. Volume 1. Translated by Thomas McCarthy. Boston: Beacon Press.

Hall, W. Scott. 1936. *The Journeymen Barbers' International Union of America*. Baltimore: Johns Hopkins University Press.

Hallpike, Christopher. R. 1972. "Social Hair." In *Reader in Comparative Religion: An Anthropological Approach*. Edited by William A. Lessa and Evon Z. Vogt. New York: Harper and Row.

Hamblin, Ken. 1996. "Even Cops are Being Polluted by Liberal Values." *New York Times*. March 28.

———. 1999. *Plain Talk and Common Sense from the Black Avenger*. New York: Simon and Schuster.

Harmon, J. H., Jr. Arnett G. Lindsay, and Carter G. Woodson. 1929. *The Negro as a Business Man*. New York: Arno Press.

Harris, Fredrick. 1994. "Something Within: Religion as a Mobilizer of African-American Political Activism." *Journal of Politics* 56, 1.

———. 1999. *Something Within: Religion in African-American Political Activism*. Oxford: Oxford University Press.

Harris, James Henry. 1985. "Laity Expectations of Ministers in the Black Urban Church." *Dissertation Abstracts International* 46, 6.

Harris, Juliette, and Pamela Johnson. 2001. *Tenderheaded: A Comb-Bending Collection of Hair Stories*. New York: Simon and Schuster.

Harris, Lyle V. 1999. "Waking and Shaking Up America; When Radio Host Tom Joyner Speaks, Corporations, Politicians and a Large Number of Atlantans Listen." *The Atlanta Journal and Constitution*. December 1, 1D.

Harris, Trudier. 1979. "The Barbershop in Black Literature." *Black American Literature Forum* 13.

Hayduk, Leslie. 1987. *Structural Equation Modeling with LISREL: Essentials and Advances*. Baltimore: Johns Hopkins University Press.

Haynes, George Edmund. 1913. *The Negro at Work in New York City: A Study in Economic Progress*. New York: Columbia University Press.

Haywood, Richette. 1997. "Can Kweisi Mfume Turn the NAACP Around?" *Ebony* 52, (January).

Heesacker, Martin, Richard E. Petty, and John T. Cacioppo. 1983. "Field Dependence and Attitude Change: Source Credibility Can Alter Persuasion by Affecting Message-Relevant Thinking." *Journal of Personality* 51, 4.

Henderson, Errol. 1996. "Black Nationalism and Rap Music." *Journal of Black Studies* 26, 3.

Henderson, Jeff. 1978. "A. Philip Randolph and the Dilemma of Socialism and Black Nationalism in the United States, 1917–1941." *Race and Class*. Volume 20.

Henry, Charles. 1990. *Culture and African American Politics*. Bloomington: Indiana University Press.

Herbst, Susan. 1994. *Politics at the Margin: Historical Studies of Public Expression Outside the Mainstream*. New York: Cambridge University Press.

Higginbotham, Evelyn Brooks. 1993. *Righteous Discontent: The Women's Movement in the Black Baptist Church, 1880–1920*. Cambridge: Harvard University Press.

Hine, Darlene Clark, Wilma King, and Linda Reed, editors. 1995. *We Specialize in the Wholly Impossible: A Reader in Black Women's History*. New York: Carlson Publishing.

Hinich, Melvin, and Michael Munger. 1996. *Ideology and the Theory of Political Choice*. Ann Arbor: University of Michigan Press.

Hochschild, Jennifer. 1995. *Facing Up to the American Dream: Race, Class, and the Soul of the Nation*. Princeton: Princeton University Press.

Hoffman, Adonis. 1995. "Why Colin Powell Won't Run for President." *The Record*. May 25.

Holden, Matthew, Jr. 1973. *The Politics of the Black "Nation."* New York: Chandler.

Holland, Bill. 1995. "Black Radio Voice Tell It Like It Was." *Billboard* 107, 49.

Holloway, Wendy, and Tony Jefferson. 1997. "Eliciting Narrative through the In-Depth Interview." *Qualitative Inquiry* 3, 1.

Holmes, Steven A. 2002. "Can We Talk? It Depends Who 'We' Is." *New York Times*. October 27.

Holt, Thomas. 1995. Afterword: Mapping the Black Public Sphere. In *The Black Public Sphere: A Public Culture Book*. Edited by The Black Public Sphere Collective. Chicago: University of Chicago Press.

Hook, Janet. 1981. "Mfume Cuts Renewed Ties to Nation of Islam." *Congressional Quarterly Weekly Report* 52, 5.

hooks, bell. 1981. *Ain't i a Woman: Black Women and Feminism*. Boston: South End Press.

———. 1989. *Talking Back: Thinking Feminist, Thinking Black*. Boston: South End Press.

———. 1992. *Black Looks: Race and Representation*. Boston: South End Press.

———. 1995a. *Killing Rage: Ending Racism*. New York: Henry Holt.

———. 1995b. Killing Rage: Ending Racism. Interview on C-Span, November 9.

———. 2000. *Feminist Theory: From Margins to Mainstream*. Second Edition. Cambridge: South End Press.

Hopkins, Dwight. 1993. *Shoes That Fit Our Feet: Sources for a Constructive Black Theology*. Maryknoll, NY: Orbis Books.

———. 2002. *Heart and Head: Black Theology-Past, Present, and Future*. New York: Palgrave.

Hopkins, Terrance. 1964. *The Exercise of Influence in Small Groups*. New Jersey: Bedminister Press.

Horkheimer, Max. 1972. *Critical Theory: Selected Essays*. Translated by Matthew J. O'Connell. New York: Herder and Herder.

Hovland, Carl I., and Walter Weiss. 1951. "The Influence of Source Credibility on Communication Effectiveness." *Public Opinion Quarterly* 15, 4.

Howard-Pitney, David. 1990. *The Afro-American Jeremiad: Appeals for Justice in America*. Philadelphia: Temple University Press.

Huckfeldt, Robert, and Carol Kohfeld. 1989. *Race and the Decline of Class in American Politics*. Chicago: University of Illinois Press.

Huckfeldt, Robert, and John Sprague. 1991. "Discussant Effects on Vote Choice: Intimacy, Structure and Interdependence." *Journal of Politics* 53, 1.

Hughes, Zondra. 2000. "The New TV Season: What's New, What's Black, What's Back." *Ebony*. October.

Hull, Gloria, Patricia Bell Scott; and Barbara Smith, editors. 1982. *All the Women Are White, All the Blacks Are Men, But Some of Us Are Brave*. New York: Feminist Press at CUNY.

Huntington, Samuel. 1981. *American Politics: the Promise of Disharmony*. Cambridge: Belknap Press.

Hurston, Zora Neale. 1942. *Dust Tracks on a Road*. New York: Harper Perennial.

Hutchinson, Earl Ofari. 2002. "'Barbershop' Reveals Black Schism." *Newsday*. October 2, A29.

Hutton, Frankie. 1992. *The Early Black Press in America, 1827 to 1860*. Westport, CT: Greenwood Publishing Group.

Inniss, Leslie, and Joe Feagin. 1995. "The Cosby Show: The View from the Black Middle Class." *Journal of Black Studies* 25, 6.

Iyengar, Shanto. 1987. "Television News and Citizen's Explanations of National Affairs." *American Political Science Review*. Volume 81.

Jackson, Derrick. 1995. "Whites Great Black Hope." *The Boston Globe*. November 9.

James, Stanlie M., and Abena P. A. Busia, editors. 1993. *Theorizing Black Feminisms: the Visionary Pragmatism of Black Women*. London: Routledge.

Jamieson, G. Harry. 1985. *Communication and Persuasion*. Dover, NH: Croom Helm.

Jenkins, J. Craig, and Charles Perro. 1977. "Insurgency of the Powerless: Farm Workers Movements (1946–1972)." *American Sociological Review* 42.

Jenkins, Timothy. 1994. "Fieldwork and the Perception of Everyday Life." *Man, New Series* 29, 2.

Johnson, Allan. 2001. "Viacom Shouldn't Miss Chance to Keep Smiley." *Chicago Tribune*. March 28, 6.

Johnson, Charles S. 1967 (1941). *Growing up in the Black Belt*. New York: Shocken Books.

Johnson, James D., et. al. 1995. "Differential Gender Effects of Exposure to Rap Music on African American Adolescent's Acceptance of Teen Dating Violence." *Sex Roles: A Journal of Research* 33, 7.

Johnson, Sharon D. 2000. "Keep the Pressure on." *Essence*. June.

Jones, James T., IV. 1995. "DJ Tom Joyner Syndicates Success: Finding Fans across the Dial." *USA Today*. April 6, 6D.

Jordan, William. 1995. "The Damnable Dilemma: African-American Accommodation and Protest during WWI." *Journal of American History* 81, 4.

———. 2001. *Black Newspapers and America's War for Democracy, 1914–1920*. Chapel Hill: University of North Carolina Press.

Joseph, Gloria, and Jill Lewis. 1986. *Common Differences: Conflicts in Black and White Feminist Perspectives*. Boston: South End Press.

Karlins, Marvin, and Herbert Abelson. 1970 (1959). *Persuasion: How Opinions and Attitudes Are Changed*. New York: Springer Publishing.

Kelley, Norman. 1996. "The Specter of Nationalism." *New Politics* 6, 1 (Summer).

Kelley, Robin D. G. 1992. "Straight from the Underground." *The Nation* 254, 22.

———. 1994. *Race Rebels: Culture, Politics, and the Black Working Class*. New York: The Free Press.

———. 1997. *Yo' Mama's Disfunktional!: Fighting the Culture War in Urban America*. Boston: Beacon Press.

Kelman, Herbert C. 1958. "Compliance, Identification, and Internalization: Three Processes of Attitude Change." *Journal of Conflict Resolution*. Volume 2.

Keyes, Alan. 1995. *Masters of the Dream: The Strength and Betrayal of Black America*. New York: William Morrow.

Kinder, Donald R.. 1983. "Diversity and Complexity in American Public Opinion." In *Political Science: The State of the Discipline*. Edited by Ada W. Finifter. Washington, DC: American Political Science Association.

Kinder, Donald R., and Thomas R. Palfrey. 1992. "On Behalf of an Experimental Political Science." In *Experimental Foundations of Political Science*. Edited by Donald R. Kinder and Thomas R. Palfrey. Ann Arbor: University of Michigan Press.

Kinder, Donald R., and Lynn Sanders. 1996. *Divided by Color: Racial Politics and Democratic Ideals*. Chicago: University of Chicago Press.

King, Corretta Scott. 1983. *The Words of Martin Luther King, Jr.* New York: Newmarket Press.

King, Gary. 1989. *Unifying Political Methodology: The Likelihood Theory of Statistical Inference*. New York: Cambridge University Press.

King, Martin Luther, Jr. 1964. *Why We Can't Wait*. New York: New American Library.

King, Mary. 1987. *Freedom Song: A Personal Story of the 1960s Civil Rights Movement*. New York: William Morrow and Company.

King, Richard H. 1992. *Civil Rights and the Idea of Freedom*. Athens: University of Georgia Press.

King, Stephen. 1975. *Communication and Social Influence*. Reading, MA: Addison-Wesley.

Kleinman, Sherryl, Martha Copp, and Karla Henderson. 1997. "Qualitatively Different: Teaching Fieldwork to Graduate Students." *Journal of Contemporary Ethnography* 25, 4.

Kluger, Richard. 1975. *Simple Justice: The History of Brown v. Board of Education*. New York: Random House.

Kranish, Michael. 1995. "Powell Still Noncommital, but Volunteers Hope for a Run." *The Boston Globe*. March 20.

Kuechler, Manfred. 1998. "The Survey Method: An Indispensable Tool for Social Science Research Everywhere." *American Behavioral Scientist* 42, 2.

Kusmer, Kenneth. 1976. *A Ghetto Takes Shape: Black Cleveland, 1870–1930*. Urbana: University of Illinois Press.

Lane, Robert. 1962. *Political Ideology: Why the American Common Man Believes What He Does*. New York: The Free Press.

Lansburg, Michele. 1992. "The ReBirth of Feminism." *The Toronto Star*. May 2.

Large, Jerry. 2002. " 'Barbershop': You Wince, You Laugh, You Respect Free Speech." *The Seattle Times*. October 2, F1.

Lau, Richard, and David Sears, editors. 1986. "Political Cognition: The 19th Annual Carnegie Symposium on Cognition." Hillsdale, NJ: L. Erlbaum Associates.

Laumann Edward O., and David R. Segal. 1971. "Status Inconsistency and Ethnoreligious Group Membership as Determinants of Social Participation and Political Attitudes." *American Journal of Sociology* 77, 1.

Lawrence, Curtis. 2002. "Belafonte Defends 'Slave' Comment in Chicago Visit." *Chicago Sun-Times*. November 14, 12.

Leach, Edmund R. 1958. "Magical Hair." *Journal of Royal Anthropological Institute* 88.

Lefever, Harry G. 1981. " 'Playing the Dozens': A Mechanism for Social Control." *Phylon* 42, 1.

Lenski Gerhard E. 1956. "Social Participation and Status Crystallization." *American Sociological Review* 21, 4.

Levine, Lawrence. 1977. *Black Culture and Black Consciousness: Afro-American Folk Thought from Slavery to Freedom*. New York: Oxford University Press.

Lichter, Linda S. 1985. "Who Speaks for Black America." *Public Opinion* 8, 4.

Lincoln, C. Eric. 1961. *The Black Muslims in America*. Grand Rapids: Eerdmans.

Lincoln, C. Eric., and Lawrence H. Mamiya. 1990. *The Black Church in the African American Experience*. Durham: Duke University Press.

Live Radio Interview of the President by Tom Joyner's Morning Radio Program. Office of the Press Secretary. September 26, 1997.

Long, J. Scott. 1983. *Covarince Structure Models: An Introduction to LISREL*. Newberry Park: Sage Publications.

Long, Rob. 1999. "Kweisi & Me." *National Review*. August 9.

Loury, Glenn. 1990. "Why Should We Care about Group Inequality?" *Social Philosophy and Policy* 5.

Loury, Glenn, and Stephen Coate. 1992. "Will Affirmative Action Politics Eliminate Negative Stereotypes." *Ms.*

Lubiano, Wahneema. 1995. "Don't Talk with Your Eyes Closed: Caught in the Hollywood Gun Sights. In *Borders, Boundaries, and Frames: Cultural Criticism and Cultural Studies*. Edited by Mae Henderson. New York: Routledge.

————, editor. 1998. *The House That Race Built: Black Americans, U.S. Terrain*. New York: Random House.

Lusane, Clarence. 1994. *African Americans at the Crossroads: The Restructuring of Black Leadership and the 1992 Elections*. Boston: South End Press.

Lyons, Schley R. 1970. "The Political Socialization of Ghetto Children: Efficacy and Cynicism." *Journal of Politics*. Volume 32.

McAdam, Doug. 1982. *Political Process and the Development of Black Insurgency, 1930–1970*. Chicago: University of Chicago Press.

McCalary, Mike. 1995. "His View of Powell from across the Street." *Daily News*. November 10.

McCarthy, John, and Mayer Zald. 1973. "The Trend of Social Movements in America: Professionalization and Resource Mobilization." Morristown, NJ: General Learning Press.

————. 1977. "Resource Mobilization and Social Movements: A Partial Theory." *American Journal of Sociology* 82.

McCartney, John. 1992. *Black Power Ideologies: An Essay in African American Political Thought*. Philadelphia: Temple University Press.

McLean, Polly E. 1997. "Age Ain't Nothing but a Number: A Cross-Cultural Reading of Popular Music in the Construction of Sexual Expression among At-Risk Adolescents." *Popular Music and Society* 21, 2.

MacDonald, J. Fred. 1992. *Blacks and White TV: African Americans in Television since 1948*. 2d Edition. Chicago: Nelson-Hall Publishers.

"McDonald's Celebrates 'Little Known' Historical Contributions of Africans and African Americans." *PR Newswire*. August 18, 2000.

McElwaine, Sandra. 1996. "Can This Man Save the NAACP?" *USA Weekend*. February 4, 15.

McGeary, Johanna. 2001. "Odd Man Out." *Time*. September 10, 24–32.

McKelly, James. 1998. "The Double Truth, Ruth: 'Do the Right Thing' and the Culture of Ambiguity." *African American Review* 32, 2.

MacLean, Nancy. 1994. *Behind the Mask of Chivalry: The Making of the Second Ku Klux Klan*. New York: Oxford University Press.

McPherson, James. 1968. *Marching Toward Freedom: The Negro in the Civil War 1861–1865*. New York: Knopf.

Malcolm X. 1965 (1964). *The Autobiography of Malcolm X, as Told to Alex Haley*. New York: Ballantine Books.

Malson, Micheline R., et al., editors. 1990. *Black Women in America: Social Science Perspectives*. Chicago: University of Chicago Press.

Mannheim, Karl. 1936. *Ideology and Utopia: An Introduction to the Sociology of Knowledge*. New York: Harcourt, Brace, and World.

Mansbridge, Jane. 1999. "Everyday Talk in the Deliberative System." In *Deliberative Politics: Essays on Democracy and Disagreement*. Edited by Stephen Macedo. New York: Oxford University Press.

Marable, Manning. 1982. "Grounding with My Sisters: Patriarchy and the Exploitation of Black Women." *Journal of Ethnic Studies* 11, 2.

————. 1995a. *Beyond Black and White: Transforming African-American Politics*. London: Verso.

———. 1995b. "History and Black Consciousness the Political Culture of Black America." *Monthly Review* 47.

Marecek, Jeanne, Michelle Fine, and Louise Kidder. 1997. "Working Between Worlds: Qualitative Methods and Social Psychology." *Journal of Social Issues* 53, 4.

Marriott, Michel. 1995. "Black Women Are Split over All-Male March in Washington." *New Tork Times*. October 14.

Martin, Tony. 1976. *Race First: The Ideological and Organizational Struggles of Marcus Garvey and the Universal Negro Improvement Association*. Westport, CT: Greenwood.

Martinez, Theresa A. 1997. "Popular Culture as Oppositional Culture: Rap as Resistance." *Sociological Perspectives* 40, 2.

Marx, Gary. 1967. *Protest and Prejudice: A Study of Belief in the Black Community*. New York: Harper & Row.

Meeks, Gregory W. 1999. "Symposium." *Insights on the News*. January 25.

Mercer, Koena. 1990. "Black Hair/Style Politics." In *Out There: Marginilization and Contemporary Cultures*. Edited by Russell Ferguson et al. Cambridge: MIT Press.

Merelman, Richard. 1995. *Representing Black Culture: Racial Conflict and Cultural Politics in the U.S.* New York: Routledge.

Meyerson, Adam. 1994. "Manna 2 Society: The Growing Conservatism of Black America." *Policy Review* 68 (Spring).

"Mfume among Blacks Arrested for Protesting Lack of Minority Clerks at U.S. Supreme Court." 1998. *Jet*. October 26.

"Mfume Charges TV 'Whitewash'." 1999. *Television Digest*. July 19.

Mfume, Kweisi, with Ron Stodghill II. 1996. *No Free Ride: From the Mean Streets to the Mainstream*. New York: One World Press.

Miller, Arthur, et. al. 1981. "Group Consciousness and Political Participation." *American Journal of Political Science*. Volume 25.

Mills, Charles W. 1998. *Blackness Visable: Essays on Philosophy and Race*. Ithaca: Cornell University Press.

Mitchell, Ellen. 2002. "Tending Barber: It's as Much about Hangin' Out as Haircuts." *Newsday*. October 3, B3.

Mitchell, Margaret King. 1993. *Uncle Jed's Barbershop*. New York: Simon and Schuster.

Mitchell, Mary A. 2002. "'Barbershop' Shows Blacks-Warts and All." *Chicago Sun-Times*. September 17.

Moody, Ann. 1965. *Coming of Age in Mississippi*. New York: Laurel.

Moore, Dhoruba. 1981. "Strategies of Repression against the Black Movement." *Black Scholar* 12, 3.

Moraga, Cherrie, and Gloria Anzaldua. 1983 (1981). *This Bridge Called My Back: Writings by Radical Women of Color*. New York: Women of Color Press

Morgan, David. 1996. "Focus Groups." *Annual Review of Sociology*. Volume 22.

Morris, Aldon. 1984. *The Origins of the Civil Rights Movement*. New York: Free Press.

Morris, Lorenzo, Joseph McCormick, and Clarence Lusane. 1995. "Million Man March: Preliminary Report on the Survey." *Ms*.

Morris, Milton. 1975. *The Politics of Black America*. New York: Harper and Row.

Morris, Philip. 2000. "Gore Swept Blacks' Votes without Even Trying." *The Plain Dealer*. December 12, 9B.

Morrison, Toni, editor. 1992. *Race-ing Justice, En-gendering Power: Essays on Anita Hill, Clarence Thomas, and the Construction of Social Reality*. New York: Pantheon Books.

Morrow, Willie. 1973. *400 Years without a Comb*. San Diego: California Curl.

Moses, Wilson Jeremiah. 1969. *The Golden Age of Black Nationalism, 1850–1925*. Hamden, CT: Archon.

———. 1982. *Black Messiahs and Uncle Toms: Social and Literary Manipulations of a Religious Myth*. State College: Pennsylvania State University Press.

———. 1990. *The Wings of Ethiopia: Studies in African-American Life and Letters*. Ames: Iowa State University Press.

Muhammad, Elijah. 1965. *Message to the Blackman in America*. Chicago: Muhammad Mosque of Islam, no. 2.

Murdock, Deroy. 2000. "NAACP Ignores the Real Needs of Black People." *Insight on the News*. February 14.

Murphy, Melvin. 1998. *Barbershop Talk: The Other Side of Black Men*. Merrifield, VA: self-published.

Myrdal, Gunnar. 1944. *An American Dilemma: The Negro Problem and Modern Democracy*. New York: Harper and Brothers.

"NAACP Buys Stock in Major Networks to Force Racial Diversity in Fall Programming Line-up as Revealed on 'BET Tonight with Tavis Smiley.'" 1999. *Business Wire*. July 22.

"NAACP President Mfume Says He Thinks it's Time to Stop Bashing Justice Clarence Thomas." 1997. *Jet*. March 3, 6.

National Negro Business League. 1901. *Proceedings*. Volume 1, 1900. Boston: J. R. Hamm.

"NBC, ABC, NAACP in Accords." 2000. *Television Digest*. January 10.

Nelsen, Hart M., Thomas W. Madron, and Raytha L. Yokley. 1975. "Black Religion's Promethean Motif: Orthodoxy and Militancy." *American Journal of Sociology* 81, 1.

"Network Walk Out on NAACP." 1999. *Television Digest*. December 6.

Newitz, Annalee. 1995. "Myth of the Million Man March." *Bad Subjects* 23 (December).

Newton, Huey P. 1973. *Revolutionary Suicide*. New York: Writers and Readers Publishing.

Niemi, Richard G., and Barbara Sobieszek. 1977. "Political Socialization." *Annual Review of Sociology*. Volume 3.

Nimmo, Don, and James Combs. 1983. *Mediated Political Realities*. New York: Longman.

Offe, Claus, and Helmut Wiesenthal. 1980. "Two Logics of Collective Action." *Political Power and Social Theory*. Volume 1.

Olson, James M., et. al. 2001. "The Heritability of Attitudes: A Study of Twins." *Journal of Personality and Social Psychology* 80, 6.

"Oral History Approach to Health." 1998. *Self*. March.

Orum, Anthony M. 1966. "A Reappraisal of the Social and Political Participation of Negroes." *American Journal of Sociology*. Volume 72.

Parish, Norm. 2000. "Tom Joyner Will Broadcast from St. Louis; Radio Personality Is Here for Annie Malone Center Benefit Weekend." *St. Louis Post-Dispatch*. May 18, B1.

Patterson, John. 2002. "Everyone Loves Barbershop-Except Jesse Jackson and Al Sharpton." *The Guardian*. October 4, 5.

Pattillo-McCoy, Mary. 1998. "Church Culture as a Strategy of Action in the Black Community." *American Sociological Review*. Volume 63 (December).

Patton, Cindy. 1995. "White Racism/Black Signs: Censorship and Images of Race Relations." *Journal of Communication* 45, 2.

Paulus, Paul, editor. 1983. *Basic Group Processes*. New York: Springer-Verlag.

Pearson, Hugh. 2002. "Sharpton Knicks Himself Cutting 'Barbershop.'" *Newsday*. October 3, A38.

Perkins, Joseph. 2000. "For Blacks, Bush Is Really a Different Kind of Republican." *The San Diego Union-Tribune*. August 11.

Perry, Huey, and Wayne Parent, editors. 1995. *Blacks and the American Political System*. Gainesville: University of Florida Press.

Persaud, Babita. 2000. "Good Morning!" *St. Petersburg Times*. May 5, 22W.

Petty, Jill. 1998. "Coloring, Styling, Perming-and Lifesaving Info." *Ms.* (July/August).

Petty, Richard E., and John T. Cacioppo. 1981. *Attitudes and persuasion: Classic and Contemporary Approaches*. Dubuque, IA: W. C. Brown.

Petty, Richard, Thomas Ostrom, and Timothy Brock, editors. 1981. *Cognitive Responses in Persuasion*. Hillsdale, NJ: Lawrence Erlbaum Associates.

Pierre, Robert E., Scott Wilson, and Jackie Spinner. 1999. "'Mfume for Mayor' Movement." *The Washington Post*. April 8, M01.

Pinderhughes, Dianne. 1987. *Race and Ethnicity in Chicago Politics: A Reexamination of Pluralist Theory*. Chicago: University of Illinois Press.

Pinkney, Alphonso. 1976. *Red, Black and Green: Black Nationalism in the United States*. Cambridge: Cambridge University Press.

Pitts, James P. 1975. "Self Direction and Political Socialization of Black Youth." *Social Science Quarterly* 56, 1.

Pitts, Leonard, Jr. 2002. "Belafonte's Off Base with Assult on Powell." *The Seattle Times*. October 27, C2.

Piven, Frances Fox, and Richard Cloward. 1977. Poor People's Movements. New York: Vintage Books.

Popkin, Samuel L. 1994. *The Reasoning Voter: Communication and Persuasion in Presidential Campaigns*. Chicago: University of Chicago Press.

Powell, Colin, with Persico, Joseph. 1995. *My American Journey*. New York: Ballantine Books.

———. 1996. "Speech of General Colin Powell at the GOP National Convention." www.pbs.org.

———. 2000. "Speech of General Colin Powell at the GOP National Convention." www.pbs.org.

Prunty, M. 1995. "In the Beauty Salon on a Saturday Afternoon." *Women and Language* 18, 1 (Spring).

Psathas, George. 1995. *Conversation Analysis: The Study of Talk-in-Interaction*. Thousand Oaks: Sage.

Purdum, Todd S. 2002. "Powell Finesses a Sour Note from Harry Belafonte, 'a Friend.'" *New York Times.* October 10, 9.

Putnam, Robert. 2000. *Bowling Alone: The Collapse and Revival of American Community.* New York: Simon and Schuster.

Radio Host Tom Joyner among Seven Inducted into the Radio Hall of Fame in Chicago." *Jet.* November 9, 1998.

Radio Interview of the President on the Tom Joyner Show." Office of the Press Secretary. November 2, 1998.

"Radio Jock and Civil Rights Group Take the Voice of the African American Community to the Nation's Leaders." 2000. *PR Newswire.* September 9.

Ramsey, Patricia G. 1987. "Young Children's Thinking about Ethnic Differences." In *Children's Ethnic Socialization.* Edited by Jean S. Phinney and Mary Jane Rotherman. Beverly Hills: Sage.

Randolph, Laura. 1995. "Why Almost Everybody Loves Colin Powell." *Ebony* 51, 1.

———. 1999. "Keeping Promises." *Ebony* 59, 9.

Ransby, Barabara, and Cheryl I. Harris. 2001. "Uncle Tom's Cabinet? A Few Black Faces at the Top Won't Quell the Outrage at the Bottom." *In These Times.* January 22, 16–17.

Ransby, Barbara, and Tracey Matthews. 1993. "Black Popular Culture and the Transcendence of Patriarchal Illusions." *Race and Class.* Volume 35.

Raspberry, William. 1998. "Josephs to the Rescue." *Raleigh News and Observer.* March 25.

Rathbun, Elizabeth A. 2000. "Boycott Threat Widened." *Broadcasting and Cable.* June 19.

Redkey, Edwin. 1969. *Black Exodus: Black Nationalist Movements 1890–1910.* New Haven: Yale University Press.

Reed, Adolph L., Jr. 1986. *The Jesse Jackson Phenomenon: The Crisis of Purpose in Afro-American Politics.* New Haven: Yale University Press.

———. 1992. "The Allure of Malcolm X." In *Malcolm X: In Our Own Image.* Edited by Joe Wood. New York: St. Martin's Press.

Reese, Laura A., and Ronald Brown. 1995. "The Effects of Religious Messages on Racial Identity and System Blame among African Americans." *Journal of Politics.* Volume 57.

"Riders on the Storm." *New York Times.* October 15, 1995.

"Robert Johnson's Statement." 2001. Blackvoices.com.

Roberts, J. Deotis. 1971. *Liberation and Reconciliation.* Philadelphia: Westminster Press.

Robinson, Dean E. 2001. *Black Nationalism in American Politics and Thought.* Cambridge: Cambridge University Press.

Robinson, Randall. 2000. *The Debt: What America Owes to Blacks.* New York: Plume Books.

Rokeach, Milton. 1968. *Beliefs, Attitudes, and Values: A Theory of Organization and Change.* San Francisco: Jossey-Bass.

———. 1973. *The Nature of Human Values.* New York: Free Press.

Rogers, Mary F. 1984. "Everyday Life as Text." *Sociological Theory.* Volume 2.

Rooks, Noliwe. 1996. *Hair Raising: Beauty, Culture, and African American Women*. New Brunswick, NJ: Rutgers University Press.

Rorty, Richard. 1994. "Feminism, Ideology, and DeConstruction: A Pragmatist View." In *Mapping Ideology*. Edited by Slavok Žižek. London: Verso.

Rose, Tricia. 1994. *Black Noise: Rap Music and Black Culture in Contemporary America*. Middleton, CT: Wesleyan University Press.

Rosenberg, Shawn W. 1985. "Sociology, Psychology, and the Study of Political Behavior: The Case of the Research on Political Socialization." *Journal of Politics* 47, 2.

Rosnow, Ralph, and Edward Robinson, editors. 1967. *Experiments in Persuasion*. New York: Academic Press.

Rothenberg, Lawrence. 1992. *Linking Citizens to Government: Interest Group Politics at Common Cause*. New York: Cambridge University Press.

Sabrosky, Judith. 1979. *From Rationality to Liberation: The Evolution of Feminist Ideology*. Westport, CT: Greenwood.

Sapiro, Virgina. 1983. *The Political Integration of Women: Roles, Socialization and Politics*. Chicago: University of Illinois Press.

Sawyer, Mary R. 1996. "The Black Church and Black Politics: Models of Ministerial Activism." *The Journal of Religious Thought* 52, 2.

"S.C. Senate Oks Removal of Confederate Flag from State Capitol Dome; NAACP Maintains Boycott." 2000. *Jet*. May 1.

Schaeffer, Nora C. 1980. "Evaluating Race-of-Interviewer Effects in a National Survey." *Sociological Methods and Research* 8, 4.

Schlosser, Joe. 1999. "NAACP Sees Boycott Ahead." *Broadcasting & Cable*. August 23.

———. 2000. "Wanted: VP of Diversity." *Broadcasting & Cable*. January 31.

Schoonmaker, Mary Ellen. 1995. "Bridging the Great Divide: Opportunity Knocks." *The Record*. November 2.

Schuman, Howard, Charlotte Steeth, and Lawrence Bobo. 1997 (1985). *Racial Attitudes in America: Trends and Interpretations*. Cambridge: Harvard University Press.

Schweninger, Loren. 1990. *Black Property Owners in the South, 1790–1915*. Urbana: University of Illinois Press.

Scott, James. 1985. *Weapons of the Weak: Everyday Forms of Peasant Resistance*. New Haven: Yale University Press.

———. 1990. *Domination and the Arts of Resistance: Hidden Transcripts*. New Haven: Yale University Press.

Searing, Donald, Gerald Wright, and George Rabinowitz. 1976. "The Primacy Principle: Attitude Change and Political Socialization." *British Journal of Political Science* 6, 1.

Sears, David, and John McConahay. 1973. *The Politics of Violence: The New Urban Blacks and the Watts Riot*. Boston: Houghton Mifflin.

Selinsky, Debbie. 2000. "Putting the 'Fun Factor' into Giving." *Success* (November).

Seltzer, Robert, and Richard Smith. 1985. "Race and Ideology: A Research Note on Measuring Liberalism and Conservatism in Black America." *Phylon* 25, 2.

Semmes, Clovis E. 1993. "Religion and the Challenge of Afrocentric Thought." *The Western Journal of Black Studies* 17, 3.

Seymour, Craig. 2002. "Film Criticized for Jabs at Black Icons." *The Atlanta Journal-Constitution.* September 20.

Shingles, Richard. 1981. "Black Consciousness and Political Participation: The Missing Link." *American Political Science Review.* Volume 75.

Shipp, E. R. 2002. "Sharpton and Jackson Are Looking Irrelevant: Why Do They Protest a Harmless Movie?" *Daily News.* September 29, 49.

Shrage, Laurie. 1994. *Moral Dilemmas of Feminism: Prostitution, Adultery, and Abortion.* New York: Routledge.

Sidran, Ben. 1971. *Black Talk.* New York: DaCapo Press.

Siegel, Paul, and Robert Hodge. 1968. "A Causal Approach to the Study of Measurement Error." In *Methodology in Social Research.* Edited by Hubert Blalockand Ann Blalock. NewYork: McGraw-Hill.

Sigelman, Lee, and Susan Welch. 1991. *Black Americans' Views of Racial Inequality: The Dream Deferred.* New York: Cambridge University Press.

Silberman, Charles E. 1964. *Crisis in Black and White.* New York: Random House.

Simon, Clea. 2000. "Radio Tracks: Joyner Brings Activism, Music to Wild." *The Boston Globe.* August 24, D1.

Sims, Muriel L. 1999. "The Fly Jock,' Tom Joyner." *Black Collegian.* February.

Singer, James W. 1981. "With a Friend in the White House, Black Conservatives are Speaking Out." *National Journal* 13, 11.

Smelser, Neil. 1962. *Theory of Collective Behavior.* London: Routledge and Kegan Paul.

"Smiley Responds to BET Firing." 2001. Blackvoices.com.

Smiley, Tavis. 1998. *The Best of Tavis Smiley on the Tom Joyner Morning Show: Thoughts on Culture, Politics and Race.* Los Angeles: Pines One Publications.

Smith, David Lionel. 1992. "Booker T. Washington's Rhetoric: Commanding Performance." *Prospects.* Volume 17.

Smith, R. Drew. 1994. "Black Religion-Based Politics, Cultural Popularization and Youth Allegiance." *Western Journal of Black Studies* 18, 3.

Smith, Richard, and Robert Seltzer. 1992. *Race, Class, and Culture.* Albany: State University of New York Press.

Smith, Robert and Peter Manning, editors. 1985. *A Handbook of Social Science Methods: Quantitative Methods: Focused Survey Research and Causal Modeling.* New York: Praeger.

Smith, Rogers. 1997. *Civic Ideals: Conflicting Visions of Citizenship in US History.* New Haven: Yale University Press.

Smith, Valerie. 1997. *Not Just Race, Not Just Gender: Black Feminist Readings.* New York: Routledge.

Smitherman, Geneva. 1977. *Talkin and Testifyin: The Language of Black America.* Boston: Houghton Mifflin.

Smitherman-Donaldson, Geneva, and Teun Van Dijk, editors. 1988. *Discourse and Discrimination.* Detroit: Wayne State University.

SNCC. 1995 (1966). "The Basis of Black Power." In *Takin' it to the Streets: A Sixties Reader.* Edited by Alexander Bloom and Wini Breines. New York: Oxford University Press.

Sobieraj, Sandra. 1995. "Mfume Called Strong, Popular Leader." *The Detroit News*. December 10.

Sook, Kristal. 1999. *Color by Fox: The Fox Network and the Revolution in Black Television*. New York: Oxford University Press.

Southgate, Minoo. 1994. "Radio in Black and White." *National Review* 46, 23.

Sowell, Thomas. 1975. *Affirmative Action Reconsidered: Was It Necessary in Academia?* Washington, DC: American Enterprise Institute for Public Policy Research.

———. 1984. *Education: Assumptions versus History*. Stanford: Hoover Institute Press.

———. 1990. *Preferential Policies: An International Perspective*. New York: William Morrow.

Spear, Allan H. 1967. *Black Chicago: The Making of a Negro Ghetto, 1890–1920*. Chicago: University of Chicago Press.

Spellman, Charles G. 1993. "The Black Press: Setting the Political Agenda during World War II." *Negro History Bulletin* 51, 1.

Spencer, Jon Michael. 1990. *Protest and Praise: Sacred Music of Black Religion*. Minneapolis: Fortress Press.

Squires, David R., and Aretha Fouch. 2001a. "Johnson: I Fired Tavis Smiley." Blackvoices.com.

———. 2001b. "Johnson Responds to View." Blackvoices.com.

Standoea, Leo. 2002. "Powell Returns Fire in Slave Slap." *Daily News*. October 10, 4.

Starling, Kelly. 1999. "National Uproar Forces Schedule Changes." *Ebony* (November).

Steele, Shelby. 1990. *The Content of Our Character: A New Vision of Race in America*. New York: St. Martin's Press.

Stone, Alfred Holt. 1908. *Studies in the American Race Problem*. New York: Doubleday, Page, and Company.

Stuckey, Sterling. 1987. *Slave Culture: Nationalist Theory and the Foundations of Black America*. New York: Oxford University Press.

Sudbury, Julia. 1998. *Other Kinds of Dreams: Black Women's Organizations and the Politics of Transformation*. New York: Routledge.

Sullivan, John L., George E. Marcus, and Daniel R. Minns. 1975. "The Development of Political Ideology: Some Empirical Findings." *Youth and Society* 7, 2.

Sullivan, Lisa. 1990. "Beyond Nostalgia: Notes on Black Student Activism." *Socialist Review* 20, 4.

Swain, Carol. 1993. *Black Faces, Black Interests: The Representation of African Americans in Congress*. Cambridge: Harvard University Press.

Tajfel, Henri. 1981. *Human Groups and Social Categories*. Cambridge: Cambridge University Press.

———. 1982. "Social Psychology of Intergroup Relations." *Annual Review of Psychology*. Volume 33.

Tajfel, Henri, and John C. Turner. 1979. "An Integrative Theory of Intergroup Conflict." In *The Social Psychology of Intergroup Relations*. Edited by William G. Austin and Steven Worchel. Monterery, CA: Brooks/Cole.

Tate, Katherine. 1991. "Black Political Participation in the 1984 and 1988 Presidential Elections." *The American Political Science Review* 85, 4.

———. 1993. *From Protest to Politics: The New Black Voters in American Elections*. New York: Russell Sage.

"Tavis Smiley Helps Keep Black Colleges from Being Placed in 'Separate but Unequal' Committee." *Jet*. April 2, 2001.

"Tavis Smiley's Commentary on the Tom Joyner Morning Show March 27, 2001." 2001. Blackvoices.com.

"Tavis Smiley's Dismissal by BET Outrages Blacks across the Nation. 2001. *Jet*. April 16.

Tedesco, Richard. 1999. "NAACP Targets February Sweeps." *Broadcasting & Cable*. November 8.

"Telephone Interview of the President for the Tom Joyner Morning Show." 2000. Office of the Press Secretary. November 2.

Thomas, Clarence. 1998. "I am a Man, a Black Man, an American." Speech to the National Bar Association. July 29.

Thomas, Tony. 1971. *In Defense of Black Nationalism*. New York: Pathfinder Press.

"To Add Minorities at Those Networks." 2000. *Jet*. January 24.

Togeby, Lise. 1995. "Feminist Attitudes: Social Interests or Political Ideology?" *Women and Politics* 15, 3.

Tolleson-Rinehart, Sue. 1992. *Gender Consciousness and Politics*. New York: Routledge.

"Tom Joyner and Tavis Smiley to Launch 42-City Campaign Encouraging African-Americans to Participate in 2000 Census; Tour to Kick-Off March 17, 2000." 2000. *Business Wire*. March 16.

"Tom Joyner Morning Show Continues Awareness Campaign with its Black Agenda 2000 Tour." 2000. *PR Newswire*. September 8.

Took, Kevin J., and David S. Weiss. 1994. "The Relationship between Heavy Metal and Rap Music on Adolescent Turmoil: Real or Artifact?" *Adolescence* 29, 115.

Tocqueville, Alexis de. 1835. *Democracy in America*. Translated by Henry Reeve. London: Saunders and Otley.

Torres, Sasha, editor. 1998. *Living Color: Race and Television in the United States*. Durham: Duke University Press.

Tripp, Luke. 1992. "The Political Views of Black Students during the Reagan Era." *Black Scholar* 22, 3.

Ture, Kwame, and Charles Hamilton. 1967. *Black Power*. New York: Vintage Books.

"Turnaround at NAACP Earns Mfume Second Term." 2001. *Los Angeles Times*. February 17.

Tyler, Bruce M. 1990. "Black Hairstyles: Cultural and Socio-Political Implications." *Western Journal of Black Studies* 14, 4.

Ugwu, Catherine, editor. 1996. *Let's Get It on: The Politics of Black Performance*. Seattle: Bay Press.

Van DeBurg, William L. 1997. *Modern Black Nationalism: From Marcus Garvey to Louis Farrakhan*. New York: New York University Press.

Van Dijk, Teun. 1998. *Ideology: A Multidisciplinary Approach*. London: Sage.

Verba, Sydney, Kay Lehman Schlozman, and Henry E. Brady. 1995. *Voice and Equality: Civic Voluntarism in American Politics*. Cambridge: Harvard University Press.

Vincent, Theodore. 1971. *Black Power and the Garvey Movement*. Berkeley: Ramparts Press.

Waitzkin, Howard. 1990. "Interpretive Analysis of Spoken Discourse: Dealing with the Limitations of Quantitative and Qualitative Methods." *The Southern Communication Journal* 58, 2.

Walker, Alice. 1983. *In Search of Our Mother's Gardens: Womanist Prose*. San Diego: Harcourt Brace Jovanovich.

———. 1997. *Anything We Love Can Be Saved: A Writer's Activism*. New York: Ballantine Books.

Walker, Juliet E. K. 1998. *The History of Black Business in America: Capitalism, Race, Entrepreneurship*. New York: Macmillan.

———, editor. 1999. *Encyclopedia of African American Business History*. Westport, CT: Greenwood Press.

Wallace, Linda. 2002. "Barbershop Isn't Offensive; It's Reassuring." *The Christian Science Monitor*. September 30, 9.

Wallace, Michele. 1978. *Black Macho and the Myth of the Superwoman*. New York: Verso.

———. 1996. "Out of Step with the Million Man March." *Ms.* 6, 4 (January).

Wallis, Jim. 1994. *The Soul of Politics: Beyond the "Religious Right" and "Secular Left."* New York: Harcourt Brace.

Walton, Hanes Jr. 1985. *Invisible Politics: Black Political Behavior*. Albany: State University of New York Press.

Washington, Booker. T. 1986 (1901). *Up From Slavery*. New York: Doubleday.

———. (1900). *The Story of My Life and Work*. Naperville, IL: J. L. Nichols.

Waters, Mary. 1999. *Black Identities: West Immigrant Dreams and American Realities*. Cambridge: Harvard University Press.

Watson, Elwood. 1998. "Guess What Came to American Politics? Contemporary Black Conservatism." *Journal of Black Studies* 29, 1.

Watts, Eric. 1997. "An Exploration of Spectacular Consumption: Gangsta Rap as a Cultural Commodity." *Communication Studies* 48, 1.

Weaver, Garrett. 1987. "The Development of the Black Durham Community, 1880–1915." Ph.D. dissertation, University of North Carolina, Chapel Hill.

Weems, Renita. 1988. *Just a Sister Away: A Womanist Vision of Women's Relationships in the Bible*. San Diego: LuraMedia

Weiss, Nancy. 1983. *Farewell to the Party of Lincoln: Black Politics in the Age of FDR*. Princeton: Princeton University Press.

Wells-Barnett, Ida B. 1969 (1892). *On Lynching: Southern Horrors, a Red Record, Mob Rule in New Orleans*. New York: Arno Press.

West, Cornel. 1982. *Prophesy Deliverance! An Afro-American Revolutionary Christianity*. Philadelphia: Westminster John Knox Press.

———. 1993. *Race Matters*. Boston: Beacon Press.

Wester, Stephen R., et. al. 1997. "The Influence of Sexually Violent Rap Music on Attitudes of Men with Little Prior Exposure." *Psychology of Women Quarterly.* Volume 21.

White, Deborah Gray. 1985. *Ar'n't I a Woman? Female Slaves in the Plantation South.* New York: Norton.

White, E. Frances. 1984. "Listening to the Voices of Black Feminism." *Radical America* 18, 2.

———. 1990. "Africa on My Mind: Gender, Counter Discourse and African-American Nationalism." *Journal of Women's History* 2, 1.

———. 2001. *Dark Continent of Our Bodies: Black Feminism and the Politics of Respectibility.* Philadelphia: Temple University Press.

"Why Are So Few Blacks Starring on TV?" 1999. *Jet.* August 9.

Wickam, DeWayne. 2002. " 'Barbershop' Flap Deflects Focus from Economic Woes." *USA Today.* October 1, 13A.

Wilcox, Clyde, and Leopoldo Gomez. 1990. "Religion, Group Identification, and Politics among American Blacks." *Sociological Analysis* 51, 3.

Williams, Delores. 1993. *Sisters in the Wilderness: The Challenge of Womanist God-Talk.* Maryknoll, NY: Orbis Books.

Williams, Gilbert A. 1998. *Legendary Pioneers of Black Radio.* Westport, CT: Praeger.

Williams, Juan. 1987. *Eyes on the Prize.* New York: Blackside.

Williams, Walter. 1996. "We've Never Been Better Off." *Conservative Chronicle.* March.

Wilson, William J. 1980a. *The Declining Significance of Race: Blacks and the Changing American Institutions.* Chicago: University of Chicago Press.

———. 1980b. *The Truly Disadvantaged: The Inner City, the Underclass, and Public Policy.* Chicago: University of Chicago Press.

"Working the Beauty Salon Network." 1996. *Publishers Weekly* 243, 16.

Yates, Miranda, and James Youniss. 1998. "Community Service and Political Identity Development in Adolescence. *Journal of Social Issues* 54, 13.

Yearwood, Lennox. 1978. "National Afro-American Organizations in Urban Communities." *Journal of Black Studies* 8, 4.

Young, Josiah U. 1986. *Black and African Theology: Siblings or Distant Cousins?* Maryknoll, NY: Orbis Books.

Zaller, John. 1992. *The Nature and Origins of Mass Opinion.* Cambridge: Cambridge University Press.

Zoroya, Gregg. 1996. "Kweisi Mfume's Job Is to Breathe New Life into the NAACP." *Los Angeles Times* Magazine. July 21, 14.

Index